THE
EIGHT

THE
EIGHT

A NOVEL
KATHERINE NEVILLE

BALLANTINE BOOKS · NEW YORK

Library of Congress Cataloging-in-Publication Data

Neville, Katherine, 1945–
    The eight.

    I. Title.
PS3564.E8517E35 1989 813'.54 87-91363
ISBN 0-345-35137-1

Design by Holly Johnson
Manufactured in the United States of America

First Edition: January 1989
10 9 8 7 6 5 4 3 2 1

Chess is Life.

—*Bobby Fischer*

Life is a kind of chess.

—*Benjamin Franklin*

THE
EIGHT

THE DEFENSE

Characters tend to be either for or against the quest. If they assist it, they are idealized as simply gallant or pure; if they obstruct it, they are characterized as simply villainous or cowardly.

Hence every typical character . . . tends to have his moral opposite confronting him, like black and white pieces in a chess game.

—Anatomy of Criticism
Northrop Frye

A flock of nuns crossed the road, their crisp wimples fluttering about their heads like the wings of large sea birds. As they floated through the large stone gates of the town, chickens and geese scurried out of their path, flapping and splashing through the mud puddles. The nuns moved through the darkening mist that enveloped the valley each morning and, in silent pairs, headed toward the sound of the deep bell that rang out from the hills above them.

They called that spring *le Printemps Sanglant,* the Bloody Spring. The cherry trees had bloomed early that year, long before the snows had melted from the high mountain peaks. Their fragile branches bent down to earth with the weight of the wet red blossoms. Some said it was a good omen that they had bloomed so soon, a symbol of rebirth after the long and brutal winter. But then the cold rains had come and frozen the blossoms on the bough, leaving the valley buried thick in red blossoms stained with brown streaks of frost. Like a wound congealed with dried blood. And this was said to be another kind of sign.

High above the valley, the Abbey of Montglane rose like an enormous outcropping of rock from the crest of the mountain. The fortress-like structure had remained untouched by the outside world for nearly a thousand years. It was constructed of six or seven layers of wall built one on top of the other. As the original stones eroded over the centuries, new walls were laid outside of old ones, with flying buttresses. The result was a brooding architectural melange whose very appearance fed the rumors about the place. The abbey was the oldest church structure standing intact in France, and it bore an ancient curse that was soon to be reawakened.

As the dark-throated bell rang out across the valley, the remaining nuns looked up from their labors one by one, put aside their rakes and hoes, and passed down through the long, symmetrical rows of cherry trees to climb the precipitous road to the abbey.

At the end of the long procession, the two young novices Valentine and Mireille trailed arm in arm, picking their way with muddy boots. They made an odd complement to the orderly line of nuns. The tall red-haired Mireille with her long legs and broad shoulders looked more like a healthy farm girl than a nun. She wore a heavy butcher's apron over her habit, and red curls strayed from beneath her wimple. Beside her Valentine seemed fragile, though she was nearly as tall. Her pale skin seemed translucent, its fairness accentuated by the cascade of white-blond hair that tumbled about her shoulders. She had stuffed her wimple into the pocket of her habit, and she walked reluctantly beside Mireille, kicking her boots in the mud.

The two young women, the youngest nuns at the abbey, were cousins on their mothers' side, both orphaned at an early age by a dreadful plague that had ravaged France. The aging Count de Remy, Valentine's grandfather, had commended them into the hands of the Church, upon his death leaving the sizable balance of his estate to ensure their care.

The circumstance of their upbringing had formed an inseparable bond between the two, who were both bursting with the unrestrained abundant gaiety of youth. The abbess often heard the older nuns complain that this behavior was unbecoming to the cloistered life, but she understood that it was better to curb youthful spirits than to try to quench them.

Then, too, the abbess felt a certain partiality to the orphaned cousins, a feeling unusual both to her personality and her station. The older nuns would have been surprised to learn that the abbess herself had sustained from early childhood such a bosom friendship, with a woman who had been separated from her by many years and many thousands of miles.

Now, on the steep trail, Mireille was tucking some unruly wisps of red hair back under her wimple and tugging her cousin's arm as she tried to lecture her on the sins of tardiness.

"If you keep on dawdling, the Reverend Mother will give us a penance again," she said.

Valentine broke loose and twirled around in a circle. "The earth is drowning in spring," she cried, swinging her arms about and nearly toppling over the edge of the cliff. Mireille hauled her up along the treacherous incline. "*Why* must we be shut up in that stuffy abbey when everything out-of-doors is bursting with life?"

"Because we are nuns," said Mireille with pursed lips, stepping up her pace, her hand firmly on Valentine's arm. "And it is our duty to pray for mankind." But the warm mist rising from the valley floor brought with it a fragrance so heavy that it saturated everything with the aroma of cherry blossoms. Mireille tried not to notice the stirrings this caused in her own body.

"We are not nuns yet, thank God," said Valentine. "We are only novices until we have taken our vows. It's not too late to be saved. I've heard the older nuns whispering that there are soldiers roaming about in France, looting all the monasteries of their treasures, rounding up the priests and marching them off to Paris. Perhaps some soldiers will come here and march me off to Paris, too. And take me to the opera each night, and drink champagne from my shoe!"

"Soldiers are not always so very charming as you seem to think," observed Mireille. "After all, their business is killing people, not taking them to the opera."

"That's not *all* they do," said Valentine, her voice dropping to a mysterious whisper. They had reached the top of the hill, where the road flattened out and widened considerably. Here it was cobbled with flat paving stones and resembled the broad thoroughfares one found in larger towns. On either side of the road, huge cypresses had been planted. Rising above the sea of cherry orchards, they looked formal and forbidding and, like the abbey itself, strangely out of place.

"I have heard," Valentine whispered in her cousin's ear, "that the soldiers do dreadful things to nuns! If a soldier should come upon a nun, in the woods, for example, he immediately takes a thing out of his pants and he puts it into the nun and stirs it about. And then when he has finished, the nun has a baby!"

"What blasphemy!" cried Mireille, pulling away from Valentine and trying to suppress the smile hovering about her lips. "You are entirely too saucy to be a nun, I think."

"Exactly what I have been saying all along," Valentine admitted. "I would far rather be the bride of a soldier than a bride of Christ."

As the two cousins approached the abbey, they could see the four double rows of cypresses planted at each entrance to form the sign of the crucifix. The trees closed in about them as they scurried along through the blackening mist. They passed through the abbey gates and crossed the large courtyard. As they approached the high wooden doors to the main enclave, the bell continued to ring, like a death knell cutting through the thick mist.

Each paused before the doors to scrape mud from her boots, crossed herself quickly, and passed through the high portal. Neither glanced up at the inscription carved in crude Frankish letters in the stone arch over the portal, but each knew what it said, as if the words were engraved upon her heart:

Cursed be He who bring these Walls to Earth
The King is checked by the Hand of God alone.

Beneath the inscription the name was carved in large block letters, "Carolus Magnus." He it was who was architect both of the building and the curse placed upon those who would destroy it. The greatest ruler of the Frankish Empire over a thousand years earlier, he was known to all in France as Charlemagne.

The interior walls of the abbey were dark, cold, and wet with moss. From the inner sanctum one could hear the whispered voices of the novitiates praying and the soft clicking of their rosaries counting off the Aves, Glorias, and Pater Nosters. Valentine and Mireille hurried through the chapel as the last of the novices were genuflecting and followed the trail of whispers to the small door behind the altar where the reverend mother's study was located. An older nun was hastily shooing the last of the stragglers inside. Valentine and Mireille glanced at each other and passed within.

It was strange to be called to the abbess's study in this manner. Few nuns had ever been there at all, and then usually for disciplinary action. Valentine, who was always being disciplined, had been there often enough. But the abbey bell was used to convene all the nuns. Surely they could not all be called at once to the reverend mother's study?

As they entered the large, low-ceilinged room, Valentine and Mireille saw that all the nuns in the abbey were indeed there—more than fifty of them. Seated on rows of hard wooden benches that had been set up facing the Abbess's writing desk, they whispered among themselves. Clearly everyone thought it was a strange circumstance, and the faces that looked up as the two young cousins entered seemed frightened. The cousins took their places in the last row of benches. Valentine clasped Mireille's hand.

"What does it mean?" she whispered.

"It bodes ill, I think," replied Mireille, also in a whisper. "The reverend mother looks grave. And there are two women here whom I have never seen."

At the end of the long room, behind a massive desk of polished cherry wood, stood the abbess, wrinkled and leathery as an old parchment, but still exuding the power of her tremendous office. There was a timeless quality in her bearing that suggested she had long ago made peace with her own soul, but today she looked more serious than the nuns had ever seen her.

Two strangers, both large-boned young women with big hands, loomed at either side of her like avenging angels. One had pale skin, dark hair, and luminous eyes, while the other bore a strong resemblance to Mireille, with a creamy complexion and chestnut hair only slightly darker than Mireille's auburn locks. Though both had the bearing of nuns, they were not wearing habits, but plain gray traveling clothes of nondescript nature.

The abbess waited until all the nuns were seated and the door had been closed. When the room was completely silent she began to speak in the voice that always reminded Valentine of a dry leaf being crumbled.

"My daughters," said the abbess, folding her hands before her, "for nearly one thousand years the Order of Montglane has stood upon this rock, doing our duty to mankind and serving God. Though we are cloistered from the world, we hear the rumblings of the world's unrest. Here in our small corner, we have received unfortunate tidings of late that may change the security we've enjoyed so long. The two women who stand beside me are bearers of those tidings. I introduce Sister Alexandrine de Forbin"—she motioned to the dark-haired woman—"and Marie-Charlotte de Corday, who together direct the Abbaye-aux-Dames at Caen in the northern provinces. They have traveled the length of France in disguise, an arduous journey, to bring us a warning. I therefore bid you hark unto what they have to say. It is of the gravest importance to us all."

The abbess took her seat, and the woman who had been introduced as Alexandrine de Forbin cleared her throat and spoke in a low voice so that the nuns had to strain to hear her. But her words were clear.

"My sisters in God," she began, "the tale we have to tell is not for the faint-hearted. There are those among us who came to Christ hoping to save mankind. There are those who came hoping to escape from the world. And there are those who came against their will, feeling no calling whatever." At this she turned her dark, luminous eyes directly upon Valentine, who blushed to the very roots of her pale blond hair.

"Regardless what you thought your purpose was, it has changed as of today. In our journey, Sister Charlotte and I have passed the length of France, through Paris and each village in between. We have seen not only hunger but starvation. People are rioting in the streets for bread. There is butchery; women carry severed heads on pikes through the streets. There is rape, and worse. Small children are murdered, people are tortured in public squares and torn to pieces by angry mobs . . ." The nuns were no longer quiet. Their voices rose in alarm as Alexandrine continued her bloody account.

Mireille thought it odd that a woman of God could recount such a tale without blanching. Indeed, the speaker had not once altered her low, calm tone, nor had her voice quavered in the telling. Mireille glanced at Valentine, whose eyes were large and round with fascination. Alexandrine de Forbin waited until the room had quieted a bit, then continued.

"It is now April. Last October the king and queen were kidnapped from Versailles by an angry mob and forced to return to the Tuilleries at Paris, where they were imprisoned. The king was made to sign a document, the 'Declaration of the Rights of Man,' proclaiming the equality of all men. The National Assembly in effect now controls the government; the king is powerless to intervene. Our country is beyond revolution. We are in a state of anarchy. To make matters worse, the assembly has discovered there is no gold in the State Treasury; the king has bankrupted the State. In Paris it is believed that he will not live out the year."

A shock ran through the rows of seated nuns, and there was agitated whispering throughout the room. Mireille squeezed Valentine's hand gently as they both stared at the speaker. The women in this room had never heard such thoughts expressed aloud, and they could not conceive such things as real. Torture, anarchy, regicide. How was it possible?

The abbess rapped her hand flat upon the table to call for order, and the nuns fell silent. Now Alexandrine took her seat, and Sister Charlotte stood alone at the table. Her voice was strong and forceful.

"In the assembly there is a man of great evil. He is hungry for power, though he calls himself a member of the clergy. This man is the Bishop of Autun. Within the Church at Rome it is believed he is the Devil incarnate. It is claimed he was born with a cloven hoof, the mark of the Devil, that he drinks the blood of small children to appear young, that he celebrates the Black Mass. In October this bishop proposed to the assembly that the State confiscate all Church property. On November second his Bill of Seizure was defended before the Assembly by the great statesman Mirabeau, and it passed. On February thirteenth the confiscation began. Any clergy who resisted were arrested and jailed. And on February sixteenth, the Bishop of Autun was elected president of the Assembly. Nothing can stop him now."

The nuns were in a state of extreme agitation, their voices raised in fearful exclamations and protests, but Charlotte's voice carried above all.

"Long before the Bill of Seizure, the Bishop of Autun had made inquiries into the location of the Church's wealth in France. Though the bill specifies that priests are to fall first and nuns to be spared, we know the bishop has cast his eye upon Montglane Abbey. It is around Montglane that many of his inquiries have centered. This, we have hastened here to tell you. The treasure of Montglane *must* not fall into his hands."

The abbess stood and placed her hand upon the strong shoulder of Charlotte Corday. She looked out over the rows of black-clad nuns, their stiff starched hats moving like a sea thick with wild seagulls beneath her, and she smiled. This was her flock, which she had shepherded for so long, and which she might not see again in her lifetime once she had revealed what she now must tell.

"Now you know as much of our situation as I," said the abbess. "Though I have known for many months of our plight, I did not wish to alarm you until I had chosen a path. In their journey responding to my call, our sisters from Caen have confirmed my worst fears." The nuns had now fallen into a silence like the hush of death. Not a sound could be heard but the voice of the abbess.

"I am an old woman who will perhaps be called to God sooner than she imagines. The vows I took when I entered the service of this convent were not only vows to Christ. Nearly forty years ago upon becoming Abbess of Montglane, I vowed to keep a secret, to preserve it with my life if necessary. Now the time has come for me to keep that vow. But in doing so, I must share some of the secret with each of you and vow you to secrecy in return. My story is long, and you must have patience if I am slow in telling. When I have finished, you will know why each of us must do what must be done."

The abbess paused to take a sip of water from a silver chalice that sat before her on the table. Then she resumed.

"Today is the fourth day of April, Anno Domini 1790. My story begins on another fourth of April many years ago. The tale was told me by my predecessor, as it was told by each abbess to her successor on the event of her initiation, for as many years as this abbey has stood. And now I tell it to you. . . ."

THE ABBESS'S TALE

On the fourth of April in the year 782, a wondrous festival was held at the Oriental Palace at Aachen to honor the fortieth birthday of the great King Charlemagne. He had called forth all the nobles of his empire. The central court with its mosaic dome and tiered circular staircases and balconies was filled with imported palms and festooned with flower garlands. Harps and lutes were played in the large halls amid gold and silver lanterns. The courtiers, decked in purple, crimson, and gold, moved through a fairyland of jugglers, jesters, and puppet shows. Wild bears, lions, giraffes, and cages of doves were brought into the courtyard. All was merriment for weeks in anticipation of the king's birthday.

The pinnacle of the festival was the day itself. On the morning of this day the king arrived in the main courtyard surrounded by his eighteen children, his queen, and his favorite courtiers. Charlemagne was exceedingly tall, with the lean grace of a horseman and swimmer. His skin was tanned, his hair and mustache streaked blond with the sun. He looked every inch the warrior and ruler of the largest kingdom in the world. Dressed in a simple woolen tunic with a close-fitting coat of marten skins and wearing his ever-present sword, he passed through the court greeting each of his subjects and bidding them partake of the lavish refreshments that were placed on groaning boards about the hall.

The king had prepared a special treat for this day. A master of battle strategy, he had a special fondness for one game. Known as the game of war, the game of kings, it was the game of chess. On this, his fortieth birthday, Charlemagne proposed to play against the best chess player in his kingdom, a soldier known as Garin the Frank.

Garin entered the courtyard with blaring trumpets. Acrobats bounced before him, young women strewed palm fronds and rose petals in his path. Garin was a slender, pale young man with serious countenance and gray eyes, a soldier in the western army. He knelt when the king rose to greet him.

The chess service was borne into the great hall on the shoulders of eight black servants dressed in Moorish livery. These men, and the chessboard they carried aloft, had been sent as a gift of Ibn-al-Arabi, the Moslem governor of Barcelona, in thanks for the king's aid against the Pyrenees Basques four years earlier. It was during retreat from this famous battle, at the Roncesvalles Pass in Navarre, that the king's beloved soldier Hruoland had been killed, hero of the "Chanson de Roland." As a result of this unhappy association, the king had never played upon the chess service, nor brought it before his people.

The court marveled at the magnificent chess service as it was set upon a table in the courtyard. Though made by Arabic master craftsmen, the pieces bore traces of their Indian and Persian ancestry. For some believed this game existed in India over four hundred years before the birth of Christ and came into Arabia through Persia during the Arabic conquest of that country in 640 A.D.

The board, wrought entirely of silver and gold, measured a full meter on each side. The pieces of filigreed precious metals were studded with rubies, sapphires, diamonds, and emeralds, uncut but smoothly polished, some the size of quails' eggs. Flashing and sparkling in the lamplight of the courtyard, they seemed to glow with an inner light that hypnotized the beholder.

The piece called Shah, or King, was fifteen centimeters high and depicted a crowned man riding upon the back of an elephant. The Queen, or Ferz, was seated within a covered sedan chair embroidered with jewels. The Bishops were elephants with saddles encrusted in rare gems; the Knights were wild Arabian steeds. The Rooks, or Castles, were called Rukhkh, the Arabic word for "chariot"; these were large camels with towerlike chairs upon their backs. The pawns, or peons, as we call them now, were humble foot soldiers seven centimeters high with small jewels for eyes and gems flecking the hilts of their swords.

Charlemagne and Garin approached the board from either side. Then the king, raising his hand aloft, spoke words that astounded those of the court who knew him well.

"I propose a wager," he said in a strange voice. Charles was not a man for wagers. The courtiers glanced at one another uneasily.

"Should my soldier Garin win a game of me, I bestow upon him that portion of my kingdom from Aachen to the Basque Pyrenees and the hand of my eldest daughter in marriage. Should he lose, he will be beheaded in this same courtyard at dawn."

The court was in commotion. It was known that the king so loved his daughters that he had begged them never to marry during his lifetime.

The king's dearest friend, the Duke of Burgundy, seized him by the arm and drew him aside. "What manner of wager is this?" he whispered. "You have proposed a wager befitting a sottish barbarian!"

Charles seated himself at the table. He appeared to be in a trancelike state. The duke was mystified. Garin was himself confused. He looked into the duke's eyes, then without a word took his place at the board, accepting the wager. The pieces were selected, and as luck would have it, Garin chose white, giving him the advantage of the first move. The game began.

Perhaps it was the tension of the situation, but it appeared as the game progressed that the two players moved their pieces with a force and precision that transcended a mere game, as if another, an invisible hand, hovered above the board. At times it even seemed as if the very pieces carried out the moves of their own accord. The players themselves were silent and pale, and the courtiers hovered about them like ghosts.

After nearly one hour of play the Duke of Burgundy observed that the king was acting strangely. His brow was furrowed, and he seemed inattentive and distracted. Garin too was possessed by an unusual restlessness, his movements quick and jerking, his forehead beaded in cold sweat. The eyes of the two men were fixed upon the board as if they could not look away.

Suddenly Charles leaped to his feet with a cry, upsetting the board and knocking all the pieces to the floor. The courtiers pushed back to open the circle. The king had flown into a black and horrible rage, tearing at his hair and beating his chest like a wild beast. Garin and the Duke of Burgundy rushed to his side, but he knocked them away. It required six nobles to restrain the king. When at last he was subdued, he looked about in bewilderment, as if he had just awakened from a long sleep.

"My lord," said Garin softly, picking up one of the pieces from the floor and handing it to the king, "perhaps we should withdraw from this game. The pieces are all in disarray, and I cannot recall a single move that was made. Sire, I fear this Moorish chess service. I believe it is possessed by an evil force that compelled you to make a wager upon my life."

Charlemagne, resting upon a chair, put one hand wearily to his forehead but did not speak.

"Garin," said the Duke of Burgundy cautiously, "you know that the king does not believe in superstitions of this sort, thinking them pagan and barbaric. He has forbidden necromancy and divination at the court—"

Charlemagne interrupted, but his voice was weak as if from strenuous exhaustion. "How can I bring the Christian enlightenment to Europe when soldiers in my own army believe in witchcraft?"

"This magic has been practiced in Arabia and throughout the East from the beginning of time," Garin replied. "I do not believe in it, nor do I understand it. But"—Garin bent over the king and looked into his eyes—*"you felt it, too."*

"I was consumed by the rage of fire," Charlemagne admitted. "I could not control myself. I felt as one feels upon the morn of battle just as the troops are charging into the fray. I cannot explain it."

"But all things of heaven and of earth have a reason," said a voice from behind the shoulder of Garin. He turned, and there stood a black Moor, one of the eight who had borne the chess service into the room. The king nodded for the Moor to continue.

"From our Watar, or birthplace, come an ancient people called the Badawi, the 'dwellers in the desert.' Among these peoples, the blood wager is considered the most honorable. It is said that only the blood wager will remove the Habb, the black drop in the human heart which the archangel Gabriel removed from the breast of Muhammed. Your Highness has made a blood wager over the board, a wager upon a man's life, the highest form of justice. Muhammed says, 'Kingdom endureth with Kufr, infidelity to al-Islam, but Kingdom endureth *not* with Zulm, which is injustice.' "

"A wager of blood is always a wager of evil," replied Charlemagne. Garin and the Duke of Burgundy looked at the king in surprise, for had he not himself proposed such a wager only an hour before?

"No!" said the Moor stubbornly. "Through the blood wager one can attain Ghutah, the earthly oasis which is Paradise. If one makes such a wager over the board of Shatranj, it is the Shatranj itself that carries out the Sar!"

"Shatranj is the name that the Moors give to the game of chess, my lord," said Garin.

"And what is 'Sar'?" asked Charlemagne, rising slowly to his feet. He towered over everyone around him.

"It is revenge," replied the Moor without expression. He bowed and stepped back from the king.

"We will play again," the king announced. "This time, there will be no wagers. We play for love of a simple game. There is nothing to these foolish superstitions invented by barbarians and children." The courtiers began to set up the board again. There were murmurs of relief coursing through the room. Charles turned to the Duke of Burgundy and took his arm.

"Did I really make such a wager?" he said softly.

The duke looked at him in surprise. "Why, yes, my lord," he said. "Do you not remember it?"

"No," the king replied sadly.

Charlemagne and Garin sat down to play again. After a remarkable battle, Garin emerged victorious. The king awarded him the property of Montglane in the Bas-Pyrenees and the title of Garin de Montglane. So pleased was the king with Garin's masterful command of chess that he offered to build him a fortress to protect the territory he had won. After many years, the king sent Garin the special gift of the marvelous chess service upon which they had played their famous game. It was called ever after "the Montglane Service."

"That is the story of Montglane Abbey," the abbess said, concluding her tale. She looked across the sea of silent nuns. "For after many years, when Garin de Montglane lay ill and dying, he bequeathed to the Church his territory of Montglane, the fortress which was to become our abbey, and also the famous chess set called the Montglane Service."

The abbess paused a moment, as if uncertain whether to proceed. At last she spoke again.

"But Garin had always believed that there was a terrible curse connected with the Montglane Service. Long before it passed into his hands he had heard rumors of evils associated with it. It was said that Charlot, Charlemagne's own nephew, had been murdered during a game played upon this very board. There were strange stories of bloodshed and violence, even of wars, in which this service had played a part.

"The eight black Moors who had first conveyed the service from Barcelona into Charlemagne's keeping had begged to accompany the pieces when they passed over to Montglane. And so the king had permitted. Soon Garin learned that mysterious night ceremonies were being conducted within the fortress, rituals in which he felt certain the Moors had been involved. Garin grew to fear his prize as if it were a tool of the Devil. He had the service buried within the fortress, and asked Charlemagne to place a curse upon the wall to guard against its ever being removed. The king behaved as though it were a jest, but he complied with Garin's wish in his own fashion, and thus we find the inscription over our doors today."

The abbess stopped and, looking weak and pale, reached for the chair behind her. Alexandrine stood and helped the abbess to her seat.

"And what became of the Montglane Service, Reverend Mother?" asked one of the older nuns who was seated in the front row.

The abbess smiled. "I have told you already that our lives are in great danger if we remain in this abbey. I have told you that the soldiers of France seek to confiscate the treasures of the Church and are, in fact, abroad in that mission even now. I have told you further that a treasure of great value and perhaps great evil was once buried within the walls of this abbey. So it should come as no surprise to you if I reveal that the secret I was sworn to hold in my bosom when first I took this office was the secret of the Montglane Service. It is still buried within the walls and floor of this room, and I alone know the precise location of each piece. It is our mission, my daughters, to remove this tool of evil, to scatter it as far and wide as possible, that it may never again be assembled into the hands of one seeking power. For it contains a force that transcends the law of nature and the understanding of man.

"But even had we time to destroy these pieces or to deface them beyond recognition, I would not choose that path. Something with so great a power may also be used as an instrument of good. That is why I am sworn not only to keep the Montglane Service hidden, but to protect it. Perhaps one day, when history permits it, we shall reassemble the pieces and reveal their dark mystery."

Although the abbess knew the precise location of each piece, it required the effort of every nun in the abbey for nearly two weeks before the Montglane Service was exhumed and the pieces cleaned and polished. It required four nuns to lift the board loose from the stone floor. When it had been cleaned, it was found to contain strange symbols that had been cut or embossed into each square. Similar symbols had been carved into the bottom of each chess piece. Also there was a cloth that had been kept in a large metal box. The corners of the box had been sealed with a waxy substance, no doubt to prevent mildew. The cloth was of midnight blue velvet and heavily embroidered with gold thread and jewels in signs that resembled the zodiac. In the center of the cloth were two swirled, snakelike figures twined together to form the number 8. The abbess believed that this cloth had been used to cover the Montglane Service so that it would not be damaged when transported.

Near the end of the second week the abbess told the nuns to prepare themselves for travel. She would instruct each, in private, regarding where she would be sent so that none of the nuns would know the location of the others. This would reduce the risk to each. As the Montglane Service contained fewer pieces than the number of nuns at the abbey, no one but the abbess would know which of the sisters had carried away a portion of the service and which had not.

When Valentine and Mireille were called into the study, the abbess was seated behind her massive writing desk and bade them take a seat opposite her. There on the desk lay the gleaming Montglane Service, partly draped with its embroidered cloth of midnight blue.

The abbess laid aside her pen and looked up. Mireille and Valentine sat hand in hand, waiting nervously.

"Reverend Mother," Valentine blurted out, "I want you to know that I shall miss you very much now that I am to go away, and I realize that I have been a grievous burden to you. I wish I could have been a better nun and caused you less trouble—"

"Valentine," said the abbess, smiling as Mireille poked Valentine in the ribs to silence her. "What is it you wish to say? You fear you will be separated from your cousin Mireille—is that what is causing these belated apologies?" Valentine stared in amazement, wondering how the abbess had read her thoughts.

"I shouldn't be concerned," continued the abbess. She handed Mireille a sheet of paper across the cherry wood desk. "This is the name and address of the guardian who will be responsible for your care, and beneath it I've printed the traveling instructions I have arranged for you both."

"Both!" cried Valentine, barely able to remain in her seat. "Oh, Reverend Mother, you have fulfilled my fondest wish!"

The abbess laughed. "If I did not send you together, Valentine, I feel certain you would single-handedly find a way to destroy all the plans I've carefully arranged, only to remain at your cousin's side. Besides, I have good reason to send you off together. Listen closely. Each nun at this abbey has been provided for. Those whose families accept them back will be sent to their homes. In some cases I've found friends or remote relatives to provide them shelter. If they came to the abbey with dowries, I return these monies to them for their care and safekeeping. If no funds are available, I send the young woman to an abbey of good faith in another country. In all cases, travel and living expenses will be provided to ensure the well-being of my daughters." The abbess folded her hands and proceeded. "But you are fortunate in several respects, Valentine," she said. "Your grandfather has left you a generous income, which I earmark for both you and your cousin Mireille. In addition, though you have no family, you have a godfather who has accepted responsibility for you both. I have received written assurance of his willingness to act in your behalf. This brings me to my second point, an issue of grave concern."

Mireille had glanced at Valentine when the abbess spoke of a godfather, and now she looked down at the paper in her hand, where the abbess had printed in bold letters, "M. Jacques-Louis David, Painter," with an address beneath it, in Paris. She had not known Valentine had a godfather.

"I realize," the abbess went on, "when it is learned I've closed the abbey, there will be those in France who will be highly displeased. Many of us will be in danger, specifically from men such as the Bishop of Autun, who will wish to know what we have pried from the walls and carried away with us. You see, the traces of our activities cannot completely be covered. There may be women who are sought out and found. It may be necessary for them to flee. Because of this, I have selected eight of us, each of whom will have a piece of the service but who also will serve as collection points where the others may leave behind a piece if they must flee. Or leave directions how to find it. Valentine, you will be one of the eight."

"I!" said Valentine. She swallowed hard, for her throat had suddenly become very dry. "But Reverend Mother, I am not . . . I do not . . ."

"What you try to say is that you are scarcely a pillar of responsibility," said the abbess, smiling despite herself. "I am aware of this, and I rely upon your sober cousin to assist me with that problem." She looked at Mireille, and the latter nodded her assent.

"I have selected the eight not only with regard for their capabilities," the abbess continued, "but for their strategic placement. Your godfather, M. David, lives in Paris, the heart of the chessboard which is France. As a famous artist, he commands the respect and friendship of the nobility, but he is also a member of the Assembly and is considered by some to be a fervent revolutionary. I believe him to be in a position to protect you both in case of need. And I have paid him amply for your care to provide him a motive to do so."

The abbess peered across the table at the two young women. "This is not a request, Valentine," she said sternly. "Your sisters may be in trouble, and you will be in a position to serve them. I have given your name and address to some who have already departed for their homes. You will go to Paris and do as I say. You have fifteen years, enough to know that there are things in life more crucial than the gratification of your immediate wishes." The abbess spoke harshly, but then her face softened as it always did when she looked at Valentine. "Besides, Paris is not so bad a place of sentence," she added.

Valentine smiled back at the abbess. "No, Reverend Mother," she agreed. "There is the opera, for one thing, and perhaps there will be parties, and the ladies, they say, wear such beautiful gowns—" Mireille punched Valentine in the ribs again. "I mean, I humbly thank the Reverend Mother for placing such faith in her devout servant." At this, the abbess burst into a merry peal of laughter that belied her years.

"Very well, Valentine. You may both go and pack. You will leave tomorrow at dawn. Don't be tardy." Rising, the abbess lifted two heavy pieces from the board and handed them to the novices.

Valentine and Mireille in turn kissed the abbess's ring and with great care conveyed their rare possessions to the door of the study. As they were about to depart, Mireille turned and spoke for the first time since they had entered the room.

"If I may ask, Reverend Mother," she said, "where will you be going? We should like to think of you and send good wishes to you wherever you may be."

"I am departing on a journey that I have longed to take for over forty years," the abbess replied. "I have a friend whom I've not visited since childhood. In those days—you know, at times Valentine reminds me very much of this childhood friend of mine. I remember her as being so vibrant, so full of life. . . ." The abbess paused, and Mireille thought that if such a thing could be said of so stately a person, the abbess looked wistful.

"Does your friend live in France, Reverend Mother?" she asked.

"No," replied the abbess. "She lives in Russia."

The following morning, in the dim gray light, two women dressed in traveling clothes left the Abbey of Montglane and climbed into a wagon filled with hay. The wagon passed through the massive gates and started across the back bowls of the mountains. A light mist rose, obscuring them from view as they passed down into the far valley.

They were frightened and, drawing their capes about themselves, felt thankful that they were on a mission of God as they reentered the world from which they had so long been sheltered.

But it was not God who watched them silently from the mountaintop as the wagon slowly descended into the darkness of the valley floor below. High on a snow-capped peak above the abbey sat a solitary rider astride a pale horse. He watched until the wagon had vanished into the dark mist. Then he turned his horse without a sound and rode away.

PAWN TO QUEEN'S FOURTH

The Queen Pawn openings—those which start with P–Q4—are "close" openings. This means that the tactical contact between the opposing forces develops very slowly. There is room for a great deal of maneuvering, and it takes time to come to grips in fierce hand-to-hand fighting with the enemy. . . . Positional chess is of the essence here.

—Complete Book of Chess Openings
Fred Reinfeld

A servant overheard in the marketplace that Death was looking for him. He raced home and told his master he must flee to the neighboring town of Samarrah, so that Death would not find him.

After supper that night, there was a knock upon the door. The master opened it and saw Death standing there, in his long black robes and hood. Death inquired after the servant.

"He is ill in bed," lied the master hastily. "He is too sick to be disturbed."

"That's odd," said Death. "Then he is surely in the wrong place. For I had an appointment with him tonight at midnight. In Samarrah."

—Legend of the Appointment in Samarrah

I was in trouble. Big trouble.

It began that New Year's Eve, the last day of 1972. I had a date with a fortune-teller. But like that fellow with the appointment in Samarrah, I'd tried to flee my own fate by avoiding it. I didn't want some palm reader telling me the future. I had enough problems in the here and now. By New Year's Eve of 1972 I had completely messed up my life. And I was only twenty-three years old.

Instead of running off to Samarrah I had run off to the data center atop the Pan Am Building in midtown Manhattan. It was a lot closer than Samarrah and, at ten P.M. on New Year's Eve, as remote and isolated as a mountaintop.

I felt as if I *were* on a mountaintop. Snow swirled around the windows that overlooked Park Avenue, the large, graceful flakes hanging in colloidal suspension. It was like being inside one of those paperweights that contain a single perfect rose or a small replica of a Swiss village. But within the glass walls of the Pan Am data center lay several acres of gleaming state-of-the-art hardware, humming softly as it controlled the routing and ticketing of airplanes all over the world. It was a quiet place to get away and think.

I had a lot of thinking to do. Three years earlier I'd come to New York to work for Triple-M, one of the largest computer manufacturers in the world. At that time Pan Am had been one of my clients. They still let me use their data center.

But now I had switched jobs, which might well prove to be the biggest mistake I'd ever made. I had the dubious honor of being the first woman ever hired into the professional ranks of that venerable CPA firm Fulbright, Cone, Kane & Upham. And they didn't like my style.

"CPA," for those who don't know, stands for "certified public accountant." Fulbright, Cone, Kane & Upham was one of the eight biggest CPA firms in the world, a brotherhood appropriately dubbed "the Big Eight."

"Public accountant" is a polite name for "auditor." The Big Eight provided this dreaded service for most major corporations. They commanded a lot of respect, which is a polite way of saying that they had their clients by the balls. If the Big Eight suggested during an audit that their client spend half a million dollars improving his financial systems, the client would be foolish to ignore the suggestion. (Or to ignore the fact that his Big Eight audit firm could provide the service *for* him—at a fee.) These things were implicitly understood in the world of high finance. There was a lot of money in public accounting. Even a junior partner could command an income of six figures.

Some people might not realize that the public accounting field is certified male only, but Fulbright, Cone, Kane & Upham sure did, and that placed *me* in something of a jam. Because I was the first woman they'd ever seen who wasn't a secretary, they treated me as if I were a commodity as rare as the dodo bird—something potentially dangerous that ought to be scrutinized with care.

Being the first woman *anything* is no picnic. Whether you're the first woman astronaut or the first woman admitted to a Chinese laundry, you must learn to accept the usual razzing, sniggering, and ogling of legs. You also have to accept working harder than anyone else and getting a smaller paycheck.

I'd learned to act amused when they introduced me as "Miss Velis, our woman specialist in this area." With press like that, people probably thought I was a gynecologist.

In fact, I was a computer expert, the best transportation industry specialist in New York. That's why they'd hired me. When the partnership of Fulbright Cone had looked me over, dollar signs had rung up in their bloodshot eyeballs; they saw not a woman, but a walking portfolio of blue-chip accounts. Young enough to be impressionable, naïve enough to be impressed, innocent enough to turn over my clients to the sharklike jaws of their audit staff—I was everything they were looking for in a woman. But the honeymoon was brief.

A few days before Christmas I was completing an equipment evaluation so a big shipping client could purchase computer hardware before year end, when our senior partner, Jock Upham, paid a visit to my office.

Jock was over sixty, tall and lean and contrivedly youthful. He played a lot of tennis, wore crisp Brooks Brothers suits, and dyed his hair. When he walked he sprang forward on the balls of his feet as if he were going for a net shot.

Jock sprang into my office.

"Velis," he said in a hearty, backslapping voice, "I've been thinking over this study you're doing. I've argued with myself about it, and I think I've finally figured out what was bothering me." This was Jock's way of saying that there was really no point in disagreeing with him. He'd already played devil's advocate with both sides, and his side, whichever he'd set his heart on, had won.

"I've nearly finished it, sir. It's due to the client tomorrow, so I hope you don't want any extensive changes."

"Nothing major," he told me as he gently set the bomb down. "I've decided that printers will be more critical to our clients than disk drives, and I'd like you to change the selection criteria accordingly."

This was an example of what's referred to in the computer business as "fixing the numbers." And it is illegal. Six hardware vendors had submitted sealed bids to our client a month earlier. These bids were based upon selection criteria that we, the impartial auditors, had prepared. We said the client needed powerful disk drives, and one vendor had come up with the best proposal. If we decided now, after the bids were in, that printers were more important than disk drives, it would throw the contract in favor of another vendor, and I could guess just which vendor that might be: the one whose president had taken Jock to lunch only that afternoon.

Clearly something of value had passed under the table. Perhaps a promise of future business for our firm, perhaps there was a little yacht or sports car in it for Jock. But whatever the deal, I wanted no part in it.

"I'm sorry, sir," I told him, "but it's too late to change the criteria now without the client's approval. We could call and tell him we want to ask the vendors for a supplement to the original bid, but of course that would mean they couldn't order the equipment until after New Year."

"That won't be necessary, Velis," said Jock. "I didn't become senior partner of this firm by ignoring my intuition. Many's the time I've acted in my clients' behalf and saved them millions in the blink of an eye, without their ever knowing about it. It's that gut-level survival instinct that has put our firm at the very top of the Big Eight, year after year." He flashed me a dimpled smile.

The odds that Jock Upham would do something for a client without taking full credit were about the same as the proverbial camel squeezing through the needle's eye. But I let it pass.

"Nevertheless, sir, we have a moral responsibility to our client to weigh and evaluate sealed bids fairly. After all, we *are* an audit firm."

Jock's dimples disappeared as if he'd swallowed them. "Surely you can't mean that you're refusing to take my suggestion?"

"If it's only a suggestion and not an order, I'd prefer not to do it."

"What if I made it an order?" said Jock slyly. "As senior partner of this firm, I—"

"Then I'm afraid I'd have to resign from the project, sir, and turn it over to someone else. Of course I'd keep copies of my working papers in case there were questions later." Jock knew what that meant. CPA firms were never audited themselves. The only people in a position to ask questions were people from the U.S. government. And *their* questions regarded illegal or fraudulent practices.

"I see," said Jock. "Well, I'll leave you to your work, then, Velis. It's clear I'll have to make this decision on my own." And he abruptly turned on his heel and left the room.

My manager, a beefy blond fellow in his thirties named Lisle Holmgren, came to see me the very next morning. Lisle was agitated, his thinning hair disheveled and his necktie skewed.

"Catherine, what the hell did you do to Jock Upham?" were the first words out of his mouth. "He's as mad as a wet hen. Called me in this morning at the crack of dawn. I barely had time to shave. He says he wants you put in a strait jacket, that you're off your rocker. He doesn't want you exposed to any clients in the future, says you're not ready to play ball with the big boys."

Lisle's life revolved around the firm. He had a demanding wife who measured success in country club fees. Though he might have disapproved of it, he toed the party line.

"I guess I lost my head last night," I said sarcastically. "I refused to throw a bid. I told him he could turn it over to someone else if that was what he wanted."

Lisle sank down on a chair beside me. He didn't say anything for a moment.

"Catherine, there are a lot of things in the business world that may seem unethical to someone of your age. But they aren't necessarily the way they look."

"This one was."

"I give you my word that if Jock Upham asked you to do something like that, he had his reasons."

"I'll bet. My guess is that he had thirty or forty grand worth of good reasons," I told him, and went back to my paperwork.

"You're slashing your own wrists, do you realize that?" he asked me. "You don't screw around with a fellow like Jock Upham. He won't go quietly back to his corner like a nice boy. He won't roll over and play dead. If you want my advice, I think you ought to march up to his office right now and apologize. Tell him you'll do anything he asks, stroke his feathers. If you don't, I can tell you right now, your career is finished."

"He wouldn't fire me for refusing to do something illegal," I said.

"He wouldn't have to fire you. He's in a position to make you so miserable you'd wish you had never set foot in this place. You're a nice girl, Catherine, and I like you. You've heard my opinion. Now I'll leave you to write your own epitaph."

That was one week ago. I had not apologized to Jock. I had not mentioned our conversation to anyone. And I'd sent my bid recommendation to the client the day before Christmas, according to schedule. Jock's candidate had not won the bid. Since then, things had been very quiet around the venerable firm of Fulbright, Cone, Kane & Upham. Until this morning, that is.

It had taken the partnership exactly seven days to figure out to what form of torture they'd subject me. This morning, Lisle had arrived in my office with the glad tidings.

"Well," he said, "you can't say I didn't warn you. That's the trouble with women, they never listen to reason." Someone flushed the toilet in the "office" next to mine, and I waited for the sounds to die away. A premonition of the future.

"Do you know what reasoning after the fact is called?" I said. "It's called rationalizing."

"Where you're going, you're going to have plenty of time to rationalize," he said. "The partnership met bright and early this morning, over coffee and jelly doughnuts, and voted on your fate. It was a close toss-up between Calcutta and Algiers, but you'll be happy to know that Algiers won. Mine was the deciding vote. I hope you appreciate it."

"What are you talking about?" I said, getting a cold, clammy feeling at the pit of my stomach. "Where the hell is Algiers? What does it have to do with me?"

"Algiers is the capital of Algeria, a socialist country on the coast of North Africa, a card-carrying member of the Third World. I think you'd better take this book and read up on it." He threw a large volume on my desk and continued. "As soon as your visa's approved, which should take about three months, you'll be spending a lot of time there. It's your new assignment."

"What have I been assigned to *do*?" I said. "Or is this just a general exile?"

"No, we actually have a project starting over there. We get work in lots of exotic places. This is a one-year gig for some minor Third World social club that meets occasionally to chat about the price of gasoline. It's called OTRAM or something. Just a minute, I'll look it up." He pulled some papers out of his jacket pocket and leafed through them. "Here it is, it's called OPEC."

"Never heard of it," I said. In December of 1972 not many people in the world had heard of OPEC. Though their ears were soon to be unplugged.

"Neither have I," Lisle admitted. "That's why the partnership thought it was such a perfect assignment for you. They want you buried, Velis, just as I said." The toilet flushed again, and with it all my hopes went down the drain.

"We received a cable from the Paris office several weeks ago asking if we had computer experts in the field of oil, natural gas, power plants—they'd take anyone we had, and we'd get a fat commission. No one on our senior consulting staff was willing to go. Energy is simply not a high-growth industry. It's considered a dead-end assignment. We were about to cable back that we had no takers when *your* name came popping up."

They couldn't force me to accept this assignment; slavery had ended with the Civil War. They wanted to push me into resigning from the firm, but I was damned if I'd let them off so easily.

"What will I be doing for these Third World good old boys?" I said sweetly. "I don't know anything at all about oil. And of natural gas, I know only what I hear from the next office." I motioned to the toilet.

"I'm glad you asked," said Lisle as he crossed to the door. "You've been

assigned to Con Edison until you leave the country. They burn everything that
floats down the East River in that power plant of theirs. You'll be an expert
in energy conversion in a few months."

Lisle laughed and waved over his shoulder as he went out. "Cheer up, Velis.
It might have been Calcutta."

∞

So here I was, sitting in the Pan Am data center in the middle of the night
boning up on a country I'd never heard of, on a continent I knew nothing about,
so I could become an expert in a field I had no interest in and go to live among
people who didn't speak my language and who probably thought women
belonged in harems. Well, they had a lot in common with the partnership of
Fulbright Cone, I thought. On both counts.

I remained undaunted. It had only taken me three years to learn everything
there was to know about the field of transportation. Learning as much about
energy seemed simpler. You dug a hole in the ground and oil came out, how
tough was that? But it would be a painful experience, if all the books I read
were as scintillating as the one before me:

> In 1950, Arabian light crude sold for $2 per bbl. And in 1972 it is
> still selling for $2 per bbl. This makes Arabian light crude one of
> the world's few significant raw materials subject to *no* inflationary
> increase in a similar period of time. The explanation for this phe-
> nomenon is the rigorous control that has been placed by world
> governments upon this fundamental raw product.

Fascinating. But what I found *truly* fascinating was what the book did not
explain. Something, indeed, that was not explained in any of the books I'd read
that night.

Arabian light crude, it seems, was a kind of oil. It was in fact the most highly
prized and sought-after oil in the world. The reason the price had remained the
same for over twenty years was that the price was not controlled by the people
who bought it or by the people who owned the land it sat beneath. It was
controlled by the people who distributed it, the infamous middlemen. And it
always had been.

There were eight large oil companies in the world. Five were American; the
remaining three were British, Dutch, and French. Fifty years earlier some of
these oilmen had decided, during a grouse shoot in Scotland, to divide up the
world's oil distribution and get off each other's toes. A few months later they
convened at Ostend with a chap named Calouste Gulbenkian, who had arrived
with a red pencil in his pocket. Taking it out, he drew what was later called

"the Thin Red Line" around a chunk of the world that contained the old Ottoman Empire, now Iraq and Turkey, and a good slice of the Persian Gulf. The gentlemen divided it up and drilled a hole. The oil gushed out in Bahrain, and the race was on.

The law of supply and demand is a moot point if you are the world's largest consumer of a product and you also control the supply. According to the charts I read, America had long been the most conspicuous consumer of oil. And these oil companies, the preponderance of them American, controlled the supply. The way they did it was simple. They contracted to develop (or find) the oil for the price of owning a healthy share, and they transported and distributed it, receiving an additional mark-up.

I sat there alone with the massive pile of books I'd assembled from the Pan Am technical and business library, the only library in New York that was open all night on New Year's Eve. I watched the snow sift down through the yellow streetlamps that ran the length of Park Avenue. And I thought.

The thought that ran through my mind over and over was one that would preoccupy better minds than mine in the months ahead. It was a thought that would keep heads of state awake and make heads of oil companies rich. It was a thought that would precipitate wars and bloodshed and economic crises and bring the major powers to the brink of a third world war. But at the time, it did not seem to me such a revolutionary concept.

The thought was simply this: What if we *didn't* control the world's supply of oil? The answer to that question, eloquent in its simplicity, would appear in twelve months' time to the rest of the world, in the form of the Handwriting on the Wall.

It was our appointment in Samarrah.

A QUIET MOVE

Positional: relating to a move, manoeuvre or style of play governed by strategic rather than tactical considerations. Thus a positional move is also likely to be a *quiet move*.

Quiet Move: a move that neither checks nor captures and which does not contain any direct threats. . . . This apparently gives Black the greatest freedom of action.

—An Illustrated Dictionary of Chess
Edward R. Brace

A phone was ringing somewhere. I picked my head up from the desk and looked around. It took me a moment before I realized that I was still at the Pan Am data center. It was still New Year's Eve; the wall clock at the far end of the room said it was a quarter past eleven. It was still snowing. I had fallen asleep for over an hour. I wondered why no one was picking up the phones.

I looked around the data center, across the expanse of white-tiled false flooring. It covered miles of coaxial cable packed like earthworms into the bowels of the building. There was no one moving anywhere; the place was like a morgue.

Then I remembered that I had told the machine operators they could take a break while I watched things for them. But that was hours ago. Now, as I grudgingly got up to cross to the switchboard, I realized that their request had seemed strange. "Do you mind if we go into the tape vault to do some crocheting?" they had asked. Crocheting?

I reached the control desk that ran the switchboards and machine consoles for this floor and hooked up with the security gates and mantraps all over the building. I pushed the button for the phone line that was flashing. I also noticed that drive sixty-three had a red light, indicating it needed to have a tape mounted. I buzzed the tape vault to call an operator onto the floor, and I picked up the phone, rubbing my eyes sleepily.

"Pan Am night shift," I said.

"You see?" said the honeyed voice with its unmistakable upper-class British accent. "I *told* you she would be working! She's *always* working." He was speaking to someone at the other end. Then he said, "Cat darling, you're *late*! We're all waiting for you. It's after eleven o'clock. Don't you realize what tonight is?"

"Llewellyn," I said, painfully stretching my arms and legs to get the kinks out. "I really can't come, I've got work to do. I know I promised, but—"

"No 'buts,' darling. On New Year's Eve we must all find out what fate has in store for us. We've all had our fortunes told, and it was too, too amusing. Now it's your turn. Harry's pushing me here, he wants to speak with you."

I groaned and pushed the buzzer again for the operator. Where *were* the goddamned operators, anyway? And why on earth would three grown men want to spend New Year's Eve in a dark, cold tape vault, knitting booties?

"Darling," boomed Harry in his deep baritone that always made me hold the receiver away from my ear. Harry had been my client when I'd worked for Triple-M, and we had remained good friends. He'd adopted me into his family and at every chance invited me to social events, cramming me down the throats of his wife, Blanche, and her brother Llewellyn. But Harry's real hope was that I'd befriend his obnoxious daughter, Lily, who was about my age. Not bloody likely.

"Darling," said Harry, "I hope you'll forgive, but I just sent Saul with the car for you."

"You shouldn't have sent the car, Harry," I said. "Why didn't you ask me before you sent Saul out in the snow?"

"Because you would have said no," Harry pointed out. Which was quite true. "Besides, Saul likes to drive around. That's his job, he's a chauffeur. With what I'm paying him, he can't complain. Anyway, you owe me this favor."

"I don't owe you any favors, Harry," I said. "Let's not forget who's done what for whom."

Two years earlier I had installed a transportation system for Harry's company that had made him the top wholesale furrier not only in New York, but in the Northern Hemisphere. "Harry's Quality Thrifty Furs" could now deliver a custom-made coat anywhere in twenty-four hours. I pushed the buzzer irritably as the red light for the tape drive glowed before me. Where *were* the operators?

"Look, Harry," I said impatiently, "I don't know how you found me, but I came here to be alone. I can't discuss it now, but I have a big problem. . . ."

"Your problem is that you're always working and you're always alone."

"My company is the problem," I said testily. "They're trying to shove me into a new career I know nothing about. They're planning to ship me overseas. I need time to think, time to figure out what I'm doing."

"I *told* you," Harry bellowed into my ear. "You should never trust those goyim. Lutheran accountants, whoever heard of such a thing? Okay, so maybe I married one, but I don't let them do my *books*, if you see what I mean. So you'll get your coat and go downstairs like a good girl. You'll come have a drink and kvetch to me about it. Besides, this fortune-teller is *incredible*! She's been working here for years, but I've never heard of her before. If I'd known about her, I'd have fired my broker and gone to her instead."

"You can't be serious," I told him in disgust.

"Have I ever kidded you? Listen, she *knew* you were supposed to be here tonight. The very first thing out of her mouth when she got to our table was, 'Where's your friend with the computers?' Can you believe that?"

"No, I'm afraid I can't," I told him. "Where are you, anyway?"

"I'm telling you, darling. This dame kept insisting you come down here. She even told me that your fortune and mine were linked together somehow. That's not all, she knew *Lily* was supposed to be here, too."

"Lily couldn't come?" I said. I was more than relieved to hear it, but I wondered how his only child could leave him alone on New Year's. She must have known how hurt he'd be.

"Daughters, what can you do with them? I need some moral support down here. I'm stuck with my brother-in-law as the life of the party."

"Okay, I'll come," I told him.

"Great. I knew you'd do it. So you'll meet Saul in front, and you'll have a big hug when you get here."

I hung up feeling more depressed than I had before. Just what I needed, an evening listening to the inanities of Harry's extremely boring family. But Harry always made me laugh. Maybe it would take my mind off my own problems.

I strode across the data center to the tape vault and swung the door open. The operators were there, passing around a little glass tube full of white powder. They looked up guiltily as I entered and held the glass tube out to me. Evidently what they'd said was "do some *cocaine*," not "crocheting."

"I'm leaving for the night," I told them. "Do you guys think you can pull it together enough to mount a tape on drive sixty-three, or should we just close down the airline for tonight?"

They scrambled over each other to respond to my request. I picked up my coat and bag and went out to the elevators.

The big black limousine was already there when I got downstairs. I could see Saul through the windows as I crossed the lobby. He jumped out of the car and ran to open the heavy glass doors.

A hatchet-faced man with big creases running down either side of his face from cheekbone to jaw, Saul was hard to miss in a crowd. He was well over six feet, nearly as tall as Harry, but as skinny as Harry was fat. Together they looked like concave and convex reflections in funhouse mirrors. Saul's uniform was lightly powdered with snow, and he took my arm so I wouldn't slip on the ice. He grinned as he put me into the backseat.

"Couldn't turn Harry down?" he said. "He's a hard man to say no to."

"He's impossible," I agreed. "I'm not sure 'no' is a word he understands. Where exactly is this mystical coven taking place?"

"Fifth Avenue Hotel," said Saul, slamming the door behind me and going around to the driver's side. He started up the engine, and we whisked away through the deepening snow.

On New Year's Eve the major thoroughfares of New York are nearly as crowded as they are in broad daylight. Taxis and limos cruise the avenues, and carousers wander the pavements in search of one more bar. The streets are littered with streamers and confetti, and a general hysteria pervades the air.

Tonight was no exception. We nearly hit a few stragglers who stumbled out of a bar into Saul's fender, and a champagne bottle flew out of an alley and bounced off the hood of the limousine.

"This is going to be a rough ride," I observed to Saul.

"I'm used to it," he replied. "I take Mr. Rad and his family out every New Year's, and it's always the same. I should get combat pay."

"How long have you been with Harry?" I asked him as we *whoosh*ed down Fifth Avenue past gleaming buildings and dimly lighted storefronts.

"Twenty-five years," he said. "I started with Mr. Rad before Lily was born. Even before he was married, in fact."

"You must like working for him," I said.

"It's a job," Saul replied. Then, after a moment, he added, "I respect Mr. Rad. I've been through some hard times with him. I remember times when he couldn't afford to pay me, but he did it anyway, even if he had to go without. He liked having a limo. He said having a driver gave him a touch of class." Saul drew up at a red light, turned, and spoke to me over his shoulder. "You know, in the old days we used to deliver the furs in the limo. We were the first furriers in New York to do that." There was a touch of pride in his voice. "Nowadays I mostly drive Mrs. Rad and her brother to go shopping when Mr. Rad doesn't need me. Or I drive Lily to the matches."

We drove on in silence until we got to lower Fifth Avenue.

"I understand Lily hasn't shown up this evening," I commented.

"No," Saul agreed.

"That's why I left work. What could possibly be so important that she couldn't spend a few hours on New Year's with her father?"

"You know what she's doing," said Saul as he pulled the car up in front of the Fifth Avenue Hotel. Perhaps it was my imagination, but his voice sounded a little embittered. "She's doing what she always does. She's playing chess."

The Fifth Avenue Hotel sat on the west side of Fifth a few blocks above Washington Square Park. I could see the trees piled with snow as thick as whipped cream, forming little peaks like gnomes' caps around the massive arch that marked the entrance to Greenwich Village.

In 1972 the public bar of the hotel had not yet been renovated. Like many New York hotel bars, it so authentically replicated a Tudor country inn that you felt you should be tying up a horse outside instead of stepping out of a limousine. The large windows overlooking the street were surmounted with heavy ornamentation in beveled and stained glass. A roaring fire in the big stone fireplace illuminated the faces of the revelers within and cast a ruby glow through the bits of stained glass, reflecting on the snowy street outside.

Harry had secured a round oak table near the windows. As we pulled up in front I could see him waving to us, leaning forward so his breath made a frosty blush against the glass. Llewellyn and Blanche were in the background, seated across the table, whispering together like a pair of blond Botticelli angels.

It was like a picture postcard, I thought as Saul helped me out of the car. The roaring fire, the crowded bar with people in their holiday cocktail attire moving about in the firelight. It didn't look real. I stood on the snow-packed pavement and watched the sparkling snow fall through the streetlamps as Saul drove off. A second later Harry came rushing out into the street to retrieve me, as if he were afraid I would melt away like a snowflake and disappear.

"Darling!" he cried, giving me a big bear hug that nearly crushed me. Harry was gigantic. He was six feet four or five, and to say he was overweight would have been kind. He was a towering mountain of flesh, with saggy eyes and jowly cheeks that made him look like a St. Bernard. He was wearing a preposterous dinner jacket of red, green, and black tartan that, if possible, made him look even bigger.

"I'm so glad you're here," he said, taking my arm and propelling me through the lobby and the heavy double doors into the bar, where Llewellyn and Blanche were waiting.

"Dear, *dear* Cat," said Llewellyn, rising from his seat to give me a peck on the cheek. "Blanche and I were just wondering would you *ever* arrive, weren't we, Dearest?" Llewellyn always called Blanche "Dearest," the name Little Lord Fauntleroy had called his mother.

"Honestly, darling," he continued, "prying you away from that computer of yours is like wresting Heathcliff from the deathbed of the proverbial Catherine. I swear, I often wonder what you and Harry would *do* if you didn't have businesses to rush to every day."

"Hello, darling," said Blanche, motioning me to bend down so she could offer me her cool porcelain cheek. "You're looking wonderful, as usual. Do sit down. What should Harry get you to drink?"

"I'm getting her an eggnog," said Harry, beaming over us all like a cheerful plaid Christmas tree. "They have wonderful eggnog here. You'll have some, then choose whatever you like after that." He plowed away into the crowd toward the bar, his head towering above everyone else's in the room.

"So Harry tells us you're going off to Europe?" said Llewellyn, sitting beside me and reaching to Blanche, who handed over his drink. They were wearing matching outfits, she in a dark green evening gown that set off her creamy complexion and he in black tie with dark green velvet evening jacket. Though they were both in their mid-forties, they were extremely youthful, but beneath the gleam and polish of the golden façades they were like show dogs, silly and inbred despite the grooming.

"Not to Europe," I replied. "To Algiers. It's a sort of punishment. Algiers is a city in Algeria—"

"I know where it is," said Llewellyn. He and Blanche had exchanged glances. "But what a coincidence, wouldn't you say, Dearest?"

"I shouldn't mention this to Harry if I were you," said Blanche, toying with her double rope of perfectly matched pearls. "He has quite an antagonism toward the Arabs. You should hear him go on."

"You won't enjoy it," added Llewellyn. "It's a dreadful place. Poverty, dirt, cockroaches. And couscous, a dreadful concoction made of steamed pasta and mutton loaded with lard."

"Have you been there?" I asked, delighted that Llewellyn had such cheery observations on the place of my impending exile.

"Not I," he said. "But I've been looking for someone to go there for me. Don't breathe a word, darling, but I believe I've found a patron at last. You may realize that I've had to rely upon Harry financially from time to time . . ."

No one knew better than I the scale of Llewellyn's indebtedness to Harry. Even if Harry had not spoken about it incessantly, the state of Llewellyn's antique shop on Madison Avenue told the story. Salespeople leaped at you when you walked in the door as if it were a used-car lot. Most successful antique stores in New York sold by appointment only—not by ambush.

"But now," Llewellyn was saying, "I've discovered a patron who collects very rare pieces. If I can locate and acquire one that he's been looking for, it might just be my ticket to independence."

"You mean what he wants is in Algeria?" I said, glancing at Blanche. She was sipping her champagne cocktail and appeared not to be listening to the conversation. "If I go at all, it won't be for three months until my visa comes through. Besides, Llewellyn, why can't you go yourself?"

"It isn't that simple," said Llewellyn. "My contact over there is an antique dealer. He knows where the piece is located, but doesn't own it. The owner is a recluse. It may require a little effort and some time. It would be simpler for someone who was already in residence. . . ."

"Why don't you show her the picture," said Blanche in a quiet voice. Llewellyn looked at her, nodded, and pulled from his breast pocket a folded color photograph that looked as if it had been torn out of a book. He flattened it on the table before me.

It showed a large carving, apparently in ivory or lightly colored wood, of a man seated on a throne-type chair, riding on the back of an elephant. Standing on the elephant's back and supporting the chair were several small foot soldiers, and around the base of the elephant's legs were larger men on horseback carrying medieval weapons. It was a magnificent carving, obviously quite old. I wasn't

certain what it was meant to signify, but as I looked at it I suddenly felt a kind
of chill. I glanced at the windows near our table.

"What do you think of it?" asked Llewellyn. "It's remarkable, isn't it?"

"Do you feel a draft?" I said. But Llewellyn shook his head. Blanche was
watching me to see what I thought.

Llewellyn went on, "It's an Arabic copy of an Indian ivory. This one is
located in the Bibliothèque Nationale in Paris. You could have a look at it if
you stop off in Europe. But I believe the Indian piece it was copied from was
really a copy of a far older piece that has not yet been found. It's called 'the
Charlemagne King.' "

"Did Charlemagne ride elephants? I thought that was Hannibal."

"It isn't a carving *of* Charlemagne. It's the King from a chess set that
supposedly *belonged* to Charlemagne. This is the copy of a copy. The original
piece is legendary. No one that I know has ever seen it."

"How do you know it exists, then?" I wanted to know.

"It exists," said Llewellyn. "The entire chess set is described in *The Legend
of Charlemagne.* My patron has already acquired several pieces from the collection, and he wants the complete set. He's willing to pay really large sums of
money for the others. But he wishes to remain anonymous. This must all be
kept very confidential, my darling. I believe the originals are made entirely of
twenty-four-karat gold and embedded with rare gemstones."

I stared at Llewellyn, uncertain whether I was hearing correctly. Then I
realized what he was setting me up to do.

"Llewellyn, there are laws about removing gold and jewels from countries,
not to mention objects of rare historical value. Are you crazy, or do you want
to get me thrown into some Arabian prison?"

"Ah. Harry is coming back," said Blanche calmly, standing up as if to stretch
her long legs. Llewellyn hastily folded the picture and returned it to his pocket.

"Not a word of this to my brother-in-law," he whispered. "We'll discuss it
again before you go off on your trip. If you're interested, there may be a great
deal of money in it for both of us." I shook my head and stood up too as Harry
arrived bearing a tray of glasses.

"Why, look," said Llewellyn aloud, "here is Harry with the eggnogs, and
he's brought one for each of us! How perfectly delightful of him." Leaning
toward me, he whispered, "I *abhor* eggnog. Pig swill, that's what it is." But he
took the tray from Harry and helped him set the glasses all around.

"Darling," said Blanche, looking at her jeweled wrist watch, "Now that
Harry is back and we're all here, why don't you run off and find the fortune-
teller. It's a quarter of twelve, and Cat should have her fortune read before the
New Year turns." Llewellyn nodded and went off, relieved that he might be
able to miss the eggnog after all.

Harry looked after him suspiciously. "You know," he told Blanche, "we've been married for twenty-five years, and every year I've been wondering who was pouring my eggnog into the plants at our Christmas parties."

"The eggnog's very good," I said. It was rich and creamy and tasted wonderfully of booze.

"That brother of yours . . ." said Harry. "In all the years I've been supporting him and he's been pouring my eggnog into the plants, this fortune-teller turns out to be the first really good idea he's had."

"Actually," said Blanche, "it was Lily who recommended her, though heaven knows how she found out there was a palm reader working at the Fifth Avenue Hotel! Perhaps she had a chess contest here," she added dryly. "They seem to be having them everywhere these days."

While Harry talked ad nauseam about getting Lily away from playing chess, Blanche resigned herself to making disparaging remarks. Each blamed the other for having produced so aberrant a creation as their only child.

Not only did Lily play chess, she thought of nothing else. She wasn't interested in business or marriage—double thorns in Harry's side. Blanche and Llewellyn abhorred the "uncultivated" places and people she frequented. To be frank, the obsessive arrogance this game engendered in her was pretty hard to take. Her total accomplishment in life was pushing a bunch of wooden pieces around a board. I found a certain justice in her family's attitude.

"Let me tell you what the fortune-teller told me about Lily," said Harry, ignoring Blanche. "She said a younger woman outside my family would play an important role in my life."

"Harry liked that, as you can imagine," said Blanche, smiling.

"She said that in the game of life pawns are the very heartbeat, and the pawn could change its ways if another woman helped out. I think she was referring to you—"

"She said, 'The pawns are the soul of chess,'" Blanche interrupted him. "It's a quotation, I believe. . . ."

"How can you remember that?" said Harry.

"Because Llew wrote it all down here on a cocktail napkin," Blanche replied. "'In the game of life the pawns are the soul of chess. And even a lowly pawn can change its dress. Someone you love will turn the tide. The woman who brings her to the fold will cut the bonds identified, and bring the end that was foretold.'" Blanche put down the napkin and took a sip of champagne without looking at us.

"You see?" said Harry happily. "I interpret this to mean that you will somehow work a miracle—get Lily to lay off chess for a while, lead a normal life."

"I shouldn't hold my breath if I were you," Blanche said somewhat coldly.

Just then Llewellyn arrived with the fortune-teller in tow. Harry stood up and stepped aside to make a place for her beside me. My first impression was that a joke was being played on me. She was downright bizarre; a real antique. All hunched over, with a bubble hairdo that looked like a wig, she peered at me through batwing eyeglasses studded with rhinestones. These were fastened about her neck with a long chain of looped colored rubber bands, such as those children make. She was wearing a pink sweater embroidered in seed-pearl daisies, ill-fitting green trousers, and bright pink bowling shoes with the name "Mimsy" stitched on the tops. She carried a Masonite clipboard that she consulted occasionally, as if keeping a running tab of strikes and spares. She was also chewing Juicy Fruit gum. I got a waft of it whenever she spoke.

"This is your friend?" she said in a high-pitched squeak. Harry nodded and handed her some money, which she tucked into her clipboard, making a brief notation. Then she sat beside me, and Harry took a seat at her other side. She looked at me.

"Now, darling," said Harry, "just nod if she's right. It may throw her off. . . ."

"Who's telling this fortune, anyway?" snapped the old lady, still studying me through her beady glasses. She sat there for quite some time, in no hurry to tell my fortune. After several moments had passed, everyone started getting restless.

"Aren't you supposed to look at my palm?" I asked.

"You're not supposed to talk!" said Harry and Llewellyn in one breath.

"Silence!" said the fortune-teller irritably. "This is a difficult subject. I'm trying to concentrate."

She was certainly concentrating, I thought. She had not taken her eyes from me since the moment she'd sat down. I glanced at Harry's watch. It was seven minutes to midnight. The fortune-teller was not moving. It seemed as if she'd turned to stone.

All around the room people were becoming agitated as the clock moved toward midnight. Their voices were raucous, and they were twisting their bottles of champagne in the icers, trying out noisemakers, and pulling out funny hats and packages of streamers and confetti. The stress of the old year was about to explode like a box of spring-loaded snakes. I remembered why I had always avoided going out on New Year's Eve. The fortune-teller seemed oblivious to her surroundings. She just sat there. Staring at me.

I glanced away from her glare. Harry and Llewellyn were leaning forward with bated breath. Blanche was sitting back in her chair calmly observing the fortune-teller's profile. When I returned my gaze to the old woman, she hadn't moved. She seemed lost in a trance and was looking right through me. Then slowly her eyes focused upon mine. As they did, I felt the same chill I had experienced earlier. Only this time it seemed to come from within.

"Do not speak," the fortune-teller suddenly whispered to me. It took a second before I realized that her lips were moving, that she was the one who'd spoken. Harry leaned farther forward so he could hear her, and Llewellyn drew up as well.

"You are in great danger," she said. "I feel danger all around me. Right now."

"Danger?" said Harry sternly. Just then a waitress arrived with an icer of champagne. Harry waved irritably for her to leave it and depart. "What are you talking about? Is this some kind of joke?"

The fortune-teller was looking down at her clipboard now, tapping her pencil against the metal frame as if uncertain whether to proceed. I was becoming annoyed. Why was this cocktail lounge soothsayer trying to frighten me? Suddenly she looked up. She must have seen the anger in my face, for she became very businesslike.

"You are right-handed," she said. "Therefore it is your left hand that describes the destiny you were born with. The right tells the direction you are moving. Give me your left hand first."

I must admit it seems strange, but as she stared at my left hand in silence, I began to have the eerie feeling she really *could* see something there. Her frail, gnarled fingers clutching my hand were like ice.

"Whoo, boy," she said in a strange voice. "This is some hand you have here, young lady."

She sat in silence looking at it, and her eyes grew wider behind the sequined glasses. The clipboard slid from her lap to the floor, but no one bent to pick it up. Repressed energy was building around our table, but no one seemed willing to speak. They all watched me as the noise swirled in the room around us.

As the fortune-teller gripped my hand in both of hers, my arm began to ache. I tried to pull my hand away, but she was holding me in a deathlike vise. For some reason this made me irrationally angry. I was also feeling a little sick from the eggnog and the reek of Juicy Fruit. With my free hand I pried her long bony fingers loose and started to speak.

"Listen to me," she interrupted in a soft voice, totally unlike the shrill squeak she'd used before. Her accent, I realized, was not American, though I couldn't place it. And although her gray hair and hunched form had made me assume she was ancient, I now saw that she was taller than she had first appeared, and her fine skin was nearly unwrinkled. I started to speak again, but Harry had hefted his big bulk out of his chair and was standing over us.

"This is too melodramatic for me," he said, placing his hand on the fortune-teller's shoulder. He'd dug into his pocket with his other hand and was thrusting some money at her. "Let's just call it a night, shall we?" The fortune-teller ignored him and bent toward me.

"I have come to warn you," she whispered. "Everywhere you go, look over your shoulder. Trust no one. Suspect everyone. For the lines in your hand reveal . . . this is the hand that was foretold."

"Foretold by whom?" I asked.

She picked up my hand again and gently traced the lines with her fingers, her eyes closed as if she were reading braille. Her voice still a whisper, she spoke as if remembering something, a poem she'd heard long ago.

"Just as these lines that merge to form a key are as chess squares, when month and day are four, don't risk another chance to move to mate. One game is real, and one's a metaphor. Untold times, this wisdom has come too late. Battle of white has raged on endlessly. Everywhere black will strive to seal his fate. Continue a search for thirty-three and three. Veiled forever is the secret door."

I was silent when she'd finished, and Harry stood there with his hands in his pockets. I hadn't a clue what she meant—but it was odd. It seemed that I had been here, in this bar, listening to these words before. I shrugged it off as déjà-vu.

"I've got no idea what you're talking about," I said aloud.

"You don't understand?" she said. And oddly, she gave me a strange smile, almost conspiratorial. "But you will," she insisted. "The fourth day of the fourth month? That means something to you?"

"Yes, but—"

She put her finger to her lips and shook her head. "You must tell no one what this means. You will soon understand the rest. For this is the hand that was foretold, the hand of Destiny. It has been written—'On the fourth day of the fourth month, then will come the Eight.' "

"What do you mean?" cried Llewellyn in alarm. He reached across the table and grasped her arm, but she pulled away from him.

Just then the room was thrown into total darkness. Noisemakers were blown all over the room. I could hear champagne corks popping, and everyone screamed, "Happy New Year!" as if with one breath. Firecrackers were going off in the streets. Against the dying embers of the fireplace, the distorted silhouettes of revelers twisted like blackened spirits out of Dante. Their screams echoed through the dark.

When the lights flooded back, the fortune-teller was gone. Harry stood beside his chair. We looked at each other in surprise across the empty space where she'd been only a moment before. Harry laughed, bent over, and kissed me on the cheek.

"Happy New Year, darling," he said, squeezing me warmly. "What a meshugge fortune you got! I guess my idea was a bust. Forgive me."

Blanche and Llewellyn were huddled together, whispering, at the opposite side of the table.

"Come on, you two," said Harry. "How about polishing off some of this champagne I just put myself in hock for? Cat, you need some, too." Llewellyn stood up and came over to give me a peck on the cheek.

"Cat dear, I must quite agree with Harry. You look as if you'd just seen a ghost." I did feel a bit drained. I wrote it off to the strain of the last few weeks and the lateness of the hour.

"What a dreadful old woman," Llewellyn went on. "All that nonsense about danger. What she said seemed to make sense to you, though. Or was that only my imagination?"

"I'm afraid not," I told him. "Chessboards and numbers and . . . what are the eight? The eight what? I couldn't make heads or tails of it." Harry handed me a glass of champagne.

"Well, no matter," said Blanche, passing me a cocktail napkin across the table. It had some scribbling on it. "Llew has written it all down there, so we'll just give it to you. Maybe it will strike a memory later. But let's hope not! It all sounded rather depressing."

"Oh, come, it's all in good fun," said Llewellyn. "I'm sorry it turned out strangely, but she *did* mention chess, didn't she? That business about 'moving to mate' and all. Rather sinister. You know the word 'mate'—'checkmate,' that is—comes from the Persian *Shah-mat*. It means 'death to the King.' Coupled with the fact she said you were in danger—are you quite certain none of that meant anything to you?" Llewellyn was pressing.

"Oh, knock it off," said Harry. "I was wrong to suggest my fortune had anything to do with Lily. Obviously the whole thing was a lot of nonsense. Just forget about it, or you'll have nightmares."

"Lily isn't the only person I know who plays chess," I told him. "In fact, I have a friend who used to play competitively. . . ."

"Indeed?" said Llewellyn a little too quickly. "Anyone I know?"

I shook my head. Blanche was about to speak when Harry handed her a glass of bubbly. She smiled and sipped her drink.

"Enough," said Harry. "Let's toast the new year, whatever it brings."

We finished off the champagne in about half an hour. Finally we collected our coats and went outside, piling into the limousine, which had magically appeared in front. Harry instructed Saul to drop me first at my apartment near the East River. When we arrived in front of my building, Harry got out and gave me a big bear hug.

"I hope your new year should be a wonderful one," he told me. "Maybe you'll do something with that impossible daughter of mine. In fact, I'm sure you will. I see it in my stars."

"I'm going to be seeing stars soon if I don't get to bed," I told him, trying to suppress a yawn. "Thanks for the eggnog and champagne."

I squeezed Harry's hand, and he watched as I went into the darkened lobby. The doorman was asleep, sitting bolt upright on a chair just inside the door. He didn't budge as I crossed the large, dimly lighted foyer and got into the elevator. The building was as silent as a grave.

I pushed the button, and the doors grumbled shut. As the elevator climbed I pulled out the cocktail napkin I'd shoved into my coat pocket and read it once again. It still didn't make any sense, so I dismissed it. I had enough problems without imagining more to worry about. But as the elevator opened and I walked down the shadowed corridor to my apartment, I wondered fleetingly how it was that the fortune-teller had known that the fourth day of the fourth month was my birthday.

FIANCHETTO

The Aufins [Bishops] are prelates wearing horns. . . . They move and take obliquely because nearly every Bishop misuses his office through cupidity.

—Quaendam Moralitas de Scaccario
Pope Innocent III
(R. 1198–1216)

O h, *merde. Merde!*" cried Jacques–Louis David. He threw his hand–tied sable brush across the floor in a frenzy of frustration and leaped to his feet. "I told you not to move. Not to *move*! Now the folds have come undone. Everything is ruined!"

He glared at Valentine and Mireille, posed on a high scaffold across the studio. They were nearly nude, draped only in translucent gauze, carefully arranged and tied beneath the bosom to resemble the fashions of ancient Greece so popular in Paris just then.

David bit the side of his thumb. His dark, disheveled hair stuck out in all directions, and his black eyes flashed wildly. The yellow–and–blue–striped foulard, tossed twice about his throat and tied in a haphazard bow, was streaked with charcoal dust. The wide tapestried lapels of his green velvet jacket were skewed.

"Now I shall have to arrange everything all over again," he complained. Valentine and Mireille did not speak. They were flushed in embarrassment, gazing with wide eyes at the open doorway behind the painter.

Jacques–Louis glanced impatiently over his shoulder. There stood a tall, well–formed young man so astonishingly handsome as to appear almost angelic. Golden hair of abundant thickness fell in ringlets tied in back with a simple ribbon. A long, purple silk cassock flowed like water over his graceful form.

His eyes, an intense, unsettling blue, rested calmly upon the painter. He smiled at Jacques–Louis with bemusement. "I hope I'm not interrupting," he said, glancing at the scaffold where the two young women stood, poised like deer about to take flight. His voice contained that soft, well–spoken assurance of the upper classes, who assume their presence will be greeted with more enthusiasm than anything they might have interrupted.

"Oh, it's only you, Maurice," said Jacques–Louis irritably. "Who let you in? They know I'm not to be disturbed when I am working."

"I hope you do not greet all your luncheon guests in this manner," replied the young man, still smiling. "Besides, this doesn't look very much like work to me. Or should I say it seems the kind of work I'd gladly put my hand to."

He looked again at Valentine and Mireille, drenched in golden light flooding through the north windows. He could see the outline of their quivering forms through the translucent cloth.

"You've put your hand to enough of that sort of work, it seems to me," said

David, picking another brush from the pewter jar on his easel stand. "But be a good fellow—go over there to the scaffold and rearrange those draperies for me, would you? I'll direct you from here. The morning light is nearly finished, anyway. Twenty minutes more and we'll break for luncheon."

"What's that you're sketching?" asked the young man. As he walked slowly to the scaffold, he seemed to move with a slight but painful limp.

"It's a charcoal and wash," David replied. "An idea I've had for some time, based on a theme of Poussin. *The Rape of the Sabine Women*."

"What a delectable thought," said Maurice as he reached the scaffold. "What would you like me to rearrange? It all looks quite charming to me."

Valentine stood on the scaffold above Maurice, one knee forward and her arms thrust out at shoulder height. Mireille, on her knees beside Valentine, held her arms forward in a beseeching gesture. Her dark red hair tumbled over one shoulder, barely concealing her naked bosom.

"That red hair must be pulled away," David called from across the studio, squinting his eyes at the scaffold and swishing his brush through the air as he gave directions. "No, not so far. Only to cover the left breast. We must see the right breast completely exposed. Completely exposed. Pull that drapery down farther. After all, they are trying to seduce soldiers from battle, not open a convent."

Maurice did as he was told, but his hand trembled as he pulled away the gauzy fabric.

"Move away. Move away, for God's sake, so I can see it. Who is the painter here?" cried David.

Maurice moved to one side and smiled weakly. He'd never seen lovelier young women in his life, and he wondered where on earth David had found them. It was known that society women queued up outside his studio hoping to be portrayed as Greek femmes fatales in one of his famous canvases, but these girls were too fresh and unsophisticated to be of the jaded Parisian nobility.

Maurice should certainly know. He'd fondled the breasts and thighs of more society women than any man in Paris, numbering among his mistresses the Duchesse de Luynes, the Duchesse de Fitz-James, the Vicomtesse de Laval, and the Princesse de Vaudemont. It was like a club to which membership was always open. Maurice had been quoted as saying, "Paris is one place where it is easier to possess a woman than an abbey."

Though he was thirty-seven, Maurice looked ten years younger, and he'd taken advantage of his youthful good looks for more than twenty years. There had been a lot of water under the Pont Neuf in that time, all of it highly enjoyable and politically expedient. His mistresses had done as much for him in the salon as in the boudoir, and though he'd had to acquire the abbey on his own, they had opened the doors to the political sinecures he coveted and would soon gain.

Women controlled France, as Maurice knew better than anyone. And though it was against French law for a woman to inherit the throne, they sought their power through other means and selected their candidates accordingly.

"Now adjust Valentine's drapery," David called impatiently. "You'll have to go up onto the scaffold, the steps are back there."

Maurice limped up the steps onto the massive scaffold, several feet above the ground. He stood behind Valentine.

"And so you are named Valentine?" he whispered in her ear. "You are quite lovely, my dear, for someone with a boy's name."

"And you are quite lecherous," Valentine replied saucily, "for someone in the purple cassock of a bishop!"

"Stop whispering," yelled David. "Fix the fabric! The light is nearly finished." As Maurice moved to touch the cloth, David added, "Ah, Maurice. I haven't introduced you. This is my niece Valentine, and her cousin Mireille."

"Your niece!" said Maurice, dropping the fabric between his fingers as if it had burned him.

"An 'affectionate' niece," he added. "She is my ward. Her grandfather was one of my dearest friends, but he passed on some years ago. The Count de Remy. Your family knew him, I believe?"

Maurice looked at David in amazement.

"Valentine," David was saying, "this gentleman arranging your draperies is a very famous figure in France. A past president of the National Assembly. May I present Monsieur Charles Maurice de Talleyrand-Périgord. The Bishop of Autun. . . ."

Mireille leaped to her feet with a gasp, pulling the fabric up to cover her bare breasts. At the same time, Valentine let out a piercing shriek that nearly split Maurice's ears.

"The Bishop of Autun!" cried Valentine, backing away from him. "It is the Devil with the cloven hoof!"

The two young women leaped from the scaffold and ran barefoot from the room.

Maurice looked across the studio at David with a wry smile. "I don't ordinarily have such effect upon the fairer sex," he commented.

"It seems your reputation has preceded you," David replied.

Seated in the small dining room beside the studio, David gazed down over the Rue de Bac. Maurice, his back to the windows, sat stiffly on one of the red-and-white-striped satin chairs surrounding the mahogany table. Several bowls of fruit and some bronze candlesticks were scattered about the table, and a service of four was set with lovely dishes patterned in birds and flowers.

"Who could have expected such a reaction?" said David, pulling at an orange rind with his fingers. "I apologize for the confusion. I've been upstairs, and they've agreed to change and come down for luncheon, at any rate."

"How does it happen that you've become guardian over all this pulchritude?" asked Maurice, twirling his wineglass and taking another sip. "It seems too much joy for one man to bear alone. And nearly wasted upon someone like yourself."

David glanced up at him quickly and replied, "I couldn't agree more. I've no idea how to manage. I have searched all over Paris for a suitable governess to continue their education. I'm at my wits' end ever since my wife left for Brussels some months ago."

"Her departure wasn't related to the arrival of your lovely 'nieces,' was it?" said Talleyrand, smiling at David's plight as he twisted the stem of his glass.

"Not at all," said David, looking very depressed. "My wife and her family are staunch Royalists. They disapprove of my involvement in the Assembly. They don't think a bourgeois painter like myself who's been supported by the monarchy should openly support the Revolution. My marriage has been under a great strain since Bastille Day. My wife demands that I renounce my post in the Assembly and discontinue my political paintings; those are the conditions she sets for her return."

"But my friend, when you unveiled *The Oath of the Horatii* in Rome, crowds came to your studio at Piazza del Popolo to strew flowers before the painting! It was the first masterpiece of the New Republic, and you are her chosen painter."

"I know that, but my wife does not." David sighed. "She took the children along to Brussels, and wanted to take my wards as well. But the terms of my agreement with their abbess was to keep them in Paris, and I'm paid a generous stipend to do so. Besides, here is where I belong."

"Their abbess? Your wards are nuns?" Maurice nearly burst out laughing. "What delicious folly! To give two young women, brides of Christ, into the care of a forty-three-year-old man who's no relation. What was this abbess thinking?"

"They aren't nuns, their vows were not taken. Unlike yourself!" David added pointedly. "It appears this dour old abbess was the one who warned them that *you* were the Devil incarnate."

"Granted my life has not been all it should be," admitted Maurice. "I am nevertheless surprised to hear it spoken of by abbesses in the provinces. I've tried to be somewhat discreet."

"If you call it discreet to litter France with unpapered brats while delivering extreme unction and claiming to be a priest, then I really can't say what might be called overt."

"I never asked to be a priest," Maurice said somewhat bitterly. "One must make do with one's inheritance. The day I remove this robe from my body for good and all, I shall feel really clean for the first time."

At that moment Valentine and Mireille entered the small dining room. They were dressed alike in the plain gray traveling clothes the abbess had provided them. Only their shining tresses added a spark of color. Both men rose to greet them, and David pulled out two chairs.

"We've been waiting nearly a quarter hour," he chastened them. "We are now ready to behave ourselves, I hope. And do try to be polite to the Monseigneur. Whatever you may have heard of him, I'm certain it would pale beside the truth. But he is our guest nonetheless."

"Have they told you I'm a vampire?" asked Talleyrand politely. "And that I drink the blood of young children?"

"Oh, yes, Monseigneur," replied Valentine. "And that you have a cloven hoof. You walk with a limp, so it must be true!"

"Valentine," said Mireille, "that is extremely rude!"

David put his head in his hands and said nothing.

"It's quite all right," said Talleyrand. "I shall explain."

He reached across and poured some wine into the glasses that sat before Valentine and Mireille, then continued. "When I was a small child, I was left by my family with a wet-nurse, an ignorant country woman. She left me atop a dresser one day, and I fell off and broke my foot. The nurse was afraid to notify my parents of the accident, so the foot was never properly set. As my mother was not enough interested to look in on me, the foot grew crookedly until it was too late to mend it. And that is the entire story. Nothing very mysterious, is there?"

"Does it give you much pain?" asked Mireille.

"The foot? No." Talleyrand smiled a little bitterly. "Only the result of the foot. I lost my right of primogeniture because of it. My mother set about giving birth to two more sons in rapid succession, passing *my* rights to my brother Archimbaud, and to Boson after him. She could not accept a crippled heir to the ancient title of Talleyrand-Périgord, could she? The last time I saw my mother was when she came to Autun to protest my being made a bishop. Though she'd forced me into the priesthood, she'd hoped I would remain buried in obscurity. She insisted I was not sufficiently pious for the post of bishop. She was quite right, of course."

"How awful!" cried Valentine in heated voice. "I should have called her an old witch for that!"

David raised his head from his hands, looked at the ceiling, and rang the bell for luncheon to be served.

"Is that what you would have done?" Maurice asked her gently. "In that case, I wish you had been there. I confess it's something I rather longed to do myself."

When everyone had been served and the valet had departed, Valentine said, "Now that you've told this story, Monseigneur, you don't seem as wicked as we'd heard. I confess I find you very good-looking."

Mireille looked at Valentine in exasperation, and David smiled broadly.

"Perhaps Mireille and I should thank you, Monseigneur, if indeed you were responsible for closing the abbeys," Valentine went on. "If not for that, we would still be at Montglane, pining away for the life in Paris we had dreamed of. . . ."

Maurice had put down his knife and fork and was looking at them.

"Montglane Abbey? In the Bas-Pyrenees? Was that the abbey you came from? But why are you no longer there? Why did you leave?"

His expression and the intensity of his questions made Valentine realize she had made a grievous error. Talleyrand, despite his good looks and charming manner, was still the Bishop of Autun, the very man against whom the abbess had warned them. If he learned that the two cousins not only knew of the Montglane Service, but had helped remove the pieces from the abbey, he would never rest until he discovered more.

Indeed, they were in great jeopardy just by the fact that he knew they had come from Montglane. Though their own pieces of the service had been carefully buried beneath the plantings in David's garden behind the studio, on the very night of their arrival in Paris, there was a further problem. Valentine had not forgotten the role she'd been assigned by the abbess, to serve as a collection point for other nuns who might have to flee and leave the pieces behind. So far that had not happened, but in the state of unrest in France, it might at any moment. Valentine and Mireille could not afford to be under the observation of Charles Maurice Talleyrand.

"I repeat," said Talleyrand sternly when the two girls sat in painful silence, "why have you left Montglane?"

"Because," Mireille replied reluctantly, "the abbey has been closed, Monseigneur."

"Closed? Why was it closed?"

"The Bill of Seizure, Monseigneur. The abbess feared for our safety—"

"In her letters to me," David interrupted, "the abbess explained she'd received an order from the Papal States instructing the abbey be closed."

"And you accepted that?" said Talleyrand. "Are you a republican or not? You know Pope Pius has denounced the Revolution. When we passed the Bill of Seizure, he threatened to excommunicate every Catholic in the Assembly! This abbess is treasonous toward France by taking such orders from the Italian papacy, which as you know is overrun with Hapsburgs and Spanish Bourbons."

"I should like to point out that I'm just as good a republican as you," David said hotly. "My family are *not* of the nobility, I am a man of the people. I stand or fall with the new government. But the closing of Montglane Abbey had nothing to do with politics."

"Everything on earth, my dear David, has to do with politics. You know what was buried at Montglane Abbey, do you not?" Valentine and Mireille turned white, but David looked at Talleyrand strangely and picked up his wineglass.

"Pah. That's an old wives' tale," he said with a scornful laugh.

"Is it?" said the other. He watched the two young women with his intense blue eyes. Then he picked up his wineglass as well and took a sip, seeming to be lost in thought. At last he picked up his fork and began to eat again. Valentine and Mireille were frozen in their places, not touching their food.

"Your nieces seem to have lost their appetites," Talleyrand commented.

David glanced over at them. "Well, what is it?" he demanded. "Don't tell me you believe in this nonsense, too?"

"No, Uncle," said Mireille quietly. "We know it is only a superstition."

"Of course, it's only an old legend, isn't it?" Talleyrand said, recovering some of his former charm. "But one that you seem to have heard yourselves. Tell me, where has this abbess of yours gone, now that she's seen fit to conspire with the pope against the government of France?"

"For God's sake, Maurice," said David irritably. "One would think you'd studied for the Inquisition. I'll tell you where she's gone, and let there be an end to it. She's gone to Russia."

Talleyrand was silent for a moment. Then he smiled slowly, as if he'd thought of something privately amusing. "I suppose you're right," he told David. "Tell me, have your charming nieces had occasion yet to visit the Paris Opéra?"

"No, Monseigneur," said Valentine hastily. "But it has been our most cherished fantasy, ever since our early childhood."

"As long ago as that?" laughed Talleyrand. "Well, perhaps something can be done about it. After luncheon, let's have a look at your wardrobes. I happen to be an expert in couture. . . ."

"The monseigneur advises half the women in Paris upon fashion," David added wryly. "It is one of his many acts of Christian charity."

"I must tell you the story of the time I arranged the coiffure of Marie-Antoinette for a masqued ball. I designed her costume as well. Even her own lovers did not recognize her, not to mention the king!"

"Oh, Uncle, *could* we ask monseigneur the bishop to do the same for us?" Valentine begged. She felt a sweeping relief that the conversation had changed to a more amenable topic, and a less dangerous one as well.

"You both look ravishing enough as it is." Talleyrand smiled. "But we will see what little we can do to improve upon nature. Luckily I've a friend who keeps among her entourage the best dressmakers in Paris—perhaps you've heard of Madame de Staël?"

Everyone in Paris had heard of Germaine de Staël, as Valentine and Mireille soon learned. As they swept in her wake into her gold-and-blue box at the Opéra-Comique, they saw the array of powdered heads turn to recognize her arrival. The cream of Parisian society filled the stacked boxes that rose to the rafters of the overheated opera house. To regard the jumbled array of jewels and pearls and laces, one would never suppose that outside in the streets, a revolution was still under way, that the royal family were languishing in the prison of their own palace, that each morning tumbrils filled with members of the nobility and clergy were sent groaning over the cobblestones to the Place de la Révolution. Within the horseshoe of the Opéra-Comique, all was splendor and festivity. And the most splendid of all, coursing into her box like a great bateau on the river Seine, was that youthful grande dame of Paris, Germaine de Staël.

Valentine had learned all about her by questioning the servants of her uncle Jacques-Louis. Madame de Staël, they'd informed her, was the daughter of the brilliant Swiss finance minister Jacques Necker, twice exiled by Louis XVI and twice recalled to his post by popular demand of the French people. Her mother, Suzanne Necker, had maintained the most powerful salon in Paris for twenty years, of which Germaine had been the star.

A millionairess in her own right, Germaine had purchased a husband at the age of twenty: Baron Eric Staël von Holstein, the impoverished Swedish ambassador to France. Following in her mother's footsteps, she had opened her own salon at the Swedish embassy and plunged headlong into politics. Her rooms were flooded with luminaries of the political and cultural milieux of France: Lafayette, Condorcet, Narbonne, Talleyrand. Germaine became a philosophical revolutionary. All the important political decisions of the day were made within the silk-lined walls of her salon, through the men whom she alone could draw together. Now, at twenty-five, she was perhaps the most powerful woman in France.

As Talleyrand limped painfully about the box, seating the three women, Valentine and Mireille studied Madame de Staël. In a low-cut gown of black-and-gold lace that accentuated her heavy arms, muscular shoulders, and thick waist, she cut an imposing figure. She wore a necklace set in heavy cameos surrounded by rubies, and the exotic gold turban that was her trademark. She leaned aside to Valentine, who was seated beside her, and whispered in her low, rumbling voice that could be heard by all.

"By tomorrow morning, my dear, everyone in Paris will be upon my doorstep, wondering who the two of you are. It will be a most delectable scandal, as I'm certain your escort understands, or he would have dressed you more appropriately."

"Madame, do our costumes not please you?" asked Valentine anxiously.

"You are both quite lovely, my dear," Germaine assured her wryly. "But white is a color for virgins, not flaming rose. And though young bosoms are always in vogue in Paris, a fichu is normally worn to cover the flesh of women under the age of twenty. As Monsieur Talleyrand well knows."

Valentine and Mireille flushed to the roots of their hair, but Talleyrand interjected, "I am liberating France in my own fashion." He and Germaine smiled at one another, and she shrugged.

"I hope you enjoy the opera," said Germaine, turning to Mireille. "It's one of my favorites, I've not seen it since my childhood. The composer, André Philidor, is the finest chess master in Europe. He's played chess and music before philosophers and kings. You may find the music old-fashioned, since Gluck has revolutionized the opera. It's difficult to listen to so much recitative. . . ."

"We have never before seen an opera, madame," Valentine chimed in.

"Never seen an opera!" said Germaine in full voice. "Impossible! But where have your family been keeping you?"

"In a convent, madame," Mireille replied politely.

Germaine stared at her for a moment, as if she'd never heard of a convent. Then she turned and glared at Talleyrand. "I see there are a few things you failed to explain to me, my friend. Had I known that David's wards were raised in a convent, I should scarcely have chosen an opera such as *Tom Jones.*" She turned back to Mireille and added, "I hope you will not be shocked. It is an English story about an illegitimate child. . . ."

"Better to have them learn the moral at an early age," laughed Talleyrand.

"That is indeed true," said Germaine between thin lips. "If they retain the Bishop of Autun as their mentor, the information may prove quite useful."

She turned back to the stage as the curtain rose.

"I believe that was the most wonderful experience of my life," Valentine said after the opera as she sat upon the thick Aubusson carpet in Talleyrand's study, watching flames lick at the glass doors of the fireguard.

Talleyrand leaned back in a large chair of blue watered silk, his feet propped on an ottoman. Mireille stood a few feet away, looking down into the fire.

"This is the first time we've had cognac, as well," Valentine added.

"Well, you are only sixteen," said Talleyrand, inhaling the aroma of the brandy in his snifter and taking a sip. "There will be time for many experiences."

"How old are *you*, Monsieur Talleyrand?" Valentine asked.

"That is not a polite question," said Mireille from the fireplace. "You should never ask people how old they are."

"And please," said Talleyrand, "call me Maurice. I'm thirty-seven, but I feel as if I'm ninety when you call me 'monsieur.' Now tell me, how did you like Germaine?"

"Madame de Staël was very charming," said Mireille, her red hair glowing against the firelight, the color of the flames.

"Is it true she's your lover?" asked Valentine.

"Valentine!" cried Mireille. But Talleyrand had exploded with laughter.

"You are remarkable," he said, tousling Valentine's hair with his fingers as she leaned against his knee in the flickering light. To Mireille he added, "Your cousin, Mademoiselle, is free of all the pretensions one finds so dull in Parisian society. I find her questions refreshing, and never take offense at them. I've found these last few weeks, dressing the two of you and escorting you about Paris, to be a tonic that's reduced the bile of my natural cynicism. But who told you, Valentine, that Madame de Staël was my lover?"

"I heard it from the servants, monsieur—I mean, Uncle Maurice. Is it true?"

"No, my dear. It is not true. Not any longer. We once were lovers, but gossip is always behind the times. She and I are good friends."

"Perhaps she cast you over because of your lame foot?" Valentine suggested.

"Blessed Mother!" cried Mireille, who was unaccustomed to swearing. "You will apologize to the monseigneur. Please forgive my cousin, Monseigneur. She did not mean to offend you."

Talleyrand was sitting silently, almost in a state of shock. Though he'd said Valentine could never offend him, no one in France had ever spoken of his deformity in public. Trembling with an emotion he could not define, he reached forward for Valentine's hands and pulled her up to sit beside him on the ottoman. Gently, he put his arms about her and embraced her.

"I am very sorry, Uncle Maurice," Valentine said. She placed her hand tenderly against his cheek and smiled at him. "I've never had the opportunity to see an actual physical deformity before. I would find it most informative if you would show me."

Mireille groaned. Talleyrand was now staring at Valentine as if he could not believe his ears. She squeezed his arm in encouragement. After a moment he said gravely, "Very well. If you'd like." Painfully he lifted his foot from the ottoman, bent down, and removed the heavy steel boot that fastened his foot into place so he was able to walk.

In the dim firelight, Valentine studied the foot. It was twisted so badly that the ball was bent underneath and the toes seemed to grow from below. From the top it truly resembled a club. Valentine picked up the foot, bent over it, and placed a little kiss on the bottom. Talleyrand sat, stunned, in his chair.

"Poor foot," she said. "Thou hast suffered so much and deserved so little of it."

Talleyrand leaned toward Valentine. Tilting her face toward his, he kissed her softly on the lips. For a moment, his golden hair and her whiter blond locks were entwined together in the firelight.

"You are the only one who has ever addressed my foot as 'thou,' " he told her with a smile. "And you've made my foot very happy."

As he gazed at Valentine with his beautiful angelic face, his golden curls haloed in the firelight, Mireille found it difficult to remember that this was the man who ruthlessly, almost single-handedly, was destroying the Catholic Church in France. The man who sought to capture the Montglane Service.

The candles had burned low in Talleyrand's study. In the dying firelight, the corners of the long room were swallowed in shadow. Glancing at the ormolu mantel clock, Talleyrand saw it was after two A.M. He roused himself from his chair, where Valentine and Mireille leaned with their hair draped across his knees.

"I promised your uncle I'd bring you home at a reasonable hour," he told them. "Look at the time."

"Oh, Uncle Maurice," pleaded Valentine, "*please* don't make us leave just yet. This is the first time we've had the chance to go out into society. Since we've arrived in Paris, we've lived just as if we'd never left the convent at all."

"Just one more story," Mireille agreed. "Our uncle won't mind."

"He'll be furious." Talleyrand laughed. "But it's already too late for me to take you home. There are drunken sans-culottes roaming the streets at this time of night, even in the better quartiers. I suggest I send the footman around to your uncle's house with a note. I'll have my valet Courtiade prepare a room for you. You'd prefer to stay together, I suppose?"

It was not entirely true that it was too dangerous to send them home. Talleyrand had a household of servants, and David's residence was not far. But he'd realized suddenly that he did not want to take them home, perhaps not ever. He'd dawdled out his tales, postponing the inevitable. These two young girls with their fresh innocence had aroused feelings he was hard-pressed to define. He'd never had a family of any sort, and the warmth he felt in their presence was a wholly new experience.

"Oh, may we really stay the night?" asked Valentine, sitting up and squeezing Mireille's arm. Mireille looked doubtful, but she too longed to stay.

"Indeed," Talleyrand said, rousing himself from his chair to pull the bell cord. "Let us hope it will not become the scandal of Paris by morning that Germaine prophesied."

The sober Courtiade, still attired in his starched livery, glanced once at the two disheveled girls and once at his master's shoeless foot, then wordlessly preceded them up the stairs to unveil the large guest bedroom.

"Could the monseigneur find us any nightclothes to wear?" asked Mireille. "Perhaps one of the serving women . . ."

"That will pose no problem," Courtiade replied politely, and he promptly laid out two silk peignoirs lavish with hand-picked lace, which certainly did not belong to any servant. Discreetly, he left the room.

When Valentine and Mireille had undressed, brushed their hair, and crawled into the big soft bed with its elaborate canopy, Talleyrand tapped upon the door.

"Is everyone quite comfortable?" he asked, putting his head in at the door.

"This is the most wonderful bed we've ever seen," replied Mireille from the thick pile of comforters. "At the convent we slept on wooden planks, to improve our posture."

"It's had a remarkable effect, as I can tell," Talleyrand said, smiling. He came over and sat on the small couch beside their bed.

"Now you must tell us one more story," said Valentine.

"It's very late . . ." Talleyrand began.

"A ghost story!" said Valentine. "The abbess would never permit us to hear ghost stories, but we used to tell them nonetheless. Do you know one?"

"Unfortunately not," Talleyrand said ruefully. "As you know, I hadn't a very normal childhood. I never heard stories of that sort." He thought for a moment. "But actually, upon one occasion in my life, I *met* a ghost."

"Not truly?" said Valentine. She squeezed Mireille's hand beneath the covers. The two looked quite excited. "A real ghost?"

"It sounds rather absurd, now that I say it," he laughed. "You must promise never to tell your uncle Jacques-Louis of this, or I'll be the laughingstock of the Assembly."

The girls wriggled under the covers and swore never to tell. Talleyrand sat on the sofa in the dim candlelight and began his story. . . .

THE BISHOP'S TALE

When I was quite a young man, before I took my vows as priest, I left my see at St. Remy, where the famous King Clovis is buried, and went off to attend the Sorbonne. After two years at this famous university, the time had come for me to announce my calling.

I knew it would be a terrible scandal for my family if I refused the profession they'd forced upon me; however, I felt totally unfit to be a priest. Privately I'd always sensed my destiny was to be a statesman.

Beneath the chapel at the Sorbonne were interred the bones of the greatest statesman France had ever known, a man I idolized. His name you will know: Armand Jean du Plessis, Duc de Richelieu, who, in a rare combination of religion and politics, had ruled this country with an iron hand for nearly twenty years until his death in 1642.

One night, near midnight, I left the warmth of my bed, threw a heavy cape over my dressing gown, and climbed down the ivy-covered walls of the student quarters, making for the Sorbonne Chapel.

Wind blew the cold leaves across the lawn, and there were strange sounds of owls and other night creatures. Though I thought myself bold, I confess I was afraid. Within the chapel, the tomb was dark and cold. There were no people praying there at that hour, and only a few candles remained burning by the crypt. I lit another and, falling upon my knees, beseeched the late priest of France to guide me. In that vast vault I could hear the beating of my own heart as I explained my plight.

No sooner was my prayer voiced than, to my utter astonishment, an icy wind blew through the vault, extinguishing all the candles. I was terrified! Swallowed in blackness, I fumbled about to find another to light. But at that moment I heard a groan, and from the tomb rose the pale murky ghost of Cardinal Richelieu! His hair, skin, and even his ceremonial robes as white as snow, he hovered above me, shimmering and completely translucent.

Had I not been kneeling already, I certainly should have fallen to the ground. My voice dried up in my throat, I could not speak. But then I heard the low groaning sound again. The cardinal's ghost was speaking to me! I felt the gooseflesh rising on my spine as he intoned his fateful words in a voice that resembled the deep ringing of a bell.

"Why hast thou awakened me?" it boomed. Wild winds swept about me, and I was still in total darkness, but my legs were too weak to permit me to get up and flee. I swallowed and tried to unloose my trembling voice to reply.

"Cardinal Richelieu," I stammered out, "I seek advice. In life, you were the greatest statesman of France, despite your priestly vocation. How did you attain such power? Please share your secret, for I wish to follow your example."

"You?" boomed the lofty, smokelike pillar, drawing itself up toward the vaulted ceiling as if sorely offended. It drifted back and forth against the walls like a man pacing the floor. With each pass it expanded in size until its diaphanous form filled the room, moving like a roiling storm about to burst. I shrank into myself. At last the ghost spoke.

"The secret that I sought remains forever mystery. . . ." The ghost was still rolling across the skies of the vault, its form dissipating as it became thinner.

"Its power lies buried with Charlemagne. I found the first key only. I had hidden it carefully. . . ."

He flickered faintly against the wall like a flame about to sputter out. I leapt to my feet and tried frantically to keep him from disappearing altogether. What had he hinted at? *What* was the secret that lay buried with Charlemagne? I shouted over the roar of wind that was consuming the ghost before my very eyes.

"Sire, blessed priest! Please tell me where to find this key you speak of."

The ghost had completely disappeared from view, but I could hear its voice like an echo bouncing off a long, long hallway.

"François . . . Marie . . . Arouet . . ." And that was all.

The wind died out, and the few candles trickled back to life again. I stood there alone in the vault. After a long time, I made my way back across the lawn to the student quarters.

The next morning I should have been inclined to believe the whole experience a bad dream, but the dead leaves and faint odor of the crypt still clinging to my cape assured me it had been real. The cardinal had told me he had found the first key to a mystery. And for some reason, I was to seek this key through the great French poet and playwright, François Marie Arouet, known as Voltaire.

Voltaire had recently returned to Paris from self-imposed exile on his estate at Ferney, purportedly to stage the production of a new play. But most believed he had come home to die. Why this cantankerous old atheistic playwright, a man born fifty years after the death of Richelieu, should be privy to the cardinal's secrets was beyond me. But I had to find out. A few weeks passed before I was able to arrange a meeting with Voltaire.

Dressed in my priestly cassock and arriving on the appointed hour, I was soon shown into the bedchamber. Voltaire hated to arise before noon and often spent the entire day in bed. He'd claimed to be at the brink of death for over forty years.

There he was, propped among the bed pillows, wearing a fluffy pink bedcap and a long white gown. His eyes like twin coals in a pallid face, his thin lips and needlelike nose, contrived to make him resemble a predatory bird.

Priests bustled about the room, and he loudly resisted their ministrations, as he'd continue to do until he breathed his last. I was embarrassed when he looked up and saw me in my novice's cassock, knowing how he loathed the clergy. Waving one gnarled hand above the bedsheets, he announced to the priests:

"Please leave us! I've been anticipating the arrival of this young man. He is an emissary direct from Cardinal Richelieu!"

Then he laughed his high, womanish cackle as the priests, glancing at me over their shoulders, scurried from the room. Voltaire invited me to be seated.

"It has always been a source of mystery to me," he said angrily, "just *why* that pompous old ghost cannot remain in its grave. As an atheist, I find it endlessly annoying that a dead priest continues to float about advising young men to visit my bedside. Oh, I can always tell when they're coming from *him*, because they have that drooly metaphysical droop about the mouth, their eyes wander vapidly, just as your own. . . . The traffic at Ferney was bad enough, but here at Paris, it's a deluge!"

I suppressed my irritation at hearing myself described in this fashion. I was both surprised Voltaire had guessed the reason for my visit—and alarmed. For he suggested others sought what I was seeking.

"I wish I could drive a stake through that man's heart once and for all," Voltaire ranted on. "Then perhaps I could have some peace." He was quite upset, and he began coughing. I could see he was choking up blood, but when I tried to help him, he waved me away.

"Doctors and priests should all be hanged at the same gallows!" he cried, reaching out for the glass of water. I handed it to him, and he took a sip.

"It's the manuscripts he wants, of course. Cardinal Richelieu can't bear it that his precious private journals have fallen into the hands of an old reprobate such as myself."

"You have the private journals of Cardinal Richelieu?"

"Yes. Many years ago, when I was a young man, I was tossed into prison for subversion against the Crown, due to some modest poem I'd scribbled about the king's romantic life. While I was moldering away, a wealthy patron of mine brought me some journals to be deciphered. They'd been in his family for ages, but were written in a secret code no one could read. As I had nothing better to do, I deciphered them and learned a good deal about our beloved cardinal."

"I thought Richelieu's writings were bequeathed to the Sorbonne?"

"That's what *you* know," Voltaire laughed wickedly. "A priest does not keep intimate journals written in code, unless he has something to hide. I knew well what sorts of things the priests of his day turned to: masturbatory thought and libidinous deed. I plunged into that journal like a horse to the feedbag, but far from the ribald confession I expected, I found merely a scholarly tract. A greater crock of nonsense I've never seen."

Voltaire began hacking and choking until I thought I must call a priest back into the room, for I wasn't yet empowered to administer the sacrament. After a dreadful sound like the death rattle, he motioned for me to bring him some shawls. Piling them on top of himself, he wrapped one about his head like an old baba and sat there shuddering beneath them.

"What did you discover in these journals, and where are they now?" I urged.

"I have them still. During my stay in prison, my patron died without heirs. They may be worth a good deal of money, due to historical value. But they are all a lot of superstitious poppycock if you ask me. Witchcraft and sorcery."

"I thought you said they were scholarly?"

"Yes, insofar as priests are capable of such objectivity. You see, Cardinal Richelieu had dedicated his life, when he wasn't leading armies against every country in Europe, to the study of power. And the object of his secret studies centered around—perhaps you've heard of the Montglane Service?"

"The chess service of Charlemagne?" I said, trying to appear calm, though my heart was now pounding against my ribs. Leaning over his bed and hanging upon his every word, I prompted him as gently as possible to go on, so not to excite another of his attacks. I'd indeed heard of the Montglane Service, but it had been lost for centuries. From what I knew of it, its value was beyond all imagining.

"I thought it was merely a legend," I said.

"Richelieu did not," the aged philosopher replied. "His journal contains twelve hundred pages of research into its origins and significance. He traveled to Aachen, or Aix-la-Chapelle, and even investigated Montglane, where he believed it had been buried, to no avail. You see, our cardinal thought this service contained the key to a mystery, a mystery older than chess, perhaps as old as civilization itself. A mystery that explains the rise and fall of civilizations."

"What sort of mystery could it be?" I asked, trying in vain to mask my excitement.

"I will tell you what he thought," Voltaire said, "though he died before he solved the puzzle. Make of it what you will, but do not bother me any further about it. Cardinal Richelieu believed the Montglane Service contained a formula, a formula hidden in the pieces of the service itself. A formula that revealed a secret of universal power . . ."

Talleyrand paused and peered through the gloomy light at Valentine and Mireille, curled in each other's arms and buried in the deep blankets of the bed. They were feigning sleep, their beautiful shimmering hair fanned out against the pillows, the long silken strands entwined. He stood up and leaned over them to pull the covers up, stroking their hair gently.

"Uncle Maurice," said Mireille, opening her eyes, "you have not finished your story. What was the formula that Cardinal Richelieu sought all his life? What was it he thought was hidden in the pieces of the service?"

"That is something we will have to discover together, my darlings." Talleyrand smiled, for he saw that Valentine's eyes were now open as well, and the two girls were trembling beneath the warm covers.

"You see, I never saw this manuscript. Voltaire died a short time later. His entire library was purchased by someone who knew well the value of Cardinal

Richelieu's journals. A person who both understood and coveted universal power.

"The person I refer to has attempted to bribe both myself and Mirabeau, who defended the Bill of Seizure, in an attempt to determine whether the Montglane Service could be confiscated by private parties of high political position and low ethical standards."

"But you refused the bribe, Uncle Maurice?" said Valentine, now sitting up in bed with the bedclothes tumbled about her.

"My price was too high for our patron, or should I say our patroness?" Talleyrand laughed. "I wanted the service for myself. And I still do."

Looking at Valentine in the dim candlelight, he smiled slowly. "Your abbess has made a great mistake," he told them. "For I've guessed what she has done, you see. She has removed the service from the abbey. Ah, do not look at me in that way, my dears. It seems coincidental, does it not, that your abbess has journeyed across a continent into Russia, as your uncle told me? You see, the person who purchased Voltaire's library, the person who attempted to bribe Mirabeau and me, the person who has sought these last forty years to lay her hands upon the service, is none other than Catherine the Great, empress of all the Russias."

A GAME
OF CHESS

But we shall play a game of Chess,
Pressing lidless eyes and
Waiting for a knock upon the door.

—*T. S. Eliot*

There was a knock upon the door. I was standing with one hand on my hip at the center of my apartment. Three months had passed since New Year's. I had nearly forgotten that night with the fortune-teller and the strange events surrounding it.

The knocking continued rather forcefully. I put another dab of Prussian blue on the large painting that stood before me and dropped the brush into a can of linseed oil. I'd left the windows open to air out the room, but my client Con Edison seemed to be burning ordure (that's French for garbage) just beneath my windows. The sills were black with soot.

I was in no mood to greet guests as I headed for the long entrance hall. I wondered why the desk hadn't rung me on the house phone, as they should have, to announce whoever was now banging on my door. I'd spent a rough enough week. I'd been trying to wind up my work with Con Edison and had spent hours fighting both with the managers of my building and with various storage companies. I was arranging for my imminent departure to Algeria.

My visa had just come through. I'd telephoned all my friends; once I left the country, I wouldn't be able to see them in over a year. There was one friend in particular whom I'd tried to reach, though he was as mysterious and inaccessible as the Sphinx. Little did I know how desperately I would need his help after the events that would soon take place.

Passing down the hallway, I glanced at myself in one of the mirrors that studded the walls. My mass of disheveled hair was streaked with vermilion paint, and there was a splash of crimson lake on my nose. I rubbed it with the back of my hand and wiped my palms on the canvas trousers and floppy work shirt I was wearing. Then I threw open the door.

Boswell the doorman was standing there, his angry fist poised in midair, wearing a navy-blue uniform with ridiculous epaulets that he'd no doubt selected himself. He looked down his long nose at me.

"Excuse me, madam," he sniffed, "but a certain powder-blue Corniche is blocking the entryway again. As you know, guests are required to leave the entrance of the building free so that deliveries can be made—"

"Why didn't you ring me on the house phone?" I interrupted angrily. I knew bloody well whose car he was talking about.

"The house phone has been out of service all week, madam. . . ."

"Well, why didn't you have the thing fixed, Boswell?"

"I am the doorman, madam. The doorman does not repair things. The custodian does that. The doorman screens the guests and makes certain that the entry—"

"All right. All right. Just send her up." There was only one person *I* knew in New York with a pale blue Corniche, and that was Lily Rad. As it was Sunday, I felt quite certain that Saul would be driving her. He could move the car while she was upstairs annoying me. But Boswell was still looking at me grimly.

"There is the matter of the small animal, madam. Your guest insists upon bringing the small animal into the building, although she has repeatedly been told—"

But it was too late. At that moment a bundle of fluff came tearing around the corner of the corridor from the elevators. It made a beeline for my apartment, whizzed between Boswell and me, and disappeared down my entrance hall. It was the size of a feather duster and made sharp little squeaks as it flew along the ground. Boswell looked at me with great disdain and did not speak.

"Okay, Boswell," I said with a shrug. "Let's just pretend we didn't see that, shall we? He won't make any trouble, and he'll be gone as soon as I can find him."

Just then Lily came waltzing around the same corner. She was draped in a sable cape with long puffy tails hanging from it. Her blond hair was tied in three or four large ponytails that frizzed out in different directions, so you couldn't see where her hair ended and the cape began. Boswell sighed and closed his eyes.

Lily completely ignored Boswell, gave me a fleeting peck on the cheek, and breezed between the two of us to enter my apartment. It wasn't easy for a person of Lily's bulk to breeze anywhere, but she carried her weight with a certain style. As she passed, she tossed off in her throaty torch-song voice, "Tell that doorman of yours not to get his bowels in an uproar. Saul is driving around the block until we leave."

I watched Boswell go, let out the groan I'd been suppressing, and closed the door. With regret, I went back into my apartment to face another Sunday afternoon, shattered by my least favorite person in New York, Lily Rad. I vowed this time I would get rid of her quickly.

My apartment consisted of one large room with a very high ceiling and a bath off the long entrance hall. Within the large room were three sets of doors enclosing a closet, a butler's pantry, and a pullman bed that folded into the wall. The room was a maze of giant trees and wild exotic plants forming junglelike pathways. Everywhere were piles of books, stacks of Moroccan pillows, and eclectica wrung from Third Avenue junk shops. There were hand-painted parchment lamps from India, majolica pitchers from Mexico, enameled French pottery birds, and chunks of Prague crystal. The walls were covered with half-finished paintings still damp with oil, old photos in carved frames, and antique mirrors. From the ceiling hung wind chimes, mobiles, and lacquered paper fish. The only piece of furniture in the room was an ebony parlor grand piano that stood near the windows.

Lily was pacing through the maze like an unleashed panther, pawing things aside as she searched for her dog. She tossed her cape of tails on the floor. I was astounded to discover that beneath it she was wearing practically nothing. Lily was built like a Maillol sculpture with tiny ankles and curving calves expanding as they moved upward to a billowing overabundance of gelatinous flesh. She had squeezed this mass into a skimpy purple silk dress that ended where her thighs began. As she moved she resembled an unmolded aspic, quivering and translucent.

Lily turned over a pillow and unearthed the silky little ball of fluff that traveled with her everywhere. She picked it up and cootchy-cooed it in her sultry voice.

"There is my darling Carioca," she purred. "Him was hiding from his mumsy. Him bad wittle doggy-woggy." I felt ill.

"A glass of wine?" I suggested as Lily put Carioca back on the floor. He ran around yapping in an annoying fashion. I went to the butler pantry and pulled a bottle of wine out of the refrigerator.

"I suppose you got that dreadful chardonnay from Llewellyn," Lily commented. "He's been trying to give it away for years."

She took the glassful I handed her and had a swig. Meandering through the trees, she paused before the painting I'd been working on when her arrival had blasted my Sunday all to hell.

"Say, do you know this fellow?" she said suddenly, referring to the man in the painting, a man on a bicycle dressed all in white, riding over a skeleton. "Did you model it after that guy downstairs?"

"What guy downstairs?" I asked, sitting on the piano bench and looking at Lily. Her lips and fingertips were enameled in Chinese lacquer red. Against her pale skin it lent an aura of the white bitch-goddess who'd lured the Green Knight or the Ancient Mariner to life-in-death. But then I thought it was àpropos. Caissa, the muse of chess, was no less ruthless than the muse of poetry. Muses had a way of killing those whom they inspired.

"The man on the bicycle," Lily was saying. "He was dressed like that— hooded and all muffled up. Though I only saw him from the back. We nearly ran him over. Had to drive up onto the sidewalk."

"Really?" I said, surprised. "I painted it from my imagination."

"It's frightening," said Lily, "like a man riding to his own death. There was something sinister about the way that man was lurking around your building, too. . . ."

"What did you say?" Something had rung a bell deep in my subconscious. *Behold a pale horse, and his name that sat upon him was Death.* Where had I heard that?

Carioca had stopped yapping and was now making suspicious little grunting sounds. He was digging the pine shavings out of one of my orchids and tossing them about the floor. I walked over, picked him up, and tossed him into the coat closet, shutting the door behind him.

"How dare you throw my dog into your closet!" Lily said.

"Dogs are only permitted in this building if they're confined to a box," I explained. "I haven't any boxes. Now tell me what good tidings brought you here? I haven't seen you in months." Mercifully, I thought.

"Harry's throwing you a farewell dinner," she said, sitting on the piano bench and tossing down the rest of her wine. "He says you can name the date. He's preparing the entire meal himself."

Carioca's little claws were tearing at the inside of my closet door, but I ignored it.

"I'd love to come to dinner," I said. "Why don't we make it this Wednesday? I'll probably be leaving by next weekend."

"Fine," said Lily. Now thuds could be heard from the closet as Carioca hurled his minuscule body against the door. Lily moved slightly from her seat on the piano bench.

"May I take my dog out of the closet, please?"

"Are you leaving?" I said hopefully.

I plucked my pile of brushes from the oil can and went over to the sink to rinse them off, as if she'd already departed. Lily was silent for a moment. Then she said, "I was just wondering, have you planned anything for this afternoon?"

"My plans don't seem to be working out today," I said from the pantry as I poured liquid soap into the hot water and it formed lathery bubbles.

"I was wondering whether you'd ever seen Solarin play," she said, smiling weakly and looking over at me with large gray eyes.

I put the brushes into the water and stared at her. This sounded suspiciously like an invitation to a chess match. Lily took great pride in never attending chess matches unless she herself was a contender.

"Who's Solarin?" I asked.

Lily looked at me in total amazement, as if I'd just asked who was the queen of England. "I had forgotten that you don't read the papers," she said. "Everyone is talking about it. This is the political event of the decade! He's supposed to be the finest chess player since Capablanca, a 'natural.' But he's just been let out of Soviet Russia for the first time in three years. . . ."

"I thought Bobby Fischer was supposed to be the world's best player," I said as I twirled my brushes in the hot lather. "What was all the shooting about in Reykjavík last summer?"

"Well, at least you've heard of Iceland," said Lily, standing up and coming over to lean against the pantry door. "The fact is, Fischer hasn't played since. There are rumors that he won't defend his title, that he'll never play in public again. The Russians are agog. Chess is their national sport, and they're all clawing each other trying to scramble to the top. If Fischer fails to defend, there are simply no contenders for the title outside Russia."

"So whichever Russian comes out best has a clear shot at the title," I said. "And you think this guy . . ."

"Solarin."

"You think Solarin will be it?"

"Maybe. Maybe not," Lily said, waxing to her theme. "That's the amazing thing about it. Everyone believes he's the best, but he doesn't have the backing of the Russian Politburo. An absolute must for any Russian player. In fact, for the last few years the Russians *haven't let him play!*"

"Why not?" I put the brushes into the drying rack and wiped my hands on a towel. "If they're so hot on winning that it's a matter of life and death . . ."

"He's not of the Soviet mold, apparently," said Lily as she pulled the wine bottle out of the fridge and poured herself another glass. "There was some brouhaha at a tournament in Spain three years ago. Solarin was whisked off in the dead of night, recalled to Mother Russia. At first they said he'd been taken ill, then they said he'd had a nervous breakdown. All sorts of stories and then—silence. Nothing's been heard of him since. Until this week."

"What happened this week?"

"This week, out of a clear blue sky, Solarin arrives in New York, simply *embedded* in a cadre of KGB men. He marches into the Manhattan Chess Club and says he wants to enter the Hermanold Invitational. Now this is outrageous on several counts. An invitational means you must be invited to attend. Solarin wasn't invited. Second, it's a zone five invitational, zone five being the USA. As opposed to zone four, which is the USSR. You can imagine the consternation when they saw who he was."

"Why couldn't they just refuse his entry?"

"Bloody hell!" said Lily with glee. "John Hermanold, the sponsor of the tournament, used to be a theatrical producer. Since the Fischer sensation in Iceland there's been an upsurge in the chess market. There's money in it now. Hermanold would commit murder to get a name like Solarin's on the ticket."

"I don't understand how Solarin got out of Russia for this tournament if the Soviets don't want him to play."

"My darling, that is the question," Lily said. "And the KGB bodyguard certainly suggests that he comes with government blessings, doesn't it? Oh, it's a fascinating mystery. That's why I thought you'd like to go today. . . ." Lily paused.

"Go where?" I said sweetly, though I knew perfectly well what she was leading up to. I enjoyed watching her squirm. Lily had made such press out of her total indifference to the competition. "I don't play the man," she'd been quoted as saying, "I play the board."

"Solarin is playing this afternoon," she said hesitantly. "It's his first public play since that thing in Spain. The game today is sold out, the tickets are being scalped for a fortune. It starts in an hour, but I think I could get us in—"

"Gee, thanks," I cut in. "But I'll pass. I really find chess pretty boring to watch. Why don't you go by yourself?"

Lily gripped her wineglass and sat stiffly on the piano bench. When she spoke it was with some strain.

"You know I can't do that," she said quietly.

I felt certain this was the first time Lily had ever had to ask a favor of anyone. If I accompanied her to the game, she could pretend she was merely doing a favor for a friend. If she showed up alone asking for a ticket, the chess columns would have a heyday. Solarin might be news, but in New York chess circles Lily Rad's appearance at a game might be bigger news. She was one of the top-ranked women players in the United States, and surely the most flamboyant.

"Next week," she said between tight lips, "I play the winner of today's game."

"Ah. Now I see," I told her. "Solarin might be the winner. And since you've never played him, and *undoubtedly* never read up on his style of play . . ."

I walked over to the closet and opened the door. Carioca slunk out furtively. Then he ran over to my foot and started wrestling with a loose thread on my canvas espadrilles. I looked down at him for a moment, then scooped him up with my toe and drop-kicked him into a pile of pillows. He wriggled with pleasure and ripped out a few feathers with his sharp little teeth.

"I can't imagine why he's so attached to you," said Lily.

"Simply a question of who's to be master," I said. Lily was silent.

We watched Carioca screw around in the pillows as if it were something of interest. Though I knew very little of chess, I recognized when I held center board. I didn't feel that the next move should be mine.

"You *have* to go with me," Lily said at last.

"I think you've phrased that wrong," I pointed out.

Lily stood up again and came over to me. She looked me right in the eye. "You've no idea how important this tournament is to me," she said. "Hermanold has swung the chess commissioners to permit this tournament to be ranked, by inviting every GM and IM in zone five. Had I placed well and picked up points, I could have gone into the big leagues. I might have even won it. If Solarin hadn't shown up."

The complexities of seeding chess players were mysterious, as I knew. The award of titles such as grand master (GM) and international master (IM) was even more so. You'd think with a game as mathematical as chess, the guidelines for supremacy would be a little clearer, but it operated like a good old boys' club. I could understand Lily's exasperation, but something puzzled me.

"What difference would it make if you came in second?" I said. "You're still one of the top-ranked women in the United States—"

"Top-ranked *women*! Women?" Lily looked as if she were about to spit on the floor. I remembered that she made a big point of never playing against women. Chess was a man's game, and to win at it you had to beat men. Lily had been waiting over a year for the IM title she felt she'd already earned. This tournament was important, I now realized, because they could no longer withhold the title if she came in first over people who outranked her.

"You understand nothing," Lily said. "This is a 'knockout' tournament. I'm paired against Solarin in his second game, assuming we both win our first, which we will. If I play him and lose, I'm out of the tournament altogether."

"You don't think you can beat him?" I said. Though Solarin was such a big deal, I was still surprised Lily would admit the possibility of defeat.

"I don't know," she said honestly. "My chess coach thinks not. He thinks Solarin could cream me all over the board. He could pull my pants down. You don't understand what it feels like to lose at chess. I hate to lose. I hate it." Her teeth were gritted and her hands folded into tight little balls.

"Don't they have to pair you against people with the same rank as yours at the onset?" I asked. It seemed I had read something about that.

"There are only a few dozen players in the United States who are seeded at over twenty-four hundred points," Lily replied gloomily. "And they're obviously not all in this tournament. Though Solarin's last seeding was over twenty-five hundred, there are only five people between my rank and his who are here. But playing him so early on, I won't have a chance to warm up in other games."

Now I understood. The theatrical producer who was running this tournament had invited Lily because of her publicity value. He wanted to sell tickets, and Lily was the Josephine Baker of chess. She had everything but the ocelot and the bananas. Now that he had a bigger drawing card in the form of Solarin, Lily could be sacrificed as a dispensable commodity. He'd pair her off against Solarin early and wipe her out. It meant nothing that this tournament could serve as a vehicle for her title. Suddenly it occurred to me that the chess world wasn't much different from the world of certified public accounting.

"Okay, you've explained it," I said. I headed off down the hallway.

"Where are you going?" Lily said, raising her voice.

"I'd like to take a shower," I called back over my shoulder.

"A shower?" She sounded a little hysterical. "What on earth for?"

"I'll have to bathe and change," I said, pausing at the bathroom door to turn and look at her, "if we're going to make that chess game in an hour."

Lily looked at me in silence. She had the grace to smile.

I felt absurd riding in an open car in mid-March when snow clouds were closing in and the temperature had dropped to thirty. Lily was swathed in her fur cape. Carioca was busily tearing off the tassels and scattering them on the floorboards. I was wearing only a black wool coat, and I was freezing.

"Is there a lid to this thing?" I asked against the wind.

"Why don't you let Harry make up a fur for you? After all, it's his business, and he adores you."

"It won't help me much right now," I told her. "Now explain why this game is a closed session at the Metropolitan Club. I'd think the sponsor would want to get as much publicity as possible from Solarin's first game in years on Western soil."

"You certainly understand sponsors," Lily agreed. "But Solarin's playing Fiske today. Having a public match instead of a quiet, private one might backfire. Fiske is more than a little crazy."

"Who's Fiske?"

"Antony Fiske," she said, drawing up her fur. "A very big player. He's a British GM, but he's registered in zone five because he used to live in Boston when he was playing actively. I'm surprised he accepted, since he hasn't played in years. At his last tournament he had the audience cleared from the room. He thought the room was bugged and there were mysterious vibrations in the air that interfered with his brain waves. All chess players are tottering on the brink. They say Paul Morphy, the first U.S. champion, died sitting up fully clothed in a bathtub floating with women's shoes. Madness is the occupational hazard of chess, but you won't find me going nuts. It only happens to men."

"Why to men?"

"Because chess, my dear, is such an Oedipal game. Kill the King and fuck the Queen, that's what it's all about. Psychologists love to follow chess players about to see if they wash their hands too much, sniff at old sneakers, or masturbate between sessions. Then they write it all up in the *Journal of the AMA*."

The powder-blue Rolls Corniche pulled up in front of the Metropolitan Club at Sixtieth Street, just off Fifth Avenue. Saul let us out. Lily handed Carioca to him and bounded ahead of me up the canopied ramp that ran along the edge of a cobbled courtyard and led to the entrance. Saul had not spoken during our trip, but now he winked at me. I shrugged my shoulders and followed Lily.

The Metropolitan Club is a weary remnant of old New York. A private men's residential club, it seemed nothing had changed within its walls since the last century. The faded red carpeting in the foyer could have used some shampooing, and the dark beveled wood of the reception desk needed a little wax. But the main lounge made up in charm for what the entrance lacked in polish.

Opening off the lobby, it was an enormous room with thirty-foot ceilings carved in palladio and encrusted with gold leaf. A single chandelier dropped on a long cord from the center. Two walls were composed of tiered balconies whose ornately sculptured railings overlooked the center like a Venetian courtyard. The third wall contained gold-veined mirrors to the ceiling, reflecting the other two. The fourth side was separated from the lobby by high louvered screens in red velvet. Scattered across the marble floor, checkered black and white like a chessboard, were dozens of small tables surrounded by leather chairs. At the far corner was an ebony piano beside a Chinese lacquered screen.

As I was studying the decor, Lily called to me from the balcony just above. Her fur cape was dangling over the side. She waved me toward the wide expanse of marble steps that swept up in a curve from the foyer to the first balcony where she stood.

Upstairs, Lily motioned me into a small card room and followed me inside. The room was moss-green with large French windows overlooking Fifth Avenue and the park. There were several workmen bustling about removing leather-topped card tables and green baize gaming tables. They gave us abrupt glances as they stacked the tables against a wall near the door.

"This is where the game will take place," Lily told me. "But I'm not sure whether anyone has arrived. We have half an hour yet." Turning to a passing workman, she said, "Do you know where John Hermanold is?"

"Maybe in the dining room." The man shrugged. "You could call upstairs and have him paged." He looked her up and down unflatteringly. Lily was dangling out of her dress, and I was glad I'd come in conservative gray flannels. I started to remove my coat, but the workman stopped me.

"Ladies ain't allowed in the gaming room," he told me. To Lily he added, "Nor in the dining room, neither. You'd best go downstairs and phone up there."

"I'm going to murder that bastard Hermanold," Lily whispered between clenched teeth. "A private *men's* club, for God's sake?" She went off down the corridor in search of her prey, and I turned back into the room and plopped down on a chair amid the hostile glances of the laborers. I didn't envy Hermanold when Lily found him.

I sat there in the gaming room gazing through the dirty windows that overlooked Central Park. There were a few limp flags hanging outside, and the flat winter light diluted their already faded colors.

"Excuse me," said a haughty voice behind me. I turned to see a tall, attractive

man in his fifties with dark hair and silvery temples. He was wearing a navy
blazer with an elaborate crest, gray trousers, and a white turtleneck sweater. He
reeked of Andover and Yale.

"No one is permitted into this room until the tournament begins," he said
firmly. "If you have a ticket, I can seat you downstairs until then. Otherwise
I'm afraid you'll have to leave the club." His initial attractiveness had begun
to wane. Pretty is as pretty does, I thought. But aloud I said, "I prefer to remain
here. I'm waiting for someone to bring my ticket—"

"I'm afraid not," he said abruptly. He actually put his hand beneath my
elbow. "I've made commitments to the club that we'd observe the rules. Furthermore, there are security considerations. . . ."

I seemed to be remaining in my seat, though he was tugging at me with all
the dignity he could muster. Hooking my ankles around the legs of my chair,
I smiled up at him. "I promised my friend Lily Rad that I would wait," I told
him. "She's looking for—"

"Lily Rad!" he said, releasing my arm as if it were a hot poker. I settled back
with a sweet expression. "Lily Rad is *here*?" I continued smiling and nodded.

"Permit me to introduce myself, Miss, er . . ."

"Velis," I said, "Catherine Velis."

"Miss Velis, I am John Hermanold," he told me. "I am the tournament
sponsor." He grabbed my hand and shook it heartily. "You've no idea what an
honor it is, having Lily come to this game. Do you know where I might find
her?"

"She went off looking for you," I said. "The workmen told us you were in
the dining room. She's probably gone up there."

"To the dining room," Hermanold repeated, clearly envisioning the worst.
"I'll just go off and find her, shall I? Then we'll round you up, and I'll buy you
both a drink downstairs." And he popped out the door.

Now that Hermanold was such an old chum, the workmen skirted around
me with grudging respect. I watched as they removed the stacked gaming tables
from the room and started setting up rows of chairs facing the windows, leaving
an aisle down the center. Then, oddly, they got down on the floor with tape
measures and began adjusting the furniture so it was squared to some invisible
standard they seemed to be tracing.

I was watching these maneuvers with such curiosity that I didn't notice a man
who slipped silently into the room until he passed close by my chair. He was
tall and slender with very pale blond hair cut long and swept back to curl at
the collar. He was wearing gray trousers and a loose white linen shirt open to
reveal the strong neck and good bones of a dancer. He moved swiftly to where
the workmen were puttering about and spoke to them in low tones. Those
who'd been measuring the floor got up at once and went over to him. When

he extended his arm to point at something, they scurried at once to carry out his wishes.

A large scoreboard in front was relocated several times, the arbiters' table was removed farther from the playing area, and the chess table itself was adjusted back and forth until it was absolutely equidistant from either wall. During these strange maneuverings, I noticed the workmen voiced no complaint. They seemed in awe of the newcomer and were reluctant to look him in the eye as they carefully carried out his orders. Then I realized that not only was he aware of my presence, he was asking them about me. He gestured in my direction and finally turned to look at me. As he did so, I felt a shock. There was something at once familiar and strange about him.

His high cheekbones, narrow aquiline nose, and strong jawline formed angular planes that caught the light like marble. His eyes were a pale, greenish gray, the color of liquid mercury. He looked like a magnificent piece of Renaissance sculpture chiseled of stone. And like stone, too, there was something cold and impenetrable about him. I was fascinated by him as a bird is charmed by a snake and completely taken off my guard when he unexpectedly left the workmen and crossed the room to where I sat.

When he reached my chair, he took me by the hands and pulled me to my feet. With one hand beneath my elbow, he started with me toward the door before I realized what was happening and whispered in my ear, "What are you doing here? You should not have come." There was the faintest trace of an accent. I was shocked by his behavior. After all, I was a total stranger to him. I stopped in my tracks.

"Who *are* you?" I said.

"It makes no difference who *I* am," he said, his voice still low. He looked into my face with those pale green eyes as if he were trying to remember something. "What matters is that I know who *you* are. It was a grave mistake for you to come here. You are in great danger. I feel danger all around me, even now."

Where had I heard that before?

"What are you talking about?" I said. "I'm here for the chess tournament. I'm with Lily Rad. John Hermanold told me I could—"

"Yes, yes," he said impatiently. "I know all that. But you must leave at once. Please don't ask me to explain. Just leave this club as quickly as possible . . . please do as I say."

"This is ridiculous!" I said, my voice rising. He quickly glanced over his shoulder at the workmen and looked back at me. "I have no intention of leaving until you tell me what you mean. I've no idea who you are. I've never seen you before in my life. What right—"

"Yes, you have," he said quietly. He placed his hand ever so gently on my shoulder and looked into my eyes. "And you will see me again. But now, you must leave at once."

Then he was gone. He'd turned on his heel and left the room as silently as he'd arrived. I stood there a moment and realized that I was trembling. Glancing over at the workmen, I saw they were still puttering about and hadn't seemed to notice anything strange. I went to the door and stepped out onto the balcony, my mind tangled from this strange encounter. And then I remembered. He'd reminded me of the fortune-teller.

Lily and Hermanold were calling to me from the lounge below. They stood on the black-and-white marble tiles beneath me, looking like oddly costumed chess pieces on a cluttered board. There were other guests moving about them.

"Come down," called Hermanold, "I'll buy you that drink."

I walked along the balcony to the red-carpeted marble staircase and descended to the lobby. My legs still felt a little weak. I wanted to get Lily alone and tell her what had happened.

"What will you have?" asked Hermanold as I approached the table. He pulled up a chair for me. Lily was already seated. "We should have some champagne. It isn't every day we have Lily's presence at someone else's chess game!"

"It isn't *any* day," Lily said irritably as she tossed her fur over the back of her chair. Hermanold ordered the champagne and launched into a self-glorification that seemed to set Lily's teeth on edge.

"The tournament is going very well. We'll be playing to full houses every day. All that advance publicity has really paid off. But even *I* couldn't have foreseen the luminaries we'd attract. First Fiske coming out of retirement, and then the blockbuster. Solarin's arrival! And yourself, of course," he added, patting Lily on the knee. I longed to interrupt and ask about the stranger upstairs, but I couldn't get a word in edgewise.

"Too bad I couldn't have had the big hall at the Manhattan for today's game," he told us as the champagne arrived. "We would have really packed them in for this one. But I was afraid of Fiske, you know. We've got medics standing by just in case. I thought it best to play him off early, eliminate him up front. He'd never make it through the tournament in any case, and we've already got the press, just by his coming."

"It sounds so exciting," said Lily. "The chance of seeing two grand masters and a nervous breakdown, all at one game." Hermanold glanced at her nervously as he poured our drinks. He wasn't certain whether she was joking. But I was. That bit about eliminating Fiske early had struck home.

"Maybe I'll stay for the game after all," she went on sweetly, sipping her champagne. "I'd planned to *leave*, once I got Cat settled in. . . ."

"Oh, you mustn't!" said Hermanold, looking genuinely alarmed. "I mean, I'd hate for you to miss this. It's the game of the century."

"And the reporters you've phoned up would be *so* disappointed if they didn't find me here as you'd promised. Wouldn't they, darling John?" She threw down a mouthful of champagne as Hermanold turned a little pink.

I saw my opportunity and interjected, "The man I saw upstairs just now, was that Fiske?"

"In the gaming room?" said Hermanold, looking worried. "I hope not. He's supposed to be resting before the game."

"Whoever it was, he was very strange," I told him. "He came in and started having the workmen move the furniture about. . . ."

"Oh, Lord," Hermanold said. "That *must* have been Fiske. The last time I dealt with him he insisted on having a person or chair put out of the room as each piece was removed from the board. It restored his sense of 'balance and harmony,' he said. Hates women as well, doesn't like them in the room when he's playing. . . ." Hermanold patted Lily's hand, but she pulled it away.

"Maybe that's why he asked *me* to leave," I said.

"He asked you to leave?" said Hermanold. "That was uncalled for, but I'll have a talk with him before the game. He's got to be made to understand that he can't carry on as he did in the old days when he was a star. He hasn't played a major tournament in over fifteen years."

"Fifteen?" I said. "He must have quit when he was twelve years old. The man I saw upstairs just now was young."

"Really?" said Hermanold, puzzled. "Who could it have been, then?"

"A tall, slender man, very pale. Attractive but icy-looking, . . ."

"Oh, that was Alexei." Hermanold laughed.

"Alexei?"

"Alexander Solarin," Lily said. "You know, darling, the one you were dying to see. The 'blockbuster'?"

"Tell me more about him," I said.

"I'm afraid I can't," Hermanold was saying. "I didn't even know what he looked like until he arrived and tried to register for the tournament. The man's a mystery. He doesn't meet people, doesn't permit photographs. We have to keep the cameras out of the game rooms. He finally gave a press interview at my insistence. After all, what's the use of *having* him here if we can't publicize the fact?"

Lily glared at him in exasperation and let out a loud sigh. "Thanks for the drink, John," she said, tossing her fur over her shoulder.

I was on my feet as soon as Lily. I walked out of the lounge and up the stairs with her. "I didn't want to talk in front of Hermanold," I whispered as we moved along the balcony, "but about this guy Solarin . . . There's something strange going on here."

"I see it all the time," said Lily. "In the chess world you meet people who are either pricks or assholes. Or both. I'm certain this Solarin is no exception. They can't bear to have women in the game—"

"That's not what I'm talking about," I interrupted. "Solarin didn't tell me to leave because he wanted to get rid of a *woman*. He told me I was in great danger!" I had grabbed her arm, and we stood there at the railing. The crowd was thickening in the lounge below.

"He told you what?" said Lily. "You've got to be kidding. Danger? At a chess game? The only danger at this one is falling asleep. Fiske likes to beat you into the ground with draws and stalemates."

"I'm telling you he warned me that I was in danger," I said again, drawing her back near the wall so some people could pass by. I lowered my voice. "Do you remember that fortune-teller you sent Harry and me to see at New Year's?"

"Oh, no," said Lily. "Don't tell me you believe in the mystic powers?" She smiled.

People were beginning to drift down the balcony and brush past us into the gaming room. We joined the flow, and Lily picked out some seats near the front to one side, where we'd have a good view but remain inconspicuous. If that were possible in the getup she was wearing. When we were seated, I leaned over and whispered, "Solarin used almost the same words as that fortune-teller. Didn't Harry mention it to you, what she told me?"

"I never saw her," Lily said, pulling a small pegboard chess set out of a pocket in her cape. She set it up in her lap. "She was recommended to me by a friend, but I don't believe in that shit. That's why I didn't go."

People were taking their seats around us, and Lily was getting a lot of stares. A group of reporters had entered the room, one with a camera around his neck. They caught sight of Lily and headed in our direction. She bent over her pegboard and said in a low voice, "We are *seriously* involved in a conversation about chess. Should anyone inquire."

John Hermanold had entered the room. He swiftly approached the reporters and collared the one with the camera just before he reached us.

"Excuse me, but I'll have to take that camera," he told the reporter. "Grand Master Solarin does not want cameras in the tournament hall. Please take your seats back here so we can start the game. There will be time for interviews after."

The reporter grudgingly handed his camera over to Hermanold. He and his companions moved to the seats the promoter had designated.

The room quieted to hushed whispers. The arbiters came in and sat at their table, followed quickly by the man I now knew to be Solarin and an older graying man I presumed was Fiske.

Fiske looked nervous and high-strung. One eye was twitching slightly, and he kept moving his graying mustache around as if he were shaking off a fly. He had thin hair, a little greasy, that was brushed back but kept falling over his forehead in loose strands. He wore a maroon velour jacket that had seen better days and had not been brushed in some time. It was sashed like a bathrobe.

His baggy brown trousers were wrinkled. I felt sorry for him. He seemed totally out of place and despondent.

Beside him, Solarin looked like the alabaster statue of a discus thrower. He stood at least a head taller than Fiske, who was hunched over. He moved gracefully to one side, pulled out a chair for Fiske, and helped him into his seat.

"Bastard," Lily hissed. "He's trying to win Fiske's confidence, gain the upper hand before the game even begins."

"Don't you think you're being a little severe?" I said aloud. Several voices shushed me from the row behind.

A boy came over with the box of pieces and started setting them up, the white pieces before Solarin. Lily explained that the color-drawing ceremony had taken place the prior day. A few more people shushed us, so we fell silent.

As one of the arbiters read the rules, Solarin looked out at the audience. His profile to me, I now had the opportunity to study him in detail. He was more open and relaxed than earlier. Now that he was in his element, about to play chess, he looked young and intense, like an athlete on the brink of competition. But then his glance fell upon Lily and me, and his face tightened, his eyes riveted upon me.

"Whoo," said Lily. "I see what you meant when you said icy. I'm glad I got a look at this before I saw it over a chessboard."

Solarin was looking at me as if he could not believe I was still there. As if he wanted to get up and drag me out of the room. I suddenly had the slow, sinking feeling that I'd done something terribly wrong by staying. The pieces were set up, and his clock started, so at last he moved his eyes to the chessboard. He pushed his King's pawn forward. I noticed that Lily, sitting beside me, made the same move on her lap pegboard. A boy standing near the easel chalked up the move: P–K4.

The play went on uneventfully for a while. Solarin and Fiske each had a pawn and a Knight out. Solarin slid his King's Bishop forward. A few people in the audience muttered. One or two stood up to go out for coffee.

"It looks like *Giuoco Piano*." Lily sighed. "This could be a very long game. That defense is never played in tournaments, it's as old as the hills. It's even mentioned in the Göttingen Manuscript, for Christ's sake." For a girl who never read a word about chess, Lily was a gold mine of erudition.

"It lets Black develop his pieces, but it's slow slow slow. Solarin is making it easy on Fiske, letting him get in a few moves before obliterating him. Call me if anything happens in the next hour or so."

"How am *I* supposed to know if anything happens?" I whispered back.

Just then Fiske made a move and stopped his clock. There was a brief murmur among the crowd, and a few people who'd been leaving paused to look back at the easel. I looked up in time to see Solarin smile. It was a strange smile.

"What happened?" I asked Lily.

"Fiske is more adventurous than I thought. Instead of moving a Bishop, he's taken the 'Two Knights' Defense.' The Russians love it. It's far more dangerous. I'm surprised he'd choose it against Solarin, who's known for . . ." She bit her lip. After all, Lily never researched other players' styles. Did she.

Solarin now advanced his Knight and Fiske his Queen's pawn. Solarin took the pawn. Fiske then took Solarin's pawn with his Knight, so they were even. I thought. It seemed to me that Fiske was in good shape, with his pieces sitting at center board and Solarin's all trapped at the back. But Solarin now took Fiske's Bishop with his own Knight. A large rumble ran through the room. The few people who'd left dashed back in with their coffees and looked at the easel as the boy chalked up the move.

"*Fegatello!*" cried Lily, and this time no one shushed her. "I don't believe it."

"What's *Fegatello?*" There seemed to be more mysterious buzz words in chess than in data processing.

"It means 'fried liver.' And Fiske's liver *will* be fried, if he uses his King to take that Knight." She chewed on her finger and looked down at the pegboard in her lap as if the game were going on there. "He'll lose something for sure. His Queen and Rook are forked there. He can't get at the Knight with any other piece."

It seemed illogical to me that Solarin would make such a move. Was he trading a Knight for a Bishop only in order to get the King to move one space?

"Once Fiske has moved the King, he can no longer castle it," said Lily as if she'd read my mind. "The King will be shoved out into center board and be scrambling for the rest of the game. He'd be better off to move the Queen and throw away the Rook."

But Fiske did take the Knight with his King. Solarin slid his Queen out and checked. Fiske tucked his King away behind some pawns, and Solarin moved his Queen back to threaten the Black Knight. Things were definitely picking up, but I couldn't tell where they were moving. Lily seemed confused as well.

"There's something odd here," she whispered to me. "This is not Fiske's style of play."

Something strange *was* going on. Watching Fiske, I noticed that he refused to look up from the board after he'd made a move. His nervousness had certainly increased. He was visibly perspiring, large dark circles of sweat had appeared beneath the arms of his maroon jacket. He seemed ill, and though it was Solarin's move, Fiske concentrated upon the board as if it were his hope of heaven.

Solarin's clock was running now, but he too was watching Fiske. He seemed to have forgotten that a game was going on, so intently was he staring at his opponent. After a very long time Fiske looked up from the board at Solarin, but his eyes slid away; he looked back to the board again. Solarin's eyes narrowed. He picked up a piece and shoved it forward.

I was no longer paying attention to the moves. I was watching the two men, trying to figure out what was happening between them. Lily was sitting beside me with open mouth studying the board intently. Suddenly Solarin stood up from the board and pushed his chair back. A commotion started behind us as people whispered to their neighbors. Solarin punched the buttons to stop both clocks and bent over Fiske to say something. An arbiter ran over to the table quickly. He and Solarin exchanged a few words, and the arbiter shook his head. Fiske just sat there hanging his head and looking at the chessboard, his hands in his lap. Solarin said something to him again. The arbiter went back to the judges' table. The judges all nodded, and the center judge stood up.

"Ladies and gentlemen," he said. "Grand Master Fiske is not feeling well. As a kindness, Grand Master Solarin has stopped the clock and agreed to a brief recess so that Mr. Fiske can have a breath of fresh air. Mr. Fiske, you will seal your next move for the arbiters, and we will resume play in thirty minutes."

Fiske wrote his move with trembling hand and put it in an envelope, sealing it and handing it to the arbiter. Solarin marched swiftly out of the room before the reporters could grab him and strode off down the hall. The room was in a great deal of agitation, everyone buzzing and whispering in small groups. I turned to Lily.

"What happened? What's going on?"

"This is incredible," she said. "Solarin can't stop the clocks. The arbiter has to do that. It's completely against the rules, they should have called the game. The arbiter stops the clocks if everyone agrees to a recess. But only *after* Fiske has sealed his next move."

"So Solarin gave Fiske some free time off the clock," I said. "Why did he do that?"

Lily looked at me, her gray eyes nearly colorless. She seemed surprised by her own thoughts. "He *knew* it wasn't Fiske's style of play," she said. She was silent for a moment, then went on, replaying it in her mind. "Solarin offered Fiske an exchange of Queens. He didn't have to within the parameters of the game. It was almost as if he were offering Fiske a test. Everyone knows how Fiske hates to lose his Queen."

"So Fiske accepted?" I asked.

"No," said Lily, still lost in her own thoughts. "He didn't. He picked up his Queen, then put it down. He tried to pretend it was *j'adoube*."

"What's *j'adoube*?"

"I touch, I adjust. It's quite legitimate to adjust a piece in the middle of play."

"So what was wrong?" I said.

"Nothing at all," said Lily. "But you must say, *'J'adoube,' before* you touch the piece. Not after you've already moved it."

"Maybe he didn't realize . . ."

"He's a grand master," Lily said. She looked at me for a long time. "He realized."

Lily sat there looking at her pegboard. I didn't want to disturb her, but everyone had left the room by now, and we were alone. I sat beside her, trying to figure out with my limited knowledge of chess exactly what all of this meant.

"Do you want to know what I think?" Lily said at last. "I think Grand Master Fiske was cheating. I think he's wired to a transmitter."

If I had known then how right she was, it might have changed events that were soon to follow. But how could I have guessed at the time what had really been happening—only ten feet away from me—as Solarin was studying the board?

Solarin had been looking down at the chessboard when he'd first noticed it. At first it had been only a flash at the corner of his eye. But the third time he'd noticed it, he had associated it with the move. Fiske had put his hands in his lap every time Solarin stopped his clock and Fiske's started. Solarin had looked at Fiske's hands the next time he made a move. It was the ring. Fiske had never worn a ring before.

Fiske was playing recklessly. He was taking chances. He was playing more interesting chess in a way, but every time he took a risk Solarin looked at his face. And it was not the face of a risk taker. That was when Solarin started watching the ring.

Fiske was wired. There was no question. Solarin was playing someone or something else. It wasn't in the room, and it surely wasn't Fiske. Solarin looked up at his KGB man, who sat against the far wall. If he were to take a gamble and lose the bloody game, he'd be out of the tournament. But he needed to know who wired Fiske. And why.

Solarin started playing dangerous chess to see if he could establish a pattern in Fiske's responses. This nearly drove Fiske up the wall. Then Solarin got the idea to force an exchange of Queens that had nothing to do with the game. He moved his Queen into position, offering her, opening her up, heedless of the outcome. He would force Fiske into playing his own game or revealing that he was a cheat. That was when Fiske fell apart.

For a moment it seemed that Fiske would actually accept the exchange, take his Queen. Then Solarin could call in the judges and resign the game. He wouldn't play against a machine, or whatever Fiske was wired to. But Fiske had backed off and instead asked for *j'adoube*. Solarin jumped up and leaned over Fiske.

"What the hell do you think you're doing?" he whispered. "We'll recess now until you've come to your senses. Do you realize that's the KGB over there? One word of this to them and your chess-playing days are over."

Solarin waved to the arbiters with one hand as he stopped the clocks with the other. He told the arbiter Fiske was ill and would seal his next move.

"And it had better be a Queen, sir," he said, bending over Fiske again. Fiske would not look up. He was twisting his ring in his lap as if it were too tight. Solarin stormed out of the room.

The KGB man met him in the hall with a questioning look. He was a short, pale man with heavy eyebrows. His name was Gogol.

"Go have a slivovitz," said Solarin. "Let me take care of this."

"What's happened?" Gogol asked. "Why did he ask for *j'adoube*? It was irregular. You shouldn't have stopped the clocks, they might have disqualified you."

"Fiske is wired. I must know to whom, and why. All you could do is to make him more frightened. Go away and pretend you don't know anything. I can take care of it."

"But Brodski is here," said Gogol in a whisper. Brodski was in the upper echelons of the secret service and well outranked Solarin's guard.

"Invite him to join you, then," Solarin snapped. "Just keep him away from me for the next half hour. I want no action on this. No action, do you understand me, Gogol?"

The bodyguard looked frightened, but he went off down the hallway to the stairs. Solarin followed as far as the end of the balcony, then ducked into a doorway and waited for Fiske to leave the gaming room.

Fiske walked quickly along the balcony and down the wide stairs, hurrying across the foyer. He did not look over his shoulder to see Solarin watching him from above. He went outside and crossed the courtyard, past the massive wrought-iron gates. In the far corner of the court, diagonal to the club entrance, was a door leading to the smaller Canadian Club. Fiske entered and went up the steps.

Solarin moved silently across the court. He pushed open the glass door of the Canadian Club just in time to see the door of the men's room swing shut behind Fiske. He paused for a moment, then moved carefully up the few short steps to the door, slipped inside, and remained motionless. Fiske stood across the room, eyes closed, his body swaying against the urinal wall. Solarin watched silently as Fiske dropped to his knees. He began to sob—low, dry sobs—then, leaning over, his stomach heaved once, and he vomited into the porcelain basin. When it was finished he leaned his forehead in exhaustion against the bowl.

From the corner of his eye, Solarin saw Fiske's head jerk up as he heard the sound of the faucet. Solarin stood motionless at the sink, watching cold water splash into the basin. Fiske was an Englishman; he would feel humiliated at someone watching him vomit like an animal.

"You will need this," Solarin said aloud, not turning from the basin.

Fiske looked about, unsure whether Solarin was addressing him. But the room seemed to be empty except for the two of them. Hesitantly he rose from his knees and walked toward Solarin, who was wringing a paper towel into the basin. The towel smelled of damp oatmeal.

Solarin turned and sponged Fiske's forehead and temples. "If you submerge your wrists, it will cool the blood throughout your body," he said, unfastening Fiske's cuffs. He tossed the damp towel into the trash bin. Fiske silently dropped his wrists into the water-filled basin, keeping his fingers, Solarin noticed, from getting wet.

Solarin was scribbling with a pencil stub on the back of a dry paper towel. Fiske glanced over, his wrists still submerged, and Solarin showed him the writing. It read, "Is the transmission one way or two?"

Fiske looked up, and the blood flooded back into his face. Solarin was looking at him with an intent expression, then he bent over the paper again and added for clarification, "Can they hear us?"

Fiske took a deep breath and closed his eyes. Then he shook his head in the negative. He took his hand from the bowl and reached for the paper towel, but Solarin handed him another one.

"Not this towel," he said, taking out a small gold lighter and setting fire to the towel on which he'd written his note. He let it burn nearly all the way down, then carried it to a toilet, tossed it in, and flushed. "You are certain?" he asked, returning to the sink. "It is important."

"Yes," said Fiske uncomfortably. "It . . . was explained to me."

"Fine, then we can speak." Solarin still held the gold lighter in his hand. "In which ear is it planted, the left or the right?" Fiske tapped his left ear. Solarin nodded. He opened the bottom of the lighter and removed a small hinged object, which he pried apart. It was a pincerlike tweezer.

"Lie on the floor and place your head in such a position that it will not move, your left ear up toward me. Do not move about suddenly, I don't wish to perforate your eardrum."

Fiske did as he was told. He seemed almost relieved to place himself in Solarin's hands and never questioned why a fellow grand master would be adept at removing hidden transmitters. Solarin squatted and bent over Fiske's ear. After a moment he pulled out a small object, which he turned about in the pincers. It was slightly larger than a pinhead.

"Ah," said Solarin. "Not so small as ours. Now tell me, my dear Fiske, who put it there? Who is behind all of this?" He dropped the small transmitter into his palm.

Fiske sat up abruptly and looked at Solarin. For the first time he seemed to realize who Solarin was: not only a fellow chess player, but a Russian. He had a KGB escort prowling about the building somewhere to reinforce this terrible fact. Fiske moaned aloud and dropped his head into his hands.

"You must tell me. You see that, don't you?" Solarin glanced down at Fiske's ring. He picked up the hand and studied the ring closely. Fiske looked up in fear.

It was an oversized signet with a crest on the surface, made of a goldlike metal with the surface inset separately. Solarin pressed the signet, and there was a low whirring click that was barely perceptible even at so close a range. Fiske could press the ring in a code to communicate what move had last been made, and his associates would send his next move through the transmitter in his ear.

"Were you warned not to remove this ring?" Solarin asked. "It is large enough to contain a small explosive as well as a detonator."

"A detonator!" cried Fiske.

"Enough to remove most of this room," Solarin replied, smiling. "At least, the part where we are seated. Are you an agent of the Irish? They're very good at small bombs, like letter bombs. I should know, most of them are trained in Russia." Fiske looked green, but Solarin continued, "I've no idea what your friends are after, my dear Fiske. But if an agent should betray *my* government as you've betrayed those who sent you, they'd have a means to silence him quickly and completely."

"But . . . I am not an agent!" Fiske cried.

Solarin looked into his face for a moment, then he smiled. "No, I don't believe you are. My God, but they have made a sloppy job of this." Fiske twisted his hands as Solarin thought silently for a moment.

"Look, my dear Fiske," he said. "You are in a dangerous game. We could be disturbed here at any moment, and then both our lives would greatly depreciate in value. The people who've asked you to do this are not very nice. Do you understand? You must tell me everything you can about them, and quickly. Only then can I help you." Solarin stood up and gave his hand to Fiske, pulling him to his feet. Fiske looked down at the ground uncomfortably as if he were about to cry. Solarin placed his hand gently on the older man's shoulder.

"You were approached by someone who wanted you to win this game. You must tell me who and why."

"The director . . ." Fiske's voice trembled. "When I . . . many years ago I became ill and could no longer play chess. The British government gave me a position teaching mathematics at university, a government stipend. Last month the director of my department came to me and asked me to see some men. I don't know who they were. They told me that in the interest of national security I must play chess in this tournament. I would be under no stress at all. . . ." Fiske began laughing and started to look about the room wildly. He was twisting the ring on his hand. Solarin took Fiske's hand in his, letting his other hand rest on Fiske's shoulder.

"You would be under no stress," said Solarin calmly, "because you would not really be playing. You'd be following instructions from someone else?"

Fiske nodded, tears in his eyes, and had to swallow hard several times before he could continue. He seemed to be breaking apart before Solarin's eyes.

"I told them I couldn't do it, not to choose me," he said, his voice rising. "I begged them not to make me play. But they had no one else. I was completely in their control. They could cut off my stipend at any time they wished. They told me that . . ." He gulped down air, and Solarin became alarmed. Fiske could not focus his thoughts, and he twisted the ring as if it pinched his hand. He was looking around the room with wild eyes.

"They wouldn't listen to me. They said they must have the formula at all cost. They said—"

"The formula!" said Solarin, gripping Fiske's shoulder forcefully. "They said the *formula*?"

"Yes! Yes! The bloody formula, that's what they wanted."

Fiske was practically shrieking. Solarin loosened his grasp of the older man's shoulder and tried to calm him by stroking him gently. "Tell me about the formula," he said carefully as if treading on eggs. "Come, my dear Fiske. Why was this formula of interest to them? How did they think you would be able to obtain it by playing in this tournament?"

"From you," Fiske said weakly, looking at the floor. Tears were running down his face.

"From me?" Solarin stared at Fiske. Then he glanced abruptly at the door. He thought he had heard a footfall outside.

"We must speak quickly," he said, lowering his voice. "How did they know that I would be here at this tournament? No one knew I was coming."

"*They* knew," said Fiske, looking at Solarin with crazed eyes. He twisted the ring abruptly. "Oh, God, let me be! I told them I couldn't do it! I *told* them I would fail!"

"Leave that ring alone," Solarin said sternly. He grasped Fiske by the wrist and twisted his hand around. Fiske grimaced. "*What* formula?"

"The formula you had in Spain," cried Fiske. "The formula you wagered against the game in Spain! You said you would give it to anyone who beat you! You said so! I *had* to win, so you would give me the formula."

Solarin stared at Fiske in disbelief. Then he dropped his hands and stepped away. He began to laugh.

"You said so," Fiske repeated dully, pulling on the ring.

"Oh, no," said Solarin. He threw back his head and laughed until tears came to his eyes. "My dear Fiske," he said, choking with laughter, "not *that* formula! Those fools arrived at the wrong conclusion. You've been the pawn of a bunch of *patzers*. Let's go outside and . . . What are you doing?!"

He had not noticed that Fiske, becoming more and more anguished, had twisted the ring loose. Now Fiske pulled the ring from his finger with one violent wrench and tossed it into an empty basin. He was babbling aloud and screamed, "I won't! I won't!"

Solarin stared for one brief second as the ring bounced into the basin. He leaped for the door as he started to count. One. Two. He hit the door and crashed through. Three. Four. Taking the steps at one leap, he landed at the bottom, tore across the small foyer. Six. Seven. Smashing the outer door open, he plowed into the courtyard, six long strides. Eight. Nine. He took a midair dive and landed on his belly on the cobblestones. Ten. Solarin's arms were over his head and muffled his ears. He waited. But there was no explosion.

He looked up from beneath his arms and saw two pairs of shoes in front of him. He looked higher up to see two of the arbiters standing over him, staring down in amazement.

"Grand Master Solarin!" said one of the judges. "Are you hurt?"

"No, I'm quite all right," Solarin said, pulling himself to his feet with dignity and dusting himself off. "Grand Master Fiske is ill in the lavatory. I was just coming for medical aid. I tripped. These cobblestones are very slippery, I'm afraid." Solarin wondered if he'd been mistaken about the ring. Perhaps its removal meant nothing, but he couldn't be sure.

"We had better go and see if there's anything we can do," said the judge. "Why did he go to the men's room at the Canadian Club? Why not the one at the Metropolitan? Or to the first-aid station?"

"He's very proud," Solarin replied. "Doubtless he didn't want anyone to see him being ill." The judges had not yet asked Solarin what *he* was doing in the same out-of-the-way restroom. Alone with his opponent.

"Is he very ill?" asked the other judge as they walked toward the entrance.

"Simply an upset stomach," Solarin replied. It didn't seem sensible to go back in there, but he hadn't much choice.

The three men went up the stairs, and the first judge opened the men's room door. He turned back quickly with a gasp.

"Don't look!" he said. He was quite pale. Solarin pushed past him and looked into the room. Hanging by his own necktie from the toilet partition was Fiske. His face was black, and from the angle of his head his neck was clearly broken.

"Suicide!" said the judge who'd told Solarin not to look. He himself was standing there wringing his hands as Fiske had done only a few moments earlier. When he had been alive.

"He's not the first chess master who's gone that way," replied the other judge. He fell awkwardly silent as Solarin turned and glared at him.

"We'd better call the doctor," the first judge added hastily.

Solarin walked over to the basin where Fiske had tossed the ring. It was no longer there. "Yes, let's get a doctor," he replied.

But I knew nothing of these events as I sat in the lounge waiting for Lily to return with our third round of coffee. If I'd known what was going on behind the scene—sooner instead of later—the next events might never have transpired at all.

It had been forty-five minutes since our recess had begun, and I was beginning to feel a little puckered around the bladder from all the coffee. I wondered what was going on. Lily arrived at the table and smiled conspiratorially.

"Guess what," she whispered. "I ran into Hermanold back in the bar, looking ten years older and conferring heavily with the tournament physician! We can adjourn permanently as soon as we finish our cafe, darling. There's not going to be a game today. They're going to announce it in a few minutes."

"Fiske was really sick? Maybe that's why he was playing so strangely."

"He's not sick, darling. He's over his illness. Rather abruptly, too, I might add."

"He's resigned?"

"In a manner of speaking. He hanged himself in the men's room just after the break."

"*Hanged* himself!" I said, and Lily shushed me as several people looked around. "What are you talking about?"

"Hermanold said he thought the pressure was too much for Fiske. The doctor had other ideas. The doctor said it was really hard for a man weighing a hundred forty pounds to break his neck by hanging himself from a six-foot-high partition."

"Could we pass on this coffee and get out of here?" I kept thinking about Solarin's green eyes as he bent over me. I felt ill. I needed to get outside.

"Very well," said Lily loudly. "But let's hurry back. I don't want to miss a second of this exciting match." We crossed the room briskly. When we reached the lobby, two reporters jumped up.

"Oh, Miss Rad," said one as they approached us, "what's going on, do you know? Will the game resume today?"

"Not unless they bring a trained monkey in to replace Mr. Fiske."

"You don't think much of his playing, then?" said the other reporter, scribbling in his notebook.

"I don't think of his playing at all," Lily replied smugly. "I only think of my own playing, as you know. As for the game," she added, bulldozing her way to the door with reporters trailing behind, "I've seen enough to know how it will end." She and I plowed through the double doors to the courtyard and headed down the ramp to the street.

"Where the hell is Saul?" Lily said. "The car is always supposed to be parked in front, he knows that."

I looked down the street and saw Lily's big blue Corniche sitting at the end of the block across Fifth Avenue. I pointed it out to her.

"Great, just what I need, another parking ticket," she said. "Come on, let's get out of here before all hell breaks loose inside." She grabbed my arm, and we raced off down the street in the bitterly cold wind. As we reached the end of the block, I realized the car was empty. Saul was nowhere to be seen.

We crossed the street, looking up and down for Saul. When we reached the car we found the key still in the ignition. Carioca seemed to be missing.

"I don't believe this!" Lily fumed. "In all these years, Saul has never left the car unattended. Where the hell could he be? And where's my dog?"

I heard a rustling sound that seemed to come from beneath the seat. I opened the door and bent over, reaching underneath. A little tongue slobbered all over my hand. I hauled Carioca out, and as I was straightening up I saw something that made my blood run cold. There was a hole in the driver's seat.

"Look," I said to Lily. "What's this hole here?"

Just then, as Lily was leaning forward to examine it, we heard a "thunk," and the car shook slightly. I glanced over my shoulder, but there was no one nearby. Pulling myself out of the car, I dropped Carioca on the seat. I examined the side of the car facing the Metropolitan Club. There was another hole that hadn't been there a second earlier. I touched it. It was warm.

I looked up at the windows of the Metropolitan Club. One of the French windows off the balcony was open, just above the American flag. The sheer drapery was blowing out the window, but no one was there. It was one of the windows of the gaming room, the one just behind the arbiters' table. I was positive.

"Jesus," I whispered to Lily. "Someone's shooting at the car!"

"You can't be serious," she said. She came around and looked at the bullet hole in the side, then followed my gaze along the line of trajectory to the open French window. There had been no people on the bitterly cold street, and no cars had passed by when we'd heard the thunk. That didn't leave many other possibilities.

"Solarin!" said Lily, grabbing my arm. "He warned you to leave the club, didn't he? That bastard is trying to bump us off!"

"He warned me that I was in danger if I *stayed* at the club," I told her. "So now I've *left* it. Besides, if someone wanted to shoot us, it would be pretty hard to miss from this distance."

"He's trying to scare me away from this tournament!" Lily insisted. "First he kidnaps my chauffeur, then he shoots at my car. Well, I'm not so easily scared off."

"Well, I am!" I told her. "Let's get out of here."

The haste with which Lily moved her bulk around to the driver's side suggested she agreed with me. She started the car up and screeched out into Fifth Avenue, tossing Carioca across the seat.

"I'm starving," she yelled over the whine of wind that came across the windscreen.

"You want to eat *now*?" I yelled back. "Are you crazy? I think we should go to the police at once."

"No way," she said firmly. "If Harry finds out about any of this, he'll imprison me so I can't play in this tournament. You and I are going to get something to eat and figure this one out for ourselves. I can't think unless I'm fed."

"Well, if we don't go to the police, then let's go back to my place."

"There's no kitchen at your place," she said. "I need red meat to get my brain cells working."

"Just head for my apartment. There's a steak house a few blocks away on Third Avenue. But I warn you, once you've been fed I'm going directly to the police."

Lily pulled up in front of The Palm restaurant on Second Avenue in the forties. She shuffled through her big shoulder bag and pulled out her pegboard chess set, stuffing Carioca into the bag in its place. He stuck his head out the top and drooled down the side.

"They don't let dogs into restaurants," she explained.

"What am I supposed to do with this?" I said, holding up the chess set she'd dropped in my lap.

"Keep it," she said. "You're a computer genius, and I'm a chess expert. Strategy is our bread and butter. I'm sure we can figure this out if we put our heads together. But first, it's time for you to learn a little chess."

Lily stuffed Carioca's head down into the bag and closed the flap. "Have you heard the expression, 'The pawns are the soul of chess'?"

"Mm. Sounds familiar, but I can't place it. Who said it?"

"André Philidor, the father of modern chess. He wrote a famous chess book around the time of the French Revolution, in which he explained that using the pawns en masse could make them just as powerful as the major pieces. No one had ever thought of that before. They used to sacrifice the pawns just to get them out of the way so they didn't block the action."

"Are you trying to say you think we're a couple of pawns that somebody's trying to get out of the way?" I found the idea strange but interesting.

"Nope," said Lily, getting out of the car and tossing her bag over her shoulder. "I'm trying to say it's time for us to join forces. Until we find what game it is we're playing."

We shook hands on it.

AN EXCHANGE
OF QUEENS

Queens never make bargains.

—Through the Looking-Glass
Lewis Carroll

ST. PETERSBURG, RUSSIA   AUTUMN 1791

The troika sluiced across the snowy fields, its three horses blowing steamy billows through their nostrils. Beyond Riga the snow had been so deep on the roads that they had changed from the dark carriage to this wide, open sleigh with its three horses harnessed abreast, the leather straps studded with silver bells and the wide, arklike sides tattooed with the imperial crest in nails of solid gold.

Here, only fifteen versts from Petersburg, the trees were still hung with ocher leaves, and peasants were still laboring in the partly frozen fields, though the snow already lay thick on the thatched roofs of the stone cottages.

The abbess lay back in her pile of furs and looked at the open countryside as it rushed past. By the European Julian calendar it was already November 4, exactly one year and seven months from the date—dare she think of it—when she'd determined to withdraw the Montglane Service from its hiding place of a thousand years.

But here in Russia, by the Gregorian calendar, it was only October 23. Russia was backward in many things, thought the abbess. A country that operated by a calendar, a religion, and a culture that were all her own. In centuries, these peasants she saw along the road had changed neither their costume nor their custom. The craggy faces with their black Russian eyes that turned as her carriage passed bespoke an ignorant people, still bound by primitive superstition and ritual. The gnarled hands clutched the same pickaxes and hacked at the same frozen soil that their ancestors had known a thousand years before. Despite the ukases dating from the days of Peter I, they still wore their thick hair and black beards uncut, tucking the loose ends into their sheepskin jerkins.

The gates of St. Petersburg lay open across the snowy expanse. The driver, dressed in the white livery and gold braid of the Imperial Guard, stood on his platform at the front of the troika with legs spread wide and lashed the horses onward. As they passed within the city, the abbess saw snow sparkling on the cupolas and high domes rising across the river Neva. Children skated on the frozen surface and, even so late in the year, the peddlers' colorful booths were strung out along the waterfront. Mongrel dogs in splotched colors barked as her sleigh passed by, and little yellow-haired children with dirty faces ran beside the runners to beg for coins. The driver whipped the horses ahead.

As they crossed the frozen river, the abbess reached into her traveling case and fingered the embroidered cloth she carried with her. She touched her rosary and said a brief Ave. She felt the weight of the grim responsibility that lay before her. It was she, and only she, who bore the burden of placing this powerful force into the right hands, hands that would protect it from the greedy or ambitious. The abbess knew it was her mission. She had been chosen for this task from birth. All her life she had awaited the events that would bring it to pass.

Today, after nearly fifty years, the abbess would see the childhood friend to whom she had unburdened herself so many years ago. She thought back to that day and to the young girl so much like Valentine in spirit, fair and fragile, a sickly child in a back brace who'd willed herself through illness and despair to a happy, healthy childhood, little Sophia Anhalt-Zerbst, the friend whom she had remembered over so many years, thought of fondly so often, written her secrets to nearly every month of her adult life. Though their paths had taken them far apart, the abbess still remembered Sophia as a girl chasing butterflies across the courtyard of her parents' home in Pomerania, her golden hair shining in the sunlight.

As the troika crossed the river and approached the Winter Palace, the abbess felt a momentary chill. A cloud had passed over the sun. She wondered what sort of person her friend and protectress would be, now that she was no longer little Sophia of Pomerania. Now that she was known throughout Europe as Catherine the Great, Czarina of all the Russias.

Catherine the Great, Empress of all the Russias, sat before her dressing table and looked into the mirror. She was sixty-two years old, of less than average height, overweight, with an intelligent forehead and heavy jaw. Her ice-blue eyes, usually sparkling with vitality, were flat and gray this morning, ringed red with weeping. For two weeks she had been shut into her chambers, refusing even to admit her family. Beyond the walls of her apartment the entire court was in mourning. Two weeks earlier, on October 12, a black-clad messenger had arrived from Jassy with the news that Count Potëmkin was dead.

Potëmkin, who had put her on the throne of Russia, handing her the tassel from the hilt of his sword to wear when, astride a white horse, she'd led the mutinous army to overthrow her husband, the czar. Potëmkin, who had been her lover, minister of state, general of her armies, and confidant, the man she described as "my only husband." Potëmkin, who'd expanded her empires by a third, extending them to the Caspian and the Black Sea. He had died on the road to Nicolayev like a dog.

He was dead of eating too much pheasant and partridge, gorging himself on rich cured hams and salted beef, drinking too much kvass and ale and cranberry liquor. Dead of satisfying the plump noblewomen who trailed behind him like camp followers, waiting for a crumb from his table. He'd tossed away fifty million rubles on fine palaces, costly jewels, and French champagne. But he had made Catherine the most powerful woman in the world.

Her ladies-in-waiting flitted about her like silent butterflies, powdering her hair and stringing ribbons through her shoes. She stood, and they draped the gray velvet robes of state over her shoulders, laden with the decorations she always wore in court: the crosses of St. Catherine, St. Vladimir, St. Alexander Nevsky; the ribbons of St. Andrew and St. George crossing her bosom, swaying with their heavy gold medals. She threw back her shoulders to display her excellent posture and descended from her chambers.

Today, for the first time in ten days, she would appear in court. Met by her personal bodyguard, she marched between the lines of soldiers through the long corridors of the Winter Palace, past the windows where years earlier she'd watched her ships sail down the Neva toward the sea to meet the Swedish fleet attacking St. Petersburg. Catherine gazed out of the windows thoughtfully as she passed.

Within the court waited the mass of vipers who called themselves diplomats and courtiers. They conspired against her, plotted her downfall. Her own son Paul planned her assassination. But also arrived at Petersburg was the one person who might save her, a woman who held within her hands the power that Catherine had lost with the death of Potëmkin. For just this morning her oldest friend from childhood had arrived at St. Petersburg, Helene de Roque, the Abbess of Montglane.

Weary after her appearance in court, Catherine retired to her private audience chamber leaning on the arm of her current lover, Plato Zubov. The abbess was waiting there in the company of Plato's brother Valerian. She rose when she saw the empress and crossed the room to embrace her.

Spry for her age and thin as a wintry reed, the abbess sparkled at the sight of her friend. As they embraced, she glanced at Plato Zubov. Wearing a sky-blue coat and skintight breeches, he was so bedecked with medals he looked as if he might topple over. Plato was young, with delicate, pretty features. There could be no mistake regarding his role at court, and Catherine stroked his arm as she spoke to the abbess.

"Helene," she sighed. "How often I have longed for your presence. I can scarcely believe you are here at last. But God has listened to my heart and brought my childhood friend to me."

She motioned the abbess to be seated in a large, comfortable chair and herself took a chair nearby. Plato and Valerian stood each behind one of the women.

"This calls for a celebration. However, as you may know, I am in mourning and cannot have a fête for your arrival. I suggest we dine together tonight in my private chambers. We can laugh and enjoy ourselves pretending for a moment that we are young girls again. Valerian, have you opened the wine as I instructed?"

Valerian nodded and went to the sideboard.

"You must try this claret, my dear. It is one of the treasures of my court. It was brought to me from Bordeaux by Denis Diderot many years ago. I value it as if it were a fine gem."

Valerian poured the dark red wine into small crystal tumblers. The two women sipped the wine.

"Excellent," said the abbess, smiling at Catherine. "But no wine can compare with the elixir produced in these old bones by seeing you again, my Figchen."

Plato and Valerian glanced at each other at the use of such familiarity. The empress, born Sophia Anhalt-Zerbst, had been nicknamed "Figchen" as a child. Because of Plato's exalted position, he had made so bold in bed as to call her "mistress of my heart," but in public he always referred to her as "Your Majesty," as did her own children. Oddly, the empress had not seemed to notice the effrontery of this French abbess.

"Now you must tell me why you chose to remain so long in France," said Catherine. "When you closed the abbey, I'd hoped you might come at once to Russia. My court is filled with your expatriate countrymen, especially since your king has been captured at Varennes trying to flee France, and is now held prisoner by his own people. France is a hydra with twelve hundred heads, a state of anarchy. This nation of shoemakers has reversed the very order of nature!"

The abbess was surprised to hear so enlightened and liberal a ruler speak out in this manner. Though it could not be denied France was dangerous, was it not this same czarina who'd befriended the liberal Voltaire and Denis Diderot, proponents of class equality and opponents of territorial warfare?

"I could not come at once," the abbess replied to Catherine's question. "I was concerned with certain business—" She looked sharply at Plato Zubov, who stood behind Catherine's chair stroking her neck. "I cannot speak of these matters with anyone but you."

Catherine studied the abbess for a moment. Then she said casually, "Valerian, you and Plato Alexandrovitch may leave us now."

"But my beloved Highness . . ." said Plato Zubov in a voice that closely approximated the whine of a small child.

"Do not fear for my safety, my dove," said Catherine, patting his hand, which still rested upon her shoulder. "Helene and I have known one another for nearly sixty years. No harm will come to us by being left alone for a few moments."

"Is he not beautiful?" Catherine asked the abbess when the two young men had left the room. "I know you and I have not chosen the same path, my dear. But I hope you will understand when I tell you I feel like a small insect warming its wings in the sun after a cold winter. There is nothing to raise the sap of an old tree like the caress of a young gardener."

The abbess sat in silence, wondering again whether her initial plan had been well chosen. After all, though their correspondence had been warm and frequent, she had not seen her childhood friend in many years. Were the rumors about her true? Could this aging woman, steeped in sensuality, jealous of her own power, be trusted with the task that lay ahead?

"Have I shocked you into silence?" Catherine laughed.

"My dear Sophia," said the abbess, "I do believe you enjoy shocking people. You remember when you were only four years old, during your presentation at court to King Frederick William of Prussia, you refused to kiss the hem of his coat."

"I told him the tailor had cut his jacket too short!" Catherine said, laughing until tears came to her eyes. "My mother was furious with me. The king told her I was entirely too bold."

The abbess smiled benevolently at her friend.

"Do you remember when the Canon of Brunswick looked at our palms to predict our futures?" she asked softly. "He found three crowns in yours."

"I remember it well," replied the other. "From that day forward, I never doubted I would rule a vast empire. I always believe in the mystic prophecies when they complement my own desires." She smiled, but this time the abbess did not return her smile.

"And do you remember what the canon found in *my* hand?" said the abbess.

Catherine was silent for a moment. "I remember it as if it were yesterday," she replied at last. "It is for that very reason I've awaited your arrival with such a sense of urgency. You cannot imagine my frenzy of anticipation when you did not come for so long. . . ." She paused hesitantly. "Do you have them?" she said at last.

The abbess reached into the folds of her abbatial gown, where a large leather traveling wallet was strapped to her waist. She withdrew the heavy gold carving, caked with jewels. It portrayed a figure dressed in long robes and seated in a small pavilion with draperies drawn back. She handed the piece to Catherine, who held it in her cupped hands in disbelief, turning it about slowly.

"The Black Queen," whispered the abbess as she watched Catherine's expression closely. The empress's hands closed about the gold and jewel-encrusted chess piece. Gripping it tightly, she held the piece to her bosom and looked at the abbess.

"And the others?" she said. Something in her voice made the abbess wary.

"They are hidden safely, where they can do no harm," was the reply.

"My beloved Helene, we must reassemble them at once! You know the power that this service holds. In the hands of a benevolent monarch, there is nothing that cannot be accomplished through these pieces—"

"You know," interrupted the abbess, "that for forty years I have ignored your entreaties to search for the Montglane Service, to remove it from the walls of the abbey. Now I shall tell you why. I have always known precisely where the service was hidden—" The abbess held up her hand as Catherine was about to erupt with an exclamation. "I also knew the danger of taking it from its hiding place. Only a saint could be trusted with such a temptation. And you are no saint, my dear Figchen."

"What do you mean?" cried the other. "I've united a fragmented nation, brought enlightenment to an ignorant people. I've wiped out the plague, built hospitals and schools, eliminated warring factions that would split Russia apart, making her prey to her enemies. Do you suggest I am a despot?"

"I thought only of your own welfare," said the abbess calmly. "These pieces have the power to turn even the coolest head. Remember that the Montglane Service nearly split the Frankish empire apart. After Charlemagne's death, his sons went to war over it."

"A territorial skirmish," sniffed Catherine. "I cannot see how the two things were related."

"Only the strength of the Catholic Church in central Europe has kept this dark force a secret for so long. But when the news came to me that France had passed the Bill of Seizure to confiscate Church property, I knew my worst fears might come to pass. When I learned that French soldiers were proceeding to Montglane, I was positive. Why to Montglane? We were far from Paris, hidden deep in the mountains. There were wealthier abbeys close at hand that would be simpler to loot. No, no. It was the service they were after. I spent my time in careful calculation, to remove the service from the abbey walls and scatter it across Europe so it could not be reassembled for many years—"

"Scattered!" cried the empress. Leaping to her feet with the chess piece still clutched to her bosom, she paced the room like a caged animal. "How could you have done such a thing? You should have come to me, called upon me for aid!"

"I tell you I could not!" said the abbess, her voice brittle and frail from the exhaustion of her journey. "I learned that there were others who knew of the location of the service. Someone, perhaps a foreign power, had bribed members of the French Assembly to pass the Bill of Seizure, and had directed their attentions toward Montglane. Does it not seem coincidental that two of the men this dark power tried to bribe were the great orator Mirabeau and the Bishop of Autun? One was the author of the bill, the other its most ardent defender. When Mirabeau fell ill this April, the bishop could not be dragged from the bedside of the dying man until he breathed his last. No doubt he was desperate to obtain any correspondence that might incriminate them both."

"How do you come to know these things?" murmured Catherine. Turning from the abbess, she crossed to the windows and gazed at the darkening sky, where snow clouds gathered upon the horizon.

"I have their correspondence," the abbess replied. Neither woman spoke for a moment. At last the abbess's voice came softly in the dim light. "You asked what mission had kept me so long in France, and now you know. I had to discover who it was that had forced my hand, who had caused me to wrench the Montglane Service from its hiding place of a thousand years. Who was the enemy that stalked me like a hunter until I was flushed out from the cover of the Church to seek across a continent another safe refuge for this treasure entrusted to my care?"

"And have you learned the name you sought?" said Catherine carefully, turning to face the abbess across the expanse of space.

"Yes, I have," replied the abbess calmly. "My dear Figchen, it was you."

"If you knew all this," said the stately czarina as she and the abbess strolled along the snow-covered path to the Hermitage the next morning, "I do not understand why it is that you came to Petersburg at all."

A troop of Imperial Guard marched at twenty paces to either side of them, trampling the snowy fields beneath their high-fringed Cossack boots, but far enough away that the two women could speak freely.

"Because, despite all evidence to the contrary, I trusted you," said the abbess with a little twinkle in her eye. "I knew you feared the government of France would crumble, the country would fall into a state of anarchy. You wanted to assure the Montglane Service would not fall into the wrong hands, and you suspected that I would not concur with the measures you were prepared to take. But tell me this, Figchen, how did you plan to relieve the French soldiers of their booty, once they'd removed the service from Montglane? Short of invading France with Russian troops?"

"I had a cadre of soldiers hidden in the mountains, to stop the French troops at the pass," said Catherine with a smile. "They were not in uniform."

"I see," said the abbess. "And what inspired you to such dire measures?"

"I suppose I must share with you what I know," the empress replied. "As you are aware, I purchased the library of Voltaire upon that gentleman's death. Contained within his papers was a secret journal written by Cardinal Richelieu, explaining in code his researches into the history of the Montglane Service. Voltaire had broken the code, and I was thus able to read what he discovered.

The manuscript is locked into a vault at the Hermitage, where I'm taking you now. I intend to show it to you."

"And what was the significance of this document?" asked the abbess, wondering why her friend had not mentioned this before.

"Richelieu had traced the service to the Moor who'd given it as a gift to Charlemagne, and even beyond that. As you know, Charlemagne had fought many crusades against the Moors both in Spain and in Africa. But on this occasion, he'd defended Córdoba and Barcelona *against* the Christian Basques who threatened to topple the Moorish seat of power. Though the Basques were Christian, they had sought for centuries to smash the Frankish kingdom and to seize control of Western Europe, most specifically the Atlantic seaboard and the mountains in which they had held sway."

"The Pyrenees," the abbess said.

"Indeed," replied the czarina. "The Magic Mountains, they called them. You know that these same mountains were once the home of the most mystical cult that has been known since the birth of Christ. The Celtic peoples came from there, and were driven northward to settle in Brittany and, at last, in the British Isles. Merlin the Magician came from these mountains, and also the secret cult we know today as Druids."

"This much I did not know," said the abbess, looking ahead at the snowy path as she walked, her thin lips pursed together, her wrinkled face resembling a stone fragment from an ancient tomb.

"You'll read it in the journal, for we are nearly there," said the other. "Richelieu claims the Moors invaded this territory and learned the terrible secret which had been protected for centuries, first by the Celts and then the Basques. These Moorish conquerors then transcribed their knowledge into a code which they themselves invented. In effect, they coded the secret into the gold-and-silver pieces of the Montglane Service. When it became clear that the Moors might lose their grasp of power in the Iberian Peninsula, they sent the chess service on to Charlemagne, of whom they were in awe. As the mightiest ruler in the history of civilization, they thought he alone might be its protector."

"And you believe this story?" asked the abbess as they approached the massive facade of the Hermitage.

"Judge for yourself," Catherine said. "I know the secret is older than the Moors, older than the Basques. Older, indeed, than the Druids. I must ask you, my friend, have you ever heard of a secret society of men who sometimes call themselves the Freemasons?"

The abbess grew pale. She paused outside the door they were about to enter. "What do you say?" she said faintly, grasping her friend by the arm.

"Ah," said Catherine. "Then you know that it is true. When you have read the manuscript, I will tell you my story."

THE EMPRESS'S TALE

When I was fourteen years old, I left my home in Pomerania, where you and I grew up side by side. Your father had recently sold his estates adjoining ours and returned to his native France. I shall never forget my sadness, my dear Helene, at not being able to share with you the triumph we had so long discussed together, the fact that I might soon be chosen successor to a queen.

I was at that time to journey to the court of the Czarina Elizabeth Petrovna at Moscow. Elizabeth, a daughter of Peter the Great, had seized power through a political coup, casting all her opponents into prison. As she'd never married and was past childbearing age, she'd selected her obscure nephew, the Grand Duke Peter, to succeed her. I was to be his bride.

En route to Russia, my mother and I were to stop at the court of Frederick II in Berlin. Frederick, the young emperor of Prussia whom Voltaire had already dubbed "the Great," wished to sponsor me as his candidate in uniting the kingdoms of Prussia and Russia through marriage. I was a better choice than Frederick's own sister, whom he could not bear to sacrifice to such a fate.

In those days the Prussian court was as sparkling as it was to become sparse in Frederick's later years. Upon my arrival, the king took great pains to charm me and make me feel at ease. He clothed me in gowns of his royal sisters and seated me at his side each evening at dinner, amusing me with tales of the opera and ballet. Though a mere child, I was not deceived. I knew he planned to use me as a pawn in a larger game, a game he played across the chessboard of Europe.

After some time I learned that at the Prussian court existed a man who'd recently returned from spending nearly ten years at the court in Russia. He was court mathematician to Frederick, and his name was Leonhard Euler. I made so bold as to request a private audience with him, thinking he might share his personal insights about the country I was so soon to visit. I could not have foreseen that our meeting would one day change the course of my life.

My first meeting with Euler was in a small antechamber of the great court at Berlin. This man of simple tastes but brilliant mind awaited the child who was soon to be queen. We must have made an odd couple. He stood alone in the room, a tall, fragile man with a neck like a long bottle, large dark eyes, and a prominent nose. He looked at me in cockeyed fashion, explained by the fact he had been blinded in one eye by close observation of the sun. For Euler was an astronomer as well as mathematician.

"I am unaccustomed to talking," he began. "I come from a country where if you speak you are hanged." This was my first introduction to Russia, and I assure you it served me well in later years. He told me how the Czarina

Elizabeth Petrovna kept fifteen thousand dresses and twenty-five thousand pairs of shoes. She would hurl her shoes at the heads of her ministers if she disagreed with them slightly and send them to the gallows on a whim. Her lovers were legion and her drinking more excessive than her sexual habits. She did not permit opinions that varied from her own.

Dr. Euler and I spent a good deal of time together once I'd overcome his initial reserve. We took quite a liking to one another, and he admitted that he longed to keep me at the Berlin court to take me as a pupil in mathematics, a field in which I showed strong promise. Of course, this was impossible.

Euler even admitted that he did not care much for the Emperor Frederick, his patron. There was a good cause for this, other than Frederick's poor grasp of mathematical concepts. Euler revealed his reason to me on the last morning of my stay at Berlin.

"My little friend," he said as I came into his laboratory on that fateful morning to bid him adieu. I remember he was polishing a lens with his silk scarf, as he was accustomed to do when working out a problem. "There is something I must tell you before you depart. I've studied you carefully these last days, and believe I can trust you with what I have to say. It will place us both in great danger, however, if you reveal these comments unwisely."

I assured Dr. Euler that I would guard any confidence with my life. To my surprise, he told me that might indeed be necessary.

"You are young, you are powerless, and you are a woman," said Euler. "For these reasons, Frederick has selected you as his tool in the vast, dark empire that is Russia. Perhaps you are unaware that for twenty years that great country has been ruled exclusively by women: first Catherine the First, widow of Peter the Great; then Anna Ivanovna, Ivan's daughter; Anna of Mecklenburg, who was regent to her son Ivan the Sixth; and now Elizabeth Petrovna, Peter's daughter. Should *you* follow in this powerful tradition, you will find yourself in great danger."

I listened politely to the gentleman, though I began to suspect that the sun had blinded more than his eye.

"There is a secret society of men who feel their mission in life is to alter the course of civilization," Euler told me. We sat there in his study, surrounded by telescopes, microscopes, and musty books scattered across the mahogany tables and littered over with a thick disarray of papers. "These men," he continued, "claim to be scientists and engineers, but in effect they are mystics. I will tell you what I know of their history, for it may be of great importance to you.

"In the year 1271, Prince Edward of England, son of Henry the Third, went off to the shores of North Africa to fight in the Crusades. He landed at Acre, a city near Jerusalem of ancient heritage. There, we know little of what he did, only that he was involved in several battles and met with the Moslem Moors who were chieftains. The following year Edward was recalled to England, for his father had died. Upon his return he became King Edward the First, and the rest of his story is known from history books. What is *not* known is that he brought something with him from Africa."

"What was it?" I was more than curious to know.

"He brought with him the knowledge of a great secret. A secret that goes back to the dawn of civilization," Euler replied. "But my story gets ahead of itself.

"Upon his return, Edward established in England a society of men with whom, presumably, he shared this secret. We know little of them, but we can follow their movements to some degree. After the subjugation of the Scots, we know that society spread to Scotland, where it lay quiet for a time. When the Jacobites fled Scotland at the beginning of our century, they brought the society and its teachings with them into France. Montesquieu, the great French poet, had been indoctrinated into the order during a sojourn in England and with his aid was established the Loge des Sciences at Paris in the year 1734. Four years later, before he became king of Prussia, our own Frederick the Great was initiated into the secret society at Brunswick. In the same year, Pope Clement the Twelfth issued a bill to suppress the movement, which had by now spread to Italy, Prussia, Austria, and the Lowlands as well as France. So strong was the society by then that the Parliament of Catholic France refused to register the pope's order."

"Why do you tell me these things?" I asked Dr. Euler. "Even if I understood the ends these men held dear, what would it have to do with me? And what could I do about it? Though I aspire to great things, I am still a child."

"From my knowledge of their goals," said Euler softly, "if these men are not defeated, they may defeat the world. You may be a child today, but soon you will be the wife of the next czar of Russia, the first male ruler of that empire in two decades. You must listen to what I have to say, etch it upon your mind." He took me by the arm.

"Sometimes these men call themselves the Brotherhood of Freemasons, sometimes Rosicrucians. Whatever the name they choose, they have one thing in common. Their origins are in North Africa. When Prince Edward established this society upon Western soil, they called themselves the Order of the Architects of Africa. They consider that their predecessors were the architects of ancient civilization, that they cut and laid the stones of the pyramids of Egypt, they built the Hanging Gardens of Babylon, the Tower and Gates of Babel. They knew the mysteries of the ancients. But I believe they were the architects of something else, something more recent and perhaps more powerful than any . . ."

Euler paused and regarded me with a look I shall never forget. It haunts me today, nearly fifty years later, as if it had happened a moment ago. I see him

with terrifying vividness even in my dreams, and can feel his breath upon my
neck as he leaned forward to whisper to me:

"I believe that they were also the architects of the Montglane Service. And
consider themselves to be its rightful heirs."

When Catherine finished her tale, she and the abbess sat without speaking
in the large library at the Hermitage, where they had brought the manuscript
of Voltaire's journals. There at the vast table with thirty-foot walls of books
rising around them, Catherine watched the abbess as a cat watches a mouse. The
abbess was gazing out of the broad windows overlooking the lawn, where the
cadre of Imperial Guard stamped and blew upon their fingers in the cold
morning air.

"My late husband," Catherine added softly, "was a devotee of Frederick the
Great of Prussia. Peter used to wear a Prussian uniform at court in Petersburg.
On our wedding night, he spread toy Prussian soldiers across our bed and made
me drill the troops. When Frederick brought the Order of Freemasons into
Prussia in force, Peter joined their group and pledged his life to supporting
them."

"And so," commented the abbess, "you overthrew your husband, imprisoned
him, and arranged his assassination."

"He was a dangerous maniac," Catherine said. "But I was not implicated in
his death. Six years later, in 1768, Frederick built the Grand Lodge of African
Architects at Silesia. King Gustavus of Sweden joined the order, and despite
Maria Theresa's attempts to drive these vermin from Austria, her son Joseph the
Second joined as well. I brought my friend Dr. Euler back to Russia as quickly
as possible when I learned of these events.

"The old mathematician was, by now, completely blind. But he had not lost
his inner vision. When Voltaire died, Euler pressed me to acquire his library.
It contained important documents that Frederick the Great badly wanted. When
I succeeded in bringing the library to Petersburg, here is what I found. I have
saved it to show you."

The empress extracted from Voltaire's manuscript a parchment document,
handing it to the abbess, who unfolded it carefully. It was addressed from
Frederick, Prince Regent of Prussia, to Voltaire, dated in the same year Frederick had entered the Order of Freemasons:

> Monsieur, there is nothing I wish so much as to possess all your
> writings. . . . If there be among your manuscripts any that you wish
> to conceal from the eyes of the public, I engage to keep them in the
> profoundest secrecy. . . .

The abbess looked up from the paper. Her eyes had a faraway look. Slowly she folded the letter and handed it back to Catherine, who returned it to its hiding place.

"Is it not clear he refers to Voltaire's decryption of Cardinal Richelieu's diary?" asked the empress. "He sought to acquire this information from the moment he joined the secret order. Now perhaps you will believe me. . . ."

Catherine picked up the last of the leather-bound volumes and fanned through the pages until she reached a place near the end, reading aloud those words the abbess had already etched upon her mind, the words the long-dead Cardinal Richelieu had taken such care to inscribe in a code known only to himself:

> For I found at last, that the secret discovered in Ancient Babylonia, the secret transmitted into the Persian and Indian Empires and known only by the elect and chosen few, was in fact the secret of the Montglane Service.
>
> This secret, like the sacred name of God, was never to be inscribed in any writing. A secret so powerful that it caused the fall of civilizations and the death of kings, it could never be communicated to any except the initiated among the sacred orders, to men who had passed the tests and taken the oaths. So terrible was this knowledge that it could only be entrusted to the highest echelons of the Elite.
>
> It is my belief that this secret took the shape of a formula, and that this formula was the cause of the downfall of the Kingdoms of all time, Kingdoms that stand only as legends in our history today. And the Moors, despite their initiation into the secret knowledge, and despite their fear of it, did transcribe this formula into the Montglane Service. They built the sacred symbols into the squares of the board itself and into the pieces, retaining the key that only true Masters of the Game could use to unlock it.
>
> This I have gleaned from my reading of the Ancient Manuscripts collected from Chalons, Soissons, and Tours and translated by myself.
>
> May God have mercy upon our souls.
>
> > Ecce Signum,
> > Armand Jean du Plessis,
> > Duc de Richelieu & Vicar of
> >   Lucon, Poitou & Paris,
> > Cardinal of Rome
> > Prime Minister of France
> > Anno Domini 1642

"From his memoirs," Catherine said to the silent abbess when she'd finished reading, "we learn that 'the Iron Cardinal' had planned to journey soon to the See of Montglane. But he died, as you know, in December of the same year, after putting down the insurrection at Roussillon. Can we doubt for an instant that he knew these secret societies existed, or that he planned to lay his hands upon the Montglane Service before it could fall into other hands? Everything he did was aimed at power. Why should he change at so ripe an age?"

"My dear Figchen," said the abbess with a faint smile that did not reflect the inner turmoil she felt at hearing these words, "your point is well taken. But all these men are dead. During their lifetimes, they may have sought. But they did not find. Surely you cannot say you fear the ghosts of dead men?"

"Ghosts can rise again!" Catherine said forcefully. "Fifteen years ago, the British colonies in America overthrew the yoke of empire. Who were the men involved? Men named Washington, Jefferson, Franklin—Freemasons all! Today, the King of France is in prison, his crown about to roll along with his head. Who are the men behind it? Lafayette, Condorcet, Danton, Desmoulins, Brissot, Sieyès, and the king's own brothers, including the Duc d'Orleans—Freemasons all."

"A coincidence—" the abbess began, but Catherine cut her off.

"Was it coincidence that, of the men I tried to employ to pass the Bill of Seizure in France, the one who accepted my terms was none other than Mirabeau—a member of the Freemasons? Of course, he could not know I planned to relieve him of the treasure when he took the bribe."

"The Bishop of Autun declined?" said the abbess with a smile, looking at her friend across the thick portfolios of journals. "And what reason did he give?"

"The amount he asked to cooperate with me was outrageous," the czarina fumed, rising to her feet. "That man knew more than he was willing to reveal to me. You know that in the assembly they call this Talleyrand 'the Angora Cat'? He purrs, but he has claws. I do not trust him."

"You trust a man whom you are able to bribe, but mistrust one whom you are not?" said the abbess. With a slow, sad look, she drew her robes around her and stood up to face her friend across the table. Then she turned as if to depart.

"Where are you going?" cried the czarina in alarm. "Do you not see why I have taken these actions? I am offering you my protection. I am sole ruler of the largest country on earth. I place my power in your hands. . . ."

"Sophia," the abbess said calmly, "I thank you for your offer, but I do not fear these men as you do. I am willing to believe, as you claim, that they are mystics, perhaps even revolutionaries. Has it ever occurred to you that these societies of mystics which you've studied so closely may have an end in mind that you've not foreseen?"

"What do you mean?" said the empress. "It's clear from their actions they want to topple monarchies into the dust. What could their aim be, but to control the world?"

"Perhaps their aim is to free the world." The abbess smiled. "At the moment, I do not have enough evidence to say one way or the other, but I do have sufficient facts at hand to say this: I see from your words that you are driven to act out the destiny that was written in your hand from birth—the three crowns in your palm. But I must act out my own."

The abbess turned her hand palm upward and held it out to her friend across the table. There, near the wrist, the life line and the line of destiny twisted together to form a figure eight. Catherine looked down at it in icy silence, then slowly traced the figure with her fingertips.

"You seek to give me your protection," said the abbess softly. "But I am protected by a greater power than you."

"I knew it!" Catherine cried hoarsely, tossing the other's hand aside. "All this talk of lofty aims and goals means only one thing: You've made a pact with another without consulting me! Who is it, in whom you've placed your misguided trust? Tell me his name, I demand it!"

"Gladly." The abbess smiled. "It is He who placed this sign upon my hand. And in this sign, I reign absolute. You may be the ruler of all the Russias, my dear Figchen. But please do not forget who *I* really am. And by whom I was chosen. Remember that God is the greatest chess master of all."

THE KNIGHT'S WHEEL

King Arthur dreamed a wonderful dream, and that was this: that him seemed he sat upon a chaflet in a chair, and the chair was fast to a wheel, and thereupon sat King Arthur in the richest cloth of gold . . . and suddenly the king thought the wheel turned up-so-down, and he fell among the serpents, and every beast took him by a limb; and then the king cried as he lay in his bed and slept, "Help."

—Le Morte d'Arthur
Sir Thomas Malory

Regnabo, Regno, Regnavi, Sum sine regno.
(I shall reign, I reign, I have reigned, I am without reign.)

—*Inscription on the Wheel of Fortune*
The Tarot

T he morning after the chess tournament was a Monday. I got up groggily from my lumpy Murphy bed, shoved it back into the wall, and went off to the shower to prepare for another day at Con Edison.

Rubbing myself with my toweling robe, I padded barefoot back down the hall and searched for the telephone amid my collection of artisana. After my dinner at The Palm with Lily and the strange event that followed it, I'd decided we were indeed a pair of pawns in someone else's game, and I wanted to bring some heavier pieces out on my side of the board. I knew precisely where to begin.

Lily and I had agreed over dinner that Solarin's warning to me had somehow been related to the bizarre happenings of the day, but after that point our opinions had diverged. She was convinced Solarin was behind everything else that had gone on.

"First, Fiske dies under mysterious circumstances," she pointed out as we sat amid the palm trees at one of the closely packed wooden tables. "How do we know Solarin didn't kill him? Then Saul disappears, leaving my car *and my dog* prey to vandals. Obviously Saul was kidnapped, or he'd never have left his post."

"That's obvious," I said with a grin as I watched her wolf down a slab of raw beef. I knew Saul wouldn't have dared to face Lily again unless *something* dire had happened to him. Lily moved on to demolish a huge salad and three baskets of bread as our conversation continued.

"Then someone takes a potshot at us," she said between munches, "and we both agree the bullet came from the open windows of the gaming room."

"There were *two* bullets," I pointed out. "Maybe someone shot at Saul and scared him away before we got there."

"But the pièce de résistance," said Lily, still munching bread and ignoring me, "is that I have discovered not only method and means, but *motive!*"

"What are you talking about?"

"I know *why* Solarin is doing these nefarious things. I figured it out between the prime rib and the salad."

"Do clue me in," I said. I could hear Carioca clawing at Lily's belongings within her satchel bag, and I suspected it would only be a matter of time till our fellow diners heard it, too.

"You know about the scandal in Spain, of course?" she said. I had to rack my brain on that one.

"You mean Solarin being recalled to Russia a few years back?" She nodded, and I added, "That's all you told me."

"It was over a formula," said Lily. "You see, Solarin had dropped out of the chess rat race pretty early. He only played at tournaments from time to time. He has grand master ranking, but he actually studied to be a physicist; that's what he does for a living. During the competition in Spain, Solarin had made a bet with another player, promising him some secret formula if that player beat him in the tournament."

"What was the formula?"

"I don't know. But when his wager was reported in the press, the Russians panicked. Solarin disappeared overnight and was never heard from again until now."

"A physics formula?" I asked.

"Maybe a recipe for a secret weapon. That would explain everything, wouldn't it?" I couldn't see that it would explain *any*thing, but I let her rattle on.

"Fearing that Solarin will pull the same trick again at *this* tournament, the KGB race in and bump Fiske off, then try to scare me away as well. If either of us had won a game off Solarin, he might give us the secret formula!" She was thrilled with how well her explanation fit the circumstances, but I wasn't buying it.

"That's a great theory all right," I agreed. "There are only a few loose ends to be tied up. For example, what happened to Saul? Why would the Russians have let Solarin out of the country if they suspected he'd try the same trick again—assuming it *was* a trick? And why on *earth* would Solarin want to pass a weapons formula either to you or to that doddering old relic Fiske, may his soul rest in peace?"

"Well, okay, not everything fits perfectly," she admitted. "But at least it's a start."

"As Sherlock Holmes once said, 'It is a capital mistake to theorize before one has data,' " I told her. "I suggest we both do a little research on Solarin. But I still think we should go to the police. After all, we have two bullet holes to prove our point."

"Never," cried Lily in agitation, "will I admit that I'm not up to solving this mystery on my own. Strategy is my middle name."

So we agreed, after many heated words and a shared hot-fudge sundae, that we would part for a few days and do some research into Grand Master Solarin's background and modus operandi.

Lily's chess coach had been a grand master himself. Though she had to practice heavily before her own match on Tuesday, Lily thought he might have some insight into Solarin's character that she could glean during training. Meanwhile she'd check up on Saul. If he hadn't been kidnapped (which I think would have disappointed her dramatic flair), she would find out from his own lips why he'd deserted his post.

I had plans of my own, and I didn't care to share them with Lily Rad just yet.

I had a friend in Manhattan who was even more mysterious than the elusive Solarin. A man who was listed in no phone book and had no mailing address. He was one of the legends of data processing and, though barely thirty years old, had written definitive texts on the subject. He'd been my mentor in the computer business when I'd first arrived in the Big Apple three years earlier, and he'd bailed me out of some sticky situations in the past. His name, when he chose to use it, was Dr. Ladislaus Nim.

Nim was not only a master of data processing, but an expert in chess. He'd played against Reshevsky and Fischer and had held his own. But his real expertise was in his panoramic knowledge of the game, and that was why I wanted to find him. He had committed to memory all of the world championship games in history. He was a walking biographical encyclopedia of the lives of the grand masters. He could regale you for hours with stories of the history of chess, when he chose to be charming. I knew he would be able to pull together the threads of the bag I seemed to be holding. Once I found him.

But wanting to find Nim and finding him were two different things. His phone answering service made the KGB and CIA seem like gossipy blabbermouths. They wouldn't even admit they knew who he *was* when you called, and I'd been calling for weeks now.

I'd wanted to reach Nim, simply to say good-bye, when I'd learned I was leaving the country. Now I *had* to reach him, and not only because of the pact I'd made with Lily Rad. Because now I *knew* that these seemingly disconnected things—Fiske's death, Solarin's warning, Saul's disappearance—were all in some way connected. They were connected to *me*.

I knew it because at midnight when I'd left Lily at The Palm restaurant, I had decided to begin a little research right away. Instead of going directly home, I had taken a cab to the Fifth Avenue Hotel to confront that fortune-teller who'd somehow, three months earlier, given me the same warning that Solarin had given me that very afternoon. Though *his* warning had been swiftly followed on the heels by firm evidence, I found their closely worded language a bit too coincidental. And I wanted to know why.

That was why I needed to talk to Nim, right away, with no delays. You see, there *was* no fortune-teller at the Fifth Avenue Hotel. I spoke with the manager of the hotel bar for over half an hour to make absolutely sure I had my facts straight. He'd worked there for fifteen years and gave me his assurances repeatedly. There had never been any fortune-teller working at the Fifth Avenue

Hotel bar. Not even on New Year's Eve. The woman who'd known that I was due to arrive there, who'd waited for Harry to call me at the data center, who'd had my fortune all prepared in iambic pentameter, who'd used the same words Solarin would use three months later in warning—the woman who had even, I recalled, known what my birth date was—had simply never existed.

Of course, she *had* existed. I had three eyewitnesses to prove it. But by now even the testimony of my *own* eyes was becoming suspect, in my eyes.

So on Monday morning, my hair dripping into my toweling robe, I unearthed my telephone and tried to reach Nim one more time. This time I was in for a surprise.

When I called the number of his answering service, the New York Telephone Company came on the line with a recorded message, telling me the number had been changed to one with a Brooklyn prefix. I dialed the new number, thinking it odd that Nim had switched the location of his service. After all, I was one of only three people in the world who had the honor of knowing the *old* number. One couldn't take too many precautions.

The second surprise came when the service picked up.

"Rockaway Greens Hall," said the woman who answered the phone.

"I'm trying to reach Dr. Nim," I told her.

"I'm afraid we have no one here by that name," she said sweetly. This was a pleasant treatment compared with the vicious denials I normally got from Nim's answering service. But another surprise was yet to come.

"Dr. Nim. Dr. Ladislaus Nim," I repeated clearly. "This is the number Manhattan information gave me."

"Is . . . is that a *man's* name?" said the woman with a gasp.

"Yes," I told her a little impatiently. "May I leave a message? It's very important that I reach him."

"Madam," said the woman, a tone of coldness creeping into her voice. "This is a Carmelite convent! Someone is playing a joke on you!" And she hung up.

I knew Nim was reclusive, but this was absurd. In a fit of fury, I decided I was going to run him to earth for once and all. As I was already late for work, I pulled out my hair dryer and started blowing my hair right in the middle of the living room as I paced about trying to think what to do next. Then I had an idea.

Nim had installed some of the major systems for the New York Stock Exchange some years back. Surely the folks who worked on their computers would know of him. Perhaps he even dropped in from time to time to look at his handiwork. I gave the DP manager there a call.

"Dr. Nim?" he said. "Never heard of him. Are you sure he worked here? I've been here three years, but I've never heard the name."

"All right," I said in complete exasperation, "I've had enough of this. I want to speak to the president. What's *his* name?"

"The . . . New . . . York . . . Stock . . . Exchange . . . does . . . not . . . *have* . . . a . . . president!" he informed me with a sneer. Shit.

"Well, what *does* it have?" I nearly screamed over the phone. "*Some*body must run things around there."

"We have a chairman," he told me in disgust, and mentioned the fellow's name.

"Fine, then forward this call to him, please."

"Okay, lady," he said. "I guess you think you know what you're doing."

I did indeed. The chairman's secretary was extremely polite, but I knew I was on the right track by the way she fielded my questions.

"Dr. Nim?" she said in a little-old-lady voice. "No . . . no, I don't believe I know the name. The chairman is out of the country right now. Could I possibly take a message?"

"That's fine," I told her. It was the best I could expect, as I knew from long experience with the man of mystery. "Should you hear from a Dr. Nim, please tell him that Miss Velis is awaiting his call at the Rockaway Greens Convent. And further, that if I do not hear from him by evening, I shall be forced to take the vows."

I gave the poor confused woman my phone numbers, and we signed off. It would serve Nim right, I thought, if the message fell into the hands of a few scions at the NYSE before it reached his. I'd like to see him explain his way out of that one.

Having accomplished as much as one might with so difficult a task, I pulled on a tomato-colored pantsuit for my day at Con Edison. I fumbled about in the bottom of my closet looking for something to put on my feet, cursing loudly. Carioca had chewed up half the shoes in there and disarranged the rest. I finally found a pair that matched, threw on my coat, and went to breakfast. Like Lily, there were certain things I found hard to face on an empty stomach, and Con Ed was one of them.

La Galette was the local French bistro, half a block from my apartment at the end of Tudor Place. It had checkered tablecloths and pink geraniums in pots. Its back windows overlooked the United Nations building. I ordered freshly squeezed orange juice, black coffee, and a prune Danish.

When my breakfast arrived I opened my briefcase and pulled out some notes I'd taken the prior night before I'd hit the sack. I thought it possible I could make some sense of the chronology of events.

Solarin had a secret formula and had been hauled back to Russia for a while.

Fiske had not played tournament chess in fifteen years. Solarin had given me a warning, using the same language as a fortune-teller I'd seen three months earlier. Solarin and Fiske had an altercation during the game and broke for a recess. Lily thought Fiske was cheating. Fiske wound up dead under suspicious circumstances. There were two bullets in Lily's car, one that was there before we arrived and one that was pumped in while we were standing there. And last, Saul and the fortune-teller had both disappeared.

Nothing seemed to fit, yet there were plenty of clues to indicate everything was somehow related. I knew the random probability of so many coincidences was zero.

I'd finished my first cup of coffee and was halfway through my prune Danish when I saw him. I had been gazing out the big glass windows at the blue-green curve of the United Nations when something caught my eye. A man passed by outside the windows, dressed completely in white, a hooded sweatsuit with a scarf muffling the lower half of his face. He was pushing a bicycle.

I was frozen in my seat, the glass of orange juice halfway to my lips. He started to descend the steep spiral stairs flanked by a stone wall that ran to the square opposite the UN. I put down my glass and jumped to my feet. I threw some money on the table, stuffed my papers back into the briefcase, grabbed the case and coat, and flew out the glass doors.

The stone steps were slippery, coated with ice and rock salt. I tugged my coat over my arm, fumbling with the briefcase as I catapulted down the stairs. The man with the bicycle was disappearing around the corner. As I was yanking my other arm into the sleeve, I caught the tip of my high-heeled shoe on the ice, ripped it loose, and toppled down two steps onto my knees. Above me, a quotation from Isaiah was carved into the stone wall:

> They shall beat their swords into plowshares and their spears into pruning hooks. Nation shall not lift up sword against nation. Neither shall they learn war any more.

Fat chance. I pulled myself up, dusting ice from my knees. Isaiah had a lot to learn about men and nations. There hadn't been a day in over five thousand years that war had not blossomed on our planet. Vietnam protestors were clotting the square already. I had to plow through them as they waved their little dove-footed peace signs at me. I'd like to see them beat a ballistic missile into a plowshare.

I skidded around the corner on my broken heel, bouncing into the side of IBM's Systems Research Institute. The man was now a full block ahead of me, astride his bicycle and pedaling. He'd reached the crossing to UN Plaza and paused for the light to change.

I tore along the pavement, my eyes streaming with cold, still trying to button my coat and close my briefcase as the strong wind hit me. Halfway down the block I saw the traffic light change as he pedaled leisurely across the street. I increased my pace, but the light turned red again just as I reached the crossing, and cars started pouring by. My eyes were glued on the retreating figure across the street.

He was off his bicycle again and was steering it up the steps into the plaza. Trapped! There was no exit from the sculpture garden, so I could calm down. As I did so, and waited for the light to change, I suddenly realized what I was doing.

The day before I'd been near witness to a possible murder and been within a few feet of a flying bullet, all within the public quarters of New York City. Now I was trailing after an unknown man, simply because he looked like the man in my painting, bicycle and all. But how could it be that he precisely resembled my painting? I thought that over and had no answer, but I checked the street both ways when the light changed before stepping off the curb.

Entering the wrought-iron gates of UN Plaza, I walked up the steps. Across the white concrete floor, seated on a stone bench, was an old woman in black feeding the pigeons. A black shawl wrapped around her head, she bent forward, tossing grain to the silvery birds that clustered, cooed, and swirled around her in a great white cloud. And before her stood the man on the bicycle.

I froze and watched them, uncertain what to do. They were speaking to each other. The old woman turned, looked in my direction, and said something to the man. Nodding briefly, but without looking back, he turned with one hand guiding his bicycle and quickly descended the far steps toward the river. I collected my wits and ran after him. A huge explosion of pigeons rose from the terrace, obscuring my view. I headed for the stairs and threw my arm across my face as they wheeled around me.

At the bottom facing the river was a huge bronze peasant donated by the Soviets. He was beating his sword into a plowshare. Before me lay the icy East River, the big Coca-Cola sign of Queens on the opposite bank with fiery furnaces billowing smoke around it. To the left lay the garden, its broad tree-lined lawn blanketed with snow. Not a footprint disturbed its smooth surface. Along the river ran a gravel path, separated from the garden by a row of smaller sculptured trees. There was no one there.

Where had he gone? There was no exit from the garden. I doubled back slowly and went up the steps to the plaza. The old woman had also disappeared, but I glimpsed a shadowy figure going into the visitors' entrance. Outside on the bicycle rack was his bicycle. How could he have come past me? I wondered as I hurried inside. The floor was deserted except for a guard who was standing, chatting up a young receptionist at the oval reception desk.

"Excuse me," I said, "has a man in a white sweatsuit come in here just now?"

"Didn't notice," said the guard, annoyed by the interruption.

"Where would you go in here if you wanted to hide from someone?" I asked. That got their attention. They both studied me as if I were a potential anarchist. I hastened to explain, "I mean, if you wanted to be alone, to have some privacy?"

"The delegates go to the Meditation Room," said the guard. "It's very quiet. It's just over there." He motioned to a door across the wide marble floor, checkered pink and gray in chessboard squares. Beside the door was a blue-green stained-glass window by Chagall. I nodded my thanks and crossed the floor. When I entered the Meditation Room, the door closed soundlessly behind me.

It was a long, darkened room resembling a crypt. Near the doors were several rows of small benches, one of which I nearly tripped over in the gloom. At the center was a coffin-shaped slab of stone illuminated by a pencil-thin spotlight that spread across its surface. The room was completely silent, cool, and damp. I felt my pupils expanding as I adjusted to the light.

I sat on one of the little benches. The straw squeaked. Setting my briefcase beside the bench, I looked at the stone slab. Suspended in midair like a monolith floating in open space, it quavered mysteriously. It had a tranquilizing effect, almost hypnotic.

When the door behind me opened soundlessly, letting in a small stream of light and closing again, I started to turn as in slow motion.

"Do not cry out," a voice whispered behind me. "I shall not harm you, but you must be silent."

My heart pounded against my ribs as I recognized the voice. I leaped at once to my feet and spun about, my back to the slab.

There in the dim light stood Solarin, his green eyes mirroring twin luminous images of the stone slab. I'd jumped to my feet so suddenly, the blood had drained from my brain. I put my hands behind me and leaned against the slab for support. Solarin stood facing me calmly. Still dressed in the slim gray trousers he'd been wearing the day before, he was now wearing a dark leather jacket that made his skin seem paler than I'd remembered.

"Sit down," he said in a low voice. "Here beside me. I have only a moment."

My legs weak, I did as he asked. I said nothing.

"I tried to warn you yesterday, but you would not listen. Now you know I was telling the truth. You and Lily Rad will stay away from this tournament. If you do not wish to end as Fiske has."

"You don't believe he committed suicide," I whispered back.

"Don't be a fool. His neck was broken by an expert. I was the last to see him alive. He was quite healthy. Two minutes later, he was dead. And articles were missing—"

"Unless you killed him," I interrupted. Solarin smiled. His smile was so absolutely dazzling, it completely transformed his face. He leaned toward me and placed both hands on my shoulders. I felt a kind of warm glow passing through his fingers.

"I'm at great risk if we are seen together, so please listen to what I have to say. I didn't put those bullets in your friend's car. But the disappearance of her chauffeur was no accident."

I looked at him in amazement. Lily and I had agreed to tell no one. How had Solarin known unless he'd done it?

"Do you know what happened to Saul? Do you know who *did* fire the gun?"

Solarin looked at me and said nothing. His hands were still resting on my shoulders. Now they tightened as he gave me his warm, beautiful smile again. He looked like a young boy when he smiled.

"They were right about you," he said quietly. "You are the one."

"*Who* was right? You know things you aren't telling me," I said irritably. "You warn me, but you don't tell me why. Do you know the fortune-teller?"

Solarin pulled his hands abruptly from my shoulders and slapped on the mask again. I realized I was pushing my luck, but I couldn't stop now.

"You *do* know," I said. "And who was that man on the bicycle? You must have seen him if you were following me! Why do you follow me around giving me warnings, but keep me completely in the dark? What do you want? What does all of this have to do with me?" I stopped to catch my breath and glared at Solarin. He was watching me closely.

"I don't know how much to tell you," he said. His voice was very soft, and for the first time I could hear the trace of a distinct Slavic accent beneath his formal, clipped pronunciation of English. "Anything I tell you may only place you in further jeopardy. I must ask you only to believe me, for I have risked a great deal just to speak with you."

Much to my surprise, he reached out and touched my hair gently as if I were a small child. "You must stay away from that chess tournament. Trust no one. You have powerful friends on your side, but you don't understand what game you are playing. . . ."

"What side?" I said. "I'm not playing any game."

"Yes, you are," he replied, looking down at me with an infinitely tender expression as if he wanted to wrap his arms around me. "You are playing a game of chess. But don't worry. I am a master of this game. And I am on your side."

He stood up and moved toward the door. I followed him in a daze. As we reached the door Solarin flattened his back against the wall and listened as if he expected someone to come bursting in. Then he looked back at me as I stood there, still confused.

He placed one hand inside his jacket and motioned with his head for me to go out first. I caught the glimpse of a gun that he was holding inside his jacket. I swallowed hard and passed quickly through the door, not looking back.

Bright winter light flooded through the glass walls of the lobby. I walked quickly to the exit. Wrapping my coat around me, I crossed the broad icy plaza and hurried down the steps to East River Drive.

I was halfway down the street, braced against the bitter wind, when I skidded to a halt before the gates of the delegates' entrance. I had left my briefcase beside the bench in the Meditation Room. It contained not only my library books, but my notes from the prior day's events.

Marvelous. It would be just my luck to have Solarin find those papers and believe I was investigating his past in far more detail than he'd suspected. Which of course was precisely what I planned to do. I cursed myself for a fool, turned on my broken heel, and went marching back to the UN Plaza.

I entered the lobby. The receptionist was busily engaged with a visitor. The guard was nowhere in sight. I assured myself that my fear of returning to the room alone was ridiculous. The entire lobby was empty—I could see all the way up the spiral staircase. There was no one about.

Walking boldly across the lobby, I glanced over my shoulder as I reached the Chagall window. I pulled open the door of the room and looked inside.

It took a second for my eyes to adjust to the light, but even from where I stood I could see that things were not as I'd left them. Solarin was gone. So was my briefcase. And lying face upward on the stone slab was a body. I stood there at the door, ill with fear. The long, outstretched body on the slab was dressed in a chauffeur's uniform. My blood turned to ice. There was a pounding in my ears. Taking a deep breath, I stepped into the room and let the door swing shut behind me.

I walked over to the slab and looked down at the white, pasty face shining in the spotlight. It was Saul all right. And he was very dead. I felt sick to my stomach and deathly afraid. I had never seen a dead person before, not even at a funeral. I started to choke up as if I were going to cry.

But suddenly something else strangled the first sob before it left my throat: Saul hadn't crawled up on that slab himself and just stopped breathing. Somebody had put him there, and that somebody had been in the room within the last five minutes.

I bolted through the door to the lobby. The receptionist was still explaining things to a visitor. I briefly considered alerting someone, then decided against it. I might have trouble explaining how the chauffeur of a friend of mine just happened to get murdered there, how I just happened to stumble upon the body. How I'd coincidentally been present at the site of a mysterious death the day before. How my friend, the chauffeur's employer, had been there, too. And how we'd failed to report the two bullet holes that had appeared in her car.

I beat my retreat from the UN and literally plummeted down the steps again to the street. I knew I should go straight to the authorities, but I was terrified. Saul had been killed in that room only moments after I'd left it. Fiske had been killed only a few minutes after the chess recess. In both cases the victims were in public places with people very close by. And in both cases Solarin had been there. Solarin had a gun, didn't he? And he'd been there. Both times.

So we were playing a game. Well, if so, I was going to find out the rules on my own. It wasn't only fear and confusion I felt as I beat it down the icy street to my safe, warm office. It was determination. I had to break through the shroud of mystery surrounding this game, identify the rules and the players. And soon. Because the moves were getting too close for comfort. Little did I know that thirty blocks away, a move was about to take place that would soon alter the course of my life. . . .

"Brodski is furious," said Gogol nervously. As soon as he'd seen Solarin come through the entrance, he had risen from the soft, comfortable chair where he'd been having tea in the lobby of the Algonquin. "Where have you been?" he asked, his pale skin as white as a pillowcase.

"Out for a breath of air," replied Solarin calmly. "This isn't Soviet Russia, you know. People in New York go for walks all the time without first notifying the authorities of their intended movements. Did he think I was going to defect?"

Gogol did not return Solarin's smile. "He's upset." He looked about nervously, but there was no one else in the lobby except an elderly woman having tea at the far end. "Hermanold told us this morning that the tournament may be indefinitely postponed until they get to the bottom of Fiske's death. His neck was broken."

"I know," said Solarin, taking Gogol by the elbow and moving him over to the table where the tea sat cooling. He motioned for Gogol to sit down and finish his tea. "I saw the body, remember?"

"That's the problem," said Gogol. "You were alone with him just before the accident. It looks bad. We weren't to draw attention to ourselves. If there's going to be an investigation, they'll surely begin by questioning you."

"Why don't you let me worry about that?" said Solarin.

Gogol picked up a sugar cube and put it between his teeth. He sucked his tea through it meditatively and was silent.

The old woman at the far end of the lobby was hobbling over to their table. She was dressed in black and moved painfully with a cane. Gogol glanced up at her.

"Excuse me," she said sweetly as she came up to the two men. "I'm afraid they didn't give me any saccharin with my tea, and I can't take sugar. Do you gentlemen have any packets of saccharin I could borrow?"

"Certainly," said Solarin. Reaching over to the sugar bowl on Gogol's tray, he pulled out several pink packets and handed them to the old woman. She thanked him kindly and left.

"Oh, no," Gogol said, looking toward the elevators. Brodski was marching across the room, making his way through the maze of tea tables and flowered chairs. "I was to take you up at once when you returned," he told Solarin under his breath. He stood up, nearly upsetting his tea tray. Solarin remained seated.

Brodski was a tall, well-muscled man with a tanned face. He looked like a European businessman in his navy pin-striped suit and silk twill tie. He approached the table aggressively, as if arriving at a business meeting. He halted before Solarin and extended his hand. Solarin shook it without standing. Brodski took a seat.

"I've had to notify the Secretary of your disappearance," Brodski began.

"I hardly disappeared. I went for a walk."

"To do a little shopping, eh?" said Brodski. "That's a nice briefcase. Where did you buy it?" He fingered the briefcase sitting on the floor beside Solarin, which Gogol had not even noticed. "Italian leather. Just the thing for a Soviet chess player," he added ironically. "Do you mind if I look inside?"

Solarin shrugged, and Brodski pulled the case onto his lap and opened it. He started going through the things inside.

"By the way, who was that woman who was leaving your table as I arrived?"

"Just an old lady," Gogol said. "She wanted some sweetener for her tea."

"She must not have needed it very badly," mused Brodski as he flipped through the papers. "She left as soon as I arrived." Gogol glanced at the table where the old woman had been seated. She was gone, but her tea things were still there.

Brodski put the papers back into the briefcase and returned it to Solarin. Then he looked at Gogol with a sigh.

"Gogol, you are a fool," he said casually as if discussing the weather. "Our precious grand master has given you the slip three times now. Once when he interrogated Fiske just before the murder. Once when he went out to pick up this briefcase, which now contains nothing but a clipboard, some pads of blank paper, and two books on the petroleum industry. Obviously anything of value has already been removed from it. And now, under your very nose, he has passed a note to an agent right here in this lounge." Gogol flushed beet red and put down his teacup.

"But I assure you—"

"Spare me your assurances," said Brodski curtly. He turned to Solarin. "The Secretary says that we must have a contact within twenty-four hours or we'll be recalled to Russia. He cannot risk breaking our cover if this tournament is canceled. It would make a bad appearance to say that we were merely remaining in New York to shop for used Italian briefcases," he sneered. "You have twenty-four hours to reach your sources, Grand Master."

Solarin looked Brodski in the eye. Then he smiled coldly. "You may inform the Secretary that we have already made contact, my dear Brodski," he said.

Brodski said nothing, waiting for Solarin to proceed. When Solarin remained silent, he said in a purring voice, "Well? Do not keep us in suspense."

Solarin looked at the briefcase on his lap. At last he looked back up at Brodski, his face a mask.

"The pieces are in Algeria," he said.

By noon I was a complete basket case. I'd tried frantically to reach Nim, to no avail. I kept seeing Saul's horrible body floating on that slab and trying to think what it all meant, how it fit together.

I was locked in my office at Con Ed overlooking the entrance to the UN, listening to every radio bulletin and watching for the police cars to pull up in front of the plaza when the body was found. But nothing like that had happened.

I'd tried to reach Lily, but she was out. Harry's office told me he had driven to Buffalo to look at shipments of damaged furs and wouldn't be back until late that night. I considered calling the police to leave an anonymous message about Saul's body, but they'd find out soon enough. A dead body couldn't lie around the UN long without someone noticing.

A little after noon I sent my secretary out for sandwiches. When the phone rang I answered it. It was my boss Lisle. He sounded unpleasantly cheerful.

"We have your tickets and itinerary, Velis," he said. "The office is expecting you in Paris next Monday. You'll spend the night there and go on to Algiers in the morning. I'll have the tickets and papers delivered to your apartment this afternoon, if that's all right?" I told him it was fine.

"You don't sound very chipper, Velis. Having second thoughts about your trip to the Dark Continent?"

"Not at all," I said as confidently as I could. "I could use a break. New York is beginning to get on my nerves."

"Very well, then. Bon voyage, Velis. Don't say I didn't warn you."

We rang off. A few minutes later the secretary came in with the sandwiches and some milk. I closed my door and tried to eat, but I couldn't put down more than a few bites. I couldn't get interested in my books about the history of the oil business, either. I just sat and stared at my desk.

Around three o'clock the secretary knocked at my door and entered, carrying a briefcase.

"A man dropped this off with the guard downstairs," she told me. "He left a note with it." I took the note with trembling hand and waited until she'd left.

I rifled through my desk for a paper knife, slit the envelope, and yanked out the paper.

"I have removed some of your papers," it said. "Please do not go to your apartment alone." It wasn't signed, but I recognized the cheery tone. I put the paper in my pocket and opened the briefcase. Everything was intact. Except, of course, my notes on Solarin.

$$\infty$$

At six-thirty I was still in my office. The secretary was sitting out in front typing, though nearly everyone else had left the building. I'd given her reams of work so I wouldn't be alone, but I was wondering how I would get to my apartment. It was only a block away; it seemed foolish to call a cab.

The janitor came in to clean up. He was dumping an ashtray into my wastebasket when my phone rang. I practically knocked it off the desk in my haste to grab the receiver.

"Working rather late, aren't you?" said the old familiar voice. I almost wept in relief.

"If it isn't Sister Nim," I said, trying to get my voice under control. "I'm afraid you've called too late, I was just packing my things to leave for retreat. I'm a card-carrying member of the Nuns for Jesus now."

"That would surely be both a pity and a waste," said Nim cheerfully.

"How did you know to find me here so late?" I asked.

"Where else would someone with your unbounded dedication be on a winter's evening?" he said. "You must by now have burned up the world's supply of midnight oil. . . . How are you, my dear? I understand you've been trying to reach me." I waited until the janitor left before replying.

"I'm afraid I'm in serious trouble," I began.

"Naturally. You are always in trouble," Nim said coolly. "That's one of the things I find so enchanting about you. A mind like mine grows weary through continual encounter with the expected."

I glanced at the secretary's back through the glass wall of my office.

"I'm in *terrible* trouble," I hissed into the phone. "Two people have been killed practically under my nose in the last two days! I've been warned it had something to do with my presence at chess games—"

"Whoa," said Nim. "What are you doing, speaking through a cheesecloth? I can barely hear you. You've been warned about what? Speak up."

"A fortune-teller predicted that I would be in danger," I told him. "And now I am. These murders—"

"My dear Cat," said Nim, laughing. "A *fortune*-teller?"

"She wasn't the only one," I said, grinding my fingernails into my palms. "Have you heard of Alexander Solarin?" Nim was silent for a moment.

"The chess player?" he said at last.

"He's the one who told me . . ." I started in a weak voice, realizing that this all sounded too fantastic to be believed.

"How do you know Alexander Solarin?" said Nim.

"I was at a chess tournament yesterday. He came up and told me I was in danger. He was quite insistent about it."

"Perhaps he mistook you for someone else," Nim said. But his voice still sounded remote, as if he were lost in thought.

"Maybe," I admitted. "But then this morning at the United Nations, he made it clear—"

"One moment," Nim interrupted. "I believe I see the problem. Fortune-tellers and Russian chess players are following you about, whispering mysterious warnings in your ear. Dead bodies are dropping out of the air. What have you had to eat today?"

"Um. I had a sandwich and some milk."

"Paranoia induced by a clear case of food deprivation," said Nim cheerfully. "Get your things together. I'll meet you downstairs in five minutes with my car. We're going to have a decent meal, and these fantasies will rapidly disappear."

"They aren't fantasies," I said. Though I was relieved that Nim was coming to fetch me. At least I'd be able to get home safely.

"I'll be the judge of that," he replied. "From where I stand you look entirely too thin. But that red suit you are wearing is quite attractive."

I glanced around my office, then looked out into the darkened street in front of the UN. The street lamps had just come on, but most of the sidewalk was deep in shadow. I saw a dark figure standing at the pay phone near the bus stop. It raised its arm.

"Incidentally, my dear," said Nim's voice through the phone, "if you're concerned about danger, I'd suggest you stop frolicking about in lighted windows after dark. Just a suggestion, of course." And he hung up.

Nim's dark green Morgan pulled up in front of Con Edison. I ran out and jumped in the passenger side, which was on the left. The car had running boards on the side, and the floorboards were made of wood. You could see the pavement go by between the gaps.

Nim was wearing faded jeans, an expensive Italian leather bomber jacket, and a white silk scarf with fringes. His coppery hair tossed in the wind as we pulled away from the curb. I wondered why I had so many friends who preferred to drive with the top down in winter. He swung the car around, the warm glow of the street lamps catching his curls with flickers of gold.

"We'll stop by your place so you can change into something warm," said Nim. "If you like, I'll go in first with a mine sweeper." Nim's eyes, due to a strange genetic twist, were of two different colors, one brown and one blue. I always had the feeling that he was looking at me and through me at the same time. A feeling I was not especially fond of.

We pulled up before my building. Nim stepped out and greeted Boswell, pressing a twenty-dollar bill into his palm.

"We'll only be a few moments, my good fellow," said Nim. "Could you possibly watch the car for me while we're inside? It's something of a family heirloom."

"Certainly, sir," Boswell said politely. Damned if he didn't come around and help me out of the car as well. It was amazing what money would buy.

I picked up my mail at the desk. The envelope from Fulbright Cone containing my tickets was there. Nim and I got into the elevator and went upstairs.

Nim looked at my door and said that no mine sweepers were necessary. If anyone had entered my apartment, he'd done it with a key. Like most apartments in New York, mine had a door of two-inch steel with double dead bolts.

Nim preceded me down the entrance hall into the living room.

"I might suggest that a maid one day per month would do wonders here," he commented. "While useful as a tool in crime detection, I can think of no other purpose for you to maintain so large a collection of dust and memorabilia." He blew a cloud off a pile of books and picked one up, leafing through it.

I fumbled in my closet and pulled out some khaki corduroy trousers and an Irish fisherman's sweater of undyed wool. When I left for the bathroom to change, Nim was sitting at the piano idly tinkling at the keys.

"Do you play this thing?" he called down the hall to me. "I notice the keys are clean."

"I was a music major," I called back from the bathroom. "Musicians make the best computer experts. Better than engineers and physicists combined." Nim had done his degrees in engineering and physics, as I knew. There was silence from the living room as I changed clothes. When I came back down the hall in stocking feet, Nim was standing in the center of the room staring at my painting of the man on the bicycle, which I'd left turned to the wall.

"Careful of that," I told him. "It's wet."

"You did this?" he said, still staring at the painting.

"That's what got me into all the trouble," I explained. "I painted this, then I saw a man who looked exactly like the painting. So I followed him. . . ."

"You did what?" Nim looked up at me abruptly.

I sat on the piano bench and started telling him the story, beginning with Lily's arrival with Carioca. Was it only yesterday? This time Nim did not interrupt me. From time to time he glanced down at the painting as I spoke, then looked back at me. I finished by telling him about the fortune-teller and my trip to the Fifth Avenue Hotel last night, when I'd discovered she had never existed. When I was through, Nim stood there thinking. I stood up and went over to the closet, dug out some old riding boots and a pea jacket, and started tugging the boots on over my cords.

"If you don't mind," Nim said thoughtfully, "I'd like to borrow this painting of yours for a few days." He'd picked up the painting and was holding it gingerly by the back stretcher brace. "And do you still have that poem from the fortune-teller?"

"It's somewhere around here," I said, motioning to the general chaos.

"Let's have a look," he said.

I sighed and started rummaging through the pockets of my coats in the closet. It took about ten minutes, but I finally found the cocktail napkin where Llewellyn had written the prophecy, deep in a lining.

Nim took the paper from my hand and stuffed it into his own pocket. Lifting the wet painting, he draped his free arm over my shoulder and we headed for the door.

"Don't worry about the painting," he told me as we went down the hallway. "I'll return it within the week."

"You may as well keep it," I said. "The movers are coming to pack my things on Friday. That was the reason I'd called you at first. I'm leaving the country this weekend. I'll be gone for a year. My company is sending me abroad on business."

"That firm of hacks," said Nim. "Where are they sending you?"

"Algeria," I said as we reached the door.

Nim halted cold and glared at me. Then he began to laugh. "My dear young woman," he said, "you never fail to amaze me. You've regaled me for nearly an hour with tales of murder, mayhem, mystery, and intrigue. Yet you've managed to miss the main point."

I was completely confused. "Algeria?" I said. "What does it have to do with any of this?"

"Tell me," said Nim, putting his hand under my chin and turning my face up to his, "have you ever heard of the Montglane Service?"

THE KNIGHT'S TOUR

Knight: You play chess, don't you?

Death: How did you know that?

Knight: I have seen it in paintings and heard it sung in ballads.

Death: Yes, in fact I am quite a good chess player.

Knight: But you can't be better than I am.

—The Seventh Seal
Ingmar Bergman

The midtown tunnel was nearly deserted. It was after seven-thirty in the evening, and you could hear the loud whine of the Morgan's engine echoing off the walls.

"I thought we were going to dinner," I yelled over the noise.

"We are going," said Nim mysteriously, "to my place on Long Island, where I practice being a gentleman farmer. Though there aren't any crops at this time of year."

"You have a farm on Long Island?" I said. It was odd, but I'd never visualized Nim actually *living* anywhere. He seemed to appear and disappear, rather like a ghost.

"Indeed I do," he replied, peering at me in the darkness with his bicolored eyes. "As you may be the only living person to testify. I guard my privacy carefully, as you know. I plan to prepare dinner for you myself. After we dine, you can spend the night."

"Now just one minute. . . ."

"Obviously it's hard to confuse you with reason or logic," said Nim. "You've just explained you're in danger. You've seen two men killed in the last forty-eight hours, and you've been warned you're somehow involved. You don't seriously propose to spend the night alone in your apartment?"

"I have to go to work in the morning," I told him.

"You'll do no such thing," said Nim with finality. "You will stay away from your known haunts until we get to the bottom of this. I have a few things to say on the subject."

As the car careened through the open countryside, wind whistling around us, I tucked the blanket closer and listened to Nim.

"First I'm going to tell you about the Montglane Service," he began. "It's a very long story, but let me start by explaining that it was originally the chess service of Charlemagne. . . ."

"Oh!" I said, sitting up straighter. "I *have* heard of it, but I didn't know the name. Lily Rad's uncle Llewellyn told me about it when he heard I was going to Algeria. He says he'd like me to get him some of the pieces."

"No doubt he would." Nim laughed. "They're extremely rare and worth a fortune. Most people don't believe they even exist. How did Llewellyn hear of them? And what makes him think they're in Algeria?" Nim was speaking in

135

a light, casual manner, but I could tell he was paying close attention to my response.

"Llewellyn's an antique dealer," I explained. "He has a client who wants to collect these pieces at any cost. They have a contact who knows where the pieces are."

"I doubt that very much," said Nim. "Legend has it that they've been buried away for well over a century, and were out of circulation for a thousand years before that."

As we drove through the black night, Nim told me a bizarre tale of Moorish kings and French nuns, of a mysterious power that had been sought for centuries by those who understood the nature of power. And, finally, how the entire service had disappeared underground, never to be seen again. It was believed, Nim told me, that it had been hidden somewhere in Algeria. Though he didn't say why.

By the time he'd finished this improbable tale, the car was moving through a deep thicket of trees, and the road dipped very low. When it came up again we could see the milk-white moon hovering low over a black sea. I could hear owls calling to each other in the woods. It certainly seemed a long way from New York.

"Well," I sighed, pulling my nose out of the blanket, "I've already told Llewellyn I'd have no part in it, that he was crazy to think I'd try to smuggle a chess piece that big, made of gold, with all those diamonds and rubies—"

The car swerved sharply, and we nearly ran off into the sea. Nim slowed down and brought us under control.

"He had one?" he said. "He *showed* you one?"

"Of course not," I said, wondering what was going on. "You told me yourself they've been lost for a century. He showed me a photograph of something like it made of ivory. In the Bibliothèque Nationale, I think."

"I see," said Nim, calming down a bit.

"I don't see what all this has to do with Solarin and people getting murdered," I told him.

"I'll explain," Nim said. "But you're sworn not to repeat this to anyone."

"That's just what Llewellyn said."

Nim looked across at me in disgust. "Perhaps you'll be more cautious when I explain that the reason Solarin has contacted you, the reason you've been threatened, could be due to these very chess pieces."

"That's impossible," I pointed out. "I'd never even heard of them. I *still* know practically nothing about them. I haven't anything to do with this silly game."

"But perhaps," said Nim sternly as the car shot along the dark coast, "someone thinks you do."

∞

The road curved slightly away from the sea. On either side manicured hedges, ten feet high, enclosed large estates. From time to time I caught moonlit glimpses of huge manor houses set back on sweeping snow-covered lawns. I had never seen anything like it near New York. It reminded me of Scott Fitzgerald.

Nim was telling me about Solarin.

"I don't know much except what I've read in the chess journals," he said. "Alexander Solarin is twenty-six years old, a citizen of the Union of Soviet Socialist Republics, raised in the Crimea, the womb of civilization but grown quite uncivilized in recent years. He was an orphan raised in a state-sponsored home. At the age of nine or ten he beat the pants off a headmaster at chess. Apparently he'd learned to play at the age of four, taught by fishermen on the Black Sea. He was popped at once into the Pioneers' Palace."

I knew what that was. The Palace of Young Pioneers was the only advanced institute in the world that devoted itself to churning out chess masters. In Russia chess was not only the national sport, it was an extension of world politics, the most cerebral game in history. The Russians thought their long hegemony confirmed their intellectual superiority.

"So if Solarin was in the Pioneers' Palace, that meant he had strong political backing?" I said.

"Should have meant," Nim replied. The car swung out toward the sea again. Spray from the waves was licking at the road, and there was a thick residue of sand on the pavement. The road dead-ended into a wide drive with large double gates of sculptured wrought iron. Nim punched a few buttons on his dashboard, and the gates swung open. We drove into a jungle of tangled foliage, mountainous curlicues of snow like the Snow Queen's domain in the *Nutcracker*.

"In fact," Nim was saying, "Solarin refused to throw games to the preferred players, a strict rule of political etiquette among the Russians in tournament play. It's been widely criticized, but it doesn't stop them doing it."

The drive was unplowed, and it seemed no cars had been through in some time. Trees arched above like spans of a cathedral, closing off the garden from view. At last we came to a big circle drive with a fountain at the center. The house loomed before us in the moonlight. It was immense, with large gables overlooking the drive and chimneys cluttering the roofs.

"So," said Nim as he turned off the car engine and looked across at me in the moonlight, "our friend Mr. Solarin enrolled in the school of physics and dropped out of chess. Except for the occasional tournament, he hasn't been a major contender since the age of twenty."

Nim helped me out of the car, and we labored, carrying the painting, to the front door, which he opened with a key.

We stood in an enormous entrance hall. Nim switched on the light, a large cut-crystal chandelier. The floors here and in the rooms opening off the hall were of hand-cut slate, polished so it shone like marble. The house was so cold I could see my breath, and ice had formed thin layers on the edges of the slate tiles. He led me through a succession of darkened rooms into a kitchen at the back of the house. What a marvelous place it was. The original gas jets were still mounted in the walls and ceiling. Setting the painting down, he lit the carriage lamps around the walls. They cast a cheery golden glow over everything.

The kitchen was huge, perhaps thirty by fifty feet. The back wall was French windows opening onto a snowy lawn, the sea beyond crashing up with wild foam in the moonlight. At one end of the room were ovens large enough to cook for a hundred people, probably wood burning. At the opposite end was a gigantic stone fireplace that filled the entire wall. Before it was a round oak table that would seat eight or ten, its surface cut and battered with years of use. Around the room were arrangements of comfortable chairs and overstuffed sofas covered in bright flowery chintzes.

Nim went to the woodpile stacked against the fireplace wall and broke up a bed of kindling, swiftly piling heavy logs on top. After a few minutes the room glowed warmly with an inner light. I pulled off my boots and curled up on a sofa as Nim uncorked some sherry. He handed me a glass and poured another for himself, taking a seat beside me. After I'd peeled off my coat, he tipped his glass toward mine.

"To the Montglane Service and the many adventures it will bring you," he said, smiling, and took a sip.

"Yum. This is delicious," I said.

"It's an amontillado," he replied, swirling it in his glass. "People have been bricked into walls still breathing, for sherries inferior to this one."

"I hope that's not the sort of adventure you're planning for *me*," I told him. "I really have to go to work tomorrow morning."

" 'I died for Beauty, I died for Truth,' " quoted Nim. "Everyone has something he believes himself willing to die for. But I've never met anyone willing to risk death to put in an unnecessary day's work at Consolidated Edison!"

"Now you're trying to frighten me."

"Not at all," Nim said, stripping off his leather jacket and silk scarf. He was wearing a brilliant red sweater that looked unexpectedly splendid with his hair. He stretched his legs out. "But if a mysterious stranger approached me in a deserted room at the United Nations, I'd be inclined to pay attention. Especially if his warnings were consistently followed close at heel by the untimely deaths of others."

"Why do you think Solarin singled me out?" I asked.

"I was hoping you could tell *me* that," said Nim, sipping his sherry meditatively and gazing into the fire.

"What about that secret formula he claimed to have had in Spain?" I suggested.

"A red herring," Nim said. "Solarin is purportedly a maniac for mathematical games. He'd developed a new formula for the Knight's Tour, and wagered it against anyone who beat him. Do you know what a Knight's Tour is?" he added, seeing my confusion. I shook my head in the negative.

"It's a mathematical puzzle. You move the Knight to every square of the chessboard without landing on the same square twice, using regular Knight moves: two squares horizontal and one vertical or the reverse. Through the ages, mathematicians have tried to come up with formulas to do it. Euler had a new one. So did Benjamin Franklin. A Closed Tour would be one in which you wound up on the same square you started from."

Nim stood up, walked over to the ovens, and started hauling down pots and pans, lighting gas jets on the stove as he spoke.

"Italian journalists in Spain thought Solarin might have hidden another formula within the Knight's Tour. Solarin likes games with many layers of meaning. Knowing he was a physicist, they naturally jumped to conclusions that would make good press."

"Exactly. He's a physicist," I said, pulling a chair over near the stove and bringing along the bottle of amontillado. "If the formula he had wasn't important, why would the Russians smuggle him out of Spain so fast?"

"You'd have an excellent career in the paparazzi," said Nim. "That was exactly *their* line of reasoning. Unfortunately, Solarin's field of physics is acoustics. It's obscure, unpopular, and totally unrelated to national defense. They don't even offer a degree in it in most schools in this country. Perhaps he's designing music halls in Russia, if they're still building any."

Nim banged a pot down on the stove and marched off into the pantry, returning with an armload of fresh vegetables and meat.

"There were no tire marks in your drive," I pointed out. "And there's been no new snow in days. So where did the fresh spinach and exotic mushrooms come from?"

Nim smiled at me as if I'd passed an important test. "You have the correct investigative abilities, I'll say that. Just what you're going to need," he commented, putting the food down into the sink and washing it. "I have my caretaker do the shopping. He arrives and departs by the side entrance."

Nim unwrapped a loaf of fresh dilled rye bread and opened a crock of trout mousse. He slathered up a big slice and handed it to me. I'd never finished breakfast and had barely touched my lunch. It was delicious. Dinner was even more so. We had thinly sliced veal smothered in kumquat sauce, fresh spinach with pine nuts, and fat red beefsteak tomatoes (impossibly rare at this time of year) broiled and stuffed with lemon apple sauce. The wide, fan-shaped mushrooms were sautéed lightly and served as a side dish. The main course was followed by a salad of red and green baby lettuce with dandelion greens and toasted hazelnuts.

After Nim had cleared away the dishes, he brought a pot of coffee and served it with a splash of Tuaca. We moved to big squishy chairs near the fire, which had burned down to glowing charcoal. Nim had located his jacket draped over a chair and pulled out the cocktail napkin from the fortune-teller. He looked at Llewellyn's printing on the napkin for a very long time. Then, handing it to me, he got up to stir the fire.

"What do you notice that is unusual about this poem?" he asked. I looked at it but didn't see anything odd.

"Of course you know that the fourth day of the fourth month is my birthday," I said. Nim nodded soberly from the hearth. The firelight turned his hair a brilliant reddish gold. "The fortune-teller warned me not to tell anyone about that," I added.

"As usual, you kept your word at all cost," Nim observed wryly, throwing a few more logs on the fire. He went over to a table in the corner and pulled out some paper and a pen, returning to sit beside me.

"Take a look at this," he said. Printing in neat block letters on the paper, he copied out the poem into separate lines. Previously it had been scrambled across the napkin. Now it read:

> Just as these lines that merge to form a key
> Are as chess squares; when month and day are four;
> Don't risk another chance to move to mate.
> One game is real and one's a metaphor.
> Untold times this wisdom's come too late.
> Battle of White has raged on endlessly.
> Everywhere Black will strive to seal his fate.
> Continue a search for thirty-three and three.
> Veiled forever is the secret door.

"What do you see here?" said Nim, studying me as I studied his printed version of the poem. I wasn't certain what he was driving at.

"Look at the structure of the poem itself," he said a little impatiently. "You've a mathematical mind, try to put it to some use."

I looked at the poem again, and then I saw it.

"The rhyming pattern is unusual," I said proudly.

Nim's eyebrows went up, and he snatched the paper away from me. He looked at it a moment and started to laugh. "So it is," he said, handing it back to me. "I hadn't noticed that myself. Here, take the pen and write down what it is."

I did so, and I wrote:

"Key-Four-Mate (A-B-C), Metaphor-Late-Endlessly (B-C-A), Fate-Three-Door (C-A-B).

"So the rhyming pattern is like so," said Nim, copying it below my writing on the paper. "Now I want you to apply numbers instead of letters and add them up." I did so beside where he'd printed the letters, and it looked like this:

$$
\begin{array}{ll}
\text{ABC} & 123 \\
\text{BCA} & 231 \\
\text{CAB} & \underline{312} \\
& 666
\end{array}
$$

"That was the number of the Beast in the Apocalypse: 666!" I said.

"So it was," said Nim. "And if you add the rows horizontally, you'll find they add to the same number. And that, my dear, is known as a 'magic square.' Another mathematical game. Some of those Knight's Tours that Ben Franklin developed had secret magic squares hidden within them. You've quite a knack for this. Found one your first time out that I hadn't seen myself."

"You didn't see it?" I said, rather pleased with myself. "But then what *was* it you wanted me to find?" I studied the paper as if searching for a hidden rabbit in a drawing from a child's magazine, expecting it to pop out at me sideways or upside down.

"Draw a line separating the last two sentences from the first seven," said Nim, and as I was drawing the line he added, "Now look at the first letter of each sentence."

I traced my eye slowly down the page, but as I moved toward the bottom a horrible chill had started to come over me, despite the warm and cheery fire.

"What's wrong?" Nim said, looking at me strangely. I stared at the paper, speechless. Then I picked up the pen and wrote what I saw.

"J-A-D-O-U-B-E / C-V," said the paper, as if speaking to me.

"Indeed," Nim was saying as I sat, frozen, beside him. "*J'adoube*, the French chess term meaning I touch, I adjust. That is what a player speaks when he is about to adjust one of his pieces during a game. Followed by the letters 'C.V.,' which are your initials. It suggests that this fortune-teller was sending you a message of some sort. She wants to get in touch with you, perhaps. I realize . . . What on *earth* is making you look so dreadful?" he said.

"You don't understand," I told him, my voice limp with fear. "*J'adoube* . . . was the last word that Fiske said in public. Just before he died."

Needless to say, I had nightmares. I was following the man on the bicycle up a long winding alley that wove up a steep hill. The buildings were so closely packed that I couldn't see the sky. It grew darker as we penetrated deeper into the maze of ever-narrowing cobbled streets. As I turned each corner, I caught a glimpse of his bicycle disappearing into the next alley. At the end of a cul-de-sac, I cornered him. He was waiting for me like a spider in its web. He turned, pulling the muffler from his face to expose a blanched white skull with gaping sockets. The skull began to grow flesh before my eyes until it slowly took on the grinning face of the fortune-teller.

I woke up in a cold sweat and threw back the comforter. I sat up in bed, shaking. The fireplace in the corner of my room still had a few glowing embers. Peeking out the window, I saw snowy lawns below. At center was a large marble basin like a fountain and beneath it a larger pool big enough for swimming. Beyond the lawn was the winter sea, pearly gray in the early-morning light.

I couldn't remember everything that had happened the night before, Nim had poured so much Tuaca down me. Now my head hurt. I got out of bed and staggered into the bathroom, turning on the hot-water tap. I managed to find some bubblebath called "Carnations and Violets." It smelled pretty bad, but I dumped it into the tub, and it formed a thin layer of foam. As I sat in the hot tub, our conversation started to come back in bits and pieces. Soon I was terrified all over again.

Outside my bedroom door was a small pile of clothes: an oiled-wool sweater from Scandinavia and some flannel-lined yellow rubber duck boots. I pulled them on over my clothes. As I went downstairs I could smell the delicious aroma of breakfast already cooking.

Nim was standing at the stove, his back to me, wearing a plaid shirt and jeans and yellow boots like mine.

"How do I get to a phone to call my office?" I asked.

"There are no phones here," he said. "But Carlos, my caretaker, came by this morning to help me clean up. I asked him to place a call in town to your office to tell them you won't be in. I'll drive you back this afternoon and show you how to safeguard your apartment. Meanwhile, let's have something to eat and go look at the birds. There's an aviary here, you know."

Nim whipped up some eggs poached in wine, thick Canadian bacon, and fried potatoes, with some of the finest coffee I'd had on the eastern seaboard. After breakfast, with very little conversation, we went out through the French windows to look at Nim's property.

The land ran nearly a hundred yards along the sea, out to the end of a point. It was all open with only a row of thick high hedges at either end to separate it from adjoining properties. The oval basin of the fountain and the larger swimming pool beneath were still partly filled with water, with floating barrels to break up the ice.

Beside the house was an enormous aviary with a Moorish dome constructed of wire mesh and painted white. Snow sifted through the latticework and gathered on twigs of the small trees that grew inside. Birds of every variety perched in the branches, and large peacocks strolled about on the ground, dragging their lovely feathers through the snow. When they screamed out their awful cry, they sounded like women being knifed. It jarred my nerves.

Nim unlocked the mesh door and escorted me inside the open dome, pointing out the various species as we moved through the snowy maze of trees.

"Birds are often more intelligent than people," he told me. "I keep falcons here as well, in a separate section closed off from the others. Carlos feeds them red meat twice a day. The peregrine is my favorite. As with many other species, it's the female that does the hunting." He pointed out a small speckled bird perched atop a birdhouse at the back of the aviary.

"Really? I didn't know that," I said as we went over to take a closer look. The bird's narrow-set eyes were large and black. I felt she was appraising *us*.

"I've always felt," said Nim as he looked at the falcon, "that *you* have the killer instinct."

"I? You must be joking."

"It hasn't been properly fostered yet," he added. "But I plan to begin its cultivation. It has been latent in you entirely too long, in my opinion."

"But *I'm* the one people are trying to kill," I pointed out.

"As in any game," said Nim, looking down at me and ruffling my hair with one gloved hand, "you may choose whether to react to a threat defensively or aggressively. Why don't you opt for the latter, and threaten your opponent?"

"I don't know who my opponent *is*!" I said, extremely frustrated.

"Ah, but you do," Nim replied cryptically. "You have known from the very beginning. Shall I prove it to you?"

"You do that." I was getting upset again and didn't feel like talking as Nim led me out of the aviary. He locked it and took my hand as we headed back to the house.

He removed my coat, sat me on a sofa near the fire, and pulled off my boots. Then he walked over to the wall where he'd propped my painting of the man on the bicycle. He brought it over and set it on a chair before me.

"Last night, after you'd gone to bed," said Nim, "I looked at this painting for a very long time. I'd had a feeling of déjà-vu, and it bothered me. You know how I must wrestle problems to the ground. This morning, I solved it."

He walked over to an oak counter that ran beside the ovens and opened a drawer. Out of it he pulled several packs of playing cards. He brought them over and sat beside me on the sofa. Opening each pack, he extracted a joker from the deck and tossed it on the table. I looked silently at the cards before me.

One was a jester with cap and bells, riding a bicycle. Both he and his cycle were posed in precisely the same position as the man in my painting. Behind his bicycle was a tombstone that said RIP. The second was a similar jester, but he was two mirror images, like my man riding his bicycle over an inverted skeleton. The third was a fool from a tarot deck, walking along blithely, about to step over a precipice.

I looked up at Nim, and he smiled.

"The jester in the card deck has traditionally been associated with Death," he said. "But it is also a symbol of rebirth. And of the innocence that mankind possessed before the Fall. I like to think of him as a knight of the holy grail, who must be naïve and simple in order to stumble upon the good fortune he is seeking. Remember that his mission is to save mankind."

"So?" I said, though I was more than a little unnerved at the resemblance between the cards before me and my painting. Now that I saw the prototypes, the man on the bicycle even seemed to have the jester's hood and his oddly spiraled eyes.

"You asked who your opponent was," Nim replied quite seriously. "I think, just as in these cards and in your painting, the man on the bicycle is both your opponent and your ally."

"You can't be talking about a real person?" I said.

Nim nodded slowly and watched me as he spoke. "You've seen him, haven't you?"

"But that was only a coincidence."

"Perhaps," he agreed. "But coincidences can take many forms. For one, it may have been a lure by someone who *knew* of this painting. Or it may have been another kind of coincidence," he added with a smile.

"Oh, no," I said, for I knew perfectly well what was coming. "You *know* I don't believe in prescience or psychic powers or all that metaphysical mumbo-jumbo."

"No?" said Nim, still smiling. "But you'd be hard-pressed to come up with another explanation for how you'd executed a painting before you'd seen the model. I'm afraid I must confess something to you. Like your friends Llewellyn, Solarin, and the fortune-teller, I think you have an important role in the mystery of the Montglane Service. How else can you explain your involvement? Could it be that in some fashion you've been predestined—even chosen—to play a key—"

"Forget it," I snapped. "I am *not* chasing around after this mythical chess set! People are trying to kill me, or at least involve me in murders, don't you get it?" I was practically screaming.

"I 'get it' all right, as you so charmingly put it," Nim replied. "But you are the one who seems to have missed the point. The best defense is a good offense."

"No way," I told him. "It's obvious you've set me up as the fall guy. You want to get your hands on this chess service, and you need a patsy. Well, I'm already into this up to my neck, right here in New York. I'm not about to go trotting off to some foreign country where I know nobody I could turn to for help. Maybe you're bored and you need a new adventure, but what happens to *me* if I get into trouble over there? You don't even have a damned phone number I can call. Perhaps you think the Carmelite nuns will rush to my aid the next time I get shot at? Or the chairman of the New York Stock Exchange might follow me around picking up the dead bodies I leave in my wake?"

"Let's not get hysterical," said Nim, always the calm voice of reason. "I am not at a loss for contacts on any continent, though you don't know that because you're too busy avoiding the issue. You remind me of those three monkeys who try to avoid evil by shutting off their sensory perceptions."

"There is no American consulate in Algeria," I said between gritted teeth. "Perhaps you have contacts at the Russian embassy who'd be glad to help me out?" Actually this was not entirely impossible, as Nim was part Russian and part Greek. But so far as I knew, he had less than a nodding acquaintance with the countries of his ancestry.

"As a matter of fact, I do have contacts with a few of the embassies in the country of your destination," he said with what looked suspiciously like a smirk, "but we'll get to that later. You must agree, my dear, that you are involved in this little escapade whether you like it or not. This quest for the holy grail has become a stampede. You'll have no bartering power whatever, unless you get to it first."

"Just call me Parsifal," I said glumly. "I should have known better than to come to you for help. Your way of solving problems has been to find more difficult ones that make the first look sweet by comparison."

Nim stood up, pulled me to my feet, and looked down at me with a smile of great complicity. He placed his hands on my shoulders.

"*J'adoube,*" he said.

SACRIFICES

People do not care to play chess on the edge of a precipice.

—Madame Suzanne Necker
Mother of Germaine de Staël

N o one realized what sort of day it would be.

Germaine de Staël did not know as she said farewell to the embassy staff. For today, September 2, she would attempt to flee France under diplomatic protection.

Jacques-Louis David did not know as he hastily dressed for an emergency session of the National Assembly. For today, September 2, enemy troops had advanced to within 150 miles of Paris. The Prussians had threatened to burn the city to the ground.

Maurice Talleyrand did not know as he and his valet, Courtiade, pulled his costly leather-bound books from the shelves of his study. Today, September 2, he planned to smuggle the valuable library across the French border in preparation for his own imminent flight.

Valentine and Mireille did not know as they walked in the autumn garden behind David's studio. The letter they'd just received told them the first pieces of the Montglane Service were in jeopardy. They could not guess that this letter would soon place them in the eye of the tornado that was about to sweep across France.

For no one knew that precisely five hours from now, at two o'clock the afternoon of September second, the Terror would begin.

9:00 AM

Valentine dangled her fingers in the small reflecting pool at the rear of David's studio. A large goldfish nibbled at her. Not far from where she sat, she and Mireille had buried the two pieces of the service they'd brought with them from Montglane. And now there might be more to join those.

Mireille stood beside her, reading the letter. Around them the dark chrysanthemums glistened smoky amethyst and topaz in the foliage. The first yellow leaves fluttered to the water's surface, giving off the scent of autumn despite the torpid late-summer heat.

"There can only be one explanation of this letter," said Mireille, and she read aloud:

My Beloved Sisters in Christ,

As you may know, the Abbey of Caen has been closed. During the great unrest in France, our Directrice, Mlle. Alexandrine de Forbin, has found it necessary to join her family in Flanders. However, Sister Marie-Charlotte Corday, whom you may also remember, has remained behind at Caen to attend unexpected business matters which may arise.

Though we have never met, I introduce myself. I am Sister Claude, a Benoit nun of the late convent at Caen. I was personal secretary to Sister Alexandrine, who visited some months ago at my home in Épernay before departing for Flanders. At that time, she pressed me to convey her tidings in person to Sister Valentine, should I find myself at any time soon in Paris.

I am presently in the Cordeliers quarter of that city. Please meet me at the gates of l'Abbaye Monastery at precisely two o'clock today, as I do not know how long I shall remain here. I think you understand the importance of this request.

—Your Sister in Christ
Claude of the Abbaye-aux-Dames, Caen

"She comes from Épernay," said Mireille when she'd finished reading the letter. "It is a city east of here, on the Marne River. She claims that Alexandrine de Forbin stopped there en route to Flanders. Do you know what lies between Épernay and the Flemish border?"

Valentine shook her head and looked at Mireille with large eyes.

"The fortresses of Longwy and Verdun are there. And half the Prussian army. Perhaps our dear Sister Claude brings us something more valuable than the good tidings of Alexandrine de Forbin. Perhaps she brings us something that Alexandrine found was too dangerous to take across the Flemish border, with armies warring there."

"The pieces!" said Valentine, leaping to her feet and frightening the goldfish. "The letter says that Charlotte Corday has stayed behind at Caen! Caen may have been a collection point at the northern border." She paused to think this through. "But if so," she added in confusion, "why was Alexandrine attempting to leave France by the east?"

"I do not know," Mireille admitted, pulling her red hair loose from its ribbon and bending to the fountain to splash water on her hot face. "We shall never know what the letter means unless we meet Sister Claude at the appointed hour. But why has she chosen the Cordeliers, the most dangerous quarter of the city? And you know that l'Abbaye is no longer a monastery. It has been converted into a prison."

"I am not afraid to go there alone," said Valentine. "I promised the abbess I would assume this responsibility, and now the time has come to prove myself. But you must stay here, my cousin. Uncle Jacques-Louis has forbidden us to leave the grounds in his absence."

"Then we will have to be very clever in our escape," Mireille replied. "For I will never let you go into the Cordeliers without me. You may be sure of that."

10:00 AM

The carriage of Germaine de Staël swept through the gates of the Swedish embassy. Atop the carriage stacks of trunks and wig boxes were piled, guarded by the coachman and two liveried servants. Within the coach Germaine was ensconced with her personal maids and many jewelry cachets. She wore the official costume of an ambassadress, replete with colored ribbons and epaulettes. The six white horses plowed through the already steaming streets of Paris, bound for the city gates. Their splendid cockades displayed the Swedish colors. The doors of the coach were emblazoned with the crest of the Swedish Crown. The window draperies were drawn shut.

Lost in her own thoughts within the insufferable heat and darkness of the coach, Germaine did not look out the window until, inexplicably, her coach came to a sudden jarring stop before reaching the city gates. A maid leaned forward and opened the window sash.

Outside, a mob of ragged women milled about, carrying rakes and hoes as if they were weapons. Several leered at Germaine through the window, their hideous mouths like jagged holes with blackened and missing teeth. Why did the rabble always have to look so rabblesque? thought Germaine. The hours she'd labored in political intrigue, lavishing her considerable fortune upon bribes to the right officials—and all for the sake of miserable wretches such as these. Germaine leaned out the window, one massive arm resting upon the ledge.

"What transpires here?" she called out in her booming, authoritarian voice. "Let my carriage pass at once!"

"No one is permitted to leave the city!" cried a woman from the mob. "We guard the gates! Death to the nobility!" This cry was picked up by the crowd, which was growing larger. The screeching hags nearly deafened Germaine with their racket.

"I am the Swedish ambassadress!" she called out. "I am on an official mission to Switzerland! I command you to let my carriage pass!"

"Ha! She commands it!" cried a woman near the carriage window. She turned upon Germaine and spat into her face as the crowd cheered.

Germaine withdrew a lace handkerchief from her bodice and wiped the spittle away. Tossing the handkerchief out the window, she cried, "There is the handkerchief of the daughter of Jacques Necker, the finance minister whom you loved and revered. Covered with the spit of the people! . . . Animals," she said, turning to her ladies-in-waiting, who shuddered in a corner of the coach. "We shall see who is master of this situation."

But the mob of women had pulled the horses free of their yokes. Harnessing themselves to the carriage instead, they began to draw it through the streets, away from the city gates. The teeming mob had now grown to huge proportions. They pressed against the coach, moving it along slowly like a swarm of ants maneuvering a crumb of cake.

Germaine clung fiercely to the door, crying oaths and threats out the window with great savagery, but the screams of the mob drowned her voice. After what seemed an eternity, the carriage settled before the imposing facade of the large building surrounded by guards. When Germaine saw where she'd been taken, her stomach filled with ice. They had taken her to the Hotel de Ville. Headquarters of the Paris Commune.

The Paris Commune was more dangerous than the rabble surrounding her carriage, as Germaine knew. They were madmen. Even the other assembly members feared them. Delegates from the streets of Paris, they imprisoned, tried, and executed members of the nobility with a haste that belied the very concept of liberty. To them, Germaine de Staël represented just another noble throat to be hacked in two by the guillotine. And she knew it.

The doors of the coach were pried open, and Germaine was dragged by dirty hands into the street. Holding herself upright, she made her way through the throng with an icy stare. Behind her, her servants babbled with fear as the mob tore them from the coach and shoved them along with the broom and shovel handles. Germaine herself was half dragged up the sweeping steps of the Hotel de Ville. She gasped as a man suddenly leaped forward and shoved the sharp tip of a pike beneath her bosom, slashing her ambassadorial gown. One slip and she would be run clean through. She held her breath as a policeman stepped forward and shoved the pike aside with his sword. Grasping Germaine by the arm, he hurled her into the dark entryway of the Hotel de Ville.

11:00 AM

David reached the Assembly out of breath. The enormous room was filled to the rafters with men crying aloud. The secretary was standing at the central podium, screaming to make himself heard. As David worked his way across the floor to his seat, he could barely make out what the speaker was saying.

"On August twenty-third, the fortress of Longwy fell to enemy troops! The Duke of Brunswick, commander of the Prussian armies, issued a manifesto demanding that we release the king and restore all royal powers, or his troops would raze Paris to the ground!"

The noise on the floor was like a wave washing over the secretary and drowning out his words. Each time the wave subsided slightly, he tried to continue.

The National Assembly held its tenuous power over France only so long as it kept the king imprisoned. But the Brunswick Manifesto had demanded release of Louis XVI as a pretext for Prussian armies to invade France. Beleaguered by pressing debt and mass desertions within the French armies, the new government, so recently come to power, was in danger of toppling overnight. To make matters worse, each delegate suspected the others of treason, of collusion with the enemy that battled at the border. It was, thought David as he watched the secretary fighting to keep order, the womb from which anarchy is born.

"Citizens!" cried the secretary. "I bring you terrible news! The fortress of Verdun, this morning, fell to the Prussians! We must take arms against—"

The Assembly was seized with hysteria. Chaos broke out across the floor, and men scurried about like cornered rats. The fortress of Verdun was the last stronghold between the enemy armies and Paris! The Prussians could be at the city gates by suppertime.

David sat silently in his place, trying to hear. The words of the secretary were completely lost in the bedlam. David could see the man's mouth flap open and shut soundlessly in the cacophony of voices.

The Assembly had become a seething mass of madmen. From the Mountain, the street rabble tossed papers and fruit down upon the moderates in the Pit. These Girondins in their lace cuffs, who'd once been considered liberals, looked up, their faces drained pale with fear. They were known to be Republican Royalists, who supported the three estates: the nobility, the clergy, and the bourgeoisie. Now that the Brunswick Manifesto had been issued, their lives were in the gravest danger even here on the Assembly floor. And they knew it.

Those who supported restoration of the king might well be dead men before the Prussians reached the gates of Paris.

Now Danton had taken the podium, as the speaker stepped to one side. Danton, the lion of the Assembly, with his large head and burly body, his broken nose and lip disfigured by the kick of a bull which he'd survived in childhood. He lifted his massive hands and called for order.

"Citizens! It is a satisfaction for the minister of a free state to announce to them that their country is saved! All are stirred, all are enthusiastic, all burn to enter the contest . . ."

In the galleries and aisles of the great Assembly hall, men stood in groups and one by one fell silent as they listened to the rousing words of the powerful leader. Danton called them forth, challenged them not to be weak, fomented them to rebel against the tide that swept toward Paris. He roused them to a fever pitch, demanding that they defend the frontiers of France, arm the entrenchments, guard the gates of the city itself with pikes and lances. The heat of his speech ignited a flame within the listeners. Soon there were cheers and cries from the Assembly hall, punctuating each word that fell from his lips.

"The cry we sound is not the alarm of danger, it commands the charge against the enemies of France! . . . We have to dare, to dare again, always to dare—and France is saved!"

The Assembly went mad. A riot ensued on the floor as men tossed papers into the air and cried aloud: "*L'audace! L'audace!* To dare, to dare!"

As pandemonium swept the floor, David's eyes passed across the gallery and settled upon one man. A thin, pale man dressed impeccably in starched foulard, creaseless morning coat, and carefully powdered wig. A young man, with a cold face and emerald-green eyes that glittered like a snake's.

David watched as the pale young man sat silently, unmoved by Danton's words. And as he watched this man, David knew that there was only one thing that would save his country, torn by a hundred warring factions, bankrupted, and threatened by a dozen hostile powers outside her borders. What France needed was not the histrionics of a Danton or a Marat. France needed a leader. A man who found his strength in silence until his abilities were needed. A man upon whose pale thin lips the word "virtue" fell more sweetly than greed or glory. A man who would restore the natural, pastoral ideals of the great Jean-Jacques Rousseau, upon which the Revolution had been founded. The man who sat in the gallery was that leader. His name was Maximilien Robespierre.

1:00 PM

Germaine de Staël sat on a hard wooden bench within the offices of the Paris Commune. She had been sitting there for over two hours. Everywhere uneasy men stood about in groups, not speaking. A few men sat on the bench alongside her, and others had found seats upon the floor. Through the open doors beyond this improvised waiting room, Germaine could see figures moving about, stamping papers. From time to time someone would come outside and call a name. The man whose name was called would grow pale, others would clap him on the back with whispered entreaties of "Courage," and the man would disappear through the doors.

She knew what was happening on the other side of the doors, of course. The members of the Paris Commune were holding summary trials. The "accused," who was probably accused of nothing except his parentage, would be asked a few questions about his background and fealty to the king. If the fellow's blood was a bit too blue, it would be spilled on the streets of Paris by dawn. Germaine did not deceive herself regarding her own chances. She had only one hope, and she nurtured this thought as she awaited her fate: they would not guillotine a pregnant woman.

As Germaine waited, fingering the broad ribands of her ambassadorial dress, the man beside her suddenly collapsed, head in hands, and began to weep. The other men glanced nervously in his direction, but no one made a move to comfort him. They looked away uneasily, as they might have averted their eyes from a cripple or a beggar. Germaine sighed and stood up. She did not want to think of the weeping man on the bench. She wanted to find a way to save herself.

Just then she caught a glimpse of a young man, pressing his way through the crowded waiting room with a handful of papers. His curly brown hair was tied back in a ribbon, his lacy jabot rather wilted. He had a frazzled but passionate air of intensity. Germaine realized suddenly that she knew him.

"Camille!" she called out. "Camille Desmoulins!" The young man turned to her, and his eyes lighted with surprise.

Camille Desmoulins was the enfant célèbre of Paris. Three years earlier, while still a Jesuit student, he'd leaped onto a table at the Cafe Foy one hot July night and challenged his fellow citizens to storm the Bastille. He was now the hero of the Revolution.

"Madame de Staël!" said Camille, working his way through the crowd to take her hand. "What brings you here? Surely you've not engaged in some misdeed against the State?" He smiled broadly, his charming poetic face so out of place in this room darkened with fear and the very smell of death. Germaine attempted to return his smile.

"I've been captured by the 'Women Citizens of Paris,' " she replied, trying to muster some of the diplomatic charm that had served her so well in the past. "It seems that an ambassador's wife who attempts to pass the city gate is now considered an enemy of the people. Don't you find it ironic, when we've fought so hard for liberty?"

Camille's smile faded. He glanced down uncomfortably at the man seated on the bench behind Germaine, who was still weeping. Then he took Germaine by the arm to lead her aside.

"You mean you were trying to leave Paris without a pass and an escort? Dear God, madame. You're fortunate you were not summarily shot!"

"Don't be absurd!" she cried. "I have diplomatic immunity. If I were imprisoned, it would be tantamount to a declaration of war against Sweden! They must be mad to think they can hold me here." But her momentary bravado waned when she heard Camille's next words.

"Don't you know what is happening just now? We are at war already, and under imminent attack. . . ." He lowered his voice as he realized the news was not yet common knowledge and would doubtless cause pandemonium. "Verdun has fallen," he said.

Germaine stared at him for a moment. Suddenly the gravity of her situation became clear to her. "Impossible," she whispered. Then, as he shook his head, she asked, "How close to Paris have . . . Where are they now?"

"Fewer than ten hours would be my guess, even with full artillery. Already the order is out to shoot anyone approaching the city gates. To attempt to leave now would incur a mandatory charge of treason." He looked at her sternly.

"Camille," she said rapidly, "do you know why I was so anxious to join my family in Switzerland? If I delay my departure much longer, I shan't be able to travel at all. I am with child."

He searched her eyes in disbelief, but Germaine's boldness had returned. Taking his hand, she pressed it upon her stomach. Through the thick folds of fabric, he knew she was telling the truth. He smiled his sweet boyish smile again and turned rather pink.

"Madame, with luck I may be able to have you returned to the embassy tonight. Even God himself could not get you through the city gates before we've turned back the Prussians. Let me take the matter up with Danton."

Germaine smiled in relief. Then, as Camille pressed her hand, she said, "When my child is born safely in Geneva, I shall name it after you."

2:00 PM

Valentine and Mireille approached the gates of l'Abbaye Prison in the carriage they had hired after their escape from David's studio. A crowd was gathering in the congested street, and several other carriages had been halted before the prison entrance.

The crowd was a ragged mob of sans-culottes, armed with rakes and hoes and swarming over the carriages near the prison gates, banging on the doors and windows with their fists and implements. The roar of their angry voices echoed down the narrow stone-walled street as prison guards perched atop the carriages tried to beat the crowd back.

The driver of Valentine and Mireille's carriage leaned down from his perch and looked in the window at them.

"I cannot come any closer," he told them. "Else we'll be jammed into the *allée* and unable to move. Besides, I do not like the look of this crowd."

Just then Valentine spotted a nun in the throng who was wearing the Benoit habit of the Abbaye-aux-Dames at Caen. She waved out the carriage window, and the older nun returned her gesture but was locked into the crowd that now was tightly packed into the narrow *allée* with its high stone walls.

"Valentine, no!" cried Mireille as her little fair-haired cousin threw open the door and leaped into the street.

"Monsieur, please," Mireille begged the driver, stepping from the carriage and looking up at him with pleading eyes, "can you hold the carriage? My cousin will only be a moment." She prayed that this was true, watching carefully for Valentine's fleeing form, which was being swallowed up in the ever-thickening crowd as she worked her way toward Sister Claude.

"Mademoiselle," said the driver, "I must turn the carriage by hand. We are in danger here. Those coaches they've stopped up ahead are carrying prisoners."

"We have come to meet a friend," Mireille explained. "We will bring her back here at once. Monsieur, I implore you to wait for us."

"These prisoners," said the driver, looking out over the crowd from his high seat, "they are all priests who've refused to take an oath of fealty to the State. I fear for them and for us as well. Get your cousin back while I turn the horse. And waste no time."

With this, the old man jumped from his high seat and, grabbing the horse's reins, began to pull him around to turn the carriage in the narrow alley. Mireille hastened into the crowd, her heart throbbing.

The crowd closed about her like a dark sea. She could no longer see Valentine in the press of bodies that swarmed into the alley. Shoving her way frantically through the mob, she felt hands pulling and tearing at her from every side. Panic began to rise in her throat as the vile smell of unwashed human flesh crushed ever closer.

Suddenly, through the forest of thrashing limbs and weapons, she caught a glimpse of Valentine, only a few feet from Sister Claude, her hand extended to reach the older nun. Then the crowd closed back again.

"Valentine!" Mireille screamed. But her voice was drowned out by thundering screams, and she was carried forward with the wave of bodies toward the half dozen closed carriages that were jammed against the prison gates—carriages that contained the priests.

Mireille struggled frantically to move in the direction of Valentine and Sister Claude, but it was like fighting a riptide. Each time she beat her way a few feet ahead, she was carried closer to the carriages against the prison walls, until at last she was hurled against the spokes of a carriage wheel and clung to it desperately, trying to stabilize herself. She was pulling herself up against the carriage wall when the carriage door was flung open, as if by an explosion. As the writhing sea of arms and legs rose about her, Mireille clung fiercely to the carriage wheel to keep from being thrust back into the mob.

Priests were dragged bodily from the carriage and into the streets. One young priest, his lips pale from fright, looked into Mireille's eyes for a single instant as he was torn from the carriage; then he disappeared into the mob. An older priest followed him, leaping from the open door and beating at the mob with his cane. He screamed frantically for help from his guards, but they were now turned to brutal beasts themselves. Siding with the mob, they dropped from the roof of the carriage and tore at the cassock of the poor priest, ripping it to shreds as he fell beneath the feet of his persecutors and was trampled against the cobblestones.

As Mireille clung to the carriage wheel, the terrified priests were dragged one by one from the carriages. They ran to each other like frightened mice, battered and stabbed at by iron pikes and rakes at every side. Almost gagging from fear, Mireille screamed Valentine's name over and over as she watched the horror around her. And then, her fingernails bleeding as she held on savagely to the spokes of the carriage, she herself was dragged back into the crowd and flung against the nearby wall of the prison.

She fell against the stone wall and then to the cobbled pavement. Thrusting her hand out to break her fall, Mireille felt something warm and wet. She lifted her head as she lay sprawled upon the hard rocks and brushed her red hair back from her face. She was looking into the open eyes of Sister Claude, who lay crushed against the wall of l'Abbaye Prison. Blood ran down the aged woman's face where her wimple had been torn away, revealing a huge gash in her forehead. The eyes looked vacantly into space. Mireille drew herself back and screamed with all her strength, but no sound came from her choked throat. For the warm, wet place where her hand rested was a gaping hole where Claude's arm had been ripped from the socket.

Mireille shoved herself away from Claude, trembling in horror. She wiped her hand frantically against her dress to remove the blood. Valentine. Where was Valentine? Mireille got to her knees and tried to claw her way up the wall to her feet as the mob surged wildly about her like an angry, mindless beast. Just then she heard a moan and realized that Claude's lips were parted. The nun was not dead!

Mireille leaned forward on her knees and grasped Claude by the shoulders as blood gushed from her gaping wound.

"Valentine!" she cried. "Where is Valentine? Please God, can you understand me? Tell me what has become of Valentine!"

The old nun moved her withered lips soundlessly and rolled her vacant eyes up toward Mireille. Mireille bent forward until her hair touched the nun's lips.

"Inside," Claude whispered. "They have taken her inside the abbey." Then she fell back unconscious.

"My God, are you certain?" said Mireille, but there was no reply.

Mireille tried to stand. The mob whirled about her, crying for blood. Everywhere pikes and hoes slashed through the air, and the screams of the killers and the dying mingled together to drown out her thoughts.

Leaning against the heavy doors of l'Abbaye Prison, Mireille banged as loudly as she could, slamming her fists into the wood until her knuckles bled.

There was no response from within. Exhausted and racked with pain and despair, she tried to force her way back through the crowd to the carriage she prayed was still there. She must find David. Only David could help them now.

Suddenly she froze in the middle of the wild swirl of bodies and looked through a small crack that had parted in the crowd. People were pulling back as something moved toward them, in Mireille's direction. Flattening herself against the wall again and working her way slowly along it, she was able to make out what it was. The carriage she had arrived in was being dragged through the stifling alley by the mob. And propped on a pike driven into the wooden seat was the severed head of her driver, his silver hair drenched in blood, his aged face a mask of terror.

Mireille bit her arm to keep from screaming. As she stood and stared wildly at the hideous head moving high above the crowd, she knew that she could not go back to find David. She had to get inside the walls of l'Abbaye Prison now. She knew with leaden certainty that if she did not get to Valentine at once, it would be too late.

3:00 PM

Jacques-Louis David passed through a cloud of rising steam, where women were tossing buckets of water to cool the hot pavement, and entered the Café de la Régence.

Inside the club, the cloud that enveloped him was even thicker with the smoke of dozens of men puffing pipes and cigars. His eyes burned, and his linen shirt, open to the waist, stuck to his skin as he forced his way through the overheated room, ducking as waiters with trays of drinks held aloft hurried between the tightly packed tables. At each table men were playing cards, dominoes, or chess. The Café de la Régence was the oldest and most famous gaming club in France.

As David made his way to the back of the room, he saw Maximilien Robespierre, his chiseled profile like an ivory cameo as he calmly studied his chess position. His chin resting upon one finger, his double-knotted foulard and brocade waistcoat still uncreased, he seemed to notice neither the noise swirling about him nor the excruciating heat. As always, the cold detachment of his demeanor suggested he played no part in his surroundings but was merely an observer. Or a judge.

David did not recognize the older man who sat across from Robespierre. Wearing an old-fashioned coat of pale blue with beribboned culottes, white stockings, and pumps in the style of Louis XV, the elderly gent moved a piece on the board without glancing at it. He looked up with watery eyes as David approached.

"Excuse me for disturbing your play," said David. "I have a favor to request of Monsieur Robespierre that cannot wait."

"That's quite all right," said the older man. Robespierre continued to study the board in silence. "My friend has lost the game, at any rate. It's mate in five. You may as well resign, my dear Maximilien. Your friend's interruption was well timed."

"I do not see it," Robespierre said. "But your eyes are better than mine when it comes to chess." Leaning back from the board with a sigh, he looked up at David. "Monsieur Philidor is the finest chess player in Europe. I consider it a privilege to lose to him, only to have the opportunity to play at the same table."

"But you are the famous Philidor!" said David, pressing the older man's hand warmly. "You are a great composer, monsieur. I saw a revival of *Le Soldat Magicien* when I was just a boy. I shall never forget it. Permit me to introduce myself, I am Jacques-Louis David."

"The painter!" said Philidor, rising to his feet. "I admire your work as well, as does every citizen in France. But I'm afraid you are the only person in this country who remembers *me*. Though once my music filled the Comédie-Française and the Opéra-Comique, I must now play exhibition chess like a trained monkey to support myself and my family. Indeed, Robespierre has been so kind to secure me a pass to leave for England, where I can earn a good deal for providing that sort of spectacle."

"That is exactly the favor I've come to request of him," said David as Robespierre gave up studying the chessboard and stood as well. "The political situation in Paris is so dangerous just now. And this hellish unbroken heat has done nothing to improve the tempers of our fellow Parisians. It's this explosive atmosphere that has made up my mind to ask . . . though the favor is not, of course, for myself."

"Citizens always require favors for someone other than themselves," Robespierre interjected coolly.

"I request the favor in behalf of my young wards," David said stiffly. "As I'm sure you can appreciate, Maximilien, France is not safe for young women of tender age."

"If you cared so much for their well-being," sniffed Robespierre, looking at David with glittering green eyes, "you'd not permit them to be squired about town on the arm of the Bishop of Autun."

"I quite disagree," Philidor chimed in. "I'm a great admirer of Maurice Talleyrand. I predict he'll one day be regarded as the greatest statesman in the history of France."

"So much for prophecy," said Robespierre. "It's fortunate you do not have to make your living telling fortunes. Maurice Talleyrand has spent weeks trying to bribe every official in France to get him back to England where he can pretend to be a diplomat. He wishes only to save his neck. My dear David, all the nobility in France are scrambling to depart before the Prussians arrive. I shall see what I can do at the Committee meeting tonight regarding your wards, but I promise nothing. Your request is rather late."

David thanked him warmly, and Philidor offered to accompany the painter to the street, as he was leaving the club as well. As the famous chess master and the painter pushed their way through the crowded room, Philidor commented, "You must try to understand that Maximilien Robespierre is different from you and me. As a bachelor, he's had no exposure to the responsibilities that come with child-rearing. How old are your wards, David? Have they been in your care for long?"

"A little over two years only," David replied. "Prior to that, they were apprenticed as nuns at the Abbey of Montglane. . . ."

"Montglane, did you say?" said Philidor, lowering his voice as they reached the club entry. "My dear David, as a chess player, I can assure you I know a good deal of the history of Montglane Abbey. Don't you know the story?"

"Yes, yes," said David, trying to control his irritation. "All a lot of mystical poppycock. The Montglane Service does not exist, and I'm surprised you should give credence to such a thing."

"Give credence?" Philidor took David's arm as they stepped out onto the blazing hot pavement. "My friend, I *know* it exists. And a great deal more. Well over forty years ago, perhaps before you were even born, I was a visitor at the court of Frederick the Great in Prussia. Whilst there, I made the acquaintance of two men of such powers of perception as I shall never forget. One, you will have heard of—the great mathematician, Leonhard Euler. The other, as great in his own way, was the aged father of Frederick's young court musician. But this musty old genius has been fated, I'm afraid, to a legacy buried in dust. Though no one in Europe has heard of him since, his music, which he performed for us one evening at the king's request, was the finest I've heard in all my years. His name was Johann Sebastian Bach."

"I've not heard the name," David admitted, "but what do Euler and this musician have to do with the legendary chess service?"

"I shall tell you," Philidor said, smiling, "only if you agree to introduce me to these wards of yours. Perhaps we'll get to the bottom of a mystery I've spent a lifetime trying to unravel!"

David agreed, and the great chess master accompanied him on foot through the deceptively quiet streets along the Seine and across the Pont Royal toward his studio.

The air was still; no leaf stirred on any tree. Heat rose in waves from the baking pavement, and even the leaden waters of the Seine coursed silently beside them as they walked. They could not know that twenty blocks away, in the heart of the Cordeliers, a bloodthirsty mob was battering down the doors of l'Abbaye Prison. And Valentine was inside.

In the still, warm silence of that late afternoon, as the two men walked together, Philidor began his tale. . . .

THE CHESS MASTER'S TALE

At the age of nineteen, I left France and journeyed to Holland to accompany upon the hautebois, or oboe, a young pianist, a girl who, as a child prodigy, was to perform there. Unfortunately I arrived to discover the child had died a few days earlier of smallpox. I was stranded in a foreign country with no money and now no hope of an income. To support myself, I went to the coffee houses and played chess.

From the age of fourteen, I'd studied chess under the tutelage of the famous Sire de Legal, France's best player and perhaps the finest in Europe. By eighteen, I could beat him with the handicap of a Knight. As a result, as I soon discovered, I could better every player I encountered. In The Hague, during the Battle of Fontenoy, I played against the Prince of Waldeck as the battle raged around us.

I traveled through England, playing at Slaughter's Coffee House in London against the best players they had to offer, including Sir Abraham Janssen and Philip Stamma, beating them all. Stamma, a Syrian possibly of Moorish ancestry, had published several books on chess. He showed these to me, as well as books written by La Bourdonnais and Maréchal Saxe. Stamma thought that I, with my unique powers of play, should write a book as well.

My book, published several years later, was entitled *Analyse du Jeu des Eschecs*. In it I proposed the theory "The pawns are the soul of chess." In effect, I showed that the pawns were not only objects to be sacrificed, but could be used strategically and positionally against the opposing player. This book created a revolution in chess.

My work came to the attention of the German mathematician Euler. He'd read of my blindfold play in the French *Dictionnaire* published by Diderot, and he persuaded Frederick the Great to invite me to his court.

The court of Frederick the Great was held at Potsdam in a large, stark hall, glittering with lamplight but barren of the artistic wonders one finds at other European courts. Indeed, Frederick was a warrior, preferring the company of other soldiers to courtiers, artists, and women. It was said he slept upon a hard wooden pallet and kept his dogs beside him at all times.

The evening of my appearance, Kapellmeister Bach of Leipzig had arrived with his son Wilhelm, having journeyed there to visit another son, Carl Philipp Emanuel Bach, harpsichordist to King Frederick. The king himself had written

eight bars of a canon and had requested the elder Bach to improvise upon this
theme. The old composer, I was told, had a knack for such things. He'd already
developed canons with his own name and the name of Jesus Christ buried within
the harmonies in mathematical notation. He'd invented inverse counterpoints of
great complexity, where the harmony was a mirror image of the melody.

Euler added the suggestion that the old kapellmeister invent a variation that
reflected within its structure "the Infinite"—that is to say, God in all His
manifestations. The king seemed pleased by this, but I felt certain Bach would
demur. As a composer myself, I can tell you it's no small chore to embroider
upon another's music. I once had to compose an opera upon themes of Jean-
Jacques Rousseau, a philosopher with a tin ear. But to hide a secret puzzle of
this nature within the music . . . well, it seemed impossible.

To my surprise, the kapellmeister hobbled his short, square body to the
keyboard. His massive head was covered in a fat, ill-fitting wig. His foreboding
eyebrows, grizzled with gray, were like eagles' wings. He had a severe nose,
heavy jaw, and a perpetual scowl etched into his hard features that suggested
a contentious nature. Euler whispered to me that the elder Bach did not care
much for "command performances" and would doubtless make a joke at the
king's expense.

Bending his shaggy head over the keys, he began to play a beautiful and
haunting melody that seemed to rise endlessly like a graceful bird. It was a sort
of fugue, and as I listened to the mysterious complexities, I realized at once what
he'd accomplished. Through a means unclear to me, each stanza of the melody
began in one harmonic key but ended one key higher, until at the end of six
repetitions of the king's initial theme, he'd ended in the key where he'd begun.
Yet the transition or where it occurred, or how, was imperceptible to me. It
was a work of magic, like the transmutation of base metals into gold. Through
its clever construction, I could see that it would go endlessly higher into infinity
until the notes, like the music of the spheres, could only be heard by angels.

"Magnificent!" murmured the king when Bach slowly ended his play. He
nodded to the few generals and soldiers who sat on wooden chairs in the sparsely
furnished hall.

"What is the structure called?" I asked Bach.

"I call it *Ricercar*," the old man said, his dour expression unaltered by the
beauty of the music he'd wrought. "In Italian, it means 'to seek.' It's a very old
form of music, no longer in fashion." As he said this he looked wryly at his
son Carl Philipp, who was known for writing "popular" music.

Picking up the king's manuscript, Bach scrawled across the top the word
Ricercar, the letters widely spaced. He turned each letter into a Latin word, so
that it read "Regis Iussu Cantio Et Reliqua Canonica Arte Resoluta." Roughly,
this means a song issuing from the king, the remaining resolved through the art
of the canon. A canon is a musical structure where each part comes in one

measure after the last but repeats the entire melody in overlapping fashion. It gives the appearance of going on forever.

Then Bach scribbled two Latin phrases in the margin of the music. When translated they read:

> As the Notes increase, the King's Fortune increases.
> As the Modulation ascends, the King's Glory ascends.

Euler and I complimented the aging composer upon the cleverness of his work. I was then requested to play three games of blindfold chess simultaneously against the king, Dr. Euler, and the kapellmeister's son Wilhelm. Though the older man did not play chess himself, he enjoyed watching the game. At the conclusion of the performance, where I won all three games, Euler took me aside.

"I'd prepared a gift for you," he told me. "I've invented a new Knight's Tour, a mathematical puzzle. I believe it to be the finest formula yet discovered for the tour of a Knight across a chessboard. But I should like to give this copy to the old composer tonight, if you don't mind. As he likes mathematical games, it will amuse him."

Bach received the gift with a strange smile and thanked us genuinely. "I suggest you meet me at my son's cottage tomorrow morning before Herr Philidor departs," he said. "I may then have time to prepare a little surprise for both of you." Our curiosity was piqued, and we agreed to arrive at the appointed time and place.

The next morning Bach opened the door of Carl Philipp's cottage and squired us inside. He seated us in the small parlor and offered us tea. Then he took a seat at the small clavier and began to play a most unusual melody. When he'd finished both Euler and I were completely confused.

"That is the surprise!" said Bach with a cackle of glee that dispelled the habitual gloom from his face. He saw that Euler and I were both totally at sea.

"But have a look at the sheet music," Bach said. We both stood and moved to the clavier. There on the music stand was nothing other than the Knight's Tour that Euler had prepared and given him the prior evening. It was the map of a large chessboard with a number written in each square. Bach had cleverly connected the numbers with a web of fine lines that meant something to him, though not to me. But Euler was a mathematician, and his mind moved faster than mine.

"You've turned these numbers into octaves and chords!" he cried. "But you must show me how you've done it. To turn mathematics into music—it is sheer magic!"

"But mathematics *are* music," Bach replied. "And the reverse is also true. Whether you believe the word 'music' came from 'Musa,' the Muses, or from 'muta,' meaning mouth of the Oracle, it makes no difference. If you think 'mathematics' came from 'mathanein,' which is learning, or from 'Matrix,' the womb or mother of all creation, it matters not. . . ."

"You've done a study of words?" said Euler.

"Words have the power to create and kill," Bach said simply. "That Great Architect who made us all, made words, too. In fact, He made them first, if we may believe St. John in the New Testament."

"What did you say? The Great Architect?" said Euler, growing a little pale.

"I call God the Great Architect, because the first thing He designed was sound," Bach replied. " 'In the Beginning was the Word,' you remember? Who knows? Perhaps it was not only a word. Perhaps it was music. Maybe God sang an endless canon of His own invention, and through it, the universe was wrought."

Euler had grown paler yet. Though the mathematician had lost the sight of one eye by studying the sun through a glass, he peered with his other eye at the Knight's Tour that sat upon the clavier stand. Running his fingers over the endless diagram of tiny numbers inked across the chessboard, he seemed lost in thought for several moments. Then he spoke.

"Where have you learned these things?" he asked the sage composer. "What you describe is a dark and dangerous secret, known only to the initiated."

"I initiated myself," said Bach calmly. "Oh, I know that there are secret societies of men who spend their lives trying to unravel the mysteries of the universe, but I am not a member. I seek truth in my own fashion."

Saying this, he reached over and plucked Euler's formulaic chess map from the piano. With a nearby quill he scratched two words across the top: *Quaerendo invenietis*. Seek, and ye shall find. Then he handed the Knight's Tour to me.

"I do not understand," I told him in some confusion.

"Herr Philidor," said Bach, "you are both a chess master, like Dr. Euler, and a composer, like myself. In one person, you combine two valuable skills."

"Valuable in what way?" I asked politely. "For I must confess, I've found neither to be of great value from a financial standpoint!" I smiled at him.

"Though it is hard to remember sometimes," Bach said, chuckling, "there are greater forces at work in the universe than money. For example—have you ever heard of the Montglane Service?"

I turned suddenly to Euler, who had gasped aloud.

"You see," said Bach, "that the name is not unfamiliar to our friend the Herr Doktor. Perhaps I can enlighten you as well."

I listened, fascinated, while Bach told me of the strange chess service, belonging at one time to Charlemagne and reputed to contain properties of great power. When the composer finished his summary, he said to me:

"The reason I asked you gentlemen here today was to perform an experiment. All my life I have studied the peculiar powers of music. It has a force of its own that few would deny. It can tranquilize a savage beast or move a placid man to charge in battle. At length, I learned through my own experiments the secret of this power. Music, you see, has a logic of its own. It is similar to mathematical logic, but in some ways different. For music does not merely communicate with our minds, but in fact *changes* our thought in some imperceptible fashion."

"What do you mean by that?" I asked. But I knew that Bach had struck a chord within my own being that I could not quite define. Something I felt I'd known for many years, something buried deep inside me that I felt only when I heard a beautiful, haunting melody. Or played a game of chess.

"What I mean," said Bach, "is that the universe is like a great mathematical game that is played upon a tremendous scale. Music is one of the purest forms of mathematics. Each mathematical formula can be converted into music, as I've done with Dr. Euler's." He glanced at Euler, and the latter nodded back, as if the two shared a secret to which I was not yet privy.

"And music," Bach continued, "can be converted into mathematics, with, I might add, surprising results. The Architect who built the universe designed it that way. Music has power to create a universe or to destroy a civilization. If you don't believe me, I suggest you read the Bible."

Euler stood in silence for a moment. "Yes," he said at last, "there are other architects in the Bible whose stories are quite revealing, are they not?"

"My friend," said Bach, turning to me with a smile, "as I've said, seek and ye shall find. He who understands the architecture of music will understand the power of the Montglane Service. For the two are one."

David had listened closely to the story. Now, as they approached the fretted iron gates of his courtyard, he turned to Philidor in dismay.

"But what does it all mean?" he asked. "What do music and mathematics have to do with the Montglane Service? What do any of these things have to do with power, whether on earth or in the heavens? Your story only serves to support my claim that this legendary chess service appeals to mystics and fools. Much as I hate to tie such appellations to Dr. Euler, your story suggests he was easily prey to fantasies of this sort."

Philidor paused beneath the dark horse chestnut trees that hung low over the gates of David's courtyard. "I have studied the subject for years," the composer whispered. "At long last, though I've never been interested in biblical scholastics, I took it upon myself to read the Bible, as Euler and Bach had suggested. Bach died soon after our meeting, and Euler immigrated to Russia, so I was never again to meet the two men to discuss what I had found."

"And what did you find?" said David, extracting his key to unlock the gates.

"They'd directed me to study architects, and so I did. There were only two architects of note within the Bible. One was the Architect of the universe. That is, God. The other was the architect of the Tower of Babel. The very word 'Bab-El' means, I discovered, 'Gate of God.' The Babylonians were a very proud people. They were the greatest civilization since the beginning of time. They built hanging gardens that rivaled the finest works of nature. And they wanted to build a tower that would reach to heaven itself, a tower that would reach to the sun. The story of this tower is the one, I felt sure, that Bach and Euler alluded to.

"The architect," Philidor continued as the two men passed through the gates, "was one Nimrod. The greatest architect of his day. He built a tower higher than any known to man. But it was never completed. Do you know why?"

"God smote him down, as I recall," David said as he crossed the court.

"But *how* did He smite him down?" asked Philidor. "He did not send a bolt of lightning, a flood, or a plague, as was His custom! I shall tell you how God destroyed the work of Nimrod, my friend. God confused the languages of the workers, which until then had been one language. He struck down the language. He destroyed the Word!"

Just then David noticed a servant running across the courtyard from the house. "What am I to take it that all this means?" he asked Philidor with a cynical smile. "Is this how God destroys a civilization? By making men mute? Confusing our language? If so, we French will never have to worry. We cherish our language as if it were worth more than gold!"

"Perhaps your wards will be able to help us solve this mystery, if they truly lived at Montglane," replied Philidor. "For I believe that it is this power, the power of the music of language, the mathematics of music, the secret of the Word with which God created the universe and struck down the empire of Babylon—this, I believe, is the secret that is contained within the Montglane Service."

David's servant had rapidly approached and stood, wringing his hands, at a respectful distance from the two men as they crossed the court.

"What is it, Pierre?" asked David in surprise.

"The young ladies," Pierre said in a worried voice. "They have disappeared, monsieur."

"What?!" cried David. "What do you mean?"

"Since nearly two o'clock, monsieur. They received a letter by the morning post. They went into the garden to read it. At luncheon we sent to look for them, but they were gone! Perhaps—there is no other way to explain it—we think they ascended the garden wall. They have not returned."

4:00 PM

Even the cheers of the crowd outside l'Abbaye Prison could not drown out the deafening screams from within. Mireille would never again be able to erase the sound from her mind.

The crowd had long grown weary of battering at the gates of the prison and had taken seats atop the carriages that were splashed with the blood of the massacred priests. The alley was littered with torn and trampled bodies.

It had been close to an hour now that the trials had been going on inside. Some of the stronger men had boosted their compatriots up onto the high walls surrounding the prison court, and these, scrambling over, had tugged the iron spikes from the stone buttresses to use as weapons and dropped down into the courtyard.

A man standing on the shoulders of another cried out, "Open the gates, citizens! There is justice to be done today!"

The crowd had cheered at the sound of a bar being shot back. One of the massive wooden gates swung open, and the crowd, throwing their full force against the gate, had crushed inside.

But the soldiers with muskets had kept back the bulk of people and forced the gates closed again. Now Mireille and the others waited for reports from those who sat on the walls watching the process of the mock trials and reporting the carnage to those who, like Mireille, waited below.

Mireille had pounded upon the prison gates and tried to scale the wall along with the men, but to no avail. She waited in exhaustion beside the gates, hoping that they would open again even for a second so that she could slip through.

Her wish was at last fulfilled. At four o'clock Mireille looked up to see an open carriage in the alley, the horse carefully picking its way over the broken bodies. The women citizens who sat on the abandoned prison wagons set up a cheer as they saw the man who sat in the back, and again the alley was alive with noise as the men jumped from their high perches on the walls and the hideous old hags clambered from the carriage tops to swarm over his coach. Mireille leaped to her feet in astonishment. It was David!

"Uncle, Uncle!" she cried, clawing her way through the crowd with tears streaming down her face. David caught sight of her, and his face grew grave as he stepped from the carriage and plowed through the crowd to embrace her.

"Mireille!" he said as the throng moved about him, patting him on the back and setting up cheers of welcome. "What has happened? Where is Valentine?" His face was filled with horror as he held Mireille in his arms and she sobbed uncontrollably.

"She is inside the prison," cried Mireille. "We came to meet a friend . . . we . . . I do not know what's happened, Uncle. Perhaps it is too late."

"Come, come," David said, making his way through the crowd with his arm around Mireille and patting several of those whom he recognized as they fell back to open a path for him.

"Open the gates!" cried some of the men from the walls into the courtyard. "Citizen David is here! The painter David is outside!"

After several moments one of the massive gates swung open and a rush of unwashed bodies crushed David against the gate; then they were swept inside, and the gates were forced shut again.

The courtyard of the prison was awash in blood. On a small grassy stretch of what had once been the monastery garden, a priest was held to the ground, his head bent backward over a wooden block. A soldier whose uniform was splashed with blood was chopping ineffectively at the priest's neck with a sword, attempting to sever the head from the body. But the priest was not yet dead. Each time he tried to raise himself, blood spurted from the wounds at his throat. His mouth was open in a silent scream.

All around the courtyard people were scurrying back and forth, stepping over the bodies that lay twisted in horrifying positions. It was impossible to tell how many had been butchered there. Arms, legs, and torsos were tossed into the manicured hedges, and entrails were heaped in piles along the herbaceous borders.

Mireille clutched David's shoulder and began to scream and gasp for breath, but he grasped her forcefully and whispered harshly in her ear, "Contain yourself, or we are lost. We must find her at once."

Mireille fought for control as David looked with haggard eyes around the courtyard. The sensitive painter's hands shook as he reached out to a man beside him and tugged at the fellow's sleeve. The man wore the tattered uniform of a soldier, not a prison guard, and his mouth seemed to be smeared with blood, though he bore no visible wound.

"Who is in charge here?" said David. The soldier laughed, then motioned to a long wooden table near the entrance to the prison, where several men were seated. A crowd milled about the table facing the men.

As David helped Mireille across the courtyard, three priests were dragged down the open steps from the prison and hurled onto the ground in front of the table. The crowd jeered at them, and the soldiers used their bayonets to drive the jeerers back. The soldiers then dragged the priests to their feet and held them facing the table.

The five men seated behind the table spoke one by one to the priests. One man glanced through some papers on the table, jotted something down, then shook his head.

The priests were turned around and marched toward the center of the courtyard, their faces deathly white masks of horror as they saw what awaited them. The crowd within the courtyard set up a deafening cheer as they saw fresh victims being dragged to the sacrifice. David clutched Mireille tightly and propelled her toward the table where the judges sat, blocked now from view by the crowd that waited, cheering, for the execution.

David came to the table just as the men upon the walls called out the verdict to the mob outside.

"Death to Father Ambrose of San Sulpice!" was the first cry, greeted by screams and cheers.

"I am Jacques-Louis David," he cried to the nearest judge, over the noise that echoed off the walls of the courtyard. "I am a member of the revolutionary tribunal. Danton has sent me here—"

"We know you well, Jacques-Louis David," said a man from the far end of the table. David turned to face him and gasped aloud.

Mireille looked down the table at the judge who sat there, and her blood ran cold. This was the sort of face she saw only in her nightmares, the face imagined when she thought of the abbess's warning. It was a face of purest evil.

The man was hideous. His flesh was a mass of scars and suppurating sores. A filthy rag was tied about his forehead, dripping with a dirty-colored liquid that trickled down his neck and matted his greasy hair. As he leered at David, Mireille thought that the pustulating wounds that covered his skin must have oozed up from the evil that lay within him, for here was the Devil incarnate.

"Ah, it is you," David was whispering. "But I thought that you were . . ."

"Ill?" the man replied. "Yes, but never too ill to serve my country, citizen."

David worked his way down the table toward the hideous man, though he seemed to fear coming too close. Pulling Mireille in his wake, he whispered in her ear, "You must say nothing. We are in danger."

Reaching the end of the table, David leaned forward to the judge and spoke.

"I've come at Danton's wish, to help with the tribunal," he said.

"We need no assistance, citizen," snapped the other. "This prison is only the first. There are enemies of the State confined in every prison. When we've dispatched these judgments, we will move on to the others. There is no lack of volunteers where the bringing of justice is concerned. Go tell Citizen Danton that I am here. The matter is in good hands."

"Fine," said David, tentatively reaching out to pat the filthy man upon his shoulder as another cry went up from the crowd behind them. "I know you are an honored citizen and Assembly member. But there is just one problem. I'm certain you can help me."

David squeezed Mireille's hand, and she stood silently, holding her breath for his next words.

"My niece happened to be passing the prison here this afternoon, and was accidentally brought inside in the confusion. We believe . . . I hope that nothing has happened to her, for she is a simple girl with no understanding of politics. I must ask to search for her inside the prison."

"Your niece?" said the other, leering at David. He reached into a bucket of water that sat beside him on the ground and withdrew a wet rag. He tore away the rag that was already circling his brow, tossing it into the bucket, then wrapped the dripping rag about his brow and knotted it. Water ran down his face, trickling over the pus that oozed from his open sores. Mireille could smell the rot of death within this man more strongly than the stench of blood and fear that pervaded the courtyard. She was weakened by it and thought that she might faint as another cheer went up behind her. She tried not to think what each chorus of cheers must mean.

"You need not bother to search for her," said the horrid man. "She is next before the tribunal. I know who your wards are, David. Including this one." He nodded toward Mireille without looking at her. "They are of the nobility, offspring of the de Remy blood. They were from the Abbey of Montglane. We have already interrogated your 'niece' within the prison."

"No!" cried Mireille, tearing free from David's grasp. "Valentine! What have you done with her?" She reached across the table and clutched at the evil man, but David pulled her back.

"Don't be a fool," he hissed at her. She was breaking away again when the foul judge raised his hand. There was a commotion above as two bodies were thrown down the steps of the prison behind the table. Mireille tore away and ran behind the table and across the walks as she saw Valentine's blond hair tumble free, her frail body rolling down the steps beside that of a young priest. The priest picked himself up and helped Valentine to her feet as Mireille threw herself into Valentine's arms.

"Valentine, Valentine," cried Mireille, looking at her cousin's bruised face and cut lips.

"The pieces," whispered Valentine, her eyes wild as she looked about the courtyard. "Claude told me where the pieces are. There are six of them. . . ."

"Do not worry about that," Mireille said, cradling Valentine in her arms. "Our uncle is here. We are going to have you released. . . ."

"No!" cried Valentine. "They are going to kill me, my cousin. They know about the pieces . . . you remember the ghost! De Remy, de Remy," she babbled, mindlessly repeating her own family name. Mireille tried to quiet her.

Just then Mireille was grasped by a soldier, who held her struggling in his arms. She looked wildly toward David, who had leaned over the table and was speaking frantically to the horrible judge. Mireille struggled and tried to bite the soldier as two men came and picked up Valentine, hauling her before the table. Valentine stood before the tribunal, held by both soldiers. For a moment she looked across the distance at Mireille, her face pale and frightened. Then she smiled, and her smile was like a burst of sunshine through a dark cloud. Mireille stopped struggling for a moment and smiled back. Then suddenly she heard the voice of the men behind the table. It rang like a whip crack against her mind and echoed off the walls of the courtyard.

"Death!"

Mireille tore against the soldier. She screamed and cried out to David, who had crumpled upon the table in tears. Valentine was dragged across the cobbled courtyard in slow motion to the grassy stretch beyond. Mireille fought like a wildcat against the iron arms that bound her. Then, suddenly, something struck her from the side. She and the soldier fell to the ground together. It was the young priest who'd tumbled down the prison steps with Valentine, and who had come to her rescue, barreling into them as the soldier held her. As the two men wrestled upon the ground, Mireille made her escape and ran to the table where David was a crumpled wreck. She grabbed the filthy shirt of the judge and screamed into his face:

"Stop the order!"

Glancing over her shoulder, she saw Valentine pinned to the ground by two burly men who'd removed their coats and rolled up the sleeves of their shirts. There was not a moment to lose. "Release her!" she cried.

"I will," said the man, "but only if you tell me what your cousin refused to reveal. Tell me where the Montglane Service is hidden. I know with whom your little friend was speaking before she was arrested, you see. . . ."

"If I tell you," Mireille said in haste, glancing back to Valentine again, "you will release my cousin?"

"I must have them!" he said fiercely. He regarded her with hard, cold eyes. The eyes of a madman, thought Mireille. Inwardly she shrank from him, but she returned his gaze steadily.

"If you release her, I will tell you where they are."

"Tell me!" he screamed.

Mireille could feel his foul breath upon her face as he bent toward her. David moaned beside her, but she paid no notice. Taking a deep breath and begging Valentine's forgiveness, she said slowly, "They are buried in the garden behind our uncle's studio."

"Aha!" he cried. His eyes burned with an inhuman flame as he leapt to his feet and leaned across the table to Mireille. "You would not dare to lie to me. For if you did, I would hunt you to the very ends of the earth. These pieces must be mine!"

"Monsieur, I beg you," cried Mireille. "What I have told you is the truth."

"Then I believe you," he told her. Raising his hand aloft, he looked across the lawn to where the two men held Valentine to the ground, awaiting their orders. Mireille watched the dreadful face, contorted beyond imagining, and vowed that as long as she lived, as long as he lived, she would never forget. She would etch his face into her mind, this man who held the life of her beloved cousin so ruthlessly in his hands. She would always remember.

"Who are you?" she said as he faced the lawn without looking at her. Slowly he turned to face her, and the hatred in his eyes chilled her to the bone.

"I am the rage of the people," he whispered. "The nobility will fall, the clergy will fall, and the bourgeoisie. They will be trampled beneath our feet. I spit upon you all, for the suffering that you have caused will be turned against you. I will bring the very heavens down around your ears. I shall have the Montglane Service! I shall own it! It will be mine! If I do not find it where you say, I shall hunt you down—you will pay!"

His venomous voice rang in Mireille's ears.

"Proceed with the execution!" he screamed, and the crowd at once set up their hideous cry. "Death! The verdict is death!"

"No!" screamed Mireille. A soldier grabbed at her, but she tore away. In a wild frenzy, she ran blindly across the courtyard, her skirts trailing through the pools of blood that soaked into the cracks between the cobblestones. She saw through the sea of screaming faces the sharpened two-pronged axe rise over Valentine's prostrate body. Valentine's hair, silvery in the summer heat, fanned out on the grassy stretch where she lay.

Mireille flew through the mass of bodies, closing in upon the horrible sight, closing in to see the kill at first hand. With a flying leap, she threw herself in midair across Valentine's body, just as the axe fell.

THE FORK

One must always put oneself in a position to choose between two alternatives.

—*Talleyrand*

On Wednesday evening I was in a taxi, going across town to meet Lily Rad at an address she'd given me on Forty-seventh Street between Fifth and Sixth avenues. It was called the Gotham Book Mart, and I'd never been there before.

The afternoon before, Tuesday, Nim had driven me into town and given me a quick lesson in how to trigger my apartment door to tell if anyone had been inside in my absence. In preparation for my trip to Algeria, he'd also given me a special phone number that dialed into his computer Centrex at any hour. (Quite a commitment for a man who didn't believe in using telephones himself!)

Nim knew a woman in Algiers named Minnie Renselaas, widow of the late Dutch consul to Algeria. She was apparently wealthy and well connected and could help me find out anything I needed to know. With this information in hand, I'd reluctantly agreed to inform Llewellyn that I would try to locate the chess pieces of the Montglane Service in his behalf. I felt bad about doing this, as it was a lie, but Nim had convinced me that finding that damned chess set was the only way I could assure myself any peace of mind. Not to mention length of life.

But for three days now I'd been worried about something other than my life or the (possibly nonexistent) chess service. I'd been worried about Saul. There'd been no notice of his death in the newspapers.

There were three articles about the UN in Tuesday's paper, but they all dealt with world hunger or the Vietnam War. Not one hint had appeared to suggest they had found a body on a stone slab. Who knows, perhaps they never dusted the Meditation Room. But it seemed more than strange. Furthermore, though there'd been a brief note about Fiske's death and a one-week postponement of the chess tournament, there was no suggestion that he hadn't died of natural causes.

Wednesday was the night of Harry's dinner party. I hadn't spoken with Lily since Sunday, but I felt certain the family would have heard of Saul's death by now. After all, he'd been in their employ for twenty-five years. I dreaded the confrontation. It would seem more like a wake, if I knew Harry. His staff were all like family to him. I wondered how I could avoid revealing what I knew.

As my taxi turned off Sixth Avenue I saw all the shopkeepers out on the streets lowering the chain-mail grates that protected their windows from burglary. Within the stores, clerks were removing lavish jewelry from the displays.

I realized that I was at the very heart of the diamond district. As I embarked from my taxi I saw men standing about in groups on the pavement wearing stiff black coats and high felt hats with flat brims. Some had dark beards shot with gray, so long they rested on their chests.

The Gotham Book Mart was about a third of the way down the block. I made my way through the clusters of men into the building. The entrance was a small carpeted lobby like a Victorian house, with stairs to the second floor. To the left were two steps down to the bookstore.

There were wooden floors, and the low ceilings were circuited with tin hot-air ducts running the length of the room. At back were entrances to several other rooms, all completely jammed from floor to ceiling with books. Piles were about to collapse in a tumble at every turn, and the narrow aisles were jammed with readers who grudgingly made way for me to pass and then resumed their places, presumably without missing a line.

Lily was standing in the very back room wearing a brilliant red fox coat and wool knit stockings. She was deep in conversation with a wizened old gent half her size. He was dressed in the same black coat and hat as the men on the street outside, but he had no beard, and his dark face was mapped with weathered lines. His thick gold-rimmed spectacles made his eyes look large and intense. He and Lily made an odd couple.

As Lily saw me approaching she put her hand on the old gentleman's arm and said something to him. He turned to me.

"Cat, I'd like you to meet Mordecai," she said. "He's a very old friend of mine and knows a great deal about chess. I thought we could question him about our little problem."

I assumed she was referring to Solarin. But I'd learned a few things myself over the last few days and was more interested in getting Lily aside to discuss Saul before I had to beard the family lions in their den.

"Mordecai is a grand master, though he doesn't play any longer," Lily was saying. "He coaches me in tournament play. He's famous. He's written books about chess."

"You flatter me," said Mordecai modestly, smiling at me. "But actually, I've made my living as a diamond merchant. Chess is my avocation."

"Cat was at the tournament with me on Sunday," Lily told him.

"Ah," said Mordecai, studying me more closely through his thick glasses. "I see. So you were a firsthand witness of the event. I suggest you ladies join me over a cup of tea. There's a place just down the street where we could talk."

"Well . . . I wouldn't like to be late for dinner. Lily's father will be disappointed."

"I insist," Mordecai said charmingly but with finality. Taking my arm, he steered me toward the door. "I myself have pressing engagements this evening, but I should be very sorry not to hear your observations on the mysterious death of Grand Master Fiske. I knew him well. I hope your opinion may be less farfetched than those my . . . friend Lily has put forth."

There was some confusion as we tried to pass back through the first room. Mordecai had to relinquish his hold on my arm as we proceeded single file through the narrow aisles, Lily breaking the way. It was a relief to get back to the cold air of the street after the cluttered bookstore. Mordecai took my arm again.

Most of the diamond merchants had dispersed by now, and the shops were dark.

"Lily tells me you're a computer expert," said Mordecai, propelling me down the street.

"Are you interested in computers?" I asked.

"Not exactly. I'm impressed with what they can do. You might say that I am a student of formulas." At this he cackled merrily, his face split into a wide grin. "I used to be a mathematician, did Lily tell you?" He looked back over his shoulder where Lily was trailing, but she shook her head and caught up with us. "I was a student of Herr Professor Einstein for one semester in Zurich. He was so smart that none of us could understand a word he said! Sometimes he would forget what he was talking about and go drifting out of the room, but no one ever laughed. We all respected him very much."

He paused to take Lily's arm too as we crossed the one-way street.

"Once I was ill in Zurich," he continued. "Dr. Einstein came to visit me. He sat at my bedside, and we talked about Mozart. He was very fond of Mozart. Professor Einstein was an excellent violinist, you know." Mordecai smiled at me again, and Lily squeezed his arm.

"Mordecai's had an interesting life," she told me. I noticed that Lily was on her good behavior around him. I'd never seen her so subdued.

"But I chose not to follow a career as a mathematician," said Mordecai. "They say you must have a calling for it, much as for the priesthood. I chose to be a merchant instead. However, I am still interested in things that pertain to mathematics. Here we are."

He pulled Lily and me through a double door that led upstairs. As we started up, Mordecai added, "Yes, I have always considered computers to be the *eighth* wonder of the world!" Then he laughed his cackly laugh again. As I ascended the stairs, I wondered whether it was merely a coincidence that Mordecai had expressed an interest in formulas. And in the back of my mind I heard a refrain: "On the fourth day of the fourth month, then will come the eight."

The small cafeteria was on a mezzanine overlooking a huge bazaar of little jewelry shops. Everything downstairs was closed for the evening, but the cafeteria was jam-packed with the old men who'd been chatting on the streets less than half an hour earlier. They'd taken off their hats, but each still wore a small skull cap. Some had long curling locks at the sides of their faces, as did Mordecai.

We found a table, and Lily offered to go for the tea while we talked. Mordecai held a chair for me and went around to sit at the other side of the table.

"These earlocks are called *payess*," he told me. "A religious tradition. Jews are not supposed to cut their beards or shave the earlocks because it says in Leviticus, 'Ye shall not round the corners of your heads, neither shalt thou mar the corners of thy beard.' " Mordecai smiled again.

"But you have no beard," I said.

"No," said Mordecai ruefully. "As it says elsewhere in the Bible, 'My brother Esau is an hairy man, but I am a smooth man.' I should like to grow a beard, as I think it would make me look rather dashing. . . ." His eyes twinkled. "But all I can raise is the proverbial field of chaff."

Lily arrived with a tray and set steaming mugs of tea around the table as Mordecai continued.

"In ancient times the Jews used to leave the corners of their fields unharvested, just as the corners of the beards, for the elderly of the village to glean and for wanderers who were passing through. Wanderers have always been highly regarded in the Jewish faith. There is something mystical connected with the concept of wandering. My friend Lily tells me *you* are about to depart on a trip?"

"Yes," I said. But I was uncertain what his reaction would be if I told him I was going to spend a year in an Arab country.

"Do you take cream with your tea?" asked Mordecai. I nodded and started to rise, but he was already on his feet. "Allow me," he said.

As soon as he'd departed I turned to Lily.

"Quick, while we're alone," I whispered, "how is your family taking the news about Saul?"

"Oh, they're really pissed off at him," she said, passing the spoons around. "Especially Harry. He keeps calling him an ungrateful bastard."

"Pissed off!" I said. "It wasn't Saul's fault he got bumped off, was it?"

"What are you talking about?" said Lily, looking at me strangely.

"Surely you can't believe Saul arranged his own murder?"

"Murder?" Lily's eyes were getting bigger by the moment. "Look, I know I got a little carried away, imagining he'd been kidnapped and all. But he came back to the house after that. He resigned! Just flat up and left us. After twenty-five years of service!"

"I'm telling you he's dead," I insisted. "I saw him. He was laid out on a slab at the UN Meditation Room on Monday morning. Somebody killed him!"

Lily was sitting there with her mouth open, the spoon in her hand.

"There's something definitely weird about this," I continued.

Lily shushed me and glanced past my shoulder. Mordecai was arriving with some little packets of cream.

"It was like pulling teeth to get these," he said, sitting between Lily and me. "There is no such thing as friendly service anymore." He glanced at Lily and then at me. "Well, what's been going on here? You look as if someone just walked over your grave."

"Something like that," said Lily in a muffled voice, her face white as a sheet. "My father's chauffeur seems to have . . . passed away."

"Ah, I'm sorry to hear that," said Mordecai. "He was in your family's service a long time, wasn't he?"

"Since before I was born." Her eyes were glazed, and her thoughts seemed a million miles away.

"He was not a young man, then? Hopefully he didn't leave a family to provide for?" Mordecai was looking at Lily with a strange expression.

"You can tell him. Tell him what you told me," she said.

"I don't really think—"

"He knows about Fiske. Tell him about Saul."

Mordecai had turned to me with a polite expression. "Some drama is involved, I take it?" he said in a light tone. "My friend Lily seems to think Grand Master Fiske did not die a natural death, and perhaps you are of the same opinion?" He sipped his tea casually.

"Mordecai," said Lily, "Cat told me that Saul was murdered."

Mordecai put down his spoon without looking up. He sighed. "Ah. That was exactly what I was afraid you were going to tell me." He looked at me with big sorrowful eyes from behind the thick glasses. "Is it true?"

I turned to Lily. "Listen, I don't really think—"

But Mordecai interrupted in a polite voice.

"How does it happen that you are the first to hear of this," he asked me, "when Lily and her family seem to know nothing about it?"

"Because I was there," I said.

Lily started to speak, but Mordecai shushed her.

"Ladies, ladies," he said, turning to me. "Perhaps you could start at the beginning. If you would be so kind?"

So I found myself telling the story I'd told Nim all over again. Solarin's warning at the chess match, Fiske's death, Saul's mysterious disappearance, the bullet holes in the car, and finally Saul's dead body at the United Nations. Of course I left out a few choice items such as the fortune-teller, the man on the bicycle, and Nim's story of the Montglane Service. The last I'd sworn to keep secret, and the others sounded too bizarre to be repeated.

"You've explained everything very well," he said when I'd finished. "I think we may safely assume that the deaths of Fiske and Saul are somehow related.

Now we must determine what events or persons tie them together and establish a pattern."

"Solarin!" Lily said. "All the circumstances lead right to him. He's surely the obvious link."

"My dear child, why Solarin?" asked Mordecai. "What would be his motive?"

"He wanted to bump off everyone who might beat him. So he wouldn't have to give them the weapons formula."

"Solarin isn't a weapons physicist," I chimed in. "He got his degree in acoustics."

Mordecai looked at me strangely. Then he went on. "Yes, that's quite true. Actually, I know Alexander Solarin. I have never told you that." Lily sat silently with her hands in her lap, obviously hurt that there was any secret her revered chess master had not shared with her.

"It was many years ago, when I was still active as a diamond merchant. I went to visit a friend in Russia as I was returning from the Amsterdam bourse. A young boy was introduced to me, about sixteen years old. He'd come to my friend's house for chess instruction—"

"But Solarin attended the Palace of Young Pioneers," I interjected.

"Yes," said Mordecai, giving me his look again. It was becoming too obvious that I'd done my homework, so I shut up. "But in Russia, everyone plays chess with everyone. There is nothing else to do, really. So I sat down to play a game with Alexander Solarin. I was foolish enough to think I might teach him a thing or two. Of course he beat me, and badly. That boy is the finest chess player I've ever faced across a board. My dear," he added to Lily, "it is possible that you or Grand Master Fiske *might* have won a game of him. But not likely."

We were all quiet for a moment. The sky outside had turned to black, and except for the three of us, the cafeteria was empty. Mordecai looked at his pocket watch and picked up his cup, finishing off the last of the tea.

"Well, what of it?" he said cheerfully to break the silence. "Have you thought of another motive for someone to wish the deaths of so many people?"

Lily and I both shook our heads in complete befuddlement.

"No solutions?" he said, standing and picking up his hat. "Well, I'm rather late for a dinner engagement, and so are both of you. I shall think through the problem further when I have some free time, but I'd like to suggest what my initial analysis of the situation might be. You can mull it over. I'd like to suggest that the death of Grand Master Fiske had little to do with Solarin, and less to do with chess."

"But Solarin was the only one who was *there*, just before each murder was discovered!" Lily cried.

"Not so," said Mordecai, smiling cryptically. "There was another person who was also present on both occasions. Your friend Cat!"

"Now just a minute," I began. But Mordecai interrupted me.

"Don't you find it rather odd that the chess tournament has been postponed for one week 'in condolence for the unfortunate death of Grand Master Fiske,' but that no mention has been made in the press that foul play may have been involved? Do you not think it strange that you *saw* the dead body of Saul two days ago in so public a place as the United Nations building, yet no publicity has appeared whatever in the media? What explanation can you give for these strange circumstances?"

"A cover-up!" cried Lily.

"Perhaps," Mordecai said, shrugging his shoulders. "But you and your friend Cat have done a little concealing of evidence yourselves. Can you help me understand why you failed to go to the police when bullets were fired into your car? Why Cat failed to report the eyewitness encounter with a dead body that has subsequently vanished into thin air?"

Lily and I both started speaking at once.

"But I told you why I wanted to . . ." she mumbled.

"I was afraid to . . ." I stammered.

"Please," said Mordecai, holding up his hand. "These mutterings would presumably sound weaker to the police than they do to me. And the fact that your friend Cat was present in all instances seems even more suspicious."

"What are you suggesting?" I asked. I kept hearing Nim whisper, "But perhaps, my dear, someone thinks you *do* know something."

"I suggest," said Mordecai, "that although *you* may have nothing to do with these events, *they* have something to do with you."

With that, he bent down to kiss Lily on the forehead. He turned to me, and as he shook my hand formally, he did the oddest thing. He winked at me! Then he whisked off down the stairs and into the dark night.

A PAWN
ADVANCES

Then she brought the chess-board and played with him; but Sharrkan, instead of looking at her moves, kept gazing at her fair mouth, and putting Knight in place of Elephant, and Elephant in place of Knight.

She laughed and said to him, "If thy play be after this fashion, thou knowest naught of the game."

"This is only our first," replied he. "Judge not by this bout."

—The Thousand Nights and One Night
Translated by Sir Richard Burton

Only a single flame burned in the small brass candlestick within the foyer of Danton's house. Just at midnight someone in a long black cape pulled the bell-cord outside. The concierge shuffled through the foyer and peeped through the slot. The man on the steps wore a floppy low-brimmed hat that concealed his face.

"For God's sake, Louis," said the man, "open the door. It's me, Camille." The bolt shot back, and the concierge drew the door open.

"One cannot be too cautious, monsieur," the older man apologized.

"I quite understand," said Camille Desmoulins gravely as he stepped across the threshold, removing his broad-brimmed hat and running his hands through his thick curly hair. "I've just returned from La Force Prison. You know what has happened—" Desmoulins stopped with a jolt as he noticed a flicker of movement in the dark shadows of the foyer. "I say, who's there?" he said in fright.

The figure rose in silence, tall, pale, and elegantly attired despite the intense heat. He stepped out of the shadows and extended a hand to Desmoulins.

"My dear Camille," said Talleyrand, "I hope I've not alarmed you. I'm waiting for Danton to return from committee."

"Maurice!" said Desmoulins, taking his hand as the concierge withdrew. "What brings you to our home so late?" As Danton's secretary, Desmoulins had shared these quarters with his employer's family for years.

"Danton has kindly agreed to secure me a pass to leave France," Talleyrand explained calmly. "So that I may return to England and resume my negotiations. As you know, the Britons have refused to recognize our new government."

"I shouldn't bother to wait for him here tonight," said Camille. "You've heard what's happened in Paris today?"

Talleyrand shook his head slowly and said, "I've heard the Prussians were turned away and are in retreat. I understand they're returning to their homeland because they've all come down with the dysentery." He laughed. "There's not an army that can march three days drinking the wines of Champagne!"

"It's true the Prussians have been routed," agreed Desmoulins, not joining in the laughter. "But what I speak of is the massacre." From Talleyrand's expression, he realized he had not heard the news. "It began this afternoon at l'Abbaye Prison. Now it's moved to La Force and La Conciergerie. Already over five hundred people are dead, as near as we can count. There's been mass butchery, even cannibalism, and the Assembly cannot stop it—"

"I've heard nothing of this!" Talleyrand exclaimed. "But what is being done?"

"Danton is at La Force even now. The committee has set up extemporaneous trials at every prison, to try to slow the tide. They've agreed to pay the judges and executioners six francs a day and meals. It was the only hope they had to appear to be in control. Maurice, Paris is in a state of anarchy. People are calling it the Terror."

"Impossible!" cried Talleyrand. "When news of this gets out, all hope of a rapprochement with England may be abandoned. We'll be fortunate if they do not join the Prussians in declaring war. All the more reason for me to depart at once."

"You may do nothing without a pass," Desmoulins said, taking him by the arm. "Only this afternoon Madame de Staël was arrested for attempting to leave the country under diplomatic immunity. She was fortunate I was at hand to save her neck from the guillotine. They had taken her to the Paris Commune." Talleyrand's face showed he understood the gravity of the situation. Desmoulins went on.

"Have no fear, she is safe at the embassy tonight. And *you* should be safely at home as well. This is no night for a member of the nobility or the clergy to be abroad. You are in double jeopardy, my friend."

"I see," said Talleyrand quietly. "Yes, I quite see."

It was nearly one o'clock in the morning when Talleyrand returned to his house on foot, crossing the darkened quarters of Paris without a carriage to reduce the chance his movements might be observed. As he made his weary way through the ill-lighted streets, he saw some groups of theatergoers returning home and the last stragglers from the casinos. Their laughter echoed back to him as the open carriages meandered past, filled with revelers and champagne.

They were dancing at the edge of the abyss, thought Maurice. It was only a matter of time. Already he could see the dark chaos into which his country was slipping. He had to get away, and quickly.

He was alarmed, approaching the front gates of his gardens, to see a light flickering across the inner court. He'd given strict orders that all the shutters be closed and draperies drawn, that no light show to suggest he was at home. It was dangerous to be at home these days. But when he went to insert his key, the massive iron gate opened a crack. Courtiade the valet was standing there, and the light was from a small candle in his hand.

"For God's sake, Courtiade," Talleyrand whispered, "I told you there must be no light. You nearly frightened me to death."

"Excuse, Monseigneur," said Courtiade, who always called his master by his religious designation, "I hope I have not overstepped my bounds by disobeying yet another instruction."

"What have you done?" Talleyrand asked as he slipped through the gate and the valet locked it behind him.

"There is a visitor, Monseigneur. I took it upon myself to permit the person inside to wait for you."

"But this is serious." Talleyrand stopped and took the valet by the arm. "Madame de Staël was stopped by a mob this morning and taken to the Paris Commune. She nearly lost her life! No one must know that I am planning to leave Paris. You must tell me who it is you've let inside."

"It is Mademoiselle Mireille, Monseigneur," said the valet. "She came alone, only a short time ago."

"Mireille? Alone at this hour of the night?" Talleyrand hastened across the courtyard with Courtiade.

"Monseigneur, she arrived with a portmanteau. Her gown is badly damaged. She could barely speak. And I could not fail to note that there seemed to be—what looks like blood upon the garment. A good deal of blood."

"My God," murmured Talleyrand, limping as quickly as he could through the garden and entering the wide, darkened foyer. Courtiade motioned to the study, and Talleyrand hurried down the hall and through the broad doors. Everywhere were half-packed crates of books in preparation for his departure. At center, Mireille lay on the peach velvet settee, her face pale in the dim light of the candle that Courtiade had placed beside her.

Talleyrand knelt with some difficulty and took her limp hand in both of his, rubbing her fingers vigorously.

"Shall I bring the salts, sire?" asked Courtiade with a concerned face. "The servants have all been dismissed, as we were to leave in the morning. . . ."

"Yes, yes," said the master, never taking his eyes from Mireille. His heart was cold with fear. "But Danton did not come with the passes. And now this . . ."

He glanced up at Courtiade, who still held a candle aloft. "Well, get the salts, Courtiade. Once we rouse her, you'll have to go round to David's. We must get to the bottom of this, and quickly."

Talleyrand sat silently beside the settee looking down at Mireille, his mind trembling with a hundred dreadful thoughts. Picking up the candle from the table, he held it closer to her still form. Blood was matted in her strawberry hair, her face was streaked with dirt and blood. Gently he smoothed her hair away from her face and bent to place a kiss upon her forehead. As he looked down at her, something stirred within him. It was odd, he thought. She'd always been the serious one, the sober one.

Courtiade returned with the salts, handing the little crystal vial to his master. Lifting Mireille's head carefully, Talleyrand waved the uncorked bottle beneath her nose until she began to cough.

Her eyes opened, and she stared at the two men in horror. Suddenly she sat up as she realized where she was. She clutched wildly at Talleyrand's sleeve in a frenzy of panic. "How long have I been unconscious?" she cried. "You have not told anyone that I was here?" Her face was absolutely white, and she gripped his arm with the strength of ten.

"No, no, my dear," said Talleyrand in a soothing voice. "You have not been here long. As soon as you're feeling a bit better, Courtiade will make you a hot brandy to calm your nerves, and then we'll send round for your uncle."

"No!" Mireille nearly screamed. "No one must know that I am here! You must tell no one, least of all my uncle! That is the very first place they would think to look for me. My life is in terrible danger. Swear to me that you will tell no one!" She tried to leap to her feet, but Talleyrand and Courtiade restrained her in alarm.

"Where is my portmanteau?" she cried.

"It is just here," said Talleyrand, patting the leather bag. "Just beside your couch. My dear, you must calm yourself and lie back. Please rest until you are well enough to speak. It is so late at night. Wouldn't you want us at least to send for Valentine, to let her know you're safe?"

At the mention of Valentine's name, Mireille's face took on such an expression of horror and grief that Talleyrand drew away in fear.

"No," he said softly. "It cannot be. Not Valentine. Tell me that nothing has happened to Valentine. Tell me!"

He had grasped Mireille by the shoulders and was shaking her. Slowly she focused her eyes upon him. What he read in their depths jarred him to the very roots of his being. He wrenched her shoulders forcefully, his voice hoarse.

"Please," he said, "please say that nothing has happened to her. You must tell me that nothing has happened to her!" Mireille's eyes were completely dry as Talleyrand continued to shake her. He seemed not to know what he was doing. Slowly Courtiade reached forward and placed his hand gently upon his master's shoulder.

"Sire," he said softly. "Sire . . ." But Talleyrand was staring at Mireille like a man who has lost his senses.

"It is not true," he whispered, biting off each word like a bitter taste in his mouth. Mireille only looked at him. Slowly he relaxed his grasp upon her shoulders. His arms fell to his sides as he looked into her eyes. His face was completely blank. He was numb from the pain of what he could not bring himself to believe.

Drawing away from her, he stood up and walked to the fireplace, his back to the room. Opening the face of his rare ormolu clock that sat upon the mantel, he inserted the gold key. Slowly, carefully, he began to wind the clock. Mireille could hear it ticking in the darkness.

∞

The sun had not yet risen, but the first pale light filtered through the sheer silk draperies of Talleyrand's boudoir.

He had been up half the night, and it had been a night of horror. He could not bring himself to admit that Valentine was dead. He felt as if his heart had been torn out, and he knew no way to come to terms with such a feeling. He was a man with no family, a man who had never felt need for another human being. Maybe it was better so, he thought bitterly. If you never feel love, you never feel loss.

He could still see Valentine's pale blond hair glowing in the firelight as she bent to kiss his foot, as she stroked his face with her slender fingers. He thought of the funny things she had said, how she loved to shock him with her naughtiness. How could she be dead? How could she?

Mireille had been totally incapable of speaking of the circumstances of her cousin's death. Courtiade had made a hot bath for her, made her drink a hot spiced brandy into which he had slipped some laudanum, so she might sleep. And Talleyrand had given her the massive bed in his own boudoir, its arcaded canopy hung with pale blue silks. The color of Valentine's eyes.

He himself had stayed up half the night, reclining on a nearby chaise of blue watered silk. Many times Mireille had nearly succumbed to the stupor of sleep but awakened in chills, her eyes vacant, crying Valentine's name aloud. At these times he'd comforted her, and when she sank into sleep again, he'd returned to his improvised bed beneath the shawls Courtiade had provided him.

But there was no one to comfort him, and as the dawn turned rosy through the French windows overlooking the garden, Talleyrand still tossed sleeplessly on his sofa, his golden ringlets disheveled, his blue eyes cloudy from lack of sleep.

Once during the night, Mireille had cried out, "I will go with you to l'Abbaye, my cousin. I will never let you go into the Cordeliers alone." And he had felt the hard, cold chill pierce his spine as he heard those words. My God, was it possible she had died at l'Abbaye? He could not even contemplate the rest. He resolved to get the truth from Mireille once she was rested—regardless the pain it cost them both.

As he lay there on the chaise, he heard a sound, a light footstep.

"Mireille?" he whispered, but there was no response. Reaching over, he pulled aside the bed hangings. She was gone.

Drawing his silk dressing gown about him, Talleyrand limped toward his dressing room. But as he passed the French windows, he saw through the opaque silk curtains a figure outlined against the rosy light. He pulled back the draperies to the terrace. Then he froze.

Mireille was standing, her back to him, looking out over his gardens and the small orchard beyond the stone wall. She was completely nude, and her creamy skin shimmered with a silken glow in the morning light. Just as he remembered from the first morning he'd seen them standing on the scaffolding of David's studio. Valentine and Mireille. The shock of this memory was so immediate and so painful that it seemed like a spear running him through. But at the same time there was something else. Something slowly surfacing from the dull, throbbing red pain of his consciousness. And as it surfaced, it seemed to him more horrible than anything he could imagine. What he felt at that precise moment was lust. Passion. He wanted to grasp Mireille there on the terrace, in the first wet dawn of the morning, to plunge his flesh into hers, to throw her to the ground, to bite her lips and bruise her body, to expend his pain into the dark, fathomless well of her being. And as this idea dawned on him, Mireille, sensing his presence, turned to face him. She blushed deeply. He was horribly humiliated and tried to cover his embarrassment.

"My dear," he said, hastily removing his dressing gown and crossing to wrap it about her shoulders, "you'll catch a chill. The dew is quite heavy at this time of year." Even to himself he sounded like a fool. And worse. When his fingers grazed her shoulders as he draped her with his silken robe, he felt a jolt of electricity go through him of a sort he had never felt before. He controlled the urge to spring away, but Mireille was looking up at him with those fathomless green eyes. He looked away in haste. She must not know what he was thinking. It was deplorable. He thought of everything he could to help him quench the feeling that had rushed upon him so suddenly. So violently.

"Maurice," she was saying as she lifted her slender fingers to brush away an unruly lock of his blond hair, "I want to speak of Valentine now. May I speak of Valentine?" Her strawberry hair was floating against his chest in the light morning breeze. He could feel it burning through the thin fabric of his night-shirt. He was so close he could smell the sweet aroma of her skin. He closed his eyes, struggling for self-control, unable to look into her eyes, afraid of what she might see there. The ache he felt inside was overwhelming. How could he be such a monster?

He forced himself to open his eyes and look at her. He forced himself to smile, though he felt his lips twisting into a strange contortion.

"You called me Maurice," he said, the forced smile still there. "Not 'Uncle Maurice.'" She was so incredibly beautiful, her lips half-parted like dark crushed rose petals. . . . He wrenched his thoughts away. Valentine. She wanted to speak of Valentine. Gently but firmly, he placed his hands on her shoulders.

He could feel the heat of her skin through the thin silk of his robe. He could see the blue vein pulsing against her long white throat. Below, he could see the shadow between her young breasts. . . .

"Valentine loved you very deeply," Mireille was saying in a choked voice. "I knew all her thoughts and feelings. I know she wanted to do those things with you that men do with women. Do you know which things I mean?" She was looking up at him again, her lips so close, her body so . . . He was not certain he had heard correctly.

"I—I'm not sure—I mean, certainly I know," he stammered, staring at her. "But I never imagined . . ." He cursed himself again for being a fool. What on earth was she saying?

"Mireille," he said firmly. He wanted to be benevolent, paternal. After all, this girl who stood before him was young enough to be his daughter, no more than a child, really. "Mireille," he said again, striving for the right way to lead the conversation back to safer ground.

But she had raised her hands to his face, sliding her fingers into his hair. She pulled his mouth down to hers. My God, he thought, I must be mad. This cannot be happening.

"Mireille," he said again, his lips brushing hers, "I cannot . . . we cannot . . ." He felt the floodgates crumbling as he pressed his lips to hers and felt the heat beating in his loins. No. He could not. Not this. Not now.

"Do not forget," Mireille was whispering against his chest as she touched him through the thin fabric of his gown, "I loved her, too." He moaned and pulled the robe from her shoulders as he buried himself in her warm flesh.

He was drowning, drowning. Sinking into a pool of dark passion, his fingers sweeping like cool deep waters over the silk of Mireille's long limbs. They lay in the thick tousled bedclothes where he had carried her from the terrace, and he felt himself falling, falling. When their lips met, he felt the surge as if his blood were rushing into her body, their blood was mingling. The violence of his passion was unbearable. He tried to remember what he was doing, and why he should not do it, but he longed only to forget. Mireille rose to him with a passion darker, more violent than his own. He had never experienced anything like this. He did not want it ever to end.

Mireille looked at him, her eyes dark green pools, and he knew she felt the same. Each time he touched her, caressed her, she seemed to fall deeper and deeper into his body, as if she too wanted to be inside him, in every bone, every nerve, every sinew. As if she wanted to pull him down to the bottom of the dark pool, where they could drown together in the opium of their passion. The pool of Lethe, of forgetfulness. And as he swam in the pools of her deep green eyes, he felt the passion racking him like a dark storm, he heard the song of the ondines calling, calling from the bottom of the depths.

Maurice Talleyrand had made love to many women, so many he could no longer count them all, but as he lay in the soft, rumpled linen of his bed with Mireille's long limbs entwined in his, he could no longer remember a single one. He knew he could never recapture what he had felt. It had been total ecstasy, of a kind few humans ever experience. But what he now felt was total pain. And guilt.

Guilt. For when they had moved in the tumbled counterpane together, folded in each other's arms, in a passionate embrace more powerful than any he'd ever known—he had gasped out "Valentine." Valentine. Just at the moment when the surge of passion had consumed. And Mireille had whispered, "Yes."

He looked down at her. Her creamy skin and tangled hair were so beautiful against the cool linen sheets. She looked up at him with those dark green eyes. Then she smiled.

"I did not know what it would be like," she said.

"And did you like it?" he asked, ruffling her hair gently with his hand.

"Yes. I liked it," she said, still smiling. Then she saw that he was troubled.

"I'm sorry," he said softly. "I didn't mean to. But you are so very beautiful. And I wanted you so very much." He kissed her hair and then her lips.

"I don't want you to be sorry," said Mireille, sitting up in bed and looking at him seriously. "It made me feel, just for a moment, as if she were still alive. As if it had all been a bad dream. If Valentine were alive, she would have made love with you. So you shouldn't be sorry that you called me by her name." She had read his thoughts. He looked at her slowly, then he smiled back.

He lay back in bed and pulled Mireille on top of him. Her long, graceful body felt cool against his skin. Her red hair tumbled over his shoulders. He drank in her perfume. He wanted to make love to her again. But he concentrated with difficulty to calm the stiffening in his loins. There was something he wanted more. First.

"Mireille, there is something I want you to do," he said, his voice muffled in her hair. She lifted her head to look at him. "I know it is painful for you, but I want you to tell me about Valentine. I want you to tell me everything. We must contact your uncle. You spoke out in your sleep last night about going to l'Abbaye Prison—"

"You cannot tell my uncle where I am," Mireille interrupted, sitting up in bed abruptly.

"At the very least, we must give Valentine a decent burial," he argued.

"I do not even know," said Mireille, choking on the words, "if we can find her body. If only you will vow to help me, I will tell you how Valentine died. And *why* she died."

Talleyrand looked at her strangely. "What do you mean, *why* she died?" he said. "I had presumed you were caught in the confusion at l'Abbaye Prison. Surely—"

"She died," said Mireille slowly, "because of this."

She got up from the bed and crossed the room to her portmanteau, which Courtiade had left beside the dressing room door. With effort she picked it up and carried it back, placing it upon the bed. She opened it and motioned for Talleyrand to look inside. Within, covered in dirt and strewn with grasses, were eight pieces of the Montglane Service.

Talleyrand reached inside the battered leather case and extracted a piece, holding it in both hands as he sat beside Mireille in the jumbled quilts. It was a large gold elephant, measuring nearly the length of his hand in height. Its saddle was encrusted as thickly as a carpet with polished rubies and black sapphires. Its trunk and golden tusks were raised aloft in battle position.

"The Aufin," he whispered. "This is the piece we now call the Bishop, adviser to the King and Queen."

One by one, he extracted the pieces from the satchel and spread them across the bed. A silver camel, and a gold. Another golden elephant, a prancing Arabian steed, its legs wildly thrashing the air, and three peons bearing various weapons, each small foot soldier the length of his finger, all encrusted with amethyst and citrine, tourmaline and emerald and jasper.

Slowly Talleyrand picked up the stallion and turned it in his hands. Wiping the base free of dirt, he saw a symbol pressed into the dark gold metal. He studied it closely. Then he showed it to Mireille. It was a circle with an arrow's shaft cut into one side.

"Mars, the red planet," he said. "God of war and destruction. *'And there went out another horse that was red: and power was given to him that sat thereon to take peace from the earth, and that they should kill one another: and there was given unto him a great sword.'* "

But Mireille did not seem to hear him. She sat, staring at the symbol on the base of the stallion Talleyrand held in his hands. She did not speak but seemed to be in a trance. At last he saw her lips moving and bent to hear her.

"And the name of the sword was Sar," she whispered. Then she closed her eyes.

Talleyrand sat in silence for over an hour, his dressing gown wrapped loosely about him, as Mireille sat unclothed in the jumbled pile of bedsheets unfolding her story.

She told him the abbess's tale, as nearly as she could recall it, and what the nuns had done to remove the service from the abbey walls. She recounted how they had scattered the pieces across Europe and how she and Valentine were to serve as a collection point should any nun need their help. Then she told him of Sister Claude and how Valentine had rushed to meet her in the *allée* outside the prison.

When Mireille reached the point in her tale where the tribunal had sentenced Valentine to death, when David had crumpled to the ground, Talleyrand interrupted her. Mireille's face was streaming with tears, her eyes were swollen and her voice choked.

"You mean to say that Valentine was not killed by the mob?" he cried.

"She was sentenced! That horrible man," Mireille sobbed. "I shall never forget his face. That hideous grimace! How he *enjoyed* the power he held over life and death. May he rot in those pustulating sores that cover him. . . ."

"What did you say?" Talleyrand grabbed her by the arm and shook her. "What was this man's name? You must remember!"

"I asked his name," said Mireille, looking at him through her tears, "but he would not tell me. He only said, 'I am the rage of the people!' "

"Marat!" cried Talleyrand. "I should have guessed. But I cannot believe—"

"Marat!" Mireille said. "Now that I know, I shall never forget it. He claimed he would hunt me down if he didn't find the pieces where I'd told him. But I shall hunt him down instead."

"My dearest girl," said Talleyrand, "you've taken the pieces from their hiding place. Marat will move heaven and earth to find you now. But how did you escape from the prison courtyard?"

"Uncle Jacques-Louis," Mireille told him. "He was close by the evil man when the order was given, and he flew at him in a terrible rage. I threw myself across Valentine's body, but they dragged me away just as . . . as . . . ." Mireille struggled to go on. "And then I heard my uncle crying my name, calling for me to flee. I ran blindly from the prison. I cannot tell you how I was able to pass through the gates. It's all a horrible dream to me, but I found myself in the *allée* once again, and I flew for my life to the garden at David's."

"You are a very brave child, my dear. I wonder if I would have the strength myself to do as you've done."

"Valentine died because of the pieces," Mireille sobbed, trying to calm herself. "I could not let him have them! I had them in my hands before he could leave the prison. I took a few clothes from my room at David's, and this leather case, and I fled. . . ."

"But you could not have left David's later than six in the evening. Where were you between that time and the time you arrived here, well after midnight?"

"Only two of the pieces were buried in David's garden," replied Mireille.

"Those that Valentine and I brought with us from Montglane: the golden elephant and the silver camel. The other six were brought from another abbey by Sister Claude. Sister Claude had only arrived in Paris yesterday morning, as I knew. She hadn't much time to hide them, and it was too dangerous to bring them when she came to meet us. But Sister Claude died and told only Valentine where they were located."

"But you have them!" Talleyrand spread his hand out over the bejeweled pieces that still lay scattered among the bedclothes. He thought he could feel a warmth radiating from them. "You told me at the prison there were soldiers and members of the tribunal and others swarming everywhere. How could you have discovered their location from Valentine?"

"Her last words were 'Remember the ghost.' And then she spoke her name several times."

"The ghost?" said Talleyrand, confused.

"I knew at once what she meant. She was referring to your story of the ghost of Cardinal Richelieu."

"Are you certain? Well, you must be, for here are the pieces before us. But I cannot imagine how you found them from that scanty information."

"You told us you'd been a priest at St. Remy, which you left to attend the Sorbonne, where you saw Cardinal Richelieu's ghost in the chapel. Valentine's family name, as you know, is de Remy. But I recalled at once that Valentine's great-grandfather, Gericauld de Remy, was buried in the Sorbonne chapel, not far from the tomb of Cardinal Richelieu! This was the message she was trying to give me. The pieces were buried there.

"I returned through the darkened quarters to the chapel, where I found a votive candle burning at the grave of Valentine's ancestor. By the light only of this candle, I searched the chapel. It was hours before I found a loose floor tile, partially hidden behind the baptismal font. Lifting it, I exhumed the pieces from the earthen floor beneath. Then I fled as quickly as possible here to the Rue de Beaune." Mireille paused, out of breath with her story.

"Maurice," she said, laying her head against his chest so that he could hear the throbbing of her pulse, "I think there was another reason Valentine mentioned the ghost. She was trying to tell me to turn to *you* for help, to trust you."

"But what can I do to help you, my dear?" said Talleyrand. "I am myself a prisoner here in France until I can secure a pass. Possession of these pieces places us both in greater jeopardy, surely you can see that."

"But not if we knew the secret, the secret of the power they contain. If we knew that, then *we* would hold the upper hand. Would we not?"

She looked so brave and serious, Talleyrand could not help but smile. He bent over her and placed his lips upon her naked shoulders. And despite himself, he felt the surge rising in him again. Just then there was a soft tap at the bedroom door.

"Monseigneur," said Courtiade through the closed door, "I do not wish to disturb you, but there is a person in the courtyard."

"I'm not at home, Courtiade," said Talleyrand. "You know that."

"But Monseigneur," said the valet, "it is a messenger from Monsieur Danton. He has brought the passes."

At nine o'clock that night, Courtiade was lying upon the study floor, his stiff jacket folded over a chair, the sleeves of his starched shirt rolled back. He was hammering the last false partition into the book crates that were scattered across the room. Loose books were stacked everywhere. Mireille and Talleyrand sat, drinking brandy, amid the piles.

"Courtiade," said Talleyrand, "you will proceed to London tomorrow with these crates of books. When you arrive there, ask for Madame de Staël's property brokers, and they will arrange to give you the keys and show you to the quarters we've secured. Whatever you do, let no one handle these crates but yourself. Do not let them out of your sight, and do not unpack them until Mademoiselle Mireille and I arrive."

"I've told you," Mireille said firmly, "I cannot go with you to London. I only wish to get the pieces of the service out of France."

"My dearest girl," said Talleyrand, stroking her hair, "we've been over all of this before. I insist you use my pass. I'll get another soon enough. You simply cannot remain in Paris any longer."

"My first task was to keep the Montglane Service from the hands of that horrible man, and from others who might misuse it," Mireille said. "Valentine would have done the same. Others may be coming here to Paris, seeking refuge. I must remain here to help them."

"You are a brave young woman," he told her. "Nevertheless, I shall not permit you to stay at Paris alone, and you cannot return to your uncle's house. We must both decide what to do with these pieces when we reach London—"

"You misunderstand," said Mireille coolly, rising from her chair. "I did not say that I planned to stay in Paris." Removing a piece of the Montglane Service from the leather satchel near her chair, she crossed to Courtiade and handed it to him. It was the Knight, the rearing gold stallion she'd studied only that morning. Courtiade carefully accepted the piece. She felt the fire passing through her arm into his as she handed it to him. Carefully he fitted it into the false partition and packed straw wadding around it.

"Mademoiselle," said the serious Courtiade with a twinkle in his eye, "it fits perfectly. I stake my life that your books will arrive safely in London."

Mireille stretched out her hand, and Courtiade shook it warmly. Then she turned back to Talleyrand.

"I don't understand at all," he said irritably. "First you refuse to go to London on grounds you must stay in Paris. Then you claim you do not plan to remain here. Please make yourself clearer."

"You will go to London with the pieces," she informed him in a surprisingly authoritative voice. "But I have another mission. I shall write the abbess, telling her of my plans. I've money of my own, and Valentine and I were orphans. By rights, her estate and title must go to me. Then I shall request she send another nun to Paris until I have completed my work."

"But where will you go? What will you do?" said Talleyrand. "You are a young woman alone, with no family. . . ."

"I've given that a good deal of thought since yesterday," Mireille said. "I have unfinished business to conduct before I can return to France. I am in danger—until I can understand the secret of these pieces. And there is only one way to understand it. That is to go to their place of origin."

"Good God," fumed Talleyrand. "You've told me they were given to Charlemagne by the Moorish governor of Barcelona! But that was nearly a thousand years ago. I should think the trail would be a bit cold by now. And Barcelona is scarcely in the outskirts of Paris! I'll not have you running about Europe by yourself!"

"I do not plan to go to a country in Europe." Mireille smiled. "The Moors did not come from Europe, they came from Mauretania, from the bottom of the Sahara Desert. One must always begin at the source in order to find the meaning. . . ." She looked at Talleyrand with her fathomless green eyes, and he looked back in amazement.

"I shall go to Algeria," she said. "For that is where the Sahara begins."

THE CENTER BOARD

Skeletons of mice are often to be found in coconuts, for it is easier to get in, slim and greedy, than to get out, appeased but fat.

—Chess Is My Life
Viktor Korchnoi (Russian GM)

Tactics is knowing what to do when there is something to do. Strategy is knowing what to do when there is nothing to do.

—*Savielly Tartakover (Polish GM)*

n the cab, en route to Harry's, I was more confused than ever. Mordecai's statement that I'd been present on both funereal occasions only reinforced the sickening feeling that this circus had something to do with *me*. Why had Solarin and the fortune-teller both warned *me*? Why had *I* painted a man on a bicycle, and why was he making guest appearances in real life?

I wished I'd asked Mordecai further questions; it seemed he knew more than he was letting on. For example, he'd admitted he had met Solarin years earlier. How did we know he and Solarin hadn't remained in contact?

When we arrived at Harry's, the doorman raced out to open the front door for us. We had barely spoken on our trip over. Going up in the elevator, Lily finally said, "Mordecai seemed quite taken with you."

"A very complex person."

"You've no idea," she said as the doors swished open on her floor. "Even when I beat him at chess, I always wonder what combinations he *might* have played. I trust him more than anyone, but he's always had a secretive side. Speaking of secretive, don't mention Saul's death until we know more about it."

"I really should go to the police," I said.

"They're going to wonder why it took you so long to get around to mentioning it," Lily pointed out. "You may delay your trip to Algiers with a ten-year prison sentence."

"Surely they wouldn't think that *I* . . ."

"Why not?" she said as we reached Harry's door.

"There they are!" cried Llewellyn from the living room as Lily and I came into the large marble foyer and handed the maid our coats. "Late as usual. Where have you two been? Harry's having a fit in the kitchen."

The foyer had a chessboard floor of black-and-white squares. Around the curved walls were marble pillars and Italian landscapes in gray-green tones. At the center splashed a little fountain, surrounded by ivy.

At either side were wide, curving marble steps, scrolled at the edges. Those at the right led down to the formal dining room, where a dark mahogany table was set for five. To the left was the living room, where Blanche was seated in a heavy chair of deep red brocade. A hideous Chinese chest, lacquered in red with gold handles, dominated the far end of the room. The overblown, costly dregs of Llewellyn's antique shop peppered the rest of the room. Llewellyn himself was crossing the room to greet us.

"Where have you two been?" said Blanche as we descended the stairs. "We were to have cocktails and hors d'oeuvres an hour ago." Llewellyn gave me a little peck and left to tell Harry we'd arrived.

"We were just chatting," said Lily, tossing her bulk in another overstuffed chair and picking up a magazine.

Harry came dashing out of the kitchen, bearing aloft a large tray of appetizers. He was wearing a chef's apron and a big floppy hat. He looked like a gigantic advertisement for self-rising dough.

"I heard you'd arrived," he said, beaming. "I let most of the staff off so they wouldn't kibitz while I was cooking. So I brought the hors d'oeuvres myself."

"Lily said they were *chatting* all this time, can you imagine?" said Blanche as Harry put the tray down on a side table. "The entire dinner might have been ruined."

"Let them alone," Harry said, winking at me, his back to Blanche. "Girls that age *should* be schmoozing a little." Harry harbored the delusion that, if exposed to me enough, some of my personality would "rub off" on Lily.

"Now look," he said, dragging me over to the hors d'oeuvres tray. "This one is caviar and smetana, this one is egg and onion, and this one is my own secret recipe for chopped liver with schmaltz. My mother gave it to me on her deathbed!"

"It smells wonderful," I told him.

"And this one is lox with cream cheese, in case you shouldn't care for the caviar. I want half of these gone before I come back. Dinner will be in thirty minutes." He beamed at me again and breezed out of the room.

"Lox, my God," said Blanche as if she felt a headache coming on. "Give me one of those." I handed her one and took some myself.

Lily went over to the hors d'oeuvres tray and wolfed down a few. "Do you want some champagne, Cat? Or can I fix you something else?"

"Champagne is fine," I told her just as Llewellyn returned.

"I'll pour," he said, going behind the bar. "Champagne for Cat, and what will it be for my charming niece?"

"Scotch and soda," said Lily. "Where's Carioca?"

"The little darling is tucked away for the evening. No need to have him rummaging about in the hors d'oeuvres." As Carioca tried to bite Llewellyn on the ankles whenever he saw him, his attitude was understandable. While Lily sulked, Llewellyn handed me a flute of champagne fizzing with bubbles. Then he returned to the bar to mix the Scotch and soda.

After the prescribed half hour and many hors d'oeuvres, Harry came out of the kitchen in a dark brown velvet dinner jacket and motioned us all to be seated. Lily and Llewellyn were at one side of the mahogany table, Blanche and Harry at either end. I had the remaining side to myself. We sat down, and Harry poured the wine.

"Let's all toast the departure of our beloved friend Cat, for her first long stay away from us since we have known her." We all clinked glasses back and forth, and Harry continued.

"Before you go, I'll give you a list of the very best restaurants in Paris. You go to Maxim's or the Tour d'Argent, mention my name to the maître d' and you'll be served like a princess."

I had to tell him. It was now or never.

"Actually, Harry," I said, "I'll only be in Paris for a few days. After that, I'm going to Algiers."

Harry glanced at me, his wineglass aloft. He put the wineglass down. "Algiers?" he said.

"That's where I'm going to work," I explained. "I'll be there for a year."

"You're going to live with the Arabs?"

"Well, I'm going to Algeria," I said. Everyone at the table was silent, and I frankly appreciated their not trying to intervene on my behalf.

"Why are you going to Algeria? You have suddenly lost your mind? Or is there some other reason that seems to be escaping me?"

"I'm going to develop a computer system for OPEC," I told him. "It's an oil consortium. It stands for Organization of Petroleum Exporting Countries. They produce and distribute oil, and one of their bases is in Algiers."

"What kind of oil consortium is it," said Harry, "run by a bunch of people who don't know how to dig a hole in the ground? For four thousand years the Arabs have been wandering around in the desert letting their camels shit wherever they liked, and producing absolutely nothing! How can you—"

With perfect timing, Valerie the maid came in with a big urn of chicken soup on a little cart. She pushed it over to Blanche and began dishing up.

"Valerie, what are you doing?" said Harry. "Not now!"

"Monsieur Rad," said Valerie, who was from Marseilles and knew how to handle men, "I have been wiz you for ten years. And in all zat time, I haf never let you tell me *when* I shall serve the zoup. Why shall I begeen now?" And she kept on ladling with remarkable aplomb.

Valerie had gotten around to me by the time Harry recovered.

"Valerie," he said, "since you insist on serving the soup, I'd like to hear your opinion on something."

"Veree well," she said, pursing her lips and moving around to serve Harry.

"You know Miss Velis here quite well?"

"Quite well," agreed Valerie.

"Do you know that Miss Velis here just informed me that she is planning to move to Algeria, to live among the Arabs? What do you think of that?"

"Algerie, it is a marvelous country," said Valerie, moving around to serve

Lily. "I have a brozzaire who leeves zaire. I have visite him many times." She nodded at me across the table. "You weel like eet very much."

She served Llewellyn and departed.

The table was silent. The sound of soup spoons could be heard scraping across the bottom of bowls. Finally Harry spoke.

"How do you like the soup?" he said.

"It's wonderful," I told him.

"You won't get any soup like this in Algeria, I can tell you that."

This was Harry's way of admitting that he had lost. You could hear the relief pass like a heavy sigh around the table.

The dinner was wonderful. Harry had made potato pancakes with home-made applesauce that was just a little sour and tasted of oranges. There was a big roast that crumbled into its own juices; you could cut it with a fork. There was a noodle casserole he called "kugel" that had a crusty top. There were lots of vegetables and four different kinds of bread served with sour cream. For dessert we had the best apple strudel I had ever eaten, thick with raisins and steaming hot.

Blanche, Llewellyn, and Lily had been unusually silent during dinner, making idle chitchat that seemed halfhearted. Finally Harry turned to me, refilling my wineglass, and said, "If you get into trouble, you'll be sure to call me? I'm concerned for you, darling, with nobody to turn to but some Arabs and those goyim you work for."

"Thanks," I said. "But Harry, try to realize that I'm going to a civilized country on business. I mean, it's not exactly like going on a jungle trek—"

"What do you mean?" Harry interrupted. "The Arabs are still cutting people's hands off for stealing. Besides, even a civilized country isn't so safe anymore. I don't let Lily drive the car herself in New York even, for fear she'll get mugged. You heard, I suppose, that Saul up and quit? That ingrate."

Lily and I glanced at each other and looked away again. Harry was still carrying on.

"Lily is still in this meshugge chess tournament, and I have no one to drive her there. I worry myself sick that she'll be out in the streets. . . . Now I hear that some player died in the tournament even."

"Don't be ridiculous," said Lily. "This is a very important tournament. If I qualify here, I could play in the interzonals against the biggest players in the world. I'm certainly not going to back out just because some crazy old guy got himself bumped off."

"Bumped off?!" said Harry, and his glance snapped back to me before I had time to adjust my expression to one of naïveté. "Great! Terrific! Exactly what

I've been worrying about. Meanwhile, you're running down to Forty-sixth Street every five minutes to play chess with that doddering old fool. How are you ever going to meet a husband?"

"Are you talking about Mordecai?" I asked Harry.

A deafening silence fell over the table. Harry had turned to stone. Llewellyn had closed his eyes and was toying with his napkin. Blanche was looking at Harry with an unpleasant little smile. Lily was staring at her plate and tapping her spoon on the table.

"Did I say something wrong?" I asked.

"It's nothing," Harry mumbled. "Don't worry about it." But he said nothing further.

"It's all right, darling," said Blanche with forced sweetness. "It's something we don't speak about very often, that's all. Mordecai is Harry's father. Lily is very fond of him. He taught her to play chess when she was quite young. I believe he did it just to spite me."

"Mother, that's ridiculous," said Lily. "I asked him to teach me. You know that."

"You were barely out of diapers at the time," Blanche said, still looking at me. "In my opinion he is a horrible old man. He has not been in this apartment since Harry and I were married twenty-five years ago. I am astounded that Lily would introduce you to him."

"He's my grandfather," said Lily.

"You could have told me first," Harry chimed in. He looked so thoroughly wounded that for a moment I thought he was going to cry. Those St. Bernard eyes had never been droopier.

"I'm really sorry," I said. "It was my fault. . . ."

"It was *not your fault*," said Lily. "So just shut up. The *problem* is that no one here has ever understood that I want to play chess. I do not *want* to be an actress or marry a rich man. I do not *want* to mooch off other people as Llewellyn does. . . ." Llewellyn looked up briefly with a dagger in his eye, then looked back down at the table again.

"I want to play chess, and no one understands that but Mordecai."

"Every single time *that man's* name is mentioned in this house," said Blanche, sounding slightly shrill for the first time, "it drives this family a little farther apart."

"I don't see why I have to sneak downtown like some kind of culprit," said Lily, "just to see my own—"

"What sneaking?" Harry said. "Have I ever asked you to sneak? I sent you in the car whenever you wanted to go. No one ever said you should sneak anywhere."

"But perhaps she *wanted* to sneak," said Llewellyn, speaking for the first time. "Perhaps our darling Lily wanted to sneak over with Cat to discuss the tournament *they attended together* last Sunday, the one where Fiske was killed. After all, Mordecai is an old cohort of Grand Master Fiske. Or *was*, I should say."

Llewellyn was smiling as if he'd just found a place for his dagger. I wondered how he'd come so close to the mark. I tried a little bluff.

"Don't be silly. Everyone knows Lily never attends tournaments."

"Oh, why lie about it?" said Lily. "It was probably in the papers that I was there. There were enough reporters crawling around."

"Nobody ever tells me anything!" Harry bellowed. His face was very red. "What the hell is going on around here?" He scowled at us all with thunder in his face. I'd never seen him so angry.

"Cat and I went to the tournament on Sunday. Fiske was playing a Russian. Fiske died, and Cat and I left. That's all there was to it, so don't make a big production."

"Who's making a production?" said Harry. "Now that you've explained it, I'm satisfied. Only you could have satisfied me a little earlier, that's all. But you're not going to any more tournaments where people are getting bumped off."

"I'll try to arrange for everybody to stay alive," Lily said.

"What did the brilliant Mordecai have to say about Fiske's death?" asked Llewellyn, unwilling to let it drop. "Surely he had an opinion on the subject. He seems to have an opinion on everything."

Blanche put her hand on Llewellyn's arm, as if that were really about enough.

"Mordecai thought Fiske was murdered," Lily said, pushing back her chair and standing up. She dropped her napkin on the table. "Anyone care to move to the drawing room for a little after–dinner arsenic?"

She walked out of the room. There was an uncomfortable silence for a moment, then Harry reached over and patted me on the shoulder.

"I'm sorry, darling. It's your farewell party, and we're all screaming at each other like a bunch of yentas. Come, let's have a cognac and talk about something more cheerful."

I agreed. We all went to the living room for a nightcap. After a few minutes Blanche complained of a headache and excused herself. Llewellyn took me aside and said, "Do you remember the little proposition I'd made you about Algiers?" I nodded, and he added, "Come into the study for a moment and we'll discuss it."

I followed him through the back corridor into the study, which was all done in soft brown plumpy furniture with dim lighting. Llewellyn closed the door behind us.

"Are you willing to do it?" he asked.

"Look, I know it's important to you," I told him. "And I've thought it over. I'll try to find these chess pieces for you. But I'm not going to do anything illegal."

"If I can wire you the money, could you buy them? I mean, I could put you in touch with someone who'd . . . remove them from the country."

"Smuggle them, you mean."

"Why put it that way?" said Llewellyn.

"Let me ask you a question, Llewellyn," I said. "If you have someone who knows where the pieces are, and you have someone who'll pay for them, and you have someone else who'll smuggle them out of the country, what do you need *me* for?"

Llewellyn was silent for a moment. It was clear he was thinking about how to reply. At last he said, "Why not be honest about it? We've tried already. The owner will not sell to my people. Refuses even to meet with them."

"Then why would he deal with me?" I wanted to know.

Llewellyn smiled strangely. Then, cryptically, he said, "It's a she. And we have cause to believe she'll only deal with another woman."

Llewellyn hadn't been very clear, but I thought it best not to press the issue as I had motives of my own that might accidentally slip out in conversation.

When we returned to the living room, Lily was sitting on the sofa with Carioca in her lap. Harry was standing near the atrocious lacquered secretary at the far end of the room, speaking on the phone. Though his back was to me, I could tell by the stiffness of his stance that something was wrong. I glanced at Lily, and she shook her head. Carioca's ears had perked up when he saw Llewellyn, and a little growl shook his fluffy body. Llewellyn hastily excused himself, giving me a peck on the cheek, and departed.

"That was the police," said Harry, hanging up the phone and turning to me with a devastated expression. His shoulders were hunched, and he seemed about to weep. "They've dredged a body from the East River. They want me to come down to the morgue and identify it. The deceased"—he choked on the words— "had Saul's wallet and chauffeur's license in his pocket. I have to go."

I turned green. So Mordecai had been right. Someone *was* trying to cover up, but how had Saul's body wound up in the East River? I was afraid to look at Lily. Neither of us said a word, but Harry didn't seem to notice.

"You know," he was saying, "I *knew* something was wrong last Sunday night. When Saul came back here, he shut himself up in his room and wouldn't speak to anyone. He didn't come out at dinner. You don't think he could have committed suicide? I should have insisted on speaking to him . . . I blame myself for this."

"You don't know for certain that it's Saul they found," said Lily. She glanced at me with pleading eyes, but I didn't know if she was pleading for me to tell the truth or to keep my mouth shut. I felt horrible about the whole thing.

"Do you want me to go with you?" I suggested.

"No, darling," said Harry, heaving a big sigh. "Let's hope Lily's right and there's been a mistake. But if it is Saul, I'll have to stay down there a while. I'd want to claim the . . . I'd want to make arrangements for him in a funeral home."

Harry kissed me good-bye, apologizing again for the sadness of the evening, and finally left.

"God, I feel awful," said Lily when he'd gone. "Harry loved Saul like a son."

"I think we should tell him the truth," I said.

"Don't be so goddamned noble," said Lily. "How the hell are we going to explain that you saw Saul's body two days ago at the UN and forgot to mention it even over dinner? Remember what Mordecai said."

"Mordecai seemed to have some presentiment that these murders were being covered up," I told her. "I think I should talk to him about it."

I asked Lily for Mordecai's number. She dropped Carioca into my lap and went over to the secretary to get some paper. Carioca licked my hand. I wiped it off.

"Can you believe the shit that Lulu drags into this house?" she said, referring to the hideous red-and-gold secretary. Lily always called Llewellyn "Lulu" when she was angry. "The drawers stick, and these ugly brass handles are too much." She jotted Mordecai's number on a piece of stationery and handed it to me.

"When are you leaving?" she asked.

"For Algeria? On Saturday. I doubt we'll have much time to talk before then, though."

I stood up and tossed Carioca to Lily. She held him up and rubbed her nose against his as he wriggled to escape.

"I won't be able to see you before Saturday anyway. I'll be closeted with Mordecai playing chess until the tournament begins again next week. But in case we get any news about Fiske's death or . . . or Saul . . . how will I reach you?"

"I don't know what my address will be. I think you should wire my office here and they'll forward the mail."

We agreed to that. I went downstairs, and the doorman got me a taxi. As my cab swept through the bitter black night, I tried to go over everything that had happened so far, to make some sense of it. But my mind was like a knotted skein of yarn, and my stomach had cold little lumps of fear. I rode in the quiet desperation of total panic to the front door of my apartment house.

Tossing some money to the taxi driver, I raced into the building and through the lobby. I frantically pushed the elevator button. Suddenly I felt a tap on my shoulder. I nearly jumped three feet in the air.

It was the front desk man, holding my mail in his hand.

"I'm sorry if I startled you, Miss Velis," he said apologetically. "I didn't want you to forget your mail. I understand you'll be leaving us this weekend?"

"Yes, I've given the manager the address of my office. You can forward all my mail there after Friday."

"Very good," he said, and bade me good night.

I didn't go directly to my apartment. I pushed the button for the roof. No one but the building residents knew about the storm door that led to the broad, tiled expanse of terrace that overlooked all of Manhattan. There below me, as far as I could see, lay the sparkling lights of the city I was soon to leave. The air was clean and crisp. I could see the Empire State and Chrysler buildings shimmering in the distance.

I stayed up there for about ten minutes until I felt I had my stomach and my nerves under control. Then I took the elevator back down to my floor.

The single hair I'd left on the door was unbroken, so no one had been inside. But when I'd unlocked all the bolts and stepped into the hallway, I knew something was wrong. I'd not yet switched on the hall lights, but from the main room at the end of the hall a faint light was glowing. I never left the lights on when I went out.

I flicked on the hall lights, took a deep breath, and walked slowly down the hallway. Across the room on the piano was a small cone-shaped lamp that I used for reading music. It had been flipped to shine on the ornate mirror above the piano. Even from twenty-five feet away, I could see what the lamp illuminated. On the mirror was a note.

I moved in a daze across the room, picking my way through the jungle. I kept thinking I heard rustling behind the trees. The little light glowed like a beacon, drawing me to the mirror. I made my way around the massive piano and stood before the note. I could feel the same familiar chill pass down my spine as I read it.

> I have warned you but you
> will not listen. When you
> meet with danger,
> you should not hide your head
> in the sand—there is a lot of sand in
> Algeria.

I stood there for a long time looking at the note. Even had the little Knight at the bottom not given me a hint, I recognized the handwriting. It was Solarin's.

But how had he entered my apartment without disturbing the booby trap? Could he scale an eleven-story wall and come through the window?

I racked my brain trying to make sense of the whole thing. What did Solarin want of me? Why was he willing to take such risks as breaking into my apartment just to communicate with me? He'd gone out of his way twice to speak with me, to warn me, each time only shortly before someone was killed. But what did it have to do with me? Moreover, if I was in danger, what did he expect me to *do* about it?

I went back down the hall and locked my door again, putting on the chain. Then I went through the apartment, checking behind the trees, in the closets and butler pantry, to make certain I was alone. I tossed my mail on the floor, pulled down the Murphy bed, and sat on the edge as I removed my shoes and stockings. It was then that I noticed it.

Across the room, still glowing in the soft lamplight, was the note. But the lamp had not been trained precisely on the center of the note. It shone on one side only. I stood up again, stockings in hand, and went back to look at it. The light was carefully pointed at one side of the note—the left side—so that it shone on the first word of each line only. And the first words combined to form a new sentence:

I will meet you in Algeria.

At two o'clock in the morning I was lying in bed staring at the ceiling. I couldn't shut my eyes. My brain was still ticking away like a computer. There was something wrong, something missing. There were many pieces to a puzzle, but I couldn't seem to put them together. Yet I was certain they would fit somehow. I ran over it again for the thousandth time.

The fortune-teller had warned me I was in danger. Solarin had warned me I was in danger. The fortune-teller had left an encrypted message in her prophecy. Solarin had left a hidden message in his note to me. Were the fortune-teller and Solarin somehow connected?

There was one thing I'd overlooked because it hadn't made sense. The fortune-teller's encrypted message had read "*J'adoube* CV." As Nim had pointed out, it seemed she wanted to contact me. If this were true, why hadn't I heard from her since? Three months had passed, and she had disappeared off the map.

I dragged myself out of bed and turned the lights back on. Since I couldn't sleep, I might as well try to figure the damned thing out. I went to the closet and fumbled about until I found the cocktail napkin and the folded piece of paper where Nim had written the poem in iambic lines. I walked to the butler

pantry and poured myself a stiff shot of brandy. Then I plopped down in a pile
of pillows on the floor.

Pulling a pencil out of a nearby jar, I started counting off letters and circling
them as Nim had shown me. If the bloody woman wanted so much to communicate with me, maybe she already *had*. Maybe there was something else hidden
in this prophecy. Something I hadn't seen before.

Since the first letter of each line had yielded a message, I tried writing down
the last letter of each line. Unfortunately that spelled "yrereyeer."

That didn't strike me as symbolically significant, so I tried all the first letters
of the second words in each line, the third words, and so forth. I got things like
"aargtobaf," and "tcaitwwsi." This set my teeth on edge. I tried the first letter
of the first sentence and the second letter of the second and got "jrngleher."
Nothing seemed to work. I took a slug of brandy and kept plodding away like
this for an hour.

It was nearly three-thirty in the morning when it occurred to me to try odd
and even numbers. Taking the odd-numbered letters of each sentence, I finally
hit pay dirt. Or at least I hit something that looked like a word. The first letter
of the first sentence, the third letter of the next, then the fifth, the seventh, and
I got: "JEREMIAHH." Not only a word, but a name. I dragged myself around
the room, plowing through piles, until I turned up a musty old Gideon Bible.
I flipped through the directory until I found Jeremiah, the twenty-fourth book
of the Old Testament. But my message said "Jeremiah-H." What was the "H"
for? I thought about that for a moment until I realized that "H" is the eighth
letter of the alphabet. So what?

Then I noticed that the *eighth* sentence of the poem read "Continue a search
for a thirty-three and three." I was damned if that didn't sound like chapter and
verse.

I looked up Jeremiah 33:3. Bingo.

Call unto me and I will answer thee, and shew thee great and mighty
things, which thou knowest not.

So I'd been right. There had been another message hidden in the prophecy.
The only problem was, this message was fairly useless to me as things stood.
If the old dirt bag had wanted to "shew" me things that were great and mighty,
then where the hell *were* these things? I knewest not.

It was refreshing to learn that a person who'd never yet been able to complete
a *New York Times* crossword puzzle could excel in decrypting fortunes from
a cocktail napkin. On the other hand, I was getting pretty frustrated. While each
layer I unveiled seemed to have some meaning, in the sense that it was English

and contained a message, the messages didn't seem to lead anywhere. Except to other messages.

I sighed, looked at the goddamned poem, slugged down the rest of my brandy, and decided to start again. Whatever it was, it *had* to be hidden in the poem. That was the only place it could be.

It was five A.M. when I got it through my thick head that perhaps I shouldn't be looking for letters any longer. Perhaps the message was spelled out in words, as it had been in Solarin's note to me. And just as the idea struck me—perhaps the third glass of brandy helped—my eyes fell upon the first sentence of the prophecy.

Just as these lines that merge to form a key . . .

When the fortune-teller had spoken those words, she'd been looking at the lines of my hand. But what if the lines of the poem *itself* formed the key to the message?

I picked up the poem for one last pass. Where was the key? I'd decided by now to take these cryptic clues in their literal sense. She'd said the lines *themselves* formed a key, just as the rhyming pattern, when added up, had produced "666," the number of the Beast.

It's hard to claim I had a sudden flash of insight, when I'd been studying the damned thing for five hours, but that's what it felt like. I knew, with an assurance that belied my lack of sleep and alcohol-to-blood ratio, that I had found the answer.

The rhyming pattern of the poem not only added up to 666. *It was the key to the hidden message.* My copy of the poem was so scribbled over by now, that it looked like a map of intergalactic relationships in the universe. Flipping the page over to write on the back, I copied out the poem and rhyming pattern again. The pattern had been 1-2-3, 2-3-1, 3-1-2. I selected the word from each sentence that corresponded to that number. The message said: JUST-AS-ANOTHER-GAME-THIS-BATTLE-WILL-CONTINUE-FOREVER.

And I knew, with the unshakable confidence my drunken stupor afforded, exactly what that meant. Hadn't Solarin told me we were playing a game of chess? But the fortune-teller had warned me three months earlier.

J'adoube. I touch thee. I adjust thee, Catherine Velis. Call unto me and I will answer thee, and shew thee great and mighty things which thou knowest not. For there is a battle going on, and you are a pawn in the game. A piece on the chessboard of Life.

I smiled, stretched my legs, and reached for the phone. Though I couldn't contact Nim, I could leave a message on his computer. Nim was a master of encryption, perhaps the world's foremost authority. He'd lectured and written books on the subject, hadn't he? No *wonder* he'd grabbed that note out of my hand when I'd first noticed the rhyming pattern. He'd guessed at once that it was a key. But the bastard had waited until I figured it out for myself. I dialed the number and left my farewell message:

A pawn advances to Algiers.

Then, as the sky was growing light outside, I decided to go to bed. I didn't want to think anymore, and my brain agreed with me. I was kicking the mail away that I'd thrown in a pile on the floor, when I noticed an envelope that had no stamp and no address. It had been hand-delivered, and I didn't recognize the complex, loopy writing that spelled out my name. I picked it up and slashed it open. Inside was a large card on heavy paper. I sat down on the bed to read it.

My dear Catherine,

I enjoyed our brief meeting. I will not be able to speak with you prior to your departure, as I am leaving the city myself for a few weeks.

Based upon our chat, I've decided to send Lily to join you in Algiers. Two heads are better than one, when it comes to problem-solving. Wouldn't you agree?

By the way, I forgot to ask . . . did you enjoy your meeting with my friend the fortune-teller? She sends you a greeting: Welcome to the Game.

With fondest regards,
Mordecai Rad

THE MIDDLE GAME

Here and there in the ancient literatures we encounter legends of wise and mysterious games that were conceived and played by scholars, monks, or the courtiers of cultured princes. These might take the form of chess games in which the pieces and squares had secret meanings in addition to their usual functions.

—The Glass Bead Game
Hermann Hesse

I play the game for the game's own sake.

—*Sherlock Holmes*

I t was one of those lavender-blue twilights shimmering with the unfolding of spring. The sky itself seemed to hum as my plane circled through the thin mist rising off the Mediterranean coast. Beneath me lay Algiers.

"Al-Djezair Beida," they called it. The White Isle. It seemed to have risen dripping from the sea like a fairyland city, a mirage. The seven fabled peaks were packed with clustered white buildings tumbling over each other like the decorative frosting on a wedding cake. Even the trees had mystical, exotic shapes and colors not of this world.

Here was the white city that lit the way into the Dark Continent. Down there, below the gleaming facade, lay the scattered pieces of the mystery I'd traveled halfway around the globe to discover. As my plane dipped over the water, I felt I was about to land, not in Algiers, but on the first square: the square that would lead me into the very heart of the game.

The airport at Dar-el-Beida (the White Palace) is just at the edge of Algiers, its short runway lapped by the Mediterranean Sea.

Before the flat two-story building, a row of palm trees waved like long feathers in the cool musty breeze as we stepped off the plane. The scent of night-blooming jasmine pervaded the air. Across the front of the low glass airport had been tacked a hand-painted ribbon: these curlicues, dots, and dashes that resembled Japanese brush painting were my first glimpse of classical Arabic. Beneath the sculptured letters, the printed words translated: *"Bienvenue en Algérie."*

Our luggage had been piled on the pavement so we could identify our pieces. A porter put mine on the metal cart as I followed the stream of passengers into the airport.

Joining the Immigrations line, I thought how far I'd come since that night barely a week ago when I'd stayed up to unravel the fortune-teller's prophecy. And I'd come the distance alone.

It had not been by choice. That very first morning after deciphering her poem, I'd tried frantically to contact everyone among my motley crew of friends, but there seemed to be a conspiracy of silence. When I'd called Harry's apartment, Valerie the maid told me that Lily and Mordecai were closeted somewhere studying the mysteries of chess. Harry had left town to convey Saul's body to obscure relatives he'd located in Ohio or Oklahoma—somewhere in the Interior. Llewellyn and Blanche, taking advantage of Harry's absence, had jogged off to London on an antique-buying spree.

Nim was still cloistered, so to speak, and returning none of my urgent phone messages. But on Saturday morning, as I was wrestling with the movers who were doing their damnedest to gift-wrap my garbage, Boswell had appeared at my apartment door with a box in his hands from "the charming gentleman who was here the other evening."

The box was full of books, with a note attached that read "Pray for guidance, and wash behind your ears." It was signed "the Sisters of Mercy." I'd stuffed the whole pile into my shoulder travel bag and forgotten them. How was I to know that those books, ticking away in my satchel like a time bomb, would have so great an impact upon the events that were soon to follow? But Nim knew. Perhaps he'd always known. Even before he'd placed his hands on my shoulders and said, *"J'adoube."*

Included in the eclectic mix of musty old paperbacks was *The Legend of Charlemagne*, as well as books on chess, magic squares, and mathematical pursuits of every possible flavor and variety. There was also a boring book on stock market projection called *The Fibonacci Numbers*, written by, of all people, Dr. Ladislaus Nim.

It's hard to claim that I became an expert on chess in the six-hour plane trip from New York to Paris, but I did learn a lot about the Montglane Service and the role it had played in the collapse of Charlemagne's empire. Though never mentioned by name, this chess service was involved in the deaths of no fewer than half a dozen kings, princes, and assorted courtiers, all smashed over the head with the pieces "of massy gold." Wars were started over some of these homicides, and upon Charlemagne's death, his own sons had torn the Frankish Empire to shreds in a battle for possession of the mysterious chess service. Nim had printed a note in the margin there: "Chess—the most dangerous game."

I had learned a little about chess on my own in the prior week, even before reading the chess books he'd included: enough to know the difference between tactics and strategy. Tactics were short-term moves to position yourself. But strategy was how you won the game. This information was to come in quite handy by the time I reached Paris.

The partnership of Fulbright Cone had lost none of its patina of time-tested treachery and corruption with my crossing the Atlantic. The language of the game they were playing might have changed, but the moves were still the same. From the moment I arrived at the Paris office, they'd announced the whole deal might be off. They had failed, it seemed, to get a signed contract from the boys at OPEC.

Apparently they'd been kept waiting for days at various ministries in Algiers, jetting back and forth from Paris at great expense and coming up empty-handed with every trip.

Now the senior partner, Jean Philippe Petard, planned to get involved. Cautioning me to do nothing at all until he arrived in Algiers at the week's end, Petard assured me that the French partnership would surely find *something* for me to do once the dust had settled. His tone implied some light typing, floors and windows, and perhaps a few toilets to clean might be in order. But I had other plans.

The French partnership might not have a signed contract with the client, but *I* had a plane ticket to Algiers and a week to spend down there with no immediate supervision.

As I walked out of the Paris office of Fulbright Cone and hailed a cab back to Orly, I decided that Nim had been right about sharpening up my killer instincts. I'd been using tactics for close maneuvers too long, and I couldn't see the board for the pieces. Could it be time to remove those pieces that were cluttering up the view?

I'd been standing in the Immigrations line at Dar-el-Beida for nearly half an hour before my turn came. We were crawling like ants through the narrow lanes with their metal guardrails before reaching the gates to passport control.

At last I was facing the glass booth. The passport officer was perusing my Algerian visa, with its official little red-and-white sticker and the big sprawling signature nearly covering the blue page. He looked at it for quite a while before glancing up at me with what seemed a strange expression.

"You are traveling alone," he said in French. It was not a question. "You have a visa for *affaires*, madame. For whom will you be working?" (*Affaires* meant "business." How like the French to kill two birds with one stone.)

"I'll be working for OPEC," I started to explain in my poor French. But before I could continue, he stamped "Dar-el-Beida" all over my visa in haste. He motioned with a nod of his head to a porter who'd been lolling against a nearby wall. The porter came over as the Immigrations officer flipped quickly through the rest of my visa and slid the Customs declaration through the slot to me.

"OPEC," said the officer. "Very well, madame. Just write on this form any gold or money you are carrying. . . ."

As I was completing the form, I noticed he mumbled something to the porter, jerking his head toward me. The porter glanced at me, nodded, and turned away.

"And your place of residence during your stay?" asked the officer as I slid my completed declaration back under the glass partition.

"The Hotel El Riadh," I replied. The porter had walked to the back of the Immigrations aisles and, glancing once at me over his shoulder, was now knocking on the smoked-glass door of the solitary office that stood against the back wall. The door opened, and a burly man came out. They were both looking at me now; it was *not* my imagination. And the burly guy had a gun on his hip.

"Your papers are in order, madame," the Immigrations officer was telling me calmly. "You may proceed now to Customs."

I mumbled my thanks, picked up my papers, and passed through the narrow aisle toward a sign that read "Douanier." From afar, I saw my luggage stacked on a stopped conveyor belt. But just as I headed toward the place, the porter who'd been eyeing me came strolling over.

"Pardon, madame," he said in a soft, polite voice that no one else could hear. "Would you come with me?" He motioned to the smoked-glass door of the office. The burly man was still standing at the door, fondling the gun at his hip. My stomach slid up into my throat.

"Certainly not!" I told him loudly and in English. I turned back to my luggage and tried to ignore him.

"I'm afraid I must insist," the porter said, placing a firm hand on my arm. I tried to remind myself that in business circles I was known for nerves of stainless steel. But I could feel the panic rising.

"I don't understand the problem," I said, this time in French, as I removed his hand from my arm.

"Pas de problème," he said quietly, never taking his eyes from mine. "The *chef du sécurité* would like to ask you a few questions, that is all. This procedure will take merely a moment. Your baggages will be perfectly safe. I myself shall attend them."

It wasn't my baggage I was worried about. I was reluctant to leave the brightly lighted floor of the Douanier to enter an unmarked office guarded by a man with a gun. But I seemed to have little choice. He escorted me to the office, where the gunman stepped aside to let me enter.

It was a tiny room, barely large enough to hold the metal desk and two chairs that were set up facing it. The man behind the desk rose to greet me as I entered.

He was about thirty years old, well muscled, tanned, and handsome. He moved around the desk like a cat, muscles rippling against the lean lines of his impeccably tailored charcoal business suit. With his thick black hair swept back from the forehead, olive skin, chiseled nose, and full mouth, he might have passed for an Italian gigolo or a French film star.

"That will be all, Achmet," he said in a silky voice to the armed thug still holding the door behind me. Achmet withdrew, shutting the door softly after himself.

"Mademoiselle Velis, I believe," said my host, motioning me to take a seat opposite his desk. "I've been expecting you."

"I beg your pardon?" I remained standing and looked him in the eye.

"I'm sorry, I don't mean to be mysterious." He smiled. "My office reviews all visas about to be issued. We don't have many *women* applying for a business visa; in fact, you may be the first. I must confess, I was curious to meet such a woman."

"Well, now that you've satisfied your curiosity," I said, turning back toward the door.

"My dear mademoiselle," he said, anticipating my thought of escape, "please *do* have a seat. I'm really not an ogre, I won't eat you. I am the head of security here. People call me Sharrif." He flashed his white teeth in a dazzling smile as I turned back and reluctantly took the thrice-proffered chair opposite him. "May I mention that I find your safari outfit *most* becoming? Not only chic, but appropriate for a country with two thousand miles of desert. Do you plan to visit the Sahara during your stay, mademoiselle?" he added casually, as he took his own seat behind the desk.

"I'll go wherever my client sends me," I told him.

"Ah, yes, your client," the slick one rambled on. "Dr. Kader: Emile Kamel Kader, the petroleum minister. An old friend. You must give him my warmest regards. It was he who sponsored your visa, as I recall. May I see your passport, please?" His hand was already out for it, and I caught a flash of gold cuff link that he must have seized at Customs. Not many airport officials make that kind of dough.

"This is merely a formality. We select people at random from each flight for a more thorough search than that conducted at Customs. It might not happen to you again in twenty trips or a hundred. . . ."

"In *my* country," I told him, "people are only hauled into private offices at airports if they're suspected of smuggling something." I was pushing my luck, and I knew it. But I was not deceived by the glitz of his chameleonlike story, his gold cuff links, or his movie-star teeth. I was the only person to be called in and searched from my entire airplane. And I'd seen the faces of the airport officials as they whispered about me from afar. It was me they were after all right. And not only because they were curious about my being a woman on business in a Moslem country.

"Ah," he said, "you fear I believe you to be a smuggler? Unhappily for me, it is the state law that only women officials may search a lady traveler for contraband! No, it is only your passport I wish to see—at least for *now*."

He pored over it with great interest. "I'd *never* have guessed your age. You look to be no more than eighteen, yet I see from your passport you've just had a birthday. Twenty-four, in fact. But how very interesting—did you know that your birthday, April fourth, is an Islamic holy day?"

At that moment, the words of the fortune-teller suddenly leapt to mind. When she'd told me not to mention my birthday, I'd forgotten about things like passports and driver's licenses.

"I hope I haven't alarmed you," he added, looking at me strangely.

"Not at all," I replied casually. "Now if you're finished . . ."

"Perhaps you'd be interested to know more," he went on, smooth as a cat, as he reached forward and pulled my handbag across the table. No doubt just another "formality," but I was becoming extremely uncomfortable. *You are in danger,* said a voice deep inside me. *Trust no one, look always over your shoulder, for it is written: On the fourth day of the fourth month—then will come the Eight.*

"April fourth," Sharrif was saying to himself as he removed tubes of lipstick, a comb, and a brush from my shoulder bag and placed them carefully on his desk like the labeled evidence for a murder trial. "In al-Islam, we call this 'the Day of Healing.' We have two ways of counting time: the Islamic year, which is a lunar year, and the solar year, which begins on March twenty-first of the Western calendar. There are many traditions for each.

"When the solar year begins," he went on, dragging notebooks, pens, and pencils out of my bag and classifying them in rows, "Muhammad has told us we must recite from the Qu'ran ten times each day for the first week. The second week, we must rise each day, blow our breath upon a bowl of water, and drink from that same bowl, for seven days. *Then*—on the *eighth* day—" Sharrif looked up at me suddenly, as if he expected to catch me picking my nose. He smiled casually, and so, I hoped, did I.

"That is, the eighth day of the second week of this magical month, when all Muhammad's rituals have been fulfilled, whatever the person's ills, he will assuredly be healed. This would be April fourth. Persons born upon this day are believed to have great powers to heal others—almost as if . . . But of course, as a Westerner, you can scarcely be interested in such superstitions."

Was it only my imagination that he was watching me as a cat does a mouse? I was adjusting my facial expression when he let out a little cry that made me jump.

"Ah!" he said, and with a flick of the wrist tossed something across the table so that it came to rest just in front of me. "I see that you are interested in chess!"

It was Lily's little pegboard chess set that had remained forgotten in a corner of my shoulder bag. And Sharrif was pulling out all the books and piling them in a stack on the desk as he carefully read the titles.

"Chess—mathematical games—Ah. *The Fibonacci Numbers*!" he cried, wearing that smile that made me think he had something on me. He was tapping the boring book that Nim had written. "So you're interested in mathematics?" he said, looking at me intently.

"Not really," I said, on my feet and trying to stuff my belongings back into my shoulder bag as Sharrif handed me my possessions one by one. It was hard to imagine how one skinny girl could carry so much useless crap halfway around the world. But there it was.

"What exactly do you know about the Fibonacci numbers?" he asked as I continued loading my bag.

"They're used for stock market projection," I muttered. "The Eliott Wave theorists project bull and bear markets with them—a theory developed by a guy named R. N. Eliott in the thirties—"

"Then you're not acquainted with the author?" interrupted Sharrif. I felt my skin go slightly green as I glanced up, my hand frozen over the book.

"Leonardo Fibonacci, I mean," Sharrif added, looking at me seriously. "An Italian born in Pisa in the twelfth century, but educated here—in Algiers. He was a brilliant scholar of the mathematics of the famous Moor al-Kwarizmi, after whom the algorithm is named. Fibonacci introduced Arabic numerals into Europe, which replaced the old Roman numbers. . . ."

Damn. I should have *known* that Nim wouldn't give me a book just for idle reading, even if he wrote it himself. Now I wished I'd really known what was in it before Sharrif's little inquisition began. A light bulb was going off in my head, but I couldn't read the Morse code it was flashing.

Hadn't Nim pressed me to learn about magic squares? Hadn't Solarin developed a formula for the Knight's Tour? Weren't the fortune-teller's prophecies riddled with numbers? So why was I such a lunkhead that I couldn't put two and two together?

It was a Moor, I recalled, who'd given the Montglane Service to Charlemagne in the first place. I was no genius at math, but I'd worked around computers long enough to learn that the Moors had introduced nearly every important mathematical discovery into Europe, ever since they'd first hit Seville in the eighth century. The quest for this fabled chess set obviously had something to do with math—but what? Sharrif had told me more than I'd told *him*, but I couldn't piece it together. Prying the last book loose from his fingers, I deposited it in my leather pouch.

"As you're going to be in Algeria for a year," he said, "perhaps we could have a game of chess sometime. I myself was once a contender for the Persian junior title. . . ."

"Here's a Western expression you might enjoy learning," I told him over my shoulder as I headed for the door. "Don't call us—we'll call you."

I opened the door. Achmet the thug glanced at me in surprise, then at Sharrif, who was only just rising from the chair behind his desk. I slammed the door behind me, and the glass shuddered. I didn't look back.

I made my way swiftly to Customs. Opening my bags for the Douanier, I could see from his indifference, and the slight disarray of the contents, that he'd seen them before. He shut them up and marked them with chalk.

The rest of the airport was nearly deserted by now, but luckily the currency exchange was still open. After changing some money, I flagged down a porter and went outside for a cab. The heaviness of the balmy air struck me again. The dark scent of jasmine pervaded everything.

"The Hotel El Riadh," I told the driver as I hopped in, and we sped off along the amber-lighted boulevard leading toward Algiers.

The driver's face, old and gnarled as a redwood burl, peered at me inquisitively from the rearview mirror. "Has madame been before in Algiers?" he asked. "If not, may I give her a brief tour of the city for a price of one hundred dinars? This would include the journey to El Riadh, of course."

El Riadh was over thirty kilometers the other side of Algiers, and a hundred dinars was only twenty-five dollars, so I agreed. It could cost more than that to get to Kennedy Airport from midtown Manhattan at rush hour.

We were passing along the main boulevard. A stately row of fat date palms ranged on one side. High arched colonial colonnades fronted the buildings on the other, facing the port of Algiers. You could smell the dank, salty flavor of the sea.

At the center of the port, across from the stately Hotel Aletti, we branched off onto a steep, sweeping boulevard that ascended the hill. As the street rose, the buildings seemed to become larger and to close in about us at the same time. Imposing, whitewashed colonial structures from before the war, looming in the darkness like ghosts that whispered together high above our heads. They were so close they folded out the starry night from view.

The air was completely dark now and silent. A few sparse streetlights cast the shadows of twisted trees against the stark white walls as the road grew ever narrower and steeper, winding its way into the very heart of Al-Djezair. The Isle.

Halfway up the hill, the pavement widened slightly and flattened into a circular plaza with a leafy fountain at the center, which seemed to mark the central point of this vertical city. Coming around the curve, I could see the twisted maze of streets that formed the upper tier of the city. As we swept through the curve, the headlights of a car that had been behind us stayed with us, as my taxi's weak beams penetrated the suffocating darkness of the upper city.

"Someone is following us," I said to the driver.

"Yes, madame." He glanced back at me in the rearview mirror, smiling nervously. His gold front teeth flashed briefly in the reflection of the pursuing headlights. "They have been following us since the airport. You are perhaps a spy?"

"Don't be ridiculous."

"You see, the car that follows us is the special car of the *chef du sécurité*."

"The head of security? He interviewed me at the airport. Sharrif."

"The very man," said my driver, becoming visibly more nervous by the minute. Our car was now at the top of the city, and the road narrowed into a fine ribbon that ran dangerously along the ledge of the steep cliff overlooking Algiers. My driver looked down as the pursuing car, long and black, swung around the curve just beneath us.

The entire city was spread out over the corrugated hills, a maze of tortuously twisted streets that ran like fingers of lava down to the crescent of lights that marked out the port. Ships glittered in the black waters of the bay beyond, floating up and down on the tideless sea.

The driver was hitting the gas. As our car swung around the next bend, Algiers disappeared completely, and we were swallowed in darkness. Soon the road slid down into a black hollow, a thick and impenetrable forest where the heavy smell of pine nearly eradicated the dank saltiness of the sea. Not even the thin, watery moonlight could sift through the massive interlacings of the trees.

"There is little we can do now," said my driver, still glancing behind us, checking his mirrors as he tore through the deserted forest. I wished he would keep his eyes on the road.

"We are now in the area called 'Les Pins.' There is nothing between us and the El Riadh but pines. This is what you call the shortcut." The road through the pines kept going up and down hills like a roller coaster. As the driver got up more steam, I thought I felt the taxi actually leave the ground a few times, coming over the top of a sharp rise. You couldn't see a damned thing.

"I've got plenty of time," I told him, hanging on to the armrest so my head wouldn't smash against the ceiling. "Why don't you slow down?" The lights came up behind us after every hill.

"This man Sharrif," said the driver, his voice trembling. "Do you know for what purpose he interrogated you at the airport?"

"He did *not* interrogate me," I said somewhat defensively. "He only wanted to ask me a few questions. There aren't many women who come to Algiers on business, after all." Even to myself, my laugh sounded a little forced. "Immigrations can question whoever they like, can't they?"

"Madame," said the driver, shaking his head and looking at me oddly in the mirror, as now and then the lights of the other car caught in his eyes, "this man Sharrif does not work for immigrations. His job is not to welcome people to Algiers. He does not have you followed to make certain you arrive home safely." He permitted himself this small joke, though his voice was still shaking. "His job is somewhat more important than that."

"Really?" I said, surprised.

"He did not tell you," said my driver, still watching his mirror with a frightened eye. "This man Sharrif, he is the head of the secret police."

The secret police, as described by my driver, sounded like a mix of the FBI, the CIA, the KGB, and the Gestapo. The driver seemed more than relieved by the time we pulled up in front of the Hotel El Riadh, a low, sleek building surrounded by thick foliage with a small free-form pool and fountain at the entrance. Tucked away in a grove of trees near the edge of the sea, its long drive and sculptural entrance twinkled with lights.

As I stepped out of the cab, I saw the headlights of the other car curve away and slip back into the dark forest beyond. My driver's gnarled old hands were shaking as he picked up my bags and started to carry them into the hotel.

I followed him inside and paid him. When he left I gave my name to the desk clerk. The clock behind the desk said a quarter to ten.

"I am desolate, madame," said the concierge. "I have no reservation for you. And unhappily, we are fully booked." He smiled and shrugged, then turned his back on me and went about his paperwork. Just what I needed at this hour. I'd noticed there wasn't exactly a line of taxis lined up outside the isolated El Riadh, and jogging back to Algiers through the police-riddled pine forests with my luggage on my back was not my idea of fun.

"There must be some mistake," I told the concierge loudly. "My reservation here was confirmed over a week ago."

"It must have been another hotel," he said with that polite smile that seemed to be a national fixture. Damn if he didn't turn his back on me again.

It occurred to me there might be a lesson for the astute executette in all of this. Maybe this back-turning indifference was merely a prelude, a warm-up to the act of bartering, Arabic style. And maybe you were supposed to barter for *everything*: not just high-powered consulting contracts, but even a confirmed hotel reservation. I decided my theory was worth a try. I yanked a fifty-dinar note from my pocket and slapped it on the counter.

"*Would* you be so kind to keep my bags behind the desk? Sharrif, the *chef du sécurité*, is expecting to find me here—please tell him I'm in the lounge when he arrives." This was not a complete myth, I reasoned. Sharrif *would* expect to find me here, since his thugs had followed me to the very door. And the concierge would scarcely telephone a guy like Sharrif to check out his cocktail plans.

"Ah, please forgive me, madame," cried the concierge, glancing down quickly at his register and, I noted, pocketing the money with a deft movement. "I suddenly see that we *do* have a reservation in your name." He penciled it

in and looked up with the same charming smile. "Shall I have the porter take
your baggage to your room?"

"That would be very nice," I told him, handing the porter a few bills as he
came trotting up. "Meanwhile I'll have a look around. Please send my key to
the lounge when he's finished."

"Very good, madame," the concierge said, beaming.

Throwing my satchel over my shoulder, I made my way through the lobby
toward the lounge. Near the hotel entrance the lobby had been low-slung and
modern, but as I turned the corner it opened up into a vast space like an atrium.
Whitewashed walls curved in sculptural flights of fancy, soaring to the fifty-foot
domed ceiling. There were holes cut out that looked up into the starry sky.

Across the magnificent sweep of lobby, suspended about thirty feet up the
far wall, was the terrace lounge that seemed to float in space. From the lip of
the terrace plunged a waterfall that seemed to spring from nowhere. It tumbled
down, a wall of water breaking in spray here and there as it encountered jutting
stone slabs embedded in the back wall. At the bottom it was caught in a large
frothing pool set into the polished marble floor of the lobby.

At either side of the waterfall, open stairways rose from the lobby to the
lounge, twisting skyward like a double helix. I crossed the lobby and started
up the left stairway. Wild flowering trees grew through holes cut into the walls.
Beautifully colored woven tapis tossed over the stairwells tumbled down fifteen
feet to fall in lovely folds at the bottom.

The floors were of gleaming marble set in dazzling patterns of various hues.
Here and there were intimate seating arrangements with thick Persian carpets,
copper trays, leather ottomans, lavish fur rugs, and brass samovars for tea.
Though the lounge was large with sweeping plate-glass windows overlooking
the sea, it had a feeling of intimacy.

Sitting on a soft leather ottoman, I gave my order to a waiter, who recommended the local freshly brewed beer. The windows of the lounge were all open,
and a damp breeze blew across the high stone terrace outside. The sea lapped
softly, seeming to stroke my mind into submission. I felt relaxed for the first
time since I'd left New York.

The waiter brought my beer on a tray, already poured. Beside it was my
room key.

"Madame will find her room off the formal gardens," he told me, pointing
to a dark space beyond the terrace that I couldn't quite make out in the thin
moonlight. "One follows the maze of shrubbery to the moonflower tree, which
will have strongly scented blossoms. Room forty-four is just behind the tree.
It has a private entrance."

The beer tasted like flowers, not sweet but rather aromatic with a light woody
flavor. I ended up ordering another. As I was sipping it I thought about Sharrif's
strange line of questioning, then decided to dismiss all surmises until I'd had

more time to bone up on the subject I now realized Nim had *tried* to prepare me for. Instead I thought about my job. What strategy would I use when I went tomorrow morning, as I'd already planned, to visit the ministry? I remembered the problems the partnership of Fulbright Cone had encountered in trying to get our contract signed. It was an odd story.

The minister of industry and energy, a fellow named Abdelsalaam Belaid, had agreed to a meeting a week earlier. It was to be an official ceremony to sign the contract, so six partners had flown to Algiers at great expense, with a case of Dom Pérignon, only to discover upon their arrival at the ministry that the Minister Belaid was "out of the country on business." They reluctantly agreed to meet with his second in command instead, a chap named Emile Kamel Kader (the same Kader who'd approved my visa, as Sharrif had noticed).

While waiting in one of the interminable rows of anterooms until Kader was free to see them, they noticed a cluster of Japanese bankers coming down the corridor and stepping onto an elevator. And in their midst was none other than Minister Belaid: the one who was out of town on business.

The partners of Fulbright Cone were not used to being stood up. Especially not six of them at once, and certainly not so blatantly. They were prepared to complain of this to Emile Kamel Kader once they were admitted to his chambers. But when at last they were shown in, Kader was bouncing around the office in a pair of tennis shorts and a polo shirt, swishing a racket through the air.

"So sorry," he tells them, "but it's Monday. And on Mondays I always play a set with an old college chum. I couldn't disappoint him." And off he went, leaving six full partners of Fulbright Cone with their fingers in their ears.

I looked forward to meeting the chaps who could pull off a Mexican standoff like this with the partners of my illustrious firm. And I assumed it was yet another manifestation of the Arabic bartering methodology. But if six partners couldn't get a contract signed, how was I going to do any better?

I picked up my beer glass and wandered out onto the terrace. I gazed over the darkened garden that spread between the hotel and the sea, as the waiter had said, like a maze. There were crunchy white gravel paths separating beds of exotic cactus, succulents, and shrubbery, tropical and desert foliage jumbled all together.

At the garden's edge bordering the beach was a flat marble terrace with an enormous swimming pool, glittering like a turquoise jewel from lamps set beneath the water's surface. Separating the pool from the sea was a sculptured twist of curved white walls laced with oddly shaped arches through which you caught glimpses of the dim sandy beach beyond and the white waves rocking back and forth. At the edge of the cobweblike wall was a high brick tower with an onion dome at top, the kind from which the muezzin chants his call to evening prayer.

My eyes were drifting back toward the garden when I saw it. It was only a glimpse, a flicker of light from the pool, caught on the spokes and rim of one wheel of the bicycle. Then it vanished into the dark foliage.

I froze on the top step of the stairway, my eyes scanning the garden, the pool, and the beach beyond, my ear trained to pick up a sound. But I heard nothing. No movement. Suddenly someone placed a hand on my shoulder. I nearly jumped out of my skin.

"Excuse, madame," said my waiter, looking at me strangely. "The concierge wishes me to inform you that he received some mail for you this afternoon before your arrival. He'd overlooked to mention it earlier." He handed me a newspaper in a brown wrapper and an envelope that looked like a telex. "I wish you a pleasant evening," he said, and departed.

I looked down into the garden again. Perhaps my imagination was playing tricks on me. After all, even if I'd seen what I thought, people undoubtedly rode bicycles in Algeria as well as anywhere else.

I went back to the lighted lounge and sat down with my beer. I opened the telex, which said: "Read your newspaper. Section G5." It was unsigned, but when I unwrapped the paper I guessed who'd sent it. It was the Sunday edition of *The New York Times*. How had it reached me so quickly across so many miles? The Sisters of Mercy moved in strange and mysterious ways.

I turned to Section G5, the sports section. There was an article about the chess tournament:

CHESS TOURNEY CANCELED

GM SUICIDE QUESTIONED

The suicide last week of Grand Master Antony Fiske, which raised eyebrows in New York chess circles, has now provoked a serious inquiry by the New York Homicide Department. The City Coroner's Office, in a statement issued today, pronounced it impossible that the 67-year-old British GM died by his own hand. The death was due to a "snapped cervical column resulting from pressure exerted simultaneously upon the vertebra prominens (C7) and beneath the chin." There is no way a man can accomplish such a fracture "unless he stands behind his own back while breaking his neck," according to tournament physician Dr. Osgood, first to examine Fiske and to voice suspicions regarding the cause of death.

Russian GM Alexander Solarin was engaged in play with Fiske when he noticed the latter's "strange behavior." The Soviet embassy has requested diplomatic immunity for the controversial GM, who has again made waves by declining to accept it. (See article page A6.) Solarin was the last to see Fiske alive and has filed a statement with the police.

Tournament sponsor John Hermanold issued a press release explaining his decision to cancel the tournament. He today alleged that GM Fiske has had a long history of struggle with drug abuse and suggested police poll drug informants for possible leads to the unexplained homicide.

To assist in the investigation, tournament coordinators have supplied the police with names and addresses of the 63 persons, including judges and players, who were present at Sunday's closed session at the Metropolitan Club.

(See next Sunday's *Times* for an in-depth analysis: "Antony Fiske, Life of a GM.")

So the cat was out of the bag, and New York homicide had its nose to the ground. I was thrilled to learn *my* name was now in the hands of the Manhattan fuzz but relieved they could do nothing about it, short of extraditing me from North Africa. I wondered if Lily also had escaped the inquisition. Solarin, undoubtedly, had not. To learn more of his plight I flipped to page A6.

I was surprised to find a two-column "exclusive interview" under the provocative heading SOVIETS DENY INVOLVEMENT IN DEATH OF BRITISH GM. I whizzed through the gushy parts describing Solarin as "charismatic" and "mysterious," summarizing his checkered career and impromptu recall from Spain. The meat of the interview told me a lot more than I'd expected.

First, it was not Solarin who'd denied involvement. Until now I hadn't realized he'd been alone with Fiske in a lavatory only seconds before the murder. But the Soviets had realized it and had worked themselves into a lather, demanding diplomatic immunity and banging the proverbial shoe on the table.

Solarin had refused the immunity (no doubt he was familiar with the procedure) and stressed his desire to cooperate with local authorities. When questioned about Fiske's possible drug abuse, his comment made me laugh: "Perhaps John (Hermanold) has insider's information? The autopsy makes no mention of chemicals in the body." Suggesting Hermanold was either a liar or a dealer.

But when I'd read the description of the actual murder from Solarin's perspective, I was astounded. By his own testimony, there was practically no way anyone could have got inside the lavatory to kill Fiske except himself. There wasn't time, and there wasn't opportunity, since Solarin and the judges had blocked the only avenue of escape. Now I found myself wishing I'd gotten more detail on the physical layout of the premises before leaving New York. It was still possible if I could get hold of Nim. He could go over to the club and case the joint for me.

Meanwhile I was getting drowsy. My internal clock told me it was four in the afternoon New York time, and I hadn't slept in twenty-four hours. Picking up my room key and mail from the tray, I went back outside and down the steps into the garden. At the near wall I found the lusciously scented moonflower tree with its black-glazed foliage, rising above the garden. Its trumpet-shaped waxy flowers were like upside-down Easter lilies, opening by moonlight to exude their heavy, sensual aroma.

I went up the few steps to my room and unlocked the door. The lamps were already lit. It was a large room with floors of baked clay tile, stucco walls, and large French windows overlooking the sea beyond the moonflower tree. There was a thick woolly bedspread like the fleece of a lamb, a small carpet of the same material, and a few sparse furnishings.

In the bath were a large tub, a sink, a toilet, and a bidet. No shower. I turned on the tap, and reddish-colored water ran out. I let it run for several minutes, but it didn't change color or get any warmer. Great. Ice-cold rust would be fun to bathe in.

Leaving the water to run, I went back into the bedroom and opened the closet. My clothes were all unpacked and hanging neatly inside, with the bags stacked at the bottom. They seem to enjoy rifling through your belongings here, I thought. But I had nothing to hide that could be concealed in a piece of luggage. I'd learned my lesson with the briefcase.

Picking up the phone, I got hold of the hotel operator and gave him the number of Nim's computer in New York. He told me he'd call me back when he'd made the connection. I took off my clothes and went back to the bath, which was now about three inches deep in iron filings. With a sigh, I stepped into the dreadful mess and lowered myself down as gracefully as possible.

The phone was ringing as I was scraping the scummy soap off my body. Wrapping the threadbare towel around me, I slogged into the bedroom and picked up the receiver.

"I am desolate, madame," the operator told me, "but your number does not respond."

"How can they not respond?" I wanted to know. "It's the middle of the day in New York. This is a business number we're calling." Besides, Nim's computer was connected twenty-four hours a day.

"No, madame, it is the *city* that does not respond."

"The city? New York *City* doesn't answer?" They couldn't have wiped it off the map in the one day since I'd left. "You can't be serious. There are ten million people in New York!"

"Perhaps the operator has gone to bed, madame," he replied with calm reason. "Or, as it's so early, perhaps she has gone to dinner."

Bienvenue en Algérie, I thought. Thanking the operator for his time, I put the phone back into its cradle and went about the room turning off the lights. Then I went to the large French windows and threw them open to fill the room with the heavy scent of the moonflower tree.

I stood looking at the stars over the sea. From here they seemed as remote and cold as stones pasted on a cloth of midnight blue. And I felt my own remoteness, how far I was from the people and things I knew. How I had slipped, without even feeling it, into another world.

At last I went back inside and crawled between the damp linen sheets and drifted off to sleep, looking at the stars hanging over the coast of the African continent.

When I heard the first sound and opened my eyes to darkness, I thought I'd been dreaming. The luminous dial of the clock beside my bed said twenty minutes past midnight. But there was no clock in my apartment in New York. Slowly I realized where I was and turned to go back to sleep when I heard the sound again, just outside my window: the slow, metallic clicking of the gears of a bicycle.

Like an idiot, I'd left the windows open facing the sea. There, hidden within the tree and backlit by the moonlight, was the outline of a man, one hand on the handlebars of a bicycle. So it had not been my imagination!

My heart was beating with slow, heavy thuds as I dropped silently from the far side of my bed and half crawled through the shadows toward the windows to slam them shut. There were two problems, I realized quickly. First, I had no idea where the window locks were located (if they existed!), and second, I wasn't wearing any clothes. Damn. It was too late now to go prancing around the room looking for haberdashery. I reached the far wall, flattened myself against it, and tried to find the locks so I could slam the damned things shut.

Just then I heard the gravel crunch as the shadowy figure outside moved toward the window, propping his bicycle against the outer wall.

"I had no idea you slept in the nude," he whispered. There was no mistaking the soft Slavic accent. It was Solarin. I could feel the blush all over my body, radiating heat in the darkness. Bastard.

He was throwing his leg over the windowsill. Jesus Christ, he was coming inside! With a gasp, I fled for the bed, snatched off a sheet, and threw it around me.

"What the hell are *you* doing here?" I cried as he climbed into the room, pulled closed the windows, and locked them.

"Didn't you get my note?" he said, drawing the shutters and moving toward me in the darkness.

"Do you have any *idea* what time it is?" I was babbling as he came nearer. "How did you get here? Yesterday you were in New York. . . ."

"So were you," said Solarin, switching on the light. He looked me up and down with a grin and sat uninvited on the edge of my bed as if he owned the place. "But now we're both here. Alone. In this charming seaside setting. It's very romantic, don't you think?" His silvery green eyes glittered in the lamp-light.

"Romantic!" I fumed, wrapping up my sheet with dignity. "I don't want you near me! Every time I see you, someone gets bumped off. . . ."

"Be careful," he said, "the walls may have ears. Put some clothes on. I'll take you somewhere we can talk."

"You must be crazy," I told him. "I'm not setting one foot out of here, especially not with *you*! And another—" But he'd stood up and moved swiftly to me, grabbing the front of my sheet in one hand as if he were about to unwind me. He was looking down at me with a wry smile.

"Get dressed or I'll dress you myself," he said.

I felt the blood creeping up into my neck. I extricated myself and marched to the closet with as much dignity as possible, grabbing some clothes. Then I beat a hasty retreat to the bathroom to change. I was really fizzing as I slammed the door. That bastard thought he could appear out of nowhere, scare me out of sleep, and intimidate me into . . . If only he weren't so damned good-looking.

But what did he want? Why was he following me around like this—halfway around the world? And what, I wondered, was he doing with that bicycle?

I put on jeans and a floppy red cashmere sweater with my old frayed espadrilles. When I came out Solarin was sitting in the rumpled bedsheets playing chess with Lily's pegboard set, which he'd found, no doubt, by rifling through my belongings. He looked up and smiled.

"Who's winning?" I asked.

"I am," he said seriously. "I always win." He stood up, glancing once more at his position on the board, then went over to my closet and pulled out a jacket, holding it for me to slip on.

"You look very nice," he told me. "Not as attractive as your first outfit, but better suited for a midnight stroll along the beach."

"You're crazy if you think I'm taking a hike on a deserted beach with you."

"It's not far," he said, ignoring me. "I am taking you down the beach to a cabaret. They have mint tea and belly dancing. You'll love it, my dear. In Algeria, the women may be veiled, but the belly dancers are men!"

I shook my head and followed him out the door, which he locked with my confiscated key. He pocketed the key.

The moonlight was very bright, tipping Solarin's hair in silver and turning his eyes translucent. We walked out along the narrow sliver of beach and saw the glittering curve of coastline running down to Algiers. The waves lapped gently on the dark sand.

"Did you read the newspaper I sent you?" he asked.

"*You* sent it? But why?"

"I wanted you to know they'd discovered Fiske was murdered. Just as I told you."

"Fiske's death has nothing to do with me," I said, kicking the sand out of my shoes.

"It has everything to do with you, as I keep telling you. Did you think I came six thousand miles just to peek in your bedroom window?" he said a little impatiently. "I've told you you're in danger. My English isn't perfect, but I seem to speak it better than you understand."

"The only person I seem to be in danger of is *you*," I snapped. "How do I know *you* didn't kill Fiske? The last time I saw you, if you'll recall, you stole my briefcase and left me with the body of my friend's chauffeur. How do I know you didn't kill Saul, *too*, and leave me holding the bag?"

"I *did* kill Saul," Solarin said quietly. When I stopped dead in the sand, he looked at my face with curiosity. "Who else could have done it?"

I seemed to be speechless. My feet were rooted to the ground, and my blood had turned to Jell-O. I was strolling down a deserted beach with a murderer.

"You ought to thank me," Solarin was saying, "for taking your briefcase away with me. It could have implicated you in his death. I had bloody hell trying to get it back to you."

His attitude infuriated me. I kept seeing Saul's white face on that stone slab, and now I knew Solarin had put him there.

"Gee, thanks a lot," I said in fury. "What the hell do you *mean*, you killed Saul? How can you bring me out here and tell me you murdered an innocent man?"

"Keep your voice down," said Solarin, looking at me with steely eyes and grasping me by the arm. "Would you have preferred he kill me instead?"

"Saul?" I said with what I hoped was a snort of disdain. I shrugged his hand off my arm and started back up the beach, but Solarin grabbed me again and spun me around.

"Protecting you, as you Americans would say, is starting to be a genuine pain in the ass," he told me.

"I don't need any protection, thank you," I snapped back. "Least of all from murderers. So go back and tell whoever sent you—"

"Look," Solarin said fiercely. Then he had his hands on my shoulders. He was rubbing my shoulders with a motion like gnashing teeth, gazing up at the moon and taking a deep breath. Counting to ten, no doubt.

"Look," he said more calmly. "What if I told you that it was *Saul* who killed Fiske? That *I* was the only one who was in a position to know this, and that's why Saul came after *me*? *Then* would you hear me out?"

His pale green eyes searched mine, but I couldn't think. My mind was a muddle. Saul, a murderer? I closed my eyes and tried to think, but still nothing was coming out.

"Okay, shoot," I said—briefly regretting my choice of words. Solarin smiled down at me. Even by moonlight his smile was radiant.

"Then we'll have to walk," he said, keeping one hand on my shoulder and steering me back along the beach. "I can't think, speak, play chess—unless I'm able to move." We walked along in silence a few moments while he collected his thoughts.

"I think I'd better start back at the beginning," Solarin said at last. I merely nodded for him to continue.

"First, you should understand that I had no interest in that chess tournament where you saw me play. It was arranged by my government, as a sort of cover so I could come to New York where I had urgent business to conduct."

"What sort of business?" I asked.

"We'll get to that." We were strolling along the sand, kicking at the waves, when Solarin suddenly bent down and picked up a small, dark seashell that had lain half-buried in the sand. It glowed opalescent in the moonlight.

"Life exists everywhere," he mused, handing me the delicate shell. "Even at the very bottom of the sea. And everywhere it is extinguished through the stupidity of man."

"That clam didn't die by having its neck broken," I pointed out. "Are you some kind of professional killer? How can you be in a room with a man for five minutes and snuff him out?" I tossed the shell as far as I could out into the waves. Solarin sighed, and we went on walking.

"When I realized Fiske was cheating at the tournament," he went on at last, with some strain in his voice, "I wanted to know who'd put him up to it, and why."

So Lily had been right about that, I thought. But I said nothing.

"I guessed there were others behind it, so I stopped the game and followed him to the lavatory. He confessed this, and more. He told me *who* was behind it. And why."

"Who was it?"

"He didn't say it directly. He didn't know himself. But he told me the men who'd threatened him had known that *I* would be at the tournament. There was only one man who knew I was coming: the man my government had made these arrangements with. The tournament sponsor . . ."

"Hermanold!" I cried.

Solarin nodded and continued. "Fiske also told me that Hermanold, or his contacts, were after a formula I'd jokingly wagered against a game in Spain. I'd said if anyone beat me, I would give him a secret formula—and these fools, thinking the offer would still be open, decided to pit Fiske against me in a way where he couldn't lose. If anything went wrong with Fiske's play against me, I believe Hermanold had arranged to meet with him at the men's room of the Canadian Club, where they wouldn't be seen. . . ."

"But Hermanold didn't plan to meet him there at all," I guessed. The pieces were coming together now, but I still couldn't see the whole picture. "He'd arranged for someone *else* to meet Fiske, that's what you're saying. Someone whose presence wouldn't be missed among the people at the game?"

"Exactly," Solarin agreed. "But they didn't expect *me* to follow Fiske over there. I was just on his heels as he went inside. His murderer, lurking in the corridor outside, must have heard every word we said. By then it was too late merely to threaten Fiske. The game was up. He had to be dispatched, immediately."

"Termination with extreme prejudice," I said. I looked out at the dark sea and thought about it. It *was* possible, at least tactically. And I had a few pieces of my own that Solarin couldn't have known. For example, Hermanold had *not* expected Lily to come to the match, as she never attended them. But when Lily and I arrived at the club, Hermanold had pressed her to stay, becoming alarmed when she'd threatened to leave (with her car and chauffeur). His actions could have more than one explanation, if he was counting on Saul to carry out some job. But why Saul? . . . Maybe Saul knew more about chess than I'd thought. Maybe *he* had been sitting outside in the limousine, playing Fiske's moves for him via transmitter! When it came right down to it, how well had I *really* known Harry's chauffeur?

Now Solarin was filling me in on all the moves—how he'd first noticed the ring Fiske was wearing, how he'd followed him to the men's room across the way, how he'd learned of Fiske's contacts in England and what they were after. How he'd fled from the room when Fiske pulled the ring off, thinking it contained an explosive. Though he *knew* Hermanold was behind Fiske's arrival at the tournament, it could *not* have been Hermanold himself who'd murdered Fiske and removed the ring from the sink. He hadn't left the Metropolitan Club, as I was a witness.

"Saul wasn't in the limousine when Lily and I came back," I admitted reluctantly. "He *did* have the opportunity, though I've no idea what his motive might have been. . . . In fact, based upon your description of events, he'd have had *no* opportunity to get *out* of the Canadian Club and back to the car, since you and the judges blocked his only avenue of escape. That would explain his absence when Lily and I were looking for him." It would explain a little more than that, I thought. It would explain the bullets fired into our car!

If Solarin's story held water, and Hermanold had hired Saul to dispatch Fiske, he couldn't afford to have Lily and me *return* to the club hunting down our chauffeur! If he'd gone upstairs to the gaming room and seen us hesitating by the car, he'd have to do something to frighten us away!

"So it was *Hermanold* who went upstairs to the gaming room while it was empty, pulled out a gun, and shot at our car!" I cried, grasping Solarin by the arm. He was staring at me in amazement, wondering how I'd arrived at that conclusion.

"That would *also* explain why Hermanold told the press that Fiske was a drug addict," I added. "It would divert attention from himself and place it on some nameless drug dealer!" Solarin started to laugh.

"I know a fellow named Brodski who'd love to hire you," he said. "You've a mind designed for espionage. Now that you know everything *I* know, let's go have a drink."

At the far end of the long curve of beach, I could now make out a large tent set up in the sand, its shape outlined in strings of twinkling lights.

"*Not* so fast," I said, still holding him by the arm. "Assuming Saul *did* dispatch Fiske, that still leaves a few questions unanswered. What *was* that formula you had in Spain that you claim they wanted so much? What sort of business were you coming to New York for? And how did Saul wind up at the United Nations?"

The red-and-white-striped tent loomed large on the beach, maybe thirty feet high at midpole. Two big palm trees sat in brass pots at the entrance, and a long carpet of blue-and-gold scrolls ran out into the sand, covered by a floppy canvas marquee, facing the sea. We walked toward the entrance.

"I had a business meeting with a contact at the United Nations," Solarin said. "I hadn't realized Saul was tailing me—until *you* got between us."

"Then you *were* the man on the bicycle!" I cried. "But your clothes were—"

"I met with my contact," he interrupted. "She saw you were following me and Saul was just behind *you*. . . ." (So that old woman with the pigeons was his "business" contact!) "We stirred up those birds as camouflage," Solarin went on, "and I ducked down the steps behind the UN until you'd passed by me. Then I doubled back to go after Saul. He'd gone inside the building, I wasn't certain where. I pulled off my sweatsuit in the elevator going downstairs, for I had my other clothes on underneath. When I came back upstairs, I saw you going into the Meditation Room. I had no idea that Saul was already there— listening to every word we said."

"*In* the Meditation Room?" I cried. We were only yards from the tent now, dressed in jeans and sweaters and looking pretty tacky. But we strolled up to the front as if arriving by limousine at El Morocco.

"My dear," said Solarin, stroking my hair as Nim sometimes would do, "you are very naïve. Though *you* might not have understood the warnings I gave you, Saul most surely did. When you left, and he came out from behind that stone slab and attacked me, I knew he'd heard enough that *your* life would be in danger as well. I removed your briefcase so his cohorts would not know you'd been there. Later my business contact passed me a note at my hotel, telling me how to return it."

"But how did she know . . ." I began.

Solarin smiled and ruffled my hair again as the majordomo came forward to greet us. Solarin tipped him a hundred-dinar note. The majordomo and I both stared. In a country where fifty cents was a good tip, we'd obviously get the best table in the house.

"I'm a capitalist at heart," Solarin whispered in my ear as we followed the man through the tent flap and into the enormous cabaret.

The entire floor, as far as you could see, was covered in straw matting laid directly on the sand. Over these were large Persian carpets in rich colors scattered with fat mirrored pillows embroidered in brilliant designs. Separating the tables were clustered oases of thick palm trees in pots, mixed with fat clumps of peacock and ostrich plumes that shimmered in the soft light. Brass lanterns peppered with punched-out designs swung from the tent poles here and there, sprinkling odd light patterns across the twinkling mirrored pillows. It was like walking into a kaleidoscope.

At center was a big round stage with spotlights and a group of musicians playing wild, frenzied music of a sort I'd never heard before. There were long oval drums in brass, big bagpipes made of animal skins with the fur still hanging from them, flutes, clarinets, and chimes of every variety. The musicians danced about in a strange, circular stepping motion as they played.

Solarin and I were seated in a deep pile of cushions near a copper table just before the stage. The loudness of the music prevented me from asking him any questions, so I ruminated as he yelled out an order into the ear of a passing waiter.

What *was* this formula Hermanold wanted? Who was the woman with the pigeons, and how had she known where Solarin could find me to return my briefcase? What business did Solarin have in New York? If Saul was last seen on a stone slab, how had he wound up in the East River? And finally, what had all this to do with *me*?

Our drinks arrived just as the band took a break. Two big snifters of amaretto, warmed like brandies, were accompanied by a pot of tea with a long spout. The waiter poured the tea into shot glasses he held far away, balanced in tiny saucers. The steamy liquid flew through the air from spout to glass without spilling a drop. When the waiter left, Solarin toasted me with his glass of mint tea.

"To the game," he said with a mysterious smile.

My blood ran cold. "I have no idea what you're talking about," I lied, trying to remember what Nim had said about turning every attack to one's advantage. What did *he* know about the goddamned game?

"Of course you do, my dear," he said softly, picking up my snifter and touching the rim to my lip. "If you didn't, I wouldn't be sitting here having drinks with you."

As the amber liquid slid down my throat, a little trickled onto my chin. Solarin smiled and wiped it away with one finger, setting the glass back on the tray. He wasn't looking at me, but his head was close enough that I could hear every word he whispered.

"The most dangerous game imaginable," he murmured so softly no one could overhear us, "and we were chosen, each of us, for the parts we play. . . ."

"What do you *mean*, chosen?" I said, but before he could answer there was a crash of cymbals and kettledrums as the musicians trotted back onto the stage.

They were followed by a cadre of male dancers in cossacklike tunics of pale blue velvet, the pants tucked into high boots and blossoming out at the knee. Around their waists were heavy twisted cords with tassels at the ends that swung from their hips and bounced as they stepped about in a slow, exotic rhythm. The music rose, sinuous and undulating from clarinets and reed pipes, like the melody that brings a cobra in a stiff, swaying column from the basket.

"Do you like it?" Solarin was whispering in my ear. I nodded my head in affirmation.

"It's Kabyle music," he told me as the music wove patterns around us. "From the High Atlas Mountains that run through Algeria and Morocco. This dancer at center, you see his blond hair and pale eyes? And the nose like a hawk, the strong chin like the profile of an old Roman coin. These are the markings of the Kabyle; they are not anything like the Bedouin. . . ."

An older woman had risen from the audience and danced onto the stage, much to the amusement of the crowd, which coaxed her on with catcalls that must have meant the same in any language. Despite her dignified bearing, her long gray paneled robes and stiff linen veil, she moved with a light step and exuded a sensuality that was scarcely lost upon the male dancers. They danced about her, swinging their hips in and out toward hers so the tassels of their tunics touched her fleetingly, like a caress.

The audience was thrilled by this display, and ever more so when the dignified silver-haired woman danced sinuously toward the lead dancer, extracted some loose bills from the folds of her gown, and slipped them discreetly between the ropes of his belt quite near the groin. For the benefit of the audience, he rolled his eyes suggestively toward the ceiling with a wide grin.

People were on their feet, clapping wildly in time to the music, which escalated as the woman danced to the stage rim in circular steps. Just at the platform's edge, with the light behind her, her hands aloft clapping out a farewell flamenco, she turned our way . . . and I froze.

I glanced quickly at Solarin, who was watching me carefully. Then I leaped to my feet just as the woman, a dark silhouette against the silvery light, stepped from the stage and was swallowed into the jumbled darkness of mingled crowd, ostrich plumes, and palm fronds. The palms moved in the glittering flash of mirrored light.

Solarin's hand was like steel on my arm. He stood beside me, his body pressed the length of mine.

"Let me go," I hissed between gritted teeth, for a few people nearby were glancing at us casually. "I said let me go! Do you know who that *was*?"

"Do *you*?" he hissed back into my ear. "Stop attracting attention!" When he saw I was still struggling, he wrapped his arms around me in a deathlike embrace that might have appeared affectionate.

"You'll place us in danger," he was whispering in my ear, so close I could inhale the mingled scent of mint and almonds on his breath. "Just as you did by coming to that chess tournament—just as you did by following me to the United Nations. You've no idea what risk she's taken by coming here to see you. Nor what sort of reckless game you're playing with other people's lives."

"No, I *don't*!" I practically cried aloud, for the pressure of his grip was hurting me. The dancers were still whirling to the wild music onstage, which was washing over us in waves of rhythm. "But that was the fortune-teller, and I'm going to find her!"

"The fortune-teller?" said Solarin, looking puzzled but not loosening his grip. His eyes gazing into mine were as green as the dark, dark sea. Anyone watching us might have thought we were lovers.

"I don't know if she tells fortunes," he said, "but she certainly knows the future. It was she who summoned me to New York. It was she who had me follow you to Algiers. It was she who chose you—"

"Chose!" I said. "Chose me for what? I don't even *know* this woman!"

Solarin took me off guard by loosening his grip. The music swirled around us like a throbbing haze of sound as he grasped me by the wrist. Raising my hand, palm up, he pressed his lips to the soft place at the base of my palm where the blood beat closest to the skin's surface. For a second I felt hot blood coursing up, up through my veins. Then he lifted his head and looked into my eyes. My knees felt a little weak as I stared back at him.

"Look at it," he whispered, and I realized his finger was tracing a pattern at the base of my wrist. I looked down slowly, not wanting to take my eyes away from him just at that moment.

"Look at it," he whispered again as I stared at my wrist. There, at the base of my palm just where the large blue artery pulsed with blood, two lines twisted together in a snakelike embrace to form a figure eight.

"You've been chosen to unravel the formula," he said softly, his lips barely moving.

The formula! I held my breath as he looked deeply into my eyes. "What formula?" I heard myself whispering.

"The formula of the Eight . . ." he began, but just then he stiffened, his face freezing into a mask again as he glanced once, quickly, over my shoulder, his eyes focusing upon something behind me. He dropped my wrist and stepped back as I turned to look over my shoulder.

The music was still beating out its primal rhythm, the dancers whirling in exotic frenzy. Far across the stage, against the glittering glare of floodlights, a shadowy form was watching. As the spotlight trailed around the curve of stage following the dancers, it fell upon the dark figure for an instant. It was Sharrif!

He nodded to me once, politely, before the light passed on. I glanced quickly back at Solarin. Where he'd stood only a moment before, a palm frond swayed slowly in space.

THE ISLE

One day a mysterious colony quitted Spain and settled on the tongue of land on which it is to this day. It arrived from no one knew where, and spoke an unknown tongue. One of its chiefs, who understood Provençale, begged the commune of Marseilles to give them this bare and barren promontory on which, like the sailors of ancient times, they had run their boats ashore. . . .

—The Count of Monte Cristo
Alexander Dumas,
describing Corsica

I have a premonition that some day this little island will astonish Europe.

—The Social Contract
Jean-Jacques Rousseau,
describing Corsica

I t was just past midnight when Mireille left Talleyrand's house under cover of darkness and disappeared into the smothering velvet of the hot Parisian night.

Once he understood he could not overcome her resolution to leave, Talleyrand had provided her a strong, healthy horse from his stable and the small pouch of coins they'd been able to scrape together at that hour. Attired in the mismatched pieces of livery that Courtiade had assembled to serve as her disguise, her hair bound up in a queue and lightly powdered like a boy's, she'd departed unobtrusively through the service court and made her way through the darkened streets of Paris toward the barricades at the Bois de Boulogne—the road to Versailles.

She could not permit Talleyrand to accompany her. His aristocratic profile was known to all of Paris. Furthermore, the passes Danton had sent, they'd discovered, were not valid until the fourteenth of September—nearly two weeks hence. The only solution, they'd all agreed, was for Mireille to depart alone, for Maurice to remain in Paris as though nothing had happened, and for Courtiade to leave that same night with the boxes of books and to wait at the Channel until his pass permitted him to cross to England.

Now, as her horse picked its way through the close darkness of the narrow streets, Mireille had time at last to consider the perilous mission that lay before her.

From the moment when her hired carriage had been stopped before the gates of l'Abbaye Prison, events had engulfed her so she'd only had time to act instinctively. The horror of Valentine's execution, the sudden terror for her own life as she'd fled through the burning streets of Paris, Marat's face and the grimaces of the onlookers as they watched the massacre—it was as if a lid had been lifted for an instant from the thin eggshell of civilization so she could glimpse the horror of man's bestiality beneath that fragile veneer.

From that instant, time had stopped and events were unleashed that swallowed her like the wild rampaging of a fire. Behind each wave that assaulted her was a backlash of emotion more powerful than any she'd known. This passion still burned within her like a dark flame—a flame that had only been intensified by the brief hours spent in Talleyrand's arms. A flame that fired her desire to grasp the pieces of the Montglane Service before anything else.

It seemed an eternity since Mireille had seen Valentine's sparkling smile across the length of that courtyard. Yet it was only thirty-two hours. Thirty-two, thought Mireille as she moved through the deserted street alone: the number of pieces on a chessboard. The number she must collect to decipher the riddle—and to avenge the death of Valentine.

She had met few people on the narrow side streets of Paris en route to the Bois de Boulogne. Even here in the countryside under the full moon, though still far from the barricades, the thoroughfares were nearly empty. By now most Parisians had learned of the prison massacres, which were still under way, and decided to remain within the relative security of their own homes.

Though she must head east to Lyons to reach her destination at the port of Marseilles, Mireille had gone west toward Versailles for a reason. The Convent of St.-Cyr was there: the convent school founded in the prior century by Madame de Maintenon, consort of Louis XIV, for the education of daughters of the nobility. It was at St.-Cyr that the Abbess of Montglane had stopped en route to Russia.

Perhaps the proctoress would give Mireille shelter there—help her contact the Abbess of Montglane for the funds she needed—help her escape from France. The reputation of Montglane's abbess was the only pass to freedom Mireille possessed. She prayed it would work a miracle.

The barricades at the Bois were piled with stones, sacks of earth, and broken pieces of furniture. Mireille could see the Place before it, thick with people with their ox carts, carriages, and animals, waiting to flee as soon as the gates were opened. Approaching the Place, she dismounted and stayed within her horse's shadow, so her disguise would not be penetrated in the flickering light of the torchères that illuminated the square.

There was a commotion at the barrier. Taking her horse by the reins, Mireille mingled with the large group that filled the Place. Beyond in the torchlight, she could see soldiers clambering up to raise the barricade. Someone was coming through from outside.

Near Mireille a group of young men milled about, craning their necks for a better view. There must have been a dozen or more, all dressed in laces, velvets, and shiny high-heeled boots pasted with glittering glass stones like gems. These were the *jeunesse dorée*, the "gilded youth," whom Germaine de Staël had pointed out to Mireille so often at the Opéra. Mireille heard them complaining loudly to the mixed crowd of nobles and peasants that packed the square.

"This revolution has become quite impossible!" cried one. "There really is no reason to hold French citizens hostage now that the filthy Prussians have been driven away."

"I say, *soldat*!" cried another, waving a lacy handkerchief at a soldier high above them on the barricade. "We've a party to attend at Versailles! How long do you intend us to be patient here?" The soldier turned his bayonet toward the waving handkerchief, which quickly disappeared from view.

There was commotion in the crowd about who might be coming through the barricades. It was known that highwaymen plied the roads through every forest region now. The "chamber-pots," groups of self-deputized inquisitioners, traveled the highways in strangely designed vehicles from which they derived their nickname. Though acting in no official capacity, they were instilled with the zeal of newly appointed citizens of France—halting a traveler, swarming over his coach like locusts, demanding to see his papers, and, if displeased with the interrogation, making a "citizen's arrest." To save trouble, this might include stringing him up from the nearest tree as a lesson to others.

The barricades opened, and a cluster of dust-coated fiacres and cabriolets passed through. The crowd from the square closed around them to learn what they could from the weary passengers who'd just arrived. Holding the reins of her horse, Mireille moved toward the first halted post chaise, the door of which was opening to release passengers.

A young soldier, dressed in the scarlet and dark blue of the army, leaped out into the midst of the crowd to help the coachman remove boxes and trunks from the roof of the post chaise.

Mireille was close enough to observe firsthand that he was a young man of extraordinary beauty. His long chestnut hair was unbound, swinging loose to his shoulders. His large dark eyes of blue-gray, shadowed with thick lashes, intensified the pale translucence of his skin. His narrow Roman nose turned down slightly. His lips, beautifully molded, curved into an expression of disdain as he glanced once at the noisy crowd and turned away.

Now she saw him helping someone to descend from the carriage, a beautiful child of no more than fifteen years who was so pale and fragile that Mireille felt frightened for her. The girl resembled this soldier so perfectly that Mireille felt certain they were brother and sister, and the tenderness with which he helped his young companion from the carriage supported this. Both were of slight build but well formed. They made a romantic-looking couple, thought Mireille—like hero and heroine in a fairy tale.

All the passengers coming from the carriages seemed shaken and frightened as they brushed the dust from their traveling clothes, but none more so than the young girl near Mireille, who was white as a sheet and trembling as if about to swoon. The soldier tried to help her through the crowd as an old man near Mireille reached out and grasped him by the arm.

"What is the state of the Versailles Road, friend?" he asked.

"I should not attempt Versailles tonight," the soldier replied politely, but loudly enough for all to hear. "The chamber-pots are out in force, and my sister is badly shaken. The trip has cost us nearly eight hours, for we've been halted a dozen times since we left St.-Cyr. . . ."

"St.-Cyr!" cried Mireille. "You've come from St.-Cyr? But that is where I'm headed!" At this, both the soldier and his young sister turned to Mireille, and the child's eyes opened wide.

"But—but it is a *lady*!" cried the young girl, staring at Mireille's costume of livery and powdered hair. "A lady dressed as a *man*!"

The soldier looked Mireille over with appreciation. "So you're bound for St.-Cyr?" he said. "Let us hope you did not plan to join the convent!"

"Have you come from the convent school at St.-Cyr?" she said. "I must reach there myself—tonight. It is a matter of grave importance. You must tell me how things stand."

"We cannot idle here," said the soldier. "My sister is not well." And hoisting their one bag onto his shoulder, he parted the way through the crowd.

Mireille followed close by, tugging the reins of her horse. As the three of them reached the edge of the crowd, the young girl turned her dark eyes upon Mireille.

"You must have a powerful reason for reaching St.-Cyr tonight," she said. "The roads are unsafe. You are brave to travel, a woman alone, at times like these."

"Even with so magnificent a steed," agreed the soldier, slapping Mireille's horse upon the flank, "and even in disguise. Had I not taken leave from the army when they closed the convent school to escort Maria-Anna home—"

"They have closed St.-Cyr?!" cried Mireille, clutching his arm. "Then indeed my last hope has deserted me!" Little Maria-Anna tried to comfort Mireille with a touch on her arm.

"Had you friends at St.-Cyr?" she asked with concern. "Or family? Perhaps it was someone I knew. . . ."

"I sought shelter there," Mireille began, uncertain how much she should reveal to these strangers. But she had little choice. If the school were closed, her only plan was demolished, and she must form another. What matter whom she confided in, when her plight was desperate?

"Though I did not know the proctoress there," she told them, "I'd hoped she might help me contact the abbess of my former convent. Her name was Madame de Roque."

"Madame de Roque!" cried the young girl. Though small and frail, she'd grasped Mireille's arm with great force. "The Abbess of Montglane!" She glanced once quickly at her brother, who set their bag upon the ground, his blue-gray eyes trained upon Mireille as he spoke.

"Then you've come from Montglane Abbey?" When Mireille nodded, cautious now, he added quickly, "Our mother knew the Abbess of Montglane—

they've long been close friends. In fact, it was upon the advice of Madame de Roque that my sister was sent to St.-Cyr eight years ago."

"Yes," whispered the child. "And I *myself* know the abbess quite well. During her visit at St.-Cyr two years ago, she spoke with me in confidence on several occasions. But before I proceed . . . were you, mademoiselle, one of the last . . . remaining at Montglane Abbey? If so, you'll understand why I've asked this question." And she glanced again at her brother.

Mireille felt her heart pounding in her ears. Was it mere coincidence that she'd stumbled upon those who were familiar with the abbess? Could she dare hope that they were privy to the abbess's confidence? No, it was too dangerous to leap to this conclusion. But the child seemed to sense Mireille's concerns.

"I see from your face," she said, "you prefer not to discuss this matter here in the open. And of course, you are quite right. But further discussion may benefit us both. You see, before she left St.-Cyr, your abbess entrusted me with a special mission. Perhaps you understand to what I refer. I offer that you accompany us to the nearby inn, where my brother has secured us lodgings for the night. We can speak in more confidence there. . . ."

The blood was still throbbing in Mireille's temples as a thousand thoughts passed through her mind. Even if she trusted these strangers enough to go with them, she'd be trapped in Paris, when Marat might be turning the city upside down in quest of her. On the other hand, she had no assurance that she could escape from Paris unaided. And where could she turn for shelter if the convent was closed?

"My sister is right," said the soldier, still watching Mireille. "We cannot remain here. Mademoiselle, I offer you our protection."

Mireille thought again how remarkably handsome he was, with his abundant chestnut hair hanging free and his large sad eyes. Though slender, and of nearly the same height as she, he gave the impression of great strength and assurance. At last, Mireille decided that she trusted him.

"Very well," she said with a smile, "I shall come with you to your inn, where we will talk."

At these words, the child smiled brightly and pressed her brother's arm. They looked into each other's eyes with great love. Then the soldier lifted their bag again and took the horse's reins as his sister locked her arm in Mireille's.

"You will not be sorry, mademoiselle," said the child. "Permit me to introduce myself. My name is Maria-Anna, but my family call me Elisa. And this is my brother Napoleone—of the family Buonaparte."

∞

At the inn, the three young people sat around a table of splintered wood on stiff wooden chairs. On the table a single candle burned, and beside it a loaf of hard black bread and a pitcher of ale provided their meager repast.

"We come from Corsica," Napoleone was telling Mireille, "an island that does not easily adapt itself to the yoke of tyranny. As Livy said nearly two thousand years ago, we Corsicans are as rugged as our land, being ungovernable as wild beasts. Not forty years ago, our leader Pasquale di Paoli drove the Genoese from our shores, liberated Corsica, and hired the famous philosopher Jean-Jacques Rousseau to draft us a constitution. This freedom was short-lived, however. For in 1768 France bought the isle of Corsica from Genoa, landed thirty thousand troops on the rock the following spring, and drowned our throne of liberty in a sea of blood. I tell you these things, for it was this history—and our family's role in it—that brought us into contact with the Abbess of Montglane."

Mireille, who was about to question the purpose of this historical saga, now sat attentively silent. She broke off a piece of the tough black bread to chew as she listened.

"Our parents fought bravely beside Paoli to repel the French," Napoleone went on. "My mother was a great heroine of the revolution. She rode bareback by night through the wild Corsican hills, French bullets whizzing about her ears, to bring munitions and supplies to my father, and the soldiers fighting at Il Corte—the Eagle's Nest. She was seven months pregnant with *me* at the time! As she's always said, I was born to be a soldier. But when I was born, my country was dying."

"Your mother was a brave woman indeed," said Mireille, trying to visualize this wild revolutionary on horseback as an intimate friend of the abbess.

"You remind me of her." Napoleone smiled. "But I neglect my tale. When the revolution proved unsuccessful and Paoli was exiled to England, the old Corsican nobility selected my father to represent our island in the States-General at Versailles. This was in 1782—the year and the place that our mother Letizia met the Abbess of Montglane. I shall never forget how elegant our mother looked, how all the boys commented upon her beauty when, returning from Versailles, she visited us at Autun. . . ."

"Autun!" cried Mireille, nearly upsetting her goblet of ale. "Were you at Autun when Monseigneur Talleyrand was there? When he was bishop?"

"No, that was after my time, for I soon went on to the military school at Brienne," he replied. "But he is a great statesman whom I should like one day to meet. I've read many times the work he prepared with Thomas Paine: the Declaration of the Rights of Man—one of the finest documents of the French Revolution. . . ."

"Continue with your story," hissed Elisa, jabbing her brother in the ribs, "for the mademoiselle and I do not wish to discuss politics all night."

"I am trying to," Napoleone said, glancing at his sister. "We don't know the exact circumstances of Letizia's meeting with the abbess, only that it took place at St.-Cyr. But we know it must have left an impression upon the abbess—for she's never failed our family since that time."

"Ours is a poor family, mademoiselle," Elisa explained. "Even when my father was alive, money ran through his fingers like water. The Abbess of Montglane has paid for my education since that day, eight years ago, when I entered St.-Cyr."

"The abbess must have felt a great bond with your mother," said Mireille.

"More than a bond," Elisa agreed, "for until the abbess left France, never a week passed that she and my mother were not in communication. You'll understand when I tell you of the mission with which the abbess entrusted me."

It had been ten years, Mireille thought. Ten years since these two women had met, women so different in background and outlook. One raised on a wild and primitive island, fighting beside her husband in the mountains, bearing him eight children—the other a cloistered woman of God, high born and well educated. What could be the nature of their relationship that inspired the abbess to confide a secret to the child now sitting before Mireille—who, when the abbess last saw her, could not have been older than twelve or thirteen?

But already, Elisa was explaining. . . .

"The message the abbess gave me for my mother was so secret that she herself did not wish to communicate it in writing. I was to repeat it only face to face when next I saw her. At the time, neither the abbess nor I suspected this would be two long years—that the Revolution would so disrupt our lives and all hope of travel. I fear for not having delivered this message earlier—perhaps it was critical. For the abbess told me there were those who conspired to relieve her of a secret treasure, a treasure known only to a few—which was hidden at Montglane!"

Elisa's voice had dropped to a whisper, though the three were completely alone in the room. Mireille tried to show no reaction, but her heart beat so loudly, she felt certain the others must hear it.

"She'd come to St.-Cyr, so close to Paris," Elisa continued, "in order to learn the identity of those who'd tried to steal it. In order to protect the treasure, she told me, she'd had it removed by the nuns of the abbey."

"And what was the nature of this treasure?" asked Mireille with faint voice. "Did the abbess tell you?"

"No," Napoleone replied for his sister, watching Mireille closely now. His long oval face was pale in the dim light, which glimmered against his dark chestnut hair. "But you know the legends surrounding those monasteries in the Basque mountains. There's always a sacred relic supposed to be hidden there. According to Chrêtien de Troyes, the holy grail is cached away at Monsalvat, also in the Pyrenees—"

"Mademoiselle," interrupted Elisa, "that is precisely why I wished to speak with you. When you told us you came from Montglane, I thought perhaps *you* could shed some light upon the mystery."

"What was the message the abbess gave you?"

"On the last day of her stay at St.-Cyr," replied Elisa, leaning over the table so the golden light caught the outline of her face, "the abbess called me into a private chamber. She said: 'Elisa, I entrust you with a secret mission, for I know you are the eighth child born to Carlo Buonaparte and Letizia Ramolino. Four of your siblings died in infancy; you are the first girl to survive. This makes you very special to me. You were named after a great ruler, Elissa, whom some called "the Red." She founded a great city named Q'ar that later gained world fame. You must go to your mother and tell her the Abbess of Montglane says: "Elissa the Red has risen—the Eight return." That is my only message, but Letizia Ramolino will know what it signifies—and what she must do!' "

Elisa paused and looked at Mireille. Napoleone also tried to gauge her reaction—but Mireille could glean no sense from the message. What secret could the abbess be communicating that was related to the fabled chess pieces? Something flickered in her mind, but she could not yet make it out. Napoleone reached over to refill her ale tankard, though she'd been unaware of having drunk any.

"Who was this Elissa of Q'ar?" she asked in confusion. "I know neither the name nor the city she founded."

"But I do," said Napoleone. Leaning back, his face in shadow, he extracted a well-worn book from his pocket. "Our mother's favorite admonition has always been, 'Page through your Plutarch, leaf through your Livy,' " he said with a smile. "I've done better than that, for I've found our Elissa here in Vergil's *Aeneid*—though the Romans and Greeks preferred to call her Dido. She came from the city of Tyre in ancient Phoenicia. But she fled that city when her brother, king of Tyre, murdered her husband. Landing on the shores of North Africa, she founded the city of Q'ar, named after the great goddess Car who'd protected her. This city we now know as Carthage."

"Carthage!" cried Mireille. Her mind racing, she began to put the pieces together. The city of Carthage, now called Tunis, lay not five hundred miles from Algiers! All lands known as the Barbary States—Tripoli, Tunis, Algeria, and Morocco—had one thing in common. They'd been ruled by the Berbers, ancient ancestors of the Moors, for five thousand years. It could not be an accident that the abbess's message pointed directly to the very land for which she was bound.

"I can see this means something to you," Napoleone said, interrupting her thoughts. "Perhaps you could tell us."

Mireille bit her lip and looked into the candle flame. They'd confided in her, while she had thus far revealed nothing. Yet to win a game like the one she was playing, she knew she needed allies. What harm would it do to reveal a portion of what she knew, to get closer to the truth?

"There *was* a treasure at Montglane," Mireille said at last. "I know, because I helped to remove it with my own hands." The two Buonapartes exchanged glances, then looked back at Mireille.

"This treasure was a thing of great value, and also great danger," she went on. "It was brought to Montglane nearly a thousand years ago—by eight Moors whose ancestry rose from those same shores of North Africa you describe. I myself am headed there, to discover what secret lies behind this treasure. . . ."

"Then you *must* accompany us to Corsica!" cried Elisa, leaning forward in excitement. "Our island is halfway to your destination! We offer you my brother's protection en route, and the shelter of our family once we arrive."

What she said was true, thought Mireille—and there was something else to consider. In Corsica, while still technically on French soil, she'd be far from the clutches of Marat, who even now might be hunting her through the streets of Paris.

But there was something more. As she watched the candle sputter down into a pool of hot wax, she felt the dark flame rekindle in her mind. And she heard Talleyrand's whispered words as they sat in the rumpled bedsheets—as he held the thrashing stallion from the Montglane Service in his hand: "And there went out another horse that was red . . . and power was given to him that sat thereon to take peace from the earth, and that they should kill one another . . . and there was given unto him a great sword . . ."

"And the name of the sword is Revenge," said Mireille aloud.

"The sword?" said Napoleone. "What sword is that?"

"The red sword of retribution," she replied.

As the light slowly faded from the room, Mireille saw again the letters she'd seen, day after day, for all the years of her childhood—carved over the portal of Montglane Abbey:

> Cursed be He who bring these Walls to Earth
> The King is checked by the Hand of God alone.

"Perhaps we have released more than an ancient treasure from the walls of Montglane Abbey," she said softly. Despite the heat of the night, she felt the cold creep into her heart as if touched by icy fingers. "Perhaps," she said, "we have also raised an ancient curse."

CORSICA   OCTOBER 1792

The isle of Corsica, like the isle of Crete, is set like a jewel, as the poet sang, "in the midst of the wine-dark sea." From twenty miles off the coast, though it was now near winter, Mireille could smell the strong scent of the macchia, that underbrush of sage, broom, rosemary, fennel, lavender, and thorn that covered the island in thick abundance.

As she stood on the deck of the small boat plying its way over the choppy sea, she could see thick mists shrouding the high and craggy mountains, partly obscuring the treacherous winding roads, the fan-shaped waterfalls that spread like lace over the surface of the rock. So thick was the veil of heavy fog, she could barely make out where the water ended and the isle began.

Mireille was wrapped in heavy woolen robes, taking the bracing air as she watched the island loom before her. She was ill, seriously ill, and it was not the roughness of the tossing sea that caused it. She'd been violently nauseated ever since they'd left Lyons.

Elisa stood beside her on the deck, holding her hand as the boatmen scurried about bringing in the sails. Napoleone had gone below to collect their few belongings before they touched the docks.

Perhaps it had been the water in Lyons, thought Mireille. Or perhaps the roughness of their journey through the Rhone valley, where warring armies had raged in battle all around them, trying to carve up Savoy—part of the kingdom of Sardinia. Near Givors, Napoleone had sold her horse, which they'd brought along hitched to their post chaise, to the Fifth Army Regiment. The officers had lost more horses than men in the heat of battle, and Mireille's had brought a tidy sum—enough to pay for her journey and more.

During all this, Mireille's sickness had gone from bad to worse. Little Elisa's face grew graver each day as she spoon-fed soup to "the mademoiselle" and applied cold compresses to her head at every stop. But the soup never stayed down long, and the mademoiselle had begun to be seriously worried herself, long before their ship cut free of the port of Toulon and headed across the rough and angry sea toward Corsica. When she'd glimpsed herself in a convex glass on board ship, she'd looked pale, wan, and ten pounds underweight, instead of fat and expanded in the glass's round shape. She'd stayed on deck as much as possible, but even the cold salt air had not restored the feeling of healthy vigor that Mireille had always taken for granted.

Now, as Elisa squeezed her hand, the two of them huddled on the small ship's deck, Mireille shook her head to clear her thoughts and swallowed to keep down the wave of nausea. She couldn't afford to be weak now.

And as if the heavens themselves had heard, the dark mist lifted slightly and

the sun broke through, forming pools of light that licked the broken surface
of the water like stepping-stones of gold, preceding her a hundred yards into
the port of Ajaccio.

∞

Napoleone was on deck, leaping to shore and helping lash their ship to
the stone pier the minute they'd struck down. The port of Ajaccio was bustling
with motion. Many warships hovered just outside the harbor. French soldiers
were crawling over the hawsers and racing upon the decks as Mireille and Elisa
looked about them in wonderment.

The French government had ordered Corsica to attack Sardinia, her neighbor.
Even as they moved supplies from the ship, Mireille heard the French soldiers
and the Corsican National Guard bickering among themselves about the propri-
ety of this attack—which appeared to be imminent.

Mireille heard a shout beneath her on the quay. Peering down, she saw
Napoleone dashing through the crush of bodies toward a small, slender woman
clutching the hand of a tiny child in each of hers. As Napoleone swept her into
his arms, Mireille caught a flash of red-chestnut hair, white hands that fluttered
up like doves about his neck, the children released and bobbing free about the
entwined form of mother and son.

"Our mother, Letizia," whispered Elisa, looking up at Mireille with a smile.
"And my sister Maria-Carolina, who is ten, and little Girolamo, who was just
a baby when I left for St.-Cyr. But Napoleone has always been Mother's
favorite. Come, I shall introduce you." And they went down into the crowded
port.

Letizia Ramolino Buonaparte was a tiny woman, thought Mireille. Though
slender as a reed, she gave the impression of substance. From afar she watched
Mireille and Elisa approach, her pale eyes as translucent as blue ice, her face
tranquil as a blossom floating on a still pool. Though everything about her
seemed placid, her presence was so commanding that Mireille felt it penetrate
even the pandemonium of the crowded port. And she felt she had known Letizia
before.

"Madame Mère," said Elisa, embracing her mother, "I present our new
friend. She comes from Madame de Roque—the Abbess of Montglane."

Letizia looked at Mireille for a long while without speaking. Then she put
forth her hand.

"Yes," she said in a low voice, "I've been expecting you."

"Expecting me?" said Mireille in surprise.

"You have a message for me—do you not? A message of some importance."

"Madame Mère, we *do* have a message!" Elisa chimed in, tugging her
mother's sleeve. Letizia glanced at her daughter, who, at fifteen, was already

taller than she. "I *myself* have met with the abbess at St.-Cyr, and she gave me this communication for you. . . ." Elisa bent to her mother's ear.

Nothing could have transformed this impervious woman more astonishingly than these whispered words. Now, as she listened, her face grew dark. Her lips trembled with emotion as she stepped back, putting her hand on Napoleone's shoulder for support.

"Mother, what is it?" he cried, grasping her hand and looking into her eyes with alarm.

"Madame," urged Mireille, "you must tell us the meaning this message holds for you. My future actions—my very life—may depend upon it. I was bound for Algiers, but stopped here only because of my chance meeting with your children. This message may be . . ." But before she could speak further, Mireille was overcome by another wave of nausea. Letizia reached out to her just as Napoleone stepped in to catch her beneath the arm, lest she fall.

"Forgive me," Mireille said faintly, cold sweat beading her brow, "I fear I must lie down—I'm not myself."

Letizia seemed almost relieved at the distraction. She carefully felt the fevered brow and palpitating heart. Then, assuming nearly military bearing, she ordered and shooed children about as Napoleone carried Mireille up the steep hill to their cart. By the time Mireille had been placed in the back of the cart, Letizia seemed to have recovered her demeanor enough to broach the subject again.

"Mademoiselle," she said carefully, glancing quickly to be certain they were not overheard, "though I've been braced for such news these thirty years—I find myself unprepared for this message. Despite what I've told my children for their own protection, I have known your abbess since I was Elisa's age—my mother has been her closest confidante. I shall answer all your questions. But first we must contact Madame de Roque and discover how you fit in with her plans."

"I cannot wait that long!" cried Mireille. "I *must* go to Algiers."

"Nevertheless, I override your decision," Letizia said, climbing into the cart and picking up the crop as she motioned for her children to follow suit. "You are not well enough to travel, and in attempting to do so, you may place others in more danger than yourself. For you do not understand the nature of this game you play, any more than the stakes."

"I come from Montglane," snapped Mireille. "I have touched the pieces with my own hands." Letizia had whipped about to stare at her, and Napoleone and Elisa paid close attention as they lifted little Girolamo into the cart. For they themselves had never learned precisely what the treasure was.

"You know nothing!" Letizia cried fiercely. "Elissa of Carthage did not heed the warnings, either. She died by fire—immolated on a funeral pyre, like that fabulous bird from which the Phoenicians derive their identity."

"But Mother," said Elisa, helping Maria-Carolina into the cart, "according to the story, she *threw* herself on the pyre when Aeneas deserted her."

"Perhaps," Letizia said cryptically, "and perhaps there was another reason."

"The phoenix!" whispered Mireille, hardly noticing as Elisa and Carolina wedged themselves in beside her. Napoleone had joined his mother on the driver's seat. "And did Queen Elissa then *rise* from her own ashes—like that mythical bird of the desert?"

"No," chirped Elisa, "for her shade was later seen in Hades by Aeneas himself."

Letizia's blue eyes still rested on Mireille as if she were lost in thought. At last she spoke—and Mireille felt a chill pass through her as she heard the words.

"But she has risen *now*—like the pieces of the Montglane Service. And we may well tremble, all of us. For this is the end that was foretold."

Turning away, she flicked her crop lightly at the horse, and they rode off in silence.

The house of Letizia Buonaparte was a small, whitewashed two-story edifice on a narrow street in the hills above Ajaccio. Two olive trees were trained up the front wall, and despite the heavy mist, a few ambitious bees still worked on the thick, late-blooming hedge of rosemary that half covered the door.

No one had spoken on the trip back. But unloading themselves from the cart, Maria-Carolina was assigned the task of settling in Mireille, while the others went bustling about preparing supper. Still dressed in Courtiade's old shirt, which was too large, and a skirt of Elisa's, which was too small, her hair still thick with dust from the trip, her skin sticky from illness—Mireille felt enormous relief when ten-year-old Carolina appeared with two copper jugs of hot water for her bath.

Having bathed and changed into heavy woolens they'd found to fit her, Mireille felt somewhat better. For dinner, the table was groaning with local specialties: bruccio—a goat cream cheese, little cakes of corn meal, breads made from chestnuts, preserves from cherries that grew wild on the island, sage honey, small Mediterranean squid and octopus they caught themselves, wild rabbit prepared in Letizia's special sauce, and that new transplant to Corsica—potatoes.

After they'd dined and the smaller children were in bed, Letizia poured little cups of apple brandy all around, and the four "adults" stayed near the brazier of hot coals in the dining room.

"Before anything else," Letizia began, "I wish to apologize for my short temper, mademoiselle. My children have told me of your bravery in leaving Paris during the Terror, at night and alone. I've asked Napoleone and Elisa to hear what I'm about to say. I want them to know what I expect of them—which is to consider you, as I do, a member of our family. Whatever the future may bring, I expect them to come to your aid as one of our own."

"Madame," said Mireille, warming her apple brandy beside the brazier, "I've come to Corsica for one reason—to hear from your own lips the meaning of the abbess's message. The mission I'm engaged in is one that was thrust upon me by events. The last of my family was destroyed because of the Montglane Service—and I pledge every drop of blood, every breath in my body, every hour I spend on this earth, to discovering the dark secret that lies behind these pieces."

Letizia looked at Mireille, her red-gold hair shimmering in the brazier's glow, the youth of her face so bitterly contrasted with the weariness of her words— and she felt a pang in her heart at what she had determined to do. She hoped the Abbess of Montglane would agree that it was right.

"I will tell you what you wish to know," she said at last. "In my forty-two years, I've never discussed what I am about to say. Have patience, for it's not a simple story. When I've finished, you'll understand the terrible burden I've carried all these years—which I now pass on to you."

MADAME MÈRE'S TALE

When I was a child of eight, Pasquale Paoli liberated the isle of Corsica from the Genoese. My father having died, my mother remarried a Swiss named Franz Fesch. In order to marry her, he had to renounce his Calvinist faith and become a Catholic. His family cut him off without a penny. It was this circumstance that set the wheels in motion for the Abbess of Montglane to enter our lives.

Few people know that Helene de Roque descends from an old and noble family of Savoy—but her family held property in many lands, and she herself had traveled widely. In the year I met her, 1764, she'd already achieved the position of abbess at Montglane, though she was not yet forty. She was acquainted with the family of Fesch and—as a noble of partly Swiss origin, though Catholic—she was held in high esteem by these thoroughly bourgeoise people. Knowing the situation, she took it upon herself to arbitrate between my stepfather and his family and reestablish familial relations—an act that at the time appeared purely unselfish.

My stepfather Franz Fesch was a tall, lean man with a craggy, charming face. Like a true Swiss, he spoke softly, volunteered his opinions rarely, and trusted almost no one. He was naturally grateful that Madame de Roque had arranged a reconciliation with his family, and he invited her to our home in Corsica. We could not have guessed that this had been her objective all along.

I shall never forget the day she arrived at our old stone house, perched high in the Corsican mountains nearly eight thousand feet above the sea. To reach it, one had to traverse the most rugged terrain of treacherous cliffs, steep ravines, and impenetrable macchia that in places formed walls of undergrowth six feet high. But the abbess was scarcely daunted by this journey. As soon as the formalities were dispensed with, she introduced the subject she'd come to discuss.

"I come hither not only by your gracious invitation, Franz Fesch," she began, "but because of a matter of great urgency. There is a man—a Swiss like yourself, and like yourself converted to the Catholic faith. I fear him greatly, for he has my movements followed. I believe he seeks to learn of a secret that I guard—a secret that goes back perhaps a thousand years. All his activities suggest this, for he's studied music, even writing a dictionary of music—and composing an opera with the famous André Philidor. He's befriended the philosophes Grimm and Diderot, both patronized by the court of Catherine the Great in Russia. He even corresponded with Voltaire—a man he despises! And now, though too ill to travel much himself, he's engaged the services of a spy who is headed here to Corsica. I ask your assistance: that you act in my behalf, as I have done for you."

"Who is this Swiss?" asked Fesch with great interest. "Perhaps I know him."

"Whether or not you know him, you'll know his name," the abbess replied. "It is Jean-Jacques Rousseau."

"Rousseau! Impossible!" cried my mother, Angela-Maria. "But he is a great man! His theories of natural virtue are those upon which the Corsican revolution was founded! In fact, Paoli has chartered him to write our constitution—it was Rousseau who said, 'Man is born free, but is everywhere in chains.'"

"It is one thing to speak of the principles of freedom and virtue," said the abbess dryly, "and another to act upon them. Here is a man who says all books are instruments of evil—yet he writes six hundred pages at a sitting. He says children should be nourished physically by their mothers and intellectually by their fathers—yet he deserts his own on the steps of a foundling home! More than one revolution will be launched in the name of the 'virtues' he preaches— yet he seeks a tool of such power that it would place *all* men in chains . . . except its possessor!" The abbess's eyes glowed like the coals of this brazier. Fesch regarded her cautiously.

"You'd like to know what it is I want," said the abbess with a smile. "I understand the Swiss, monsieur. I am nearly one myself. I go to the point at once. I want information and cooperation. I understand you can give me neither—until I tell you what is the secret I guard, that is buried at Montglane Abbey."

For most of that day, the abbess proceeded to tell us a long and miraculous tale of a legendary chess service, said to have belonged to Charlemagne and believed to have been buried within Montglane Abbey for a thousand years. I say "believed"—for no one living had actually *seen* it, though many had sought to learn its location and the secret of its reputed powers. The abbess herself feared, as had each of her predecessors, that the treasure might have to be exhumed during *her* tenure. And she would be responsible for opening Pandora's box. As a result, she'd come to fear those who crossed her path too closely, as a chess player watches with mistrust all pieces that may pin him—including his own—and plans his counterattacks in advance. It was to this end she'd come to Corsica.

"Perhaps I know what Rousseau seeks here," said the abbess, "for this isle's history is both ancient and mysterious. As I've said, the Montglane Service passed into Charlemagne's hands through the Moors of Barcelona. But in the year 809 A.D.—five years before Charles's death—another group of Moors took the island of Corsica.

"There are nearly as many sects in the Islamic faith as in the Christian," she continued with a wry smile. "As early as Muhammed's death, his own family went to war, splitting the faith apart. The sect that settled Corsica were the Shia, mystics who preached Talim, a secret doctrine that included the coming of a Redeemer. They founded a mystical cult with a lodge, secret rites of initiation, and a grand master—upon which the current Society of Freemasons have based their rituals. They subdued Carthage and Tripoli, establishing powerful dynasties there. And one of their order, a Persian from Mesopotamia who was called Q'armat after the ancient goddess Car, raised an army that attacked Mecca and stole the veil of the Kaaba and the sacred black stone that lay inside. At last they spawned the Hashhashin, a group of drug-inspired political murderers from which we drive the name 'assassins.'

"I tell you these things," said the abbess, "for this ruthless, politically motivated Shi'ite sect that landed on Corsica *knew* of the Montglane Service. They'd studied the ancient manuscripts of Egypt, Babylon, and Sumer, which spoke of the dark mysteries to which they believed the service held a key. And they wanted to get it back.

"During the centuries of war that followed—these clandestine mystics were repeatedly thwarted in their attempts to locate and retrieve the service. At last, the Moors were driven altogether from their strongholds in Italy and Spain. Split by internal factions, they ceased to be a major force in history."

Through all the abbess's speech, my mother had been strangely silent. Her usually forthright, open personality now seemed veiled and guarded. Both Fesch and I noticed this, and now he spoke—perhaps to draw her out:

"My family and I are held in thrall by the tale you've told," he said. "But naturally, you would expect us to wonder what the secret is that Monsieur Rousseau might seek upon our island—and why you've chosen *us* as confidants in your attempt to thwart him."

"Though Rousseau, as I've said, may be too ill to travel," replied the abbess, "he would surely appoint his agent to visit one of his few fellow Swiss residing here. As for the secret he seeks—perhaps your wife, Angela-Maria, could tell us more. Her family roots go back very far on the isle of Corsica—if I'm not mistaken, even to before the Moors. . . ."

In a flash, I understood why the abbess had come! My mother's sweet, fragile face flushed dark red as she glanced once, quickly, at Fesch and once at me. She twisted her hands in her lap and seemed uncertain which way to turn.

"I do not mean to disconcert you, Madame Fesch," the abbess said in a calm voice, which nonetheless managed to convey a sense of urgency. "But I'd hoped the Corsican sense of honor would require, for my favor, a favor in return. I admit I tricked you in providing a service where none had been requested. But now I hope my efforts will not have been in vain." Fesch looked confused, but I was not. I'd lived on Corsica since my birth—and I knew the legends of my mother's family, the Pietra-Santas, who counted their stay on this isle from the dim twilight of its very beginnings.

"Mother," I said, "these are only old myths, or so you've always told me. What difference if you share them with Madame de Roque, when she's done so much for us?" At this, Fesch put his hand over my mother's and pressed it, to show his support.

"Madame de Roque," said my mother in a trembling voice, "I owe you my gratitude, and mine are a people who honor their debts. But the story you've told has frightened me. Superstition runs deep in our blood. Though most families on this isle descend from Etruscany, Lombardy, or Sicily—mine were the first settlers. We come from Phoenicia, an ancient people from the eastern coast of the Mediterranean Sea. We colonized Corsica sixteen hundred years before the birth of Christ."

The abbess was nodding her head slowly as my mother continued.

"These Phoenicians were traders, merchants, known in the ancient histories as 'the People of the Sea.' The Greeks called them Phoinikes—meaning 'blood red'—perhaps for the purple-red dyes they produced from shells, perhaps for the legendary firebird, or the palm tree, both named Phoinix: 'red like fire.' There are those who think they came from the Red Sea and were called after their homeland. But none of these is true. We were named for the color of our hair. And all later tribes of the Phoenicians, such as the Venetians, were known by this flame-red sign. I dwell upon this, for red things, the color of flame and blood, were worshiped by these strange and primitive peoples.

"Though the Greeks called them Phoinikes, they called *themselves* the People of Khna—or Knossos—and later the Canaanites. From the Bible, we know they worshiped many gods, the gods of Babylon: the god Bel, whom they called Ba'al; Ishtar, who became Astarte; and Mel'Quarth, whom the Greeks called Car, meaning 'Fate' or 'Destiny,' and whom my people called the Moloch."

"The Moloch," whispered the abbess. "It was the pagan worship of this god that the Hebrews deplored, but were accused of indulging in. They threw their living children into the fire to placate the god. . . ."

"Yes," said my mother, "and worse. Though most ancient people believed that revenge belonged only to the gods, the Phoenicians believed it belonged to them. The places they founded—Corsica, Sardinia, Marseilles, Venetia, Sicily—are places where treachery is only a means to an end; where retaliation means justice. Even today their descendants ravage the Mediterranean. Those Barbary pirates did not descend from the Berbers, but from Barbarossa—'red beard'—and even now at Tunis and Algiers, they hold twenty thousand Europeans in bondage for the ransom by which they make their fortunes. These are the true descendants of Phoenicia: men who rule the seas from island fortresses, who worship the god of thieves, live by treachery, and die by the vendetta!"

"Yes," said the abbess with excitement. "Just as the Moor told Charlemagne, it was the chess service itself that would carry out the Sar—revenge! But what is it? What can the dark secret be, sought by the Moors and perhaps even known to the Phoenicians? What power is contained within these pieces—perhaps once known, now lost forever without this buried key?"

"I am not sure," my mother replied, "but from what you've told me, I may have a clue. You said there were eight Moors who brought the chess service to Charlemagne, and refused to be parted from it—following it even to Montglane, where they were believed to practice secret rituals. I know what this ritual may have been. My ancestors the Phoenicians practiced rites of initiation like the ones you've described. They worshiped a sacred stone, sometimes a stele or monolith, believed to contain the voice of the god. Like the black stone of the Kaaba at Mecca, like the Dome of the Rock at Jerusalem, there was a *masseboth* at every Phoenician shrine.

"In our legends, there's the tale of a woman named Elissa, who came from Tyre. Her brother was king, and when he murdered her husband, she stole the sacred stones and fled to Carthage on the shores of North Africa. Her brother hunted her—for she'd stolen his gods. In our version of the tale, she sacrificed herself on the pyre to placate the gods and save her people. But even as she did, she claimed she would rise again like a phoenix from the ashes—on the day when the stones began to sing. And that would be a day of retribution for the Earth."

The abbess sat in silence for a long time when my mother had completed her tale. Nor did my stepfather and I choose to interrupt their thoughts. At last, the abbess spoke what she was thinking.

"The mystery of Orpheus," she said, "who sang the rocks and stones to life. The sweetness of his singing was such that even the desert sands wept blood-red tears. Though these may be only myths, I feel myself that this day of retribution is near at hand. If the Montglane Service rises, may heaven protect us all, for I believe it contains the key to open the mute lips of Nature, to unleash the voices of the gods."

∞

Letizia looked around the small dining room. The coals in the brazier had burned to ashes. Her two children sat silently watching her, but Mireille was more intent.

"And did the abbess say how she thought the service might bring such a thing to pass?" she asked.

Letizia shook her head. "No, but her other prediction came true—the one about Rousseau. For the autumn after her visit, his agent arrived—a young Scot named James Boswell. Under the pretext of writing a history of Corsica, he befriended Paoli and dined with him every night. The abbess had begged us to report to her his movements and to caution those of Phoenician ancestry not to share with him the old tales. But this was scarcely necessary, for we are by nature a clannish and secretive people who do not easily talk to strangers unless, like the abbess, we owe them a strong debt. As she also predicted, Boswell contacted Franz Fesch, but was put off by my stepfather's cool reception and jokingly called him a typical Swiss. When *The History of Corsica and Life of Pasquale Paoli* was later published, it was hard to imagine he'd learned much to take to Rousseau. And now, of course, Rousseau is dead. . . ."

"But the Montglane Service has risen," said Mireille, standing up and looking Letizia in the eye. "Though your tale explains the abbess's message and the nature of your friendship—it explains little else. Do you expect me, madame, to accept this story of singing stones and vengeful Phoenicians?

"I may have red hair like Elissa of Q'ar—but there is a brain beneath mine! The abbess of Montglane is no more a mystic than I, and would be no more satisfied with this tale. Besides, there was more to her message than the part you've explained—she told your daughter that when you received this news you would *know what to do*! What did she mean by that, Madame Buonaparte? . . . *And how was it connected with the formula?*"

At these words Letizia grew ashen white and put her hand to her breast. Elisa and Napoleone were riveted to their chairs, but Napoleone whispered in the silence, "What formula?"

"The formula that Voltaire knew of—that Cardinal Richelieu knew of— that Rousseau undoubtedly knew of—and that your mother most certainly knows of!" cried Mireille, her voice rising with every note. Her green eyes burned like dark emeralds as she stared at Letizia, who still sat there, in shock.

Mireille crossed the room with two swift strides and, grasping Letizia by the arms, pulled her to her feet. Napoleone and Elisa jumped up as well, but Mireille held up one hand to ward them off.

"Answer me, madame—these pieces have already killed two women before my eyes. I've seen the hideous and evil nature of one who seeks them—who hunts *me* even now, and would kill me for what I know. The box has been opened, and Death is on the loose. I've seen it with my own eyes—just as I've seen the Montglane Service—and the symbols that are carved into it! I *know* there is a formula. Now tell me *what the abbess wants you to do!*" She was nearly shaking Letizia, her face set with grim fury as she saw again before her eyes the face of Valentine—Valentine, who'd been murdered for the pieces.

Letizia's lips were trembling—she was weeping, this woman of steel who never shed a tear. Even as Mireille clutched her, Napoleone slid his arm about his mother and Elisa touched Mireille's arm gently.

"Mother," said Napoleone, "you must tell her. Tell her what she wants to know. My God, you have braved a hundred French soldiers with guns! What horror is it so terrible you cannot even speak of it?"

Letizia was trying to speak, her dry lips running with salt tears as she struggled to check her sobs.

"I swore—we all swore—we would never speak of it," she said. "Helene— the abbess *knew* there was a formula, before she had seen the service. And if she had to be the first to bring it to light after these thousand years, she told me she would *write it down*—write down the symbols on the pieces and the board—and somehow she'd send them to *me!*"

"To you?" said Mireille. "Why to you? You were only a child at the time."

"Yes, a child," Letizia said, smiling through her tears. "A child of fourteen— who was about to be married. A child who bore thirteen children of her own and watched five of them die. I am still a child, for I did not understand the danger of my promise to the abbess."

"Tell me," said Mireille softly. "Tell me what you promised her to do."

"I'd studied the ancient histories for all my life. I promised Helene that, when she had the pieces in her hands—I'd go to my mother's people in North Africa—I'd go to the ancient mufti of the desert. And I would decipher the formula."

"You know people there who can help you?" Mireille said with excitement. "But madame, that is where I'm bound. Oh, let me perform this service. It is my only wish! I know I've been ill—but I am young, and I'll recover quickly. . . ."

"Not until we communicate with the abbess," said Letizia, recovering a bit of her former aplomb. "Besides, it would take more than one evening for you to learn what I've learned in forty years! Though you think you're strong, you're not strong enough to travel—I think I've seen enough of this sort of illness to predict that in six or seven months it will run its course. Just enough time for you to learn—"

"Six or seven months!" Mireille cried. "Impossible! I cannot stay here in Corsica that long!"

"I'm afraid so, my dear," said Letizia with a smile. "You see, you're not ill at all. You are with child."

LONDON   NOVEMBER 1792

Six hundred fifty miles north of Corsica, the father of Mireille's child, Charles Maurice de Talleyrand-Périgord, sat on the frozen banks of the river Thames—fishing.

Beneath him on the stubbled grasses were spread several woolen shawls covered by oilcloth. His culottes were rolled above the knee, tied with grosgrain ribbon, his shoes and stockings placed carefully beside him. He was wearing a thick leather jerkin and fur-lined boots, with a broad-brimmed hat designed to keep the snows from his collar.

Behind him, beneath the snowy branches of a large oak, stood Courtiade, a straw basket of fish over one arm and his master's velvet cutaway folded neatly over the other. Lining the straw basket to soak up the blood of the fish were the yellowed leaves of a French newspaper already two months old, which had been tacked to the study walls until only that morning.

Courtiade knew what the newspaper said and was relieved when Talleyrand had suddenly ripped it from the wall, stuffed it into the basket, and announced it was time to go fishing. His master had been unusually quiet since the news had first arrived from France. They'd read it aloud together:

WANTED FOR TREASON

Taillerand, former Bishop of Autun, has emigrated . . . try to get information from relatives or friends who may harbor him. This description . . . long face, blue eyes, average nose with a slight upward tilt. Taillerand-Périgord has a limp, either in the right or left foot . . .

Courtiade's eyes followed the dark outlines of the barges moving up and down the bleak gray waters of the Thames. Chunks of ice broken from the riverbanks bounced like baubles sucked away by the swift current. Talleyrand's line floated out among the reeds between crevices of sooty ice. Even in the cold air, Courtiade could smell the rich and salty scent of fish. The winter, like many things, had come too soon.

It was September 23, scarcely two months ago, that Talleyrand had arrived in London at the small house on Woodstock Street that Courtiade had prepared for his arrival. It had been none too soon, for the prior day the committee had opened the king's "iron cupboard" at the Tuilleries—and found the letters from Mirabeau and LaPorte that revealed the many bribes that changed hands from

Russia, Spain, and Turkey—even from Louis XVI—to dedicated members of the Assembly.

Mirabeau was lucky; he was dead, thought Talleyrand as he reeled in his line and motioned for Courtiade to bring him more bait. That great statesman whose funeral had been attended by three hundred thousand—now they'd thrown a veil over his bust in the Assembly and removed his ashes from the Panthéon. For the king, matters would go far worse. Already his life hung by the merest thread, incarcerated with his family in the tower of the Knights Templar—that powerful Order of the Freemasons who were clamoring for him to be brought to trial.

Talleyrand too had been brought to trial, in absentia, and found guilty. Though they had no hard evidence against him in his own hand, LaPorte's confiscated letters suggested that his friend the bishop, as former president of the Assembly, would be willing to serve the king's interests—for a price.

Talleyrand strung his fish hook through the bit of suet Courtiade handed him and with a sigh tossed his line back into the dark waters of the Thames. All his precautions to leave France with a diplomatic pass had been in vain. A wanted man now in his own country, the doors of the British peerage had been slammed against him. Even the Émigrés here in England loathed him for having betrayed his own class by supporting the Revolution. Most dreadful of all, he was now completely without funds. Even those mistresses of his upon whom he'd once relied for financial support were now destitute in London, making straw hats to sell or writing novels.

Life was bleak. He saw the thirty-eight years of his existence swept under by the current like the bait he'd just tossed into the black waters, leaving not a trace. But still he held the pole. Though he spoke of it rarely, he could not forget his ancestry descended from Charles the Bald, grandson of Charlemagne. Adalbert of Périgord had put Hugh Capet on the throne of France; Taillefer the Ironcutter was a hero of the Battle of Hastings; Hélie de Talleyrand had put Pope John XXII in the Shoes of the Fisherman. He was descended from that long line of king makers whose motto was "Reque Dieu": We serve none but God. When life was bleak, the Talleyrands of Périgord were more likely to throw down the gauntlet than to throw in the towel.

He reeled in his line, cut the bait, and tossed it into Courtiade's basket. The valet helped him to his feet.

"Courtiade," Talleyrand said, handing over his pole, "you know that in a few months it will be my thirty-ninth birthday."

"Certainly," replied the valet. "Would the monseigneur wish me to prepare a celebration?"

At this, Talleyrand threw back his head and laughed. "By the end of this month I must relinquish my house on Woodstock Street and take a smaller place in Kensington. By year end with no source of income, I shall have to sell my library. . . ."

"Perhaps the monseigneur has overlooked something," said Courtiade politely, helping Talleyrand to remove his things and holding his velvet cutaway. "Something that might have been provided by fate against the difficult situation in which he now finds himself—I refer to those items currently located behind the books of the monseigneur's library at Woodstock Street."

"Not a day has passed, Courtiade," Talleyrand replied, "that I've not thought the same thing myself. I do not believe, however, that they were meant to be sold."

"If I may make so bold," pursued Courtiade, folding Talleyrand's clothes and picking up his shiny pumps from the riverbank, "has the monseigneur heard news of late from Mademoiselle Mireille?"

"No," he admitted, "but I'm not yet prepared to write her epitaph. She's a brave girl, and she's on the right course. What I meant was, this treasure now in my possession may be of more value than its pure weight in gold—else why has it been pursued by so many for so long? The age of illusion is ended now in France. The king has been weighed in the balance and—like all kings—found wanting. His trial would be merely a formality. But anarchy cannot replace even the weakest rule. What France needs now is a leader, not a ruler. And when he comes, I shall be the first to recognize him."

"The monseigneur means a man who will serve God's will, and restore peace to our land," said Courtiade, kneeling to pack some ice into the basket of fish.

"No, Courtiade," Talleyrand sighed. "If God wanted peace on earth, we should surely have it by now. I quote a savior who once said: 'I came not to bring peace, but a sword.' The man I describe will understand the value of the Montglane Service—which is summed up in one word: power. It is this I offer to the man who will one day soon lead France."

As Talleyrand and Courtiade made their way along the frozen banks of the Thames, the valet hesitantly put forth the question that had been in his mind ever since they'd received that French paper, now lying crumpled beneath melting ice and ripe fish:

"How does the monseigneur plan to locate such a man, when the charge of treason prevents him from returning to France?"

Talleyrand smiled, clapping his hand upon the valet's shoulder with unaccustomed familiarity. "My dear Courtiade," he said, "treason is merely a question of dates."

PARIS   DECEMBER 1792

The date was December 11. The event was the trial of Louis XVI, king of France. The charge was treason.

The Jacobin Club was already packed when Jacques-Louis David entered the front doors. The last of the stragglers from the first day's court hearings were trailing behind him, and a few clapped him on the shoulders. He caught snatches of their conversation—the ladies in their boxes at the trial drinking flavored liqueurs, the hawkers selling ices through the Convention Hall, the mistresses of the Duc d'Orleans whispering and giggling behind their lacy fans. And the king himself, presented with the letters from his iron cupboard, pretending he'd never seen them—denying his own signature—pleading a poor memory when confronted with multiple charges of treason against the State. He was a trained buffoon, the Jacobins all agreed. And most had decided on their vote even before entering the large oak doors of the Jacobin Club.

David was crossing the tiled floors of the former monastery where the Jacobins held their rallies when someone touched his sleeve. He turned to look into the cold, glittering green eyes of Maximilien Robespierre.

Impeccably outfitted as always, in a silver-gray suit with high-boned collar and carefully powdered hair, Robespierre looked paler than the last time David had seen him, and perhaps more severe. He nodded to David and, reaching inside his jacket, extracted a small box of pastilles. He took one and offered the box to David.

"My dear David," he said, "we've not seen you about, these many months. I heard you were working on a painting of the Jeu de Paume. I know you're a dedicated artist, but you must really not absent yourself so long—the Revolution needs you."

This was Robespierre's subtle way of pointing out that it was no longer safe for a revolutionary to stay away from the action. It might be construed as lack of interest.

"I heard, of course, about the fate of your ward at l'Abbaye Prison," he added. "Permit me to express my deepest sympathy, though belated. You know, I suppose, that Marat was chastised by the Girondins before the entire Assembly? When they cried out for his punishment, he stood in the Mountain and pulled out a pistol, flourishing it at his temple as if he meant to do himself in! A disgusting display, but it bought him his life. The king might do well to follow his example."

"You think the Convention will vote for the king's death?" said David, changing the subject from the painful thought of Valentine's death, which he'd barely been able to keep from his mind all these months.

"A live king is a dangerous king," said Robespierre. "Though I'm not a proponent of regicide, there can be no question from his correspondence that he was engaged in treason against the State—as was your friend Talleyrand! Now you see that my predictions about him were true."

"Danton sent me a note requesting my presence tonight," David said. "It seems there's some question of putting the king's fate to a popular vote."

"Yes, that's why we're meeting," said Robespierre. "The Girondins, those bleeding hearts, are supporting it. But if we permit all their provincial constituents to cast a vote, it will be a landslide return of the monarchy, I fear. And speaking of Girondins, I should like you to make the acquaintance of that young Englishman coming toward us—a friend of André Chénier the poet. I've invited him here this evening so his romantic illusions of the Revolution may be shattered by seeing the left wing in action!"

David saw the tall, gangly youth approach them. He had sallow skin, thin lank hair that he pushed back from his forehead, and the habit of stooping forward as if ambling over an open pasture. He was dressed in an ill-fitting brown frock coat that looked as if he'd picked it up in a ragbag. And instead of a foulard, he wore about his neck a knotted black handkerchief, rather the worse for wear. But his eyes were bright and clear, his weak chin counterbalanced by a strong and prominent nose, his young hands already marked with the calluses of those who'd grown up in the country and had to do for themselves.

"This is young William Wordsworth, a poet," said Robespierre as the youth came up to them and took David's proffered hand. "He's been in Paris for over a month now—but this is his first visit to the Jacobin Club. I present Citizen Jacques-Louis David, former president of the Assembly."

"Monsieur David!" Wordsworth cried, pressing David's hand warmly. "I had the great honor to see your painting displayed in London when I was down from Cambridge—*The Death of Socrates*. You are an inspiration to someone like myself, whose greatest wish is to record history in the making."

"A writer, are you?" said David. "Then as Robespierre will agree, you've arrived just in time to witness a great event—the fall of the French monarchy."

"Our own British poet, the mystical William Blake, has published last year a poem, 'The French Revolution,' in which he proclaims, as in the Bible, a visionary prophecy of the Fall of Kings. Perhaps you've read it?"

"I'm afraid I devote myself to Herodotus, Plutarch, and Livy," said David with a smile. "In these, I find adequate subject matter for my paintings, being neither a mystic nor a poet."

"That's odd," Wordsworth said. "For in England we'd believed those behind this French Revolution were the Freemasons, who must surely be counted mystics."

"It's true most of us belong to that society," agreed Robespierre. "In fact, the Jacobin Club itself was first founded by Talleyrand as an Order of the Freemasons. But here in France we Freemasons are scarcely mystics—"

"Some are," David interrupted. "Marat, for example."

"Marat?" said Robespierre with raised eyebrow. "Surely you jest. Whatever gave you that idea?"

"In fact, I came here tonight not only at Danton's behest," David admitted reluctantly. "I came to see you, for I thought perhaps you could help me. You referred to the—accident—that befell my ward at l'Abbaye Prison. You know that her death was no accident. Marat purposely had her questioned and executed because he believed she knew something about . . . Have you ever heard of the Montglane Service?"

At these words, Robespierre grew pale. Young Wordsworth glanced back and forth between the two men with an expression of confusion.

"Do you know what you're speaking of?" Robespierre whispered, drawing David aside, though Wordsworth followed them, now paying close attention. "What could your ward have known of such matters?"

"Both my wards were former novices at the Abbey of Montglane—" David began, but was again interrupted.

"Why have you never mentioned this before?" said Robespierre, his voice trembling. "But of course—this explains the devotion the Bishop of Autun lavished upon them from the moment of their arrival! If only you'd told me this earlier—before I let him slip through my fingers!"

"I never believed the story, Maximilien," David said. "I thought it was only a legend, a superstition. Marat believed it, though. And Mireille, attempting to save her cousin's life, told him the fabled treasure actually *existed*! She told him that she and her cousin *had* a portion of the treasure, and had buried it in my garden. But when he arrived the next day with a deputation to dig for it . . ."

"Yes? Yes?" Robespierre said fiercely, his fingers nearly crushing David's arm. Wordsworth was hanging on every word.

"Mireille had disappeared," whispered David, "and near the small fountain in the garden, there was a place where the earth had been freshly churned."

"Where is this ward of yours now?" Robespierre nearly cried in his agitation. "She must be brought in for questioning. At once."

"That is how I wished you might help me," said David. "I have now lost hope that she will return at all. With your contacts, I'd thought you might learn her whereabouts and whether anything has—befallen her."

"We shall find her if we have to turn France upside down," Robespierre assured him. "You must give me a full description, with as much detail as possible."

"I can do better than that," David replied. "I've a painting of her in my studio."

CORSICA   JANUARY 1793

But the subject of the painting, as fate would have it, was not destined to remain long on French soil.

It was well after midnight, near the end of January, when Mireille was roused from a deep sleep by Letizia Buonaparte, in the small room she shared with Elisa in their house in the hills above Ajaccio. Mireille had been in Corsica for three months now—and had learned at Letizia's side much, but not all, of what she'd stayed to learn.

"You must dress quickly," said Letizia in a low voice to the two girls, who were still rubbing the sleep from their eyes. Beside Letizia in the darkened room were her two small children, Maria-Carolina and Girolamo, already dressed, like Letizia, for travel.

"What is it?" Elisa cried.

"We must flee," said Letizia in a calm and steady voice. "The soldiers of Paoli have been here. The king of France is dead."

"No!" Mireille cried, sitting up abruptly.

"He was executed ten days ago at Paris," said Letizia, pulling clothes from the wardrobe in their room so they could dress quickly. "And Paoli has raised troops, here on Corsica, to join forces with Sardinia and Spain—to overthrow the French government."

"But my mother," complained Elisa, unwilling to leave her warm bed, "what has this all to do with us?"

"Your brothers Napoleone and Lucciano have spoken out against Paoli this afternoon in the Corsican Assembly," said Letizia with a wry smile. "Paoli has placed the vendetta traversa upon them."

"What is that?" Mireille said, climbing from bed and pulling clothes over her head as Letizia handed them to her.

"The collateral revenge!" Elisa whispered. "It is customary in Corsica, when someone has injured you, to bring the revenge against his entire family! But where are my brothers now?"

"Lucciano is in hiding with my brother, Cardinal Fesch," Letizia replied, handing Elisa her clothes. "Napoleone has fled the island. Now come, we've not enough horses to make it to Bocognano tonight, even with the children riding double. We must steal some and reach there before dawn." She left the room, pushing the smaller children ahead of her. As they whimpered in fear in the darkness, Mireille heard Letizia say in a firm voice, "*I* am not crying, am I? So what have you invented to cry about?"

"What's at Bocognano?" Mireille whispered to Elisa as they hastened from the room.

"My grandmother, Angela-Maria di Pietra-Santa, lives there," replied Elisa. "This means that matters are very grave indeed."

Mireille was flabbergasted. At last! She would finally see the old woman she'd heard so much about—friend of the Abbess of Montglane—

Elisa threw her arm about Mireille's waist as they hurried into the dark night.

"Angela-Maria has lived in Corsica all her life. From her own brothers, cousins, and grandnephews, she could raise an army that would wipe out half this isle. That is why Mother turns to her—it means she accepts the collateral revenge!"

The village of Bocognano was a walled fortress tucked high in the rugged and craggy mountains, nearly eight thousand feet above the sea. It was close to dawn when they crossed the last bridge on horseback, single file, the raging torrent boiling with mist below them. As they climbed the final hill, Mireille saw the pearly Mediterranean stretched out to the east, the little islands of Pianosa, Formica, Elba, and Monte Cristo that seemed to be floating in the sky, and beyond them the shimmering coastline of Tuscany just rising from the mist.

Angela-Maria di Pietra-Santa was not happy to see them.

"So!" said the little gnomelike woman, her hands on her hips as she stepped out of her small stone house to meet the weary riders. "Again they are in trouble, these sons of Carlo Buonaparte! I should have guessed that one day they would bring us to this."

If Letizia was surprised to hear that her mother knew the reason for their arrival, she did not show it. Her face still calm and tranquil, showing no emotion, she leapt from her horse and went to embrace her knotty and irate parent on either cheek.

"Well, well," snapped the older woman, "enough of the formalities. Get these children off their horses, for they look half-dead already! Don't you feed them? They all look like plucked chickens!" And she bustled about, pulling the younger ones from the horses by their feet. When she reached Mireille, she stopped and watched her dismount. Then she went over and grasped Mireille's chin roughly, turning her face this way and that to have a good look.

"So this is the one you've told me about," she tossed over her shoulder to Letizia. "The one with child? The one from Montglane?"

Mireille was nearly five months pregnant now, and her health had recovered, as Letizia had said it would.

"She must be removed from the island, Mother," replied Letizia. "We can no longer protect her, though I know the abbess would wish us to do so."

"How much has she learned?" demanded the old woman.

"As much as I could teach her in so short a time," Letizia said, her pale blue eyes resting briefly on Mireille. "But not enough."

"Well, let's not stand here clacking about for all the world to hear!" cried the old woman. She turned to Mireille and threw her withered arms about her in an embrace. "You come with me, young lady. Perhaps Helene de Roque will curse me for what I'm about to do—but if so, she should answer her correspondence more promptly! I've not heard a reply in the whole three months you've been here.

"Tonight," she went on in a mysterious whisper, leading Mireille toward the house, "under cover of darkness, I've arranged for a ship to take you to a friend of mine, where you'll be safe until the traversa is over."

"But madame," said Mireille, "your daughter has not finished my education. If I must go away and hide until this battle is over, it will delay my mission even further. I cannot afford to wait much longer."

"Who's asking you to wait?" She patted Mireille's small stomach and smiled. "Besides, I need you to go where I'm sending you—and I don't think you'll mind. The friend who protects you has been told you're coming, though he didn't expect you quite so soon. His name is Shahin—quite a dashing name. In Arabic, it means 'Peregrine Falcon.' He will continue your education in Algiers."

POSITIONAL ANALYSIS

Chess is the art of analysis.

—*Mikhail Botvinnik*
Soviet GM/World Champion

Chess is imagination.

—*David Bronstein*
Soviet GM

Wenn ihr's nicht fühlt, ihr werdet's nicht erjagen. (If you don't feel it, you'll never get it.)

—Faust
Johann Wolfgang Göethe

The coast road swung in long curves above the sea, each turn revealing a breathtaking view of rocky surf below. Small flowering succulents and lichen tumbled over the sheer rock faces, washed by sea spray. Ice plants were blooming in brilliant fuchsias and golds, the spiky leaves forming lacy patterns as they clambered down the salt-crusted rock. The sea shimmered metallic green—the color of Solarin's eyes.

I was distracted from this view, however, by the tangle of thoughts that had jammed my brain since the night before. I was trying to sort them out as my cab swept along the open corniche toward Algiers.

Every time I put two and two together—I kept coming up with eight. There were eights everywhere. First the fortune-teller had pointed it out with regard to my birthday. Then Mordecai, Sharrif, and Solarin had invoked it like a magical sign: not only was there an eight etched in the palm of my hand, but Solarin said there was a *formula* of the Eight—whatever that was supposed to mean. Those had been his last words before disappearing into the night, leaving Sharrif as my escort home—and *no key* to get back into my hotel room, since Solarin had pocketed it.

Sharrif had naturally been curious to know who my handsome companion had been at the cabaret and why he'd disappeared so suddenly. I explained how flattering it was to a simple girl like me to have not one, but *two* dates, only a few hours after landing on the shores of a new continent—and left him to his own thoughts as he and his thugs chauffeured me home in the squad car.

My key was at the desk when I arrived, and Solarin's bike was no longer propped outside my window. Since my night of peaceful sleep had been shot to hell anyway, I decided to waste the rest of it doing a little research.

Now I knew there was a formula, and it wasn't just a Knight's Tour. As Lily had imagined, it was another sort of formula—a formula that not even Solarin had deciphered. And it had something to do, I was certain, with the Montglane Service.

Nim had tried to warn me, hadn't he? He'd sent enough books about mathematical formulas and games. I decided to start with the one Sharrif had seemed most interested in, the one Nim himself had written—the Fibonacci numbers. I'd stayed up reading it until nearly dawn, and my determination had paid off, though I wasn't certain exactly how. The Fibonacci numbers, it seems, were used for a little more than stock market projections. Here's how they work:

Leonardo Fibonacci had decided to take numbers starting with "one": by adding each number to the one preceding, he produced a string of numbers that had very interesting properties. So one plus zero makes one; one and one = two; two and one = three; three and two = five; five and three = eight . . . and so on.

Fibonacci was something of a mystic, having studied among the Arabs who believed all numbers had magical properties. He discovered that the formula describing the relationship between each of his numbers—which was one-half the square root of five minus one ($\frac{1}{2} (\sqrt{5} - 1)$)—also described the structure of everything in nature that formed a spiral.

According to Nim's book, botanists soon learned that every plant whose petals or stems were spiral conformed to the Fibonacci numbers. Biologists knew that the nautilus shell and all spiral forms of marine life followed the pattern. Astronomers claimed the relationships of planets in the solar system—even the shape of the Milky Way—were described by the Fibonacci numbers. But I'd noticed something else, even before Nim's book spelled it out. Not because I knew anything about mathematics, but because I'd been a music major. You see, this little formula had *not* been invented by Leonardo Fibonacci but discovered two thousand years earlier—by a guy named Pythagoras. The Greeks called it the *aurio sectio:* the golden mean.

Simply put, the golden mean describes any point on a line where the ratio of the smaller part to the larger part is the same as the ratio of the larger part to the whole line. This ratio was used by all ancient civilizations in architecture, painting, and music. It was considered by Plato and Aristotle to be the "perfect" relationship to determine whether something was aesthetically beautiful. But to Pythagoras, it meant a great deal more than that.

Pythagoras was a fellow whose devotion to mysticism made even Fibonacci look like a patzer. The Greeks called him "Pythagoras of Samos" because he'd come to Crotona from the island of Samos, fleeing political problems. But according to his own contemporaries, he was born in Tyre, a city of ancient Phoenicia—that country we now call Lebanon—and traveled widely, living in Egypt for twenty-one years and Mesopotamia for twelve, arriving at last in Crotona well past the age of fifty. There he founded a mystical society, thinly disguised as a school, where his students learned the secrets he'd gleaned from his wanderings. These secrets centered around two things: mathematics and music.

It was Pythagoras who discovered that the base of the Western music scale was the octave because a plucked string divided in half would give the same sound exactly eight tones higher than one twice as long. The frequency of vibration of a string is inversely proportional to its length. One of his secrets was that a musical fifth (five diatonic notes, or the golden mean of an octave), when repeated twelve times in ascending sequence, should return to the original note eight octaves higher. But instead, when it got there it was off by an eighth of a note—so the ascending scale, too, formed a spiral.

But the biggest secret of all was the Pythagorean theory that the universe is constructed of numbers, each having Divine properties. These magical ratios of numbers appeared everywhere in nature, including—according to Pythagoras—in the sounds made by the vibrating planets as they moved through the black void. "There is geometry in the humming of the strings," he said. "There is music in the spacing of the spheres."

So what did this have to do with the Montglane Service? I knew that a chess set had eight pawns and eight pieces to a side; and the board itself had sixty-four spaces—eight squared. There was a formula all right. Solarin had called it the formula of the Eight. What better place to hide it than in a chess set comprised entirely of eights? Like the golden mean, like the Fibonacci numbers, like the ever-ascending spiral—the Montglane Service was greater than the sum of its parts.

I yanked a piece of paper out of my briefcase in the moving cab and drew a figure eight. Then I turned the paper sideways. It was the symbol for infinity. I heard the voice pounding in my head as I stared at the shape hovering before me. The voice said: *Just as another game . . . this battle will continue forever.*

But before I joined the fray, I had a bigger problem: to stay in Algiers at all I had to be certain I had a job—a job with enough éclat to make me mistress of my own fate. I'd had a taste of North African hospitality from my pal Sharrif, and I wanted to be sure in any future arm wrestling my credentials matched his. Then, too, how was I to hunt for the Montglane Service when, by the end of the week, my boss Petard would be hanging over my shoulder?

I needed space, and there was only one person who could arrange that for me. I was on my way to sit in the interminable rows of waiting rooms to try to get in to meet him. He was the man who'd approved my visa but stood up Fulbright Cone's partnership for a tennis match, the man who'd foot the bill for a major computer contract if only they could get him to sign the paper. And somehow I felt his support would be indispensable to the success of the many endeavors ahead of me. Though at the time, I could not have imagined to what degree. His name was Emile Kamel Kader.

My taxi came into the bottom of Algiers along the vast sweep of open port. Facing the sea was the high arcade of white arches that fronted the government buildings. We pulled up before the Ministry of Industry and Energy.

As I entered the marble lobby, enormous, dark, and cold, my eyes slowly adjusted to the light. Clusters of men stood about, some dressed in business suits, others in flowing white robes or black djellabas—those hooded robes that protected against the drastic swings in desert climate. A few were wearing headcloths in red-and-white checks that looked like Italian tablecloths. All eyes turned to gape at me as I entered the lobby, and I could see why. I seemed to be one of the few people in the place wearing pants.

There was no building directory or information desk, and there were three truckloads of guys for every available elevator. Besides, I didn't relish riding up and down with the bug-eyed oglers, when I wasn't sure what department I was looking for. So I headed for the wide marble stairs that led to the next floor. I was waylaid by a swarthy fellow in a business suit.

"May I assist you?" he said abruptly, placing his body squarely between me and the staircase.

"I have an appointment," I said, trying to push past him, "with Monsieur Kader. Emile Kamel Kader. He'll be expecting me."

"The minister of petrol?" said the fellow, looking at me in disbelief. To my horror, he nodded politely and said, "Certainly, madame. I shall conduct you to him."

Shit. I hadn't much choice but to let him escort me back to the elevators. The fellow had his hand under my elbow and was clearing a path for me through the throng as if I were the Queen Mother. I wondered what would happen when he discovered I had no appointment.

To make matters worse, it suddenly occurred to me as he commandeered a private elevator just for the two of us, that I wasn't as competent at fast talking in French as I was in English. Oh, well, I could plan my strategy as I waited in the anterooms for the many hours that Petard had told me were de rigueur. It would give me time to think.

When we got off the elevator on the top floor, a bevy of white-robed desert dwellers milled about near the reception desk, waiting to have their briefcases checked for firearms by the little turbaned receptionist. He sat behind the high desk with portable radio blaring music, casually passing inspection on each case with a wave of his hand. The crowd around him was fairly impressive. Though their clothes looked like bedsheets, the gold-and-ruby cabochon fingerwear would have made Louis Tiffany faint dead away.

My escort was dragging me through the throng, pardoning himself as he plowed among the shroudlike array. He spoke a few words in Arabic to the receptionist, who leapt up from behind his desk and trotted past us down the corridor. At the end, I saw him pause to speak to a soldier with a rifle slung over his shoulder. They both turned to stare at me, and the soldier disappeared around the corner. After a moment the soldier returned and motioned with a wave of the hand. The chap who'd escorted me from the lobby nodded and turned to me.

"The minister will see you now," he said.

Taking a last quick glance at the Ku Klux Klan around me, I picked up my briefcase and trotted down the hall after him.

At the end of the corridor, the soldier motioned me to follow him. He goose-stepped around the corner and down another, longer hallway toward a pair of carved doors that must have been twelve feet high.

The soldier stopped, stood at attention, and waited for me to go through. Taking a deep breath, I opened one of the doors. Inside was a tremendous foyer that had dark gray marble floors emblazoned with a pink marble star at center. The open doors opposite revealed an enormous office with wall-to-wall Boussac carpeting in black with squares of fat rosy chrysanthemums. The back wall of the office was a curved sweep of multipaned French windows, all opened so the sheer draperies floated back into the room. The tips of tall date palms beyond partially masked a view of the water.

Leaning on the wrought-iron railing of the balcony, his back to me, was a tall, slender man with sand-colored hair who was looking out to sea. He turned as I came in.

"Mademoiselle," he said warmly, coming around the desk to greet me with outstretched hand. "Permit me to introduce myself. I am Emile Kamel Kader, the minister of petroleum. I've looked forward to meeting you."

This entire introduction was delivered in English. I nearly fell on the floor. *Quel* relief.

"You're surprised at my English," he said with a smile, and not the "official" kind I'd received from the locals. This was one of the warmest smiles I'd ever seen. He continued to press my hand for a bit too long.

"I grew up in England and attended Cambridge. But everyone in the ministry speaks *some* English. It is, after all, the language of oil."

He also had the warmest voice, rich and golden like honey pouring into a spoon. His coloring reminded me of honey, too: amber eyes, wavy ash-blond hair, and skin that was golden olive. When he smiled, which he did often, the weblike crinkles appeared around his eyes, traces of being too often in the sun. I thought of the tennis match and smiled back.

"Please do be seated," he said, putting me on a beautifully carved rosewood chair. Going to his desk, he pushed the intercom and said a few words in Arabic. "I'm having tea brought up," he told me. "You're at the El Riadh, I understand. The food there is mostly tinned, quite unpalatable, though the hotel is lovely. I'll take you to lunch after our interview, if you haven't any plans? Then you can see a bit of the city."

I was still confused about this warm reception, and I suppose my face showed it, for he added: "You're probably wondering why you were shown into my office so quickly."

"I have to admit, I'd been told it would take a little longer."

"You see, mademoiselle . . . may I call you Catherine? . . . Fine, and you must call me Kamel, my so-called Christian name. In our culture, it's considered very rude to refuse a woman anything. Unmanly, actually. If a woman says she has an appointment with a minister, you don't leave her moldering in waiting rooms, you show her in at once!" He laughed in his wonderful golden voice. "You may get away with murder during your stay here, now that you know the recipe for success."

Kamel's long Roman nose and high forehead made him look as if his profile had been copied from a coin. Something about him looked familiar.

"Are you Kabyle?" I said suddenly.

"Why, yes!" He looked very pleased. "How did you know?"

"Just a guess," I said.

"A very good guess. A great portion of the ministry are Kabyle. Though we make up less than fifteen percent of Algeria's population, we Kabyle hold eighty percent of the high official posts. The golden eyes always give us away. It comes of looking at so much money." He laughed.

He seemed to be in such a good mood, I decided it was time to broach a most difficult subject—though I wasn't exactly sure how to go about it. After all, the partnership had been thrown out of his office for disrupting a tennis match. What would prevent *me* from being tossed out on my ear for foot-in-mouth disease? But I was in the inner sanctum—a chance like this might not come again soon. I decided to press my advantage.

"Look, there's something I must discuss with you before my colleague arrives at the end of the week," I began.

"Your colleague?" he said, taking a seat behind his desk. Was it only my imagination that he seemed suddenly guarded?

"My manager, to be precise," I said. "My firm has decided since we don't have a signed contract yet, they need this manager on site to supervise things. In fact, I'm countermanding orders by coming here today. But I've read the contract," I added, whipping a copy from my briefcase and slapping it on his desk, "and frankly I couldn't see that it called for so much supervision."

Kamel glanced at the contract and back at me. He folded his hands in prayerful attitude and bowed his head over them as if thinking. Now I was sure I'd gone too far. At last, he spoke.

"So you believe in breaking the rules?" he said. "That is interesting—I should like to know *why*."

"This is a 'blanket contract' for the services of one consultant," I told him, gesturing at the still untouched packet on the desk between us. "It says I'm to do analyses of petroleum resources, both underground and in the can. All I need is a computer to do that—and a signed contract. A boss might only get in the way."

"I see," said Kamel, still not smiling. "You've given me an explanation without answering my question. Let me ask you another. Are you familiar with the Fibonacci numbers?"

I decided not to let out a gasp. "A little," I admitted. "They're used for stock market projection. Could you tell me what your interest is in a subject so—shall I say erudite?"

"Certainly," said Kamel, pushing the button on his desk. A few moments later a serf came in bearing a leather folder, handed it to Kamel, and departed.

"The Algerian government," he said, taking out a document and handing it to me, "believes our country has only a limited supply of petroleum, enough to last perhaps eight more years. Maybe we will find more in the desert, maybe not. Oil is our only major export at this time; it completely supports the country paying for all our imports, including food. We've very little arable land here, as you'll see. We import all our milk, meat, grain products, lumber . . . even sand."

"You import sand?" I said, looking up from the document I'd begun reading. Algeria had hundreds of thousands of square miles of desert.

"Industrial-grade sand, to use in manufacturing. The sand in the Sahara is not suitable quality for industrial purposes. So we are completely dependent upon oil. We have no reserves, but we do have a very large strike of natural gas. So large that we may in time become among the world's biggest exporters of this product—if only we can find a way to transport it."

"What does this have to do with my project?" I said, quickly scanning the pages of the document, which, though written in French, had no reference either to petrol or *gaz naturel*.

"Algeria is a member country of the OPEC cartel. Each member country currently negotiates contracts and sets petroleum prices on its own, with different terms for different countries. Much of this is subjective and sloppy bartering. As the host country of OPEC, we propose to swing our members over to the concept of collective bartering. This will serve two purposes. First, it will dramatically increase the price per barrel of oil, while retaining the fixed cost of development. Second, we can reinvest this money in technological advance, much as the Israelis have done with Western funds."

"You mean in weapons?"

"No," said Kamel with a smile, "though it's true we all seem to spend plenty in that department. I was referring to industrial advances, and more than that. We can bring water to the desert. Irrigation is the root of all civilization, you know."

"But I see nothing in this document that reflects what you're telling me," I said.

Just then the tea arrived, wheeled in on a cart by a valet wearing white gloves. He poured the now familiar mint tea in a steaming spurt through the air. It hit the tiny glasses with a hiss.

"This is the traditional way of serving mint tea," Kamel explained. "They crush spearmint leaves and soak them in boiling water. It contains as much sugar as it can absorb. In some quarters it's thought to be a health tonic; in others, an aphrodisiac." He laughed as we tilted our glasses toward one another and sipped the heavily scented tea.

"Perhaps we could continue our conversation now," I said as soon as the door had closed behind the valet. "You've got an unsigned contract with my firm that says you want to calculate oil reserves; you've got a document here that says you want to analyze the import of sand and other raw materials. You want to project some kind of trend, or you wouldn't have brought up the Fibonacci numbers. Why so many different stories?"

"There is only one story," said Kamel, setting down his teacup and looking at me closely. "Minister Belaid and I reviewed your résumé closely. We agreed you'd be a good choice for this project—your track record shows you are willing to throw the rule book out the window." He smiled broadly as he said this. "You see, my dear Catherine, I have already refused a visa for your manager, Monsieur Petard—only this morning."

He pulled the copy of my vaguely worded contract across the desk, took out a pen, and slashed his name across the bottom of the page. "Now you have a signed contract that explains your mission here," he said, handing it to me across the desk. I stared at the signature for a moment, and then I smiled. Kamel smiled back.

"Great, boss," I said. "Now will somebody please explain what I'm supposed to be doing?"

"We want a computer model," he said softly. "But prepared in the utmost secrecy."

"What's the model to do?" I clutched the signed contract to my chest, wishing I could see Petard's face when he opened it in Paris—the contract the entire partnership couldn't get signed.

"We would like to predict," Kamel said, "what the world will do, economically, when we cut off their supply of petroleum."

The hills of Algiers are steeper than those of Rome or San Francisco. There are places where it's even hard to stand up. I was winded by the time we reached the restaurant, a small room on the second floor of a building overlooking an open plaza. It was called El Baçour, which Kamel explained meant "The Camel's Saddle." In the tiny entrance and bar, hard leather camel saddles were scattered about, each embroidered in beautifully colored patterns of leaves and flowers.

The main room had tables with crisply starched white tablecloths and white lace curtains blowing gently in the breeze from the open windows. Outside, the tops of wild acacias tapped against the open windowpanes.

We took a table in a round window alcove, where Kamel ordered pastilla au pigeon: a pie with crispy crust dipped in cinnamon and sugar, stuffed with a delectable combination of ground pigeon meat, minced scrambled eggs, raisins, toasted almonds, and exotic spices. As we worked our way through the traditional five-course Mediterranean lunch—the crisp home-grown wines flowing like water—Kamel regaled me with stories of North Africa.

I'd not realized the incredible cultural history of this country I now called home. First came the Tuaregs, Kabyle, and Moors—those tribes of the ancient Berber who'd settled the coast—followed by the Minoans and Phoenicians, who'd formed garrisons there. Then the Roman colonies; the Spaniards, who'd taken the Moorish lands after winning back their own; and the Ottoman Empire, which held token sway over the Barbary Coast pirates for three hundred years. From 1830 onward, these lands had been under French rule until—ten years before my arrival—the Algerian revolution had ended outside rule.

In between, there'd been more dynasties of deys and beys than I could count, all with exotic-sounding names and more exotic practices. Harems and beheadings seemed to be the order of the day. Now that Muslim rule was in force, things had calmed down a bit. Though I'd noticed Kamel had drunk his share of red wine with the tournedos and saffron rice, and white wine to chase the salad, he still professed to be a follower of al-Islam.

"Islam," I said as they served the syrupy black coffee and dessert. "It means 'Peace,' doesn't it?"

"In a way," said Kamel. He was cutting up the rahad lakhoum into squares: a jellylike substance coated with powdered sugar and flavored with ambrosia, jasmine, and almonds. "It is the same word as 'shalom' in Hebrew: peace be with you. In Arabic, it's 'salaam,' accompanied by a deep bow until the head touches the earth. It signifies total prostration to the will of Allah—it means complete submission." He handed me a square of rahad lakhoum with a smile. "Sometimes submission to the will of Allah means peace—sometimes not."

"More often not," I said. But Kamel looked at me seriously.

"Remember that of all the great prophets in history—Moses, Buddha, John the Baptist, Zarathustra, Christ—Muhammed was the only one who actually went to war. He raised an army of forty thousand and, leading it himself on horseback, attacked Mecca. And won it back!"

"How about Joan of Arc?" I asked with a smile.

"She didn't found a religion," he replied. "But she had the right spirit. However, the jihad isn't what you Westerners think. Have you ever read the

Koran?" When I shook my head, he said, "I'll have a good copy sent to you—in English. I think you'd find it interesting. And different than you might imagine."

Kamel picked up the tab, and we went out to the street. "Now for that tour of Algiers I promised you," he said. "I'd like to begin by showing you the Poste Centrale."

We headed down to the big central post office on the waterfront. En route he said, "All the phone lines are run through the Poste Centrale. It's another of those systems we've inherited from the French, where everything runs into the center and nothing can get back out again—just like the streets. The international calls are put through by hand. You'll enjoy seeing it—especially as you're going to have to deal with this archaic phone system to design the computer model I've just signed for. Much of the data you'll be collecting will come via phone lines."

I wasn't certain how the model he'd described to me would require telecommunications, but we'd agreed not to speak of it in public, so I said only, "Yes, I had some trouble placing a long-distance call last night."

We went up the steps to the Poste Centrale. Like all the other buildings, it was large and dark with marble floors and high ceilings. Elaborate chandeliers hung from the ceiling like a bank office designed in the 1920s. Everywhere were large framed photos of Houari Boumédienne, the president of Algeria. He had a long face, large sad eyes, and a heavy Victorian mustache.

There was a lot of empty space in all the buildings I'd seen, and the poste was no exception. Though Algiers was a big city, there never seemed to be as many people about as there was space to fill, even on the streets. Coming from New York, this made an impression upon me. As we crossed the poste, the sound of our clicking heels echoed off the walls. People spoke in hushed whispers, as if it were the public library.

At the far corner, in an open space by itself, sat a tiny switchboard no larger than a kitchen table. It looked as if it had been designed by Alexander Graham Bell. Behind it was a small tight-faced woman in her forties, with a concoction of bright hennaed hair piled on top of her head. Her mouth was a slash of blood-red lipstick, a color they hadn't made since the Second World War, and her flowered voile dress was vintage, too. A large box of chocolates with loose wrappers sat on top of the switchboard.

"If it isn't the minister!" said the woman, pulling a plug out of her switchboard and standing up to greet him. She put both her hands out, and Kamel took them in his. "I got your chocolates," she said, motioning to the box. "Swiss! You never do anything second-rate." She had a low, gravelly voice, like that of a chanteuse in a Montmartre dive. There was some of the roustabout in her personality, and I liked her at once. She spoke French like the Marseilles sailors that Harry's maid Valerie could imitate so well.

"Therese, I'd like you to meet Mademoiselle Catherine Velis," Kamel told her. "The mademoiselle is doing some important computer work for the ministry—for OPEC, in fact. I thought you'd be a good person for her to know."

"Ahhh, OPEC!" said Therese, making big eyes and shaking her fingers. "Very big. Very important. This one must be a clever one!" she said of me. "You know this OPEC, she will make a big splash pretty soon, you listen to me."

"Therese knows everything." Kamel laughed. "She listens in on all the transcontinental phone calls. She knows more than the ministry."

"Oh, of course," she said. "Who would take care of matters if I were not here?"

"Therese is *pied noir*," Kamel told me.

"That means 'black foot,'" she said in English. Then, lapsing again into French, she explained, "I was born with my feet in Africa, but I am not one of these Arabs. My people come from the Lebanon."

I seemed destined to remain confused about the genetic distinctions that were made in Algeria. Though it all seemed very important to them.

"Miss Velis had some trouble placing a phone call last night," Kamel told her.

"What time was it?" she wanted to know.

"About eleven P.M.," I said. "I tried to call New York from the El Riadh."

"But I was here!" she exclaimed. Then, shaking her head, she informed me, "These 'types' that work in the hotel switchboards are very lazy. They cut off connections. Sometimes you must wait eight hours to put a call through. Next time you let me know, and I will arrange everything. You wish to make a call tonight? Tell me when, and it is done."

"I want to send a message to a computer in New York," I told her, "to let someone know I've arrived. It's a voice recorder, you talk the message and it's digitally recorded."

"Very modern!" said Therese. "I can do it in English for you, if you'd like."

We agreed, and I wrote down the message to Nim, telling him I'd arrived safely and would go to the mountains soon. He would know what that meant: that I was going to meet Llewellyn's antique dealer.

"Excellent," said Therese, folding the note. "I will send this off at once. Now that we've met, your calls will always receive top priority. Come and visit me again sometime."

As Kamel and I left the poste, he said, "Therese is the most important person in Algeria. She can make or break a political career just by unplugging someone she doesn't like. I think she likes you. Who knows, she might even make you president!" He laughed.

We were walking along the waterfront back to the ministry, and he commented casually, "I noticed in the message you sent that you planned to go to the mountains. Was there somewhere specific you wanted to go?"

"Only to meet a friend of a friend," I said noncommittally. "And to see a bit of the country."

"I ask, because the mountains here are the home of the Kabyle. I grew up there, and I know the area quite well. I could send a car for you or drive you myself, if you'd like." Though Kamel's offer was as casual as his offer to show me Algiers, I noted another tone beneath it I couldn't identify.

"I thought you grew up in England?" I said.

"I went there when I was fifteen to attend public school. Before that, I ran barefoot through the hills of the Kabyle like a wild goat. You should really have a guide. It's a magnificent region, but easy to get lost. Road maps of Algeria aren't all they should be."

He was doing a bit of a sales pitch, and I thought it might be impolitic to decline his offer. "It *might* be best if I went there with you," I said. "You know, last night when I came from the airport, I was followed by Sécurité. A fellow named Sharrif. Do you think that means anything?"

Kamel had stopped in his tracks. We were standing at the port, and the giant steamers rocked gently up and down on the slow tide.

"How do you know it was Sharrif?" he said abruptly.

"I met him. He . . . had me brought to his office at the airport as I was going through Customs. He asked me a few questions, was very charming, then released me. But he had me followed—"

"What sorts of questions?" Kamel interrupted. His face was very gray. I tried to remember everything that had passed, recounting it all to Kamel. I even told him the taxi driver's commentary.

Kamel was silent when I'd finished. He seemed to be thinking something over. At last he said, "I'd appreciate it if you'd mention this to no one else. I'll look into it, but I shouldn't be too concerned. It's probably a case of mistaken identity."

We walked along the port back toward the ministry. As we reached the ministry entrance, Kamel said, "Should Sharrif contact you again for any reason, tell him you've informed me of all this." He put his hand on my shoulder. "And tell him that *I* will be taking you into the Kabyle."

THE SOUND OF THE DESERT

But the Desert hears, though men do not hear, and will one day be transformed into a Desert of sound.

—Miguel de Unamuno y Jugo

Mireille stood on the Erg and surveyed the vast red desert.

South of her lay the dunes of Ez-Zemoul El Akbar, rolling in waves over a hundred feet high. From this distance in the morning light, they looked like blood-red talons rippling the sand.

Behind her rose the Atlas Mountains, still purpled with shadow and shrouded in low-hanging snow clouds. They brooded over this empty desert—a wilderness larger than any on earth—a hundred thousand miles of deep sands the color of crumbled brick, where nothing moved but crystals borne by the breath of God.

"Sahra," it was called. The South. The Wasteland. Kingdom of the Aroubi—the Arab, Wanderer in the Wilderness.

But the man who'd brought her here was not an Aroubi. Shahin had fair skin with hair and eyes the color of old bronze. His people spoke the tongue of the ancient Berber who'd ruled this barren desert for over five thousand years. They'd come, he said, from the mountains and the Ergs—that stately range of mesas separating the mountains behind her from the sands that spread before her. This chain of mesas they had named "Areg": the Dune. And they called themselves the Tou-Areg. Those who are bound to the Dune. The Touareg knew a secret as ancient as their lineage, a secret buried in the sands of time. This was the secret Mireille had traveled so many months, so many miles, to find.

It was only a month since the night she'd gone with Letizia to the hidden Corsican cove. There she took a small fishing boat across the raging winter sea to Africa, where her guide Shahin, the Falcon, waited at the docks of Dar-el-Beida to take her into the Maghreb. He was dressed in a long black haik, his face shrouded in the indigo litham, a double veil through which he could see but not be seen. For Shahin was one of the "Blue Men," those sacred tribes of the Ahaggar where only the men wore veils against the desert winds, tinting their skin an unearthly shade of blue. The nomads called this special sect Maghribi—Magicians—those who could unfurl the secrets of Maghreb, the Sunset-land. They knew where the key to the Montglane Service was to be found.

This was why Letizia and her mother had sent her into Africa, why Mireille had crossed the High Atlas in winter—three hundred miles through blizzards and treacherous terrain. For once she found the secret, she'd be the only living person who'd touched the pieces—and knew the key to their power.

The secret was not hidden beneath a rock in the desert. Nor was it tucked inside a musty library. It lay hidden within the softly whispered tales of these nomadic men. Moving across the sands by night, passing from mouth to mouth, the secret had moved as the sparks of a dying bonfire are scattered across the silent sands and buried in darkness. The secret was hidden in the very sounds of the desert, in the tales of her people—in the mysterious whispers of the rocks and stones themselves.

Shahin lay on his belly in the brush-covered trench they'd dug in the sand. Overhead, the falcon circled in a slow, lazy spiral, scanning the brush for motion. Beside Shahin, Mireille squatted low, scarcely breathing. She watched her companion's tense profile: the long narrow nose, hooked like the peregrine for which he was named, the pale yellow eyes, grim mouth, and softly wrapped headcloth, with long braided hair tumbling down his back. He'd removed his traditional black haik and wore, like Mireille, only a soft hooded wool djellaba dyed a clear bright russet from the juice of the abal bush, the color of the desert. The falcon that circled above could not distinguish them from the sands and brush that formed their camouflage.

"It is a hurr—a Sakr falcon," Shahin whispered to Mireille. "Not so swift or aggressive as the peregrine, but smarter and with better vision. He'll make a good bird for you."

Mireille must catch and train a falcon, he'd told her, before they crossed the Ez-Zemoul El Akbar at the lip of the Great Eastern Erg—the broadest, highest range of dunes on earth. This was not only the test of worth customary among the Touareg—whose women both hunted and ruled—it was also a necessity for survival.

For ahead of them lay fifteen days, perhaps twenty, in the dunes, blazing by day and freezing by night. They could only press their camels at one mile per hour as the dark red sands slipped away beneath them. At Khardaia they'd bought provisions: coffee and flour, honey and dates—and bags of stinking dried sardines to feed the camels. But now that they'd left the salt marshes and stony Hammada with its last trickle of dying springs, they'd have no other food, unless they could hunt. And no species on earth possessed the endurance, eyesight, tenacity, and predatory spirit to hunt this wild and barren land—except the falcon.

Mireille watched as the falcon seemed to hover effortlessly above them on the hot desert breeze. Shahin reached inside his pack and withdrew the tame pigeon they'd brought. He bound a thin string to its leg; the other end he wrapped about a stone. Then he released the bird into the air. The pigeon beat upward into the sky. In an instant the falcon had spotted it and seemed to stop in midair, gathering itself. It plummeted swiftly as a bullet and struck. Feathers flew out in all directions as the two birds tumbled to earth.

Mireille began to move forward, but Shahin restrained her with a hand.

"Let him taste the blood," he whispered. "The blood erases memory and caution."

The falcon was on the ground tearing at the pigeon when Shahin began to tug at the string. The falcon fluttered up a bit but settled back in the sand, confused. Shahin tugged the string again—so it appeared that the pigeon, crippled, was flapping across the sand. As he'd predicted, the falcon quickly returned to gorge on the warm flesh.

"Move up as close as possible," Shahin whispered to Mireille. "When he's at one meter, catch him by the leg."

Mireille looked at him as if he were mad but moved as close as she could to the edge of the brush, still squatting for the spring. Her heart was beating as Shahin tugged the pigeon closer and closer. The falcon was within feet of her, still worrying its prey, when Shahin tapped her on the arm. Without a beat, she dove through the brush and grasped the falcon's leg. It wheeled, beating its wings against her, and with a cry drove its sharp-toothed beak into her wrist.

Shahin was out of the brush beside her in an instant, catching the bird, hooding it with expert motions, and shackling it with a length of silken cord to the leather band he'd already bound to her left wrist.

Mireille sucked at the blood that gushed forth from her other, wounded wrist, splattering her face and hair. Clucking his tongue, Shahin tore loose a strip of muslin and bound up where the falcon had torn the flesh away. The bird's beak had come precariously close to an artery.

"You caught him so you could eat," he said with a wry smile, "but he's nearly eaten *you*." Taking her bandaged arm, he placed that hand against the blinded falcon that now clung with its talons to the strap on her other wrist.

"Stroke him," he counseled her. "Let him know who is master. It requires one moon and three quarters to break a hurr—but if you live with him, eat with him, stroke him, talk to him—even sleep with him—he'll be yours by the new moon. What name will you give him, so he can learn it?"

Mireille looked proudly at the wild creature that clung trembling to her arm. For a moment she forgot the throbbing in her wounded wrist. "Charlot," she said. "Little Charles. I've captured a little Charlemagne of the skies."

Shahin looked at her silently with his yellow eyes, then slowly pulled up his indigo veil so it covered the lower half of his face. When he spoke, the veil rippled in the dry desert air.

"Tonight we will place your mark upon him," he said, "so he knows he is yours alone."

"My mark?" said Mireille.

Shahin slipped a ring from his finger and pressed it into her hand. Mireille glanced down at the signet, a block of heavy gold in her palm. Emblazoned on the top was a figure eight.

Silently she followed Shahin down the steep embankment to where their camels waited in the gully of the dune, kneeling on folded legs. She watched as he placed his knee in the camel's saddle and the beast rose with one movement, lifting him like a feather. Mireille followed suit, holding the falcon aloft on her wrist, and they swept away across the rust-red sands.

The embers glowed low in the fire as Shahin leaned forward to place the ring in the coals. He spoke little and smiled rarely. She'd not learned much about him in the month they'd spent together. They concentrated on survival. She only knew they would reach the Ahaggar—those lava mountains that were home to the Kel Djanet Touareg—before her child was born. Of other topics, Shahin was reticent to speak, responding to all her queries with "Soon you will see."

She was surprised, therefore, when he removed his veils and spoke, as they watched the golden ring gathering heat amid the coals.

"You are what we call a *thayyib*," said Shahin, "a woman who has known a man only once—yet you are with child. Perhaps you noticed how those at Khardaia looked at you when we stopped there. Among my people there is a story. Seven thousand years before the Hegira, a woman came from the east. She traveled thousands of miles alone across the salt desert until she reached the Kel Rela Touareg. She had been cast out by her own people, for she was with child.

"Her hair was the color of the desert, like yours. Her name was Daia, which means 'the wellspring.' She sought shelter in a cave. The day her child was born, water sprang forth from the rock of the cave. It flows there even today, at Q'ar Daia—the cave of Daia, goddess of the wells."

So this Khardaia, where they'd stopped for camels and supplies, was named for the strange goddess Q'ar—just like Carthage, thought Mireille. Was this Daia—or Dido—the same legend? Or the same person?

"Why do you tell me this?" asked Mireille, stroking Charlot perched on her arm as she gazed into the fire.

"It is written," he said, "that one day a Nabi, or Prophet, will come from the Bahr al-Azraq—the Azure Sea. A Kalim—one who talks with spirits, who follows the Tarikat, or mystic path to knowledge. This man will be all these things, and he will be a Za'ar—one who has fair skin, blue eyes, and red hair. It is a portent to my people, which is why they stared at you."

"But I am not a man," said Mireille, looking up, "and my eyes are green—not blue."

"It is not you I speak of," Shahin said. Bending over the fire, he pulled out his *bousaadi*—a long thin knife—and extracted the glowing ring from the hot coals. "It is your son we've awaited—he who will be born beneath the eyes of the goddess—just as it was foretold."

Mireille didn't question how Shahin knew her unborn child would be male. Her mind was brimming with a million thoughts as she watched him wrap a strip of leather over the glowing ring. She permitted herself to think of the child in her swollen belly. At nearly six months, she could feel him moving inside her. What would become of him, born in this vast, treacherous wilderness—so far from his own people? Why did Shahin believe he'd fulfill this primitive prophecy? Why had he told her the story of Daia—and what did it have to do with the secret she sought? She shook these thoughts from her mind as he handed her the hot ring.

"Touch him quickly but firmly on the beak—just here," he instructed as she took the leather-wrapped ring, still glowing hot. "He feels it not much, but he will remember. . . ." Mireille looked at the hooded falcon that sat trustingly on her arm, its talons digging into the thick wristband. The beak was exposed, and she held the hot ring only inches away. Then she paused.

"I cannot," she said, pulling the ring away. The reddish glow flickered in the cold night air.

"You must," Shahin said firmly. "Where will you get the strength to kill a *man*—if you haven't force enough to place your mark upon a bird?"

"Kill a man?" she said. "Never!" But even as she spoke, Shahin smiled slowly, his eyes glittering gold in the strange light. The Bedouin were right, she thought, when they said there was something terrible about a smile.

"Do not tell me you will not kill this man," Shahin said softly. "You know his name—you speak it nightly in your sleep. I can smell the revenge in you, as one can find water by scent. This is what brought you here, what keeps you alive—revenge."

"No," said Mireille, though she felt the blood beating behind her eyelids as her fingers tightened on the ring. "I came here to find a secret. You know that. Instead, you tell me myths of some red-haired woman who has been dead thousands of years. . . ."

"I never said she was dead," said Shahin abruptly, his face expressionless. "She lives, like the singing sands of the desert. Like the ancient mysteries, she speaks. The gods could not bear to see her die—they turned her into living stone. For eight thousand years she has waited, for you are the instrument of her retribution—you and your son—just as it was foretold."

I will rise again like a phoenix from the ashes on the day when the rocks and stones

begin to sing . . . and the desert sands will weep blood-red tears . . . and this will be
a day of retribution for the Earth. . . .

Mireille heard Letizia's voice whispering in her mind. And the abbess's reply:
The Montglane Service contains the key to open the mute lips of Nature—to
unleash the voices of the gods.

She looked out over the sands, a pale and eerie pink in the firelight, swimming beneath the vast sea of stars. In her hand was the glowing golden ring.
Murmuring softly to the falcon, she took a deep breath and pushed the hot bezel
against its beak. The bird flinched, trembled, but did not move as the acrid smell
of burning cartilage filled her nostrils. She felt ill as she dropped the ring on
the ground. But she stroked the falcon's back and folded wings. The soft feathers
shifted against her fingertips. On the beak was a perfect figure eight.

Shahin reached out, placing his big hand on her shoulder as she stroked the
falcon. It was the first time he'd touched her, and now he looked into her eyes.

"When she came to us from the desert," he said, "we called her Daia. But
now she lives at the Tassili, where I am taking you. She stands over twenty feet
tall, towering a mile above the valley of Djabbaren, above the giants of the
earth—whom she rules. We call her the White Queen."

They'd moved alone through the dunes for weeks, pausing only to flush
small game, releasing one of the falcons to hunt it down. This was the only fresh
food they'd had. Milk from the camels with its sweaty, saltlike taste was their
only drink.

It was noon of the eighteenth day when Mireille came over the rise, her camel
slipping in the soft sand—and caught her first glimpse of the *zauba'ah,* those
wild whirlwind pillars that ravaged the desert. Nearly ten miles away, they
reared a thousand feet into the sky, columns of red-and-ocher sand slanting
heavily into the wind. The sand at their base whipped a hundred feet in the air,
a churning sea of rocks, sand, and plants in a wild kaleidoscope like colored bits
of confetti. At three thousand feet they cast off a huge red cloud that covered
the sky, arching over the pillars and obliterating the midday sun.

The tentlike scaffolding that shrouded her from the desert glare flapped high
above the camel saddles like the sails of a boom crossing the sea of the desert.
This was the only sound Mireille heard, this dry flapping—while in the distance
the desert tore itself silently to shreds.

Then she heard the sound—a slow hum, low and frightening like a mysterious Oriental gong. The camels began prancing, pulling against their leads,
thrashing wildly in the air. The sand was slipping away beneath their feet.

Shahin leapt off his camel, grabbing the reins to pull it about as it kicked
out at him.

"They're afraid of the singing sands," he cried to her, grasping her reins as she clambered down to help pull the scaffolding apart. Shahin was blindfolding the camels as they lurched against him, crying with their hoarse, braying voices. He hobbled them with a *ta'kil*—shackling the foreleg above the knee—and forced them down into the sand as Mireille lashed down their gear. The hot wind picked up its pace as the singing sands grew louder.

"They are ten miles away," Shahin was screaming, "but they move very fast. In twenty minutes, perhaps thirty, they'll be upon us!"

He was hammering tent posts into the ground, tacking down tent canvas over their belongings as the camels brayed frantically, clawing on their hobbled forelegs for purchase in the moving sands. Mireille cut the *sibaks*, the silken cords that bound the falcons to their perches, grabbed the birds, and shoved them into a sack, pushing it under the lip of the flattened tent. Then she and Shahin crawled beneath the canvas that was already half buried in heavy, bricklike sand.

Under the canvas, Shahin was wrapping muslin over her head and face. Even here, under the tent, she could feel the harsh grit stinging her skin, forcing its way into her mouth, nose, and ears. She flattened into the sand and lay there trying not to breathe as the sound grew louder—like the roar of the sea.

"The serpent's tail," said Shahin, throwing his arm across her shoulders to form a pocket of air for her to breathe as the sands crushed down ever heavier upon them. "He rises to guard the gate. This means—if Allah wills us to live—we will reach the Tassili tomorrow."

ST. PETERSBURG, RUSSIA   MARCH 1793

The Abbess of Montglane sat in the vast drawing room of her apartments at the Imperial Palace in St. Petersburg. The heavy tapestries that covered the doors and windows shut out all light and seemed to lend the room a sense of security. Until this morning, the abbess had believed she *was* secure, that she'd prepared for every eventuality. Now she realized she'd been mistaken.

Around her were the half-dozen *femmes de chambre* that the Czarina Catherine had assigned to wait upon her. Seated silently, their heads bowed over their tatting and embroidery, they watched her from the corners of their eyes so they could report her every move. She moved her lips, mumbling an Act of Hope and an Apostle's Creed so they would think she was deep in prayer.

Meanwhile, seated at the inlaid French writing table, she opened the pages of her leather-bound Bible and secretly read for the third time a letter the French ambassador had smuggled to her only that morning—his last act before the arrival of the sleigh that would carry him back to France in exile.

The letter was from Jacques-Louis David. Mireille was missing—she'd fled from Paris during the Terror and perhaps even left the shores of France. But Valentine, sweet Valentine, was dead. And where were the pieces? the abbess wondered in desperation. That, of course, the letter did not say.

Just at that moment, there was a loud crash in the outer foyer—and a clatter of metal followed by agitated cries. Rising above all was the stentorian voice of the czarina.

The abbess folded the pages of her Bible over the letter. The *femmes de chambre* were glancing at one another uneasily. The door to the inner chamber flew open. The covering tapestry was ripped from the wall, falling to the floor in a clatter of brass rings.

The ladies leapt up in confusion—sewing baskets upset, yarns and fabrics spilling over the floor, as Catherine barreled into the room, leaving a bevy of confused guards collecting themselves in her wake.

"Out! Out! Out!" she cried, crossing the room as she pounded a stiff roll of parchment against her open palm. The ladies-in-waiting scurried from her path, strewing bits of thread and cloth in their trail as they tripped over one another trying to reach the door. There was brief congestion in the foyer as women and guards collided in an attempt to escape the sovereign wrath; then the outer doors slammed shut with a clang—just as the empress reached the writing desk.

The abbess smiled up at her calmly, the Bible closed on the desk before her. "My dear Sophie," she said sweetly, "after these many years, you've come to say Matins with me. I suggest we begin with the Act of Contrition. . . ."

The empress slammed the rolled parchment down on the abbess's Bible. Her eyes were blazing with fire. "*You* begin with the Act of Contrition!" she cried. "How *dare* you defy me? How *dare* you refuse to obey? My will is the law of this State! This State, that has given you shelter for over a year—despite the advice of my counsellors and against my own better judgment! How dare you refuse my command?!" Snatching up the parchment, she yanked it open before the abbess's face. "Sign it!" she screamed, grabbing a plume from the inkwell and splattering ink across the desk with trembling hand, her face black with fury. "Sign it!!"

"My dear Sophie," said the abbess calmly, taking the parchment from Catherine's fingers, "I have no idea what you are talking about." She surveyed the paper as if she'd never seen it before.

"Plato Zubov told me you refused to sign it!" she cried as the abbess continued to read. The pen still dripped from between the czarina's fingers. "I demand to know what reason you give—before I cast you into prison!"

"If I'm to be cast into prison," said the abbess with a smile, "I fail to see what difference my excuse would make—even though it might be of vital interest to you." She looked back at the paper.

"What do you mean?" asked the empress, putting the pen back into the inkstand. "You know perfectly well what this paper is—to refuse to sign it is an act of treason against the State! Any French émigré wishing to continue my protection will sign this oath. That nation of dissolute scoundrels has assassinated their king! I've expelled Ambassador Genet from my court—I've severed all diplomatic relations with that puppet government of fools—I've forbidden French ships entry to any Russian port!"

"Yes, yes," said the abbess a little impatiently. "But what has this all to do with me? I'm hardly an émigré—I left long before the doors of France were closed. Why should I sever all relations with my country—even friendly correspondence that does nobody any harm?"

"In refusing, you suggest you're in league with those devils!" said Catherine in horror. "Do you realize they *voted* to execute a king? By what right do they take such liberty? Those street scum—they murdered him in cold blood, like a common criminal! They cropped his hair and stripped him to his shirt-sleeves and carried him in a wooden tumbril through the streets for the rabble to spit upon! On the scaffold, when he tried to speak—to forgive the sins of his own people before they butchered him like a cow—they forced his head down on the block and set the tambours rolling. . . ."

"I know," the abbess said quietly. "I know." She put the parchment on the desk and stood to face her friend. "But I cannot cease communication with those in France, despite any ukase you may devise. There is something worse— something more dreadful than the death of a king—perhaps than the death of *all* kings."

Catherine looked at her in astonishment as the abbess reluctantly opened the Bible before her and extracted the letter from between the pages, handing it to her.

"Some pieces of the Montglane Service may be missing," she said.

Catherine the Great, Czarina of all the Russias, sat at the black-and-white-tiled chessboard across from the abbess. She picked up a Knight and placed it at the center. She looked fatigued and ill.

"I don't understand," she said in a low voice. "If you've known where the pieces were all this time, why didn't you tell me? Why didn't you trust me? I thought they had been scattered. . . ."

"They *were* scattered," the abbess replied, studying the board, "but scattered by hands that I thought I controlled. Now it seems I was mistaken. One of the players is missing, along with some pieces. I must recover them."

"Indeed you must," the empress agreed. "And now you see you should have turned to me in the first place. I've agents in every country. If anyone can get those pieces back, I can."

"Don't be absurd," said the abbess, sliding her Queen forward and picking off a pawn. "Eight pieces were in Paris when this young woman disappeared. She'd never be fool enough to carry them with her. She's the only one who knows where they've been hidden—and she'd trust none but a person she *knew* was sent by me. To this end, I've written to Mademoiselle Corday, who used to manage the convent at Caen. I've asked her to journey to Paris in my behalf—to pick up the trail of the missing girl before it is too late. If she should die, all knowledge of those pieces dies with her. Now that you've exiled my postman, Ambassador Genet, I can no longer communicate with France unless you help me. My last letter has left with his diplomatic pouch."

"Helene, you are too clever for me by half," said the czarina with a broad grin. "I should have guessed where the rest of your mail was coming from—the parts I was unable to confiscate."

"Confiscate!" said the abbess, watching Catherine remove her Bishop from the board.

"Nothing of interest," said the czarina. "But now that you've shown enough faith in me to reveal the contents of this letter, perhaps you'll go a step further and permit me to assist you with the service, as I originally offered. Though I suspect it's only the removal of Genet that's caused you to confide in me—I am still your friend. I want the Montglane Service. I must have it before it falls into hands far less scrupulous than mine. You've placed your life in my hands by coming here, but until now you've never shared with me what you know. Why should I not confiscate your letters, when you've shown no trust in *me*?"

"How could I trust you that far?" cried the abbess fiercely. "Don't you think I've used my eyes? You've signed a pact with your *enemy*, Prussia, for another partition of your *ally*, Poland. Your life is threatened by a thousand foes, even within your court. You must know your son Paul is drilling Prussian-looking troops on his estate at Gatchina, planning a coup. Every move you make in this dangerous game suggests you might seek the Montglane Service to serve your own ends—power. How do I know you'd not betray me as you've betrayed so many others? And though you may be on my side, as I long to believe—what would happen if we brought the service here? Even your power, my dear Sophie, will not extend beyond the grave. If *you* should die, I tremble to think of the use to which your son Paul might put these pieces!"

"You need not fear Paul," the czarina sniffed as the abbess castled her King. "His power will never extend beyond those poor miserable troops he marches about in their silly uniforms. It's my grandson Alexander who'll be czar when I'm dead. I've trained him myself, and he will do my bidding—"

Just then the abbess put her finger to her lips and motioned to a tapestry that hung against the far wall. The czarina, following her gesture, raised herself stealthily from her chair. Both women stared at the tapestry as the abbess continued speaking.

"Ah, what an interesting move," she said, "and one that poses problems. . . ."

The czarina was marching across the room with powerful stride. She yanked the heavy tapestry aside with a single gesture. There stood Crown Prince Paul, his shamed face as purple as a cabbage. He glanced at his mother in shock, then down at the floor.

"Mother, I was just coming to pay you a visit. . . ." he began, but could not fix her with his eyes. "I mean, Your Majesty, I was . . . coming to see her reverend mother the abbess on a matter . . ." He fumbled with the buttons of his jacket.

"I see that you are as quick-witted as your late father," she snapped. "To think that I bore in my womb a crown prince whose greatest talent appears to be snooping about at doorways! Leave us at once! The very sight of you disgusts me!"

She turned her back on him, but the abbess saw the look of bitter hatred that crossed Paul's face as he glared at his mother's back. Catherine was playing a dangerous game with this boy; he was not half the fool she believed him to be.

"I pray the Reverend Mother and Her Majesty will both excuse my most ill-timed disturbance," he said softly. Then, bowing low to his mother's back, he stepped backward once and exited the room in silence.

The czarina did not speak but stood near the doorway, her eyes fastened on the chessboard.

"How much do you think he overheard?" she asked at last, reading the abbess's thoughts.

"We must assume that he heard all," said the abbess. "We must act at once."

"What, because a foolish boy has learned he's not the man who will be king?" Catherine said with a bitter smile. "I'm certain he's guessed that long before now."

"No," said the abbess, "because he has learned about the service."

"But surely it's safe enough until we've formed a plan," Catherine said. "And the one piece you've brought *here* is in my vaults. We can dispatch that, if you'd like, to a place where no one would ever think to look. Workmen are pouring another concrete base for the last wing of the Winter Palace. It's been under construction these last fifty years—I dread to think of the bones that must already be buried there!"

"Could we do it ourselves?" said the abbess as the czarina crossed the room.

"Surely you're jesting." Catherine took her seat beside the chessboard once again. "What, the two of us—sneak out in the dead of night to hide a little chess piece only six inches high? I hardly think there's cause for such alarm."

But the abbess was no longer looking at her. Her gaze rested upon the chessboard that sat between them, scattered with their half-played game, a gaming table of black-and-white tile that she had brought with her from France. Slowly she raised her hand and, with a brush of her arm, swept the pieces aside so a few toppled to the soft Astrakhan carpet beneath. She rapped on the board with her knuckles. There was a dull, thick tone as if padding lay beneath the surface—as if something were separating the thin enamel tiles from something buried underneath. The czarina's eyes widened as she put out her hand to touch the surface of the board. She rose from the table, her heart pounding, and stepped to a nearby brazier whose coals had long ago crumbled to ashes. She picked up a heavy iron poker and, lifting it over her head, brought it down with all her might across the chess table. A few of the tiles cracked. Casting aside the poker, she ripped out the broken pieces with her bare hands and the cotton batting that lay under the tiles. Beneath the wadding, she saw a dull glow that seemed to radiate with an inner flame. The abbess sat on her chair beside the board, her face grim and pale.

"The board of the Montglane Service!" whispered the czarina, staring at the carved squares of silver and gold that showed through the gaping hole. "You've had it all this time. No wonder you've been silent. We must remove these tiles and wadding, pry it loose from the table so I may bathe my eyes in all its radiance. Ah, how I ache to see it!"

"I had imagined it in my dreams," the abbess said. "But when at last it was raised from the earth, when I saw it glowing in the dim light of the abbey, when I felt the chiseled stones and strange magical symbols with my fingertips—I felt a force run through me more terrifying than anything I'd known. Now you understand why I wish to bury it—tonight—where no one will find it again until the other pieces can be retrieved. Is there anyone we can trust to help us in this mission?"

Catherine looked at her for a long moment, feeling for the first time in many years the loneliness of the role she'd chosen for her life. An empress could afford no friends, no confidants.

"No," she said to the abbess with a mischievous, girlish grin, "but we've engaged in dangerous caprices long before this—have we not, Helene? Tonight at midnight, we can sup together—and perhaps a brisk walk in the gardens will do us good?"

"We may wish to take *several* walks," agreed the abbess. "Before I ordered this board built into the table, I had it cut carefully into four pieces—so it could be moved without the aid of too many assistants. I foresaw this day. . . ." Using the iron poker as a crowbar, Catherine had already begun to crack loose the fragile tiles. The abbess lifted the pieces away to reveal larger portions of the magnificent board. Each square contained a strange mystical symbol, in alternating silver and gold. The edges were embellished with rare uncut gems, polished like eggs and set into oddly sculpted patterns.

"After we dine," said the abbess, looking up at her friend, "we will read my . . . confiscated letters?"

"Of course—I'll have them brought to you," said the empress, looking with marveling eyes at the board. "They weren't very interesting. They're all from a friend of yours of years ago—mostly chatting about the weather in Corsica. . . ."

THE TASSILI   APRIL 1793

But Mireille was already thousands of miles away from the shores of Corsica. And as she came over the last high wall of the Ez-Zemoul El Akbar, she saw before her, across the sands, the Tassili—home of the White Queen.

The Tassili n'Ajjer, or Plateau of Chasms, loomed from the desert, a long ribbon of blue stone running three hundred miles from Algeria into the kingdom of Tripoli, skirting the edge of the Ahaggar Mountains and the lush oases that dotted the southern desert. Within these plateau canyons lay the key to the ancient mystery.

As Mireille followed Shahin from the bleak desert into the mouth of the narrow western defile, she felt the temperature drop rapidly—and for the first time in nearly a month, she smelled the rich scent of fresh water. Entering the defile with its high rock walls, she saw the narrow trickle of flatwash over broken stone. The banks were thick with pink oleander whispering in the shade, and a few sparse date palms dotted the riverbed, their feathery fronds reaching up toward the shimmering fragment of sky.

As their camels climbed through the narrow gorge, the neck of blue rock slowly widened into a rich and fertile valley where high rivers fed the orchards of peach, fig, and apricot trees. Mireille, who'd eaten nothing for weeks but lizard, salamander, and buzzard baked in coals, plucked peaches from the trees as they moved among the thick branches, and the camels filched big mouthfuls of dark green leaves.

Each valley opened into dozens of other valleys and twisted gorges, each with its own climate and vegetation. Formed millions of years ago by deep underground rivers cutting their way through many-colored layers of rock, the Tassili was sculpted like the caves and chasms of a subterranean sea. The river cut gorges whose lacy walls of pink-and-white stone resembled coral reefs, wide valleys of spiral needles thrusting toward the sky. And surrounding these castlelike mesas of petrified red sandstone were the massive plateaus of blue-gray, fortresslike walls, hurtling from the floor of the desert a mile into the sky.

Mireille and Shahin encountered no one until, high above the ledges of Aabaraka Tafelalet, they came to Tamrit—the Village of Tents. Here, thousand-year-old cypresses towered over the deep, cold riverbed, and the temperature dropped so drastically that Mireille could scarcely remember the 120-degree heat of their month in the dry and barren dunes.

At Tamrit they'd leave behind their camels and proceed on foot with only the provisions they could carry. For now they'd entered that portion of the Labyrinth where, according to Shahin, the switchbacks and ledges were so treacherous that even wild goats and mouflon rarely ventured there.

They made arrangements for their camels to be watered by the People of the Tents. Many had come out to stare wide-eyed at Mireille's red tresses—now turned to flame by the setting sun.

"We must rest here for the night," Shahin told her. "The Labyrinth can only be negotiated in daylight. Tomorrow we start. At the heart of the Labyrinth is the key. . . ." He raised his arm to point to the end of the gorge, where the rock walls swept away in a curve already hidden in blue-black shadow as the sun slipped under the rim of the canyon.

"The White Queen," whispered Mireille, looking up at the contorted shad-ows that made the twisted rock seem to writhe with motion. "Shahin, you don't really believe there's a woman of stone up there, do you—I mean, a living person?" She felt a chill pass over her as the sun dipped down and the air became palpably cold.

"I know it," he whispered back, as if someone might be listening. "They say sometimes at sunset, when no one is near, she has been heard from a great distance—singing a strange melody. Perhaps . . . she will sing for you."

At Sefar the air was cold and clear. Here they encountered their first rock carvings—though these were not the oldest—small devils with horns like goats, frisking about the walls in bas-relief. These were painted about 1500 B.C. The higher they climbed, the more difficult the access became and the more ancient the paintings—the more magical, mysterious, and complex.

Mireille felt she was moving back in time as she ascended the steep ledges that were carved from the sheer canyon walls. As they turned through each curve of canyon, the paintings splashed across the dark rock face told the story of the ages of men whose lives had mingled with these chasms—a tide of civilization, wave after wave—going back eight thousand years.

Art was everywhere—carmine and red ocher and black and yellow and brown—carved and crayoned on the steep walls, burned with wild color into the dark recesses of fissures and caves—thousands and thousands of paintings, as far as the eye could see. Unfolded here in the wilds of nature, painted at angles and heights that could only be reached by an expert mountain climber or—as Shahin had said, by a goat—they told the story not only of man—but of life itself.

On the second day they saw the chariots of the Hyksos—the sea people who'd conquered Egypt and the Sahara two thousand years before Christ, and whose superior weaponry—horse-drawn vehicles and body armor—had helped them prevail over the painted camels of the indigenous warriors. The tableaux of their conquest read like an open book as they passed across the canyon walls like predators across the vast red desert. Mireille smiled to herself, wondering what her uncle Jacques-Louis would think, gazing upon the work of all these anonymous artists, whose names were buried in the dim mists of time yet whose works had endured these thousands of years.

Each night when the sun sank beneath the canyon rim, they had to seek shelter. When there were no caves nearby, they wrapped themselves in wool blankets that Shahin tacked into the canyon with tent pegs—so they wouldn't roll over the cliffs in their sleep.

On the third day they reached the caves of Tan Zoumaitok—so dark and deep they could only see by the light of torches made from scrub brush they pulled from the cracks of the rock. Here in the caves were colored pictures, perfectly preserved, of faceless men with coin-shaped heads, speaking with fish that walked upright on legs. For the ancient tribes, said Shahin, believed their ancestors had moved from the sea to land as fish, walking on legs from the primeval ooze. Here too were depictions of the magic they'd used to appease the spirits of nature—a spiral dance performed by *djenoun*, or genii who seemed to be possessed—moving counterclockwise in ever-narrowing circles about the central shape of a sacred stone. Mireille looked at the image for a long time, Shahin standing beside her wordlessly, before they moved on.

On the morning of the fourth day, they approached the summit of the plateau. As they rounded the bend of the gorge, the walls expanded and opened into a wide, deep valley completely covered with paintings. Everywhere, on every face of rock, was color. This was the Valley of Giants. More than five thousand paintings filled the walls of the gorge from top to bottom. Mireille stopped breathing for a moment as her eyes wandered over the vast array of art—the most ancient they'd seen—washed with a color, rendered with a clarity and simplicity, as if they'd been painted only yesterday. Like the frescoes of the great masters, they were timeless.

She stood there a long time. The stories on these walls seemed to enfold her, to draw her into another world, primitive and mysterious. Between the earth and the sky was nothing but color and form—color that seemed to move in her blood like a drug as she stood on the high ledge, suspended in space. And then she heard the sound.

At first she thought it was the wind—a high-pitched hum like air blowing through the narrow neck of a bottle. Looking up, she saw a high cliff—perhaps a thousand feet above—that jutted out over the dry, wild gorge. A narrow crack seemed to appear from nowhere in the rock face. Mireille glanced at Shahin. He too was looking at the cliff where the sound was coming from. He drew his veils over his face and nodded for her to precede him on the thin ribbon of trail.

The trail ascended sharply. Soon it became so steep, and the ledge itself so fragile, that Mireille—well past seven months—struggled to keep both her breath and her balance. Once, her feet slipped out from under her, and she toppled to her knees. The pebbles that crumbled beneath her pitched three thousand feet into the gorge below. Swallowing with a dry throat, she picked herself up—for the ledge was so narrow Shahin could not help her—and continued on without looking down. The sound became ever louder.

It was three notes, played over and over in different combinations—higher and higher pitches. The closer she came to the fissure in the rock, the less it sounded like the wind. The beautiful, clear tone resembled a human voice. Mireille continued to pick her way up the crumbling ledge.

The shelf was five thousand feet from the valley floor. Here, what had appeared from below as a narrow crevice in the rock was in fact a gigantic fissure—the entrance to a cave, or so it seemed. Twenty feet across and fifty feet high, it ran like a huge rip in the stone, between the ledge and the summit. Mireille waited for Shahin to catch up with her, and, taking his hand, they stepped through the opening.

The sound became deafening, swirling around them from all sides and echoing off the enclosing walls of the fissure. It seemed to move through every particle of her body as Mireille forged through the dark crevasse. At the end, she saw a flicker of light. She plowed through the darkness as the music seemed to swallow her. At last she reached the end, still holding on to Shahin, and stepped out.

What she'd thought was a cave was in fact another small valley, its ceiling open to the sky. Light flooded from above, illuminating everything with a wash of eerie white. On the sweep of curving concave walls were the giants. Twenty feet high, they floated above her in pale, ethereal colors. Gods with spiral rams' horns growing from their heads, men in puffy suits with hoses running from mouth to chest, their faces concealed beneath globular helmets with only grates where their features should have been. They sat on chairs with strange backs that supported their heads; before them were levers and circular gadgets like the dials of clocks or barometers. They all performed functions strange and alien to Mireille, and at their center floated the White Queen.

The music had stopped. Perhaps it had been a trick of the wind—or of her mind. The figures shone brilliantly in the wash of white light. Mireille looked at the White Queen.

High on the wall loomed the strange and terrible figure—larger than any other. Like a divine nemesis, she rose upon the cliff in a cloud of white—her strong face barely suggested with a few violently slashed lines—her hooked horns like question marks that seemed to spring forth from the wall. Her mouth was an open wail, like a tongueless person struggling to speak. But she did not speak.

Mireille stared at her with a numbness approaching terror. Surrounded by silence more frightening than sound, she glanced at Shahin, who stood motionless beside her. Swathed in his dark haik and blue veils, it seemed he too had been carved from the timeless rock. In the brilliant wash of light, surrounded by the cold walls of the gorge, Mireille was terrified and confused as she turned her eyes slowly back to the wall. And then she saw it.

The White Queen's upraised hand held a long staff—and around this staff were twined the forms of serpents. Like the caduceus of healing, they formed a figure eight. She thought she heard a voice, but it did not come from the curved stone wall—it came from within. The voice said, *Look again. Look closely. See.*

Mireille looked at the figures ranging across the wall. They were all figures of men—all but the White Queen. And then, as if a veil had been torn from her eyes, she saw it all differently. It was no longer a panorama of men engaged in strange and indecipherable acts—it was *one* man. Like a moving picture that began in one place and ended in another, it showed the progression of this man through many phases—a transmutation from one thing to another.

Beneath the transforming wand of the White Queen, he moved across the wall, passing from stage to stage just as the round-head men had come as fish from the sea. He dressed in ritual clothing—perhaps for protective purposes. He moved levers in his hands, as a navigator steering a ship or a chemist grinding at a mortar. And at last, after many changes, when the great work was complete, he rose from his chair and joined the White Queen, crowned for his efforts with the sacred spiral horns of Mars—god of war and destruction. He'd become a god.

"I understand," said Mireille aloud—and the sound of her voice echoed back and forth from the walls and floor of the abyss, shattering the sunlight.

It was at that moment she felt the first pain. She doubled over as it seized her, and Shahin grasped her and helped her to the ground. She was cold with sweat, and her heart beat frantically. Shahin ripped off his veils and put his hand to her stomach as the second contraction wrenched her body.

"It is time," he said softly.

THE TASSILI   JUNE 1793

From the high plateau above Tamrit, Mireille could see twenty miles across the outer dunes. The wind lifted her hair so it floated out behind her, the color of the red sand. The soft fabric of her caftan was unlaced, and at her breast the child was nursing. As Shahin had predicted, he'd been born beneath the eyes of the goddess—and it was a boy. She'd named him Charlot, after her falcon. He was now nearly six weeks old.

Against the horizon she saw the soft red plumes of rising sand that marked the riders from Bahr-al-Azrak. When she narrowed her eyes she could make out four men on camels, sliding down the inside curl of a massive feathered dune, like small chips of wood sucked into the curve of an ocean wave. Heat baked off the dune in hot patterns, obscuring the figures when they moved into its path.

It would take them nearly a day to reach Tamrit, so far into the canyons of the Tassili, but Mireille did not need to wait for their arrival. She knew they were coming for her. She'd felt it for many days now. Kissing her son on the top of his head, she wrapped him in the sack she'd slung about her neck and started back down the mountain—to wait for the letter. If not today, it would come soon enough. The letter from the Abbess of Montglane, telling her she must return.

THE MAGIC MOUNTAINS

What is the future? What is the past? What are we? What is the magic fluid that surrounds us and conceals the things we most need to know? We live and die in the midst of marvels.

—*Napoleon Bonaparte*

S o we went up into the Magic Mountains, Kamel and I. Journeying into the Kabyle. The deeper we penetrated into that lost domain, the more I lost touch with everything that seemed real to me.

No one knows precisely where the Kabyle begins or ends. A labyrinthine maze of high peaks and deep gorges sandwiched between the Medjerdas north of Constantine and the Hodnas below Bouïra, these vast front ranges of the High Atlas—the Grand and Petite Kabylie—wander over thirty thousand kilometers, tumbling at last down the sheer rock corniche near Bejaïa into the sea.

As Kamel drove his black ministry Citroën along the twisting dirt road between columns of ancient eucalyptus, the blue hills rose above us, majestic, snow-capped, and mysterious. Beneath them spread the Tizi-Ouzou—Gorge of the Gorse—where wild Algerian heather bathed the wide valley in brilliant fuchsia, the heavy blossoms swaying like sea waves with every sultry breeze. The scent was magical, flooding the air with heady fragrance.

The clear blue waters of the Ouled Sebaou rippled through knee-deep heather beside the road. This river, fed by spring snow melt, meandered three hundred miles to Cap Bengut, watering the Tizi-Ouzou throughout the long hot summer. It was hard to imagine we were only thirty miles from the mist-bound Mediterranean and ninety miles to our south spread the largest desert in the world.

Kamel had been strangely silent during the four hours since he'd picked me up at my hotel. He'd taken long enough to bring me here—nearly two months since he'd promised. In that time, he'd sent me on every sort of mission—some resembling a wild-goose chase. I'd inspected refineries, gins, and mills. I'd seen women with veiled faces and bare feet sitting on the floors of *semoule* plants separating couscous; I'd had my eyes scalded in the fiber-filled hot air of textile plants, my lungs burned out inspecting extrusion sites; and I'd nearly toppled headfirst into a vat of molten steel from the precarious scaffolding at a refinery. He'd sent me everywhere in the western part of the state—Oran, Tlemcen, Sidi-bel-Abbès—so I could collect the data I needed as a base for his model. But never to the east, where the Kabyle was.

For seven weeks I'd loaded data on every industry into the big computers at Sonatrach, the oil conglomerate. I'd even put Therese the phone operator to work collecting government statistics on oil production and consumption in other countries, so I could compare balances of trade and see who'd be hit the hardest. As I'd pointed out to Kamel, it wasn't easy jerry-rigging a system in a country where half the communications went through a World War I switchboard and the other half came by camel. But I'd do my best.

On the other hand, I seemed farther than ever from my goal—to track down the Montglane Service. I'd heard nothing from Solarin or his sidekick, the mysterious fortune-teller. Therese had sent every message I could devise to Nim, Lily, and Mordecai, with no results. There was an information blackout where I was concerned. And Kamel had sent me so far afield, I almost felt he *knew* what I was planning. Then only this morning he'd shown up at my hotel, offering "that trip I promised you."

"You grew up in this region?" I said, rolling down the tinted window for a better view.

"In the back range," Kamel replied. "Most of the villages there are on high peaks and have a lovely view. Was there anywhere particular you wanted to go, or shall I just give you the grand tour?"

"Actually, there's an antique dealer I'd like to visit—a colleague of a friend in New York. I promised to see his shop, if it isn't out of your way. . . ." I thought it best to be casual, as I didn't know much about Llewellyn's contact. I couldn't find the village on any map—though, as Kamel said, Algerian *cartes geographiques* were pretty sparse.

"Antiques?" said Kamel. "There aren't many. Anything of value has been put into museums long ago. What's the name of the shop?"

"I don't know. The village is called Ain Ka'abah," I told him. "Lewellyn said it was the only antique store in town."

"How very unusual," said Kamel, still watching the road. "Ain Ka'abah is the village I come from. It's a tiny place, far from the beaten path, but there's no antique shop there—I'm certain."

Pulling my address book from my satchel, I leafed through it until I located my hastily scribbled notes from Llewellyn.

"Here it is. No street address, but it's on the north side of town. It seems they specialize in antique *carpets*. The owner's name is El-Marad." Perhaps I only imagined that Kamel turned slightly green at these words. His jaw was locked, and his voice seemed strained when he spoke.

"El-Marad," he said. "I know him. He's one of the biggest traders in the region, which is famous for its carpets. Are you interested in buying one?"

"Actually, I'm not," I said, careful now. Kamel wasn't telling me everything, though I could see from his face something was wrong. "My friend in New York just asked me to stop in and chat. I could always come later on my own, if it's a problem."

Kamel didn't speak for several minutes. He seemed to be thinking. We came to the end of the valley and started up the road into the mountains. Rolling meadows of spring grass were dotted with flowering fruit trees. Little boys stood beside the road selling bunches of wild asparagus, fat black mushrooms, and fragrant narcissus. Kamel pulled off the road and bartered for several minutes in a strange language—some Berber dialect like the soft chirping of birds. Then he put his head back in the window, handing me a bunch of the sweetly scented flowers.

"If you're going to meet El-Marad," he said, recovering his former smile, "I hope you know how to barter. He's as ruthless as a Bedouin, and ten times as rich. I haven't seen him—in fact, I've not been home—since my father died. My village has many memories for me."

"We don't have to go," I repeated.

"Of course we'll go," said Kamel firmly, though his tone was far from enthusiastic. "You'd never find the place without me. Besides, El-Marad will be surprised to see me. He's been head of the village since my father's death." Kamel clammed up again, looking rather grim. I wondered what was going on.

"So what's he like, this carpet trader?" I said to break the ice.

"In Algeria, you can learn much about a man from his name," said Kamel as he wound expertly along roads that were becoming ever more tortuous. "For example, 'Ibn' means 'son of.' Some are place names, like Yamini—Man of the Yemen; or Jabal-Tarik—Mountain of Tarik—or Gibraltar. The words 'El,' 'Al,' and 'Bel' refer to Allah or Ba'al—that is, God—like Hanniba'al: Ascetic of God; Al'a-ddin: Servant of Allah; and so forth."

"So what does El-Marad mean—God's Marauder?" I laughed.

"Closer than you think," said Kamel with an uncomfortable laugh. "The name is neither Arabic nor Berber—it's Akkadian, the language of ancient Mesopotamia. Short for al-Nimarad, or Nimrod, an early king of Babylon. He was the builder of the Tower of Babel, which was meant to rise to the sun, to the gates of heaven. For that's what Bab-el means—the Gate of God. And Nimrod means the Rebel—One who trespasses upon the gods."

"Quite a name for a carpet trader." I laughed. But of course, I'd noticed the resemblance to the name of someone *else* I knew.

"Yes," he agreed, "if that were *all* he was."

Kamel wouldn't explain what he meant about El-Marad, but it was no accident that he'd grown up in the one village of hundreds where this carpet trader made his home.

By two, when we reached the little resort of Beni Yenni, my stomach was crying aloud with hunger pains. The tiny inn at the top of a mountain was far from posh, but the dark Italian cypresses twisting against ocher walls and red-tiled roofs made a charming setting.

We had lunch on the small slate terrace surrounded by a white railing that jutted from the mountaintop. Eagles skimmed the valley floor below, glints of gold sparkling from their wings as they passed through the thin blue mist rising from the Ouled Aissi. Around us we could see the treacherous terrain: twisting roads like thin frayed ribbons about to slip from the mountainside, whole villages that looked like crumbling reddish boulders, balanced precariously at the pinnacle of each high hill. Though already June, the air was cool enough for my pullover, at least thirty degrees colder than the coast we'd left that morning. Across the valley I could see snow capping the Djurdjura Massif and low-hanging clouds that looked suspiciously heavy—just in the direction we were headed.

We were the only people on the terrace, and the waiter was somewhat surly as he carried our drinks and luncheon from the warm kitchen. I wondered if anyone was staying at the inn, which was state-subsidized for members of the ministry. The tourist traffic in Algeria was hardly sufficient to support even the more accessible resorts along the coast.

We sat in the brisk air drinking bitter red byrrh with lemon and crushed ice. We ate in silence. Hot broth of pureed vegetables, crispy baguettes, and poached chicken with mayonnaise and aspic. Kamel still seemed deep in thought.

Before departing Beni Yenni, he opened the car trunk and brought out a thick pile of wool lap rugs. Like me, he was concerned about the impending weather. The road became precarious almost at once. How could I guess this was nothing compared with what we were soon to encounter?

It was only an hour's drive from Beni Yenni to Tikjda, but it seemed like an eternity. We spent most of it in silence. At first the road wound down to the valley floor, crossed the little river, and headed back up over what seemed to be a low, undulating hill. But the farther we went, the steeper it became. The Citroën was straining when we reached the top. I looked down. Before me was a chasm two thousand feet deep—a maze of jagged, gaping gorges torn from the rock. And our road—what there was of it—was a crumbling mass of ice-crusted gravel about to collapse at the spine of the ridge. To add to the thrill, this narrow ledge cut from broken rock, torqued and crimpled like a sailor's knot, also *dropped* down the sheer rock face at a fifteen percent grade—all the way into Tikjda.

As Kamel moved the big, catlike Citroën over the edge and onto the crumbling path, I shut my eyes and said a few prayers. When I opened them again, we'd swung around the curve. The road now seemed connected to nothing at all, suspended in space among the clouds. Gorges dropped a thousand feet or more at either side of us. Snow-tipped mountains seemed to spring like stalagmites from the valley floor. A wild, whirling wind screeched up the walls of the black ravines, sucking snow across our path and obscuring the road. I would have suggested turning around—but there was no place to do it.

My legs were shaking as I braced my feet against the floorboards, prepared for the shock when we lost the road altogether and hurtled out into space. Kamel slowed to thirty miles, then twenty—until we were crawling along at ten.

Oddly, the snow got heavier as we descended the steep incline. Occasionally, coming around a sharp turn, we'd encounter a hay wagon or broken-down truck abandoned in the road.

"For God's sake, it's *June*!" I said to Kamel as we edged our way carefully around an especially high drift.

"It's not even snowing yet," he said quietly, "just blowing a bit. . . ."

"What do you mean, *yet*?" I said.

"I hope you like his carpets," said Kamel with a wry smile. "Because these may cost you more than money. Even if it doesn't snow, even if the road doesn't collapse—even if we get to Tikjda before dark—we still have to cross the bridge."

"Before *dark*?" I said, flapping open my unwieldy and useless map of the Kabyle. "According to this, Tikjda is only thirty miles from here—and the bridge is just beyond."

"Yes," agreed Kamel, "but maps only show *horizontal* distances. Things that look close in two dimensions can be very far in reality."

We reached Tikjda just at seven. The sun, which mercifully we could see at last, was balanced on the last ridge, prepared to sink behind the Rif. It had taken three hours to go thirty miles. Kamel had marked Ain Ka'abah on the map near Tikjda—it looked as if we could jog there from here—but that turned out to be quite misleading.

We left Tikjda, having stopped only to fill our car with gas and our lungs with fresh mountain air. The weather had changed for the better—the sky was peach, the air like silk, and far off in the distance beyond the prism-shaped pines rolled a cool blue valley. At its center, perhaps six or seven miles away, rising purple and gold in the last of the setting sun, was an enormous square-shaped mountain, the top cut off flat like a mesa. It stood completely alone in the middle of the wide valley.

"Ain Ka'abah," said Kamel, motioning through the car window.

"Up there?" I said. "But I don't see any road. . . ."

"There is no road—only a footpath," he replied. "Several miles over marshy ground in the dark, then up the trail. But before we get there, we must cross the bridge."

The bridge was only five miles from Tikjda—but four thousand feet below. At dusk—that most difficult time for clear vision—it was hard to see through the purple shadows cast by the high cliffs. But the valley to our right was still brilliantly flooded with light, turning the mountain of Ain Ka'abah into a block of gold. Directly before us was a view that took my breath away. Our path hurtled down, down, nearly to the valley floor—but five hundred feet above the rocks, suspended over the plunging torrent of a river, was the bridge. Kamel slowed the car as we dropped and dropped toward the canyon floor. At the bridge, he stopped.

It was a flimsy, shaky bridge that seemed to be built of Tinkertoys. It might have been constructed ten years before or a hundred. The surface, high and narrow, was barely wide enough to admit one car, and ours might be the last. The river pounded and tore at the invisible supports beneath, a raging torrent of water falling swiftly from the gorges above.

Kamel edged the sleek black limousine out onto the rough surface. I felt the bridge shudder beneath us.

"You'll find this hard to imagine," said Kamel in a whisper, as if the vibration of his voice might prove the last straw, "but at high summer, that river is just a dry trickle through the marshland—nothing but loose gravel and tundra through the hot season."

"How long is the hot season—about fifteen minutes?" I asked, my mouth dry from fear as the car creaked forward. A log or something hit the pilings below, and the bridge trembled as if we were having an earthquake. I hung on to my armrest until it stopped.

When the front wheels of the Citroën passed onto solid ground, I started breathing again. My fingers stayed crossed until I felt the rear wheels touch earth, too. Kamel stopped the car and looked across at me with a wide grin of relief.

"The things women ask of men," he said, "just to do a little shopping!"

The valley floor looked too soft to put the car down, so we left it on the last stony ledge below the bridge. Goat trails crisscrossed the marshes cutting through the high rough grass. You could see their dung and deep hoofprints in the sloshy mud.

"Lucky I wore the right footgear," I said, looking ruefully at my thin, strappy gold sandals, unsuited to any purpose.

"The exercise will do you good," said Kamel. "Kabyle women hike every day—with sixty pounds of hods on their backs." He grinned at me.

"I must trust you because I like your smile," I told him. "There's no other explanation for why I'm doing this."

"How can you tell a Bedouin from a Kabyle?" he asked as we slugged through the wet grasses.

I laughed. "Is this an ethnic joke?"

"No, I'm serious. You can tell a Bedouin because he never shows his teeth when he laughs. Impolite to show the back teeth—bad luck, actually. Watch El-Marad and see."

"He's not Kabyle?" I said. We were winding our way across the dark flat river valley. The mountain of Ain Ka'abah towered over us, still catching the last of the sun. Where the sweet grasses had been trodden down, we could glimpse wildflowers in purple, yellow, and red, just closing for the night.

"No one knows," said Kamel, breaking the way before me. "He came to the Kabyle years ago—I've never learned from where—and settled at Ain Ka'abah. A man of mysterious origins."

"I gather you don't much care for him," I said.

Kamel walked ahead in silence. "It's hard to like a man," he said at last, "whom you hold responsible for your father's death."

"Death!" I cried, racing ahead through the grass to catch up with him. One of my sandals was pulled off and disappeared in the grass. Kamel paused while I hunted for it. "What do you mean?" I muttered from the deep grass.

"They had a business venture together, my father and El-Marad," he said while I retrieved my sandal. "My father went to England for a negotiation. He was robbed and murdered by thugs in the streets of London."

"So this El-Marad didn't actually have a hand in it?" I said, catching up to him as we went on.

"No," said Kamel. "In fact, he paid my tuition from the proceeds of my father's business, so I could remain in London. He kept the business, however. I never sent him a thank-you note. That's why I said he'd be surprised to see me."

"Why do you hold him responsible for your father's death?" I pressed.

It was clear Kamel didn't want to speak about it. Each word was a strain. "I don't know," he said quietly, as if sorry he'd brought it up. "Perhaps I think he should have gone instead."

We didn't speak for the rest of the way across the valley. The road to Ain Ka'abah was a long spiral that wound around the mountain. It was half an hour from bottom to top—the last fifty yards were wide stairs hewn from the stone and well worn by the passing of many feet.

"How do the people who live here eat?" I asked as we puffed to the top. Four-fifths of Algeria was desert, there was no timber, and the only arable land was two hundred miles away along the sea.

"They make carpets," Kamel replied, "and silver jewelry, which they trade. There are precious and semiprecious stones in the mountain—carnelian and opal, and a bit of turquoise. Everything else is imported from the coast."

The village of Ain Ka'abah had a long road down the center with stucco houses at either side. We stopped on the dirt road outside a large house with a thatched roof. Storks had made a nest in the chimney, and there were several perched on the roof.

"That is the weavers' cottage," said Kamel.

As we walked down the street, I noticed that the sun had completely disappeared. It was a lovely lavender twilight—but already the air was growing chilly.

There were a few carts on the road with loads of hay, several donkeys, and

a few small flocks of goats. I assumed it was easier to get donkey carts up the
hill than a Citroën limousine.

At the end of town, Kamel paused in the road outside a large house. He stood
there looking at it for a long time. The house was stucco like the others, but
perhaps twice as wide, with a balcony running across the front. A woman stood
on the balcony, beating carpets. She was dark and dressed in colorful clothes.
Beside her sat a small child with golden curls, wearing a white dress and
pinafore. The top of the child's hair was braided in thin plaits that fell in loose
ringlets below. She ran downstairs when she saw us and came up to me.

Kamel called up to the mother, who stood looking down at him for a
moment in silence. Then she saw me and broke into a smile, showing several
gold teeth. She went into the house.

"This is the house of El-Marad," said Kamel. "That woman is his senior wife.
The child is a very late one—the woman gave birth long after they thought
she was barren. This is considered to be a sign from Allah—the child is
'chosen.' "

"How do you know all this when you've been gone ten years?" I said. "This
child's only five or so." Kamel took the little girl by the hand as we went toward
the house and looked down at her with affection.

"I'd never seen her before," he admitted, "but I keep track of what happens
in my village. This child was considered quite an event. I should have brought
her something—after all, she's hardly responsible for the way I feel toward her
father."

I rummaged about in my floppy bag to see if I had anything that might fill
the bill. A piece of Lily's pegboard chess set came loose in my hand—just a piece
of plastic—the White Queen. It looked like a miniature doll. I handed it to
the child. In great excitement she hurried indoors to show her mother the toy.
Kamel smiled at me in thanks.

The woman came out and took us into the darkened house. She held the chess
piece in her hand, chattered to Kamel in Berber, and kept looking at me with
sparkling eyes. Perhaps she was asking him about me. She touched me from time
to time with featherlike fingers.

Kamel said a few words to her, and she departed.

"I asked her to bring her husband," he told me. "We can go into the shop
and sit there. One of the wives will bring us coffee."

The carpet shop was a large room, taking up the better part of the main floor.
Carpets were piled everywhere, folded in stacks and rolled in long tubes against
the walls. There were carpets six deep spread across the floors, and others were
hanging from the walls and tossed over the inner balcony of the second floor.
We sat cross-legged on hassocks on the ground. Two young women came in,
one bearing a tray with a samovar and cups, the other carrying a stand to put

the tray on. They set up everything and poured us coffee. They giggled when they looked at me and swiftly looked away again. After a few moments they left.

"El-Marad has three wives," Kamel told me. "The Islamic faith permits as many as four, but it's unlikely he'll take another at this late date. He must be close to eighty."

"But you haven't any wives?" I asked.

"A minister is only permitted one, by state law," Kamel replied. "So one must be more cautious." He grinned at me but still seemed very quiet. It was clear he was under strain.

"They seem to find something very amusing about me, these women. They giggle when they look at me," I said to clear the air.

"Perhaps they've never seen a Western woman before," said Kamel. "Certainly they've never seen a woman wearing trousers. Probably there are many questions they would like to ask you, but they're too shy."

Just then the curtains beneath the balcony parted, and a tall, imposing man entered the room. He was over six feet tall, with a long sharp nose, hooked like a hawk, craggy eyebrows over piercing black eyes, and a mane of dark hair streaked with white. He wore a long red-and-white-striped caftan of fine light wool and walked with a vigorous step. He didn't look more than fifty. Kamel stood to greet him, and they kissed on either cheek and touched their fingers to their foreheads and breasts. Kamel said a few words in Arabic to him, and the man turned to me. His voice was higher-pitched than I'd expected and soft—almost a whisper.

"I am El-Marad," he told me. "Any friend of Kamel Kader is welcome in my home." He motioned for me to take a seat, and he sat opposite, cross-legged, on ottomans on the floor. I could see no sign of the strain Kamel had mentioned between the two men, who, after all, had not spoken in at least ten years. El-Marad had spread his robes around him and looked at me with interest.

"I present Mademoiselle Catherine Velis," Kamel said with polite formality. "She's come from America to do work for OPEC."

"OPEC," said El-Marad, nodding at me. "Luckily, we do not have petrol here in the mountains, or we too would have to change our way of life. I hope you will enjoy your stay in our land, and that through your work—if Allah wishes—we may all prosper."

He raised his hand, and the mother came in, holding the little girl by the hand. She gave her husband the chess piece, and he held it out to me.

"You've given my daughter a gift, I understand," he said to me. "You place me in your debt. Please choose the carpet you would like to take with you." He waved his hand again, and the mother and child vanished as silently as they'd come.

"No, please," I said. "It's only a plastic toy." He was looking at the piece in his hand and seemed not to hear me. Now he looked up at me with eagle eyes beneath forbidding brows.

"The White Queen!" he whispered, glancing once quickly at Kamel, then back at me. "Who sent you?" he demanded. "And why have you brought *him*?"

This took me completely by surprise, and I looked at Kamel. Then, of course, I understood. He knew what I was there for—perhaps the chess piece was some sort of signal that I'd come from Llewellyn. But if so, it was a signal Llewellyn had never mentioned.

"I'm terribly sorry," I said to smooth things over. "A friend of mine, an antique dealer in New York, asked me to come and see you. Kamel was kind enough to bring me here."

El-Marad said nothing for a moment but glared at me from beneath his beetled brow. He kept toying with the chess piece in his hand as if it were a string of prayer beads. At last he turned to Kamel and said a few words in Berber. Kamel nodded and rose to his feet. Looking down at me, he said:

"I think I'll go for a breath of fresh air. It seems there's something El-Marad would like to say to you in private." He smiled at me, to show he didn't mind the rudeness of this strange man. To El-Marad he added, "But Catherine is *dakhil-ak*, you know. . . ."

"Impossible!" cried El-Marad, rising to his feet as well. "She is a woman!"

"What is that?" I said, but Kamel had disappeared out the door, and I was left alone with the carpet trader.

"He says you are under his protection," El-Marad said, turning back to me when he was certain Kamel had gone. "A Bedouin formality. A man who is pursued may grasp the skirt of another man in the desert. The burden of protection is mandatory upon him, even if they are not of the same tribe. It is rarely offered unless requested—and *never* given to a woman."

"Maybe he thought leaving me alone with you called for dire measures," I suggested.

El-Marad stared at me in amazement. "You are very brave to make jests at a time like this," he said slowly, walking around me in a circle, sizing me up. "He did not tell you that I educated him like my own son?" El-Marad stopped pacing and gave me another tiresome stare. "We are *nahnu malihin*—on terms of salt. If you share your salt in the desert with someone, it's worth more than gold."

"So you *are* a Bedouin," I said. "You know all the desert customs, and you never laugh—I wonder if Llewellyn Markham knows that? I'll have to drop him a note and let him know the Bedouin aren't as polite as the Berbers."

At the mention of Llewellyn's name, El-Marad grew pale. "So you *are* from him," he said. "Why didn't you come alone?"

I sighed and looked at the chess piece in his hand. "Why don't you tell me where they are?" I said. "You know what I came for."

"Very well," he said. He sat down, shooting a squirt of coffee from the samovar into a little cup and sucking at it. "We've located the pieces and tried to purchase them—to no avail. The woman who owns them will not even see us. She lives in the Casbah of Algiers, but she is very rich. Though she does not own the entire set, we've cause to believe she has many pieces. We can collect the funds to purchase them—if you can get in to see her."

"Why won't she see *you*?" I said, repeating the question I'd asked Llewellyn.

"She lives in a harem," he said. "She is sequestered—the very word 'harem' means 'forbidden sanctuary.' No man is permitted but the master."

"So why not negotiate with her husband?" I asked.

"He no longer lives," said El-Marad, putting his coffee cup down with an impatient gesture. "He is dead, and she is rich. His sons protect her, but they are not *her* sons. They do not know she has the pieces. *No* one knows this."

"Then how do *you* know?" I demanded, raising my voice. "Look, I offered to perform this simple service for a friend, but you're giving me no help at all. You haven't even told me this woman's name or her address."

He paused and looked at me carefully. "Her name is Mokhfi Mokhtar," he said. "There are no street addresses in the Casbah, but it's not large—you'll find her. And when you do, she'll sell to you if you tell her the secret message I am going to give you. It will open every door."

"Okay," I said with impatience.

"Tell her that *you* are born on the Islamic holy day—the Day of Healing. Tell her you are born, by the Western calendar—on April fourth. . . ."

Now it was my turn to stare. My blood went cold, and my heart was pumping. Even Llewellyn didn't know the date of my birthday.

"Why should I tell her that?" I asked as calmly as possible.

"It is the day of Charlemagne's birthday," he told me softly, "the day when the chess service was raised from the ground—an important day associated with the pieces we seek. It is said that the one who is destined to put the pieces together again, to reunite them after all these years, will be born on this day. Mokhfi Mokhtar will know the legend—and she will see you."

"Have you ever seen her?" I asked.

"Once, many years ago . . ." he said, his face changing as he looked into the past. I wondered what this man was really like—a man who'd do business with a flake like Llewellyn—a man Kamel thought had stolen his father's business and maybe sent to his death, but who'd financed Kamel's education so he could become one of the most influential ministers in the country. He lived here like a hermit a million miles from nowhere, with a bevy of wives—yet he had business contacts in London and New York.

"She was very beautiful then," he was saying. "She must be quite old by now. I met her, but only for a moment. Of course, I did not know then that she had the pieces—that one day she would be . . . But she had eyes like yours. That I do recall." He snapped back to attention. "Is that all you wish to know?"

"How do I get the money, if I *can* buy the pieces?" I asked, bringing the subject back to business.

"We will arrange that," he said brusquely. "You may contact me through this postal box." And he handed me a slip of paper with a number on it. Just then, one of the wives popped her head in through the drapery, and we saw Kamel standing behind her.

"Finish your business?" he asked, stepping into the room.

"Quite so," said El-Marad, standing and helping me to my feet. "Your friend drives a hard bargain. She can claim the *al-basharah* for yet another carpet." He pulled two rolled carpets of uncombed camel hair from a stack. The colors were beautiful.

"What's that I've claimed?" I said with a smile.

"The gift claimed by one who brings good news," said Kamel, hoisting the carpets on his back. "What good news did you bring? Or is that a secret, too?"

"She brings a message from a friend," El-Marad said smoothly. "I can send a donkey boy down with you, if you'd like," he added. Kamel said that would be much appreciated, so we sent for the boy with the cart. El-Marad accompanied us to the street as the boy came up.

"*Al-safar zafar!*" said El-Marad, waving us on our way.

"An old Arabic proverb," Kamel explained. "It means, 'Voyaging is victory.' He wishes you well."

"Not as much of a curmudgeon as I'd originally thought," I told Kamel. "But I still don't trust him."

Kamel laughed. He seemed much more relaxed. "You play the game well," he said.

My heart stopped, but I kept on walking through the dark night. I was happy he couldn't see my face. "What do you mean?" I said.

"I mean you got two free rugs from the shrewdest carpet trader in Algeria. His reputation would be ruined if this news got out."

We walked on in silence for a while, listening to the squeaking wheels of the donkey cart that moved through the darkness before us.

"I think we should go ahead to the ministry quarters in Bouira for the night," said Kamel. "It's about ten miles from here, down the road. They'll have nice rooms for us, and we could go back to Algiers from there tomorrow—unless you'd prefer to double back through the mountains tonight?"

"Not on your life," I told him. Besides, at the ministry quarters they probably had hot baths and other luxuries I hadn't enjoyed in months. Though the El

Riadh was a charming hotel, the charm had worn thin after two months of cold water with iron filings.

It wasn't until Kamel and I were back in the car with our carpets, had tipped the donkey boy, and were on the highway to Bouira that I pulled out my Arabic dictionary to look up some words that had been puzzling me.

As I'd suspected, Mokhfi Mokhtar wasn't a name at all. It meant the Hidden Elect. The Secret Chosen One.

THE
CASTLE

Alice: It's a great huge game of chess that's being played all over the world. . . . Oh what fun it is! How I *wish* I was one of them! I wouldn't mind being a Pawn, if only I might join—though of course I should *like* to be a Queen best.

Red Queen: That's easily managed. You can be the White Queen's Pawn if you like, as Lily's too young to play—and you're in the Second Square to begin with. When you get to the Eighth Square you'll be a Queen. . . .

—Through the Looking-Glass
Lewis Carroll

On the Monday morning after our trip to the Kabyle, all hell broke loose. It started the night before when Kamel dropped me at my hotel—and dropped a bomb in parting. It seems there was an OPEC conference coming up soon, at which he planned to present the "findings" of my computer model—a model that wasn't built yet. Therese had collected more than thirty tapes of data for me on barrels per month by country. I had to format these and load my own data by keypunch to produce trends on production, consumption, and distribution. Then I had to write the programs that would analyze it—all before this conference took place.

On the other hand, with OPEC no one ever knew what "soon" meant. The dates and locations of each conference were kept in darkest secrecy until the final hour—on the assumption that such piss-poor planning would prove less convenient to the schedules of terrorists than to the OPEC ministers. It was open season on OPEC in some circles, and a number of ministers had been snuffed out in recent months. It was a testimonial to the importance of my model that Kamel had even hinted at a forthcoming meeting. I knew I was under the gun to deliver data.

To make matters worse, when I arrived at the Sonatrach data center, high on the central hill of Algiers, there was a message in an official envelope pinned to the console where I did my work. It was from the Ministry of Housing— they'd found me a real apartment at last. I could move in tonight; in fact, I *must* move in tonight, or I'd lose it. Housing was rare in Algiers—I'd already waited two months for this one. I'd have to race home, pack, and move as soon as the whistle blew quitting time. With all this going on, how was I going to accomplish my own goal to hunt down Mokhfi Mokhtar of the Casbah?

Though office hours in Algiers are seven in the morning to seven at night, the buildings are shut during the three hours of lunch and siesta. I decided to use those three hours to begin my search.

As in all Arabic cities, the Casbah was the oldest quarter, which had once been fortified for protection. The Casbah of Algiers was a mazelike puzzle of narrow cobbled streets and ancient stone houses tumbling ramshackle down the steepest of the hills. Though it only covered about 2,500 square yards of mountainside, it was crammed with dozens of mosques, cemeteries, Turkish baths, and dizzying flights of stone steps branching off like arteries at every angle. Of the million residents in Algiers, nearly twenty percent lived in this tiny quarter: robed, veiled figures that slipped silently in and out of the deep shadows of hidden doorways. One could be swallowed in the Casbah without a trace. It was the perfect setting for a woman calling herself "the secret chosen."

Unfortunately it was also the perfect place to get lost. Though it was only a twenty-minute hike from my office to the Palais de la Casbah at the upper gate, I spent the next hour like a rat in a maze. No matter how many crooked streets I headed up, I kept finding myself back at the Cemetery of Princesses—a circular loop. No matter how many people I asked about local harems, I got the same blank stares—drug-induced, no doubt—and a few outrageous insults or bum steers. At the name Mokhfi Mokhtar, people laughed.

At the end of the "siesta," exhausted and empty-handed, I made a pass by the Poste Centrale to see Therese at her switchboard. It was unlikely my quarry would be listed in the phone directory—I hadn't even seen phone lines in the Casbah—but Therese knew everyone in Algiers. Everyone but the one I was looking for.

"Why would anyone have so ridiculous a name?" she asked me, letting the switchboard buzzers ring as she offered me some pastel bonbons. "My girl, I am happy you came by here today! I've a telex for you. . . ." She rifled through a sheaf of papers on the shelf of her switchboard. "These Arabs," she muttered. "With them, everything is *b'ad ghedoua*—'later than tomorrow'! If I tried to send this to you at the El Riadh, you'd be lucky to get it next month." She produced the telex and handed it to me with a flourish. Dropping her voice to a whisper, she added, "Even though this comes from a convent—I suspect it is written in code!"

Sure enough, it was from Sister Mary Magdalene, of the Convent of St. Ladislaus in New York. She'd certainly taken long enough to write. I glanced through the telex, exasperated that Nim would be so hokey:

> PLEASE ASSIST WITH NY TIMES X-WORD PUZZLE STOP ALL SOLVED BUT
> WHAT FOLLOWS STOP WORD OF ADVICE FROM HAMLET TO HIS GIRL-
> FRIEND STOP WHO STANDS IN POPES SHOES STOP BOUNDARY OF TAMER-
> LANE EMPIRE STOP WHAT ELITE DO WHEN HUNGRY STOP MEDIEVAL
> GERMAN SINGER STOP REACTOR CORE EXPOSED STOP WORK BY TCHAI-
> KOVSKY STOP LETTERS ARE 9-9-7-4-5-8-9
>
>   REPLY REQUESTED SISTER MARY MAGDALENE
>   CONVENT OF ST. LADISLAUS NY NY

Wonderful—a crossword puzzle. I hated them, as Nim knew perfectly well. He'd sent this just to torture me. Just what I needed, another mindless chore from the king of trivia.

I thanked Therese for her diligence and left her at the many tentacled switchboard. In fact, my decryption quotient must have increased in the last few months, for I *had* figured out some of the answers just standing there in the Poste Centrale. The advice Hamlet gave Ophelia, for example, was "Get thee to a nunnery." And what the elite did when hungry was "meet to eat." I'd have to chop up the messages to fit the length of the letters he'd provided, but it was clearly tailored for a simple mind like mine.

But when I went back to the hotel that evening at eight there was another surprise in store for me. There in the twilight, parked at the hotel entrance, sat Lily's powder-blue Rolls Corniche—surrounded by ogling porters, waiters, and chamber boys, all stroking the chrome and touching the soft leather dashboard.

I scurried past, trying to imagine I hadn't seen what I'd seen. I'd sent Mordecai at least ten telegrams in the last two months, begging him *not* to send Lily to Algiers. But that car didn't get here by itself.

When I went to the front desk to collect my key and notify the concierge I was moving, I got another jolt. Leaning against the marble counter and chatting with the desk clerk was the attractive but sinister Sharrif—head of the secret police. He spotted me before I could make a quick exit.

"Mademoiselle Velis!" he cried, flashing his movie star smile. "You've arrived just in time to assist us with a small investigation. Perhaps you noticed the car of one of your countrymen as you came in just now?"

"That's odd—it looked British to me," I told him casually as the desk man handed me my key.

"But with New York license plates!" said Sharrif, raising an eyebrow.

"New York is a big city. . . ." I began to stroll off toward my room, but Sharrif wasn't finished.

"When it came through the Douanier this afternoon, someone had it registered to *you* at this address. Perhaps you can explain?"

Shit. I was going to murder Lily when I found her. She'd probably bribed her way into my room already.

"Gee, that's great," I told him. "An anonymous gift from a fellow New Yorker. I've been needing a car—and rentals are so hard to get." I was headed for the garden, but Sharrif was on my heels.

"Interpol is checking the plates for us now," he told me, sprinting along to keep pace with me. "I can't believe the owner would pay duty in cash—it's one hundred percent of the car's value—and have it delivered to someone he didn't even know. Only a hired lackey showed up to collect it and bring it here. Besides, no Americans are registered at this hotel but you."

"And not even me," I said, stepping outside and crossing the crunchy gravel of the garden. "I'm checking out in half an hour to move to Sidi-Fredj, as I'm sure your *jawasis* have told you." *Jawasis* were spies—or stool pigeons—for the secret police. The innuendo was not lost on Sharrif. Squinting his eyes, he

grabbed me by the arm, and I jerked to a stop. I looked down with disdain at
the hand on my elbow and carefully pried it loose.

"My *agents*," he said, always a stickler for semantics, "have already checked
your quarters for visitors—as well as this week's entry lists from Algiers and
Oran. We're waiting for the lists from the other ports of entry. As you know,
we share borders with seven other countries and the coastal zone. It would make
things so much simpler if you'd just tell us whose car that is."

"What's the big deal?" I said, moving on again. "If the duty's paid and the
papers are in order, why should I look a gift horse in the mouth? Besides, what
difference does it make to *you* whose car that is? There isn't any quota on
imported vehicles in a country that doesn't manufacture any—is there?"

He was at a loss to answer that one. He could hardly admit his *jawasis* were
tailing me everywhere and reporting each time I sneezed. Actually I was just
trying to make things difficult for him until I could find Lily myself—but it
did seem odd. If she wasn't in my room and hadn't registered at the hotel, where
was she? Just then, my question was answered.

At the far side of the pool was the decorative brick minaret that separated
the garden from the beach. I heard a suspiciously familiar voice—the sound of
little dog claws tearing at the wooden door and a slobbering growl that, once
heard, was hard to forget.

In the waning light across the pool, I saw the door push open a crack—and
a ferocious-looking ball of fluff burst forth. Skirting the poolside at top speed,
it tore toward us. Even in the clearest light, it would be hard at first glance to
recognize exactly what sort of animal Carioca *was*—and I saw Sharrif stare in
amazement as the beast barreled into him at ankle height, sinking his pointed
little teeth into Sharrif's silk-stockinged leg. Sharrif let out a cry of horror,
jumping about on his good leg and trying to shake Carioca off the other. With
a grab, I plucked the little beast away, pinning him with one arm to my chest.
He wriggled and licked me on the chin.

"What in God's name *is* that?" cried Sharrif, glaring at the writhing angora
monster.

"He's the owner of the car," I said with a sigh, realizing the jig was up.
"Would you like to meet his better half?"

Sharrif followed me, limping and pulling up his trouser cuff to check his
injured leg. "That creature might well be rabid," he complained as we reached
the minaret. "Animals like that often attack people."

"Not rabid—just a severe critic," I told him.

We pushed through the door that was ajar and ascended the darkened
stairwell of the minaret to the second floor. It was a large room with window
seats of pillows all around. Lily was ensconced amid the cushions like a pasha,
her feet propped up and wads of cotton between her toes—carefully applying
blood-red lacquer to her toenails. Wearing a microscopic minidress with pranc-

ing pink poodles, she glanced up at me with an icy stare, her frizzy blond hair falling into her eyes. Carioca yapped to be put down. I squished him into silence.

"It's about *time*," she began in indignation. "You wouldn't *believe* the problems I've had getting here!" She looked at Sharrif behind my shoulder.

"*You've* had problems?" I said. "Permit me to introduce my escort—Sharrif, head of the secret police."

Lily let out a big sigh.

"How many times must I tell you," she said, "we do *not* need the police. We can handle this ourselves—"

"He's not the police," I interrupted. "I said the secret police."

"What's that supposed to mean—no one should know he's a policeman? Oh, damn. I've smudged my polish," said Lily, fussing with her foot. I dropped Carioca in her lap, and she glared again.

"I take it you know this woman," Sharrif said to me. He was standing beside us and put out his hand. "May I please see your papers? There is no record of your entry into this country, you've registered an expensive car under an assumed name, and you own a dog that is clearly a civic hazard."

"Oh, go take a laxative," said Lily, pushing Carioca away and dropping her feet to stand up and face him. "I paid bloody hell to ship that car into this country, and how do you know I came here illegally? You don't even know who I am!" She was hobbling around the room on her heels so the cotton between her toes wouldn't smudge the polish. She extracted some papers from a pile of expensive leather bags and waved them before Sharrif's face. He snatched them away, and Carioca barked.

"I've stopped in your despicable country on my way to Tunisia," she informed him. "I happen to be a major chess master, and I'm playing an important tournament there."

"There isn't a chess tourney in Tunisia until September," Sharrif said, perusing her passport. He looked up at her with suspicion. "Your name is Rad—are you by chance related to—"

"Yes," she snapped. I remembered Sharrif was a chess nut. He'd no doubt heard of Mordecai, maybe even read his books.

"Your visa isn't stamped for entry to Algeria," he pointed out. "I'm taking it with me until I get to the bottom of this. Mademoiselle, you're not to leave these premises."

I waited until the door below slammed shut.

"You certainly make friends quickly in a new country," I said as Lily came back to sit on the window seat. "What are you going to do now that he's taken your passport?"

"I have another one," she said glumly, picking the cotton from between her toes. "I was born in London to an English mother. British citizens can hold dual citizenship, you know." I didn't know, but I had some bigger questions.

"Why did you register your damned car to *me*? And how *did* you get in, if you didn't come through Immigrations?"

"I chartered a sea plane in Palma," she said. "They dropped me here near the beach. I had to have the name of a resident to register the car to, since I was shipping it ahead. Mordecai told me to arrive here as unobtrusively as possible."

"Well, you've certainly done *that*," I said wryly. "I doubt anyone in the country has guessed you're here except Immigrations at every border, the secret police, and probably the president! What the hell are you supposed to be doing here, or did Mordecai forget that part?"

"He told me to come rescue you—*and* he told me Solarin would play Tunisia this month, the bloody liar! I'm starving. Maybe you can find me a cheeseburger or something substantial to eat. There's no room service here—I don't even have a phone."

"I'll see what I can do," I told her. "But I'm checking out of this hotel. I've got a new apartment at Sidi-Fredj, about half an hour's walk down the beach. I'll take the car to move my things and whip up some dinner for you over there in an hour. You can leave when it's dark and slip out by the beach. The hike would do you good."

Lily grudgingly agreed, and I went off to collect my belongings with the keys to the Rolls in my pocket. I was sure Kamel could handle her illegal entry—and while I was stuck with her, at least I'd have a car. Then, too, I hadn't heard from Mordecai since his cryptic message about the fortune-teller and the game. I'd have to pump Lily about how much she'd learned from him in my absence.

The ministry apartment at Sidi-Fredj was wonderful—two rooms with vaulted ceilings and marble floors, fully furnished with even the linens, and a balcony overlooking the port and the Mediterranean beyond. I bribed the alfresco restaurant beneath my terrace to bring up food and wine and sat outside on a chaise to decipher Nim's crossword puzzle while I watched for Lily to come down the beach. The message read as follows:

Advice from Hamlet to his girlfriend	(9)
Who stands in Pope's Shoes	(9)
Boundary of Tamerlane Empire	(7)
What Elite do when Hungry	(4)
Medieval German Singer	(5)
Reactor Core Exposed	(8)
Work by Tchaikovsky	(9)

I had no intention of spending as much time on this exercise as I'd spent on the fortune-teller's cocktail napkin, but I had the advantage of a musical education. There were only two kinds of German troubadours: Meistersingers and Minnesingers. I also knew everything Tchaikovsky ever wrote—there weren't that many works with nine letters.

My first attempt read: "Get thee to, Fisherman, Caspian, Meet, Minne, Meltdown, *Joan of Arc*." That was close enough for shooting. Another boundary of Tamerlane's empire was the steppes of Russia, which like the Caspian had seven letters. And a nuclear reactor that was melting down went "critical"— which had eight. So the message was "Get thee to the Fisherman Steps; Meet Minne; Critical!" Though I didn't know what *Joan of Arc* had to do with it, there *was* a place in Algiers called Escaliers de la Pêcherie—Fisherman's Steps. And a quick glance at my address book told me that Nim's friend Minnie Renselaas, wife of the Dutch consul—whom he'd told me to phone if I needed help—lived at number one of these same Fisherman's Steps. Though I didn't need help so far as *I* knew, it seemed critical to him that I meet her. I tried to remember the plot of Tchaikovsky's *Joan of Arc*, but all I recalled was her burning at the stake. I hoped Nim didn't have that fate in store for me.

I knew the Fisherman's Steps—an endless flight of stone that ran between the Boulevard of Anatole France and a street called Bab el Oued, or Rivergate. The Mosque of the Fisherman was up at the top near the entrance to the Casbah—but nothing that resembled a Dutch consulate. *Au contraire*, the embassies were far across town in a residential area. So I went back inside, picked up the phone, and called Therese, still on duty at nine at night.

"Of course I know Madame Renselaas!" she yelled in her gravelly voice. We were only thirty miles apart, and on dry land, but the line sounded as if it were at the bottom of the sea. "Everyone in Algiers knows her—a very charming lady. She used to bring me Dutch chocolates and those little candies from Holland with the flower in the center. She was wife of the consul from the Netherlands, you know."

"What do you mean, she *was*?" I yelled back.

"Oh, this was before the revolution, my girl. Ten years, maybe fifteen, her husband has been dead. But she is still here—at least so they say. She has no telephone number, though, or I would know it."

"How can I reach her?" I bellowed as the line got thicker with water noises. No need to bug this—our conversation could be heard across the port. "I only have the address—number one Fisherman's Steps. But there aren't any houses near the mosque."

"No," cried Therese, "there is no number one there. Are you sure you have it right?"

"I'll read it to you," I said. "It's *wahad*, Escaliers de la Pêcherie."

"Wahad!" Therese laughed. "That means number one all right—but it's not an address—it's a person. He's the tour guide up there near the Casbah. You know that flower stall by the mosque? Ask the flower vendor for him—fifty dinars, and he gives you a tour. The name Wahad—it's like 'numero uno,' you see?"

Therese had rung off before I could ask why a tour guide was needed to find Minnie. But things were done differently in Algiers, it would seem.

I was just planning my excursion for lunchtime tomorrow when I heard the sound of doggy toenails skittering across the marble floors of the hallway outside. There was a quick knock at the door, and Lily came barging in. Both she and Carioca headed for the kitchen, from which wafted the scents of our warming dinner: grilled *rouget*, steamed oysters, and couscous.

"I have to be fed," Lily called over her shoulder. When I caught up with her she was already lifting the lids from pots and poking about with her fingers. "No need for plates," she told me, tossing scraps to Carioca, who gobbled them down.

I sighed and watched Lily stuffing herself, an experience that always put off my appetite.

"Why did Mordecai send you here, anyway? I wrote him to keep you away."

Lily turned to look at me with wide gray eyes. A chunk of lamb from the couscous dripped between her fingers. "You ought to be *thrilled*," she informed me. "It so happens we've solved this whole mystery in your absence."

"Do tell," I said, unimpressed. I went over to uncork a bottle of excellent Algerian red wine, pouring a couple of glasses as she spoke.

"Mordecai was trying to buy these rare and valuable chess pieces in behalf of a museum—when Llewellyn found out about it and started mucking up the deal. Mordecai suspects that Llewellyn bribed Saul to find out more about them. When Saul threatened to reveal his duplicity, Llewellyn panicked and hired someone to bump him off!" She was very pleased with this explanation.

"Mordecai is either misinformed or deliberately misleading you," I told her. "Llewellyn had nothing to do with Saul's death. Solarin did it. He told me so himself. Solarin is here in Algeria."

Lily had an oyster halfway to her lips, but she dropped it in the couscous pot. Reaching for the wine, she took a big slug. "Try that one more time," she said.

So I told her. The whole story, just as I'd pieced it together, holding back nothing. I recounted how Llewellyn had asked me to get him the pieces—how the fortune-teller had hidden a message in her prophecy—how Mordecai had written to reveal he knew the fortune-teller—how Solarin had shown up in Algiers and said Saul killed Fiske and tried to kill *him*. All because of the pieces. I told her I'd figured out there *was* a formula, just as she'd thought. It was hidden in the chess service everyone was looking for. I concluded by describing my visit to Llewellyn's pal the carpet trader—and the latter's tale of the mysterious Mokhfi Mokhtar of the Casbah.

When I'd finished, Lily was standing there with her mouth open—and she hadn't touched a bite. "Why haven't you told me any of this before?" she wanted to know.

Carioca was lying on his back with his paws in the air, acting sick. I scooped him up and put him in the sink, trickling a little water so he could drink.

"I didn't know most of this until I got here," I told Lily. "The only reason I'm telling you *now* is because there's something you can help me with that I can't do myself. It seems there's a chess game going on, with other people making the moves. I haven't a clue how the game is played, but you're an expert. I need to know, in order to find these pieces."

"You can't be serious," said Lily. "You mean a *real* chess game? With people as the pieces? So when somebody gets killed—it's like wiping a piece off the board?"

She went over to the sink and rinsed her hands, splashing Carioca with water. Tucking him still damp beneath her arm, she wandered off toward the living room, and I followed with the wine and glasses. She seemed to have forgotten all about food.

"You know," she said, still moving about the room, "if we could figure out who the pieces were, we might be able to work this out. I can look at any board, even in the middle of a game, and reconstruct the moves so far. For example, I think we could safely assume that Saul and Fiske were pawns. . . ."

"And you and I as well," I agreed. Lily's eyes were glowing like those of a hound with the fox's scent. I'd rarely seen her so excited.

"Llewellyn and Mordecai might be pieces—"

"And Hermanold," I added quickly. "He was the one who shot at our car!"

"We can't forget Solarin," she said. "He's a player for sure. You know, if we could go over this carefully, re-creating the events, I think I could lay out the moves on a board and come up with something."

"Maybe you should stay here tonight," I suggested. "Sharrif might send his boys by to arrest you once he has proof you're really here illegally. I could smuggle you into town tomorrow. My client Kamel can pull strings to keep you out of prison. Meanwhile we can work on the puzzle."

We stayed up half the night reconstructing events, moving chess pieces around Lily's pegboard set—using a matchstick for the missing White Queen. But Lily was frustrated.

"If only we had just a little more data," she complained as we watched the morning sky turn to lavender.

"Actually, I know a way we might get some," I admitted. "I've a very close friend who's been helping me with this puzzle—when I can reach him. He's a computer wizard who's played lots of chess, too. He has a friend in Algiers with high connections—wife of the late Dutch consul. I'm hoping to see her tomorrow. You could go with me, if we get your visa cleared up."

So we agreed and pulled down the sheets of our beds to catch a little sleep. I didn't guess that in a few hours something would happen that would transform me from an unwilling participant into a major player in the game.

$$\infty$$

La Darse was the quay at the northwest end of the port of Algiers, where the fishing boats were moored. It was a long rocky mole that connected the mainland to that small island for which Algiers was named—Al-Djezair.

The ministry parking lot was located there, but Kamel's car was missing, so I pulled the big blue Corniche into his slot, leaving a note on the dash. I felt a bit conspicuous about putting a pastel touring car amid all those sleek black limousines, but it was better than leaving it on the streets.

Lily and I went along the waterfront on the Boulevard Anatole France and crossed the Avenue Ernesto Che Guevara to the Escaliers that led to the Mosquée de la Pêcheur. Lily was only a third of the way up the steps when she sat down on the cold flat stones, dripping with sweat, though it was still the cool of the morning.

"You're trying to kill me," she informed me with a gasp. "What kind of place is this? These streets go straight up. They ought to bulldoze the whole thing and start from scratch."

"I find it charming," I told her, pulling her up by the arm. Carioca was lying bedraggled on the steps beside her, his tongue hanging out. "Besides, there's no place to park near the Casbah. So get a move on."

After much complaining and many rest stops, we reached the top where the curving street Bab el Oued separated the Fisherman's Mosque from the Casbah. To our left was the Place des Martyrs, a wide plaza full of old men on park benches, where the flower stall was located. Lily plopped down on the first empty bench.

"I'm looking for Wahad the tour guide," I told the surly flower vendor. He looked me up and down and waggled his hand. A dirty little boy came running up, dressed like a ragtag street urchin, a cigarette reeking of hemp dangling from between his colorless lips.

"Wahad, a client seeks you," the flower vendor told the little boy. I did a double take.

"*You're* the tour guide?" I said. The filthy little creature couldn't have been older than ten but was already wizened and decrepit. Not to mention riddled with lice. He scratched himself, licked his fingers to pinch out his cigarette, and tucked it behind his ear.

"Fifty dinars is my minimum for the Casbah," he told me. "For a hundred, I'll show you the city."

"I don't want a tour," I said, taking his ragged shirt gingerly by the sleeve to pull him aside. "I'm looking for Mrs. Renselaas—Minnie Renselaas, wife of the late Dutch consul. A friend told me—"

"I know who she is," he said, squinting one eye to check me out.

"I'll pay you to take me there—fifty dinars, did you say?" I was scrounging in my bag for money.

"No one goes to see the lady, unless she told me so," he said. "You got an invitation or something?"

An invitation? I felt like a fool, but I pulled out Nim's telex and showed it to him, thinking that might do the trick. He looked at it for a long while, holding it in different directions. Finally he said:

"I can't read. What does it say?" So I had to explain to the disgusting child that a friend of mine had sent it in code. I told him what I thought it said: Get thee to Fisherman's Steps. Meet Minnie. Critical.

"That's all?" he asked me, as if this conversation were an everyday event. "There's not another word? Like a secret word?"

"Joan of Arc," I told him. "It said Joan of Arc."

"That's not the right word," he told me, pulling out his cigarette again and lighting up. I glanced across the plaza at Lily on her bench. She returned a look that said I was crazy. I racked my brain, trying to think of another Tchaikovsky piece that had nine letters—clearly that was the clue—but I couldn't. Wahad was still looking at the paper in his hand.

"I can read numbers," he told me at last. "That's a phone number there." I looked down and saw that Nim had written seven numbers. I was very excited.

"It's *her* phone number!" I said. "We could call her and ask. . . ."

"No," said Wahad, looking mysterious, "that's not her phone number—it's mine."

"Yours!" I cried. Lily and the flower vendor were both looking at us now, and Lily stood up, starting to wander toward us. "But doesn't that prove . . ."

"It proves that somebody knows I can find the lady," he told me. "But I *won't*, unless you know the right word."

Stubborn little bugger. I was cursing Nim in my mind for being so cryptic, when suddenly I thought of it. Another Tchaikovsky opera that had nine letters—at least, it did if you said it in French. Lily had just reached us when I grabbed Wahad by his collar.

"Dame Pique!" I cried. "The Queen of Spades!"

Wahad smiled at me with his crooked teeth.

"That's it, lady," he told me. "The Black Queen." Crushing his cigarette on the ground, he motioned for us to cross the Bab el Oued and follow him into the Casbah.

∞

Wahad took us up and down steep streets in the Casbah that I never would have discovered on my own. Lily was huffing and puffing behind us, and I finally picked up Carioca and stuffed him in my shoulder bag so he'd stop whining. After half an hour of winding through tortuous twists and turns, we came at last to a cul-de-sac with high brick walls that shut out all the light from above. Wahad paused for Lily to catch up, and I suddenly felt a cold chill run up my spine. I felt I'd been here before. Then I realized this was like my dream that night at Nim's when I'd wakened in a cold sweat. I was terrified. I wheeled on Wahad and grabbed him by his shoulder.

"Where are you taking us?" I cried.

"Follow me," he said, and opened a heavy wooden door buried deep in the brick wall. I glanced at Lily and shrugged, then we stepped inside. There was a dark stairwell that looked as if it led down into a dungeon.

"Are you sure you know what you're doing?" I called after Wahad, who'd already disappeared into the gloom.

"How do we know we're not being kidnapped?" Lily whispered behind me as we started down the stairs. Her hand was on my shoulder, and Carioca whimpered softly in my bag. "I've heard blond women are sold at very high prices in the white slave trade. . . ."

They'd get double for her, based on volume, I thought. Aloud, I said, "Shut up and stop shoving." But I was afraid. I knew I could never find my way out of here again.

Wahad was waiting at the bottom, where I collided with him in the dark. Lily was still hanging on me as we heard Wahad turn the lock of the door. The door opened a crack, emitting a dim light.

He pulled me inside a large dark cellar where a dozen or more men sat about on the cushioned floor, playing dice. A few looked up with bleary eyes as we moved through the smoke-filled room. But no one tried to stop us.

"What's that ghastly smell?" asked Lily in hushed tones. "It's like decomposing flesh."

"Hashish," I whispered back, glancing at the large water-filled bongs that sat about the room, at the men sucking on hoses and rolling the ivory dice.

Good God, where was Wahad taking us? We followed him through the room to a door on the other side and went up a sloped and darkened passage into the back of a small shop. The shop was completely filled with birds—jungle birds on branched perches moving about in cages everywhere.

Only one large vine-covered window let in light from the outside. Glass droplets of chandeliers cast glittering gold, green, and blue prisms of color against the walls and across the veiled faces and hair of the half-dozen women who moved about the room. Like the men below, these women ignored us as if we were part of the wallpaper.

Wahad pulled me through the maze of trees and perches to a small archway at the far side of the shop, which opened onto a narrow alley. It was completely enclosed with no entrance but the way we'd come, high walls of mossy brick surrounding the little square, cobbled pavement, and a heavy door in the wall across from us.

Wahad crossed the enclosed court, pulling a rope that hung beside the door. It took a long time before anything happened. I glanced at Lily, who was still hanging on to me. She'd caught her breath, but her face was deadly white, as I'm sure was mine. My uneasiness was turning to terror.

A man's face appeared at the grate in the door. He looked at Wahad without speaking. Then his eyes moved to Lily and me where we huddled across the court. Even Carioca was silent. Wahad muttered something, and though we were twenty feet away, I could hear what he said.

"Mokhfi Mokhtar," he whispered. "I have brought her the woman."

We passed through the massive wooden door to stand in a small brick-walled formal garden. The floor was a pattern of enameled tiles in various designs. None seemed to be repeated. Soft fountains gurgled in the spotty foliage. Birds cooed and warbled in the speckled half-light. At the back of the court was a bank of many-paned French windows draped with vines. Through these windows I glimpsed a room richly furnished with Moroccan carpets, Chinese urns, and intricate tooled leathers and carved woods.

Wahad slipped away through the gate behind us. Lily whirled, crying out, "Don't let that little creep escape—we'll never get out of here!"

But he'd already vanished. The man who'd let us in was gone as well, so the two of us were left alone in the court, where the air was dark and cool and the mingled scent of colognes and sweet grasses pervaded the air. I felt in a daze as the fountains splashed musically, echoing off the mossy walls.

I noticed a shape moving behind the French windows. It flickered past the heavy drape of jasmine and wisteria. Lily clutched my hand. We stood beside the fountains and watched the silvery form as it moved through an archway into the garden, floating through the half-green light—a slim, beautiful woman whose translucent robes seemed to whisper as she moved. Her soft hair fluttered about her half-veiled face like the silvered wings of birds. When she spoke to us, her voice was as sweet and low as cool water passing over smooth stones.

"I am Minnie Renselaas," she said, standing before us like a wraith in the shimmering light. But even before she removed the opaque silver veil that masked her face, I knew who she was. It was the fortune-teller.

THE DEATH OF KINGS

For God's sake, let us sit upon the ground
And tell sad stories of the death of kings:
How some have been deposed, some slain in war,
Some haunted by the ghosts they have deposed,
Some poisoned by their wives, some sleeping killed—
All murdered; for within the hollow crown
That rounds the mortal temples of a king
Keeps Death his court . . . and with a little pin
Bores through his castle wall, and farewell king!

—Richard II
William Shakespeare

Mireille stood beneath the leafy chestnut trees at the entrance to Jacques-Louis David's courtyard and peered through the iron gates. In the long black haik, her face obscured by the muslin veil, she looked like a typical model for the famous painter's exotic canvases. More importantly, no one could recognize her in this attire. Dusty and exhausted from her arduous journey, she tugged the cord and heard the bell echo from within.

Less than six weeks ago, she'd received the abbess's letter filled with urgency and admonishment. It had taken long enough to reach her, having been sent first to Corsica, then forwarded by the only member of Napoleone and Elisa's family who hadn't fled that isle—their gnarled old grandmother, Angela-Maria di Pietra-Santa.

The letter ordered Mireille to France at once:

> In learning of your absence from Paris, I feared not only for you, but for the fate of that which God placed within your guardianship—a responsibility I discover you've spurned. I am in despair for those of your Sisters who may have fled to that city seeking your aid when you were not there to help them. You understand my meaning.
>
> I remind you that we face powerful adversaries who will halt at nothing to achieve their ends—who've organized their opposition while we've been blown by the winds of fate. The time has come to take the reins into our hands, turn the tide again in our favor, and reunite what fate has torn asunder.
>
> I urge you to Paris at once. By my direction, someone you know was sent there seeking you—with specific instructions regarding your mission, which is critical.
>
> My heart goes out to you in the loss of your cherished cousin. May God go with you in this task.

There was no date on the letter and no signature. Mireille recognized the abbess's handwriting, but she had no idea how long ago she'd written. Though stung by the accusation that she'd shirked her duty, Mireille had grasped the true meaning of the abbess's letter. Other pieces were in jeopardy, other nuns were in danger—from the same evil forces that had destroyed Valentine. She must go back to France.

Shahin agreed to accompany her as far as the sea. But her month-old son, Charlot, was too young to make the arduous trip. At Djanet, Shahin's people vowed to care for the child until her return, since they already regarded the red-haired infant as the prophet that was foretold. After a painful farewell, Mireille left him in the arms of the wet nurse and departed.

For twenty-five days they crossed the Deban Ubari, the western rim of the Libyan Desert, bypassing the mountains and treacherous dunes in a shortcut to the sea at Tripoli. There Shahin put her onto a twin-masted schooner bound for France. These ships, the fastest on earth, sailed into the wind on open sea at fourteen knots, making the course from Tripoli to Saint-Nazaire at the mouth of the Loire in a mere ten days. Mireille was back in France.

Now, as she stood before David's gate, begrimed and exhausted from travel, she looked through the bars across that courtyard she'd fled less than a year ago. But it seemed a hundred years since that afternoon she and Valentine had scaled the garden walls, giggling with excitement at their boldness, and gone into the Cordeliers to meet Sister Claude. Forcing these thoughts from her mind, Mireille tugged the bell-cord again.

At last the aging servant Pierre emerged from the gatehouse, shuffling toward the iron gates where she stood silently in the shadows of the spreading chestnuts.

"Madame," he said, not recognizing her, "the master sees no one before luncheon—and never without an appointment."

"But Pierre, surely he will consent to see *me*," said Mireille, lowering her veil.

Pierre's eyes grew large, and his chin began to tremble. He fumbled with his heavy keys to unlock the iron gates. "Mademoiselle," he whispered, "we have prayed for you every day." There were tears of joy in his eyes as he threw open the gates. Mireille embraced him quickly, then the two hurried across the courtyard.

David, alone in his studio, was whittling at a large block of wood—a sculpture of Atheism that would be torched next month at the Festival of the Supreme Being. The scent of freshly cut wood pervaded the air. Piles of shavings covered the floor, and sawdust coated the rich velvet of his jacket. He turned as the door behind him opened, then leapt to his feet, upsetting the stool, the bevel falling from his hand.

"I'm dreaming, or I've gone mad!" he cried, shedding a cloud of sawdust as he flew across the room and grasped Mireille in a powerful embrace. "Thank God you're safe!" He held her away for a better look. "When you left, Marat came with a deputation, rooting about in my garden with his ministers and delegates from the gutter like pigs searching for truffles! I had no idea those chess pieces really existed! Had you confided in me, I might have helped. . . ."

"You can help me now," said Mireille, sinking to a chair in exhaustion. "Has someone come here seeking me? I expect an emissary from the abbess."

"My dear child," David said in a worried voice, "there've been several here in Paris during your absence—young women who wrote, seeking an interview with you or Valentine. But I was sick with fear for you. I gave these notes to Robespierre, thinking it might help us find you."

"Robespierre! My God, what have you done?" cried Mireille.

"He's a close friend who can be trusted," David said hastily. "They call him 'the Incorruptible.' No one could bribe him from his duty. Mireille, I've told him of your involvement with the Montglane Service. He was also searching for you—"

"No!" Mireille screamed. "No one must know I'm here or that you've even seen me! Don't you see—Valentine was murdered for those pieces. My life is in danger as well. Tell me how many nuns there were, whose letters you gave to this man."

David was pale with fear as he searched his mind. Could she be right? Perhaps he'd miscalculated. . . .

"There were five," he told her. "I've a record of their names in my study."

"Five nuns," she whispered. "Five more dead on my account. Because I was not here." Her eyes stared vacantly into space.

"Dead!" said David. "But he never interrogated them. He found they'd vanished—every one."

"We can only pray that's true," she said, focusing her gaze on him. "My uncle, these pieces are dangerous beyond anything you can imagine. We must learn more of Robespierre's involvement, without letting him know I'm here. And Marat—where is he? For if that man learned of this, even our prayers would not help."

"He's at home, gravely ill," whispered David. "Ill, but more powerful than ever. Three months ago, the Girondins brought him to trial for advocating murder and dictatorship, for overthrowing the tenets of the Revolution— liberty, equality, fraternity. But Marat was acquitted by a frightened jury, crowned with laurel by the rabble, carried through the streets by cheering throngs and elected president of the Jacobin Club. Now he sits at home denouncing the Girondins who crossed him. Most have been arrested; the rest have fled to the provinces. He rules the State from his bath with the weapon of fear. What they say of our revolution seems true—the fire that destroys cannot build."

"But it can be consumed by a greater flame," said Mireille. "That flame is the Montglane Service. Once united, it will devour even Marat. I've returned to Paris to unleash this force. And I expect you to help me."

"But don't you hear what I've said?" David cried. "It's this very vengeance and betrayal that's torn our country apart. Where will it end? If we believe in God, we must believe in a divine justice that in time will restore sanity."

"I have no time," said Mireille. "I will not wait for God."

JULY 11, 1793

Another nun who could not wait was even then hastening toward Paris.

Charlotte Corday arrived in the city by post chaise at ten o'clock in the morning. After registering at a small hotel nearby, she headed for the National Convention.

The abbess's letter, smuggled to her at Caen by Ambassador Genet, had been long in coming but clear in its message. The pieces sent to Paris last September with Sister Claude had disappeared. Another nun had died along with Claude in the Terror—young Valentine. Valentine's cousin had disappeared without a trace. Charlotte had contacted the Girondin faction—former convention delegates now holed up at Caen—in hopes they'd know who'd been at l'Abbaye Prison, the last place Mireille had been seen before she'd vanished.

The Girondins knew nothing of a red-haired girl who'd disappeared amid that madness, but their leader, the handsome Barbaroux, sympathized with the former nun who sought her friend. The pass he gave her secured permission for a brief interview with Deputy Lauze Duperret, who met her at the Convention in the visitors' antechamber.

"I come from Caen," Charlotte began as soon as the distinguished deputy was seated opposite her at the polished table. "I seek a friend who disappeared during the prison troubles last September. Like myself, she was a former nun whose convent had been closed."

"Charles-Jean-Marie Barbaroux has done me no great service by sending you here," said the deputy, raising a cynical eyebrow. "He's a wanted man—or hadn't you heard? Does he want them to put out a warrant for *my* arrest as well? I've enough troubles of my own, as you may tell him upon your return to Caen—which I hope will be soon." He started to rise.

"Please," said Charlotte, putting out her hand. "My friend was at l'Abbaye Prison when the massacres began. Her body was never found. We've cause to believe she escaped, but no one knows where. You *must* tell me—who among the Assembly members presided over those trials?"

Duperret paused and smiled. It was not a pleasant smile. "No one escaped from l'Abbaye," he told her curtly. "A few were acquitted—I could count the number on my two hands. If you were foolish enough to come here, perhaps you'll be fool enough to interrogate the man who was responsible for the Terror. But I wouldn't recommend it. His name is Marat."

JULY 12, 1793

Mireille, now in a dress of red-and-white dotted Swiss and a straw hat with colorful streamers, descended from David's open carriage and asked the driver to wait. She hurried into the vast, crowded market quarter of Les Halles, one of the oldest in the city.

In the two days since she'd arrived at Paris, she'd learned enough to act on at once. She did not need to wait for instructions from the abbess. Not only had five nuns vanished with their pieces, but others, David told her, knew of the Montglane Service—and of her involvement. Too many others: Robespierre, Marat, and André Philidor, the chess master and composer whose opera she had seen with Madame de Staël. Philidor, said David, had fled to England. But just before leaving, he'd told David of a meeting he'd had with the great mathematician Leonhard Euler and a composer named Bach. Bach had taken Euler's formula for the Knight's Tour and turned it into music. These men thought the secret of the Montglane Service was related to music. How many others had advanced this far?

Mireille moved through the open-air markets, passing colorful arrays of vegetables, viands, and seafood that only the rich could afford. Her heart was pounding, her mind spinning. She had to act at once, while she knew *their* whereabouts but before they discovered hers. They were all like pawns on a chessboard, driven toward an unseen center in a game as inexorable as fate. The abbess had been right in saying they must gather the reins into their own hands. But it was Mireille herself who must take control. For now, she realized, she knew more than the abbess—more perhaps than anyone—about the Montglane Service.

Philidor's tale supported what Talleyrand had told her and Letizia Buonaparte had confirmed: there *was* a formula in the service. Something the abbess had never mentioned. But Mireille knew. Before her eyes still floated the strange pale figure of the White Queen—with the staff of the Eight in her upraised hand.

Mireille descended into the labyrinth, that portion of Les Halles that once had been Roman catacombs but was now an underground market. Here were booths of copper wares, ribbons, spices, and silks from the East. She passed a small cafe with tables in the narrow passageway, where a cluster of butchers still smeared with the marks of their trade sat eating cabbage soup and playing dominoes. Her glazed eyes focused on the blood on their bare arms, their white aprons. Closing her eyes, she pushed on through the narrow labyrinth.

At the end of the second passage was a cutlery shop. Looking through the wares, she tested the strength and sharpness of each before finding one that suited her—a dinner knife with a six-inch balanced blade, similar to the *bousaadi* she'd used with such skill in the desert. She had the vendor whet the blade until it could split a hair.

Only one question now remained. How would she get in? She watched the merchant wrap the sheathed knife in brown paper. Mireille paid him two francs, tucked the package under her arm, and departed.

JULY 13, 1793

Her question was answered the next afternoon, when she and David sat quarreling in the small dining room beside the studio. As a Convention delegate, *he* could secure her entry to Marat's quarters. But he refused—he was afraid. Their heated conversation was interrupted by the servant Pierre.

"A lady's at the gate, sire. She asks for you, seeking information about Mademoiselle Mireille."

"Who is it?" asked Mireille, casting a quick glance at David.

"A lady as tall as yourself, mademoiselle," Pierre replied, "and with red hair—calling herself Corday."

"Show her in," said Mireille, much to David's surprise.

So this was the emissary, thought Mireille when Pierre had departed. She remembered the cold, fierce companion of Alexandrine de Forbin, who'd come to Montglane three years ago to tell them the pieces of the Montglane Service were in jeopardy. Now she'd been sent by the abbess—but she'd come too late.

When Charlotte Corday was shown into the room, she halted, staring at Mireille in disbelief. She sat hesitantly in the chair David held for her, never taking her eyes from Mireille. Here sat the woman whose news had brought the service from the earth, thought Mireille. Though time had changed them both, they were still alike in appearance—tall, large-boned, with unbound red curls framing their oval faces—alike enough to be sisters. Yet so far apart.

"I'd come in desperation," Charlotte began. "Finding all trails to you cold, all doors closed. I must speak with you alone." She glanced uneasily at David, who excused himself. When he'd left she said, "The pieces—are they safe?"

"The pieces," said Mireille with bitterness. "Always the pieces. I marvel at the tenacity of our abbess—a woman entrusted by God with the souls of fifty women, women cloistered from the world, who believed in her as in their own lives. She told us the pieces were dangerous—but not that we'd be hunted down and killed for them! What sort of shepherd leads his own sheep to the slaughter?"

"I understand. You are devastated by the death of your cousin," said Charlotte. "But it was an accident! Caught in a mob scene with my beloved Sister Claude. You cannot permit this to corrupt your faith. The abbess has chosen you for a mission. . . ."

"I choose my *own* missions now," cried Mireille, her green eyes burning with passion. "My first, to confront the man who murdered my cousin—for it was no accident! Five more nuns have disappeared in this last year. I think he knows what has become of them, and of the pieces in their charge. And I have a score to settle."

Charlotte had put her hand to her breast. Her face was white as she stared across the table at Mireille. Her voice trembled.

"Marat!" she whispered. "I've learned of his involvement—but not this! The abbess did not know of these missing nuns."

"It would seem there are many things our abbess doesn't know," replied Mireille. "But I do. Though I do not intend to thwart her, I think you understand there are things I must accomplish first. Do you stand with me—or against me?"

Charlotte looked at Mireille across the dining table, her deep blue eyes intense with emotion. At last she reached out and placed her hand over Mireille's. Mireille felt herself trembling.

"We will defeat them," said Charlotte with great force. "Whatever you require of me, I shall be at your side—as the abbess would wish."

"You have learned of Marat's involvement," Mireille said with tension in her voice. "What more do you know of the man?"

"I tried to see him, seeking you," Charlotte replied, lowering her voice. "I was turned away from his door by a porter. But I've written him for an appointment—this evening."

"Does he live alone?" pressed Mireille with excitement.

"He shares rooms with his sister Albertine—and Simonne Évrard, his 'natural' wife. But surely you can't mean to go there yourself? If you give your name, or they guess who you are, you'll be arrested. . . ."

"I don't plan to give my name," Mireille said with a slow smile. "I'll give them yours."

∞

It was sunset when Mireille and Charlotte arrived, in the back of a hired cabriolet, at the *allée* across from Marat's quarters. The sky's reflection turned the windowpanes blood red; the waning sun licked the paving stones with copper.

"I must know what reason you gave in your letter for an interview," Mireille told Charlotte.

"I wrote him I'd come from Caen," said Charlotte, "to report the activities of Girondins against the government. I said I knew of plots laid there."

"Give me your papers," said Mireille, holding out her hand, "in case I need proof to get inside."

"I pray for you," Charlotte said, handing over the papers, which Mireille shoved into her bodice, next to the knife. "I shall wait here until your return."

Mireille crossed the street and went up the steps of the rickety stone house. She paused before the entrance, where a frayed card was tacked:

JEAN PAUL MARAT: PHYSICIAN

She took a deep breath and rapped the metal knocker against the door. The sounds echoed from the bare walls within. At last she heard shuffling footsteps approaching—the door was jerked open.

There stood a tall woman, her large, whey-colored face creased with lines. With one wrist she brushed aside a stray wisp that had pulled loose from the slovenly twist of hair. Wiping flour-covered hands on the towel tucked at her ample waist, she looked Mireille up and down, taking in the frilly dress of dotted Swiss, the beribboned bonnet, the soft curls tumbling over creamy shoulders.

"What do you want?" she snorted in disdain.

"My name is Corday. Citizen Marat expects me," said Mireille.

"He's ill," snapped the woman. She started to close the door, but Mireille shoved it open, forcing her back a pace.

"I insist upon seeing him!"

"What is it, Simonne?" called another woman who'd appeared at the end of the long corridor beyond.

"A visitor, Albertine—for your brother. I've *told* her he's ill. . . ."

"Citizen Marat would wish to see me," Mireille called out, "if he knew the news I bring from Caen—and from Montglane."

A man's voice came through a door that was ajar halfway down the hall. "A visitor, Simonne? Bring her to me at once!"

Simonne shrugged and motioned for Mireille to follow.

It was a large tiled room with only a small high window through which she glimpsed the red sky, bleeding to gray. The place reeked with astringent medicines and the stench of decay. In the corner sat a boot-shaped copper tub. There, in shadow broken only by the light of a single candle placed on a writing board across his knees, sat Marat. His head wrapped in a wet cloth, his pocked skin gleaming sickly white in the candle's glow, he busied himself over the board littered with pens and papers.

Mireille's eyes were riveted upon the man. He did not look up as Simonne ushered her into the room and gestured for her to sit on a wooden stool beside the tub. He continued writing as Mireille stared at him, her heart pounding furiously. She longed to leap at him, shove his head under the tepid water of his bath, hold him there until . . . But Simonne remained standing behind her shoulder.

"How well timed your arrival," Marat was saying, still working over his papers. "I'm just preparing a list of Girondins believed to be agitating in the provinces. If you've come from Caen, you can confirm my list. But you say you've news of Montglane as well. . . ."

He glanced up at Mireille, and his eyes widened. He was silent for a moment, then he looked at Simonne.

"You may leave us now, my dear friend," he told her.

Simonne did not budge for a moment, but at last, beneath Marat's penetrating stare, she turned and left, closing the door behind her.

Mireille returned Marat's gaze without speaking. It was odd, she thought. Here was the incarnate manifestation of evil—the man whose hideous face had haunted her tortured dreams for so long—sitting in a copper tub filled with foul-smelling salts, rotting away like a piece of rancid meat. A withered old man, dying of his own evil. She would have pitied him if there were room for pity in her heart. But there was not.

"So," he whispered, still staring at her, "you've come at last. I knew when the pieces were missing—that one day you would return!" His eyes glittered in the flickering candlelight. Mireille felt the blood turn cold in her veins.

"Where are they?" she said.

"The very question I planned to ask *you*," he told her calmly. "You've made a large mistake in coming here, mademoiselle, under an assumed name or not. You'll never leave this place alive—unless you tell me what became of those pieces you exhumed from David's garden."

"Nor will you," said Mireille, feeling her heart grow calm as she extracted the knife from her bodice. "Five of my sisters are missing. I mean to know whether they ended as my cousin did."

"Ah, you've come to kill me," Marat said with a terrible smile. "But I hardly think you'll do that. I'm a dying man, you see. I don't need doctors to tell me; I'm a physician myself."

Mireille touched the knife's edge with her finger.

Picking up a quill from the board, Marat tapped it against his bare chest. "I advise you to place the tip of the dagger here—the left side between the second and third ribs. You'll sever the aorta. Quick and sure. But before I die, you'll be interested to know that I *do* have the pieces. Not five, as you supposed—but eight. Between the two of us, mademoiselle, we could control half the board."

Mireille tried to show no expression, but her heart was beating once again. Adrenaline pumped through her blood like a drug. "I don't believe you!" she cried.

"Ask your friend Mademoiselle de Corday how many nuns came to *her* in your absence," he said. "Mademoiselle Beaumont, Mademoiselle Defresnay, Mademoiselle d'Armentieres—do these names sound familiar?"

They were all nuns of Montglane. What was he saying? None of these had come to Paris—none of these had written the letters David had turned over to Robespierre. . . .

"They went to Caen," said Marat, reading Mireille's thoughts. "They thought to find Corday. How sad. They quickly learned the woman who intercepted them was no nun."

"Woman?!" cried Mireille.

Just then there was a tap outside, and the door was thrown open. Simonne Évrard entered, bearing a platter of steaming kidneys and sweetbreads. She crossed the room, a dour expression on her face as she glanced from the corner of her eye at Marat and his visitor. She set the platter on the window ledge.

"To cool—so we may grind them for the meat loaf," she said curtly, turning her beady eyes on Mireille, who'd quickly tucked the knife in her skirt folds.

"Please do not disturb us again," Marat told her tersely. Simonne looked at him in shock, then left the room quickly, a hurt expression on her ugly face.

"Lock the door," Marat told Mireille, who glanced at him in surprise. His eyes were dark as he leaned back in the tub, his lungs rasping from the effort of breathing. "The disease is everywhere in me, my dear mademoiselle. If you want to kill me, you haven't much time. But I think you want information more—just what I want from you. Lock the door, and I'll tell you what I know."

Mireille crossed to the door, still clutching the knife, and twisted the key until she heard the lock click. Her head was throbbing. Who was the woman he'd spoken of—who'd taken the pieces from the unsuspecting nuns?

"You killed them. You and that ugly harlot," she cried. "You murdered them for the pieces!"

"I'm an invalid," he replied with a horrible smile, his white face floating in the shadows. "But like the King on a chessboard, the weakest piece can also be the most valuable. I killed them—but only with information. I knew who they were and where, when flushed out, they were likely to go. Your abbess was a fool; the names of the nuns at Montglane were a matter of public record. But no, I did not kill them myself. Nor did Simonne. I'll tell you who did when you tell me what you've done with those pieces you took away. I'll even tell you where *our* captured pieces are, though it will do you no good. . . ."

Doubt and fear gnawed at Mireille. How could she trust him, when the last time he'd given her his word, he'd murdered Valentine?

"Tell me the woman's name, and where the pieces are," she said, crossing the room to stand over the tub. "Otherwise, nothing."

"You hold the knife in your hand," said Marat in a rasping voice. "But my ally is the most powerful player in the Game. You'll never destroy her—never! Your only hope is to join forces with us and unite the pieces. Individually, they're nothing. But united, they hold a world of power. Ask your abbess if you don't believe me. She knows who the woman is. She understands her power. Her name is Catherine—she's the White Queen!"

"Catherine!" cried Mireille as a thousand thoughts flooded her mind. The abbess had gone to Russia! Her childhood friend . . . Talleyrand's tale . . . the woman who'd purchased Voltaire's library . . . Catherine the Great, czarina of all the Russias! But how could this woman be both friend to the abbess and ally of Marat?

"You're lying," she said. "Where is she now? And where are the pieces?"

"I've told you the name," he cried, his face white with passion. "But before I tell you more, you must show the same faith. Where are the pieces you dug from David's garden? Tell me!"

Mireille took a deep breath, the knife tight in her fist. "I've sent them out of the country," she said slowly. "They're safe in England." But Marat's face lit up as he heard these words. She could see the changes working in him as his expression contorted into the evil mask she remembered in her dreams.

"Of course!" he cried. "I've been a fool! You've given them to Talleyrand! My God, this is more than I'd hoped for!" He tried to raise himself from the tub.

"He's in England!" he cried. "In *England*! My God—she can get them!" He struggled to push away the board with feeble arms. Water churned in the tub. "My dear friend! To me! To me!"

"No!" cried Mireille. "You said you'd tell me where the pieces are!"

"You little fool!" He laughed and shoved the board so it toppled to the floor, splashing Mireille's skirts with ink. She heard footsteps coming down the hall, a hand rattling the doorknob. She shoved Marat back into the tub. With one hand she grasped his greasy hair, the knife poised at his breast.

"Tell me where they are!" she screamed as the sound of pounding fists upon the door drowned her words. "Tell me!"

"You little coward!" he hissed at her, spittle flecking his lips. "Do it, or be damned! You are too late . . . too late!"

Mireille stared at him as the pounding went on. Women's cries filled her ears, and she looked at the horrible face that leered at her. He wanted her to kill him, she realized in terror. *How will you have the strength to kill a man? . . . I can smell the revenge in you as one smells water in the desert,* she heard Shahin's voice whispering in her mind, drowning the cries of the women, the pounding at the door. What did he mean, she was "too late"? What did it mean that Talleyrand was in England? What did he mean, "*she* can get them"?

The bolt of the door was giving way as Simonne Évrard's heavy body thrust against it, the rotten wood splintering around the lock. Mireille looked into the pustuled face of Marat. Taking a deep breath, she plunged in the knife. Blood spurted from the wound, splashing her dress. She shoved the blade in to the hilt.

"Congratulations, the exact spot . . ." he whispered, the blood bubbling to his lips. His head fell over on his shoulder; blood spurted in great throbs with each contraction of his heart. She pulled out the knife and dropped it to the floor just as the door burst open.

Simonne Évrard hurtled into the room with Albertine just behind. Marat's sister took one look at the tub, screamed, and fainted. Simonne was shrieking as Mireille moved in a daze toward the door.

"My God! You've killed him! You've killed him!" she cried, rushing past Mireille to the tub, falling on her knees to stanch the flow of blood with her towel. Mireille kept moving out into the hallway as if in a trance. The front door burst open, and several neighbors plunged into the apartment. Mireille passed them in the hallway—moving in a daze, her face and dress splashed with blood. She heard the cries and wails coming from behind her as she moved on toward the open door. What had he meant, she was "too late"?

She had her hand on the door when the blow struck her from behind. She felt the pain and heard the sound of splintering wood. She crumpled to the ground. Pieces of the shattered chair that struck her lay scattered across the dusty floor. Her head throbbing, she struggled to rise. A man grasped her by the front of her gown, clawing her breasts, dragging her to her feet. He smashed her against the wall, where she struck her head again and slumped to the floor. This time she could not rise. She heard the trampling of feet, the warped floorboards buckling as many people dashed through the house, the sounds of screams and men's boisterous cries, the sound of a woman weeping.

She lay on the dirty floorboards unable to move. After a long time she felt hands beneath her—someone trying to lift her. Men in dark uniforms, helping her to her feet. Her head ached, she felt an awful throbbing down her neck and spine. They were holding her up under the elbows, moving her to the door as she tried to walk.

Outside, a crowd had formed, surrounding the house. Her eyes were blurred as she looked out over the mass of faces, hundreds of faces that swam like a sea of lemmings. All drowning, she thought—all drowning. The police were beating the crowd back. She heard screams and cries: "Murderess!" "Killer!"

And far in the distance, across the street, one white face floated in the open window of a waiting carriage. She struggled to focus her eyes. For a second she saw the terrified blue eyes, the pale lips, the white knuckles gripping the carriage door—Charlotte Corday. Then everything went black.

JULY 14, 1793

It was eight o'clock in the evening when Jacques-Louis David returned wearily from the Convention. Already people were setting off firecrackers and running through the streets like drunken fools as he pulled his carriage into the court.

It was Bastille Day. But somehow he couldn't capture the spirit. This morning, arriving at the Convention Hall, he'd learned that Marat had been assassinated last night! And the woman they were holding in the Bastille, the murderess, was Mireille's visitor of yesterday—Charlotte Corday!

Mireille herself had not returned last night. David was sick with fear. He was not so safe that the long arm of the Paris Commune would fail to reach him, if they discovered the anarchist plot was laid in his own dining room. If only he could find Mireille—get her out of Paris before people put two and two together. . . .

Climbing from his carriage, he brushed the dust from his tricolor cockade hat, designed by himself for Convention delegates, to represent the Spirit of Revolution. As he went to close the gates behind the carriage, a slender form slipped from the shadows and moved toward him. David shrank in fear as the man clutched him by the arm. A firecracker went off in the sky, affording him a glimpse of the pale face—the sea-green eyes of Maximilien Robespierre.

"We must speak, citizen," whispered Robespierre in a soft, chilling voice as fireworks sparkled across the evening sky. "You missed the arraignment this afternoon. . . ."

"I was in convention!" David cried in a frightened voice, for it was clear whose arraignment Robespierre was speaking of. "Why did you jump out of the shadows like that?" he added, trying to mask the real cause of his trembling. "Come inside if you wish to speak to me."

"What I have to say must not be overheard by servants and keyhole peepers, my friend," said Robespierre gravely.

"My servants are given leave tonight for Bastille Day," David said. "Why do you think I closed the gate myself?" He was shaking so, he was grateful for the darkness that surrounded them as they crossed the courtyard.

"It's unfortunate you couldn't come to the hearing," said Robespierre as they entered the darkened, empty house. "You see, the woman they arraigned was not Charlotte Corday. It was the girl whose drawing you showed me, the girl we've been hunting across France these many months. My dear David—it's your ward Mireille who assassinated Marat!"

∞

David was deathly cold despite the warm July weather. He sat in the small dining room across from Robespierre as the latter lit an oil lamp and poured him some brandy from a decanter on the sideboard. David was shaking so badly he could scarcely hold the cup in his two hands.

"I've told no one what I know, until I could speak with you," Robespierre was saying. "I need your help. Your ward has the information I want. I know why she went to see Marat—she's after the secret of the Montglane Service. I *must* know what transpired between them in their interview before his death, and whether she's had the opportunity to smuggle to others what she knows."

"But I tell you I know nothing of these awful events!" cried David, looking at Robespierre in horror. "I never believed the Montglane Service existed until that day when I left the Café de la Régence with André Philidor—you recall? *He* was the one who told me. But when I repeated his tale to Mireille . . ."

Robespierre reached across the table to grasp David's arm. "She's been here? You spoke with her? My God, why haven't you told me?"

"She said no one must know she was here," moaned David, his head in his hand. "She arrived four days ago from God knows where—dressed in mufti like an Arab . . ."

"She's been to the desert!" Robespierre said, leaping to his feet and pacing up and down. "My dear David, this ward of yours is no innocent schoolgirl. This secret goes back to the Moors—to the desert. It's the secret of the pieces she's after. She murdered Marat in cold blood for them. She's at the very heart of this powerful and dangerous game! You must tell me what else you learned from her—before it's too late."

"It was telling you the truth that caused this horror!" cried David, nearly in tears. "And I'm a dead man if they discover who she is. Marat may have been hated and feared when alive, but now that he's dead, they're going to place his ashes in the Panthéon—his heart's been enshrined as a sacred relic at the Jacobin Club."

"I know," said Robespierre in the soft voice that sent chills down David's spine. "That's why I've come. My dear David, perhaps I can do something to help you both . . . but only if you help me first. I believe your ward Mireille trusts you—she'll confide in you, whereas she wouldn't even speak to me. If I could get you into the prison in secrecy . . ."

"Please don't ask this of me!" David nearly screamed. "I'd do anything in my power to help her—but what you suggest may cost us *all* our heads!"

"You don't understand," said Robespierre calmly, sitting again, but this time beside David. He took the artist's hand in his. "My dear friend, I know you're a dedicated revolutionary. But you don't know that the Montglane Service lies at the very center of the storm that's sweeping away the monarchy throughout Europe—that will cast off the yoke of oppression forever." He reached to the sideboard and poured himself a glass of port, then continued:

"Perhaps if I tell you how *I* came to the Game, you'll understand. For there is a game going on, my dear David—a dangerous and deadly game that destroys the very power of kings. The Montglane Service must be united under the control of those—like us—who'll *use* this powerful tool in support of those innocent virtues espoused by Jean-Jacques Rousseau. For it was Rousseau himself who chose me for the Game."

"Rousseau!" David whispered in awe. "He sought the Montglane Service?"

"Philidor knew him, and so did I," said Robespierre, extracting a piece of letter paper from his pocketbook and looking about for something to write with. David, fumbling through the litter on the sideboard, handed him a drawing crayon, and Robespierre continued as he began to draw a diagram.

"I met him fifteen years ago, when I was a young lawyer attending the States General in Paris. I learned that the revered philosopher Rousseau had fallen gravely ill just outside Paris. Hastily arranging an interview, I journeyed on horseback to visit the man who, in his sixty-six years, had produced a legacy that would soon alter the future of the world. What he told me that day certainly altered *my* future—perhaps yours will be changed as well."

David sat in silence as firecrackers burst like unfolding chrysanthemums in the deepening darkness beyond the windows. And Robespierre, his head bent over his drawing, began his tale. . . .

THE ATTORNEY'S TALE

Thirty miles from Paris, near the town of Ermenonville, lay the estate of the Marquis de Girardin, where Rousseau and his mistress, Thérèse Levasseur, had been staying in a cottage since the middle of May in the year 1778.

It was June—the weather was balmy, the aroma of freshly cut grass and full-blown roses wafted across the deep lawns surrounding the château of the marquis. There was a small island, the Isle of Poplars, at the center of a lake on the estate. I found Rousseau there, dressed in the Moorish costume I'd heard he always wore: loose purple caftan, green shawl dripping with fringes, red Moroccan shoes with curling toes, a large satchel of yellow leather slung across one shoulder, and a fur-trimmed cap framing his dark, intense face. An exotic and mysterious man who seemed to move against the dappled trees and water as if to an inner music he alone could hear.

Crossing the little footbridge, I made my greeting, though I was sorry to disrupt this profound concentration. Unknown to me, Rousseau was contemplating his own meeting with eternity, which was to be only a few weeks away.

"I've been expecting you," he said quietly in greeting. "They tell me, Monsieur Robespierre, that you're a man who embraces those natural virtues I myself extol. At the threshold of death, it's comforting to know one's beliefs are shared by at least *one* fellow human being!"

I was twenty at the time, and a great admirer of Rousseau—a man who'd been driven from pillar to post, exiled from his own country, forced to depend upon the charity of others despite his fame and the wealth of his ideas. I don't know what I'd expected in coming to see him—perhaps some deep philosophical insight, an uplifting chat about politics, a romantic excerpt from *La Nouvelle Héloïse*. But Rousseau, sensing the close proximity of death, seemed to have something else on his mind.

"Voltaire died last week," he began. "Our two lives were yoked together like those horses Plato spoke of—one pulling toward the earth, the other up into the heavens. Voltaire pulled for Reason, while I've championed Nature. Between us, our philosophies will serve to rip asunder the chariot of Church and State."

"I thought you disliked the man," I said, confused.

"I hated him and I loved him. I regret never having met him. One thing is certain—I'll not long outlive him. The tragedy is, Voltaire had the key to a mystery I've spent my life trying to unravel. Due to his pigheaded adherence to the Rational, he never knew the value of what he'd discovered. Now it's too late. He's dead. And with him died the secret of the Montglane Service."

I felt the excitement growing in me as he spoke. The chess service of Charlemagne! Every French schoolboy knew the story—but was it possible it was more than a legend? I held my breath, praying he'd go on.

Rousseau had taken a seat on a fallen log and was rummaging through his satchel of yellow Moroccan leather. To my surprise, he extracted a delicate cloth of needlepoint and hand-picked lace and began working over it with a tiny silver needle as he spoke.

"When I was young," he began, "I supported myself in Paris by selling my lace and crewelwork, since no one was interested in the operas I wrote. Though

I'd hoped to be a great composer, I spent each evening playing chess with Denis Diderot and André Philidor, who, like myself, could see the bottom of their pocketbooks. In the nick of time Diderot found me a paying position as secretary to the Comte de Montaigu, French ambassador to Venice. It was the spring of 1743—I shall never forget. For in Venice that year I was to witness something I can still see as vividly as if it were yesterday. A secret at the very core of the Montglane Service."

Rousseau seemed to drift off as if moving into a dream. The needlework dropped from his fingers. I bent to pick it up and returned it to him.

"You say you *witnessed* something?" I pressed. "Something to do with the chess service of Charlemagne?"

The old philosopher slowly shook himself back to reality. "Yes . . . Venice was even then a very old city, filled with mystery," he reminisced dreamily. "Though completely surrounded by water and filled with glittering light, there was something dark and sinister about the place. I could feel this darkness pervading everything, as I wandered through the winding labyrinth of streets, passed over ancient stone bridges, moved in gliding gondolas through the secret canals where only the sound of lapping water broke the silence of my meditation. . . ."

"It seemed an easy place," I suggested, "to believe in the supernatural?"

"Precisely," he replied, laughing. "One night I went alone to the San Samuele—the most charming theater in Venice—to see a new comedy by Goldoni called *La Donna di Garbo*. The theater was like a miniature jewel: tiers of boxes rose to the ceiling, ice-blue and gold, each with a tiny hand-painted basket of fruit and flowers and sets of glittering carriage lamps so you could see the audience as well as the performers.

"The theater was packed to the rafters with colorful gondoliers, feathered courtesans, bejeweled bourgeoisie—an audience completely unlike the jaded sophisticates one found in Parisian theaters—and all participating in the play at full volume. Hissing, laughter, cheers greeted every word of dialogue so one could scarcely hear the actors.

"Sharing my box was a young fellow about the age of André Philidor—sixteen or so—but wearing the pale pancake makeup and rubied lips, the powdered wig, and plumed hat so fashionable at that time in Venice. He introduced himself as Giovanni Casanova.

"Casanova had been educated as a lawyer—like yourself—but had many other talents. The child of two Venetian thespians, troupers who'd trod the boards from here to St. Petersburg, he supported himself by playing violin at several local theaters. He was thrilled to meet someone who'd just arrived from Paris—he longed to visit that city so famous for its wealth and decadence, two traits most agreeable to his disposition. He said he was interested in the court of Louis Quinze, since the monarch was known for his extravagance, his mistresses, his immorality, and dabbling in the occult. Casanova was interested especially in this last and questioned me closely about the Societies of Free-masons so popular in Paris just then. Though I knew but little of such things, he offered to improve my education the next morning—Easter Sunday.

"We met as arranged at dawn, where a large throng had already gathered outside the Porta della Carta—that door separating the famous Cathedral San Marco from the adjoining Ducal Palace. The crowd, sheared of their colorful costumes of the prior week's *carnevale*, were all dressed in black—awaiting with hushed voices the beginning of some event.

" 'We're about to witness the oldest ritual in Venice,' Casanova told me. 'Each Easter at sunrise, the Doge of Venice leads a procession across the Piazzetta and back into St. Mark's. It's called "the Long March"—a ceremony as ancient as Venice herself.

" 'But surely Venice is older than Easter—older than Christianity,' " I pointed out as we stood amid the expectant crowd, all huddled behind velvet ropes.

" 'I never said it was a Christian ritual,' said Casanova with a mysterious smile. 'Venice was founded by the Phoenicians—whence we derive our name. Phoenicia was a civilization built upon islands. They worshiped the moon goddess—Car. As the moon controls the tides, so the Phoenicians ruled the seas, from which spring the greatest mystery of all—life.'

"A Phoenician ritual. This lit some dim memory in my mind. But just then the crowd around us fell hushed. A horn ensemble appeared on the palace steps and riffled through a fanfare. The Doge of Venice, crowned with jewels and hung with purple satins, emerged from the Porta della Carta surrounded by musicians with lutes, flutes, and lyres playing music that seemed divinely inspired. They were followed by emissaries of the Holy See in stiff white chasubles, their bejeweled miters picked with threads of gold.

"Casanova nudged me to observe the ritual closely, as the participants descended to the Piazzetta, pausing in the Place of Justice—a wall decorated with biblical scenes of judgment, where they'd strung up heretics during the Inquisition. Here were the monolithic Pillars of Acre, brought back during the Crusades from the shores of ancient Phoenicia. Did it mean something that the Doge and his companions paused to meditate at this precise spot?

"At last they moved on to the strains of the heavenly music. The cordons restraining the crowd were lowered so we could follow the procession. As Casanova and I linked arms to move with the crowd, I began to feel the faint glimmer of something—I cannot explain it. A feeling that I was witnessing something as old as time itself. Something dark and mysterious, rich in history and symbolism. Something dangerous.

"As the procession twisted its serpentine course across the Piazzetta and back through the Colonnade, I felt as if we were moving deeper and deeper into the bowels of a dark labyrinth from which there was no escape. I was perfectly safe, outside in daylight, surrounded by hundreds of people—yet I was afraid. It was some time before it dawned on me that it was the music—the movement—the ceremony itself that frightened me. Each time we paused in the Doge's wake— at an artifact or piece of sculpture—I felt the pounding in my veins grow louder. It was like a message trying to tap itself through to my mind in a secret code, but one I could not understand. Casanova was watching me closely. The Doge had paused again.

" 'This is the statue of Mercury—messenger of the gods,' " said Casanova as we came up to the dancing bronze figure. 'In Egypt, they called him Thoth—the Judge. In Greece they called him Hermes—Guide of Souls—for he conducted souls to Hell and sometimes tricked the very gods by stealing them back again. Prince of Tricksters, Joker, Jester—the Fool of the tarot deck—he was a god of theft and cunning. Hermes invented the seven-stringed lyre—the octave scale—whose music made the gods weep for joy.'

"I looked at the statue for quite some time before moving on. Here was the quick one, who could free people from the kingdom of the dead. With his winged sandals and bright caduceus—that staff of twined serpents forming the figure eight—he presided over the land of dreams, worlds of magic, the realms of luck and chance and games of every sort. Was it coincidence that his statue faced this staid procession with its wicked, grinning smile? Or was it, somewhere in the dark mists of time, *his* ritual?

"The Doge and company made many stops in this transcendental tour— sixteen in all. As we moved, the pattern began to unfold for me. It was not until the tenth stop—the Castello Wall—that I started to put it all together.

"The wall was twelve feet thick, covered in multicolored stones. The inscription, the oldest in Venetic, was translated for me by Casanova:

> If a man could say and do what he thinks,
> He'd see how he might be transformed.

"And there at the center of the wall was embedded a simple white stone, which the Doge and his entourage were regarding as if it contained some miracle. Suddenly I felt a cold chill run through me. It was as if a veil were being torn from my eyes so I could see the many parts as one. This was no mere ritual—but a *process* unfolding before us, each pause in the procession symbolizing a *step* in the path of transformation from one state to another. It was like a formula, but a formula for what? And then I knew."

Now Rousseau paused in his discourse and pulled a drawing, frayed with wear, from his yellow leather satchel. Unfolding it carefully, he handed it to me.

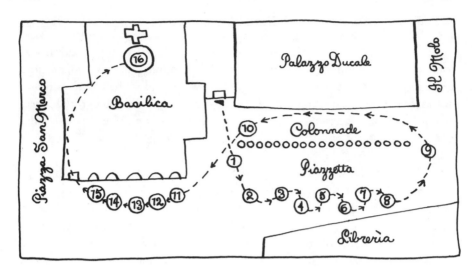

"This is the record I made of the Long March, showing the path of sixteen stops, the number of pieces of black or white on a chessboard. You'll note the course itself describes a figure eight—like the twined serpents on Hermes' staff—like the Eightfold Path the Buddha prescribed to reach Nirvana—like the eight tiers of the Tower of Babel one climbed to reach the gods. Like the formula they say was brought by the eight Moors to Charlemagne—hidden within the Montglane Service. . . ."

"A formula?" I said in astonishment.

"Of infinite power," replied Rousseau, "whose meaning may be forgotten, but whose magnetism is so strong we act it out without understanding what it means—as did Casanova and I that day thirty-five years ago in Venice."

"It seems quite beautiful and mysterious, this ritual," I agreed. "But why do you associate it with the Montglane Service—a treasure which, after all, everyone believes to be no more than a legend?"

"Don't you see?" said Rousseau in irritation. "These Italian and Greek isles all took their traditions, their labyrinthine, stone-worshiping cults from the same source—the source from which they sprang."

"You mean Phoenicia," I said.

"I mean the Dark Isle," he said mysteriously, "the isle the Arabs first named Al-Djezair. The isle between two rivers, rivers that twist together like Hermes' staff to form a figure eight—rivers that watered the cradle of mankind. The Tigris and Euphrates . . ."

"You mean this ritual—this formula came from Mesopotamia?" I cried.

"I've spent a lifetime trying to get my hands on it!" said Rousseau, rising from his seat and grasping my arm. "I sent Casanova, then Boswell, finally

Diderot, to try to get the secret. Now I send you. I choose you to track down the secret of this formula, for I've spent thirty-five years trying to understand the meaning behind the meaning. It is nearly too late. . . ."

"But monsieur!" I said in confusion. "Even if you discovered so powerful a formula, what would you do with it? You, who've written of the simple virtues of country life—the innocent and natural equality of all men. What use would such a tool be to you?"

"I am the enemy of kings!" cried Rousseau in despair. "The formula contained in the Montglane Service will bring about the end of kings—*all* kings— for all time! Ah, if only I might live long enough to have it within my grasp."

I had many questions to ask Rousseau, but already he was pale with fatigue, his brow beaded with sweat. He was putting away his lacework as if the interview were at an end. He gave me one final look as if slipping away into a dimension where I could no longer follow.

"Once there was a great king," he said softly. "The most powerful king in the world. They said he'd never die, that he was immortal. They called him al-Iksandr, the two-horned god, and pictured him on gold coins wearing the spiral ram's horns of divinity at his brow. History remembers him as Alexander the Great, conqueror of the world. He died at the age of thirty-three at Babylon in Mesopotamia—seeking the formula. So would they all die, if only the secret were ours. . . ."

"I place myself at your command," I said, helping him to the footbridge as he leaned heavily upon my shoulder. "Between us, we'll locate the Montglane Service if it still exists, and learn the formula's meaning."

"It's too late for me," said Rousseau, shaking his head sadly. "I entrust you with this chart, which I believe is the only clue we have. Legend has it that the service is buried in Charlemagne's palace at Aix-la-Chapelle—or at the Abbey of Montglane. It is your mission to find it."

Robespierre broke off suddenly and glanced over his shoulder. Before him on the table in the lamplight lay the drawing he'd made from memory of the strange Venetian ritual. David, who'd been studying it, looked up.

"Did you hear a sound?" asked Robespierre, his green eyes mirroring a sudden burst of sparkling fireworks outside.

"It is only your imagination," David said abruptly. "I shouldn't wonder you're skittish, remembering a tale like this. I wonder how much of what you've told me was the raving of senility?"

"You've heard Philidor's tale, and now Rousseau's," said Robespierre irritably. "Your ward Mireille actually possessed some of the pieces—she admitted as much at l'Abbaye Prison. You *must* accompany me to the Bastille, get her to confess. Only then can I help you."

David understood all too well the thinly veiled threat implicit in these words: without Robespierre's aid, Mireille's death warrant was as good as written—and David's as well. Robespierre's powerful influence could as easily be turned *against* them, and David was already implicated beyond his worst imagination. Now he saw clearly for the first time that Mireille had been right to warn him of this "friend."

"You *were* in this with Marat!" he cried. "Just as Mireille feared! Those nuns whose letters I gave you . . . what has become of them?"

"You still don't understand," Robespierre said impatiently. "This Game is larger than you or I—or your ward or those silly nuns. The woman I serve will make a far better ally than opponent. Remember that, if you wish to keep your head on your shoulders. What's become of the nuns, I cannot say. I only know that *she* strives to unite the pieces of the Montglane Service, just as Rousseau, for the betterment of mankind—"

"She?" said David, but Robespierre had risen as if to depart.

"The White Queen," he said with a cryptic smile. "Like a goddess, she takes what she deserves and bestows what she wishes. Mark my words—if you do as I ask, you'll be well rewarded. She'll see to that."

"I want no ally, no reward," said David bitterly, rising as well. What a Judas he was. He had little choice but to comply—but it was fear that drove him to it.

He picked up the oil lamp, accompanying Robespierre to the door, and offered to see him to the gates as there were no servants about.

"It makes no difference what you want, so long as you do it," Robespierre said tersely. "When she returns from London, I'll introduce you. I cannot reveal her name just yet, but they call her the Woman from India. . . ."

Their voices trailed away down the hall. When the room was in complete darkness, the rear door that led to the studio opened a crack. Illuminated only by the occasional flowering of fireworks outside, a shadowy figure slipped into the room and crossed to the table where the two men had been seated. In the next brief explosion of fireworks that lit the room, the tall, stately form of Charlotte Corday was bathed in light as she bent before the table. Beneath her arm was tucked a box of paints and a wad of clothing she'd stolen from the studio.

Now she looked for a long while at the maplike chart that lay open on the table before her. Carefully she folded the drawing of the Venetian ritual and tucked it in her bodice. Then she slipped into the corridor and disappeared into the shadowy night.

JULY 17, 1793

It was dark inside the prison cell. A small barred window, too high to reach, emitted a crack of light that only made the cell seem blacker. Water trickled down the mossy rock, forming puddles that reeked of mildew and urine. This was the Bastille, whose liberation four years ago had lit the torch of the Revolution. Mireille's first night here had been Bastille Day—July 14—the night after she'd killed Marat.

For three days now she'd been in this dank cell, taken out only for her arraignment and trial that afternoon. It hadn't taken them long to bring in the verdict: death. In two hours she'd leave this cell again, never to return.

She sat on the hard pallet, not touching the crust of bread or tin cup of water they'd provided as her last meal. She thought of her child, Charlot, whom she'd left in the desert. She would never see him again. She wondered what the guillotine would be like—what she'd feel when they set the tambours rolling as a signal for the blade to drop. In two hours she would know. It would be the last thing she'd ever know. She thought of Valentine.

Her head still ached from the blow she'd received when she was captured. Though the wound had healed, she could still feel the throbbing lump at the back of her head. Her trial had been more brutal than the arrest. The prosecutor had ripped open the bosom of her gown before all the court, to extract those papers of Charlotte's she had tucked there. Now the world believed her to be Charlotte Corday—and if she corrected that impression, the life of every nun from Montglane would be in jeopardy. If only she might smuggle what she knew to the outside world—what she'd learned from Marat about the White Queen.

She heard a grating sound outside the cell door, the sound of a rusty bolt being pulled back. The door opened, and when her eyes adjusted she saw two figures outlined against the dim light. One was her jailer; the other was dressed in breeches, silk hose, faille pumps, and a loose-fitting coat with foulard, a low-brimmed hat partly concealing his face. The jailer stepped inside the cell, and Mireille rose to her feet.

"Mademoiselle," said the jailer, "a portrait painter has been sent by the court to prepare a sketch of you for the records. He said you've given permission—"

"Yes, yes!" Mireille said quickly. "Show him in!" Now was her chance, she thought in excitement. If only she might convince this man to risk his life by carrying her message from the prison. She waited until the guard departed, then raced to the painter's side. He set down his box of paints and the dim oil lamp, which put out a smoky fume.

"Monsieur!" cried Mireille. "Give me a sheet of paper and something to write with. There's a message I must get to the outside—to someone I trust—before I die. Her name, like mine, is Corday. . . ."

"Don't you recognize me, Mireille?" said the painter in a soft voice. Mireille stared as he began to remove his jacket, then his hat. The red locks tumbled down over the bosom of Charlotte Corday! "Come, don't waste time. There's much to be said and done. And we must exchange garments at once."

"But I don't understand—what are you doing?" Mireille asked in a hoarse whisper.

"I've been to David's," said Charlotte, grasping Mireille's arm. "He's in league with that devil Robespierre. I overheard them. Have they been here?"

"Here?" Mireille cried in complete confusion.

"They know *you* killed Marat, and more. There's a woman behind this—they call her the Woman from India. She's the White Queen, and she's gone to London. . . ."

"London!" said Mireille. That was what Marat meant when he'd said she was too late. It was not Catherine the Great at all, but a woman in London, where Mireille had sent the pieces! The Woman from India . . .

"Make haste," Charlotte was saying. "You must undress and put on these painter's garments I stole from David's."

"Are you mad?" said Mireille. "You can carry this news along with mine to the abbess. But there's no time for tricks—they'll never work. And I've much to reveal before I must—"

"Please make haste," Charlotte replied gravely. "I've much to tell *you* and little time. Here, look at this drawing and see if it reminds you of anything." She handed Mireille the folded map Robespierre had drawn, then sat on the pallet to remove her shoes and stockings.

Mireille studied the drawing carefully. "It seems to be a map," she said, looking up as something slowly focused in her mind. "Now I remember . . . there was a cloth we exhumed with the pieces. A cloth of midnight blue, which covered the Montglane Service! The design—it was like this map!"

"Exactly," said Charlotte. "There's a tale that goes with it. Do as I say, and quickly."

"If you mean to exchange places with me, you cannot," cried Mireille. "In two hours they take me to the tumbril. You'll never escape if they find you here in my place."

"Listen carefully," Charlotte replied gravely, yanking hard to loosen the knot of her foulard. "The abbess sent me here to protect you at all costs. We knew who you were long before I risked my life coming to Montglane. If not for *you*, the Abbess would never have removed the service from the abbey. It was not your cousin Valentine she chose when she sent you two to Paris. She knew you'd never go without her, but it was *you* she wanted—you who could bring success. . . ."

Charlotte was unfastening Mireille's gown. Suddenly Mireille reached out and seized her arm. "What do you mean, she chose me?" she whispered. "Why do you say she removed the pieces because of me?"

"Don't be blind," said Charlotte ferociously. She grasped Mireille's hand and held it beneath the lantern's light. "The mark is on your hand! Your birthday is the fourth of April! You are the one who was foretold—the one who'll reunite the Montglane Service!"

"My God!" Mireille cried, tearing her hand away. "Do you realize what you are saying? Valentine died because of this! For a foolish prophecy you risk your life. . . ."

"No, my dear," Charlotte said quietly. "I *give* my life."

Mireille stared at her in horror. How could she accept so great an offer? She thought of her child again, left in the desert. . . .

"No!" she cried. "There cannot be another sacrifice on behalf of those dreaded pieces. Not after the terror they've already wrought!"

"Do you wish us both to die, then?" said Charlotte, continuing to loosen Mireille's garments, suppressing the tears as she kept her eyes averted.

Mireille put her hand beneath Charlotte's chin, pulling her face up until they looked deeply into each other's eyes. After a long moment, Charlotte spoke in trembling voice.

"We must defeat them," she said. "You're the only one who can do it. Don't you see, even now? Mireille—*you* are the Black Queen!"

Two hours had passed when Charlotte heard the grating of the bolt that signified the guards had arrived to take her to the tumbril. She was kneeling in darkness beside the pallet, praying.

Mireille had taken the oil lamp and the few sketches she'd done of Charlotte—sketches she might have to produce to get out of the prison. After their tearful parting, Charlotte had withdrawn into her own thoughts and memories. She felt a sense of completion, of finality. Somewhere inside she'd formed a small pool of calm tranquillity that even the guillotine's sharp blade would not cut away. She was about to become one with God.

The door behind her had opened and closed—all was darkness—but she heard someone breathing within the cell. What was it? Why did they not take her? She waited in silence.

There was the sound of scraping flint, a whiff of naphtha as a lantern flickered to light across the room.

"Permit me to introduce myself," said a soft voice. Something about it sent chills through her. Then she remembered—and froze, keeping her back turned. "My name is Maximilien Robespierre."

Charlotte was trembling as she kept her face turned away. She saw the lantern light move across the walls toward her, heard the chair pulled out so near the place she knelt—and another sound she couldn't identify. Was there someone else in the room? She feared to turn and look.

"You needn't introduce yourself," Robespierre was saying calmly. "I was at the trial this afternoon and the arraignment earlier. Those papers the prosecutor tore from your bodice—they were not yours."

Then she heard soft footsteps moving stealthily across the room toward them. They were *not* alone. She jumped, nearly screaming aloud, as she felt the soft hand on her shoulder.

"Mireille, please forgive what I've done!" cried the unmistakable voice of the painter David. "I *had* to bring him here—I had no choice. My dearest child . . ."

David pulled her about, burying his face in her neck. Over his shoulder, she saw the long oval face, the powdered wig, the glittering sea-green eyes, of Maximilien Robespierre. His insidious smile quickly melted into an expression of surprise, then fury, as he gingerly lifted the lantern with his fingers, holding it aloft for better light.

"You fool!" he screamed in a high-pitched voice. Wrenching the terrified David from where he knelt weeping upon Charlotte's shoulder, he flung out his hand to point at her. "I told you we'd be too late! But no—you had to wait for the trial! You actually thought she'd be acquitted! Now she's escaped us, and all because of you!"

He threw the lantern back on the table, spilling some of the oil, as he grabbed Charlotte and yanked her to her feet. Knocking David to one side, Robespierre drew back his arm in fury and slashed his hand across her face.

"Where is she?!" he screamed. "What have you done with her? You'll die in her place, no matter what she's told you—I swear it—unless you confess!"

Charlotte let the blood drip from her lip as she proudly drew herself up to look Robespierre in the eye. Then she smiled.

"That is what I intend," she said calmly.

LONDON   JULY 30, 1793

It was near midnight when Talleyrand returned from the theater. Tossing his cape on a chair in the entrance hall, he headed for the small study off the foyer to pour himself a sherry. Courtiade stepped quickly into the hall.

"Monseigneur," he said in a hushed voice, "a visitor awaits. I've put her in the study until your return. It seemed most critical. She says she brings news of Mademoiselle Mireille."

"Thank God—at last," said Talleyrand, rushing into the study.

There in the firelight stood a slender form, wrapped closely in a black velvet cape. She was warming her hands by the fire. As Talleyrand entered, she shook back the heavy hood and let the cape slip from her naked shoulders. The white-blond hair tumbled down over her half-bare breasts. He could see her trembling flesh in the firelight, the profile tipped in golden light, the retroussé nose and tilted chin, the low-cut gown of dark velvet clinging to her lovely form. He could not breathe—he felt hard fingers of pain clutching at his heart as he froze in the doorway.

"Valentine!" he whispered. Good God, how could it be? How could she return from the grave?

She turned to him and smiled, her blue eyes sparkling, the flickering firelight shining through her hair. Swiftly, with a motion like flowing water, she moved to him as he stood frozen in the doorway and knelt before him, pressing her face against his hand. He placed his other hand on her hair, stroking it. He closed his eyes. His heart was breaking. How could it be?

"Monsieur, I am in great danger," she whispered in a low voice. But it was not the voice of Valentine. He opened his eyes to gaze into the upturned face—so beautiful, so like Valentine's. But it was not she.

His eyes ran down over her golden hair, her smooth skin, the shadow between her breasts, her bare arms . . . then a jolt of shock ran through him as he saw what she clasped in her hands—what she was holding up to him in the fire's glow. It was a golden pawn, glittering with jewels—a pawn of the Montglane Service!

"I throw myself upon your mercy, sire," she whispered. "I need your aid. My name is Catherine Grand—and I come from India. . . ."

THE BLACK
QUEEN

Der Hölle Rache kocht in meinem Herzen
Tod und Verzweiflung flammet um mich her! . . .
Verstossen sei auf evig, verlassen sei auf evig,
Zertrümmert zei'n auf evig alle bande der Natur.

(The Revenge of Hell boils in my Heart,
Death and Despair blaze all around me! . . .
Cast off forever, abandoned forever,
Broken forever are all bonds of Nature.)

—*The Queen of the Night*
The Magic Flute
Emanuel Schikaneder and
Wolfgang Amadeus Mozart

S o here was Minnie Renselaas—the fortune-teller.

We were seated in her room of many-paned French windows, sheltered from the courtyard by a curtain of vines. Food came in from the
kitchen, served on the low bronze table by a bevy of veiled women who
disappeared as silently as they'd come. Lily, collapsed in a pile of cushions on
the floor, was picking at a pomegranate. I was beside her, deep in a Moroccan
leather chair, munching on a kiwi-persimmon tart. And across from me, reclining with her feet up on a green velvet divan, was Minnie Renselaas.

Here she was at last—the fortune-teller who, six months ago, had dragged
me into this dangerous game. A woman of many faces. To Nim she was a pal,
wife of the late Dutch consul. She was supposed to protect me if I got into
trouble. If one were to believe Therese, she was a popular woman about town.
To Solarin she was a business contact. To Mordecai, his ally and old friend. But
if one listened to El-Marad, she was also Mokhfi Mokhtar of the Casbah—the
woman who had the pieces of the Montglane Service. She was many things to
many people, but they all added up to one.

"You're the Black Queen," I said.

Minnie Renselaas smiled mysteriously. "Welcome to the Game," she said.

"So *that's* what that Queen of Spades stuff meant!" cried Lily, sitting bolt
upright in the cushions. "She's a player, so she knows the moves!"

"A major player," I agreed, still studying Minnie. "She's the fortune-teller
your grandfather arranged to have me meet. And if I'm not mistaken, she knows
more about this game than just the moves."

"You're not mistaken," said Minnie, still smiling like the Cheshire Cat. It
was incredible how different she looked each time I saw her. Arrayed in
shimmering silver against the dark green divan, her creamy skin unlined, she
looked much younger than the last time I'd seen her—dancing at the bistro. And
a far cry from either the tinselly fortune-teller with her rhinestone glasses, or
the antique bird woman at the United Nations, swathed in black. She was like
a chameleon. Who was she, really?

"At last you've come," she was saying in her low, cool voice that reminded
me of flowing water. There was still that trace of an accent I couldn't place.
"I've waited so long. But now you can help me. . . ."

My patience was fraying. "Help *you*?" I said. "Look, lady, I didn't ask you
to 'choose' me for this game. But I've called on you and you've answered me,

just as your poem said. Now suppose you 'shew me great and mighty things I knowest not.' Because I've just about had it with mystery and intrigue. I've been shot at, chased by the secret police, seen two people killed. Lily's wanted by Immigrations and about to be slapped in an Algerian jail—all because of this so-called game."

I was breathless from this outburst, my voice echoing from the high walls. Carioca had jumped into Minnie's lap for protection, and Lily glared at him.

"I'm glad to see you have spirit," Minnie said coolly. As she stroked Carioca, the little traitor purred in her lap like an angora cat. "However, a more valuable trait in chess is patience, as your friend Lily can tell you. I've been patient for a very long time, waiting for you. I came to New York at great risk to my life, just to meet you. Aside from that trip, I haven't left the Casbah in ten years, not since the Algerian revolution. In a sense, I'm a prisoner here. But you will set me free."

"A prisoner!" Lily and I both said at once.

"You look pretty mobile to me," I added. "Who's holding you in bondage?"

"Not 'who' but 'what,' " she said, reaching over to pour some tea without disturbing Carioca. "Ten years ago something happened—something I couldn't have foreseen—that altered a delicate balance of power. My husband died, and the revolution began."

"The Algerians threw the French out in 1963," I explained to Lily. "It was a real bloodbath." Then, turning to Minnie, I added, "With the embassies closed down, you must have been in a pickle, with no place to go but home to Holland. Surely your government could have gotten you out. Why are you still here? The revolution's been over for ten years."

Minnie set her teacup down with a bang. She brushed Carioca aside and stood up. "I'm pinned, like a backward pawn," she said, clenching her fists. "What happened in the summer of 1963 was only exacerbated by the death of my husband and the inconvenience of the revolution. Ten years ago, in Russia, workmen repairing the Winter Palace *found* the broken pieces of the board—of the Montglane Service!"

Lily and I glanced at each other with excitement. Now we were getting somewhere.

"Terrific," I said. "But how do you happen to know this? It wasn't exactly headline news. And what did it have to do with your being trapped?"

"Listen and you'll understand!" she cried, pacing up and down as Carioca jumped down to trot behind her trailing silver gown. He kept trying to pounce on the end of it as it moved before him. "If they'd captured the board, they had a third of the formula!" She yanked her skirts out of Carioca's teeth and wheeled to face us.

"You mean the Russians?" I said. "But if they're on the other team, how come you're buddy-buddy with Solarin?" But my mind was moving fast. A third of the formula, she'd said. That meant she knew how many parts there were!

"Solarin?" said Minnie with a laugh. "How do you think I learned about it? Why do you think I chose him as a player? Why do you think my life's in danger—that I must remain in Algeria—that I need the two of *you* so badly?"

"Because the Russians have a third of the formula?" I said. "Surely they're not the only players on the opposing team."

"No," agreed Minnie. "But they're the ones who discovered that *I* have the rest!"

Lily and I were bursting with excitement after Minnie left the room in search of something she wanted to show us. Carioca was bouncing around like a rubber ball until I squashed him with my foot.

Lily retrieved her pegboard chess set from my bag and was setting it up on the tooled-bronze table as we spoke. Who were our opponents? I wondered. How did the Russians know Minnie was a player, and what *did* she have that trapped her for ten years?

"You remember what Mordecai told us," said Lily. "He said he went to Russia and played chess with Solarin. That was about ten years ago, wasn't it?"

"Right. You're saying he recruited him as a player at that time."

"But which player?" Lily said, moving the pieces around the board.

"The Knight!" I cried, suddenly remembering. "Solarin put that symbol on the note he left in my apartment!"

"So if Minnie's the Black Queen, we're all on the black team—you and I, Mordecai and Solarin. The guys in the black hats are the *good* guys. If Mordecai picked Solarin, maybe Mordecai's the Black King—which makes Solarin a kingside Knight."

"You and I are pawns," I added quickly. "And Saul and Fiske . . ."

"Pawns that were knocked off the board," Lily said as she swept aside a couple of pawns. She was moving pieces around like a shell game as I tried to follow her line of thought.

But something had been nagging my mind since the moment I'd realized Minnie was the fortune-teller. Suddenly I knew what it was. It wasn't actually *Minnie* who'd dragged me into this game. It was Nim—it had been Nim all along. If it hadn't been for him, I'd never have bothered to decipher that puzzle, worry about my birthday, assume other people's deaths had anything to do with *me*—or hunt for the pieces of the Montglane Service. Now that I thought of it, it was *Nim* who'd arranged my contract with Harry's company in the first place—three years ago when we were both working for Triple-M! And it was Nim who'd sent me to Minnie Renselaas. . . .

Just then Minnie came back into the room, carrying a large metal box and a small leather-bound book tied in stiff twine. She set both on the table.

"Nim *knew* you were the fortune-teller!" I said to her. "Even when he was 'helping' me decode that message!"

"Your friend in New York?" Lily chimed in. "Which piece is he?"

"A Rook," said Minnie, studying the board Lily was adjusting.

"Of course!" Lily cried. "He's staying in New York to castle the King. . . ."

"I've only met Ladislaus Nim once," Minnie told me. "When I chose him as a player, just as I've chosen you. Though he recommended you highly, he had no idea I'd come to New York to meet you. I had to be certain you were the one I needed, that you had the skills required."

"*What* skills?" said Lily, still fiddling with the pieces. "She can't even play chess."

"No, but *you* can," Minnie said. "The two of you will make a perfect team."

"Team?!" I cried. I was as anxious to be teamed with Lily as an ox is to be yoked to a kangaroo. Though her chess was clearly better than mine, she was all over the board when it came to reality.

"So we have a Queen, a Knight, a Rook, and a bunch of pawns," Lily interjected, turning her gray eyes on Minnie. "What about the other team? How about John Hermanold, who shot at my car, or my uncle Llewellyn, or his pal the carpet trader—what's his name?"

"El-Marad!" I said. Suddenly I realized what part *he* must play. It wasn't that hard—a guy who lived like a hermit in the mountains, never leaving his place, yet conducting business all over the world, feared and hated by everyone who knew him . . . and who was after the pieces. "He's the White King," I guessed.

Minnie had turned deathly pale. She sank to a seat beside me. "You've met El-Marad?" she said, her voice nearly a whisper.

"A few days ago, in the Kabyle," I told her. "He seems to know a lot about *you.* He told me your name was Mokhfi Mokhtar, that you lived in the Casbah, and that you had the pieces of the Montglane Service. He said you'd give them to me if I told you my birthday was the fourth day of the fourth month."

"Then he knows far more than I thought," said Minnie, more than a little upset. She took out a key and started unlocking the metal box she'd brought in. "But there's obviously one thing he does *not* know, or you'd never have been permitted to see him. He doesn't know *who you are!*"

"Who *I* am?" I said, utterly confused. "I don't have anything to do with this game. Lots of people were born on my birthday—lots of people have funny squiggles on their hand. This is ridiculous. I must agree with Lily: I don't see how I can help you."

"I don't want you to help me," Minnie said firmly, opening the box as she spoke. "I want you to take my place." She leaned over the board, swept Lily's arm aside, picked up the Black Queen, and moved it forward.

Lily stared at the piece—at the board. Then suddenly she grabbed my knee.

"That's it!" she cried, jumping up and down on the pillows. Carioca took this opportunity to snatch a fluffy cheese pastry with his little teeth and drag it into his lair beneath the table. "You see? With this arrangement, the Black Queen can place White in check, forcing the King out onto the board—but only by exposing herself. The only piece to protect her is this forward pawn. . . ."

I tried to understand. There on the board, eight of the black pieces sat on black squares, the others on white. And before all, at the end of white territory, sat a single black pawn, protected by a Rook and a Knight.

"I knew you'd work well together," said Minnie with a smile, "given half a chance. This is a near perfect reconstruction of the Game to date. At least, this round." Looking at me, she added, "Why don't you ask this granddaughter of Mordecai Rad *which* is the pivotal piece around which this particular game now focuses?"

I turned to Lily, who was also smiling and tapping that forward pawn with her long red fingernail.

"The only piece that can replace a Queen is another Queen," said Lily. "That seems to be *you*."

"What do you mean?" I asked. "I thought I was a pawn."

"Exactly. But if a pawn passes the ranks of opposing pawns and reaches the eighth square on the opposite side, it can be transformed into any piece it likes. Even a Queen. When this pawn reaches the eighth square, the queening square, it can replace the Black Queen!"

"Or avenge her," said Minnie, her eyes glowing like coals. "A passed pawn penetrates Algiers—the White Isle. Just as you've penetrated white territory, you'll penetrate the mystery. The secret of the Eight."

My mood was rising and falling like a barometric reading during the monsoon. I was the Black Queen? What did it mean? Though Lily pointed out there could be *more* than one Queen of the same color on the board, Minnie had said I was to *replace* her. Did that mean she was planning to leave the Game?

Furthermore, if she needed a replacement, why not Lily? Lily had laid out the game on that little pegboard set so every person fit the pieces and every move matched the events. But I was a patzer at chess, so what was my skill? Besides, that pawn had a way to go before it got to the queening square. Though it was too late for any other pawns to pick it off, it could still get eradicated by pieces that had more flexible moves. Even *I* knew that much about chess.

Minnie had unwrapped the contents of the metal box before us. Now she withdrew a heavy cloth, which she proceeded to unfold across the vast bronze table. The cloth was dark blue, nearly black. Scattered across it were chunks of colored glass—some round, some oval—each about the size of a quarter. The cloth was heavily embroidered with strange designs in a kind of metallic thread. They looked like symbols from the zodiac. They also resembled something else I couldn't place, but which seemed familiar. At the center of the cloth was a big embroidery of two snakes swallowing each other's tails. They formed a figure eight.

"What's this?" I asked, looking over the strange cloth with curiosity.

Lily had moved closer and was feeling the fabric. "It reminds me of something," she said.

"This is the cloth," said Minnie, watching us closely, "that originally covered the Montglane Service. It was buried with the pieces for a thousand years until, during the French Revolution, both were exhumed by the nuns of Montglane Abbey in the south of France. This cloth has subsequently passed through many hands. It's said to have been sent into Russia during the time of Catherine the Great, along with the broken board I told you they'd discovered."

"How do you know all this?" I said, though I couldn't seem to take my eyes away from the dark blue velvet spread before us. The cloth of the Montglane Service—over a thousand years old and still intact. It seemed to glow dully in the greenish light filtering through the wisteria. "And how did you get your hands on this?" I added, reaching out to touch the stones Lily was already feeling.

"You know," said Lily, "I've seen a lot of uncut gemstones at my grandfather's. I think these things are *real*!"

"They are," said Minnie in a voice that made me tingle despite myself. "Everything about this dread service is real. As you've learned, the Montglane Service contains a formula—a formula of great power, a force of evil for those who understand how to use it."

"Why necessarily evil?" I said. But there was *something* about this cloth—perhaps it was my imagination, but it seemed to illuminate Minnie's face from below as she bent over it in the dim light.

"The question should be, why is evil necessary?" Minnie said coldly. "But it's existed since long before the Montglane Service. So has the formula. Take a closer look at this cloth, and you'll see." She smiled an oddly bitter smile as she poured more tea all around. Her beautiful face seemed suddenly harsh and weary. For the first time, I realized what toll this game had taken on her.

I felt Carioca drooling cheese pastry on my foot. Pulling him from beneath the table, I set him on my chair and bent over the cloth to study it better.

There in the dim light was the golden figure eight, the serpents writhing across the dark blue velvet like a twisted comet across the midnight sky. And around it were the symbols—Mars and Venus, Sun and Moon, Saturn and Mercury . . . Then I saw it. I saw what else they were!

"They're elements!" I cried.

Minnie smiled and nodded.

"The octave law," she said.

Now it all made sense. These chunks of uncut gems and golden stitching formed symbols that had been used by philosophers and scientists alike since time immemorial to describe the most basic building blocks of nature. Here were iron and copper, silver and gold—sulphur, mercury, lead, and antimony—hydrogen, oxygen, the salts, and acids. In short, everything that comprised matter, whether living or dead.

I began to pace around the room as I thought it out, and it was all coming together. "The Octave Law," I explained to Lily, who was looking at me as if I were crazy. "It's the law on which the *Periodic Table of the Elements* was built. In the 1860s before Mendeléev formed his tables, John Newlands, the English chemist, discovered that if you arrange the elements in ascending order by atomic weight, every *eighth* element will be a sort of repetition of the first—just like the eighth note of a musical octave. He named it after Pythagoras's theory because he thought the molecular properties of elements bore the same relationship to each other as notes in a musical scale!"

"And do they?" asked Lily.

"How should *I* know?" I said. "All I know about chemistry is what I learned *before* I was flunked for blowing up my high school chemistry lab."

"You've learned correctly," Minnie said, laughing. "Do you remember anything else?"

What was it? I was still standing, looking at the cloth, when it came to me. Waves and particles—particles and waves. Something about valences and electron shells danced at the outer edge of my mind. But Minnie was speaking.

"Perhaps I can refresh your memory. This formula is nearly as old as civilization itself, having been hinted at in writings as early as 4000 B.C. Let me tell you the tale. . . ." I sank onto a seat beside her as Minnie bent forward, letting her fingers trace the outline of the figure eight. She seemed lost in a trance as she began her tale.

"Six thousand years ago there were already advanced civilizations along the great rivers of the world—the Nile, Ganges, Indus, and Euphrates. They practiced a secret art that would later give birth both to religion and to science. So secret was this mysterious art that it required a lifetime to become an initiate—to be introduced to its true meaning.

"The initiation rite was often cruel and sometimes deadly. The tradition of this ritual has carried down to modern times; it still appears in the Catholic High Mass, in the cabbalistic rites, in the ceremonies of the Rosicrucians and Freemasons. But the meaning behind the tradition has been lost. These rituals are nothing other than a reenactment of the process of the formula that was known to ancient man, a reenactment that enabled him to pass on knowledge through an act. For it was forbidden to write it down." Minnie looked up at me with dark green eyes, her gaze seeming to seek something deep in me.

"The Phoenicians understood the ritual. So did the Greeks. Even Pythagoras forbade his followers to put it into writing, so dangerous was it believed to be. The great error of the Moors was that they disobeyed this command. They put the symbols of the formula into the Montglane Service. Though it's encrypted, anyone possessing all the parts can eventually work out the meaning—without undergoing the initiation which forces them to swear, on pain of death, never to use it for evil.

"The lands where this hidden science was developed—where it flourished—were named by the Arabs after the rich black silt that was deposited upon the banks of their life-giving rivers each spring, when the rite took place. They called them 'Al-Khem,' the Black Lands. And the secret science was named 'Al-Khemie'—the Black Art."

"*Alchemy?*" said Lily. "You mean, like turning straw into gold?"

"The art of transmutation, yes," Minnie said with a strange smile. "They claimed they could transform base metals such as tin and copper into rare ones like silver and gold—and much, much more."

"You're kidding," said Lily. "You mean we traveled thousands of miles and went through all these hassles just to find out the secret of this service is a pile of phony magic trumped up by a lot of primitive priests?"

I continued to study the cloth. Something started to click.

"Alchemy isn't magic," I told her, beginning to get excited. "I mean, it wasn't that originally—only recently. Actually, it was the origin of modern chemistry and physics. All the scientists of the Middle Ages studied it, and even later. Galileo helped the Duke of Tuscany and Pope Urban the Eighth with their basement experiments. Johannes Kepler's mother was nearly burned at the stake as a witch for teaching him mystical secrets. . . ." Minnie was nodding her head as I kept moving. "They say Isaac Newton spent more time cooking up chemicals in his Cambridge lab than writing the *Principia Mathematica*. Paracelsus may have been a mystic, but he was also the father of modern chemistry. In fact, we use the alchemical principles he discovered in modern smelting and cracking plants. Don't you know how they produce plastics, asphalt, and synthetic fibers from oil? They crack the molecules, take them apart with heat and catalysts—just as the ancient alchemists claimed *they* did by turning mercury into gold. In fact, there's only one problem with this story."

"Only *one?*" said Lily, always the skeptic.

"They didn't *have* particle accelerators six thousand years ago in Mesopotamia—or cracking plants in Palestine. They couldn't do much more than turn copper and brass to bronze."

"Perhaps not," Minnie said, unruffled. "But if these ancient priests of science didn't possess a rare and dangerous secret, why did they shroud it in a veil of mystery? Why require the initiate to undergo a lifetime of training, a litany of vows and promises, a cultlike ritual of pain and danger, before he was admitted to the Order. . . ."

"Of the Hidden Elect?" I said. "The Secret Chosen?"

Minnie didn't smile. She looked at me, then down at the cloth. It was a long time before she spoke, and when she did her voice went through me like a knife.

"Of the Eight," she said quietly. "Of those who could hear the music of the spheres."

Clink. The last piece fell into place. Now I knew why Nim had recommended me, why Mordecai had set me up, and Minnie "chosen" me. It wasn't just my sparkling personality, my birthdate, or my palm—though that's what they wanted me to believe. This wasn't mysticism we were talking about; it was science. And music *was* science—older than acoustics, which Solarin had studied, or physics, Nim's special province. I was a music major, so I knew. It was no accident that Pythagoras had taught it on equal footing with mathematics and astronomy. He thought sound waves washed the universe, comprised everything that existed from the largest to the smallest. And he wasn't far from wrong.

"It's waves," I said, "that hold molecules together—waves that move an electron from one shell to another, changing its valence so it can enter into chemical reactions with other molecules."

"Exactly," said Minnie with excitement. "Waves of light and sound that comprise the universe. I knew you were the right choice. You're on the right track already." With her face flushed she looked young again, and again I observed what a beauty she must have been not so many years ago. "But so are our enemies," she added. "I told you there were three parts of this formula—the board, which is now in the hands of the opposing team, and the cloth, which lies before you. The central portion is in the pieces."

"But I thought you had them," Lily cut in.

"I possess the largest cache since the service was first removed from earth— twenty pieces scattered in hiding places where I'd hoped they would not be discovered for another thousand years. But I was wrong. Once the Russians got wind of my owning the pieces, the white forces instantly suspected some might be here in Algeria where I live. And to my great misfortune they were right. El-Marad is collecting his forces. I believe he has emissaries here who'll shortly close in upon me so I can never get these pieces out of the country."

So that was what she'd meant about El-Marad not knowing who I was! Of course—he'd chosen *me* as emissary, never realizing I'd been hand-picked by the other team. But there was more to learn.

"So your pieces are here in Algeria?" I said. "Who has the others? El-Marad? The Russians?"

"They've some, I'm not certain how many," she told me. "Others were scattered or lost after the French Revolution. They may be anywhere—in Europe, the Far East, even America—perhaps never to be found again. I've spent a lifetime collecting those *I* possess. Some are safely hidden in other countries, but of the twenty, eight are hidden here in the desert—in the Tassili. You must capture the eight and bring them to me before it is too late." Her face was still flushed with excitement as she gripped me by the arm.

"Not so fast," I said. "Look, the Tassili is well over a thousand miles from here. Lily is in the country illegally, and I've a job to do of pressing urgency. Can't this wait until—"

"Nothing could be more urgent than what I ask of you!" she cried. "If you don't get those pieces, they may fall into other hands. The world could become a place not possible to imagine. Don't you see the logical extension of such a formula?"

I did. There was another process that employed transmutation of elements—the creation of transuranic elements. Elements with a higher atomic weight than uranium.

"You mean with this formula someone could cook up plutonium?" I suggested. Now I understood why Nim said the most important thing a nuclear physicist could study was ethics. And I understood Minnie's sense of urgency.

"I'll draw you a map," Minnie was saying, as if our going were a fait accompli. "You'll commit it to memory, then I'll destroy it. And there's something else I wish you to have, a document of great importance, great value." She handed me the leather-bound book tied in twine that she'd brought in with the cloth. As she started drawing the map, I searched in my bag for my nail scissors to cut the twine.

The book was small—the size of a thick paperback—and very old from the look of it. The cover was of soft Moroccan leather, well worn and stamped with markings that seemed burned in with a hot brand—like a signet cut into leather instead of wax—in the shape of figure eights. I felt something cold pass through me as I looked at it. Then I snipped through the stiff twine, and the book fell open.

It was hand-tied. The paper was as transparent as onionskin, but smooth and creamy as cloth—so thin I realized there were more pages than I'd thought, maybe six or seven hundred, all handwritten.

It was a small, tight script with flourishes typical of old-fashioned writing like the kind John Hancock had fancied. Copied on both sides of the thin paper, the ink had bled through, making it doubly hard to read. But read it I did. It was in an old style of French, and I didn't recognize some of the words, but I quickly got the message.

As Minnie murmured to Lily in the background, going over the map in detail, my heart grew cold and frightened. *Now* I understood how she'd learned all she'd been telling us.

"Cette Anno Dominii Mille Sept Cent Quatre-Vingt-Treize, au fin de Juin à Tassili n'Ajjer Saharien, je devient de racontre cette histoire. Mireille ai nun, si suis de France . . ."

As I began to read aloud, translating along the way, Lily looked up and slowly came to realize what I was reading. Minnie sat in silence, as if lost in a trance. She seemed to be hearing a voice calling from the wilderness, from the dim mists of time—a voice that spanned the millennia. In fact, it was not yet two hundred years since the document had been written:

"This year of 1793," I read,

> in the month of June at Tassili n'Ajjer in the Sahara, I begin to recount this tale. My name is Mireille, and I come from France. After passing eight years of my youth at the Abbey of Montglane in the Pyrenees, I beheld a great evil released into the world—an evil I now begin to comprehend. I shall set down its story. They call it the Montglane Service, and it began with Charlemagne, the great King who built our Abbey. . . .

THE LOST CONTINENT

At a distance of ten days' journey there is a salt mound, a spring, and a tract of uninhabited land. Beside this rises Mount Atlas, shaped like a slender cone, so tall they say the top cannot be seen, for summer or winter it's never free of clouds.

The natives are named "Atlanteans" after this mountain, which they call "Pillar of the Sky." It's said these people eat no living creature, and that they never dream.

—*"People of the Sand Belt"*
The Histories *(454 B.C.)*
Herodotus

A s Lily's big Corniche swept down from the Ergs toward the oasis at Ghardaïa, I saw the endless miles of dark red sand that stretched out beyond in all directions.

On a map, the geography of Algeria is pretty simple: it's designed like a tilted pitcher. The spout, at the bottom of the Moroccan border, appears to be pouring water into the neighboring countries of western Sahara and Mauretania. The handle is formed by two strips: a fifty-mile-thick stretch of irrigated land along the north coast and another three-hundred-mile ribbon of mountains just south of that. The rest of the country—nearly a million square miles—is desert.

Lily was driving. We'd been on the road five hours and covered 360 miles of hairpin mountain turns headed for the desert, a feat that had driven Carioca whimpering beneath the seat. I hadn't noticed. I'd been too absorbed translating aloud from the journal Minnie had given us—a tale of dark mystery, the unfolding of the Terror in France, and beneath it all the two-hundred-year-old quest of the French nun Mireille for the secret of the Montglane Service. The same quest we were on ourselves.

Now it was clear how Minnie had discovered the history of the service—its mysterious power, the formula contained in it, and the deadly game for the pieces. A game that had continued for generation after generation, sweeping the players along in its wake just as Lily and I, Solarin and Nim—and perhaps Minnie herself—had been swallowed up in it. A game played over the same terrain that we were now crossing.

"The Sahara," I said, glancing up from the book as we started the descent into Ghardaïa. "You know, this wasn't always the largest *desert* in the world. Millions of years ago, the Sahara was the world's largest inland *sea*. That's how all the crude oil and liquid natural gas were formed—the gaseous decomposition of tiny marine animals and plants. Nature's alchemy."

"You don't say?" Lily commented dryly. "Well, my fuel meter indicates we should stop for a refill of those little marine life forms. I guess we'd better do it at Ghardaïa. Minnie's map didn't show too many more towns along this route."

"I didn't see it," I said, referring to the map Minnie'd drawn and then destroyed. "I hope you've got a good memory."

"I'm a chess player," said Lily as if that explained it all.

"This town, Ghardaïa, used to be called Khardaia," I said, drawn back to the journal. "Our friend Mireille seems to have stopped here in the year 1793." I read:

> And we came into the place of Khardaia, named for the Berber Goddess Kar—the Moon—whom the Arabs called "Libya"—dripping with rain. She ruled the inland sea from the Nile to the Atlantic Ocean; her son Phoenix founded the Phoenician Empire; her father is said to be Poseidon himself. She has many names in many lands: Ishtar, Astarte, Kali, Cybelle. From her all life springs as from the sea. In this land, they call her the White Queen.

"My God," said Lily, glancing at me as she slowed the car for the turnoff to Ghardaïa. "You mean this town was named for our arch-nemesis? So maybe we're about to land on a white square!"

So involved were we in plowing through the journal for more facts that I failed to notice the dark gray Renault behind us until it hit the brakes and followed us on the turnoff to Ghardaïa.

"Haven't we seen that car before?" I asked Lily.

She nodded affirmatively, keeping her eyes on the road. "In Algiers," she said calmly. "It was parked three cars away from us in the ministry parking lot. The same two guys were inside; they passed us in the mountains maybe an hour back, so I got a good look. They haven't left us since. Think our pal Sharrif had anything to do with this?"

"Nope," I said, checking them out in my side mirror. "That's a ministry car." And I knew who had sent it.

∞

I'd been upset ever since Algiers. As we'd left Minnie in the Casbah, I phoned Kamel from a pay booth on the plaza to let him know I'd be gone a few days. He hit the ceiling.

"Are you mad?" he cried over the fuzzy line. "You know that balance of trade model is critical to me right now! I must have these figures by no later than the end of the week! This project of yours has reached the highest level of urgency."

"Look, I'll be back soon," I said. "Besides, everything's done. I've collected data from every country you specified and loaded most of it into the computers at Sonatrach. I can leave you a list of instructions on how to run the programs—they're all set up."

"Where are you right now?" Kamel interrupted, practically jumping through the line at me. "It's after one o'clock. You should've been at work hours ago. I found that ridiculous car in my parking slot with a note on it. Now Sharrif's just outside my door looking for you. Says you've been smuggling automobiles, harboring illegal immigrants—something about a vicious dog! Will you *please* explain what's going on?"

Great. If I ran into Sharrif before completing this mission, my goose was cooked. I'd have to level with Kamel—at least in part. I was getting short of allies.

"Okay," I said. "A friend of mine's in trouble. She came to visit me, but her visa isn't stamped."

"Her passport's sitting here on my desk," fumed Kamel. "Sharrif brought it. She doesn't even *have* a visa!"

"A technicality," I said quickly. "She has dual citizenship—another passport. You could get it fixed up so it looked as if she'd come in legally. You'd make Sharrif appear a fool. . . ."

Kamel's voice was becoming brittle. "It is not my ambition, mademoiselle, to make the chief of secret police appear a fool!" Then he seemed to mellow a bit. "Though it's against my better judgment, I'll try to help. Incidentally, I know who the young woman is. I knew her grandfather. He was a close friend of my father. They played chess together in England."

Well now—the plot thickened! I motioned to Lily, who tried to squeeze into the booth and press her ear to the phone with me.

"Your father played chess with Mordecai?" I repeated. "Was he a serious player?"

"Aren't we all?" Kamel replied obliquely. He was silent a moment; he seemed to be thinking. With his next words, Lily stiffened beside me, and I felt my stomach do a flip-flop. "I know what you're planning. You've seen *her*, haven't you?"

"Her who?" I said with all the naïveté I could muster.

"Don't be an idiot. I'm your friend. I know what El-Marad told you—I know what you're seeking. My dear girl, you're playing a dangerous game. These people are killers, all of them. It's not hard to guess where you're headed—I know what's rumored to be hidden there. Don't you imagine when he's certain you're missing, Sharrif will look for you there as well?"

Lily and I stared at each other across the receiver. Did this mean Kamel was a player, too?

"I'll try to cover for you," he was saying, "but I expect you back by the end of the week. Whatever you do, don't come to your office or mine before then—and don't try the airports. If you've something you need to tell me regarding your . . . project . . . it's best to communicate through the Poste Centrale."

From his tone, I guessed what *that* meant: I should pass all correspondence through Therese. I could drop Lily's passport and my OPEC instructions with her before we left.

As we rang off, Kamel wished me luck and added, "I'll try to look out for you the best I can. But if you get into *real* trouble, you may be on your own."

"Aren't we all," I replied, laughing. Then I quoted El-Marad: *"El-safar Zafar!"* Voyaging is Victory. I hoped that old Arabic proverb would prove true, but I had grave reservations. As I hung up, I felt as if my last link with reality had been cut.

∞

So the ministry car that eased into Ghardaïa behind us had been sent by Kamel, I was certain. Probably guards dispatched for our protection. We couldn't have them tagging along with us into the desert. I'd have to figure something out.

I didn't know this chunk of Algeria, but I did know that the town of Ghardaïa we were approaching was one of the famous Pentapolis, or "Five Cities of the M'zab." As Lily cruised along looking for a gas station, I saw the towns arrayed against the purple, pink, and red cliffs around us, like crystalline rock formations that had risen from the sand. These were cities that had been written of in every book on the desert. Le Corbusier said they flowed with "the natural rhythm of life." Frank Lloyd Wright had called them the most beautiful cities in the world, their sand-red structures "the color of blood—the color of creation." But the diary of the French nun Mireille had something more interesting to say of them:

> These cities were founded a thousand years ago by the Ibadites—
> "Those Possessed by God"—who believed the towns were possessed
> by the spirit of the strange Moon Goddess, and named them after
> her: the Luminous One, Melika—the Queen. . . .

"Holy shit," said Lily, pulling into the gas station. The pursuing car had passed us, made a U-turn, and doubled back for a fill-up of its own. "We're in the middle of nowhere with two mugs on our tail, a million miles of sand in front of us, and no idea what we're looking for, even when we've found it."

I had to agree with her bleak assessment. But things were soon to go from bad to worse.

"I'd better get some extra gas," Lily said, jumping from the car. She pulled out a wad of money and bought two 5-gallon cans of gas and two more of water while an attendant filled the gas-guzzling Rolls to the brim.

"You didn't need to do that," I told her when she returned from loading the extras into the trunk. "The road to the Tassili goes through the Hassi-Messaoud oil field. It's derricks and pipelines all the way."

"Not the way *we're* going," she informed me, starting the engine. "You should've looked at that map." I began to get a sick feeling at the pit of my stomach.

From here there were only two routes into the Tassili. One went east through the oil fields at Ourgla, then dipped south to enter the top of the region. Even *this* route called for four-wheel drive most of the way. But the other, maybe twice as long, went through the barren, arid Plain of Tidikelt—one of the driest, most dangerous parts of the desert, a place where the road was marked with thirty-foot-high poles so they could dig it out when it vanished, which was often. The Corniche might *look* like a tank, but it didn't have the Caterpillar belt needed to cross those dunes.

"You're not serious," I assured Lily as she pulled out of the filling station with our companions right on our tail. "Pull in at the nearest restaurant. We need to have a chat."

"And a strategy session," she agreed, glancing in the rearview mirror. "Those guys are making me nervous."

We found a little restaurant at the edge of Ghardaïa. Disembarking, we went through the cool pub at the entrance into the inner courtyard, where umbrellaed tables and stringy date palms cast shadows in the evening's red glow. The tables were all empty—it was only six P.M.—but I found a waiter and ordered some crudités and a *tadjine*, spicy ragout of lamb, with couscous.

Lily was picking at the raw vegetables in the oily array of crudités when our companions arrived and discreetly took a table some distance away.

"How do you suggest we unload those bozos?" said Lily, dropping a piece of lamb *tadjine* into Carioca's mouth as he sat on her lap.

"First let's discuss the route," I told her. "I'm guessing it's four hundred miles from here to the Tassili. But if we take the southern route, it'll be eight hundred, on a road where the food, fuel, and towns are few and far between—just endless sand."

"Eight hundred miles is nothing," said Lily. "It's all on the flat. The way *I* drive, we'll be there before morning." She snapped her fingers for the waiter and ordered six large bottles of Ben Haroun, the Perrier water of the South. "Besides, it's the only way to get where we're going. I committed this route to memory, remember?"

Before I could counter, I glanced toward the courtyard entrance and let out a muffled groan. "Don't look now," I said under my breath, "but we've got some more guests."

Two burly guys had come through the beaded curtain and were crossing the palm court to take a seat nearby. They checked us out casually, but Kamel's emissaries at our other side were getting eyestrain. They stared at the newcomers, then back at one another, and I knew why. I'd last seen one of these burly chaps fondling a gun at the airport, and the other had chauffeured me home from the bistro that same night I'd arrived in Algiers—gratis the secret police.

"Sharrif hasn't forgotten us after all," I informed Lily, picking at my food. "I never forget a face, and maybe he chose them because *they* wouldn't, either. They've both seen me before."

"But they *couldn't* have followed us on that empty road," she insisted. "I'd have noticed them just like the others."

"Tracking with your nose to the ground went out with Sherlock Holmes," I pointed out.

"You mean they stuck something on our car—like radar!" she whispered in her husky voice. "So they could tail us without being seen themselves!"

"Bingo, my dear Watson," I said in a low voice. "Shake them for twenty minutes, and I'll find the little bug and pry it off. Electronic devices are my forte."

"I've got a few techniques of my own," Lily whispered with a wink. "If you'll excuse me, I believe I'll retire to the powder room." Standing with a smile, she dropped Carioca on my lap. The thug who rose to follow her was forestalled when she called loudly to the waiter across the room, inquiring the location of *"les toilettes."* The thug resumed his seat.

I was wrestling with Carioca, who seemed to have formed a preference for *tadjine.* When at last Lily returned, she grabbed him up, stuffed him in my bag, divvied up the heavy bottles of water between us, and headed for the door.

"What's the game?" I whispered. All our dinner companions were hastily paying their tabs in our wake.

"Kid stuff," she mouthed as we headed for the car. "A steel nail file and a rock. I punctured the gas lines and tires—not big holes, just slow leaks. We'll run them around in the desert a while 'til they wear out, then hit the road."

"Two birds with one stone—and file," I said warmly as we climbed into the Corniche. "Good work!" But as we were pulling out onto the street, I noticed there were half a dozen cars parked around us in the lot, maybe those of the restaurant staff or neighboring cafes. "How did you know which one was the secret police?"

"I didn't." Lily gave me a smug smile as she took off down the street. "So to be safe, I drilled them all."

I'd been wrong when I guessed it was eight hundred miles by the southern route. The detailed sign at the edge of Ghardaïa that gave mileages to all points south (there weren't that many) said 1637 kilometers—over a thousand miles—

to Djanet at the south gate of the Tassili. And though Lily might be a fast driver, how much time could she make when we ran out of freeway?

As Lily had predicted, Kamel's bodyguards had run out of transportation after about an hour of following us through the waning light of the M'zab. And as *I'd* predicted, Sharrif's boys had stayed so far behind we weren't privileged to witness how they let their boss down by falling at the wayside. Once we were free of escorts, we pulled over in the dusk, and I crawled under the big Corniche. It took five minutes with the aid of a flashlight to find their bugging device behind the rear axle. I smashed it off with the crowbar Lily handed me.

Overlooking the sprawling Ghardaïa cemetery, breathing in the cool night air, we jumped up and down, slapping each other on the back a few times at our cleverness as Carioca pranced around us, yapping his head off. Then we jumped back in the car and hauled iron.

By now I'd changed my attitude about Minnie's choice of route. Though the northern freeway might have been simpler, we'd shaken our pursuers so they couldn't tell which direction we'd taken. No Arab in his right mind would dream that two women alone might select this route—I found it hard to visualize myself. But we'd pissed away so much time eluding these guys that by the time we left the M'zab it was after nine o'clock and quite dark. Too dark to read the book in my lap, too dark to look at the empty scenery. I caught a few catnaps as Lily barreled down the long, straight road, so I could relieve her the next shift.

By the time we crossed the Hammada and cut south through the dunes of Touat, ten hours had passed; it was already dawn. Luckily it'd been an uneventful trip—maybe *too* uneventful. I had the uneasy feeling our luck was wearing thin. I'd started thinking about the desert.

The mountains we'd crossed yesterday at midday had been a cool sixty-five degrees. Ghardaïa at sunset was maybe ten degrees warmer, and the dunes at midnight, even as late as June, were still cold with dew. But now it was dawn in the Plain of Tidikelt, the brink of the *real* desert—the one with sand and wind replacing palm trees, plants, and water—and we still had four hundred and fifty miles to go. We had no clothes but those on our backs, no food but the few bottles of bubbly water. But there was worse news up ahead. Lily interrupted my thoughts.

"There's a roadblock up there," she said in a tense voice, peering through the insect-peppered windshield splashed with strong light from the rising sun. "It looks like a border crossing. . . . I don't know what it is. Should we take a chance?"

Sure enough, there was a little kiosk with the striped barrier pole one associated with an Immigrations outpost, sitting there in the middle of the desert. It seemed strange and out of place in this vast, empty wilderness.

"We seem to have no choice," I told her. We'd passed the last cutoff a hundred miles back. This was it—the only road in town.

"Why would they have a roadblock here, of all places?" said Lily, edging the car forward, her voice tight from nerves.

"Maybe it's a sanity check," I said with false humor. "Not many people are crazy enough to go beyond this point. You know what's out there, don't you?"

"Nothing?" she guessed. Our laughter released some tension. We were both worried about the same thing: what the prisons were like in this quarter of the desert. Because that's what we'd be facing if they found out who we were—and what we'd done to the vehicular property of the OPEC minister and the head of secret police.

"Let's not panic," I said as we eased up to the barrier. The guard came out, a little mustachioed fellow who looked as if he'd been forgotten when the Foreign Legion decamped. After a lot of conversation in my mediocre French, it became clear he wanted us to produce some sort of permit before we could pass.

"A permit?!" Lily screamed, nearly spitting at him. "We need *permission* to enter this godforsaken armpit of the earth?"

I said politely in French, "And what, monsieur, is the purpose of this permit we need?"

"For El-Tanzerouft—the Desert of Thirst," he assured me, "your car must be inspected by the government and given a bill of health."

"He's afraid the car won't make it," I told Lily. "Let's cross his palm with silver, let him check a few things himself. Then we can go."

When the guard saw the color of our money and Lily shed a few tears, he decided he was important enough to give us the government kiss of approval. He looked at our cans of gas and water, marveled over the big silver hood ornament of some winged, bosomy bimbo, clucked with admiration at the bumper stickers that said "Suisse" and "F" for France. It looked as if things were tooting right along until he told us we could put up the convertible top and go.

Lily looked at me uncomfortably. I wasn't sure what the problem was. "In French, does that mean what I think?" she said.

"He told us we could split," I assured her, starting to get back into the car.

"I mean the part about the roof. Do I have to put it up?"

"Of course. This is the desert. In a few hours it's going to be one hundred degrees in the shade—only there's no shade. Not to mention the effect of sand on the coiffure. . . ."

"I can't!" she hissed at me. "There *isn't* any top!"

"We've driven over eight hundred miles from Algiers in a car that can't make it through the desert?!" I was raising my voice. The guard was in the gatehouse ready to lift the pole, but he paused.

"Of *course* the car will make it," she said indignantly, sliding into the driver's seat. "This is the best automobile ever built. But there's no roof. It was broken, and Harry said he'd have it repaired, only he never did. However, I think our more immediate problem—"

"Our immediate problem," I yelled at her, "is that you're about to drive into the biggest desert in the world with no roof over our heads! You're going to get us killed!"

Our little guard might not have understood English, but he knew *something* was going on. Just then a big semi pulled up behind us and tooted its horn. Lily waved her hand, started the ignition, and backed the Corniche to one side so the big truck could pull ahead. The guard came out again to inspect the trucker's papers.

"I don't see why you're getting so excited," said Lily. "The car *does* have air-conditioning."

"*Air*-conditioning!" I screamed again. "Air-conditioning? That's going to help a lot with sunstrokes and sandstorms! . . ." I was just warming to my theme when the guard went back into his hut to raise the gate for the trucker, who, undoubtedly, had had the sense to have *his* vehicle inspected before descending into the seventh circle of hell.

Before I knew what was happening, Lily hit the gas. Churning sand, she plowed back up onto the road and through the gate right behind him. I ducked as the iron bar came crashing down past my head and smashed into the back of the Corniche with a clang. There was a sickening sound of chewed metal as the bar scraped across the sleek rear fenders. I could hear the guard running from the gatehouse, screaming his head off in Arabic—but my own voice drowned him out.

"You almost got me decapitated!" I hollered. The car tottered dangerously toward the edge of the road. I was thrown back against my door; then, to my horror, we spun off the road and plowed into deep red sand.

Terror seized me—I couldn't see a thing. Sand was in my eyes, my nose, my throat. The red haze swirled around me. The only sounds were Carioca's hacking cough beneath the seat and the booming horn of the giant truck, which seemed dangerously close to my ear.

When we surfaced into the glittering light of day, sand sifted from the big fins of the Corniche, our wheels were on hard pavement, and the car some-how—miraculously—was thirty yards in *front* of the semi, still barreling down the road. I was furious with Lily, but also thunderstruck with amazement.

"How did we get here?" I said, pulling my fingers through my hair to loosen the gritty sand.

"I don't know why Harry ever bothered to get me a chauffeur," Lily said blithely as if nothing had happened. Her hair, face, and dress were completely coated with a thin powdery layer of sand. "I've always *loved* driving. It's great to be out here. I bet I already hold the land speed record among chess players—"

"Didn't it occur to you," I interrupted, "that even if you didn't get us killed, that little guy back there might have a phone? What if he reports us? What if he calls ahead?"

"Calls ahead *where?*" snorted Lily with disdain. "This place isn't exactly crawling with Highway Patrol."

Of course she was right. Nobody was going to get excited enough to chase after us way out here in the middle of nowhere, just because we jumped a car inspection checkpoint.

I returned to the diary of the French nun Mireille, beginning where I'd left off the day before:

> And so I went East from Khardaia across the dry Chebkha and stony plains of the Hammada, headed for the Tassili n'Ajjer that lay at the edge of the Libyan Desert. And as I departed, the sun rose over the red dunes to lead me to what I sought. . . ."

East—the direction the sun rose each morning over the Libyan border, across the canyons of the Tassili where we too were headed. But if the sun rose in the east, why hadn't I noticed that it was *now* rising, red and full, in what seemed to be the north, as we barreled down the road from the barricade at Ain Salah—into infinity?

$$\infty$$

Lily had been clipping along for hours on the endless ribbon of two-lane road that swayed like a long, long serpent among the dunes. I was growing drowsy from the heat, and Lily—who'd been behind the wheel for close to twenty hours and awake for twenty-four—was looking green around the gills and red at the tip of her nose from the blistering heat.

The temperature had been rising steadily for the last four hours since we'd crossed the barricade. Now it was ten o'clock, and the dashboard dials registered an incredible atmospheric temperature of 120 degrees Fahrenheit and an altimeter reading of five hundred feet above sea level. These couldn't be correct. I rubbed my scratchy eyes and looked again.

"Something's wrong," I told Lily. "Those plains we left may have been close to sea level, but it's been four hours since Ain Salah. We should be up a few thousand feet by now, moving into high desert. It's much hotter than it should be this early in the day as well."

"That's not all," agreed Lily in a voice thick from the swelling heat. "There should've been a turnoff at least half an hour ago, according to Minnie's directions. But there wasn't. . . ." And then I noticed the direction of the sun.

"Why did that guy say we needed a permit for our car?" I said, my voice rising a little hysterically. "Didn't he say it was for El-Tanzerouft—the Desert of Thirst? My God. . . ." Though the road signs had all been in Arabic and I wasn't too familiar with maps of the Sahara, something horrible was beginning to dawn on me.

"What's the matter?" cried Lily, looking at me nervously.

"That barricade you ran wasn't Ain Salah," I suddenly realized. "I think we took a wrong turn somewhere during the night. We're headed south into the salt desert! We're headed for Mali!"

Lily stopped the car in the middle of the freeway. Her face, already peeling badly from the sun, had crumpled in despair. She leaned her forehead against the steering wheel, and I put my hand on her shoulder. We both knew I was right. Jesus, what were we going to do now?

When we'd joked that there was nothing beyond that barricade, we'd laughed too soon. I'd heard stories about the Desert of Thirst. There was no more terrifying spot on earth. Even the famous Empty Quarter in Arabia could be crossed by camel, but this was the end of the world—a desert where no life could survive at all. It made the plateaus we'd accidentally missed seem like a lost paradise. Here, when we dropped below sea level, they said the temperatures rose so high you could fry an egg on the sand, and water turned instantly to steam.

"I think we should turn back," I told Lily, who still sat with her head inclined. "Move over and let me drive. We'll turn on the air-conditioning— you look ill."

"That'll only heat the engine more," she said thickly, raising her head. "I don't know how the hell I missed the way. You can drive, but if we turn back, you know the jig is up."

She was right, but what else could we do? I looked at her and saw her lips were cracking from the heat. I got out of the car and opened the trunk. There were two lap rugs in the back. I wrapped one around my head and shoulders, taking the other to wrap up Lily. I dragged Carioca from beneath the seat; his little tongue was hanging out, and it was nearly dry. I held his mouth up and poured some water down his throat. Then I went up to look under the hood.

I made a few trips to replenish gas and water. I didn't want to depress Lily any further, but her error last night had been a major fuck-up. Based on the way the tank guzzled down the first can of water, it didn't look like we were going to make it in this car, even if we did turn back. If that were so, we might as well go forward.

"There's a semi following us, isn't there?" I said, getting into the driver's seat and starting the car again. "If we go on, even if we break down, he'll have to show up eventually. There haven't been any exits but dirt roads in the last two hundred miles."

"I'm game if you are," she told me weakly, then looked at me with a grin that cracked her lips a little more. "If only Harry could see us now."

"Gee, we're friends at last—just as he'd always hoped." I smiled back with false bravado.

"Yeah," agreed Lily. "But what a meshugge way to die."

"We're not dead yet," I told her. But as I watched the glaring sun rising still higher in the parched white sky, I wondered how long it would be. . . .

So this was what a million miles of sand looked like, I thought as I kept the big Corniche carefully clicking along below forty, trying to keep the water from boiling off. It was like a big red ocean. Why wasn't it yellow or white or dirty gray like other deserts? The pulverized rock sparkled like crystal beneath the sun's hot glare, more glittery than sandstone, darker than cinnamon. As I listened to the engine slowly hissing our water away and watched the thermostat rise, the desert waited silently as far as the eye could see—waiting like a dark red eternity.

I had to keep stopping the car to cool it down, but the external thermostat was now climbing over 130 degrees, a temperature I found hard to imagine outside an oven. When I stopped to lift the hood I saw the cracking, flaking paint on the front of the Corniche. My shoes were all sloshy and filled with sweat, but when I bent to slip them off it wasn't perspiration I found. The skin of my swollen feet had burst from the heat—the shoes were filled with blood. I felt nausea climbing in my throat. I put the shoes back on, got back into the car without a word, and kept on driving.

I'd taken off my shirt miles back to wrap around the steering wheel where the leather had cracked and was peeling off. The blood in my brain was boiling; I felt the suffocating heat burning my lungs. If only we could make it until sunset, we could survive another day. Maybe someone would come and rescue us—maybe that semi behind us would come. But even the gigantic truck we'd passed that morning started to seem like a figment of my imagination, the memory's mirage.

It was two in the afternoon—the needle on the thermostat said it was close to 140 degrees—when I first noticed something. At first I thought my brain had sizzled and I was having hallucinations, that I was *really* seeing a mirage. I thought I saw the sand begin to move.

There wasn't a breath of wind to stir the air, so how could the sand be moving? But it was. I slowed the car a bit, then stopped completely. Lily was sleeping heavily in the back seat, she and Carioca covered with the lap rug.

I sniffed the air and listened. There was that flat, oppressive air one senses before a storm—that smothering silence, the terrifying vacuum of sound that comes only before the most horrid kinds of storms: the tornado . . . the hurricane. There was *something* coming all right, but what?

I jumped out, pulled off my blanket, and tossed it across the car's scalding hood so I could climb on top for a better view. Clambering up to a standing position, I scanned the horizon. There was nothing at all in the sky, but as far as I could see across the desert the sands were moving—crawling slowly like some living thing. I shivered despite the throbbing, aching heat.

I jumped back down and went to wake Lily, pulling off the lap rug protecting her. She sat up sluggishly, her face already badly blistered from the sun she'd taken earlier.

"We're out of gas!" she said, frightened. Her voice was cracked, her lips and tongue swollen.

"The car's still okay," I told her. "But something's coming. I don't know what."

Carioca had crept from beneath the blanket and started whining as he peered suspiciously at the moving sand around us. Lily glanced down at him, then back at me with frightened eyes.

"A storm?" she said.

I nodded. "I think so. I don't suppose we could hope for rain out here—it's got to be a sandstorm. It could be very bad."

I didn't want to rub it in that, thanks to her, we hadn't any shelter. It might not have helped if we had. In a place like this, where roads could be buried in drifts up to thirty feet, so could we. We wouldn't stand a chance even if the damned car had a roof—even crawling underneath it might not help.

"I think we should try to outrun it," I announced firmly, as if I knew what I were talking about.

"What direction's it coming from?" said Lily.

I shrugged. "Can't see it, smell it, or feel it," I told her. "Don't ask me how, but I know it's there." So did Carioca, who was scared out of his little wits. We couldn't both be wrong.

I started the car again and hit the gas as hard as I could. As we tore through the miserable heat, I felt real fear gripping me. Like Ichabod Crane fleeing the horrible headless ghost of Sleepy Hollow, I raced ahead of the storm I could neither see nor hear. The air grew more and more oppressive, smothering like a scalding blanket of fire closing over our faces. Lily and Carioca were in the front seat beside me, staring ahead through the sand-pocked windshield as the car barreled on into the relentless red glare. And then I heard the sound.

At first I thought it was my imagination, a sort of whirring in my ears that might have been caused by the sand that tore constantly against the metal car. The paint on the hood and grille had been sheared away—the sand had eaten it down to raw metal. But the sound grew louder and louder, a faint droning like a buzzsaw or a fly. I kept moving, but I was afraid. Lily heard it, too, and turned to me, but I wouldn't stop to discover what it was. I was afraid I already knew.

As the sound intensified it seemed to drown everything around us. The sand beside the road was lifting in little puffs now, whipping slight flurries across the pavement, but still the sound grew louder and louder, until it was almost deafening. Then suddenly I took my foot off the gas as Lily gripped the dashboard with her blood-red nails. The sound ripped violently over our heads, and I nearly ran off the road before I found the brakes.

"A plane!" Lily was screaming—and I was screaming, too. We were grasping each other, the tears stinging our eyes. A plane had come right over our heads and was landing before our very eyes, not a hundred yards away on a landing strip in the desert!

$$\infty$$

"Ladies," said the *fonctionnaire* of the Debnane Airstrip, "you were fortunate to find me here. We receive only this one flight a day from Air Algérie. When no private flights are scheduled, this post is otherwise closed. It's over a hundred kilometers to the next petrol, and you would not have made it."

He was replenishing our gas and water from pumps out near the runway. The huge transport plane that had buzzed over our car sat idle on the tarmac, heat melting up into the air from the hot propeller engines. Lily stood with Carioca in her arms, looking at our burly little savior as if he were the archangel Gabriel. He was, in fact, the only person within eyeshot as far as you could see. The plane's pilot had gone inside the metal quonset hut for a quick nap in the miserable heat. Dust blew across the runway; the wind was rising. My throat was aching from dryness and relief at my salvation. I decided I believed in God.

"What's this landing strip here for, out in the middle of nowhere?" Lily asked me. I communicated her question to the *fonctionnaire*.

"Mail delivery," he said, "supplies for some natural gas development crews working in trailers west of here. They just stop en route to the Hoggar, then shuttle back to Algiers." Lily had understood.

"The Hoggar," I told her, "are volcanic mountains in the south. I think they're near the Tassili."

"Ask him when they'll get this crate off the ground," said Lily, heading for the hut with Carioca trotting behind her on tippy-toe, lifting the pads of his feet gingerly off the scalding asphalt.

"Soon," the man replied to my question in French. He pointed to the desert. "We have to get her up before the sand devils hit. It won't be long." So I'd been right—there was a storm coming.

"Where are you going?" I called after Lily.

"To find out how much it'll cost to bring the car," she shot over her shoulder.

∞

It was four in the afternoon when our car was lowered down the ramp from the plane onto the tarmac at Tamanrasset. The date palms waved in the tepid breeze, and the blue-black mountains twisted into the sky around us.

"It's amazing what money will buy," I told Lily as she paid the cheerful pilot his commission and we climbed back into the Corniche.

"Don't you forget it," she retorted, pulling out through the steel mesh gates. "And the guy even gave me a frigging *map*! I'd have coughed up another grand for that, back there in the desert. Now at least we'll know where we *are* when we get lost again."

I didn't know which looked worse, Lily or the Corniche. Her pale skin was shredded from the sun, and the blue paint on the entire front half of the car had been stripped down to gray metal from the abrasion of sand and sun. But the engine was still purring like a cat. I was amazed.

"Here's where we're going." Lily pointed to a spot on the map she'd unfolded across the dashboard. "Add up the kilometers and convert them for me. Then we'll figure out the quickest route."

There was only one route—450 miles of it—and it was mountains all the way. At the junction to Djanet we stopped at a roadside *moulin* for our first meal in nearly twenty-four hours. I was ravenous and wolfed down two plates of creamed chicken soup with vegetables, sopping it up with chunks of dry baguette. A carafe of wine and a big helping of redfish and potatoes helped ease the stomach agony. I bought a quart of syrupy coffee for the road.

"You know, we should've read this diary earlier," I told Lily when we were back on the winding two-lane road headed east toward Djanet. "This nun Mireille seems to have camped all over this turf—knows everything about it. Did you know that the Greeks named these mountains 'Atlas' long before the ones up north were given that name? And the people who lived here, according to the historian Herodotus, were called Atlanteans? We're driving through the kingdom of lost Atlantis!"

"I thought it sank under the ocean," said Lily. "She doesn't mention where the pieces are hidden, does she?"

"Nope. I think she knows what happened to them, but she's gone off to look for the secret behind them—the formula."

"Well, read on, my darling. Read on. But this time tell me where to turn."

We drove through the afternoon and evening. It was midnight when we reached Djanet, and the batteries in the flashlight were exhausted from my reading. But now we knew exactly where we were headed. And why.

"My God," said Lily as I put the book away. She'd pulled the car over to the side of the road and turned off the engine. We sat, looking up at the star-spangled sky, the moonlight dripping like milk over the high plateaus of the Tassili to our left. "I can't believe this story! She crossed the desert by camel in a sandstorm, climbed these plateaus on foot, and gave birth to a kid in the middle of the mountains at the feet of the White Queen? What kind of broad *is* this?"

"We haven't exactly been tiptoeing through the tulips ourselves," I said with a laugh. "Maybe we should catch some shut-eye for a few hours until it's light."

"Look, it's a full moon. I've got some more batteries for that flashlight in the trunk. Let's drive up the road as far as we can until we get to the gap, then hit the trail. I'm wide awake from all that coffee. We can bring the blankets just in case. Let's go for it now, while no one else is around."

A dozen miles after Djanet we came to an intersection where a long dirt road branched off into the canyons. It was marked "Tamrit" with an arrow and beneath it five camel prints that read "Piste Chameliere." Camel Track. We headed up it anyway.

"How far in is this place?" I asked Lily. "You're the one who committed the trip to memory."

"There's a base camp. I think that's Tamrit, the village of tents. From there, the *touristas* go on foot to the prehistoric paintings—she said about twenty kilometers. That's thirteen miles or so."

"A four-hour hike," I told her. "But not in these shoes." We weren't exactly prepared for the rigors of cross-country travel, I thought ruefully. But it was too late to check our local directory for the nearest Saks Fifth Avenue.

We halted on the dirt trail at the turnoff to Tamrit and left the Corniche beside the road behind a clump of brush. Lily replenished the batteries and grabbed the blankets. I stuffed Carioca back in the bag, and we headed along the footpath. About every fifty yards there were little signposts by the road with lacy Arabic words and French translations beneath.

"This place is better marked than the freeways," Lily whispered. Though the only sounds for miles were the chirping of crickets and the dry crunch of gravel beneath our feet, we were both tiptoeing and whispering as clandestinely as if we were about to break into a bank. That was, of course, pretty close to what we were doing.

The sky was so clear, the moonlight so intense, we didn't even need the flashlight to read the signposts. The flat path gradually inclined as we moved southeast. We were walking through a narrow canyon alongside a gurgling stream when I noticed a cluster of signs all pointing in different directions: Sefar, Aouanrhet, In Itinen . . .

"What next?" I said, letting Carioca free to run around. He scurried instantly to the nearest tree and baptized it.

"That's it!" said Lily, jumping up and down. "There they are!" The trees she pointed to, which Carioca was still sniffing, grew from the very riverbed—a clump of gigantic cypresses at least sixteen feet around that rose so high they blackened the night sky. "First the giant trees," said Lily, "then there should be some reflecting lakes nearby."

Sure enough, not fifteen hundred feet ahead we saw the little pools, their limpid surfaces mirroring the luminous moon. Carioca had whipped ahead to one of the pools to drink. His lapping tongue broke the surface of the water into a million ripples of light.

"These point the direction," Lily said. "We continue down this canyon past something called the Stone Forest. . . ." We were moving briskly down the flat streambed when I saw another sign, pointing uphill to a narrow defile: "La Forêt de Pierre."

"This way," I said, grabbing Lily's arm and starting up the hill. There was a lot of loose slag on the incline of the defile that crumbled beneath our feet as we headed up. I heard Lily whisper "ouch!" every few yards as a stone bruised through her thin slippers. And every time a piece of slag broke loose, Carioca went tumbling head over heels—until finally I picked him up again and carried him to the top.

It was a long steep road that took us over half an hour to negotiate. At the top the canyon widened into a high, flat plateau—a valley on top of a mountain. All across the vast sweep, washed by moonlight, we could see the spiral needles of rock rising from the plateau floor like the long, twisted skeleton of a dinosaur stretched across the valley.

"The Forest of Stone!" whispered Lily. "Just where it was supposed to be." She was breathing heavily, and I was panting too from the uphill climb over loose rubble, and yet it all seemed too easy.

But perhaps I spoke too soon.

We walked through the Forest of Stone, whose beautiful twisted rocks took on hallucinogenic colors in the moonlight. At the far end of this plateau was another cluster of signs pointing in various directions.

"What now?" I said to Lily.

"We're supposed to look for a sign," she told me mysteriously.

"Here they are—half a dozen of them, at least." I pointed at the little arrows with names on them.

"Not that *kind* of sign," she told me. "A sign that will tell us where the pieces are."

"What's it supposed to look like?"

"I'm not sure," she told me, looking around in the moonlight. "It's just after the Stone Forest—"

"You're not *sure*?" I said, stifling my desire to throttle her. It'd been what you might call a rough day. "You said you had this all laid out in your brain like a game of blindfold chess—a landscape of the imagination, as you described it. I thought you could visualize every nook and cranny of this terrain?"

"I can," said Lily angrily. "I got us *this* far, didn't I? Why don't you shut up and help me solve this problem?"

"So you admit you're lost," I said.

"I am *not* lost!" cried Lily, her voice echoing back from the sparkling forest of monolithic stones that surrounded us. "I am looking for something—something specific. A sign. She said there'd be a sign that would *mean* something, just beyond this point."

"Mean something to whom?" I said slowly. Lily looked at me dumbly in the moonlight. I could see the peeling skin on her tilted nose. "I mean, a sign like a rainbow? Like a thunderbolt? Like the handwriting on the wall—*Mene, mene, tekel . . .*"

Lily and I stared at one another. It occurred to us both at once. She flicked on the flashlight, turning it toward the cliff before us at the end of the long plateau—and there it was.

A gigantic painting filled the entire wall. Wild antelope fleeing across the plains, in colors that seemed brilliant even in the unnatural light. And at their midst, a single chariot flying at top speed, bearing a huntress—a woman dressed completely in white.

We looked at the painting for a very long time, running the flashlight across the magnificent panorama to pick out each of the delicately wrought forms. The wall was high and wide, curved inward like the fragment of a broken bow. Here at the center of the wild stampede across the ancient plains was the chariot of the sky, its body shaped like a crescent moon, its two wheels of eight spokes, pulled by a troika of leaping horses, their flanks splashed with color: red, white, and black. A black man with the head of an ibis knelt at the front, holding the reins tightly as the horses bounded forward over the tundra. Behind, two serpentine ribbons streamed out, twisting together in the wind to form a figure eight. At center, towering over the figures of man and beast like a great white vengeance, was the goddess. She stood motionless while all was frenzy about her—back to us, hair flying in the breeze, her body frozen like a statue. Her arms were raised as if to strike at something. The long, long spear she held aloft was not aimed at the antelope that fled madly everywhere, but pointed upward into the starry sky. Her body itself cut the shape of a harsh, triangulated figure eight that seemed carved from stone.

"That's it," said Lily breathlessly, gazing upon the painting. "You know what that shape means, don't you? That double triangle shaped like an hourglass?" She brushed the wall with a splash of the flashlight to pick out the shape:

"Ever since I saw that cloth at Minnie's, I've been trying to think what it reminded *me* of," she went on. "And now I know. It's an ancient double-headed axe called a *labrys* that's shaped like a figure eight. It was used in Crete by the ancient Minoans."

"What does this have to do with why we're here?"

"I saw it in a chess book Mordecai showed me. The most ancient chess service ever discovered was found at the palace of King Minos on Crete—the place where the famous Labyrinth was built, named after this sacred axe. The chess service dates to 2000 B.C. It was made of gold and silver and jewels, just like the Montglane Service. And in the center was carved a *labrys*."

"Just like Minnie's cloth," I interjected. Lily was nodding and waving the flashlight around in agitation. "But I thought chess wasn't even invented until six or seven hundred A.D.," I added. "They always say it came from Persia or India. How could this Minoan chess service be so old?"

"Mordecai's written a lot himself on the history of chess," said Lily, turning the light back to the woman in white, standing in her moon-shaped chariot, her spear raised to the heavens. "He thinks that chess set in Crete was designed by the same guy who built the Labyrinth—the sculptor Daedalus. . . ."

Now things were beginning to click into place. I took the flashlight from her hands and ran it over the face of the cliff. "The moon goddess," I whispered. "The ritual of the labyrinth . . . 'There is a land called Crete in the midst of the wine-dark sea, a fair rich land begirt by water. . . .' " An island, I recalled, like the others in the Mediterranean—that was settled by the Phoenicians. That was, like the Phoenician, a labyrinthine culture surrounded by water—that worshiped the moon. I looked at the shapes on the wall.

"Why was this axe carved on the chessboard?" I asked Lily, knowing the answer in my heart before she spoke. "What did Mordecai say was the connection?" But though I was prepared, her words brought the same cold chill as that white form towering above me on the wall.

"That's what it's all about," she said quietly. "To kill the King."

The sacred axe was used to kill the King. The ritual had been the same since the beginning of time. The game of chess was merely a reenactment. Why hadn't I recognized it before?

Kamel had told me to read the Koran. And Sharrif, on the very eve of my arrival in Algiers, had mentioned the importance of my birthday to the Islamic calendar, which, like most ancient calendars, was lunar, or based upon cycles of the moon. But still I hadn't made the connection.

The ritual was the same for all those civilizations whose survival depended on the sea—and hence upon that moon goddess who pulled the tides, who caused the rivers to rise and fall. A goddess who demanded blood sacrifice. To her, they chose a living man to wed as king, but the term of his reign was set by strict ritual. He ruled for a "Great Year," or eight years—the time required for the lunar and solar calendars to cycle back together, a hundred lunar months being equal to eight solar years. At the end of that time the king was sacrificed to appease the goddess, and a new king was chosen with the new moon.

This ritual of death and rebirth was always celebrated in the spring, when the sun was smack between the zodiacal constellations of Aries and Taurus—that is, by modern reckoning, April fourth. It was the *day on which they killed the king*!

Here was the ritual of the triple goddess Car, to whose name ancient tribute was paid from Carchemish to Carcassone, from Carthage to Khartoum. In the dolmens of Karnak, in the caves of Karlsbad and Karelia, through the Carpathian mountains, her name rings even today.

The words that sprang from her name flooded my mind as I held the light and looked at her monolithic form towering above me on the wall. Why had I never heard these names before? She appeared in carmine, cardinal, and cardiac, in carnal, carnivorous, and Karma—the endless cycle of incarnation, transformation, and oblivion. She was the word made flesh, the vibration of destiny coiled like *kundalini* at the heart of life itself—the caracole, or spiral force, that formed the very universe. Hers was the force unleashed by the Montglane Service.

I turned to Lily, the flashlight shaking in my hand, and we hugged each other for warmth as the cold moonlight poured over us like an icy bath.

"I know what the spear is pointing toward," she said weakly, gesturing to the painting on the wall. "She's not aiming at the moon—that's not the sign. It's something the moonlight is falling *on*, atop that cliff." She looked as frightened as I felt about climbing up there in the dead of night. It must have been four hundred feet straight up.

"Maybe," I replied. "But we have a saying in *my* business: 'Don't work hard; work smart.' We got the message—we know the pieces are around here somewhere. But there's more to the message than that, and you figured out what it was."

"I did?" she said, looking at me with wide gray eyes. "What was it?"

"Look at the lady on the wall," I told her. "She's riding the chariot of the moon across a sea of antelope. She doesn't notice them—she's looking away from us and pointing her spear at the sky. But she's not *looking* at the sky. . . ."

"She looking directly into the mountain!" cried Lily. "It's *within* that cliff!" Her excitement calmed a bit as she looked again. "But what are we supposed to do, blow the cliff apart? I forgot to pack my nitroglycerine."

"Be reasonable," I told her. "We're standing in the Forest of Stone. How do you think those lacy, spiral stones got to look so much like trees? Sand doesn't cut stone that way, regardless of how hard it blows. It wears it down smooth, polishes it. The only thing that cuts rock into precise shapes like that is *water*. This whole plateau was formed by underground rivers or oceans. Nothing else could make it look like that. Water cuts holes in rock. . . . Are you getting my drift?"

"A labyrinth!" Lily cried. "You're saying there's a labyrinth *inside* that cliff! That's why they painted the moon goddess as a *labrys* on the side! It's a message, like a road marking. But the spear still points up. The water must have come in and formed it from the *top*."

"Maybe," I said, still grudgingly. "But take a look at this wall, how it's cut. It curves *inward*, it's been scooped out like a bowl. Exactly the way the sea cuts into a cliff. That's the way all sea grottoes are formed. You see them along every rockbound coastline from Carmel to Capri. I think the entrance is down here. At least we should check before we kill ourselves climbing that rock."

Lily took the flash, and we groped our way along the cliff for half an hour. There were several crevices, but none wide enough for us to slip through. I was beginning to think my idea was a bust when I saw a place where the smooth rock face took a slight dip. Fortunately I ran my hands into the dip. Instead of joining, as it appeared, the front portion of the rock kept sliding back. I followed it, and it kept swinging around as if curving back to join the other rock—but it never did.

"I think I've got it," I called to Lily as I disappeared into the darkness of the cleft. She followed my voice with the flashlight. When she arrived, I took the light and ran it over the surface of the rock. The cleft kept sliding back in a spiraled curve, deeper and deeper into the cliff.

The two sections of rock seemed to curl around each other like the spirals of a chambered nautilus, and we kept with them. It grew so dark that the weak beam of our flashlight hardly illuminated more than a few feet ahead.

Suddenly there was a loud noise, and I nearly jumped in the air. Then I realized it was Carioca inside my satchel, letting out a bark. It echoed like the roar of a lion.

"There's more to this cave than it appears," I told Lily, fumbling to let Carioca out. "That echo went a long way."

"Don't put him down—there may be spiders in here. Or snakes."

"If you think I'm going to let him pee in my bag, you're mistaken," I told her. "Besides, when it comes to snakes, better him than me." Lily glared at me in the faint light. I set Carioca on the floor, where he instantly did his business. I looked at her with raised eyebrow, then checked the place out.

We walked around the cave slowly; it was only ten yards around. But we didn't find a clue. After a while, Lily set down the blankets she'd been carrying and sat on the floor.

"They *have* to be here somewhere," she said. "It's too perfect that we found this place, though it isn't exactly the labyrinth I had in mind." Suddenly she sat bolt upright. "Where's Carioca?" she said.

I looked around, but he'd disappeared. "My God," I said, trying to be calm. "There's only one way out—the way we came in. Why don't you call him?" So she did. After a long, painful moment we heard his little yelps. They were coming from the curlicue entrance, much to our relief.

"I'll go get him," I told her.

But Lily was on her feet at once. "Not on your life," she said, her voice echoing in the gloom. "You're not leaving me here in the dark." She was right on my heels, which probably explains why she fell down the hole right on top of me. It seemed to take a long time to hit bottom.

Just near the end of the spiral entrance to the cave, hidden from view when we'd entered by the curve of the wall, was a steep rock slope that went thirty feet into the plateau. When I extracted my bruised body from beneath Lily's weight, I turned the beam upward. Light glittered everywhere off the crystallized walls and ceilings of the biggest cave I'd seen so far. We sat there looking at the myriad colors as Carioca bounced playfully around us, unfazed by his fall.

"Good work!" I cried, patting him on the head. "Once in a while it's lucky you're such a klutz, my furry friend!" I stood up and brushed myself off as Lily collected the blankets and the scattered items that had tumbled from my bag. We gaped at the enormous cave. No matter where we turned our beam, it seemed to go on forever.

"I think we're in trouble." Lily's voice came from the darkness behind me. "It occurs to me this ramp we slid down is too steep to get back up without a crane. It also occurs we could get terribly lost in this place unless we leave a trail of breadcrumbs behind."

She was right on both counts, but my brain was now working overtime.

"Sit down and think," I told Lily wearily. "You try to remember a clue, and I'll try to figure out how we can get out of here." Then I heard a sound—a vague whispering like dried leaves blowing across an empty alleyway.

I started to flash the light around, but suddenly Carioca was jumping up and down, yapping hysterically at the ceiling of the cave, and a deafening scream like the screeching of a thousand harpies assaulted my ears.

"The blankets!" I screamed at Lily over the noise. "Get the fucking blankets!" I grabbed Carioca, who was still bounding off the floor, pinned him under my arm, and made a dive for Lily, grabbing the blankets from her hands just as she started screaming. I threw a blanket over her head and tried to cover myself, crouching on the floor just as the bats hit.

There were thousands of them, by the sound of it. Lily and I hunkered down on the floor as they hit the blankets like tiny kamikaze pilots—thunk, thunk,

thunk. Over the sound of their beating wings, I could hear Lily's screams. She was getting hysterical, and Carioca was wriggling frantically in my arms. He seemed to want to take on the entire bat population of the Sahara single-handedly, and his high-voiced yapping, combined with Lily's screams, echoed from the high walls.

"I hate bats!" Lily yelled hysterically, gripping my arm as I raced her through the cave, peeking out from beneath my blanket to get a glimpse of the terrain. "I hate them! I hate them!"

"They don't seem too fond of *you*," I yelled over the racket. But I knew bats couldn't hurt you unless they got tangled in your hair or were rabid.

We were running in a half crouch toward one of the arteries of the big cave when Carioca wriggled loose from my grasp and hit the floor running. Bats were still soaring everywhere.

"My God!" I screamed. "Carioca, come back!" Holding my blanket above my head, I released Lily and went tearing after him, waving the flashlight around in hopes I'd confuse the bats.

"Don't leave me!" I heard Lily cry. Her footsteps were pounding after me across the broken rubble of the floor. I was running faster and faster, but Carioca turned a corner and disappeared.

The bats were gone. A long cave stretched before us like a hallway, and the bats were nowhere within earshot. I turned to Lily, who was huddled behind me trembling, her blanket draped over her head.

"He's dead," she whimpered, scanning the place for Carioca. "You turned him loose, and they killed him. What should we do?" Her voice was feeble with fear. "You always know what to do. Harry says—"

"I don't give a damn what Harry says," I lashed out. The rising wash of panic was gripping me, but I fought it down with deep breaths. There was really no point in going crazy. Huckleberry Finn got out of a cave like this, didn't he? Or was it Tom Sawyer? I started laughing.

"Why are you laughing?" said Lily frantically. "What are we going to do?"

"Turn off the flashlight, for one thing," I told her, switching it off. "So we don't run out of batteries in this godforsaken—" And then I saw it.

From the far end of the hallway where we stood, there was a faint glow. Very faint, but in the pitch-black darkness it was like the beacon of a lighthouse shining across a wintry sea.

"What's that?" Lily said breathlessly. Our hope of salvation, I thought, grabbing her arm and moving toward it. Could there be another entrance to this place?

I'm not sure how far we walked. In the dark you lose all sense of time and space. But we followed the dim glow without a flashlight, moving through the silent cave for what seemed a very long time. The glow grew brighter and brighter as we approached. At last we came to a room of magnificent dimensions—a ceiling perhaps fifty feet high and walls encrusted with strangely glittering forms. From an open hole in the ceiling poured a wonderful flood of moonlight. Lily started to cry.

"I never thought I'd be so happy just to see the sky," she sobbed.

I couldn't have agreed more. The relief washed through me like a drug. But just as I was wondering how we were going to pull ourselves fifty feet up through that hole in the roof, I heard a snuffling sound that was hard to mistake. I switched the flashlight on again. There in the corner—digging in the ground as for a bone—was Carioca.

Lily started to rush to him, but I grabbed her arm. What was he doing? We both stared at him in the eerie light.

He was digging frantically through the mound of rock and rubble on the floor. But there was something odd about that mound. I turned off the light so only the dim wash of moonlight lit the room. Then I realized what it was that bothered me. The mound *itself* was glowing—something underneath that rubble. And just above it, carved into the wall, a gigantic caduceus with a figure eight seemed to float in the pale moonlight.

Lily and I were on our knees on the ground, tearing at the stones and rubble alongside Carioca. It was only a few minutes before we unearthed the first piece. I pulled it out and held it in my hands—the perfect shape of a horse, rearing on its hind legs. It was about five inches high and much heavier than it looked. I switched the flashlight back on and handed it to Lily as we examined the piece more closely. The detail in the work was incredible. Everything was precisely tooled in a metal that seemed to be a very pure form of silver. From the flaring nostrils to the delicately wrought hooves, it was obviously the work of a master craftsman. The fringed trappings of the horse's saddle were picked out thread by thread. The saddle itself, the base of the piece—even the horse's eyes—were of polished uncut stones that glittered in luminous colors in the small spotlight.

"It's incredible," whispered Lily in the silence that was broken only by the sound of Carioca's continued digging. "Let's get the others out."

So we kept clawing through the mound until we'd extracted them all. Eight pieces of the Montglane Service sat around us in the rubble, glowing dully in the moonlight. There was the silver Knight and four small pawns, each about three inches high. They wore strange-looking togas with a panel down the front and carried spears with twisted points. There was a golden camel with a tower on its back.

But the last two pieces were the most amazing of all. One was a man sitting on the back of an elephant, its trunk upraised. It was all in gold, and similar to the picture of the ivory one Llewellyn had shown me so many months ago—but minus the foot soldiers around the base. He seemed to be carved from life, from an actual person rather than the stylized faces usual on chess pieces. It was a large, noble face with a Roman nose, but flaring nostrils like the

Negroid heads found at Ife in Nigeria. His long hair tumbled down his back, some of the locks braided and flecked with smaller jewels. The King.

The last piece was nearly as tall as the King, about six inches. It was a covered sedan chair with draperies drawn aside. Within sat a figure in a lotus position, facing outward. It wore an expression of hauteur—almost fierceness—in the almond-shaped emerald eyes. I say "it," for though the figure had a beard, it also had the breasts of a woman.

"The Queen," said Lily softly. "In Egypt and Persia, she wore a beard, indicating her power to rule. In olden days, this piece had less power than in the modern game. But her strength has grown."

We looked at each other in the pale moonlight, across the glowing pieces of the Montglane Service. And we smiled.

"We did it," Lily said. "Now all we have to do is figure out how to get out of here."

I ran the flashlight up the walls. It seemed difficult, but not impossible.

"I think I can get handholds on this rock," I told her. "If we cut these blankets into strips, we can make a rope. I can lower it once I get up there. You can tie it to my shoulder bag, and we'll haul out Carioca and the pieces."

"Great," said Lily. "But what about me?"

"I can't pull you," I said. "You'll have to climb yourself."

I took off my shoes as Lily shredded the blankets, using my nail scissors. The sky was getting light above us by the time we'd cut the thick wool blankets.

The walls were rough enough to get good toeholds, and the crevice of light extended all the way to the sides of the cave. It took nearly half an hour for me to climb up with my rope attached. When I emerged, panting, into the light of day, I was on top of the cliff through whose base we'd entered the night before. Lily tied the bag below, and I hauled first Carioca, then the pieces, to the ledge. Now it was Lily's turn. I caressed my raw feet, for the blisters had opened again.

"I'm afraid," she called up to me. "What if I fall and break my leg?"

"I'd have to shoot you," I told her. "Just do it—and don't look down."

She started up the steep cliff, feeling with her bare toes for the solid spots in the rock. About halfway up, she froze.

"Come on," I said. "You can't freeze up now." She just stood there, cleaving to the rock like a terrified spider. She didn't speak or move. I started to panic.

"Look," I told her, "why don't you imagine this as a chess game? You're pinned in a spot and can't see your way out. But there's *got* to be a way out, or you'll lose the game! I don't know what you call it when all the pieces are pinned without a place to move . . . but that's where you are now unless you find another place to put your foot."

I saw her move her hand a little. She released her hold and slipped a bit. Then slowly she started moving up again. I heaved a big sigh of relief but said nothing to distract her as she continued her upward course. After what seemed aeons, her hand clutched the top of the ledge. I grabbed the rope I'd had her tie around her waist, and tugging it, I hauled her over the top.

Lily lay there panting. Her eyes were closed. For a long time she didn't speak. Finally she opened her eyes and looked at the dawn, then at me.

"They call it *Zugzwang*," she gasped. "My God—we did it."

There was more to come.

We put on our shoes and hiked across the ledge, shinnying to the bottom. Then we passed back through the Forest of Stone. It only took two hours on the downhill hike to return to the hill that overlooked our car.

We were both punchy from exhaustion, and I was just telling Lily how much I'd like fried eggs for breakfast—an impossible delicacy in a country like this—when I felt her grab my arm.

"I don't believe this," she said, pointing down at the road where we'd left the car behind the bushes. There were two police cars parked at either side—and a third car I thought I recognized. When I saw Sharrif's two thugs crawling over the Corniche with a fine-toothed comb, I knew I was right.

"How could they get here?" she said. "I mean, it's hundreds of miles from where we shook them."

"How many blue Corniches do you think there are in Algeria?" I pointed out. "And how many roads through the Tassili that we might have taken?"

We stood there for a minute looking down through the brush at the road.

"You haven't blown all of Harry's pin money, have you?" I asked her. She looked on her last legs as she shook her head.

"Then I suggest we hoof it to Tamrit, that village of tents we passed. Maybe we can buy a few donkeys to take us back to Djanet."

"And leave my car in the hands of those villains?" she hissed.

"I should have left you hanging on the side of that rock," I said. "In *Zugzwang*."

ZUGZWANG

It is always better to sacrifice your opponent's men.

—Savielly Tartakover
Polish GM

t was just past noon when Lily and I left the corrugated high plateaus of the Tassili and descended into the plains of Admer a thousand feet below, to the outskirts of Djanet.

We found water to drink along the way from the many little rivers that irrigate the Tassili, and I'd brought along some branches laden with fresh *dhars*, those syrupy dates that stick to your fingers and your ribs. It was all we'd had to eat since last night's dinner.

We'd rented donkeys from a guide at Tamrit, the village of tents we'd passed by night at the entrance to the Tassili.

Donkeys are less comfortable to ride than horses. To my shredded feet I now added an inventory of bodily woes: a sore derriere and aching spine caused by endless hours of trotting up and down the stony dunes; torn hands from clawing my way up a cliff; a throbbing head probably caused by sunstroke. But despite all that, my spirits were high. We had the pieces at last—we were headed for Algiers. At least, so I thought.

We left the donkeys with the guide's uncle at Djanet, four hours away. He gave us a ride in his hay cart to the airport.

Though Kamel had said to avoid airports, this seemed impossible now. Our car had been discovered and was under guard, and finding a rental car in a town this size was out of the question. How were we to get back—hot-air balloon?

"It worries me, flying into the Algiers airport," said Lily as we brushed the hay from our clothes and entered the glass doors of the Djanet airport. "Didn't you say Sharrif had an office there?"

"Just inside the Immigrations gate," I confirmed. But we didn't have to worry about Algiers for long.

"There are no more flights to Algiers today," said the lady at the ticket counter. "The last one left an hour ago. There won't be another until tomorrow morning." What could you expect in a town with two million palm trees and two streets?

"Good Lord," said Lily, drawing me aside. "We *can't* stay overnight in this burg. If we tried to check into a hotel, they'd ask for identification, and I don't have any. They found our car, so they *know* we're here. I think we need a new plan."

We had to get out of here—and fast. And get the pieces back to Minnie's before anything else happened. I went back to the ticket counter with Lily on my heels.

"Are there any other flights leaving this afternoon, to anyplace at all?" I asked the ticketing agent.

"Only a chartered flight returning to Oran," she said. "It was booked by a group of Japanese students en route to Morocco. It's leaving in a few minutes from gate four."

Lily was already hoofing it toward gate four with Carioca tucked under her arm like a loaf of bread, and I was right behind her. If anyone understood money, it was the Japanese, I thought. And Lily had enough of *that* to communicate in any language.

The tour organizer, a dapper fellow in a blue blazer with a name tag that read "Hiroshi," was already shooing the boisterous students out to the runway when we arrived out of breath. Lily explained our situation in English, which I began to translate rapidly into French.

"Five hundred bucks cash," said Lily. "American dollars right in your pocket."

"Seven fifty," he snapped back.

"Done," said Lily, peeling off the crisp notes beneath his nose. He pocketed them faster than a Las Vegas dealer. We were on our way.

Until that flight, I'd always visualized the Japanese as a people of impeccable culture and high sophistication who played soothing music and performed tranquil tea ceremonies. But that three-hour flight across the desert revised my impression. These students were dashing up and down the aisles telling raucous jokes and singing Beatles songs in Japanese—a cacophonous caterwauling that made me reminisce longingly over the shrieking bats we'd just left in the caves of the Tassili.

Lily was oblivious to all this. She lost herself at the back of the plane in a round of Go with the tour director, defeating him ruthlessly in a game that is the Japanese national sport.

I was relieved when from the plane window I spotted the huge pink stucco cathedral that topped the mountainous city of Oran. Oran has a large international airport serving not only the Mediterranean cities, but the Atlantic coast and sub-Saharan Africa as well. As Lily and I disembarked from our charter flight, I thought of a problem that had never crossed my mind at the airport in Djanet: how to get past the metal detectors if we changed planes.

So when Lily and I got off the plane, I went at once to the car rental agency. I had a plausible cover: there was an oil refinery at the nearby town of Arzew.

"I'm with the Petrol Ministry," I told the rental agent, flashing my ministry badge. "I need a car to visit the refineries at Arzew. It's an emergency—the ministry car broke down."

"Unhappily, mademoiselle," said the agent, shaking his head, "there are no rental cars available for at least a week."

"A week! This is an impossible situation! I must have a car today, to inspect production rates. I demand you requisition one for me. There are cars outside on your lot. Who has reserved them? Whoever it is, this is more urgent."

"If only I'd had some warning," he said, "but those cars on the lot—they've just been returned today. Some clients have been waiting weeks for them, and they're all VIPs. Like this one . . ." He plucked a set of car keys off the desk and jangled them. "Only an hour ago, the Soviet consulate telephoned. Their petroleum liaison officer is arriving on the next flight from Algiers."

"The Russian petroleum officer?" I snorted. "You must be joking. Perhaps you'd like to telephone the *Algerian* oil minister and explain I cannot inspect production at Arzew for a full week because the Russians—who know nothing about oil—have stolen the last car?"

Lily and I looked at each other indignantly and shook our heads as the rental agent became more nervous. He was sorry he'd tried to impress me with his clientele, but sorrier yet that he'd mentioned it was a Russian.

"You're right!" cried the agent, pulling out a clipboard with some papers attached and pushing them over to me. "What business has the Soviet embassy to demand a car so fast? Here, mademoiselle—sign this. Then I'll bring the car around for you."

When the agent returned, keys in hand, I asked to use his phone to connect with the international operator in Algiers, assuring him he wouldn't be charged for the call. He put me through to Therese, and I took the phone.

"My girl!" she cried over the static on the line. "What have you done? Half of Algiers is searching for you. I should know—I've listened to the calls! The minister told me if I heard from you, I'm to tell you he can't be reached. You are *not* to go near the ministry in his absence."

"Where is he?" I asked, glancing nervously at the agent, who was listening to every word while pretending not to understand English.

"He's in conference," she said meaningfully. Shit. Did that mean the OPEC conference had begun? "Where are you if he needs to reach you?"

"I'm on my way to inspect the Arzew refineries," I told her loudly, and in French. "Our car broke down, but thanks to the fine work of the auto rental agent here at the Oran airport, we've secured another vehicle. Tell the minister I'll be reporting in to him tomorrow."

"Whatever you do, you must *not* return now!" said Therese. "That *salud* from Persia *knows* where you've been—and who sent you there. Get out of that airport as fast as you can. The airports are secured by his men!"

The Persian bastard she referred to was Sharrif, who clearly knew we'd gone to the Tassili. But how did Therese know—and more incredibly, how did she guess who'd sent me there? Then I remembered it was Therese I'd interrogated to help find Minnie Renselaas!

"Therese," I said, still watching the agent as I switched to English, "was it you who told the minister I had a meeting in the Casbah?"

"Yes," she whispered back. "I see you found her. May heaven help you now, my girl." She lowered her voice so I had to strain to hear her. "They have guessed *who you are*!" The line was silent for a moment, then I heard the disconnect signal. I put down the receiver, my heart thumping, and picked up the car keys that lay on the counter.

"Well," I said briskly, shaking the agent's hand, "the minister will be most pleased to learn we can inspect Arzew after all! I can't thank you enough for your assistance."

Outside, Lily hopped into the waiting Renault with Carioca, and I took the wheel. I laid down rubber heading for the coast road. Against Therese's advice, I was going to Algiers. What else could I do? But my brain was going a mile a minute as the car chewed up the turf. If Therese meant what I thought she did, my life wasn't worth a plugged farthing. I drove like a bat out of hell until I hit the twisting two-lane highway to Algiers.

The road went along the high corniche 250 miles east into Algiers. After passing the Arzew refineries, I stopped watching my rearview mirror so anxiously and at last pulled over and turned the driving over to Lily so I could continue with the translation of Mireille's journal.

Opening the soft leather cover, I turned the fragile leaves carefully to find the place where we'd left off. It was already afternoon, and the purple-edged sun was curving toward the dark sea, making rainbows in the spray where the water struck the cliffs. Groves of black-branched olive trees hugged the cliffs in the slanting afternoon light, their fluttering leaves moving like tinkling bits of metal.

As I turned my gaze from the moving landscape, I felt myself returning to the strange world of the written word. It was odd, I thought, how this book had become more real to me than even the very real and immediate dangers that surrounded me. This French nun Mireille had become like a companion on the road of our adventure. Her story unfolded before us—inside us—like a dark and mysterious flower.

As Lily drove in silence, I continued to translate. I felt as if I were hearing the tale of my own quest from the lips of someone who sat beside me—a woman engaged in a mission I alone could understand—as though the whispering voice I heard were my own. Somewhere in the course of my adventures, Mireille's quest had become my quest as well. I read on. . . .

> I left the prison with great trepidation. In the box of paints I carried
> was a letter from the Abbess, and a considerable sum of money she'd

enclosed to aid my mission. A letter of credit, she said, would be established for me to draw upon my late cousin's funds at a British bank. But I was resolved not to go to England yet—rather, there was another task I must accomplish first. My child was in the desert—Charlot, whom only that morning I'd believed I'd never see again. He was born under the eye of the Goddess. He was born into the Game. . . .

∞

Lily slowed the car, and I looked up from my reading. It was dusk, and my eyes were strained from the waning light. It took a moment before I realized why she'd pulled suddenly to the side of the road, dousing her lights. Through the dim light I saw police cars and military vehicles all over the road ahead—and a few passenger cars they'd pulled aside to search.

"Where are we?" I asked. I wasn't sure if they'd seen us.

"About five miles before Sidi-Fredj—your apartment and my hotel. Forty kilometers from Algiers. Half an hour and we'd have been there. What now?"

"Well, we can't stay here," I told her. "And we can't go on. No matter where we hide those pieces, they'd find them." I thought a minute. "There's a seaport a few yards ahead. It's not on any map, but I've gone there to buy fish and lobster. It's the only place we can turn off without doubling back and looking suspicious. It's called La Madrague. We can hole up there until we formulate a plan."

We edged slowly up the winding road until we came to the dirt road that trailed off the main drag. By now it was almost completely dark, but the town was only a one-block street that ran along the edge of the tiny harbor. We pulled up before the only inn in town, a sailor's hangout where I knew they had good bouillabaisse. We could see cracks of light through the closely shuttered windows and the front door, which was just a screen on loose springs.

"This is the only place for miles around with a phone," I told Lily as we sat outside in the car looking through the pub doors. "Not to mention food. It seems like we haven't eaten in months. Let's try to reach Kamel to see if he can get us out of here. But no matter how you look at it, I think we're in *Zugzwang*." I grinned at her in the gloom.

"What if we can't reach him?" she asked. "How long do you think that search party will be there? We can't stay here all night."

"Actually, if we want to abandon our car, we can hoof it down the beach. My apartment's only a few miles from here if you go on foot. We'd bypass the roadblock that way, but we'd be stuck at Sidi-Fredj with no wheels."

So we decided to try the first plan and went inside. It was perhaps the worst suggestion I'd made since we began our trek.

The pub at La Madrague was a sailors' hangout all right—but the sailors that turned to us as we entered looked like extras from a film of *Treasure Island*. Carioca burrowed into Lily's arms, making snuffling sounds as if trying to rid his nose of the evil smell.

"I just remembered," I told her as we paused at the door. "By day La Madrague is a fishing port, but by night it's the home of the Algerian Mafia."

"I sure hope you're kidding," she said, raising her chin as we started to move to the bar. "Somehow I don't think you are."

Just then my stomach did a horrible turn. I glimpsed a face that I wished was not familiar. He was smiling and raised his hand to the bartender as we arrived at the bar. The bartender leaned toward Lily and me.

"You are invited to be guests at the corner table," he whispered in a voice that didn't sound like an invitation. "Name your drinks, and I'll serve them there."

"We buy our own drinks," Lily began haughtily, but I grabbed her arm.

"We're in deep shit," I whispered in her ear. "Don't look now, but our host Long John Silver is a long way from home." And I guided her through the throng of silent sailors, who parted like the Red Sea in our path—straight toward the table of the man who waited alone at the far side of the room. The carpet trader—El-Marad.

I kept thinking about what I had nestled in my shoulder bag, and what this guy would do to us if he found out.

"We've tried the powder room trick," I said in Lily's ear. "I hope you've got something else up your sleeve. The guy you're about to meet is the White King, and I doubt he has any illusions about who we are and where we've been."

El-Marad was sitting at the table with a bunch of matchsticks spread out in front of him. He was picking them out of a box and putting them on the table in the shape of a pyramid, and he didn't rise or look up as we arrived.

"Good evening, ladies," he said in that horrible soft voice as we came up to his table. "I've been expecting you. Won't you join me in a game of Nim?" I did a double take, but apparently no pun was intended.

"It's an old British game," he continued. "In English slang, nim means 'to pinch, to filch—to steal.' But perhaps you didn't know that?" He looked up at me with those jet-black eyes that had no pupils. "It's a simple game, really. Each player removes one matchstick or more from any row in the pyramid, but from one row only. The player required to take the last matchstick loses the game."

"Thanks for explaining the rules," I said, pulling out a chair and taking a seat as Lily did likewise. "You didn't arrange that roadblock out there, did you?"

"No, but since it was there I took advantage of the fact. This was the only place to which you could detour, once you showed up."

Of course—what an idiot I'd been! There wasn't another town for miles this side of Sidi-Fredj.

"You didn't get us here to play a game," I said, looking disdainfully at his matchstick pyramid on the table. "What do you want?"

"But I *did* bring you here to play a game," he said with a sinister smile. "Or should I say, to play *the* Game? And this, if I'm not mistaken, is the granddaughter of Mordecai Rad, the expert gamesman of all time—especially those having to do with theft!" His voice was getting nasty as he looked at Lily with his hateful black eyes.

"She's also the niece of your 'business associate' Llewellyn, who introduced us," I told him. "Just what part does *he* play in this game?"

"How did you enjoy meeting Mokhfi Mokhtar?" said El-Marad. "It was she who sent you on the little mission you've just returned from, if I'm not mistaken?" He reached out and removed a matchstick from the top row, then nodded for me to make a move.

"She sends you her regards," I told him, taking two sticks from the next row. My mind was on a thousand things, but somewhere in the back I was looking at this game we were playing—the game of Nim. There were five rows of sticks, with one stick on the top and each row having one more than the row above. What was it that reminded me of something? Then I knew.

"Me?" said El-Marad, a bit uncomfortably, I thought. "Surely you're mistaken."

"You're the White King, aren't you?" I said calmly, watching his leathery skin grow pale. "She's got your number, bub. I'm surprised you'd leave those mountains where you were so safe, to make a trip like this—plopped out on the board and running for cover. It was a bad move."

Lily was staring at me as El-Marad swallowed, looked down, then took another match from the pile. Suddenly she squeezed me under the table. She'd understood what I was up to.

"You made the wrong move *there*, too," I told him, pointing at the matches. "I'm a computer expert, and this game of Nim is a binary system. That means there's a formula for winning or losing. And I've just won."

"You mean, it was all a trap?" El-Marad whispered in horror. He jumped up from the table, scattering matches everywhere. "She sent you into the desert merely to draw me out? No! I don't believe you!"

"Okay, you don't believe me," I said. "You're still safe at home on the eighth square, protected by your flanks. You're not sitting here, flushed out like a partridge . . ."

"Across from the new Black Queen," Lily chimed in gleefully. El-Marad stared at her, then back at me. I stood up as if prepared to leave, but he grabbed my arm.

"You!" he cried, his black eyes darting around wildly. "Then—she's left the Game! She's tricked me. . . ." I was moving toward the door with Lily right behind me. El-Marad caught up and grabbed me again.

"You have the pieces," he hissed. "This is all a trick to lead me astray. But you have them. You'd never have returned from the Tassili without them."

"Sure I have them," I said. "But not in a place where *you'd* ever think of looking." I had to get out of there before he guessed where they were. We were nearly at the door.

Just then Carioca jumped out of Lily's arms, skittered on the slick linoleum floor, recovered, and ran around yapping his head off as he barreled for the door. I looked up in horror as the door burst open and Sharrif, surrounded by a brigade of thugs in business suits, filled the doorway with a solid block of shoulders.

"Halt in the name of the—" he began. But before I could get my wits together, Carioca had plunged for his favorite ankle. Sharrif buckled over in pain, backed away, and went through the screen door of the pub, pulling some of his guards along with him. I plowed right after him, knocking him down as I left skid marks across his face. Lily and I headed for the car with El-Marad and half the bar on our tail.

"The water!" I screamed over my shoulder as I ran. "The water!" For we'd never make it to the car in time to lock ourselves in and start it. I didn't look back—just kept on running, straight out onto the little pier. There were fishing boats slopping around everywhere, loosely moored to the pilings. When I got to the end I looked over my shoulder.

The quay was pandemonium. El-Marad was just behind Lily. Sharrif had pried Carioca from his leg, still snapping, and was struggling with him while trying to peer into the darkness for something moving to shoot at. There were three guys pounding down the pier behind me, so I held my nose and jumped.

The last thing I saw as I hit the water was the tiny body of Carioca, lofted into the air by Sharrif and sailing toward the sea. Then I felt the cold dark waters of the Mediterranean closing around me. I felt the heavy weight of the Montglane Service pulling me down, down toward the bottom of the sea.

THE WHITE LAND

The land which warlike Britons now possess,
And therein have their mighty empire raised,
In antique times was savage wilderness,
Unpeopled, unmanured, unproved, unpraised. . . .

Ne did it then deserve a name to have,
Till that the venturous mariner that way,
Learning his ship from those white rocks to save,
Which all along the southern seacoast lay
Threatening unheedy wreck and rash decay,
For safety that same his sea-mark made,
And named it Albion.

—The Faerie Queene *(1590)*
Edmund Spenser

Ah, perfide, perfide Albion!

—*Napoleon, quoting*
Jacques Bénigne Bossuet (1692)

I t was four o'clock in the morning when the soldiers of William Pitt rapped loudly upon the door of Talleyrand's house in Kensington. Courtiade threw on his dressing gown and hastened upstairs to discover what the racket was all about. As he opened the door, he could see the flicker of lights just lit in nearby houses and a few curious neighbors peering through their draperies at the cadre of imperial soldiers standing before him on the step. Courtiade drew in his breath.

How long they'd waited in fear for this. Now it had come at last. Talleyrand was already descending the stairs wrapped closely in silken shawls that fell over his long dressing gown. His face was a mask of icy reserve as he crossed the small hall to the waiting soldiers.

"Monseigneur Talleyrand?" said the officer in charge.

"As you see." Talleyrand bowed, smiling coldly.

"Prime Minister Pitt conveys regrets he could not deliver these papers in person," replied the officer as if reciting a memorized speech. Pulling a packet of papers from his jacket, he thrust them at Talleyrand and continued. "The Republic of France, an unrecognized body of anarchists, has declared war upon the sovereign kingdom of Britain. All émigrés who support this so-called government, or who can be shown to have done so in the past, are hereby denied the shelter and protection of the house of Hanover and His Majesty George the Third. Charles Maurice de Talleyrand-Périgord, you are found guilty of seditious acts against the kingdom of Great Britain, of violating the Traitorous Correspondence Act of 1793, of conspiring, in your former capacity as assistant foreign minister of said country, against the sovereign. . . ."

"My dear fellow," said Talleyrand with a vicious laugh, looking up from the papers he'd been perusing. "This is absurd. France declared war upon England nearly a year ago! And Pitt knows full well I did everything in my power to prevent it. I'm wanted for treason in France—doesn't that say enough?" But his words were lost on the officers who stood at the door.

"Minister Pitt informs you that you have three days to quit England. Those are your deportation papers and travel permit. I wish you good morrow, Monseigneur."

Calling the command to about-face, he turned on his heel. Talleyrand watched in silence as the cadre of soldiers marched in cadence down the stone path that led from his door. Then he turned silently away. Courtiade closed the door.

"*Albus per fide decipare,*" said Talleyrand softly under his breath. "That is a quote from Bossuet, my dear Courtiade, one of the greatest orators France has ever known. He called it 'the White Land that deceives by trust': Perfidious Albion. A people who've never been ruled by their own race—first the Teutonic Saxons, then the Normans and Scots, and now the Germans, whom they loathe but are so like. They curse us, but they have short memories, for they killed a king of their own in Cromwell's day. Now they drive from their shores the only French ally who does not wish to be their master."

He stood, head bowed, his silken shawls trailing upon the floor. Courtiade cleared his throat.

"If the Monseigneur has selected a destination, I might begin the travel arrangements at once. . . ."

"Three days are not enough," said Talleyrand, bringing back his attention. "I'll go at dawn to Pitt's asking for an extension. I must secure funds and find a country that will accept me."

"But Madame de Staël . . . ?" said Courtiade politely.

"Germaine has done her best to get me to Geneva, but the government refuses. I am a traitor to everyone, it seems. Ah, Courtiade, how swiftly the streams of possibility freeze up in the winter of one's life!"

"The Monseigneur is hardly in the winter of life," Courtiade objected.

Talleyrand regarded him with cynical blue eyes. "I'm forty and a failure," he said. "Isn't that enough?"

"But not a failure in everything," said a soft voice from above.

The two men glanced up the stairway. There on the landing, leaning against the balustrade in a thin silk dressing gown, her long blond hair tumbling about her bare shoulders, stood Catherine Grand.

"The prime minister can have you tomorrow—it's soon enough," she said with a slow and sensual smile. "But tonight, you are mine."

Catherine Grand had entered Talleyrand's life four months ago, arriving at his house at midnight bearing the golden pawn of the Montglane Service. She had not left since.

She'd come in desperation, she said. Mireille had been sent to the guillotine, and with her last breath, she'd begged Catherine to take this chess piece to Talleyrand so he could hide it just as he had the others. This, at least, was her story.

She'd trembled in his arms, tears clinging to her thick lashes, her warm body pressed to his. How bitter she'd seemed at the death of Mireille, how comforting to Talleyrand in his own grief at these words—and how beautiful, as she fell on her knees to beg for mercy in her desperate plight.

Maurice had always been partial to beauty, in objects of art, in thoroughbred animals—and most especially, in women. Everything about Catherine Grand was beautiful: her flawless complexion, her magnificent body draped in impeccable clothes and jewels, the violet scent of her breath, the cascade of white-blond hair. And everything about her reminded him of Valentine. Everything but one: she was a liar.

But she was a beautiful liar. How could something so beautiful seem so dangerous, so treacherous, so foreign to his ways? The French had a saying that the best place to learn the ways of a foreigner was in bed. Maurice confessed himself only too willing to try.

The more he learned, the more she seemed perfectly suited to him in every way. Perhaps too perfectly. She loved the wines of Madeira, the music of Haydn and Mozart, and she preferred Chinese silks to French against her skin. She loved dogs, as he did, and bathed twice a day, a custom he'd always thought unique to himself. It was almost as if she'd studied his preferences—in fact, he felt certain she had. She knew more of his habits than Courtiade did. But on the subject of her past, her relationship with Mireille or her knowledge of the Montglane Service, her words rang false. That was when he'd decided to learn as much of her as she had of him. He wrote to those he could still trust in France, and his investigation began. The correspondence reaped interesting results.

She'd been born Catherine Noël Worlée—four years earlier than she claimed—to French parents at the Dutch colony of Tranquebar, India. At fifteen they'd married her off for money to an Englishman far older than herself—one George Grand. When she was seventeen, her lover, whom her husband had threatened to shoot, paid her fifty thousand rupees to leave India forever. Those funds enabled her to live lavishly in London first and later in Paris.

At Paris, suspicion had mounted that she was a spy for the British. Shortly before the Terror, her porter had been shot dead on her very doorstep, and Catherine herself had disappeared. Now, barely a year later, she'd sought out the exiled Talleyrand in London—a man without title, money, or country, with little hope that his prospects would change. Why?

As he loosened the pink silk ribbons of her gown and slipped it from her shoulders, Talleyrand smiled to himself. After all, he'd built his own career on his attractiveness to women. Women had brought him money, position, and power. How could he fault Catherine Grand for using her own considerable resources in the same fashion? But what did she want from him? Talleyrand thought he knew. There was only one thing in his possession she could be after—she wanted the Montglane Service.

But he wanted *her*. Though he knew she was too seasoned to be innocent, too driven to be genuinely passionate, too treacherous to be trusted—he wanted her with an urgency he could not control. Though everything about her was artifice and veneer, he wanted it nonetheless.

Valentine was dead. If Mireille had also been killed, then the Montglane Service had cost him the lives of the only two people he'd ever loved. Why should it not bring him something in return?

He embraced her with a terrible, urgent passion like a dry thirst. He would have her—and let the devils that tormented him be damned.

JANUARY 1794

But Mireille was far from dead—and not far from London. She was aboard a merchant ship that even now hove through the darkened waters of the English Channel as the coming storm closed fast upon them. As they churned through the choppy straits, she caught her first glimpse of the white cliffs of Dover.

In the six months since she'd left Charlotte Corday in her place at the Bastille, Mireille had traveled far. With the money sent by the abbess that she'd found in her paintbox, she'd hired a small fishing boat near the port of the Bastille to take her along the Seine until she'd found, at one of the docks on that twisted river, a ship bound for Tripoli. Secretly securing passage, she'd boarded and raised anchor in the Seine before Charlotte had even been taken to the tumbril.

As the coast of France melted away behind her, Mireille thought she could hear the groaning wheels of the cart that would now be carrying Charlotte to the guillotine. In her mind she heard the heavy steps on the scaffolding, the roll of the tambours, the swish of the blade in its long descent, the cheers of the crowd in the Place de la Révolution. Mireille felt the cold blade cutting away whatever remained of childhood and innocence, leaving only the fatal task. The task for which she'd been chosen—to destroy the White Queen and reunite the pieces.

But first there was another task. She would go to the desert to bring back her child. Given a second chance, she would overcome even Shahin's insistence to keep the infant as Kalim—a seer to his people. If he is a prophet, thought Mireille, let his destiny be twined with my own.

But now, as the North Sea winds struck the yards of sail with the first slashes of rain, Mireille wondered whether she'd been wise to tarry so long before heading to England—to Talleyrand, who had the pieces. She held Charlot's small hand in hers as he sat on her lap on the deck. Shahin stood beside them, watching another ship passing out into the turbulent English Channel. Shahin, in his long black robes, who'd refused to be parted from the little prophet he'd midwifed at birth. Now he raised his long arm toward the lowering clouds over the chalky cliffs.

"The White Land," he said quietly. "Domain of the White Queen. She is waiting—I can feel her presence even so far away."

"I pray we are not too late," said Mireille.

"I smell adversity," Shahin replied. "It always comes with storms, like a treacherous gift from the gods. . . ." He continued to watch the ship that, spreading its sails into the wind, was swallowed into the darkness of the violent Channel. The ship that—unknown to them—was carrying Talleyrand away toward the Atlantic main.

The one thought that Talleyrand had as his ship moved into the heavy darkness was not for Catherine Grand, but for Mireille. The age of illusion was ended, and perhaps Mireille's life as well. While he, at the age of forty, went to begin life anew.

After all, thought Talleyrand as he sat in his cabin assembling his papers, forty was not the end of life, nor was America the end of the world. Armed with letters of introduction to President Washington and Secretary of the Treasury Alexander Hamilton, he'd at least be in good company in Philadelphia. And of course he'd known Jefferson, who'd just resigned as Secretary of State, during the latter's tenure as ambassador to France.

Though he had little to see him through but his excellent health and what cash he'd raised from the sale of his library, he at least had the satisfaction of now having nine pieces of the Montglane Service in his possession, instead of the original eight. For despite all the connivings of the lovely Catherine Grand, he'd convinced her his hiding place would also secure the golden pawn she'd entrusted to him. He laughed when he thought of her expression at their tearful parting—when he'd tried to convince her to come with him, rather than worry about the pieces he'd left so well hidden in England!

Of course, they were in his trunks aboard the ship, thanks to the resourcefulness of the ever-alert Courtiade. Now they'd have a new home. He was thinking these thoughts as the first onslaught struck the ship.

He looked up in surprise as the ship moved violently beneath him. He was about to ring for assistance when Courtiade rushed into the cabin.

"Monseigneur, we are asked to come to the below deck at once," said the valet with his usual calm. But the swiftness of his movements as he collected the pieces of the Montglane Service from their hiding place in the trunk revealed the urgency of the situation. "The captain believes the ship will be driven upon the rocks. We are to prepare for the lifeboats. They will keep the top deck clear to work the sails, but we should be on the ready to come up at once if we cannot clear the shoals."

"*Which* shoals?" cried Talleyrand, leaping up in alarm, nearly upsetting his writing tools and inkstand.

"We've passed the Pointe Barfleur, Monseigneur," said Courtiade quietly, holding Talleyrand's morning coat as the ship tossed them back and forth. "We're driven upon the Normandy corniche." He bent to shove the pieces into a carrying case.

"My God," Talleyrand said, grasping the case. He limped toward the state-room door, leaning on the valet's shoulder as he clutched the bag. The ship took a sudden lurch to starboard, and the two men were hurled against the door. Clearing it with difficulty, they made their way along the narrow passage, where women were already sobbing hysterical commands to their children to hurry. By the time they reached the below deck, people were crammed everywhere— the shrieks, wails, and moans of their fear mingled with the pounding feet and cries of sailors on the upper deck, the sound of the Channel's waters striking in fury against the ship.

And then, in horror, they felt the ship itself falling beneath their feet as their bodies crashed into one another like eggs loose in a basket. The ship fell and continued falling as if it would never stop. Then it hit, and they heard the horrid splintering of wood. The water gushed through the jagged hole, washing them everywhere with powerful force as the gigantic ship foundered upon the rock.

∞

The icy rain slashed down upon the cobbled streets of Kensington as Mireille carefully picked her way over the slippery stones toward the grilled gates of Talleyrand's garden. Shahin followed, his long black robes drenched with rain, carefully holding little Charlot in his arms.

It had never occurred to Mireille that Talleyrand might no longer be in England. But before she'd even opened the gates, she saw with heavy heart the empty garden with its deserted gazebo, the boards across the windows of the house, the iron bar sealing the front door. Nevertheless she unfastened the gate and went along the stone path, her skirts trailing in the puddles.

Her futile banging echoed through the empty house. As the rain beat upon her bare head, she heard the hideous voice of Marat whispering, "You are too late—too late!" She leaned against the door, letting the rain wash over her in hard sheets, until she felt Shahin's hand beneath her arm, leading her away across the soggy lawn to the shelter of the gazebo.

In despair she threw herself facedown on the wooden bench that circled the inner perimeter, sobbing until she felt her heart would break. Shahin set Charlot on the floor, and the child crawled to Mireille, pulling himself up on her wet skirts to stand teetering on unsteady legs. He wrapped his tiny hand around her finger and gripped it with great force.

"Bah," said Charlot as Mireille looked into his startling blue eyes. He was frowning, his sage, serious face dripping beneath the wet hood of his little djellaba.

Mireille laughed. "Bah, *toi*," she said, pulling back the hood. She ruffled his silky red hair. "Your father has disappeared. You're supposed to be a prophet—why didn't you foresee this?"

Charlot looked at her gravely. "Bah," he said again.

Shahin sat beside her on the bench. His hawklike face, tinted the pale blue of his tribe, seemed even more mysterious in the eerie light reflecting from the violent storm that railed outside the lattices.

"In the desert," he said softly, "a man may be found by the tracks of his camel, for each beast leaves a print as recognizable as a face. Here, the path may be more difficult to follow. But a man, like a camel, has his own custom—dictated by his breeding, conformation, and gait."

Mireille laughed inwardly at the idea of tracking Talleyrand's limping foot-steps through the cobbled streets of London. But then she saw what Shahin meant.

"A wolf always returns to its known haunts?" she said.

"At least," said Shahin, "long enough to leave his scent."

But the wolf whose scent they sought had been removed—not only from London, but from the ship that was now lashed firmly to the rock that shredded it. With the other passengers, Talleyrand and Courtiade sat in the open boats hauling under oar to the darkened coastline of the Channel Islands and safe refuge from the driving storm.

It was refuge of another sort that relieved Talleyrand's mind, for this chain of little islets, nestled so close within the coastal waters of France, was in fact English and had been since the time of William of Orange.

The natives still spoke an antique form of Norman French that even the French could not comprehend. Though they paid their tithes to England for protection against plunder, they retained their ancient Norman law, coupled with the fiery independence of spirit that made them useful and brought them wealth in times of war. The Channel Isles were famous for their shipwrecks—and the great shipyards that outfitted everything from warships to privateers. It was to these yards that Talleyrand's ruined ship would mercifully be hauled for repairs. And meanwhile, though he might not rest in complete comfort here, at least he would be safe from French arrest.

Their rowboat sheered around the dark rocks of granite and *grès pourpre* that bound the coastline, the sailors pulling hard against the powerful waves until at last they sighted a stony strip of beach and hauled her in. The weary passengers went on foot in the driving rain, up mud trails that passed through high open fields of wet flax and dormant heather, into the nearest town.

Talleyrand and Courtiade, the satchel of pieces miraculously intact, adjourned to a nearby pub to warm themselves with brandy by the fire before seeking more permanent quarters. It was not clear how many weeks or months they might be stranded here waiting to continue their journey. Talleyrand inquired of the pubkeeper how fast their local shipyards could repair a ship with keel and hull as badly damaged as theirs.

"Ask the shipyard master," replied the man. "He's just come in from viewing the wreck. Having a pint in the corner there."

Talleyrand rose and crossed the room to a ruddy man in his mid-fifties who sat, both hands wrapped around his ale tankard. He looked up, saw Talleyrand and Courtiade standing there, and motioned them to be seated.

"From the wreck, are you?" said the older man, who'd overheard their conversation. "It was bound for America, they say. An unlucky place. It's where I'm from myself. I shall never fail to find amazement in how you French all flock to it, as if it were the promised land."

The man's speech indicated good breeding and education—his posture suggested he'd spent more hours in a saddle than in a shipyard. His bearing was that of one accustomed to command. Yet everything in his tone conveyed a weariness, a bitterness with life. Talleyrand resolved to know more.

"America seems a promised land to me," he said. "But I'm a man left with few options. If I return to my homeland, I'd swiftly taste the guillotine, and thanks to Minister Pitt I've recently been invited to part company with Britain as well. But I've letters of reference to some of your most distinguished countrymen—Secretary Hamilton and President Washington. Perhaps they'll find some use for an aging Frenchman out of work."

"I know them both well," his companion replied. "I served long in George Washington's command. It was he who made me brigadier and major general, and gave me command of Philadelphia."

"But I am astounded!" cried Talleyrand. If the fellow had held these posts, what on earth was he doing in obscurity, rebuilding wrecked ships in the Channel Isles and chandlering privateers? "Then perhaps you could see your way clear to write another letter in my behalf to your president? I hear he is difficult to see. . . ."

"I'm afraid I'm the one man whose reference would put you farther from his door," said the other with a grim smile. "Permit me to introduce myself. I am Benedict Arnold."

∞

The opera, the casinos, the gaming clubs, the salons . . . These were the places, thought Mireille, that Talleyrand would frequent. The places to which she must gain access in order to ferret him out in London.

But as she returned to her inn, she saw the leaflet pinned to the wall that revised all her decisions before they were made:

GREATER THAN MESMER!
An Astounding Feat of Memory!
Lauded by the French Philosophes!
Undefeated by Frederick the Great,
Phillip Stamma, or the Sire Legal!
Tonight!
BLINDFOLD EXHIBITION
by the Famous Chess Master
ANDRÉ PHILIDOR
Parsloe's Coffee House
St. James Street

Parsloe's on St. James Street was a coffee house and pub where chess was the principal activity. Within these walls one found the cream not only of the London chess world, but of European society. And the biggest attraction was André Philidor, the French chess player whose fame had spread through all of Europe.

As Mireille entered the heavy doors of Parsloe's that evening, she stepped into another world—a silent world of wealth. Before her spread an array of richly polished wood, dark green watered silk, and thick Indian carpets, lit by mellow oil lamps in smoky glass bowls.

The room was still nearly empty except for a few porters setting out the bar glasses and a solitary man, perhaps in his late fifties, who sat on an upholstered chair near the door. He was well upholstered himself, with broad midriff, heavy jowls, and a second chin that covered half his gold lace cravat. He was dressed in a velvet coat of such deep red that it nearly matched the broken veins of his nose. His beady eyes, from the depths of puffy folds, regarded Mireille with interest—and with even more interest the strange blue-faced giant who entered in purple silk robes behind her, bearing in his arms a tiny red-haired child!

Tossing down the last of his liquor, he set the glass on the table with a bang, calling to the barkeep for more. Then he fumbled to his feet and lurched toward Mireille as if crossing the unsteady deck of a ship.

"A red-haired wench, and prettier I've never seen," he said, slurring his words. "The red-gold tresses that break a man's heart, the kind that wars are started over—like Deirdre of the Sorrows." He pulled off his own foolish-looking peruke, sweeping it below his midriff in a mock bow and reviewing her figure on the way down and up. Then, in his drunken stupor, he shoved the powdered wig in his pocket, seized Mireille's hand, and kissed it gallantly.

"A woman of mystery, complete with exotic factotum! I introduce myself: I am James Boswell of Affleck, lawyer by vocation, historian by avocation, and descendant of the bonny Stuart kings." He nodded to her, suppressing a hiccup, and crooked out his arm. Mireille glanced at Shahin, whose face, as he understood no English, remained an impartial mask.

"Not the Monsieur Boswell who wrote the famous *History of Corsica*?" said Mireille in her charmingly accented English. This seemed too great a coincidence. First Philidor, then Boswell, of whom Letizia Buonaparte had had so much to say—both here at the same club. Perhaps not a coincidence after all.

"The same," said the swaying drunk, leaning against Mireille's arm as if she were to support *him*. "I suppose by your accent that you are French, and do not approve of the liberal views that I, as a young man, expressed against your government?"

"To the contrary, monsieur," Mireille assured him, "I find your views fascinating. And we in France have a new government now—more along the lines that you and Monsieur Rousseau proposed so long ago. You were acquainted with the gentleman, were you not?"

"I knew them all," he said carelessly. "Rousseau, Paoli, Garrick, Sheridan, Johnson—all the great ones, in whatever walk of life. Like a camp follower, I make my bed in the mud of history. . . ." He chucked her beneath the chin. "And other places as well," he said with a ribald laugh.

They'd reached his table, where a fresh drink was already waiting. Picking up the glass, he took another healthy swig. Mireille sized him up boldly. Though drunk, he was no fool. And it was surely no accident that two men connected with the Montglane Service were here tonight. She should be on her guard, for there might be others.

"And Monsieur Philidor, who is performing here tonight—do you know him as well?" she asked with careful innocence. But beneath the calm, her heart was pounding.

"Everyone interested in chess is interested in your famous countryman," replied Boswell, the glass halfway to his lips. "This is his first public appearance in some time. He's not been well. But perhaps you know that? As you're here tonight—shall I take it *you* play the game?" His beady eyes were now alert despite his intoxication, the double entendre too apparent.

"That is what I've come for, monsieur," said Mireille, dropping her school-girl charm and fixing him with an obtuse smile. "As you seem to know the gentleman, perhaps you'll be kind enough to introduce us when he arrives?"

"Only too charmed, I'm sure," said Boswell, though he didn't sound it. "In fact, he's here already. They're setting things up in the back room." Offering his arm, he led her to the wood-paneled chamber with brass chandeliers. Shahin followed silently.

There, several men had gathered. A tall, gangly man not much older than Mireille, with pale skin and a beaklike nose, was setting forth pieces on one of the chessboards at the center of the room. Beside these tables stood a short, sturdy fellow in his late thirties, with a luxurious head of sand-colored hair falling in loose curls about his face. He was speaking to an older man whose stooped back was turned to her.

She and Boswell approached the tables.

"My dear Philidor," he cried, slapping the older man on the shoulder with strength, "I interrupt only to introduce this ravishing young beauty from your homeland." He ignored Shahin, who watched with the black eyes of a falcon while remaining beside the door.

The older man turned and looked into Mireille's eyes. Clothed in the old-fashioned style of Louis XV—though his velvets and stockings seemed rather the worse for wear—Philidor was a man of dignity and aristocratic bearing. Though tall, he seemed as fragile as a dried flower petal, his translucent skin nearly as white as his powdered wig. He bowed slightly, pressing his lips to Mireille's hand. Then he addressed her with great sincerity.

"It's rare to find such radiant beauty beside a chessboard, madame."

"Rarer yet to find it dangling on the arm of an old degenerate like Boswell here," interjected the sandy-haired man, turning his dark, intense eyes upon Mireille. As he too bowed to kiss her hand, the tall young fellow with the hawklike nose pressed closer to be next in line.

"I have never had the pleasure of meeting Monsieur Boswell before entering this club," Mireille told her entourage. "It is Monsieur Philidor I've come to see. I am a great admirer of his."

"No more than we!" agreed the first young man. "My name is William Blake, and this young goat pawing at the earth beside me is William Words-worth. Two Williams for the price of one."

"A houseful of writers," added Philidor. "That is to say, a houseful of paupers—for these Williams both profess to be poets."

Mireille's mind was racing, trying to remember what she could of these two poets. The younger one, Wordsworth, had been at the Jacobin Club and met

David and Robespierre, who both knew Philidor as well. David had told her as much. She also recalled that Blake, whose name was already famous in France, had written works of great mysticism, some about the French Revolution. How did it all fit together?

"You've come to see the blindfold exhibition?" Blake was saying. "This feat is so remarkable that Diderot immortalized it in the *Encyclopédie*. It begins shortly. In the meanwhile, we scrape together our resources to offer you a cognac. . . ."

"I'd prefer some information," said Mireille, determined to take the upper hand. She might never again have these men together in a room, and there was surely a reason they were all here.

"You see, it's another chess game I am interested in, as Monsieur Boswell might have guessed. I know what he tried to discover in Corsica so many years ago, what Jean-Jacques Rousseau was seeking. I know what Monsieur Philidor learned from the great mathematician Euler while in Prussia, and what you, Monsieur Wordsworth, learned from David and Robespierre."

"We've no idea what you're talking about," Boswell interjected, though Philidor had grown pale and was groping for a seat.

"Yes, gentlemen, you know quite well what I am talking about," said Mireille, pressing her advantage as the four men stared at her. "I'm speaking of the Montglane Service, which you have met to discuss tonight. . . . You needn't look at me in such horror. Do you think I would be here if I didn't know your plans?"

"She knows nothing," Boswell said. "There are people arriving for the exhibition. I suggest we postpone this conversation. . . ."

Wordsworth had poured a glass of water, which he handed to Philidor, who looked as if he were about to faint. "Who are you?" the chess master asked Mireille, staring at her as if he'd seen a ghost.

Mireille took a deep breath. "My name is Mireille, and I come from Montglane," she said. "I know the Montglane Service exists, for I have held its pieces in my hands."

"You are David's ward!" exclaimed Philidor with a gasp.

"The one who disappeared!" said Wordsworth. "The one they were seeking. . . ."

"There is someone we must confer with," said Boswell hastily. "Before we go further—"

"There is no time," interrupted Mireille. "If you tell me what you know, I will confide in you as well. But now—not later."

"A bargain, I should say," mused Blake, pacing about as if lost in reverie. "I confess I'm interested in this service for reasons of my own. Whatever your cohorts' wishes, my dear Boswell, they are of no concern to me. I learned of the service in another fashion, by a voice crying in the wilderness. . . ."

"You're a fool!" cried Boswell, banging his fist drunkenly on the table. "You think the ghost of your dead brother gives you a unique patent upon this service. But there are others who understand its value—who are not drowning in mysticism."

"If you regard my motives as too pure," snapped Blake, "you should not have invited me to join your cabal tonight." With a cold smile, he turned to Mireille. "My brother Robert died some years ago," he explained. "He was all I loved on this green earth. As his spirit left his body, it spoke to me with a sigh—and told me to seek the Montglane Service, the wellspring and source of all mysteries since time began. Mademoiselle, if you know something of this object, I shall be glad to share the little *I* know. And Wordsworth, too, if I'm not misled."

In horror, Boswell turned and hurried from the room. Philidor glanced sharply at Blake, putting his hand on the younger man's arm as if to caution him.

"Perhaps at last," said Blake, "I shall lay my brother's bones to rest."

He took Mireille to a seat near the back and went off to get her cognac as Wordsworth settled Philidor at the table at center. Guests were filtering into the room as Shahin, with Charlot in his arms, came to sit behind Mireille.

"The drunken one left the building," Shahin said quietly. "I smell danger. Al-Kalim feels it, too. We must leave this place at once."

"Not yet," said Mireille. "There is something I must learn first."

Blake returned with Mireille's drink and sat beside her. The last of the guests were taking their seats when Wordsworth came back to join them. A man in front was explaining the rules of play as Philidor sat blindfolded at the board. The two poets leaned toward Mireille as Blake began in low voice.

"There's a well-known tale in England," he said, "regarding the famous French philosopher François-Marie Arouet, known as Voltaire. Around Christmas of 1725—over thirty years before I was born—Voltaire one night escorted the actress Adrienne Lecouvreur to the Comédie-Française in Paris. During the entr'acte, Voltaire was publicly insulted by the Chevalier de Rohan Chabot, who shouted across the lobby, 'Monsieur de Voltaire, Monsieur Arouet—why don't you decide what your name is?' Voltaire, never at a loss for retorts, called back, 'My name begins with me—yours ends with you.' Not long after, the chevalier had Voltaire beaten by six rogues for this retort."

"Despite the injunction against dueling," Blake continued, "the poet went to Versailles and openly demanded satisfaction from the chevalier. He was tossed into the Bastille for his pains. While pining there in his cell, he got an idea. Appealing to the authorities not to let him languish yet another stay in prison, he proposed to go into voluntary exile instead—in England."

"They say," Wordsworth chimed in, "that during his first stay in the Bastille Voltaire had deciphered a secret manuscript related to the Montglane Service. Now he conceived the notion of journeying here to present this as a sort of puzzle to our famous mathematician and scientist Sir Isaac Newton, whose works he'd read with admiration. Newton was old and weary, and had lost interest in his work, which no longer presented a challenge. Voltaire proposed to provide the required spark—a challenge not only to decipher what he himself had done, but to unravel the deeper problem of its true meaning. For they say, madame, this manuscript described a great secret buried in the Montglane Service—a formula of enormous power."

"I know," Mireille hissed irritably as she removed Charlot's fingers, which were entangled in her hair. The rest of the audience watched with eyes riveted upon the board at center, where the blindfolded Philidor listened to his opponent's moves read out as, his back to the board, he called out his replies.

"And did Sir Isaac succeed in resolving the puzzle?" she asked impatiently, feeling Shahin's tension to depart, though she could not see his face.

"Indeed," replied Blake. "That is just what we wish to tell you. It was the last thing he ever did—for the following year he was dead. . . ."

THE TALE OF THE TWO POETS

Voltaire was in his early thirties—Newton eighty-three—when the two men met at London in May of 1726. Newton had suffered a breakdown some thirty years before. He'd published little of scientific importance since.

When they met, the slender, cynical Voltaire with his rapier wit must at first have been disconcerted by Newton, fat and pink with a mane of snowy hair and a languid, almost docile manner. Though lionized by society, Newton was in fact a solitary man who spoke little and kept his deepest thoughts jealously guarded—quite the opposite of the young French admirer who'd already been twice incarcerated in the Bastille for tactlessness and rash temper.

But Newton was always tempted by a problem, whether mathematical or mystical in nature. When Voltaire arrived with his mystical manuscript, Sir Isaac eagerly took it to his chambers and disappeared for several days, leaving the poet in suspense. At last he invited Voltaire back to his study, a place filled with optical equipment and lined with walls of musty books.

"I have published only a fragment of my work," the scientist told the philosopher. "And that, only by the insistence of the Royal Society. Now I am old and rich, and may do as I like—but I still refuse to publish. Your fellow Cardinal Richelieu understood such reservations, or he'd not have written his journal in code."

"You've deciphered it, then?" said Voltaire.

"That, and more," said the mathematician with a smile, taking Voltaire to the corner of his study where sat a very large metal box that was locked. He extracted a key from his pocket and looked at the Frenchman carefully. "Pandora's box. Shall we open it?" he said. When Voltaire eagerly agreed, they turned the key in the rusty lock.

Here were manuscripts hundreds of years old, some nearly crumbling to dust through the neglect of many years. But most were well worn and Voltaire suspected by the hand of Newton himself. As Newton lifted them lovingly from the metal trunk, Voltaire glimpsed the titles in surprise: *De Occulta Philosophia, The Musaeum Hermeticum, Transmutatione Metallorum* . . . heretical books by al-Jabir, Paracelsus, Villanova, Agrippa, Lully. Works of dark magic forbidden by every Christian church. Works of alchemy—dozens of them—and beneath them, bound neatly in paper covers, thousands of pages of experimental notes and analyses in Newton's own hand.

"But you are the greatest proponent of reason in our century!" said Voltaire, staring at the books and papers in disbelief. "How can you wade in this morass of mysticism and magic?"

"Not magic," Newton corrected him, "but science. The most dangerous of all sciences, whose purpose is to alter the course of nature. Reason was invented by man only to help decipher the formulas created by God. In everything natural there is a code—and to each code a key. I've re-created many experiments of the ancient alchemists, but this document you give me says the final key is contained in the Montglane Service. If this were true, I would give everything I've discovered—everything I've invented—for one hour alone with those pieces."

"What would this 'final key' reveal that you are unable to discover yourself through research and experimentation?" asked Voltaire.

"The stone," Newton replied. "The key to *all* secrets."

When the poets paused breathlessly, Mireille turned at once to Blake. The murmurs of the audience at the progress of the blindfold play had successfully masked their voices from all.

"What did he mean—the stone?" she asked, gripping the poet's arm forcefully.

"Of course, I forget." Blake laughed. "I've studied these things myself, so I assume everyone knows. The aim of all alchemical experiments is to arrive at a solution that reduces to a cake of dry reddish powder—at least, that's how it's described. I've read Newton's papers. Though they were suppressed from publication due to embarrassment—no one really believed he'd spent so much time on such nonsense—they were fortunately never destroyed."

"And what *is* this cake of reddish powder?" pressed Mireille, so anxious she could nearly scream. Charlot was tugging on her from behind. She didn't require a prophet to tell her she'd idled here too long.

"Why, that's it," Wordsworth said, leaning forward, his eyes bright with excitement. "This cake *is* the stone. A piece of it combined with base metal turns it to gold. When dissolved and swallowed, it's supposed to heal all your ills. They call it the philosophers' stone. . . ."

Mireille's mind churned through all she knew. The sacred stones worshiped by the Phoenicians, the white stone described by Rousseau, embedded in the wall of Venice: "If a man could say and do as he thinks," read the inscription, "he'd see how he might be transformed." The White Queen floated on the wall before her eyes, transforming a man into a god. . . .

Suddenly Mireille stood up. Wordsworth and Blake jumped to their feet in surprise.

"What is it?" whispered the young Wordsworth quickly. Several people had glanced around in irritation at the disturbance.

"I must go," Mireille said, planting a kiss on his cheek as he blushed beet red. She turned to Blake and took his hand. "I am in danger—I cannot remain. But you shall not be forgotten." She turned, followed by Shahin, who rose and moved like a shadow behind her as she swept from the room.

"Perhaps we should go after her," said Blake. "But somehow I think we'll hear from her again. A remarkable woman, you agree?"

"Yes," Wordsworth said. "I see her in a poem already." Then he laughed as he saw Blake's worried expression. "Oh, not one of mine! One of yours. . . ."

Mireille and Shahin moved swiftly through the outer room, their feet sinking into the soft carpeting. The porters lounging about the bar hardly noticed as they passed like wraiths. As they went outside into the street, Shahin caught Mireille by the arm and pulled her against the darkened wall. Charlot, in Shahin's arms, gazed into the wet darkness with the eyes of a cat.

"What is it?" whispered Mireille, but Shahin put his finger to her lips. She strained her eyes in the darkness, and then she heard the sound of soft footsteps crossing the wet pavement. She saw two shadowy forms outlined in the mist.

The shadows approached stealthily to the very door of Parsloe's, only a few feet from where Shahin and Mireille waited, not breathing. Even Charlot was as silent as a mouse. The door of the club opened, emitting a crack of light— illuminating the shapes on the wet street. One was the heavy, drunken Boswell, draped in a long dark cape. The other . . . Mireille gaped with open mouth as she watched Boswell turn and offer his hand.

It was a woman, slender and beautiful, who threw back the hood of her cape. Out spilled the long blond hair of Valentine! It was Valentine! Mireille let out a muffled sob and started to step forward into the light, but Shahin restrained her with iron hand. She wheeled to him in anger, but he bent swiftly to her ear.

"The White Queen," he whispered. Mireille turned back in horror as the door of the club swung shut, leaving them once again in darkness.

THE CHANNEL ISLANDS   FEBRUARY 1794

During the weeks of his stay waiting for the repair of his ship, Talleyrand had many opportunities to get to know Benedict Arnold, the famous traitor who'd betrayed his country by becoming a spy for the British government.

It was odd, these two men sitting together over checkers or chess at the inn. Each had had a promising career, held high positions and the respect of peers and superiors alike. But both had formed enmities that had cost them their reputations and livelihoods. Arnold, returning to England after his espionage was discovered, had found that no position was waiting for him in the military. He was a subject of scorn, left to fend for himself. This explained the situation in which Talleyrand now found him.

But though Arnold could not give a letter of reference to Americans in lofty places, Talleyrand saw that he *could* provide information about the country he himself was soon to journey to. Over the weeks he'd plied the shipyard master with questions. And now, on the last day of his stay before his ship departed for the New World, Talleyrand questioned further as the two men sat at the inn over a game of chess.

"What are the social occupations in America?" said Talleyrand. "Do they have salons as in England or in France?"

"Once you've left Philadelphia or New York—which is full of Dutch immigrants—you'll find little but frontier towns. The people sit by the fire at night with a book, or have a game of chess as we're doing now. There isn't much in the way of society outside the eastern seaboard. But chess is nearly the national pastime. They say even the fur trappers carry a small set on their journeys."

"Really," said Talleyrand. "I'd no idea there was that level of intellect present in what were, until very recently, isolated colonies."

"Not intellect—but morality," Arnold said. "That's how *they* look at it, anyway. Perhaps you've read the work by Ben Franklin that's so popular in America? It's called *The Morals of Chess*—and speaks of how we might learn many lessons in life from a thorough study of the game." He laughed a little bitterly and looked up from the board into Talleyrand's eyes. "It was Franklin, you know, who was so anxious to solve the riddle of the Montglane Service."

Talleyrand looked at him sharply. "What on earth are you talking about?"

he asked. "You mean that ridiculous legend is discussed even on the opposite side of the Atlantic?"

"Ridiculous or not," Arnold said with a smile the other couldn't fathom, "they say old Ben Franklin spent a lifetime trying to decipher the puzzle. Even went down to Montglane during his tenure here as ambassador to France. It's a place in the south of France."

"I know where it is," snapped Talleyrand. "What was he seeking?"

"Why, the chessboard of Charlemagne. I thought everyone here knew of it. They said it was buried at Montglane. Benjamin Franklin was an excellent mathematician and chess player. He developed a Knight's Tour that he claimed was his idea of how the Montglane Service was laid out."

"Laid out?" said Talleyrand, feeling a frightening chill pass over him as he realized what the man's words suggested. Even in America, thousands of miles from the horrors of Europe, he'd not be safe from the grasp of the horrid service that had so affected his life.

"Yes," said Arnold, moving a piece across the board. "You must ask Alexander Hamilton, a fellow Freemason. They say Franklin deciphered a part of the formula—and turned it over to them before he died. . . ."

THE EIGHTH SQUARE

"The Eighth Square at last!" she cried. . . . "Oh, how glad I am to get here! And what *is* this on my head?" she exclaimed in a tone of dismay . . . as she lifted it off, and set it on her lap to make out what it could possibly be.

It was a golden crown.

—Through the Looking-Glass
Lewis Carroll

dragged myself out of the water and onto the stony crescent of beach that fronted the pine forest, nearly gagging from all the salt water I'd swallowed—but I was alive. And it was the Montglane Service that had saved me.

The weight of those pieces in my shoulder bag had plummeted me to the bottom before I could take a stroke, dragging me out of range of those little chunks of lead that were striking the water above me—pumped from the handguns of Sharrif's companions. Since the water was only ten feet deep, I could walk up the floor of sand, dragging the bag along with me, feeling my way among the boats until I could stick my nose out for air. Still using the bevy of fishing boats as camouflage and my satchel as an anchor, I worked my way along the shallows in the wet black night.

I opened my eyes on the beach, trying to gauge in bleary despair exactly where I'd landed. Though it was nine o'clock and nearly dark, I could see a few twinkling lights that looked like the port of Sidi-Fredj about two miles away. I could get there on foot if I weren't captured, but where was Lily?

I felt my soggy shoulder bag and fumbled inside. The pieces were all still there. God knew what else I'd lost by dragging this bag through the dreck on the bottom, but my two-hundred-year-old manuscript was tucked in a water-proof zippered pouch where I kept my makeup. If only it hadn't leaked.

I was plotting my next move when a soggy object came crawling from the water a few yards down the beach. In the deep purple light it looked like a newly hatched chicken, but the little yap it gave as it staggered to me and threw itself on my lap gave no doubt—it was a bedraggled Carioca. I had no way to dry him, since I was drenched as well. So I picked him up as I got to my feet, tucked him under my arm, and headed into the pine forest—a shortcut home.

I'd lost one shoe in the water, so I discarded the other and went barefoot over the soft carpet of pine needles, using my homing instincts to head for the port. I'd been traveling about fifteen minutes when I heard a twig snap nearby. I froze and stroked the trembling Carioca, praying he wouldn't pull the same routine he had with the bats.

But it made no difference. A few seconds later I was hit full in the face with a large floodlight. I stood there squinting into it, my heart frozen with fear. Then a soldier in khaki came around into the light and approached me. In his hands was a big machine gun with a belt of nasty-looking bullets hanging from the side. The gun was pointed at my stomach.

"Freeze!" he cried unnecessarily. "Who are you? Explain yourself! What are you doing here?"

"Taking my dog for a swim," I said. I held Carioca up in the light as proof. "I'm Catherine Velis. I'll show you my identification. . . ."

I realized the papers I was about to reach for were soaked, and I didn't want him to search my bag. I started talking fast.

"I was walking my dog over at Sidi-Fredj," I said, "when he fell off the pier. I jumped in to rescue him, but we were washed down here by the current. . . ." God, I suddenly realized there *was* no current in the Mediterranean. I hastily rattled on. "I work for OPEC, for Minister Kader. He'll vouch for me. I live just over there." I raised my arm, and he waved his gun in my face.

I decided to try another approach—the Ugly American.

"I tell you it's critical I see Minister Kader!" I said forcefully, drawing myself up with a dignity that must have looked ridiculous in my dripping-wet condition. "Do you have any idea *who I am*?!" The soldier glanced over his shoulder at his partner, obscured behind the floodlight.

"You are attending the conference, perhaps?" he said, turning back to me.

Of course! That's why these soldiers were patrolling the woods! That's what the blockade on the road was all about. That's why Kamel had sounded so urgent when he'd kept insisting I be back by the end of the week. The OPEC conference had begun!

"Absolutely," I assured him. "I'm one of the key delegates. They'll be wondering where I am."

The soldier walked around behind the strobe light and muttered with his companion in Arabic. After a few minutes they switched off the light. The older one spoke apologetically.

"Madame, we will see you to your group. The delegates are just now assembling at the Restaurant du Port. Perhaps you'd like to retire to your quarters first and change?"

I agreed that would be a very good idea. After half an hour or so, my escort and I arrived at my apartment. The guard waited outside while I quickly threw on another outfit, blow-dried my hair, and fluffed up Carioca as best I could.

I could scarcely leave the pieces in my apartment, so I dug a duffel bag from the closet, tossing them inside along with Carioca. The book Minnie had given me was damp but, thanks to its watertight compartment, mercifully not destroyed. Thumbing the pages, I gave it a once-over with the blower, too, then put it in the duffel and went out to the waiting guard, who escorted me across the port.

The Restaurant du Port was a huge building with high ceilings and marble floors, where I'd often taken lunch while still living at El Riadh. We passed through the long colonnade of key-shaped arches that ran from the plaza beside the port, then we ascended the wide flight of steps rising from the water to the brightly lighted glass walls of the restaurant. There were soldiers every thirty paces, facing the port with their hands tucked behind them, rifles slung over their backs. When we reached the entrance I peered through the glass walls to see if I could locate Kamel.

They'd rearranged the restaurant so there were five long rows of tables stretching from where we stood to the far side, perhaps a hundred feet away. Around the center floor was a raised U-shaped terrazzo with brass railings overlooking the main floor, where loftier dignitaries had been seated. Even from here the array of power was impressive. Here were not only the oil ministers, but the rulers as well, of every OPEC nation. Uniforms with gold braid, embroidered robes with leopard pillbox hats, white robes, and charcoal business suits all mingled together in a colorful mélange.

Our surly door guard relieved my soldier of his weapon and gestured to the marble terrace a few feet above the crowd. The soldier marched before me between the long rows of white-clothed tables to the short staircase at center. As we crossed I could see the horrified expression on Kamel's face from thirty paces. I went up to the table, the soldier clicked his heels, and Kamel rose to his feet.

"Mademoiselle Velis!" said Kamel. He turned to the soldier. "Thank you for bringing our esteemed associate to our table, Officer. Was she lost?" He was looking at me from the corner of his eye as if I'd soon have some explaining to do.

"In the pine forest, Minister," said the soldier. "An unfortunate mishap involving a dog. We understood she was expected at your table. . . ." He glanced at the table, completely filled with men, where no place was set for me.

"You've done quite well, Officer," Kamel said. "You may return to your post. Your swift action will not be forgotten." The soldier clicked again and departed.

Kamel was waving his hand for a passing waiter and asked him to set up another place setting. He remained standing until the chair arrived, then we took our seats. Kamel was introducing me around.

"Minister Yamini," he said, indicating the plump, pink, angelic-faced Saudi OPEC minister to my right, who nodded politely and half rose. "Mademoiselle Velis is the American expert who created the brilliant computer system and the analyses I spoke of at this afternoon's meeting," he added. Minister Yamini raised an eyebrow to show he was impressed.

"You already know Minister Belaid, I believe," Kamel went on as Abdelsalaam Belaid, who'd signed my contract, rose with a twinkle in his eye and pressed my hand. His walnut complexion and smooth skin, his silvery temples and shiny balding head, reminded me of an elegant mafia capo.

Minister Belaid turned to his right to speak to his table companion, who was busily engaged in conversation with his other neighbor. The two men broke off to look at him, and I turned green as I recognized them.

"Mademoiselle Catherine Velis, our computer expert," said Belaid in his whispering voice. The long sad face of the president of Algeria, Houari Boumédienne, looked once at me, then back at his chief minister, as if wondering what the hell I was doing there. Belaid shrugged his shoulders with a noncommittal smile.

"Enchanté," said the president.

"King Faisal of Saudi Arabia," continued Belaid, indicating the intense, hawklike man who peered at me from beneath his white headdress. He did not smile but merely nodded once in my direction.

I picked up the wineglass before me and took a healthy slug. How in God's name was I going to tell Kamel what was going on—and how was I going to get out of here to rescue Lily? With table companions like these, I could hardly excuse myself, even to go to the bathroom.

Just then there was a sudden commotion down on the main floor a few feet below us. Everyone turned to see what was going on. The floor was crowded— there must have been six hundred men filling the room. All were seated except the waiters, who were scurrying about setting forth the baskets of bread, plates of crudités, and refills of water and wine. But a tall, dark man had entered, dressed in a long white robe. His handsome face was a dark mask of passion as he moved down the long row of tables, swinging a riding crop. The waiters, cowering in clusters, were making no move to stop him. I stared in disbelief as I watched him flick the crop at tables on either side as he passed, sweeping the wine bottles in fury to the floor. All the diners sat in silence as he moved along the rows, bottles crashing to his right and left.

With a sigh, Boumédienne rose from our table and spoke quickly to the majordomo, who'd hurried to his side. Then Algeria's sad-eyed president left and descended to the floor, where he waited for the handsome man to reach him in his swift strides down the rows.

"Who is that guy?" I whispered to Kamel.

"Muammar Khaddafi. Of Libya," Kamel said quietly. "He made a speech at the conference today about how the followers of al-Islam should not drink. I see he means to follow his words with actions. He's quite mad. They say he's hired assassins in Europe to attack prominent OPEC ministers."

"I know," said the cherubic Yamini, dimpling with a smile. "My name is very high on the list." It didn't seem to concern him much. He helped himself to a stick of celery and munched it complacently.

"But why?" I whispered to Kamel. "Just because they drink?"

"Because we insist upon making the embargo economic rather than political," he replied. Lowering his voice, he said through clenched teeth, "Now that we have a moment, just what is going on? Where have you been? Sharrif has turned this country upside down looking for you. Though he'll hardly arrest you here, you're in serious trouble."

"I know," I whispered back, looking down on the floor, where Boumédienne was speaking quietly with Khaddafi, his long sad face lowered so I couldn't read its expression. The diners were picking up the wine bottles and handing them, dripping, to waiters, who surreptitiously replaced them with fresh ones.

"I've got to speak with you alone," I went on. "Your Persian pal has got my friend. Half an hour ago I was swimming down the coast. There's a wet dog in my duffel bag—and something more that might interest you. I have to get out of here. . . ."

"Good Lord," said Kamel softly. "You mean you actually have them? Here?" He looked around at the other diners, camouflaging his panic with a smile.

"So you *are* in the Game," I whispered, smiling myself.

"Why do you think I brought you here?" Kamel whispered back. "It cost me bloody hell trying to explain when you disappeared just before the conference."

"We can discuss that later. For now, I've got to get out of here and rescue Lily."

"Leave it to me—we'll do something. Where is she?"

"La Madrague," I said under my breath.

Kamel gaped at me, but just then Houari Boumédienne returned to the table and resumed his seat. Everyone smiled in his direction, and King Faisal spoke in English.

"Our Colonel Khaddafi is not the sort of fool he looks," he said, his large, liquid falcon's eyes trained on the president of Algeria. "You remember at the conference of unaligned nations, when someone complained of Castro's presence—what he said?" The king turned to Yamini, his minister, to my right. "Colonel Khaddafi said that if any country was barred from Third World participation by virtue of receiving money from the two superpowers, then we should all pack our bags and go home. He finished by reading a list of the financial and arms arrangements of half the countries present—quite accurate, I might add. I should not write him off as a religious zealot. Not at all."

Boumédienne was looking at me now. He was a man of mystery. No one knew his age, his background, or even his birthplace. Since his success spearheading the revolution ten years before, and the subsequent "coup militaire" that left him president of the country, he'd brought Algeria to the forefront of OPEC and made her the Switzerland of the Third World.

"Mademoiselle Velis," he said, addressing me directly for the first time, "in your work for the ministry, have you ever made the acquaintance of Colonel Khaddafi?"

"Never," I said.

"That's odd," said Boumédienne. "For he noticed you at our table as we were speaking below, and said something that seemed to indicate otherwise."

I felt Kamel stiffen beside me. He gripped my arm forcefully beneath the table. "Really?" he said casually. "And what was that, Mr. President?"

"Just a case of mistaken identity, I suppose," said the president in an offhand way, turning his large dark eyes on Kamel. "He asked if she was the one."

"The one?" said Minister Belaid, confused. "What's that supposed to mean?"

"I suppose," said the president casually, "he meant the one who'd prepared these computer projections we've heard so much about from Kamel Kader." Then he turned away.

I started to speak to Kamel under my breath, but he shook his head and turned to his boss, Belaid. "Catherine and I should like the opportunity to review the figures before they're presented tomorrow. Is it possible we could excuse ourselves from the banquet? Otherwise, I fear we'll be up all night working."

Belaid did not believe a word of this, as was clear from his expression. "I'd like a word with you first," he said, rising and drawing Kamel aside. I got up, too, toying idly with my napkin. Yamini leaned forward.

"It's been a pleasure having you at my table, regardless how brief a time," he assured me with a dimpled smile.

Belaid was standing near the wall whispering to Kamel as waiters rushed by bearing platters of steaming food. As I approached, he said, "Mademoiselle, we thank you for all you've accomplished in our behalf. Don't keep Kamel Kader up too late." He went back to the table.

"Can we split now?" I whispered to Kamel.

"Yes, at once," he said, taking me by the arm and hurrying me down the stairs. "Abdelsalaam received a message from the secret police that they're looking for you. They said you escaped arrest at La Madrague. He learned of it during dinner. He places you in my trust rather than turning you in at once. I hope you understand the position you put me in if you disappear again."

"For God's sake," I hissed at him as we plowed our way among the tables, "you know why I went to the desert. And you know where we're going now! It's I who should ask the questions here. Why didn't you tell me you were involved in the Game? Is Belaid a player, too? How about Therese? And what about that Muslim crusader from Libya who said he knew me—what was that all about?"

"I only wish I knew," said Kamel grimly. He tossed a nod to the guard, who bowed as we passed. "We'll take my car to La Madrague. You must tell me everything that's happened so we can help your friend."

We got into his car in the dimly lighted parking lot. He turned to me in the darkness so only the glint of his yellow eyes reflected the glow of the street lamps. I filled him in quickly on Lily's plight, then asked him about Minnie Renselaas.

"I have known Mokhfi Mokhtar since childhood," he said. "She chose my father for a mission—to form an alliance with El-Marad and penetrate white territory, the mission that resulted in his death. Therese worked for my father. Now, though she works at the Poste Centrale, she actually serves Mokhfi Mokhtar, as do her children."

"Her children?" I said, trying to visualize the flamboyant switchboard operator as a mother.

"Valerie and Michel," said Kamel. "You've met the boy Michel, I believe. He calls himself Wahad. . . ."

So Wahad was Therese's child! The plot was as thick as pea soup—and since I no longer believed in coincidences, I tucked in the back of my mind the information that Valerie was also the name of a housemaid who worked in the employ of Harry Rad. But I had bigger fish to fry than singling out the pawns.

"I don't get it," I interrupted. "If your father was sent on this mission and he failed—that means the white team got whatever pieces he was after, right? So when does the Game ever end? When someone collects all the pieces?"

"Sometimes I think this game will never be over," said Kamel bitterly, starting the car and pulling out down the long road that led past high walls of cactus on the way out of Sidi-Fredj. "But your friend's life will be, if we don't reach La Madrague soon."

"Are you enough of a big cheese to waltz in and demand they give her back?"

Kamel smiled coldly in the reflection of the dashboard lights. We were pulling up to the roadblock Lily and I had seen coming the other way. He flipped his pass out the window, and the guard motioned him by.

"The only thing El-Marad would rather have than your friend," he said calmly, "is what you claim you have in that duffel bag. And I'm not referring to the dog. Do you think it a fair trade?"

"You mean give him the pieces in exchange for Lily?" I said, aghast. Then I realized that was probably the only way we'd get in and out of there alive. "Couldn't we just give him *one* of the pieces?" I suggested.

Kamel laughed, then reached over and squeezed my shoulder. "Once he knows you have them," he said, "El-Marad will sweep us from the board."

Why hadn't we brought a bunch of soldiers with us, or even some OPEC delegates? I could've used that fanatical Khaddafi with his riding crop right about now, sweeping down on his enemies like a one-man Mongol horde. But instead I had the charming Kamel, going to his death with perfect composure and dignity, just as his father might have done ten years before.

Instead of stopping the car before the lighted pub, where our rental car still sat, Kamel proceeded down the port through the one short block of deserted town. He stopped at the end, where a flight of steps ran up the steep cliff that sheltered the tiny curve of inlet. There wasn't a soul in sight, and the wind had come up, driving scudding clouds across the broad surface of the moon. We got out, and Kamel pointed to the top of the cliff, where a small but lovely house sat among the ice plants that toppled over the rocky slope. On the sea side, the cliff sheared off and dropped a hundred feet to the water below.

"El-Marad's summer home," Kamel said softly. There were lights on in the house, and as we started our ascent of the rickety wooden stairs, I heard the commotion from within, echoing down the cliff. I could make out Lily's voice, screaming above the sloshing of the waves.

"You put one hand on me, you trashy dog assassin," she yelled, "and it's the last thing you ever do!"

Kamel glanced at me in the moonlight with a smile. "Perhaps she doesn't need our help," he said.

"She's talking to Sharrif," I told him. "He's the one who threw her dog in the drink." Carioca was already making noises inside my bag. I put my hand in and scratched him on the head. "Time to do your stuff, little fluff," I told him, extracting him from the bag.

"I think you should go back down and get the car running," whispered Kamel, handing me the car key. "Let me do the rest."

"Not on your life," I told him, my anger rising at the scuffling sounds I heard coming from the house above. "Let's take them by surprise." I put Carioca on the steps, and he bounced up them like a crazy Ping-Pong ball. Kamel and I were right behind him. I held on to the car key.

The entrance to the house was through the bank of French windows that ran along the sea side. The path leading to them, I observed, was balanced precipitously close to the ledge, separated only by a low rock wall draped with nasturtiums. This might work to our advantage.

Carioca was already squeaking his little claws across the glass doors as I came around the side and quickly glanced inside to case the joint. Three thugs were leaning against the left wall, their jackets open so you could see their shoulder holsters. The floor was slippery enamel tile in blue and gold. At the center, Lily sat on a chair with Sharrif hovering over her. She leapt up when she heard Carioca's ruckus, and Sharrif slammed her back down again. It looked like there was a bruise on her cheek. In the far corner of the room sat El-Marad in a pile of cushions. He idly moved a chess piece across the board on the low copper table before him.

Sharrif had wheeled to the windows, where we stood illuminated by the spotty moonlight. I swallowed hard and put my face up to the glass panes so he could see me.

"Five of them, three and a half of us," I whispered to Kamel, who stood silently beside me as Sharrif moved toward the door, gesturing for his cohorts to keep their weapons sheathed. "You take the thugs. I'll take El-Marad. I believe Carioca has already chosen his poison," I added as Sharrif opened the door a crack.

Glancing down at his little arch nemesis, Sharrif said, "You come in—but *it* stays outside."

I shoved Carioca to one side so Kamel and I could enter.

"You saved him!" cried Lily, beaming at me. Then, sneering at Sharrif, she added, "People who threaten defenseless animals are just trying to cover up their own impotence. . . ."

Sharrif was moving toward her as if to strike her again when El-Marad spoke softly from the corner, glancing at me with a sinister smile.

"Mademoiselle Velis," he said, "how very fortunate you've returned—and with an escort. One would have thought Kamel Kader more intelligent than to bring you to me twice. But now that we're all here . . ."

"Let's skip the pleasantries," I said, crossing the room toward him. As I passed Lily, I pressed the car key into her palm and whispered, "The door—now."

"You know what we're here for," I said to El-Marad as I kept on moving.

"And you know what I want," he told me. "Shall we call it a trade?"

I stopped beside his low table and glanced over my shoulder. Kamel had positioned himself near the thugs and was asking one of them for a light for the cigarette he had cupped in his hands. Lily was at the French windows with Sharrif just behind. She'd crouched down and was tapping on the glass with her long red fingernails as Carioca's slobbering tongue licked the other side. We were all in position—it was now or never.

"My friend the minister doesn't seem to think you're exactly scrupulous about keeping bargains," I told the carpet trader. He looked up and started to speak, but I interrupted. "But if it's the pieces you want," I said, "here they are!"

I swung the duffel bag from my shoulder and with one unbroken circle brought it up as high as my arm could reach and down, down with all its massive weight—crashing into his head. His eyes rolled back, and he started to slump sideways as I whirled to the pandemonium that was going on behind me.

Lily had shoved open the French windows, Carioca was barreling into the room, and I was swinging the blackjack of my duffel bag, running toward the thugs. The first one had his gun halfway out when I hit him. The second was doubled over with a stomach punch from Kamel. We were all in a pile on the ground as the third freed his gun from the holster and pointed it at me.

"Over here, you fool!" screamed Sharrif, beating Carioca away with rapid kicks. Lily was tearing up turf, halfway out the door. The thug raised his gun, pointed it at her, and squeezed the trigger—just as Kamel knocked him sideways, slamming him into the wall.

Sharrif screamed in high-pitched frenzy as he spun around with the force of the bullet, his hand cupped to his shoulder in pain. Carioca was following his leg around in circles, trying to get in a bite. Kamel was behind me, wrestling for the thug's gun as one of the others was rising from the floor. I raised my bag and hit him again. This time he stayed down. Then I smacked Kamel's companion in the back of the head for good measure. As he fell, Kamel pulled loose the gun.

We tore for the door; I felt a hand grab me and wrenched myself away. It was Sharrif, dog manacled to his leg but still moving. He lurched through the door behind me, blood pouring from his wound. Two of his pals were on their feet again and just behind him as I darted—not toward the stairs, but toward the steep edge of the cliff. Below I could see Kamel halfway down the steps, looking back at me in frenzy. In the moonlight I saw Lily reach bottom and head for Kamel's car.

Without thinking, I jumped over the low retaining wall and flattened myself on the ground as Sharrif and his troops tore around the side of the house and headed for the stairs. The enormous weight of the Montglane Service hung suspended from my aching hand over the side of the precipice. I nearly dropped it. I could see a hundred feet straight down, where the waves crashed against the sheer rock in the rising wind. I held my breath and slowly pulled the bag back up with all my strength.

"The car!" I heard Sharrif screaming. "They're headed for the car!" I heard the clatter of their feet going down the rickety steps and started to raise myself up when I heard something crunch close to my ear. In the pale light I peered over the top of the wall, and Carioca's long tongue lapped me in the face. I was about to get up when the clouds parted again and I saw the third thug, whom I'd thought I'd knocked cold, coming toward me rubbing his head. I ducked again, but too late.

He made a lunge toward me right over the two-foot wall. I flattened again as I heard him scream. Peeking through my fingers, I saw his unbalanced leg tottering on the ledge. Then it disappeared. I leaped back over the wall onto solid ground, grabbed Carioca, and headed for the steps.

The wind was really high now, as if a storm were coming in. To my horror, I saw Kamel's car taking off in a cloud of dust as Sharrif and his two companions ran frantically behind it, taking wild potshots at the tires. Then, to my surprise, the car doubled back, threw on the headlights, and made right for the guys on foot. The three villains dove out of the way as the car swept by them. Lily and Kamel were coming back for me!

I clattered down the steps, taking them four at a time, as fast as I could go, keeping a tight grip with one hand on Carioca, the other on the pieces. I hit bottom just as the car swept up in a cloud of dust; the door flew open, and I jumped inside. Lily took off again before I could pull it closed. Kamel was in the backseat, his gun pointed out the window. The explosion of bullets was deafening. As I struggled to slam the car door shut, I saw Sharrif and his pals tearing by us on foot toward a car that was parked just at the edge of the port. We kept on going as Kamel pumped their car full of lead.

At the best of times Lily's driving was unnerving, but now she seemed to feel she had license to kill. We fishtailed all over the dirt road out of the port and kept right on laying down rubber till we reached the main road. We all sat in breathless silence, Kamel watching out the back as she increased the speed first to eighty, then ninety. When she was about to break a hundred, I saw the OPEC blockade coming up in the distance.

"Push the red switch on the dashboard!" screamed Kamel over the sound of squealing tires. I leaned over and flipped it, and a siren came on, with a tiny red light that flashed like a beacon on the dashboard.

"Good equipment!" I called over my shoulder to Kamel as we barreled on and the guards ahead scurried out of the way. Lily slalomed between the cars as amazed faces stared at us through the windows—then we were past.

"There are *some* advantages to being a minister," said Kamel modestly. "But there's another roadblock at the far side of Sidi-Fredj."

"Damn the torpedoes and full speed ahead!" Lily cried, hitting the gas again as the big Citroën leaped ahead like a thoroughbred in the final stretch. We took the second blockade the same as we had the first, leaving them in dust.

"By the way," she said, glancing at Kamel in the rearview mirror, "we haven't been formally introduced. I'm Lily Rad. I hear you know my grandfather."

"Keep your eyes on the road," I snapped as the car wavered treacherously near the steep edge of the corniche. The wind was practically lifting the car in the air.

"Mordecai and my father were close friends," said Kamel. "Perhaps I shall meet him again one day. Please give him my warmest regards when you see him next."

Just then Kamel whipped around and stared through the rear window. Some lights were closing on us fast. "More juice," I told Lily urgently. "Now's the time to impress us with your driving skills." Kamel muttered, holding his gun poised as the car behind us turned on its siren and lights. He was trying to peer through the violent wind and dust.

"Jesus, it's a cop," said Lily, letting up on the gas slightly.

"Keep going!" Kamel snapped ferociously over his shoulder. She obediently hit the gas again, and the Citroën swerved for a moment, then recovered. The needle was pushing 200 kilometers—which I quickly converted into a speed over 120 miles per hour. They couldn't push much faster than that on these roads, no matter what kind of car they had. Especially not with the violent gusts that were now hitting us from all sides.

"There's a back route into the Casbah," said Kamel, still keeping his eye on our pursuers. "It's a good ten minutes from here, and you'll have to cut through Algiers. But I know those back streets better than our friend Sharrif. This route will bring us into the Casbah from above. . . . I know the way to Minnie's," he added quietly. "I should—it's my father's house."

"Minnie Renselaas is living in your father's house?" I cried. "But I thought you came from the mountains?"

"My father kept a house here in the Casbah, for his wives."

"His *wives*?" I said.

"Minnie Renselaas is my stepmother," said Kamel. "My father was the Black King."

∞

We ditched the car in one of the side streets that formed the mazelike upper region of Algiers. I had a million questions but was straining my eyes for Sharrif's car. I was certain we hadn't shaken them, but they were far enough behind that we could no longer see their lights when we doused ours. We leaped out of the car and headed into the labyrinth on foot.

Lily was right behind Kamel, grabbing his sleeve as I caught up to them. The streets were so dark and narrow that I stubbed my toe and nearly fell on my face trying to keep up.

"I don't get it," Lily was croaking in her hoarse whisper as I kept looking over my shoulder for our pursuers. "If Minnie was the wife of the Dutch consul—Renselaas—how could she be married to your father, too? Monogamy doesn't seem to be very popular in these parts."

"Renselaas died during the revolution," said Kamel. "She needed to stay in Algiers—my father offered her his protection. Though they loved each other deeply as friends, I suspect it was a marriage of convenience. At any rate, my father was dead within one year."

"If he was the Black King," hissed Lily, "and he got killed, why didn't the Game end? Isn't that it—Shah-mat, the King is dead?"

"The Game goes on, just as in life," Kamel said, still keeping up the clip. "The King is dead—long live the King."

I looked up at the sky between the narrow crack of buildings closing about us as we plunged deeper into the Casbah. Though I could hear the wind wailing above us, it couldn't penetrate the narrow passages we now moved through. A thin dust was sifting down on us from above, and a dark red film was moving across the face of the moon. Kamel glanced up as well.

"The sirocco," he said carefully. "It's coming; we must move quickly. I only hope this does not upset our plans."

I looked at the sky. The sirocco was a sandstorm, one of the most famous in the world. I wanted to get indoors before it hit. Kamel paused in a small cul-de-sac and extracted a key from his pocket.

"The opium den!" Lily whispered, remembering our last journey here. "Or was it hashish?"

"This is a different route," said Kamel. "A door to which I have the only key." He unlocked the door in darkness, letting me pass in first and Lily after. I heard him locking the door behind us.

It was a long, dark corridor with a dim light at the very end. I could feel thick plush carpeting beneath my feet and cool damask covering as I felt my way along the walls.

At the end we reached a large room, the floors covered in rich Persian carpets, a large gold candelabra on a marble table at the far end providing the only light. But that was adequate to pick out the opulent furnishings: low tables of dark Carrara marble, yellow silk ottomans hung with golden tassels, sofas in the deep burnished colors of aged liqueurs, and large pieces of sculpture scattered about on pedestals and tables—magnificent even to my untrained eye. In the liquid golden light, the room looked like a treasure trove found on the floor of an ancient sea. I felt as if I were passing through an atmosphere denser than water as I crossed the room slowly with Lily just behind me, to the two figures at the far side.

There in the candlelight, in a gown of gold brocade scattered with glittering coins, stood Minnie Renselaas. And beside her, holding a glass of cordial as he looked up with his pale green eyes—was Alexander Solarin.

Solarin looked at me with his dazzling smile. I'd thought of him often since that night he'd disappeared at the tent on the beach, always with the secret understanding that we'd meet again. He came forward and took my hand, then turned to Lily.

"We've never been formally introduced," he told her. She was bristling as if she'd like to slap down a gauntlet—or a chessboard—and challenge him then and there. "I am Alexander Solarin, and you are the granddaughter of one of the finest chess masters alive. I hope I can return you to him soon." Somewhat mollified by this accolade, Lily shook Solarin's hand.

"Enough," said Minnie as Kamel came up to join our group. "We haven't much time. I assume you have the pieces?" I noticed, sitting on the nearby table, a metal box I recognized as that containing the cloth.

I patted my duffel bag, and we adjourned to the table, where I set it down and extracted the pieces one by one. There they sat in the candlelight, glittering with all those colored jewels and emitting the same strange glow I'd noticed in the cave. We all stared at them in silence for a moment—the brilliant camel, the prancing horse that was the Knight, the dazzling King and Queen. Solarin bent to touch them, then glanced up at Minnie. She was the first to speak.

"At last," she said. "After all this time, they will be reunited with the others. And you are to thank for this. Through your actions, you'll redeem the fruitless death of so many, over the course of so many years. . . ."

"The *others*?" I said, glancing at her in the dim light.

"In America," she said with a smile. "Solarin will take you tonight to Marseilles, where we've arranged passage for your return." Kamel had reached inside his jacket pocket and returned Lily her passport. She took it, but we were both staring at Minnie in amazement.

"To America?" I said. "But who has the other pieces?"

"Mordecai," she said, still smiling. "He has nine more. With the cloth," she added, picking up the box and handing it to me, "you'll have more than half the formula. It will be the first time these have been united in nearly two hundred years."

"What happens when they're united?" I wanted to know.

"That is for you to discover," said Minnie, looking at me gravely. Then she gazed back down at the pieces, still glowing at the center of the table. "Now it's your turn. . . ." Slowly she turned away and put her hands on Solarin's face.

"My beloved Sascha," she said to him with tears in her eyes. "Take good care of yourself, my child. Protect them. . . ." She pressed her lips to his forehead. To my surprise, Solarin threw his arms about her and buried his face in her shoulder. We all watched in amazement as the young chess master and the elegant Mokhfi Mokhtar clung to each other in silence. Then they parted, and she turned to Kamel, pressing his hand.

"Get them safely to the port," she whispered. Without another word to Lily or me, she turned and swept from the room. Solarin and Kamel looked after her in silence.

"You must go," Kamel said at last, turning to Solarin. "I'll see she's all right. May Allah go with you, my friend." He was collecting the pieces on the table, shoving them back in my bag along with the box containing the cloth, which he took from my hands. Lily was standing there clutching Carioca to her chest.

"I don't get it," she said weakly. "You mean that's it? We're leaving? But how are we getting to Marseilles?"

"We've secured a boat," said Kamel. "Come, we haven't a moment to lose."

"But what about Minnie?" I said. "Are we going to see her again?"

"Not just now," Solarin said quickly, recovering himself. "We must go before the storm hits—get out to sea at once. The crossing is rather simple once we've cleared the port."

I was still in a daze when I found myself, with Lily and Solarin, once again in the darkened streets of the Casbah.

We were racing down through the silent passages where the houses squeezed together to shut out all the light. I could tell by the salty fish scent invading my nostrils that we were approaching the port. We came out in the wide plaza near the Mosquée de la Pêcheur, where we'd met Wahad so many days before. It felt like months. Sand was blowing across the plaza with great violence now.

Solarin grabbed my arm and hurried me across the square as Lily, with Carioca in her arms, ran quickly behind.

We'd started down the Fisherman's Steps to the port when I caught my breath and said quickly to Solarin, "Minnie called you her child—she's not *your* stepmother, too, is she?"

"No," he said softly, pulling me down the steps two at a time. "I pray I'll see her again before I die. She's my grandmother. . . ."

THE SILENCE BEFORE THE STORM

For I would walk alone,
Under the quiet stars, and at that time
Have felt whate'er there is of power in sound . . .
And I would stand,
In the night blackened with a coming storm,
Beneath some rock, listening to notes that are
The ghostly language of the ancient earth,
Or make their dim abode in distant winds.

Thence did I drink the visionary power.

—The Prelude
William Wordsworth

Talleyrand limped through the leafy forest, where shafts of sunlight, swimming with golden motes, cut through the cathedral of spring foliage. Bright green hummingbirds shot here and there, hovering to gather nectar from the brilliant blossoms of a trumpet vine that hung like a veil from an old oak. The ground was still damp beneath his feet, the trees still dripping with water from the recent shower, catching the light like diamonds scattered in the mottled foliage.

Two years and more he'd been in America. It had lived up to his expectations—but not his hopes. The French ambassador to America, a mediocre bureaucrat, understood Talleyrand's ambitious political aspirations and was also familiar with the charges of treason against him. He'd blocked his entrée to President Washington, and the doors of Philadelphia society had closed as swiftly as those in London. Only Alexander Hamilton had remained his friend and ally, though he'd been unable to secure him any work. At last, his resources exhausted, Talleyrand was reduced to selling Vermont real estate to newly arrived French émigrés. At least it kept him alive.

Now, as he tramped with his walking stick across the rough terrain, measuring the plots he'd sell tomorrow, he sighed and thought of his ruined life. What was he salvaging, really? At forty-two he'd nothing to show for his centuries of breeding, his fine education. With few exceptions the Americans were savages and criminals, cast out by the civilized countries of Europe. Even the upper classes in Philadelphia had less education than barbarians like Marat, who'd taken a medical degree, or Danton, who'd studied law.

But the majority of those gentlemen were dead, they who'd first spearheaded, then undermined the Revolution. Marat assassinated; Camille Desmoulins and Georges Danton gone to the guillotine in the same tumbril; Hébert, Chaumette, Couthon, Saint-Just; Lebas, who'd blown out his own brains rather than submit to arrest; and the Robespierre brothers, Maximilien and Augustin, whose deaths beneath the blade marked the end of the Terror. He might have met the same fate, had he remained in France. But now it was time to pick up the pieces. He patted the letter in his pocket and smiled inwardly. It was France where he belonged, in the midst of Germaine de Staël's glittering salon, weaving brilliant political intrigue. Not tramping about in the midst of this godless wilderness.

Suddenly he realized that it was quite some time since he'd heard anything but the buzzing of bees. He bent to tack his marker into the ground, then peering into the foliage called out: "Courtiade, are you there?"

There was no reply. He called again, louder this time. From the depths of the brush came the sorrowful voice of the valet.

"Yes, Monseigneur—unhappily yes, I am."

Courtiade parted his way through the underbrush and stepped into the small clearing. A big leather pouch dangled from a strap across his chest.

Talleyrand threw his arm across the valet's shoulders as they picked their way through the undergrowth back to the rocky trail where they'd left their horse and cart.

"Twenty parcels of land," he mused. "Come, Courtiade—if we sell these tomorrow, we'll return to Philadelphia with sufficient funds to pay our passage back to France."

"Then your letter from Madame de Staël bears promise you may return?" said Courtiade, his sober, impassive face breaking into the semblance of a smile.

Talleyrand reached into his pocket and withdrew the letter he'd carried these last few weeks. Courtiade looked at the handwriting and the flowery stamps engraved with the name of the French Republic.

"As usual," said Talleyrand, tapping the letter, "Germaine has leapt into the fray. As soon as she was back in France herself, she installed her new lover—a Swiss named Benjamin Constant—at the Swedish embassy under the very nose of her husband. She's created so much furor over her political activities, she was denounced on the very floor of the Convention for trying to stir up a monarchist conspiracy whilst cuckolding her husband. Now they've ordered her to remain twenty miles distant from Paris—but even there she works her magic. A woman of great power and charm, whom I shall always number among my friends. . . ." He'd nodded for Courtiade to open the letter. The valet was reading as they continued toward their horse-drawn cart.

> Your day has come, *mon cher ami.* Return soon, and reap the rewards of patience. I still have friends with their necks in one piece, who will remember your name and the services you've rendered France in the past. Affectionately, Germaine.

Courtiade looked up from the letter with undisguised joy. They'd reached the cart, where the tired old horse stood munching sweet grass. Talleyrand patted her on the neck and turned to Courtiade.

"You've brought the pieces?" he asked softly.

"They are here," replied the valet, patting the leather pouch that swung from his shoulder. "And the Knight's Tour of Monsieur Benjamin Franklin, which Secretary Hamilton had copied for you."

"That we can keep, for it bears no significance to anyone but ourselves. But the pieces are too dangerous to take back into France. That's why I wanted to bring them here, to this wilderness where no one would ever imagine them to be. Vermont—a French name, isn't it? Green Mountains." He pointed his walking stick toward the lofty range of rolling green hills that hovered above them. "Up there, atop those verdant emerald peaks so close to God. Then He can keep an eye on them in my place."

His eyes twinkled as he looked at Courtiade. But the valet's expression had again become sober.

"What is it?" asked Talleyrand. "You don't like the idea?"

"You've risked so much for these pieces, sire," the valet explained politely. "They've cost so many lives. To leave them behind seems . . ." He searched to express his thought.

"That it would all have been for nothing," said Talleyrand bitterly.

"If you will excuse my speaking so boldly, Monseigneur . . . if Mademoiselle Mireille were alive, you'd move heaven and earth to guard these pieces within your care, as she entrusted you—not abandon them to the ravages of the wilderness." He looked at Talleyrand with an expression of grave concern at what he was about to do.

"Nearly four years have passed with no word, no sign," said Talleyrand with broken voice. "Even without a shred to cling to, I never abandoned hope—not until now. But Germaine is back in France, and with her circle of informants would surely have learned if there was any trace. Her silence on the subject bodes the worst. Perhaps by planting these pieces in the soil, my hope will take root again."

Three hours later, as the two men placed the last rock upon the mound of earth deep in the heart of the Green Mountains, Talleyrand raised his head to look at Courtiade.

"Perhaps now," he said, looking down at the mound, "we may rest assured that they will not surface again for another thousand years."

Courtiade was drawing vines and brush over the burial spot. Gravely, he replied, "But at least—they will survive."

ST. PETERSBURG, RUSSIA   NOVEMBER 1796

Six months later, in an antechamber of the Imperial Palace at St. Petersburg, Valerian Zubov and his handsome brother, Plato, beloved of the Czarina Catherine the Great, stood whispering together as members of the court, dressed prematurely in black mourning attire, filed by the open doors en route to the royal chambers.

"We shall not survive," whispered Valerian, who, like his brother, was dressed in a black velvet costume bedecked with ribbons of state. "We must act now—or all is lost!"

"I cannot leave until she is dead," Plato whispered fiercely when the last group had passed. "How would it look? She might recover unexpectedly, and then all *would* be lost!"

"She will not recover!" replied Valerian, struggling to keep the agitation from his voice. "It is *haémorragie des cervelles.* The doctor told me no one recovers from brain hemorrhage. And when she dies, Paul will be czar."

"He's come to me with a truce," said Plato, sounding uncertain himself. "Only this morning—he's offered me a title and an estate. Not as splendid as the Taurida Palace, of course. Something in the countryside."

"And do you trust him?"

"No," admitted Plato. "But what can I do? Even if I chose to flee, I should never make it to the border. . . ."

The abbess sat beside the bed of the grand Czarina of all the Russias. Catherine's face was white. She was unconscious. The abbess held Catherine's hand in hers, looking at her bleached white skin that, from time to time, turned purple as she gasped in the final throes of death.

How dreadful it was, to see her lying there, this friend who'd been so vital, so alive. All the power in the world had not saved her from this awful death, her body a pale, mottled sac of fluid like a decayed fruit that dropped too late from the tree. This was the end that God designated for all—high and low, saint and sinner. *Te absolvum,* thought the abbess, if my absolution will help. But first you must awake, my friend. For I need your help more. If there is one thing you must do before you die, it is to tell me where you've hidden the one chess piece I brought to you. Tell me where you've put the Black Queen!

∞

But Catherine did not recover. As the abbess sat in her cold chambers, looking at the empty grate she was too weak with sorrow to light, she racked her mind for what she might do next.

The whole court was in mourning behind closed doors, but mourning for themselves as much as for the deceased czarina. Sick with fear for what might befall them now that the mad Prince Paul was to be crowned czar.

They said the moment Catherine breathed her last, he'd raced to her chambers to empty the contents of her desk, unopened and unread, into the blazing hearth fire. Afraid there might be among these some final disposition stating what she'd always claimed she might do—disinherit him in favor of his son Alexander.

The palace itself had been turned into a barracks. The soldiers of Paul's personal guard, arrayed in their Prussian-looking uniforms with shiny buttons, marched up and down the corridors night and day, shouting commands that could be heard over the clatter of boots. The Freemasons and other liberals whom Catherine had opposed were being let out of the prisons. Everything Catherine had done in life, Paul was resolved to overturn. It was only a matter of time, thought the abbess, before his attention turned to those who'd been her friends. . . .

She heard the creaking door of her chambers opening. Raising her eyes hopelessly toward the entrance, she saw Paul, his bulging eyes staring at her from across the room. He chuckled idiotically, rubbing his hands together—whether from satisfaction or from the icy cold of the room, she was not sure.

"Pavel Petrovich, I've been expecting you," said the abbess with a smile.

"You will call me Your Majesty—and you will *rise* when I enter your chamber!" he nearly screamed. Then, calming himself as the abbess slowly got to her feet, he crossed the room to her and looked down with hatred in his face. "Quite a difference in our positions since the last time I entered this room, wouldn't you say, Madame de Roque?" he said in challenging voice.

"Why, yes," the abbess replied calmly. "If memory serves, your mother was explaining the reasons why you would not inherit her throne—and yet, events seem to have taken a different course."

"*Her* throne?!" screamed Paul, clenching his hands in fury. "It was *my* throne—which she stole from me when I was only eight years old! She was a despot!" he cried, his face red with fury. "I know what you were plotting between you! I know what you had in your possession! I demand you tell me where the rest are hidden!" With this, he reached into the pocket of his jacket and extracted the Black Queen. The abbess drew back in fear but recovered herself at once.

"That belongs to me," she said calmly, putting forth her hand.

"No, no!" cried Paul with glee. "I want them all—for I know what they are, you see. They will all be mine! All mine!"

"I'm afraid not," the abbess said, still holding out her hand.

"Perhaps a stay in prison will jog your conscience," Paul replied, turning from her as he put the heavy chess piece back in his pocket.

"Surely you don't mean what you say," said the abbess.

"Not until after the funeral," Paul giggled, pausing at the door. "I'd hate for you to miss the spectacle. I've ordered the bones of my murdered father, Peter the Third, to be exhumed from the monastery of Alexander Nevski and brought to the Winter Palace for display beside the body of the woman who ordered his death. Above my parents' coffins as they lie in state will be a streamer that reads 'Divided in Life, Joined in Death.' Their caskets will be borne through the snowy streets of the city by a cortege of pallbearers comprised of my mother's former lovers. I've even arranged for those who assassinated my father to bear *his* casket!" He was laughing hysterically now as the abbess stared at him in horror.

"But Potëmkin is dead," she said softly.

"Yes—too late for the Serenissimus." He laughed. "*His* bones will be removed from the mausoleum at Kherson and scattered for the dogs to eat!" With that, Paul shoved open the door and turned to the abbess for a parting glance. "And Plato Zubov, my mother's most recent favorite, will receive a new estate. I'll welcome him there with champagne and a dinner on gold plate. But he'll only enjoy it for a day!"

"Perhaps he'll be my companion in prison?" suggested the abbess, anxious to learn as much of the madman's plans as she might.

"Why bother with such a fool? As soon as he's settled, I'll extend him an invitation to travel. I'll enjoy the sight of his face when he learns he must give up in one day all that he's earned so hard for so many years in her bed!"

No sooner had the drapery swung closed behind Paul than the abbess hastened to her writing desk. Mireille was alive, she knew. For the letter of credit she'd sent via Charlotte Corday had been drawn upon not once, but many times—on the bank in London. If Plato Zubov were to go into exile, he might be the one person who could communicate with Mireille through that bank. If only Paul did not change his mind, she had a chance. Though he might have one piece of the Montglane Service, he did not have all. She still had the cloth—and knew where the board was hidden.

As she prepared the letter, carefully worded lest it fall into the wrong hands, she prayed that Mireille might receive it before it was too late. When completed she slipped it into her gown so she might pass it to Zubov at the funeral. Then the abbess sat down to stitch the cloth of the Montglane Service into her abbatial robes. It might be the last chance she'd have to hide it before she went to prison.

PARIS   DECEMBER 1797

The carriage of Germaine de Staël passed through the rows of magnificent Doric columns that marked the entry to the Hotel Galliffet on the Rue de Bac. Her six white horses, lathered and pawing the gravel, drew to a halt before the front entrance. The footman leaped down and drew out the carriage steps to help his irate mistress descend. In one year she'd brought Talleyrand from obscurity in exile to this magnificent palace—and these were the thanks she received!

The courtyard was already filled with decorative trees and shrubs in pots. Courtiade paced through the snow, giving directions regarding where they should be placed on the outer lawns against the vast backdrop of the snowy park. There were hundreds of blossoming trees, enough to transform the lawns into a spring fairyland in the midst of winter. The valet looked up uncomfortably at Madame de Staël's arrival, then hurried to greet her.

"Don't try to placate me, Courtiade!" Germaine cried out even before the valet had reached her. "I've come to wring the neck of that ungrateful wretch who is your master!" And before Courtiade could stop her, she marched up the steps and entered the house through the open French windows at the side.

She found Talleyrand upstairs going over receipts in the sunny study that overlooked the courtyard. He turned with a smile as she came barreling into the room.

"Germaine—what an unexpected pleasure!" he said, rising to greet her.

"How dare you throw a soiree for that Corsican upstart without inviting me?" she cried. "Do you forget who got you back from America? Who had the charges against you dropped? Who convinced Barras you'd make a better minister of *relations extérieures* than Delacroix? Are these the thanks I receive for placing at your disposal my considerable influence? May I remember in the future how quickly the French forget their friends!"

"My dear Germaine," said Talleyrand, purring soothingly as he stroked her arm, "it was Monsieur Delacroix himself who convinced Barras I'd be a better man for the job."

"A better man for *some* jobs," Germaine cried with anger and scorn. "All Paris knows that the child his wife is carrying is yours! You've probably invited them both—your predecessor and the mistress with whom you've cuckolded him!"

"I've invited *all* my mistresses." He laughed. "Including yourself. But when it comes to cuckolding, I shouldn't begin flinging stones if I were you, my dear."

"I've received no invitation," said Germaine, glossing over his other implications.

"Of course not," he said, his brilliant blue eyes regarding her with docility. "Why waste an invitation on my best friend? How did you expect me to plan a party of this magnitude—five hundred guests—without your help? I expected you days ago!"

Germaine looked uncertain for a moment. "But the preparations are already under way," she said.

"A few thousand trees and shrubs," Talleyrand sniffed. "It's nothing com-

pared with what I have in mind." Taking her by the arm, he walked her along
the banks of French windows, pointing down to the court.

"What do you think of this—dozens of silken tents flying with ribbons and
banners, along the lawns and clustered throughout the courtyard. Amongst the
tents, soldiers in French uniforms standing in military position . . ." He walked
her back to the study door, where the marble gallery circled the lofty entrance
hall leading to a stairway of rich Italian marble. Deep red carpeting was being
laid by workmen on their hands and knees.

"And here, as the guests enter, musicians playing military tunes will move
about the gallery, proceeding up and down the stairway as 'the Marseillaise' is
sung!"

"It's magnificent!" cried Germaine, clapping her hands. "The flowers must
all be colored red, white, and blue—with streamers of the same in crepe across
the balustrades. . . ."

"You see?" Talleyrand smiled, embracing her. "What could I do without
you?"

As a special surprise, Talleyrand had arranged the dining hall so that there
were chairs at the banquet tables for only the ladies. Each gentleman stood
behind a lady's chair, serving her delicate morsels from the platters of elaborately
prepared foods that were constantly circulated by the liveried servants. This
arrangement flattered the women and afforded the men an opportunity to talk.

Napoleon was delighted with the re-creation of his Italian military camp that
had greeted him at the entrance. Dressed in simple attire devoid of decorations,
as Talleyrand had advised, he far outshone the directors of the government,
who'd arrived in the lavish plumed costumes designed by the painter David.

David himself, at the far end of the room, was assigned to serve a fair-haired
beauty whom Napoleon was anxious to meet.

"Have I seen her somewhere before?" he whispered to Talleyrand with a
smile, looking down the rows of tables.

"Perhaps," replied Talleyrand coolly. "She's been in London during the
Terror, but has just returned to France. Her name is Catherine Grand."

When the guests had risen from table and scattered to the various ballrooms
and music rooms, Talleyrand brought the lovely woman across the room. The
general was already cornered by Madame de Staël, who was plying him with
questions.

"Tell me, General Bonaparte," she said forcefully, "what sort of woman do
you most admire?"

"She who bears the most children," he replied curtly. Seeing Catherine Grand
approach on the arm of Talleyrand, he smiled.

"And where have you been keeping yourself, my beauty?" he asked when they'd been introduced. "You've a French appearance, but an English name. Are you British by birth?"

"Je suis d'Inde," replied Catherine Grand with a sweet smile. Germaine gasped, and Napoleon looked at Talleyrand with raised eyebrow. For this statement of double entendre, as she pronounced it, also meant "I am a complete nitwit."

"Madame Grand is not quite the fool she'd have us believe," said Talleyrand wryly, glancing at Germaine. "In fact, I find her one of the cleverest women in Europe!"

"A pretty woman may not always be smart," Napoleon agreed, "but a smart woman is always pretty."

"You embarrass me before Madame de Staël," said Catherine Grand. "Everyone knows that *she* is the most brilliant woman in Europe. Why, she's even written a book!"

"She writes books," said Napoleon, taking Catherine's arm, "but books will be written about you!"

David arrived at their group, greeting everyone warmly. But at Madame Grand he paused.

"Yes, the resemblance is remarkable, is it not?" said Talleyrand, guessing the painter's thoughts. "It's why I gave you the place beside Madame Grand at dinner. And tell me, whatever became of that painting you were doing of the Sabine women? I should like to purchase it, for memory's sake—if it's ever unveiled."

"I finished it in prison," David said with a nervous laugh. "It was shown at the Academy soon after. You know I was shut up for months just after the fall of the Robespierres."

"I too was put in prison at Marseilles." Napoleon laughed. "And for the same cause. Robespierre's brother Augustin was a big supporter of mine . . . but what is this painting you speak of? If Madame Grand posed for it, I should be interested to see it myself."

"Not she," David replied with trembling voice, "but someone she closely resembles. A ward of mine who—died during the Terror. There were two of them. . . ."

"Valentine and Mireille," interjected Madame de Staël. "Such lovely girls . . . they used to go about everywhere with us. The one died—but whatever became of the other, the one with red hair?"

"Dead, too, I believe," said Talleyrand. "Or so Madame Grand has claimed. You were quite a close friend of hers, were you not, my dear?"

Catherine Grand had turned pale but smiled sweetly as she struggled to recover. David shot her a sudden glance and was about to speak when Napoleon interrupted.

"Mireille? Was she the one with red hair?"

"Quite so," said Talleyrand. "They were both nuns at Montglane."

"Montglane!" Napoleon whispered, staring at Talleyrand. Then he glanced back at David. "They were your wards, you say?"

"Until they met their death," Talleyrand repeated, watching Madame Grand closely as she writhed beneath his gaze. Then he looked back at David as well. "It seems there's something bothering you," he said, taking the painter's arm.

"There is something disturbing *me*," said Napoleon, choosing his words carefully. "Gentlemen, I suggest we escort the ladies to the ballroom and retire to the study for a few moments. I should like to get to the bottom of this."

"Why, General Bonaparte?" Talleyrand said. "Do you know something of the two women of whom we speak?"

"Indeed I do. At least one of them," he replied with sincerity. "If she is the woman I believe she is, she nearly gave birth to her child at my home in Corsica!"

∞

"She's alive—and she's had a child," said Talleyrand after piecing together the stories of Napoleon and David. *My* child, he thought, pacing about his study as the other two men sat sipping a fine Madeira while seated on soft gold damask armchairs beside the glowing fire. "But where could she be now? She's been to Corsica and the Maghreb—then back into France, where she conducted this crime you tell me of." He looked at David, who sat trembling with the immensity of the tale he'd just told—the first time it had passed his lips.

"But Robespierre is dead now. There's no one in France who knows of this but *you*," he told David. "Where could she be? Why does she not return?"

"Perhaps we should confer with my mother," suggested Napoleon. "As I told you, it was she who knew the abbess, who set this entire game in motion. I believe her name is Madame de Roque."

"But—she was in Russia!" said Talleyrand, suddenly wheeling to face the others as he realized what that meant. "Catherine the Great *died* last winter— nearly a year ago! And what has become of the abbess, now that Paul is on the throne?"

"And the pieces, whose location she alone must know?" added Napoleon.

"I know where some have gone," said David, speaking for the first time since he'd concluded his horrible tale. Now he looked Talleyrand in the eye, and the latter grew uneasy. Had David guessed where Mireille was that last night she spent in Paris? Had Napoleon guessed whose magnificent horse she was riding when he and his sister encountered her at the barricades? If so, perhaps they'd guessed how she'd disposed of the gold-and-silver pieces of the Montglane Service before departing France.

He looked at David attentively, his face a mask of indifference as David continued.

"Robespierre told me before he died of the Game under way to get the pieces. There was a woman behind it—the White Queen, patroness of himself and Marat. It was she who killed those nuns who came to seek Mireille—she who captured their pieces. God knows how many she has now or whether Mireille knows of the danger to her from this quarter. But *you* should know, gentlemen. Though she resided in London during the Terror, he called her 'the Woman from India.'"

THE
STORM

Albions Angel stood beside the Stone of Night and saw
The terror like a comet, or more like the planet red
That once inclos'd the terrible wandering comets in its
    sphere . . .

The Spectre glowd his horrid length staining the
    Temple long
With beams of blood; & thus the Voice came forth and
    shook the Temple.

—America: A Prophecy
William Blake

So I have traveled throughout the land and was a pilgrim
all my life, alone and a stranger feeling alien. Then Thou
has made grow in me Thine art under the breath of the
terrible storm in me.

—*Paracelsus*

I was frankly startled to learn that Solarin was the grandson of Minnie Renselaas. But I had no time to question his genealogy as we scrambled down the Fisherman's Steps with Lily in the dark of the rising storm. Below us, the sea was hung with a mysterious reddish haze, and when I glanced uphill over my shoulder, I saw in the eerie glow of the moon the dark red fingers of the sirocco carrying tons of airborne sand, crawling down through the cracks between the mountains as if reaching out to grasp us in our flight.

We made it to the docks at the far end of the port where the private ships were moored. I could barely make out their dark forms bobbing in the sand and wind. Lily and I stumbled blindly on board our boat behind Solarin, going below at once to stash Carioca and the pieces and to escape the sand that was already burning our skin and lungs. I glimpsed Solarin unfastening the ship from its moorings as I closed the door of the little cabin and felt my way down the steps behind Lily.

The engine had started, putt-putting softly as the ship began to move. I felt around until I found a lamp-shaped object that smelled of kerosene. I lit it so we could see the interior of the small but richly appointed cabin. There was dark wood everywhere and thick carpeting, some leather swivel chairs, a double-deck bed against the wall, and a fishnet hammock filled with Mae Wests hanging in the corner. Across from the beds was a little galley with a sink and stove. But when I opened the cupboards, there was no food—just a well-stocked liquor cabinet. I uncorked a cognac, scrounged some spotty water glasses, and poured us each a stiff drink.

"I hope Solarin knows how to sail this thing," Lily said, taking a healthy slug.

"Don't be ridiculous," I told her, realizing after my first dizzying sip of brandy how long it had been since I'd eaten anything. "Sailboats don't have engines. Don't you hear that noise?"

"Well, if it's just a motorboat," said Lily, "then why's it got all those masts sticking up in the middle? Just to make it look pretty?"

Now that she mentioned it, I thought I'd remembered seeing them, too. We couldn't possibly be going to sea in a sailboat with a storm coming on. Even Solarin didn't have *that* much self-confidence. Just to be safe, I thought I'd better have a look.

I climbed the narrow steps that led to the little cockpit surrounded by cushioned seats. We'd pulled out of the port by now and were slightly ahead of the sheet of red sand still moving down over Algiers. The wind was strong, the moon clear, and in its cold light I got my first good look at the ship of our intended salvation.

It was larger than I'd thought, with beautiful decks that looked like hand-rubbed teak. Polished brass rails ran around the perimeter, and the little cockpit where I stood was loaded with gleaming state-of-the-art hardware. Not one, but two large masts rose toward the darkening sky. Solarin, with one hand on the wheel, was pulling big bundles of folded canvas from a hole in the deck.

"A sailboat?" I said, watching him as he worked.

"A ketch," he muttered, still pulling out cloth. "It was all I could steal on such short notice, but it's a good ship—thirty-seven feet and yar." Whatever that meant.

"Great. A *stolen* sailboat," I said. "Neither Lily nor I knows a thing about sailing. I sure hope *you* do."

"Of course," he sniffed. "I grew up on the Black Sea."

"So what? I live on Manhattan—an island with boats all around it. That doesn't mean I know how to steer one in a storm."

"We might be able to beat this storm if you'd stop complaining and help me get these sails up. I'll tell you what to do—I can work them myself once they're rigged. If we get off quickly, we could be past Minorca by the time this hits."

So I set to work, following his instructions. The ropes, called sheets and halyards and made of scratchy hemp, cut my fingers when I pulled on them. The sails—yards of hand-stitched Egyptian cotton—had names like "jib" or "mizzen." We lashed two to the forward mast and one to the "aft," as Solarin called it. I hauled as hard as I could as he yelled instructions at me—and tied what I hoped were the right ropes to the metal cleats embedded in the deck. When all three were up, it was remarkable how pretty the ship looked and how fast it sprang forward.

"You've done well," said Solarin as I joined him in the cockpit. "This is a fine ship. . . ." He paused and looked at me. "Why don't you go below and get some rest? You look as if you need it. The game's not over yet."

It was true. I hadn't slept since a catnap on the plane to Oran twelve hours ago, though it seemed like days. And except for that dip in the sea, I hadn't bathed, either.

But before I gave in to fatigue and hunger, there were things I needed to know.

"You said we were headed for Marseilles," I said. "Wouldn't that be one of the first places Sharrif and his cohorts would think to look for us, once they realize we're not in Algiers?"

"We'll sail in close to La Camargue," said Solarin, pushing me down onto a seat in the cockpit as we came about and the boom swept over our heads.

"Kamel has a private plane waiting for us on a landing strip nearby. It won't wait forever—it was hard for him to arrange—so it's lucky we have good wind."

"Why don't you tell me what's really going on?" I said. "Why did you never mention that Minnie was your grandmother, or that you knew Kamel? How did you get into this game in the first place? We thought it was Mordecai who drafted you."

"It was," he told me, keeping his eyes on the ever-darkening sea. "Before I came to New York, I'd only met my grandmother once, when I was just a child. I couldn't have been more than six at the time, but I'll never forget . . ." He paused as if lost in reverie. I didn't interrupt his thoughts but waited for him to resume.

"I never met my grandfather," he said slowly. "He died before I was born. She married Renselaas later—and after he died, she married Kamel's father. I only met Kamel when I came here to Algiers. It was Mordecai who came to Russia to bring me into the Game. I don't know how Minnie met him, but he's surely the most ruthless chess player since Alekhine, and far more charming. I learned a good deal of technique from him in the little time we had to play."

"But he didn't come to Russia to play chess with you," I interjected.

"No indeed." Solarin laughed. "He was after the board, and thought I could help them get it."

"And did you?"

"No," said Solarin, turning his green gaze on me with a look I couldn't fathom. "I helped them get *you*. Wasn't that enough?"

I had a few more questions, but his glance made me uncomfortable—I can't say why. The wind was stronger now, carrying the hard, stinging sand in its wake. Suddenly I felt very weary. I started to stand up, but Solarin pushed me back down.

"Watch the boom," he told me. "We're coming about again." Snapping the sail to the other side, he motioned for me to go below. "I'll call if I need you," he said.

When I came down the steep steps, Lily was sitting on the lower bunk feeding Carioca some dried biscuits soaked in water. Beside her on the bed was an open jar of peanut butter she'd somehow located with several bags of dried crackers and toast. It occurred to me Lily was suddenly looking rather trim, her sunburned nose turning to tan and her filthy microdress now clinging to svelte curves rather than gelatinous fat.

"You'd better eat," she said. "This constant chopping is making me queasy—I couldn't put down a bite."

Here in the cabin, you could really feel the sloshing of the waves. I gobbled some crackers spread thick with peanut butter, washed them down with the dregs of my cognac, and crawled on the top bunk.

"I think we'd better get some sleep," I told her. "We've got a long night ahead of us—and a longer day tomorrow."

"It *is* tomorrow," said Lily, standing up and checking her watch. She put out the lamp. I could hear the springs creaking in the bed below as she and Carioca tucked in for the night. It was the last sound I remembered before casting off into dreamland.

∞

I can't say when I heard the first crash. I was dreaming that I was on the bottom of the sea, crawling through the soft sand as waves moved all around me. In my dream, the pieces of the Montglane Service had come to life and were trying to climb out of my bag. No matter how hard I tried to shove them back again and move toward shore, my feet kept getting sucked down in the mire. I had to breathe. I was trying to get to the surface when a big wave came and shoved me under again.

I opened my eyes but at first couldn't understand where I was. I was looking through a porthole completely underwater. Then the ship rolled to the other side, and I was thrown out of my bunk, smashing into the galley across the aisle. I picked myself up off the floor, soaking wet. The water was knee deep, sloshing around the cabin. The waves were lapping into Lily's lower bunk, where Carioca sat perched on her still sleeping form, trying to keep his little paws dry. Something was terribly wrong.

"Wake up!" I screamed as the sound of pounding water and groaning beams drowned my words. I was trying to keep my bearings as I hauled her toward the hammock. Where were the pumps? Weren't they supposed to be going with all this water?

"My God," Lily groaned, trying to stand. "I'm going to be sick."

"Not now!" I half dragged her toward the fishnet hammock. Holding her up with one arm, I swept the life vests out with the other. I tossed her into the swinging hammock, then snatched at Carioca and dropped him in the hammock just as Lily's stomach started heaving. Grabbing a plastic bucket that was floating by, I shoved it in her face. She pitched her cookies, then looked up at me with rolling eyes.

"Where's Solarin?" she asked over the sound of screeching wind and water.

"I don't know," I said, tossing her a life vest and pulling on another myself as I worked my way through the deepening water. "Put that on—I'm going up to find out."

The water was surging down the steps. The door above me was banging against the wall. I grabbed it as I got outside and squeezed it shut against the heavy wash. Then I looked around—and wished I hadn't.

The ship, listing deeply to the right, was sliding backward on the diagonal

down a big hollow of water. Water was washing over the deck and filling the
cockpit. The boom was loose and swinging out over the side. And one of the
front sails, wet and heavy, had ripped loose and was dragging partly in the water.
Solarin, not six feet away, was lying half out of the cockpit, his arms dangling
across the deck as the wave of water that surged across lifted him—and started
to carry him away!

I grasped the steering wheel and made a leap for him, grabbing at his bare
foot and trouser leg as the water tore at his lifeless body . . . but the water kept
dragging him away. Suddenly my grip broke free. He was thrown across the
narrow strip of deck and smashed against the rail, then lifted again as he started
to wash overboard!

I threw myself face down across the sliding deck, using the traction of
anything—my toes, my hands—grasping at metal cleats embedded in the deck
as I tried to crawl across the slanted floor to where he lay. We were being sucked
into the belly of a wave, while another wall of water the size of a four-story
building was swelling on the other side of the gully.

I smashed into Solarin and grabbed him by the shirt, dragging him with all
my might against the water and steep incline of the deck. God knows how I
got him to the cockpit and shoved him headfirst over the side. I pulled his head
out of the water, throwing him back against the seat, and slapped him hard
several times. There was blood gushing from a wound on his head, running
down over his ear. I was screaming over the sound of the wind and water as
the boat fell faster and faster down the wall of the wave.

He opened his bleary eyes, then squeezed them shut against the spray.

"We're spinning!" I screamed. "What should we do?"

Solarin sat bolt upright, clinging to the side of the cockpit, and glanced
around quickly taking in the situation.

"Get the sails down at once. . . ." He grabbed my hands and put them on
the wheel. "Cut it to the starboard!" he cried as he struggled to stand.

"Is that left or right?" I screamed in panic.

"Right!" he screamed back, but he collapsed back onto the seat beside me,
his head bleeding profusely as water washed over us and I clung to the wheel.

I cut the wheel as hard as I could and felt the boat dip sickeningly into the
water as we fell. I kept turning as hard as I could until we lay completely on
our side. I was sure we'd turn over—there was nothing but gravity pulling us
down and down as the wall of water loomed over us, blackening the muddy
brown light of the morning sky.

"The halyards!" cried Solarin, grabbing me. I looked at him a second, then
shoved him forward onto the wheel, which he clutched with all his strength.

I could already taste the fear in my mouth. Solarin, still steering the boat into
the base of the approaching wave head on, grabbed an axe and shoved it into
my hand. I crawled over the top of the cockpit straight for the front mast. The

wave above us was growing higher as the plume at the top began to curl inward upon itself. I couldn't see a thing as water closed over the ship. The roar of thousands of tons of water was deafening. Erasing all thoughts from my mind, I half slid, half crawled toward the mast.

Grabbing it with all my strength, I hacked at the halyard until the hemp lashed free in a spiral like a ball of rattlesnakes cutting loose. The rope broke free, and I threw myself flat as the onslaught struck like a railroad train plowing into us at full force. Sails were everywhere, and I could hear the sickening sound of cracking wood. The wall of water crashed over us. Pebbles and sand were forced up my nose; water was being shoved down my throat as I fought to keep from coughing or gasping for air. I was ripped from the mast and tossed backward so I couldn't tell which way was up or down. Whatever I hit, I tried to grab hold of with all my strength, as the water kept on coming.

The front of the ship popped into the air, then down again. Dirty gray spray showered the boat as we rocked violently in and out of the waves—but we were still afloat. Sails were everywhere, dragging in the sea and flopping over the deck, some lying heavily across my legs as I pulled myself out. I started back to the rear mast, grabbing the axe embedded in a pile of sail not three feet away. It might have been my head, I thought as I ran along the side, gripping the rail for balance.

In the cockpit, Solarin was pulling sails away as he gripped the wheel. Blood splashed his wet blond hair like a crimson badge and trickled down into his collar.

"Get that sail tied down!" he bellowed after me. "Use anything you can find—just batten it down before we're hit again." He was yanking at the front sails as he stood in the cockpit. They lay sprawled everywhere like the skin of a drowned animal.

I hacked the rear halyard from the cleat, but the wind was so hard I was having quite a battle trying to get the sail down. When I'd dragged down and tied up as much as I could, I ran in a low crouch across the deck, my bare feet slapping in the water as I dug my toes in like running cleats. I was soaked to the skin, but I hauled the front jib, yanking it with all my might as it slapped in the sea and pulling it from the water that ran off the deck. Solarin was pulling in the main boom, which was dangling loose like a broken arm.

I jumped into the cockpit as Solarin wrestled with the wheel. The boat was still bobbing about like a little cork across the dark muddy void. Though the sea was rough and violent, flinging spray about and tearing us back and forth, there were no more waves like the one that had just smashed us. It was as if a strange genie had risen from a bottle on the dark sea floor, had one brief burst of wrath, then disappeared. At least I hoped so.

I was exhausted—and amazed I was still alive. I sat there still trembling with cold and fear, watching Solarin's profile as he watched the waves. He looked as intent as he had before that chessboard, as if that too were a matter of life and death. "I am a master of this game," I remembered him saying. "Who's winning?" I'd asked him, and he'd replied, "I am. I always win."

Solarin struggled in grim silence with the wheel for what seemed like hours as I sat there cold and numb, my mind empty. The wind was dropping, but the waves were still so high we moved as on a roller coaster. I'd seen these storms that came and vanished on the Mediterranean, throwing waves ten feet high up the steps of the port at Sidi-Fredj, then disappearing as if sucked off into a vacuum. I was praying that this would be one of the same.

When I could see the dark sky over us clearing to muddy brown in the distance, I spoke at last.

"If we're okay for a while," I said to Solarin, "I should go down and see if Lily's still alive."

"You can go in a moment." He turned to me, the side of his face smeared with blood and water, water dripping from his matted hair down his nose and chin. "But first I'd like to thank you for saving my life."

"I think you saved *mine*," I told him with a smile, though I was still shaking with cold and fear. "I wouldn't have begun to know what to do. . . ."

But Solarin was looking at me intently, his hands still on the wheel. Before I could react, he bent over me—his lips were warm, and water dripped from his wet hair to my face as a burst of spray came across the bow, drenching us again with stinging, whiplike fingers. Solarin leaned against the wheel, pulling me to him, his hands warm in the places where my wet shirt clung to the skin. A chill went through me like an electric current as he kissed me again, longer. The waves rolled up and down. Surely that explained the strange feeling deep in my stomach. I couldn't move as I felt his warmth penetrating deeper and deeper. At last he drew away and looked into my eyes with a smile.

"We'll drown for certain if I keep this up," he said, his lips still inches from mine. Reluctantly he put his hands back on the wheel. His brow was furrowed as he turned his attention to the sea. "You'd better go below," he said slowly as if thinking of something. He didn't look back at me.

"I'll try to find something to fix your head," I said, angry because my voice felt so weak. The sea was still wild, dark walls of water moving all around us. But that didn't explain the way I felt as I looked at his dripping hair, the places where his wet torn shirt clung to his lean, muscled body.

I was still shaken as I clambered downstairs. Of course, I thought, Solarin had embraced me in gratitude—that was all. So why did I have this strange feeling in my stomach? Why could I still see his translucent green eyes, so penetrating in the second before he'd kissed me?

I felt my way across the cabin in the dim light from the porthole. The hammock had ripped loose from the wall. Lily was sitting in the corner, holding the bedraggled Carioca in her lap. He had his paws on her chest and was trying to lick her face. He perked up when he heard me plowing through the brackish water on unsteady feet, tossing back and forth between the galley and the beds. As I moved, I plucked things out of the wash and tossed them in the sink.

"Are you okay?" I called to Lily. The place reeked of vomit. I didn't want to look too closely at the water I was wading through.

"We're going to die," she moaned. "My God, after all we've been through, we're going to die. All because of those goddamned pieces."

"Where are they?" I said in sudden panic, thinking my dream might have been a premonition after all.

"Here in the bag," she said, extracting the big satchel from the water she sat in. "When the ship took that big plunge, they came crashing across the room and hit me—and the hammock fell down. I have bruises all over. . . ." Her face was streaked with tears and dirty water.

"I'll put them away," I told her. Grabbing the bag, I stowed it under the sink, then shut the cupboard door. "I think we're going to make it. The storm's dying down. But Solarin got a nasty whack on the head. I've got to find something to clean up his cut."

"There were some medical supplies in the loo," she told me weakly, trying to rise. "My God, am I sick."

"Try to get back into bed," I told her. "Maybe the upper bunk's drier than the rest of this place. I'm going back up to help."

When I came back from the little toilet with the waterlogged box of medicaments I'd salvaged from the debris, Lily had crawled into the upper bunk and was lying on her side groaning. Carioca tried to burrow beneath her looking for a warm spot. I patted them each on their wet heads, then struggled back up the creaking steps as the ship rolled and bucked beneath me.

The sky was lighter now—the color of chocolate milk—and in the distance I could see what looked like a puddle of sunlight on the water. Was it possible the worst was over? I felt relief flooding through me as I squished onto the seat beside Solarin.

"Not a dry bandage in the house," I told him, opening the leaking tin box of medical supplies and reviewing the soggy contents. "But there's iodine and scissors. . . ." Solarin glanced down and plucked out a fat tube of lubricating ointment, handing it to me without looking up.

"You can smear that on, if you would," he told me, turning his eyes back to the water as he started to unbutton his shirt with one hand. "It will disinfect and stanch the bleeding a bit. Then, if you'd shred my shirt for binding . . ."

I helped him pull the wet shirt free from his shoulder and extract his arm as he kept his eyes on the sea. I could smell the warmth of his skin only inches away. I tried not to think of it as he spoke.

"This storm is calming down," he said as if speaking to himself. "But we've worse problems yet. The boom is cracked, and the jib is torn to shreds. We'll not make it to Marseilles. Besides, we're way off course—I'll have to get bearings. As soon as you've fixed me up, you can take the wheel while I have a look at the charts."

His face was a mask as he stared at the sea, and I tried not to look at his body, only inches away as he sat there naked to the waist. What was wrong with me? I thought. My mind must have been wobbly from the recent terror I'd undergone, but all I could think of as the ship moved over the waves was how warm his lips had been, the color of his eyes as he looked into mine . . .

"If we don't make it to Marseilles," I said, forcing my mind back, "won't the plane leave without us?"

"Yes," said Solarin, smiling strangely as he continued to watch the sea. "What an awful plight—we might be forced to put in at some remote spot. We could be stranded in complete isolation for months, with no transportation." I was up on my knees, smearing goo on his head as he spoke. "How terrible . . . what would you do, stuck with a crazy Russian who could only amuse you by playing chess?"

"I guess I'd learn to play," I told him, starting to wrap the bandage as he winced.

"I think the bandages can wait," he told me, grabbing me by the wrists, my two hands full of medicine and strips of his shirt. He lifted me to my feet and, as I stood on the seat, wrapped his arms around my legs and tossed me over his shoulder like a sack of potatoes, stepping up on the seat out of the cockpit as the ship continued to roll through the waves.

"What are you doing?" I laughed, my face muffled against his back as the blood ran to my head.

He slid me down across his body and set me on the deck. Water was running over our bare feet as we stood there facing each other, our legs absorbing the constant movement of the boat over the water.

"I'm going to show you what else Russian chess masters can do," he said, looking down at me. His gray-green eyes were not smiling. He pulled me to him so our lips and bodies met. I could feel the heat of his naked flesh through the wet cloth of my shirt. Salt water dripped from his face into my open mouth as he kissed my eyes, my face. His hands were buried in my wet hair. Through the cold wet fabric that clung to me, I could feel my own heat rising, melting me inside like ice in a hot summer sun. I gripped his shoulders and buried my face in the hard skin of his bare chest. Solarin was murmuring in my ear as the boat swayed up and down, rocking us as we moved together. . . .

"I wanted you that day in the chess club." He pulled my face back to look into my eyes. "I wanted to take you there on the floor—with all those workmen standing by. The night I went to your apartment to leave that note, I nearly stayed behind hoping you'd come home early by mistake and find me there. . . ."

"To welcome me to the Game?" I smiled.

"To hell with the Game," he said bitterly, his eyes dark green pools of passion. "They told me not to come near you—not to get involved. I haven't slept a night without thinking of this, without wanting you. My God, I should have done this months ago. . . ." He was unfastening my shirt. His hands moved over my skin as I felt the surge of power pass between us like a terrible force, washing through me and leaving me empty of all but one thought.

He lifted me in a long sweep and placed me upon the wet and crumpled sails. I felt the spray strike us with every dip of the waves. The masts above us were creaking, the sky was pale with a yellow wash. Solarin was looking down at me, his head bent over me, his lips moving over my skin like water, his hands moving over the wet places where he'd pulled my clothes away. His body melted into mine with the heat and violence of a catalyst. I clung to his shoulders as I felt his passion sweeping me.

Our bodies moved with a power as fierce and primal as the sea that rolled beneath us. I felt myself falling—falling as I heard Solarin's low moan. I felt his teeth sinking into my flesh, his body sinking into mine.

Solarin's body lay over mine in the sails, one hand tangled in my hair, his blond head dripping water on my breast that streamed down into the hollow of my belly. How strange, I thought as I put my hand on his head, that I should feel I'd known him all my life, when we'd only met three times—now four. I knew nothing of Solarin but gossip from Lily and Hermanold at the club and what little Nim had recalled from his chess journals. I hadn't the vaguest clue about where Solarin lived, what sort of life he had, who his friends were, whether he ate eggs for breakfast or wore pajamas to bed. I'd never asked him how he'd evaded his KGB guards or why they were with him in the first place. Nor did I know how it happened that he'd met his own grandmother only once before.

Suddenly I knew why I'd painted his portrait before I'd ever seen him. I might have noticed him lurking about my apartment building on that bicycle without it consciously registering. But even that was not important.

These were things I didn't really need to know—superficial relations and events that are the pivotal center of most people's lives. But not mine. In Solarin I saw beneath the mystery, the mask, the cold veneer—to what lay at the very core. And what I saw was passion, an unquenchable thirst for life—a passion to discover the truth behind the veil. It was a passion I recognized, because it matched my own.

That was what Minnie recognized and wanted in me—this passion, channeled by *her*, into a quest for the pieces. That's why she'd cautioned her grandson to protect me but not to distract me, not to get "involved." As Solarin rolled over and pressed his lips to my stomach, I felt a delicious chill move through my spine. I touched his hair. She was wrong, I thought. There was one ingredient she'd overlooked in the alchemical brew she was cooking up to defeat evil forever. The ingredient she'd forgotten was love.

The sea had died to gently rocking waves of muddy brown when at last we stirred. The sky had grown a bright flat white, glaring without the sun. We searched about for our cold wet clothes and fumbled to put them on. Without a word, Solarin picked up some scraps of his former shirt and used them to wipe the places where his blood still stained my body. Then he looked at me with his sea-green eyes and smiled.

"I've some very bad news," he said, slipping one arm around me as he raised the other to point out across the flat dark waves. There in the distance, shimmering against the glare of water, rose a miragelike form. "Land ho," he whispered in my ear. "Two hours ago, I'd have given anything to see a sight like that. But just now, I'd rather pretend it wasn't real. . . ."

The isle was called Formentera, in the southern curve of the Balearic group just off the eastern coast of Spain. This meant, I calculated quickly, we'd been driven by the storm 150 miles east of our original course and were now at a spot equidistant from Gibraltar and Marseilles. To reach the plane on that landing strip near La Camargue was now patently impossible, even if we had a boat that was seaworthy. But with our cracked boom, torn sails, and the general carnage on deck—we needed to stop for an inventory and make extensive repairs. As Solarin brought us limping on our stalwart little engine into an isolated bay at the south end of the island, I went below to roust Lily so we could form an alternate plan.

"I never thought I'd feel *relieved* to spend a night rolling about in that watery coffin," Lily gasped when she caught her first glimpse of the deck. "But this place looks like a battle zone. Thank God I was too sick to witness the catastrophe." Though her face was still sickly, she seemed to have recovered most of her former strength. She crossed the battered deck covered with debris and soggy canvas, gulping down fresh air.

"We have a problem," I told her as soon as we sat down for a pow-wow with Solarin. "We're not going to make that plane. Now we have to figure out how to get to Manhattan without taking those pieces through Customs, while bypassing Immigrations as well."

"We Soviet citizens," Solarin explained to Lily's questioning look, "don't exactly have carte blanche to travel everywhere. Besides, Sharrif will be watching all commercial airports, including, I'm sure, those at Ibiza and Majorca.

Since I promised Minnie I'd return you both safely—with the pieces—I'd like to suggest a plan."

"Shoot—I'm game for anything at this point," said Lily, pulling knots out of Carioca's wet and matted hair as he struggled to escape from her lap.

"Formentera is a small fishing island. They're used to the occasional visitor sailing over from Ibiza just for the day. This cove is very sheltered—we'll never be noticed here. I suggest we go into the local town, buy fresh clothing and supplies, and see if we can't get a new sail and the tools I'll need to repair the damage. This might be costly, but in a week or so we'd be seaworthy and could simply leave as silently as we've come, with no one the wiser."

"Sounds great," Lily agreed. "I still have plenty of soggy money we can use. I could certainly stand a change of attire and a few days' rest from all this hysteria. Once we're all shipshape, where do you propose we head?"

"New York," said Solarin, "by way of the Bahamas and the Inland Waterway."

"What?!!" Lily and I both cried in unison.

"That must be four thousand miles," I added in horror, "in a ship that barely survived three hundred in a storm."

"Actually, it's closer to *five* thousand miles by the route I propose," said Solarin with an easy smile. "But if it worked for Columbus, why shouldn't it for us? This might be the worst season for sailing the Mediterranean, but it's the mildest for crossing the Atlantic. With a decent breeze, we'll make it in under a month—and you'll both be excellent sailors by the time we've arrived."

Lily and I were too exhausted, dirty, and hungry to argue with conviction. Besides, more recent than my memory of the storm was my memory of what had happened between Solarin and me just after the storm. A month of that wouldn't be entirely unacceptable. So we set off in search of a town on the tiny island while Solarin stayed behind to clean up the wreckage.

Days of hard work and beautiful golden weather mellowed us a bit. The isle of Formentera had whitewashed houses and sandy streets, olive groves and silent springs, old women dressed in black and fishermen in striped shirts. All this, set against the backdrop of the endless azure sea, was a balm to the eye, a soothing salve to the soul. Three days of eating fresh fish from the sea and fruits ripe from the tree, of drinking good strong Mediterranean wine and breathing healthful salt air, had worked wonders on our dispositions. We had leathery tans—even Lily was getting lean and well muscled from all the work we shared around the boat.

Each night Lily played chess with Solarin. Though he never let her win, he explained after each game what mistakes she'd made, in painstaking detail. After a while she began not only to take these defeats in good grace, but to question Solarin when a move of his puzzled her. She was once again so wrapped up in chess that she hardly noticed when—beginning that first night on the isle—I elected to sleep on deck with Solarin rather than adjourn to the cabin when she turned in.

"She really has it," Solarin told me one night as we sat alone on deck, looking up at the sea of silent stars. "Everything her grandfather had—and more. She'll be a great chess player, if she can just forget she's a woman."

"What does being a woman have to do with it?" I asked.

Solarin smiled and tugged my hair. "Little girls are different from little boys," he said. "Shall I prove it to you?"

I laughed and peered at him in the pale moonlight. "You've made your point," I said.

"We *think* differently," he added, sliding over to lie with his head in my lap. He looked up at me, and I realized he was serious. "For example, to discover the formula contained in the Montglane Service, you'd probably go about it far differently than I."

"Okay," I said with a laugh. "How would *you* go about it?"

"I'd try to itemize everything I knew," he told me, reaching up to help himself to a sip of my brandy. "Then see how these 'given' items could be combined into a solution. I admit, however, I've a small advantage. For example, I may be the only person in a thousand years who's seen the cloth, the pieces, and who's also had a glimpse of the board." He glanced up as he felt me move slightly in surprise.

"In Russia," he said, "when the board surfaced, there were those who quickly arrogated for themselves the responsibility of finding the other pieces. Of course, they were members of the white team. I believe Brodski—the KGB official who accompanied me to New York—is one of them. I ingratiated myself with high government officials by suggesting, as Mordecai directed, that I knew where other pieces were and could obtain them."

He returned slowly to his initial thought. Looking up at me in the silvery light, he said, "I saw so many symbols contained in the service, it led me to believe there might not be just *one* formula, but *many*. After all—as you've already guessed—these symbols don't represent only planets and signs of the zodiac, but also elements in the Periodic Table. It seems to me you'd need a different formula to convert *each* element into another. But how do we know which symbols to combine in what sequence? How do we know *any* of these formulae really works?"

"With your theory, we wouldn't," I said, taking a sip of the brandy as my brain began to work. "There'd be too many random variables—too many permutations. I may not know much about alchemy, but I do understand formulas. Everything we've learned points to the fact there's only *one* formula. But it may not be what we think. . . ."

"What do you mean?" said Solarin, glancing up at me.

Since our arrival at the isle, none of us had mentioned those pieces stowed in their bag beneath the galley. As if by unspoken common consent, we agreed not to disturb our brief idyll by mentioning the quest that had placed our lives in such great danger. Now that Solarin had jarred me by raising the specter, I again began to probe the thought that, like a toothache, had throbbed in my head these many weeks and months.

"I mean I think there's just one formula, with a simple solution. Why hide it in such a veil of mystery if it was so difficult no one could understand it? It's like the pyramids—for thousands of years people have been going on about how *hard* it was for those Egyptians to haul all those two-thousand-ton blocks of granite and limestone with their primitive tools. And yet there they are. But what if they *didn't* move them that way? The Egyptians were alchemists, weren't they? They must have known you can dilute those stones in acid, toss them in a bucket, and slap them together again like cement."

"Go on," said Solarin, looking up at me in the moonlight with a strange smile. Even from upside down, I thought how beautiful he was.

"The pieces of the Montglane Service glow in the dark," I said, my mind racing ahead. "Do you know what you get if you break down the element mercury? Two radioactive isotopes—one that decays in a matter of hours or days into thallium, the other to radioactive gold."

Solarin rolled over and leaned on his elbow as he looked at me closely. "If I may be devil's advocate for a moment," he said, "I should point out that you reason from effect to cause. You say, if there were pieces that were transmuted, there must be a formula that did it. Even if so—why *this* formula? And why only one, rather than fifty or a hundred?"

"Because in science, as in nature, it's often the simplest solution—the obvious one—that works," I said. "Minnie thought there was only one formula. She said it had three parts: the board, the pieces, and the cloth." I stopped cold as something suddenly occurred to me. "Like rock, scissors, paper," I said. When Solarin looked puzzled, I added, "It's a children's game."

"You remind me of a child." He laughed and took another sip of my brandy. "But so were all the greatest scientists children at heart. Go on."

"The pieces cover the board—the cloth covers the pieces," I said, working it out in my mind. "So the first part of the formula may describe *what*, the second tells *how,* and the third . . . explains *when.*"

"You mean the symbols on the board describe which raw materials—elements—are used," Solarin said, rubbing the bandaged cut on his head, "the pieces tell in what proportions to combine them, and the cloth tells in what sequence?"

"Almost," I said, jittery with excitement. "As you said, those symbols describe elements in the Periodic Table. But we've overlooked the first thing we noticed. They *also* represent planets and *signs of the zodiac*! The third part tells exactly *when*—in what time, month, or year—each step of the process is to be executed!" But as soon as I said it, I knew that couldn't be it. "What difference could it make what day or month you begin or end an experiment?"

Solarin said nothing for a moment, and when he spoke it was slowly, with that clipped, formal English he used when under great strain.

"It would make a very large difference," he told me, "if you understood what Pythagoras meant when he used the phrase 'the music of the spheres.' I think you're on to something. Let's get the pieces."

Lily and Carioca were snoring in their respective bunks when I went downstairs. Solarin had remained behind to light a lamp on deck and set up the pegboard chess set he and Lily played on each night.

"What's going on?" Lily said as I fumbled around for the bag I'd stored under the galley.

"We're solving the riddle," I said cheerfully. "Care to join in?"

"Of course," she said. I could hear the mattress creaking as she climbed off the bunk. "I was wondering when you two were going to invite me to your nightly covens. What exactly is going on between you, or shouldn't I ask?" I was thankful for the darkness—my face felt hot. "Forget it," said Lily. "He's a handsome enough devil, but not my type. One of these days I'll beat his ass in chess."

We clambered up the stairs, Lily throwing on a sweater over her pajamas, and sat on the cushioned seats of the cockpit at either side of Solarin. Lily poured herself a drink as I removed the pieces and cloth from the bag and spread them out in the lamplight on the floor.

Quickly recapping for Lily what we'd discussed, I sat back, leaving the floor to Solarin. The boat was swaying, the waves lapping gently. A warm breeze stroked us as we sat beneath the universe of stars. Lily was touching the cloth, looking at Solarin with a strange expression.

"What exactly *did* Pythagoras mean by 'the music of the spheres'?" she asked him.

"He thought the universe was comprised of numbers," said Solarin, looking down at the pieces of the Montglane Service. "That just as notes of a musical scale repeat octave after octave, so all things in nature form such a pattern. He began a field of mathematical inquiry in which major breakthroughs have been made, *we* think, only in recent times. It is called harmonic analysis—the basis of my field, acoustical physics, and also a key factor in quantum physics."

Solarin stood up and started pacing. I remembered what he'd once said about having to move in order to think.

"The basic idea," he said as Lily watched him closely, "is that *any* phenomena of a periodically recurring nature can be measured. That is, any wave—whether sound, heat, or light—even the tides of the sea. Kepler used this theory to discover the laws of planetary motion, Newton to explain the law of universal gravitation and the precession of the equinoxes. Leonhard Euler used it to prove that light was a wave form whose color depended upon length. But it was Fourier, the great eighteenth-century mathematician, who revealed the method by which all wave forms—including those of atoms—could be measured." He turned to us, his eyes glowing in the dim light.

"So Pythagoras was right," I said. "The universe *is* made up of numbers that recur with mathematical precision and can be measured. Is that what you think the Montglane Service is all about—harmonic analysis of molecular structure? Measuring waves to analyze the structure of elements?"

"What can be measured can be understood," said Solarin slowly. "What can be understood can be altered. Pythagoras studied with the greatest alchemist of them all—Hermes Trismegistus, who was considered by the Egyptians to be the incarnation of the great god Thoth. It was he who defined the first principle of alchemy: 'As above, so below.' The waves of the universe operate the same as the waves of the tiniest atom—and can be shown to interact." He paused and turned to look at me.

"Two thousand years later, Fourier showed just *how* they interact. Maxwell and Planck revealed that energy itself could be described in terms of these wave forms. Einstein took the last step, and showed that what Fourier had suggested as an analytic tool was so, in reality—that matter and energy were wave forms that could be transformed into each other."

Something was working in my mind. I was staring at the cloth where Lily's fingers were running over the gold bodies of the twined serpents that formed a figure eight. Somewhere deep inside, a connection was forming between that cloth—the *labrys*/labyrinth Lily had described—and what Solarin had just said about waves. As above, so below. Macrocosm, microcosm. Matter, energy. What did it all mean?

"The Eight," I said aloud, though still lost in my thoughts. "Everything leads back to the Eight. The *labrys* is shaped like an eight. So is the spiral that Newton showed us was formed by the precession of the equinoxes. That mystical walk described in our journal—the one Rousseau took in Venice—that was an eight, too. And the symbol for infinity . . ."

"What journal?" said Solarin, suddenly alert. I stared at him in disbelief. Was it possible Minnie had shown *us* something of which her own grandson was unaware?

"A book Minnie gave us," I told him. "It's the diary of a French nun who lived two hundred years ago. She was present when the service was removed from Montglane Abbey. We haven't had time to finish it. I have it here. . . ."
I started to extract the book from my bag, but Solarin leaped forward.

"My God," he cried, "so that's what she meant when she told me *you* had the final key. Why haven't you mentioned this before?" He was touching the soft leather cover of the book I held in my hand.

"I've had a few things on my mind," I said. I opened the book to the page where the Long March—that ceremony in Venice—was portrayed. The three of us bent over it in the candlelight, and we studied it in silence for a moment. Lily smiled slowly and turned to look at Solarin with her big gray eyes.

"These are chess moves, aren't they?" she said.

He nodded. "Each move on the figure eight in this diagram," he said, "corresponds to a symbol in the same location on this cloth—probably a symbol they *saw* in the ceremony as well. And if I'm not mistaken, it tells us what *kind* of piece and where it would logically land on the board. Sixteen steps, each comprised of three pieces of information. Perhaps the very three you guessed: what, how, and when. . . ."

"Like the trigrams of the I-Ching," I said. "Each group containing a quantum of information."

Solarin was staring at me. Then he laughed. "Exactly," he said, reaching over to squeeze my shoulder. "Come, chess players. We've figured out the structure of the Game. Now let's put it all together and discover the gateway to infinity."

We labored over the puzzle all that night. Now I could see why mathematicians felt a transcendental wave of energy washing over *them* when they discovered a new formula or saw a new pattern in something they'd looked at a thousand times. Only in mathematics was there that sense of moving through another dimension, one that didn't exist in time and place—that feeling of falling into and through a puzzle, of having it surround you in a physical way.

I wasn't a great mathematician, but I understood Pythagoras when he said mathematics was one with music. As Lily and Solarin labored over the chess moves on the board and I tried to capture the pattern on paper, I felt as if I could *hear* the formula of the Montglane Service singing to me. It was like an elixir running through my veins, driving me on with its beautiful harmony as we beat ourselves into the ground trying to find the pattern in the pieces.

It wasn't easy. As Solarin had implied, when you were dealing with a formula comprised of sixty-four squares, thirty-two pieces, and sixteen positions on a cloth, the possible combinations were far more than the total number of stars in the known universe. Though it looked from our drawing as if some of the moves were Knight moves and others Rook or Bishop, we couldn't be sure. The entire pattern had to fit within the sixty-four squares on the board of the Montglane Service.

This was complicated by the fact that, even if we knew *which* pawn or Knight had made the move to a certain square, we didn't know which had been sitting on which square when the Game was first designed.

Nevertheless, I was certain there was a key even to these things, so we forged ahead with the information we *did* have. White always makes the first move, and it's usually a pawn. Though Lily complained this wasn't de rigueur historically, it seemed clear from our map the first move was a pawn's—the only piece that could make a straight vertical move at the beginning of the game.

Were the moves alternating black and white pieces, or should we assume—as in a Knight's Tour—they could be made by a single piece hopping randomly about the board? We opted for the former choice, as it narrowed the alternatives. We also decided, since this was a formula and not a game, that each piece could only move once, and each square could only be occupied once. To Solarin, the pattern didn't form a game that made any sense in actual play, but it did reveal a pattern that looked like the one on the cloth and on our map. Only, oddly, it was backward—that is, a mirror image of the procession that took place in Venice.

By dawn we'd come up with a picture that looked like Lily's image of the *labrys.* And if you left the *unmoved* pieces still on the board, they formed *another* geometric figure eight on the vertical plane. We knew we were very close:

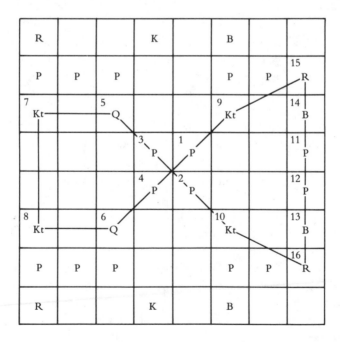

Bleary-eyed, we looked up from our figuring with a camaraderie that transcended our individual competitive streaks. Lily began laughing and rolling on the ground with Carioca jumping on her stomach. Solarin raced to me like a madman, picking me up and whirling me around. The sun was rising, turning the sea blood-red and the sky a pearly pink.

"Now all we need to do is get the board and the rest of the pieces," I told him with a wry grin. "A piece of cake, I'm sure."

"We know there are nine more in New York," he pointed out, smiling at me with an expression that suggested he had more than chess on his mind. "I think we should go have a look, don't you?"

"Aye-aye, Skipper," Lily said. "Let's rig the yardarm and jig the boom. I vote we hit the road."

"By water it is, then," said Solarin happily.

"May the great goddess Car smile upon all our nautical endeavors," I said.

"I'll hoist sail to that," said Lily. And she did.

THE
SECRET

Newton was not the first of the Age of Reason. He was the last of the magicians, the last of the Babylonians and Sumerians . . . because he looked on the universe and all that is in it *as a riddle*, as a secret which could be read by applying pure thought to certain evidence, certain mystic clues which God had laid about the world to allow a sort of philosopher's treasure hunt to the esoteric brotherhood. . . .

He regarded the universe as a cryptogram set by the Almighty—just as he himself wrapt the discovery of the calculus in a cryptogram when he communicated with Leibniz. By pure thought, by concentration of mind, the riddle, he believed, would be revealed to the initiate.

—John Maynard Keynes

We have in the end come back to a version of the doctrine of old Pythagoras, from whom mathematics and mathematical physics took their rise. He . . . directed attention to numbers as characterizing the periodicity of notes of music. . . . And now in the twentieth century we find physicists largely engaged in the periodicity of atoms.

—Alfred North Whitehead

Number, then, appears to lead towards truth.

—Plato

P aul I, Czar of all the Russias, paced about his chambers slapping a riding crop against the breeches of his dark green military uniform. He was proud of these uniforms of coarse cloth, fashioned after those used by the troops of Frederick the Great of Prussia. Paul flicked something from the lapel of his high-cut waistcoat and raised his eyes to those of his son Alexander, who stood at attention across the room.

What a disappointment Alexander had proven, thought Paul. Pale, poetic, and so handsome as to be considered pretty, there was something both mystical and vacuous floating behind those blue-gray eyes he'd inherited from his grandmother. But he had not inherited her brains. He lacked everything one looked for in a leader.

In a way this was fortunate, thought Paul. For the twenty-one-year-old lad, far from wishing to seize the throne Catherine had intended to be his, had actually announced his wish to abdicate should such a responsibility be thrust upon him. He preferred, he said, the quiet life of a man of letters—living somewhere in obscurity on the Danube rather than mingling in the seductive but dangerous court at Petersburg, where his father commanded him to remain.

Now, as Alexander stood gazing through the windows into the autumn gardens, his vacant eyes suggested there was nothing more on his mind than daydreams. In fact, however, his thoughts were far from idle. Beneath those silken curls was a mind whose workings were far more complex than Paul could ever fathom. The problem he worked on now was how to broach a certain subject without arousing Paul's suspicions—a topic that was never mentioned at Paul's court, not since the death of Catherine nearly two years ago. The topic of the Abbess of Montglane.

Alexander had a vital reason for trying to discover what had become of this old woman, who'd disappeared as into a vacuum only a few days after his grandmother's death. But before he could think how to begin, Paul had wheeled to face him, still slapping his crop like an idiotic toy soldier. Alexander tried to pay attention.

"I know you do not care to hear of the affairs of state," Paul told his son disdainfully. "But you really must show some interest. After all, one day this empire will be yours. The actions I take today will be your responsibility tomorrow. I've called you here today to tell you something in complete confidence, which may alter the future of Russia." He paused for effect. "I've decided to form a treaty with England."

"But Father, you hate the British!" said Alexander.

"Yes, I despise them," Paul said, "but I've little choice. The French, not satisfied with breaking up the Austrian Empire, expanding their borders into every surrounding country, and massacring half their own populace to keep them quiet—have now sent this bloodthirsty General Bonaparte across the sea to take Malta and Egypt!" He slammed his crop down on the leather desk, his face clouding dark like a summer storm. Alexander said nothing.

"*I* am the elected grand master of the Knights of Malta!" screamed Paul, pounding a gold medal on the dark ribbon that crossed his chest. "*I* wear the eight-point star of the Maltese Cross! That island belongs to me! For centuries we've sought a warm-water port like Malta—and now at last we almost had one. Until this French assassin came along with his forty thousand troops." He looked at Alexander as if expecting a response.

"Why would a French general try to take a country that's been a thorn in the side of the Ottoman Turks for over three hundred years?" he said, privately wondering why Paul would wish to *oppose* such a move. It could only divert those Muslim Turks his grandmother had battled for twenty years over control of Constantinople and the Black Sea.

"Can't you guess what he's after, this Bonaparte?" whispered Paul, stepping up to look Alexander in the face as he rubbed his hands together.

Alexander shook his head. "Do you think the British will serve you any better?" he asked. "My tutor La Harpe used to call England Perfidious Albion. . . ."

"That is not the issue!" cried Paul. "As usual, you mix poetry and politics, doing disservice to each. *I* know why that blackguard Bonaparte went into Egypt—no matter what he's told those fools who dole out money in the French Directory, no matter how many tens of thousands of soldiers he's landed there! Restore the powers of the Sublime Porte? Put down the Mamelukes? Bah! It's all camouflage." Alexander was still and guarded but paying close attention as his father ranted on. "Mark my words, he will not stop with Egypt. He'll move on to Syria and Assyria, Phoenicia and Babylon—the lands my mother always wanted. She even named you Alexander and your brother Constantine as a good-luck charm." Paul paused and looked about the room, his eyes falling upon a tapestry depicting a hunt scene. A wounded hart, bleeding and riddled with arrows, struggled into the forest with hunters and hounds in pursuit. Paul turned back to Alexander with a cold smile.

"This Bonaparte doesn't want territory—he wants power! He's taken as many scientists as soldiers: the mathematician Monge, Berthollet the chemist, the physicist Fourier . . . He's cleaned out the École Polytechnique and the Institut National! Why so, I ask you, if it was only conquest he thirsted after?"

"What do you mean?" whispered Alexander, the first glimmer of a thought beginning to light his mind.

"The secret of the Montglane Service is hidden there!" hissed Paul, his face a mask of fear and hatred. "That's what he's after."

"But Father," said Alexander, choosing his words with extreme caution. "Surely you don't believe those old myths? After all, the Abbess of Montglane herself—"

"Of course I believe it!" screamed Paul. His face had turned dark, and he lowered his voice to an hysterical whisper. "I myself have one of the pieces." His hands were tightened into balled fists; he'd dropped his crop on the floor. "There are others hidden here. I know it! But even two years in Ropsha Prison haven't loosened *that* woman's tongue. She's like the Sphinx. But one day she will break—and when she does . . ."

Alexander hardly heard anything further as his father ranted on about the French, the British, his plans in Malta—and the insidious Bonaparte whom he planned to destroy. It was unlikely any of these threats would bear fruit, Alexander knew, since Paul's own troops already despised him as children loathe a tyrannical governess.

Alexander complimented his father upon the brilliant political strategy, excused himself, and left the quarters. So the abbess was incarcerated at Ropsha Prison, he thought as he strode through the long halls of the Winter Palace. So Bonaparte had landed in Egypt with a boatload of scientists. So Paul had one of the pieces of the Montglane Service. It had been a productive day. Things were coming together at last.

It took Alexander nearly half an hour to reach the indoor stables, which took up an entire wing at the far end of the Winter Palace—a wing nearly as large as the mirrored hall at Versailles. The air there was steamy with the heady smell of animals and fodder. He strode down the straw-strewn corridors as pigs and chickens waddled from his path. Rosy-cheeked servants in their jerkins, dirndls, white aprons, and thick boots turned to look after the young prince as he passed, smiling to one another behind his back. His handsome face, his curly chestnut hair and sparkling blue-gray eyes, reminded them of the youthful Czarina Catherine, his grandmother, when she used to ride forth in the snowy streets on her speckled gelding, dressed in military attire.

This was the boy they wished they had as czar. The very things his father found annoying—his silence and mystique, the veiled mystery beneath his blue-gray gaze—aroused the dark strain of mysticism buried deep in their Slavic souls.

Alexander went to the groomsman to have his horse saddled, then mounted and rode forth. The servants and stable hands stood watching. Always watching. They knew the time was near at hand. He was the one they waited for, the one who was foretold since the time of Peter the Great. The silent, mysterious Alexander who was chosen not to lead them out, but to descend with them—into darkness. To become the soul of Russia.

Alexander had always felt uncomfortable around the serfs and peasants. It was almost as if they regarded him as a saint—and expected him to live up to the role.

This was also dangerous. Paul guarded zealously the throne that had been withheld from him so long. Now he took the power he'd so long lusted for—cherished it, used it, and abused it like a mistress whom one desires but cannot control.

Alexander crossed the Neva and passed the city markets, letting his big white horse break into a canter only when he'd passed the open pastureland and crossed into the wet autumn fields.

He rode for hours through the forest, as if aimlessly. The yellow leaves lay like heaps of corn husks on the ground. At last, in an empty quarter of the forest, he came to a silent glen where a maze of black branches and wet webs of golden leaves partially masked the outline of an old sod hut. He dismounted casually and began to walk his steaming horse.

The reins held lightly between his fingers, he moved over the soft, richly scented leaf mulch of the forest floor. His lean athletic form, the black military jacket with its high collar reaching nearly to his chin, the tight white breeches and stiff black boots, made him appear as a simple soldier wandering in the forest. Some water toppled from the bough of a tree. He brushed it from the fringe of his gold epaulet and drew his sword, touching it casually as if merely examining its sharpness. He glanced for an instant at the hut, where two horses grazed nearby.

Alexander looked around the silent forest. A cuckoo called three times—then nothing. Only the sound of water softly plopping from the branches of the trees. He dropped his horse's reins and walked toward the hut.

He pushed the door ajar with a creaking sound. Inside, it was nearly black. His eyes could not adjust to the light, but he could smell the bare earth floor—the scent of a tallow candle recently doused. He thought he heard something stirring in the darkness. His heart raced faster.

"Are you there?" Alexander whispered in the darkness. Then a small shower of sparks—the smell of burnt straw as a flame blazed up—a candle being lighted. Above its glow, he saw the beautiful oval face, the brilliant tumult of strawberry hair, the glittering green eyes looking up searchingly into his.

"Did you succeed?" said Mireille in a voice so low he had to strain to hear it.

"Yes. She's at Ropsha Prison," Alexander whispered back, though he'd seen no one for miles around who could hear him. "I can take you there. But there's more. He has one of the pieces, just as you feared."

"And the rest?" said Mireille quietly. Her green eyes dazzled him.

"I could learn nothing more without arousing his suspicions. It seemed a miracle he spoke as much as he did. Ah, yes—it seems that French expedition into Egypt may be more than we thought, a cover-up, perhaps. General Bonaparte has taken many scientists along."

"Scientists?" Mireille said quickly, sitting forward on her chair.

"Mathematicians, physicists, chemists," said Alexander.

Mireille had glanced over her shoulder into the dark corner of the room. Now, from the shadows, emerged the tall and slender form of a craggy, hawk-faced man dressed completely in black. He held the hand of a little boy of about five, who smiled sweetly up at Alexander. The Crown Prince smiled back.

"You heard?" Mireille asked Shahin. He nodded silently. "Napoleone is in Egypt, but not at *my* request. What does he do there? How much has he learned? I want him brought back to France. If you go now, how quickly can you reach him?"

"Perhaps he is at Alexandria, perhaps at Cairo," said Shahin. "If I pass through the Turkish Empire, I can reach him at either place within two moons. I must bring al-Kalim with me—those Ottomans will see he is the Prophet, the *Porte* will let me pass and lead me to the son of Letizia Bonaparte."

Alexander was staring in amazement at this interchange. "You speak of General Bonaparte as if you knew him," he told Mireille.

"He is a Corsican," she said curtly. "Your French is far better than his. But we haven't time to dally—take me to Ropsha before it's too late."

Alexander turned to the door, helping Mireille draw her cape around her, when he noticed little Charlot standing beside his elbow.

"Al-Kalim has something to tell you, Majesty," Shahin said, motioning to Charlot. Alexander looked down at the child with a smile.

"Soon you will be a great king," said little Charlot in his piping, childish voice. Alexander was still smiling, but his smile faded at the child's next words. "The blood on your hands will leave a smaller stain than that on your grandmother's, but for a similar deed. A man you admire will betray you—I see a cold winter and a great fire. You have helped my mother. Because of this you'll be saved from the hands of this disloyal person and live to rule twenty-five years. . . ."

"Charlot, that's quite enough!" Mireille hissed, grabbing her son by the hand as she shot a dark look at Shahin.

Alexander stood there frozen—chilled to the bone. "This child has the second sight!" he whispered.

"Then let him put it to some use," she snapped, "instead of going about casting fortunes like an old witch over a tarot." Dragging Charlot behind her, she bustled through the door leaving the astounded Prince of Russia in her wake. As he turned to Shahin and looked into the impenetrable black eyes, he heard the voice of little Charlot:

"I'm sorry, *Maman*," he piped. "I only forgot. I promise I won't do it again."

∞

Ropsha Prison made the Bastille seem a palace by comparison. Cold and damp, with no windows to let in even a crack of light, it was in every sense a dungeon of despair. For two years the abbess had survived here, drinking brackish water and eating food that was little better than pig slop. Two years of which Mireille had spent every hour, every minute, trying to discover her location.

Now Alexander slipped them into the prison and spoke with the guards, who loved him far better than his father and would do anything he asked. Mireille, still holding Charlot's hand, went through the dark corridors behind the guard's lantern, as Alexander and Shahin brought up the rear.

The abbess's cell was deep in the bowels of the prison, a small hole secured by a heavy metal door. Mireille felt a horrible cold fear. The guard admitted her, and she stepped across the room. The old woman lay there like a doll whose stuffing had been removed, her withered skin yellowed like a dead leaf in the pale lantern light. Mireille fell on her knees beside the plank and threw her arms around the abbess, lifting her to sit up. There was no substance to her at all—it seemed she might crumble away to dust.

Charlot came up and took the abbess's withered hand in his tiny one. *"Maman,"* he whispered, "this lady is very sick. She wishes we would take her out of this place before she dies. . . ." Mireille looked down at him, then glanced up at Alexander, who stood behind her.

"Let me see what I can do," he said. He stepped outside with the guard. Shahin came up beside the bed. With extreme effort, the abbess tried to open her eyelids but failed. Mireille bent her head over the old woman's breast and felt the hot tears rising behind her eyes, burning her throat. Charlot put his hand on her shoulder.

"There is something she needs to say," he told his mother quietly. "I can hear her thoughts. . . . She does not wish to be buried by others. . . . Mother," he whispered, "there is something inside her dress! Something we must have—she wants us to have it."

"Good God," murmured Mireille just as Alexander returned to the chamber.

"Come, let us take her before the guard changes his mind," he whispered urgently. Shahin bent over the bed and lifted the abbess like a feather in his arms. The four of them hurried from the prison, leaving by a door that led to a long corridor that ran beneath the earth. At last they came up into the light of day, not far from where they'd left their horses. Shahin, holding the fragile abbess in one cupped arm, swung into his saddle with ease and headed for the forest with the others just behind.

As soon as they reached an isolated spot, they drew up and dismounted. Alexander lifted the abbess down in his arms. Mireille spread her cape on the ground for the dying woman to lie upon. The abbess, her eyes still closed, was struggling to speak. Alexander brought her water in cupped hands from a nearby stream, but she was too weak to drink.

"I knew . . ." she said in a hoarse and faltering voice.

"You knew I'd come for you," said Mireille, stroking the feverish brow as the abbess struggled on. "But I'm afraid I've come too late. My dear friend— you will have a Christian burial. I shall take your confession myself, as no one else is here." Tears were streaming down her face as she knelt beside the abbess gripping her hand. But Charlot was on his knees as well, his hands on the abbatial gown that hung from her brittle frame.

"Mother, it is here in this dress—between the cloth and the lining!" he cried. Shahin came forward, drawing out his sharp *bousaadi* to cut the cloth. Mireille laid her hand on his arm to prevent him, but just then the abbess opened her eyes and spoke in a hoarse whisper.

"Shahin," she said, the smile spreading across her face as she tried to lift her hand to touch him. "You've found your prophet at last. I go to meet this Allah of yours . . . quite soon. I bring Him . . . your love . . ." She dropped her hand, and her eyes fell closed. Mireille began to sob, but the abbess's lips were still moving. Charlot leaned forward across from Mireille and pressed his lips to the abbess's forehead. "Do not cut . . . the cloth . . ." she said. Then she did not move.

Shahin and Alexander stood motionless beneath the dripping trees as Mireille threw herself across the body of the dead abbess and wept. After several minutes Charlot pulled his mother away. With his tiny hands he lifted the heavy robe of the abbess from her withered body. There on the lining of the front panel of her gown, she had drawn a jagged chessboard, written in her own blood— now brown and stained with wear. In each of the squares, a symbol had been printed with great care. Charlot looked up at Shahin, who handed him the knife. The child carefully cut free the thread that held the fabric to the lining. There, beneath the chessboard, was the heavy cloth of midnight blue—covered with glowing stones.

PARIS   JANUARY 1799

Charles Maurice Talleyrand left the offices of the Directory and limped down
the long stone steps to the courtyard where his carriage waited. It had been a
hard day of accusations and insults, hurled at him by the five directors, over
bribes he had supposedly received from the American delegation. He was too
proud to justify or excuse himself—and had too recent a memory of poverty
to admit his sins and turn over the money. He'd sat there in stony silence as
they'd frothed at the mouth. When they'd worn themselves out, he'd left
without giving any ground.

He limped wearily across the cobbled court to his carriage. He'd dine alone
tonight, open a bottle of aged Madeira, and have a hot bath. These were the
only thoughts on his mind as his driver, sighting his master, rushed toward the
carriage. Talleyrand waved him to the box and opened the door himself. As
he slipped into his seat, he heard a rustling sound within the darkness of the large
compartment. He stiffened at once.

"Do not fear," said a soft woman's voice—a voice that sent chills down his
spine. A gloved hand closed over his in the darkness. As the carriage pulled forth
into the light of the street lamps, he glimpsed the beautiful creamy skin, the
strawberry hair.

"Mireille!" cried Talleyrand, but she put her gloved fingers upon his lips.
Before he knew what was happening, he was on his knees in the rocking
carriage, showering her face with kisses, burying his hands in her hair, murmuring a thousand things as his mind fought for control. He thought he was going
mad.

"If you knew how long I'd searched for you—not here only, but in every
land. How could you let me go so long without a word, a sign? I was beside
myself with fear for you. . . ." Mireille silenced him with her lips on his, as
he drank in the perfume of her body and wept. He wept seven years of unshed
tears and drank the tears from her cheeks as they clung to each other like children
lost at sea.

They went into his house under cover of darkness, through the wide French
windows overlooking the lawns. Without pausing to shut the windows or
light a lamp, he swept her into his arms and carried her to the divan, her
long hair flowing over his arm. Undressing her without a word, he covered
her shivering body with his and lost himself in her warm flesh, her silken
hair.

"I love you," he said. It was the first time these words had ever passed his
lips.

"Your love has given us a child," whispered Mireille, looking up at him in the moonlight that streamed through the windows. He thought his heart would break.

"We shall make another," he said, and felt his passion rack him like a storm.

"I buried them," said Talleyrand as they sat at the parqueted table in the drawing room beside his bedchamber. "In the Green Mountains of America—though to do him service, Courtiade tried to convince me against it. He had more faith than I. He thought you were still alive." Talleyrand smiled at Mireille, who sat with disheveled hair, wrapped in his dressing gown, across the table. She was so beautiful, he longed to take her there again. But the conservative Courtiade sat between them, folding his serviette carefully as he listened to their talk.

"Courtiade," he said, trying to calm the violence of his feelings, "it seems I have a child—a son. His name is Charlot, after myself." He turned to Mireille. "When will I get to see this little prodigy?"

"Soon," said Mireille. "He's gone to Egypt, where General Bonaparte is quartered. How well do you know Napoleone?"

"It was I who convinced him to go there—or at least, so he'd have me believe." He described briefly his meeting with Bonaparte and David. "It was in this way I learned you might still be alive, that you were with child," he told her. "David told me about Marat." He was watching her gravely, but Mireille shook her head as if to rid herself of the thought.

"There's something more you should know," Talleyrand said slowly, his eyes meeting those of Courtiade as he spoke. "There is a woman—her name is Catherine Grand. She is somehow involved in the hunt for the Montglane Service. David told me that Robespierre called her the White Queen. . . ."

Mireille had grown very pale. Her hand was twisted around her butter knife as if she would snap it in two. For a moment she could not speak. Her lips were so pale, Courtiade had reached for the champagne to revive her. She looked into Talleyrand's eyes.

"Where is she now?" she whispered.

Talleyrand looked at his plate for a moment, then back at her with direct blue eyes. "If I'd not found you last night in my carriage," he said slowly, "she would have been in my bed."

They sat in silence, Courtiade staring at the table, Talleyrand's eyes riveted upon Mireille. She put the knife on the table and, pushing back her chair, stood up and crossed to the windows. Talleyrand rose to follow her, came up behind and wrapped his arms around her.

"I've had so many women," Talleyrand murmured in her hair. "I thought you were dead. And then after, when I learned you were not . . . If you saw her, you'd understand."

"I've seen her," said Mireille in a flat voice. She turned to look him in the eye. "That woman is behind it all. She has eight of the pieces. . . ."

"Seven," Talleyrand said. "I have the eighth." Mireille looked at him in astonishment.

"We buried it in the forest along with the others," he told her. "But Mireille, I did right to hide them, to rid us of this dreadful curse. Once, I wanted the service, too. I toyed with you and Valentine, hoping I could win your trust. But you won my love instead." He grasped her by the shoulders. He could not see what thoughts were ravaging her mind. "I tell you, I love you," he said. "Must we all be dragged down into this sinkhole of hatred? Hasn't this game cost us enough? . . ."

"Too much," said Mireille, her face a bitter mask as she pulled away. "Too much to forgive and forget. That woman has murdered five nuns in cold blood. She was responsible for Marat and Robespierre—for Valentine's execution. You forget—I saw her die, slaughtered like an animal!" Her green eyes were glazed over as if she were drugged. "I saw them all die—Valentine, the abbess, Marat. Charlotte Corday gave her life for me! This woman's treachery will not go unanswered. I tell you I will have those pieces at any cost!"

Talleyrand had taken a step back and was looking at her with tears in his eyes. He did not notice Courtiade, who'd risen and now moved across the room to place his hand on his master's arm.

"Monseigneur, she is right," he said softly. "No matter how much we long for happiness, no matter how we may wish to turn a blind eye—this game will never end until the pieces are collected and put to rest. You know it as well as I do. Madame Grand must be stopped."

"Hasn't enough blood been spilled?" asked Talleyrand.

"I no longer wish for revenge," Mireille said, seeing before her eyes the horrid face of Marat as he'd told her where to place the dagger. "I want the pieces—the Game must end."

"She gave me that one piece of her own accord," said Talleyrand. "Even brute force wouldn't convince her to part with the others."

"If you married her," said Mireille, "under French law, all her property would be yours. She would belong to you."

"Married!" cried Talleyrand, leaping away as if burned. "But I love *you*! And besides, I am a bishop of the Catholic church. With or without a See, I'm bound for life by Roman law, not French."

Courtiade cleared his throat. "The monseigneur might receive papal dispensation," he suggested politely. "There have been precedents, I believe."

"Courtiade, please do not forget in whose service you're employed," Talleyrand snapped. "It's out of the question. After all you've said of the woman, how could either of you suggest such a thing? For seven miserable pieces, you'd sell my soul."

"To end this game for once and all," said Mireille, the dark fire gleaming in her eyes, "I'd sell my own."

CAIRO, EGYPT   FEBRUARY 1799

Shahin forced down his camel near the great pyramids of Gizeh and let Charlot slide from the saddle to the ground. Now that they'd arrived in Egypt, he wanted to bring the child at once to this holy place. Shahin watched as Charlot scampered across the sands to the base of the Great Sphinx and began to climb its gigantic paw. Then he himself dismounted and crossed the sand, his dark robes billowing in the breeze.

"This is the Sphinx," Shahin told Charlot when he reached the spot. The red-haired child, now nearly six, could speak fluent Kabyle and Arabic as well as his native French, so Shahin could converse freely with him. "An ancient and mysterious figure, with the torso and head of a woman, the body of a lion. She sits between the constellations of Leo and the Virgin, where the sun rests during the summer equinox."

"If it's a woman," said Charlot, looking up at the great stone figure looming over his head, "why does it have a beard?"

"She is a great queen—the Queen of the Night," Shahin replied. "Her planet is Mercury, god of healing. The beard shows her tremendous power."

"My mother's a great queen—so you told me," Charlot said. "But *she* doesn't have a beard."

"Perhaps she does not choose to display her power," said Shahin.

They looked across the stretch of sand. In the distance sat the many tents of the encampment from which they'd come. Around them the gigantic pyramids loomed in the golden light, scattered like children's blocks forgotten on the empty plain. Charlot looked up at Shahin with wide blue eyes.

"Who left them there?" he asked.

"Many kings over many thousand years," said Shahin. "These kings were great priests. That is our name for them in Arabic—*kahin*. One who knows the future. Amongst the Phoenicians, Babylonians, and Khabiru—the people you call Hebreu—the name for priest is *kohen*. And in my tongue, Kabyle, we call him *kahuna*."

"Is that what I am?" asked Charlot as Shahin helped him down from the lion's paw where they sat. A cortege of riders was moving across the sands from the encampment in the distance, their horses making puffs of dust in the golden light.

"No," Shahin said quietly. "You are more than that."

As the horses came to a halt, one young rider at front leapt to the ground and strode across the rough ground, pulling off his gloves as he approached. His long chestnut hair swung loose at his shoulders. He went down on one knee before little Charlot as the other riders dismounted.

"So here you are," said the young man. He was dressed in the close-fitting breeches and high-cut jacket of the French army. "Mireille's child! I am General Bonaparte, young man—a close friend of your mother. But why has she not come with you? They said at the camp you'd come alone, seeking me."

Napoleon put his hand on Charlot's bright red hair and mussed it, then tucked his gloves in his waistcoat and stood up, bowing formally to Shahin.

"And you must be Shahin," he said without waiting for the child's reply. "My grandmother, Angela-Maria di Pietra-Santa, has often spoken of you as a great man. It was she who sent the boy's mother to you in the desert, I believe? It must have been five years ago or more. . . ."

Shahin gravely drew back his lower veil. "Al-Kalim brings a message of great urgency," he said in a quiet voice. "To be heard by your ears only."

"Come, come," said Napoleon, waving his hand toward the soldiers. "These are my officers. We leave at dawn for Syria—a hard march. Whatever it is can wait until tonight. I invite you to be my guests at dinner at the bey's palace." He turned as if to depart, but Charlot took the general's hand.

"This campaign is ill-fated," said the little boy. Napoleon turned to him in astonishment, but Charlot had not finished. "I see hunger and thirst. Many men will die, and nothing will be won. You must return to France at once. There you will become a great leader. You will have much power over the earth. But it will only last for fifteen years. Then it will be finished. . . ."

Napoleon pulled his hand away as his officers stood looking on uncomfortably. Then the young general threw back his head and laughed.

"They told me you were called the Small Prophet," he said, smiling down at Charlot. "In the camp, they said you told soldiers all sorts of things—how many children they would have, in what battles they would meet with glory or death. I only wish it were true such vision existed. If generals were prophets, they could avoid many pitfalls."

"There was once a general who was also a prophet," Shahin said softly. "His name was Muhammed."

"I too have read my Koran, my friend," said Napoleon, still smiling. "But he fought for the glory of God. We poor Frenchmen only fight for the glory of France."

"It is those who strive for their *own* glory who must beware," said Charlot.

Napoleon heard the officers muttering behind him as he glared at Charlot. His smile had faded. His face was dark with an emotion he struggled to control. "I'll not have insults hurled at me by a child," he said under his breath. Then, in a louder voice, he added, "I doubt my glory will burn so bright as you seem to think, my young friend—or be extinguished so quickly. I leave at dawn for my march through the Sinai, and only the command of my government will hasten my return to France."

Turning his back upon Charlot, he went to his horse and mounted, snapping a command at one of the officers that Charlot and Shahin be brought to the palace at Cairo in time for dinner. Then he rode away alone across the desert as the others looked on.

Shahin told the disconcerted soldiers that they'd make their own way, that the child still had not seen the pyramids closely. When the officers departed reluctantly, Charlot took Shahin's hand and they wandered alone across the vast plain.

"Shahin," said Charlot pensively, "why was General Bonaparte angry with what I said? Everything I told him was true."

Shahin was silent for a moment. "Imagine you were in a dark forest where you could see nothing," he said at last. "Your only companion was an owl, who could see far better than you because his eyes were equipped for the dark. This is the kind of vision you have—like the owl—to see ahead where others move in darkness. If you were they, would you not be afraid, too?"

"Maybe," Charlot admitted. "But I certainly wouldn't be angry with the owl if he warned me I was about to fall into a pit!"

Shahin looked down at the child for a moment, an unaccustomed smile hovering about his lips. Finally he spoke.

"Possessing something others do not have is always difficult—and often dangerous," he said. "Sometimes it is better to leave them in the dark."

"Like the Montglane Service," said Charlot. "My mother said it was buried in darkness for a thousand years."

"Yes," Shahin said. "Like that."

Just then they came around the side of the Great Pyramid. There on the ground before them a man was seated on a woolen robe spread in the sand, with many papyrus scrolls unfolded before him. He was gazing at the pyramid that towered above, but looked over his shoulder as Charlot and Shahin approached. His face lighted with recognition.

"The little Prophet!" he said, standing and brushing the sand from his breeches as he came to greet them. His jowly cheeks and biscuit-shaped chin crumpled into a smile as he pushed back the forelock from his brow. "I've been at the camp today, and the soldiers were laying odds General Bonaparte would reject the advice you planned to give him about returning to France! He's not much of a believer in prophecy, our general. Perhaps he thinks this ninth crusade of *his* will succeed where the other eight failed."

"Monsieur Fourier!" said Charlot, releasing Shahin's hand to run to the side of the famous physicist. "Have you discovered the secret of these pyramids? You've been here so long and worked so very hard."

"I'm afraid not." Fourier smiled and patted Charlot on the head as Shahin came up to join them. "Only the numbers in these papyri are Arabic numerals. The rest is all in gibberish we're wholly unable to read. Picture drawings and such. They say they've found some stone at Rosetta that seems to have several languages written on it. Perhaps that may help us translate all. They're taking it back to France. But by the time they decipher it, I may well be dead!" He laughed and took Shahin's hand. "If your little companion were really the prophet you claim he is, he'd be able to read these pictures and save us a good deal of trouble."

"Shahin understands some of them," said Charlot proudly, walking to the side of the Pyramid and looking at the strange array of drawings carved and painted there. "This one—the man with the head of a bird—is the great god Thoth. He was a doctor who could heal any illness. He invented writing, too. It was his job to write the names of everyone in the Book of the Dead. Shahin says each person has a secret name given him at birth, written on a stone, and handed to him when he dies. And each god has a number instead of a secret name. . . ."

"A number!" said Fourier, looking quickly at Shahin. "You can read these drawings?"

Shahin shook his head. "I know the old stories only," he said in his broken French. "My people have great reverence for numbers, endowing them with divine properties. We believe the universe is comprised of number, and it is only a question of vibrating to the correct resonance of these numbers to become one with God."

"But this is what I myself believe!" cried the mathematician. "I am a student of the physics of vibrations. I'm writing a book on what I call the 'Harmonic Theory' as it applies to heat and light! You Arabs discovered all those truths about number on which our theories are built. . . ."

"Shahin is not an Arab," Charlot interjected. "He is a Blue Man of the Touareg."

Fourier looked at the child in confusion, then turned back to Shahin. "Yet you seem familiar with what I seek—the works of al-Kwarizmi brought to Europe by the great mathematician Leonardo Fibonacci, the Arabic numerals and algebra that revolutionized our way of thought? Did these not originate here in Egypt?"

"No," said Shahin, looking at the drawings on the wall before him. "They came from Mesopotamia—Hindu numbers brought down from the mountains of Turkestan. But the one who knew the secret and wrote it down at last was al-Jabir al-Hayan, the court chemist of Harun al-Rashid in Mesopotamia—the king of the Thousand Nights and One Night. This al-Jabir was a Sufi mystic, a member of the famous Hashhashins. He recorded the secret and as a result was cursed for all time. He hid it in the Montglane Service."

THE
END GAME

In their grave corner, the players
Move their plodding pieces. The board
Detains them until dawn within its
Strictured bounds where two colors clash.

From within, the forms radiate their magic rules.
Homeric castle, nimble knight,
Armored queen, backward king,
Oblique bishop, and aggressive pawns.

When the players have departed,
When time has consumed them,
Certainly the ritual will not have ceased.

In the Orient this war burst into flame
Whose amphitheatre now is all the Earth.
Like another game, this game is infinite.

Weak king, slanted bishop, carnivorous
Queen, straightforward rook and cunning pawn.
Over the black and white they seek the path
And unleash their armed battle.

They do not know that the distinguished hand
Of the player governs their destiny.
They do not know that an unyielding force
Controls their autonomy and their days.

The player too is prisoner
(The phrase is Omar's) of another board
Of black nights and of white days.

God moves the player, and he, the piece.
What god from behind God begins to weave the plot
of dust and time and dreams and agonies?

—Chess
Jorge Luis Borges

We were approaching another isle in the midst of the wine–dark sea. A 120-mile stretch of land floating off the Atlantic seaboard, known as Long Island. On a map it looks like a giant carp whose mouth is about to flap open at Jamaica Bay and swallow Staten Island, and whose tail fins flipping up toward New Haven seem to scatter little isles like drops of water in its wake.

But as our dark ketch skimmed landward, our yards of sails unfurled in the glittering sea breeze—that long, white sand coastline rippling with little bays seemed paradise to me. Even the place names I remembered were exotic: Quogue, Patchogue, Peconic, and Massapequa—Jericho, Babylon, and Kismet. The silver needle of Fire Island hugged the crenellated shore. And somewhere around a turn and out of sight, the Statue of Liberty lifted her coppery lamp three hundred feet above New York Harbor, beckoning tempest-tossed travelers like us toward the golden door of capitalism and institutional trading.

Lily and I stood on deck with tears in our eyes, hugging each other. I wondered what Solarin thought of this land of sunshine, wealth, and freedom— so different from the darkness and fear I imagined penetrated every corner of Russia. In the month or more it had taken to cross the Atlantic and come up the coast, we'd spent days reading Mireille's journal and deciphering the formula and many nights exploring each other's minds and hearts. But not once had Solarin mentioned either his past in Russia or his plans for the future. Every moment spent with him seemed a frozen golden drop of time, like the jewels scattered on the dark cloth—as vivid and as precious. But the darkness that lay beneath could not be penetrated.

Now, as he trimmed the sails and our boat slipped toward the island, I wondered what would become of us once the Game was over. Of course, Minnie had always said the Game would never end. But deep in my heart I knew it would—for us, at least—and soon.

Boats bounced like sparkling baubles everywhere. The closer we came to the island's coast, the thicker was the water traffic—colorful flags and wind-whipped sails fluttering across the frothy water, mingling with the dark polished gleam of silent yachts and little motorboats buzzing back and forth like dragon-flies among them. Here and there we sighted the gray splash of a Coast Guard cutter putting quietly along and a scattering of big naval ships anchored near the point. So many ships, in fact, that I wondered what was going on. Lily answered my question.

"I don't know whether it's our luck or misfortune," she said as Solarin came back to take the wheel, "but this greeting committee isn't for us. You know what today is? Labor Day!"

That was it all right. And if I wasn't mistaken, it also marked the closing day of yachting season, which explained the mad confusion that swarmed around us.

By the time we reached the Shinnecock Inlet, the boats around us were so thickly packed there was hardly room to sail. The queue waiting to get into the bay was forty boats long. So we sailed on about ten miles down to the Moriches Inlet, where the Coast Guard were so busy towing boats and pulling tipsy people out of the drink, they could hardly be expected to notice one little boat like ours that had tiptoed up the Inland Waterway full of illegal immigrants and illicit contraband, about to creep in beneath their unsuspecting eyes.

The line here seemed to be moving faster as Lily and I hauled down the sails and Solarin quickly turned on the engine and strung floats around our sides to keep us from being rammed by the heavy traffic. One ship going out in the opposite direction passed close to our flanks. A passenger dressed in yachting regalia leaned over our side, passing Lily a plastic champagne glass with an invitation ribbon-tied to the stem. It requested our presence at six o'clock for martinis at the Southampton Yacht Club.

It seemed like hours that we putt-putted along in that slow procession, the tension of our situation draining all our energy as the revelers on other boats cavorted around us. As in war, I thought, it was often the last phase—the final confrontation—that decided everything. Likewise it's often the soldier with his discharge papers in his pockets who gets picked off by a sniper while boarding a plane that would've taken him home. Though there was nothing confronting us but a $50,000 Customs fine and twenty years for smuggling in a Russian spy, I couldn't forget that the Game itself was not yet over.

At last we cleared the inlet and pulled toward Westhampton Beach. There wasn't a slip in sight, so Solarin dropped Lily and me at the pier with Carioca, the bag of pieces, and several satchels containing our scanty belongings. Then he dropped anchor in the bay, stripped down to trunks, and swam back the few yards to the beach. We adjourned to a local pub so he could put on dry clothes and we could lay our plans. We were all in a daze as Lily went off to the booth to phone Mordecai with the news.

"Couldn't reach him," she said as she returned to the table. I had three Bloody Marys already waiting, complete with celery sticks. We had to get to Mordecai with these pieces. Or at least get out of here until we could find him.

"My friend Nim has a house near Montauk Point, about an hour from here,"

I told them. "The Long Island Railroad stops there. We could catch it just down the road at Quogue. I think we should leave him a message we're coming and head for the point. It's too dangerous to go dashing into Manhattan." I kept thinking of the city with its maze of one-way streets—how easy it would be to get trapped there with no way out. After all our exertions, to be pinned like pawns would be criminal.

"I have an idea," said Lily. "Why don't *I* go get Mordecai. He never strays far from the diamond district, and it's only a block long. He'll be at the bookstore where you met him, or at one of the restaurants nearby. I can stop at my place and pick up a car, then drive him out here to the island. We'll bring those pieces Minnie said he had, and I'll phone you from Montauk Point when we arrive."

"Nim doesn't have a phone," I told her, "except the one attached to his computer. I hope he picks up his messages; otherwise we'll be stranded there ourselves."

"Let's arrange a time to meet, then," Lily suggested. "How about nine o'clock tonight? That'll give me time to round him up, fill him in on our escapades and my new chess expertise . . . I mean, he's my grandfather. I haven't seen him in months."

Agreeing to what seemed a plausible plan, I phoned Nim's computer to announce I'd be arriving by train in an hour. We threw down our drinks and departed on foot for the station—Lily to continue toward Manhattan and Mordecai, Solarin, and I in the other direction.

At the flat, open platform at Quogue, Lily's train arrived before ours, around two o'clock. As she climbed aboard with Carioca tucked under her arm, she said, "If there's any problem getting there by nine, I'll leave a message on that computer number you gave me."

It did no good for Solarin and me to study the schedules. The Long Island Railroad has traditionally established its schedules using a Ouija board anyway. I sat on a green slat bench, watching the gaggles of other passengers milling around me. Solarin put the bags down and sat beside me.

He let out a sigh of frustration as he turned again to look down the empty track. "You'd think this was Siberia. I thought people in the West were punctual, that the trains always ran on time." He jumped up and was pacing up and down like a leashed animal through the thick crowd on the platform. I couldn't stand watching him, so I hefted the bag with the pieces over my shoulder and stood up, too. Just then they called our train.

Though it's only about forty-five miles from Quogue to Montauk Point, the trip took over an hour. With the hike to Quogue and the wait on the platform thrown in, it had been nearly two hours since I'd left that message on Nim's computer from the bar. Still, I didn't expect to see him—for all I knew, he might phone in for messages once a month.

So I was surprised when, descending from the train, I saw Nim's long, lean form moving down the tracks in my direction, his coppery hair blowing in the breeze, his long white scarf fluttering with every stride. When he spotted me he grinned like a madman and waved his arm, then broke into a trot, bounding around passengers as they nervously stepped out of his way to avoid a collision. When he reached me he grabbed me with both hands, then swept me into his arms, burying his face in my hair—crushing me to him until I nearly suffocated. He lifted me off my feet, spun me around in a dizzying way, then set me on the ground and held me away for a better look. There were tears in his eyes.

"My God, my God," he whispered in a broken voice, shaking his head. "I thought for sure you were dead. I haven't slept a moment since I learned how you'd left Algiers. That storm—then we completely lost track of you!" He couldn't stop looking at me. "I really thought I'd killed you by sending you off like that. . . ."

"Having you as a mentor hasn't exactly improved my health," I agreed.

He was still beaming down at me and had dragged me to him in another embrace—when suddenly I felt his body stiffen. Slowly he released me, and I looked up at his face. He was staring over my shoulder with an expression that seemed to mingle amazement and disbelief. Or perhaps it was fear—I couldn't be sure.

Quickly glancing over my shoulder, I saw Solarin descending the steps from the train behind me, carrying our collection of canvas bags. He was looking back at us, his face the same cold mask I remembered from that first day at the club. He was staring at Nim, his unfathomable green eyes glittering in the late afternoon sun. I wheeled back to Nim and started to explain, but his lips were moving as he continued to stare at Solarin as if he were a monster or a ghost. I had to strain to hear him.

"Sascha?" he whispered in a choked voice. "Sascha . . ."

I flipped back to Solarin, who still stood on the steps with passengers waiting behind him to disembark. His eyes were filled with tears—tears were streaming down his cheeks as his face crumpled.

"Slava!" he cried in a cracked voice. Dropping our bags on the ground, he leaped from the steps and flew past me, throwing himself into Nim's arms in an embrace of such power, it looked as if they would crush one another into dust. I quickly scrambled for the bag he'd dropped with the pieces. When I'd retrieved it they were still weeping. Nim's arms were wrapped around Solarin's head, grasping him frantically. First he would hold him away, look at him, then they embraced each other again as I stood there in astonishment. Passengers streamed around us like water parting around a stone, indifferent as only New Yorkers can be.

"Sascha," Nim kept murmuring, embracing him repeatedly. Solarin had buried his face in Nim's collar, his eyes closed, tears pouring down his cheeks. With one hand he clung to Nim's shoulder as if too weak to stand. I couldn't believe this.

When the last few passengers had passed, I stepped away to pick up the rest of our scattered bags that Solarin had dropped on the ground.

"Let me get those," Nim called to me, blowing his nose. When I glanced up he was coming toward me, one arm draped across Solarin's shoulders, squeezing him from time to time as if trying to make sure he was there, his eyes red from weeping.

"It seems you two have met before," I said irritably, wondering why no one had ever mentioned this to *me*.

"Not for twenty years," said Nim, still smiling at Solarin as they bent to pick up the bags. Then he turned his strange bicolored eyes on me. "I cannot believe, my dear, the joy you've brought me. Sascha is my brother."

Nim's little Morgan wasn't really big enough to hold the three of us, let alone our bags. Solarin sat on the bag with the pieces, and I sat on him, the few bags with our belongings squeezed into every nook and cranny. As he drove away from the station, Nim kept looking over at Solarin with an expression of disbelief and joy.

It was odd to see these two men, so cold and self-contained, suddenly overcome with such emotion. I could feel the power of it surging all around me as the car whizzed along, wind rattling through the wooden floorboards. It seemed as deep and dark as their Russian souls, and it belonged to them alone. No one spoke for the longest time. Then Nim reached over and squeezed me on the knee I was trying to keep clear of his stick shift.

"I suppose I should tell you everything," he said to me.

"That would certainly be refreshing," I agreed.

He smiled at me. "It's only been for your own protection—and ours—that I haven't done so earlier," he explained. "Alexander and I haven't seen one another since we were children. He was six and I was ten when we were parted...." The tears were still in his eyes, and he reached over to grasp Solarin's hair as if he couldn't keep his hands away.

"Let me tell it," said Solarin, smiling through his tears.

"We'll both tell it," Nim said. And as we wheeled along the coast in the open car toward Nim's exotic estate on the sea, they unfolded a story that for the first time revealed what the Game had cost them.

THE TALE OF TWO PHYSICISTS

We were born on the isle of Krym—that famous peninsula in the Black Sea written of by Homer. Russia had wanted to get her hands on it since the time of Peter the Great, and was still trying when the Crimean War took place.

Our father was a Greek sailor who'd fallen in love with a Russian girl and married her—our mother. He'd become a prosperous shipping merchant with a fleet of small ships.

After the war, things changed for the worse. The world was a mess—and nowhere more than on the Black Sea, surrounded by countries that considered themselves still at war.

But where we lived, life was beautiful. The Mediterranean climate of the southern coast, its olive, laurel, and cypress trees sheltered from snow and bitter wind by the close-lying mountains, the restored ruins of Tatar villages and Byzantine mosques set among the cherry orchards. It was a paradise, far from the foibles and purges of Stalin, who, as his name implied, still ruled Russia with a fist of steel.

A thousand times our father discussed leaving. And yet—though he had many contacts among the shipping fleets along the Danube and Bosporus who would have assured us safe passage—it seemed he could never bring himself to go. Go where? he asked. Surely not home to Greece—or Europe, which was still suffering the throes of postwar reconstruction. It was then that something happened, something that made up his mind. Something that was to change the course of all our lives.

It was late December of the year 1953, one night near midnight in the dark of a coming storm. We were all in bed, having shuttered the windows of our dacha and let the fires burn low. We boys, sleeping together in a bedroom on the lower floor, were the first to hear the tapping at the window that sounded different from the pomegranate tree blowing against the shutters. It was the sound of a person's hand. We opened the window and the shutters—and there outside in the storm stood a silver-haired woman dressed in a long dark cape. She smiled at us and stepped through the window to come inside. Then she knelt before us on the floor. She was so beautiful.

"I am Minerva—your grandmother," she told us. "But you must call me Minnie. I've come a long way, and I'm weary, but there is no time for rest. I'm in great danger. You must rouse your mother and tell her I have come." Then she embraced us with great dignity, and we scurried upstairs to wake our parents.

"So she's come at last—this grandmother of yours," our father growled to our mother, rubbing the sleep from his eyes. This surprised us, for Minnie had said she was *our* grandmother. How could she be the same to our mother, too?

Father put his arms about the wife he loved, who stood barefoot and trembling in the dark. He kissed her coppery hair, and then her eyes. "We've waited so long in fear," he murmured. "Now at last, it is nearly over. Get dressed. I'll go downstairs to meet her." And ushering us before him, we went down to where Minnie waited near the dying fire below. She looked up with her large eyes as he approached, and came to embrace him.

"Yusef Pavlovitch," she said, addressing our father—as she had us—in fluent Russian. "I am pursued. There's little time. We must flee, all of us. Have you a ship we could secure at Yalta or Sevastopol—now? Tonight?"

"I'm not prepared for this," he began, putting his two hands on either of our shoulders. "I can't take my family out in weather like this, across the winter seas. You should have given some warning, let me know. It's something you cannot ask of me at the final hour like this—coming in the dead of night. . . ."

"I tell you we must go!" she cried, clutching his arm and pushing us boys away. "For fifteen years you've known one day this would come—and now it has. How can you say you've had no warning? I've traveled all the way from Leningrad. . . ."

"Then you found it?" said our father, excitement in his voice.

"Of the board, there was no trace. But these I secured through other means." Drawing her cape aside, she went to the table, and in the dim firelight she set down not one, but three chess pieces—glowing in silver and gold.

"They were hidden throughout the breadth of Russia," she said. Our father stood, his eyes riveted on the pieces as we boys stepped up to touch them carefully. A golden pawn and a silver elephant, all covered with glittering jewels, and a horse of silver filigree, rearing on its hind legs, its nostrils flared.

"You must go now to the docks and secure a ship," whispered Minnie. "I'll join you with my children as soon as they've dressed and packed. But for God's sake, make haste—and take these with you." She gestured to the pieces.

"They're *my* children, and my wife," he protested. "And I must be responsible for their safety." But Minnie had closed upon us, her eyes gleaming with a fire darker than the glow of the pieces.

"If these pieces fall into the hands of others, you'll be able to protect no one!" she hissed.

Our father looked her in the eye and seemed to arrive at his decision. He nodded slowly. "I've a fishing schooner at Sevastopol," he told her. "Slava knows how to find it. I'll be ready to put to sea in two hours at most. Be there, and may God favor us in this mission." Minnie pressed his arm, and he took the stairs in a few bounds.

And so our newfound grandmother ordered us to dress at once. Our parents had come downstairs, and Father embraced Mother again, his face in her hair as if he wanted to remember her scent. He kissed her once on the forehead, then turned to Minnie, who handed him the pieces. With a grave nod, he departed into the night.

Mother was brushing her hair and looking about with bleary eyes as she commanded us boys about, sending us upstairs to collect her things. As we went up we heard her speak to Minnie in low voice.

"So you've come," she said. "May God punish you for beginning the dread Game again. I thought it was finished—over."

"It was not I who began it," Minnie replied. "Be thankful you've had fifteen years of peace, fifteen years with a husband you love and children whom you've kept always at your side. Fifteen years without danger breathing always at your shoulder. It's more than I've had. It's I who've kept you from the Game. . . ."

That was all we heard, for their voices fell to whispers. Just then we heard the footsteps outside, the hammering at the door below. We looked at each other in the dim light and started to run from the room. Suddenly Minnie appeared in the doorway, her face glowing with an otherworldly light. We could hear our mother's footsteps coming up the stairs, the sound of the door below splintering, and men's cries above the sound of thunder.

"Out the window!" said Minnie, lifting us one by one to the branches of the fig tree that grew like a vine up the south wall, a tree we'd both climbed a hundred times. We were halfway down, hanging like little monkeys from the tree, when we heard the sound of our mother's scream.

"Flee!" she cried. "Flee for your lives!" Then we heard nothing as the rain slashed down upon us, and we dropped into the darkness of the orchard below.

$$\infty$$

The big iron gates of Nim's estate swung open. Down the long drive, the arched trees shimmered in the late day sunlight. At its end was the fountain that had been frozen in winter, now surrounded by brilliant dahlias and zinnias, its tinkling water haunting like wind chimes against the wash of the nearby sea.

Nim pulled up to the front and turned to look at me. I could feel Solarin's body, tight with tension, as I sat on his lap.

"That was the last time we saw our mother," said Nim. "Minnie leapt from the second-floor window onto the soft ground beneath. The rain had already formed pools of water as she picked herself up and dragged us into the orchards. Even above the sound of the rain, we heard the sounds of our mother's screams, the trampling feet of the men inside the house. 'Search the forests!' someone cried as Minnie dragged us on toward the cliffs below." Nim paused, still looking at me.

"My God," I said, trembling from head to foot. "They captured your mother. . . . How did you escape?"

"At the end of our orchard were cliffs of stone that tumbled down toward the sea," Nim continued. "When we reached these, Minnie stepped over the edge and pulled us beneath the shelter of a broken ledge. I saw she had something in her hand, like a little leather-bound Bible. She pulled out a knife and cut away some pages, folding them quickly and stuffing them inside my shirt. Then she told me to go ahead—run to the ship as fast as I could. To tell my father to wait for her and Sascha. But we were *only* to wait for one hour. If they weren't there by then, my father and I were to escape, she said, and take the pieces to safety. At first I refused to go on without my brother." Nim looked at Solarin gravely.

"But I was only six years old," Solarin said. "I couldn't make it over the cliffs as quickly as Ladislaus, who was four years older and fleet as the wind. Minnie was afraid we'd *all* be captured if I couldn't keep up. As Slava left, he kissed me and told me to be brave. . . ." I glanced back at Solarin and saw the tears in his eyes as he recalled his childhood. "It seemed like hours we struggled down those cliffs in the storm, Minnie and I. At last we reached the docks at Sevastopol. But my father's ship was gone."

Nim got out of the car, his face a grim mask, and came around to my side, opening the door and offering me his hand.

"I myself had fallen a dozen times," Nim continued as he helped me from the car, "slipping through the mud and rocks to reach my father's ship. When he saw I'd arrived alone, he was alarmed. I told him what had happened, what Minnie had said about the pieces. My father began to cry. He sat with his head in his hands, sobbing like a child. 'What would happen if we *did* go back—if we tried to rescue them?' I asked him. 'What would happen if those pieces *were* captured by others?' He looked at me, the rain washing the streaming tears down his face. 'I vowed to your mother I'd never let it happen,' he told me, 'even if it cost us all our lives. . . .' "

"You mean, you left without waiting for Minnie and Alexander?" I said. Solarin was crawling out of the Morgan behind me, bringing the bag with the pieces.

"It wasn't so simple," said Nim sadly. "We waited for hours—well beyond the time Minnie had allotted as a reasonable measure for safety. My father was pacing up and down the deck in the rain. I climbed to the crow's nest a dozen times to see if I could catch sight of them through the storm. At last, we understood they weren't coming. They'd been captured—it was all we could imagine. When my father put out to sea, I begged him to wait just a little longer. Then he made it clear for the first time that this had been expected, even planned. It wasn't just the sea we were headed for—it was America. He'd known since the day he married my mother, perhaps even earlier—about the Game. He'd known a day might come—*would* come—when Minnie would appear, and my family would be called upon for terrible sacrifice. That day was here, and in

a few hours half his family had disappeared in the dead of night. But the first
and final vow he'd made my mother was that, even before his children, he would
save the pieces."

"Good Lord!" I said, staring at both of them as we stood together in the
drive. Solarin strolled over into the zinnias and dipped his fingers in the
splashing fountain. "I'm surprised you'd both agree to be players in a game like
this—when it destroyed your entire family in a single night!"

Nim tossed his arm casually across my shoulder, and we went to his brother,
who was gazing silently at the fountain. Solarin glanced at Nim's hand, which
rested on my shoulder.

"You've done as much yourself," he said. "And Minnie isn't even your
grandmother. But then, I gather it was Slava who first seduced you into the
Game?"

I couldn't read from his voice or face what was going on in his head, but
it wasn't that hard to guess. I evaded his eyes. Nim squeezed my shoulder.

"Mea culpa," he admitted with a smile.

"What happened to you and Minnie when you found your father's ship had
left?" I asked Solarin. "How did you survive?"

He was plucking petals from the head of a zinnia and tossing them into the
fountain bowl. "She took me off into the forest and hid me until the storm was
over," he said as if lost in thought. "For three days we worked our way slowly
along the coast toward Georgia, like a couple of peasants traveling to market.
When we were far enough from home to be safe, we sat down to discuss our
prospects. 'You're old enough to understand what I tell you,' she said. 'But not
old enough to help me in the mission that lies ahead. One day you will be—then
I'll send for you and tell you what you must do. But now, I must go back and
try to save your mother. If I take you with me, you'll only get in the way,
jeopardize my efforts.' " Solarin looked at us as one in a daze. "I understood
completely," he said.

"Minnie went back to rescue your mother from the Soviet police?" I asked.

"You did the same for your friend Lily, didn't you?" he asked.

"Minnie put Sascha in an orphanage," Nim interjected, hugging me with his
arm as he looked at his brother. "Father died soon after we succeeded in reaching
America, so I was left to fend for myself here, just as little Sascha was in Russia.
Though I was never sure, somehow I always knew in my heart that the boy
chess prodigy Solarin one read about in the papers was really my brother. By
then I called myself Nim—a private joke, since that's how I made my living,
pinch as pinch can. It was Mordecai, whom I met at the Manhattan Chess Club
one night, who discovered who I really was."

"And what happened to your mother?" I said.

"Minnie was too late to save her," said Solarin gravely, turning away. "She
barely escaped from Russia herself. I got a letter from her at the orphanage some

time later. Not really a letter, just a clipping from a newspaper—*Pravda*, I think. Though there was no date, no return address, and it was mailed from *inside* Russia, I knew who'd sent it. The article said the famous chess master Mordecai Rad would be touring Russia to speak on the status of world chess, give exhibitions, and search for young children with talent for a book he was writing about child chess prodigies. One of the places coincidentally on his route was my orphanage. Minnie was trying to contact me."

"And the rest is history," said Nim, who still had his arm draped over my shoulder. Now he put his other arm around Solarin and ushered us toward the house.

We passed through big sunny rooms filled with bowls of cut flowers and polished furniture that glowed in the afternoon sun. In the enormous kitchen, sunshine slanted sideways to fall in pools on the slate tiled floor. The flowered chintz sofas were even more cheerful than I'd remembered.

Nim released us but put his hands on my shoulders as he looked down at me with affection.

"You've brought me the greatest gift of all," he said. "That Sascha is here is a miracle—but the best miracle is that you're alive. I should never have forgiven myself if something had happened to you." He embraced me again, then went off to the pantry.

Solarin had dropped the bag with the pieces and gone to the windows, where he stood looking across the green lawns toward the sea. Boats still fluttered like white doves across the water. I went to stand beside him.

"It's a beautiful house," he said softly, watching the fountain on the back lawn as it splashed from one level to another and tumbled into the turquoise swimming pool. Solarin was silent a moment, then he added, "My brother's in love with you."

I felt a cold ball like a fist tightening in my stomach. "Don't be ridiculous," I said.

"It must be discussed," he replied, turning to look at me with that pale green gaze that always made me feel weak. He started to put his hand on my hair, but just then Nim returned from the pantry with a champagne bottle and a fistful of glasses. He came over and set them on the low table before the windows.

"We've so much to discuss—so much to remember," he told Solarin as he started to unwrap the champagne. "It's still impossible for me to believe you're here. I don't think I'll ever let you go again. . . ."

"You may have to," said Solarin, taking me by the hand and leading me to a seat on one of the sofas. He sat beside me as Nim poured the champagne. "Now that Minnie's left the Game, someone has to go back to Russia and get the board."

"Left the Game?" said Nim, pausing with the bottle in midair. "How could she? It's not possible."

"We have a new Black Queen." Solarin smiled, watching his face. "One you seem to have chosen yourself."

Nim turned to stare at me. Understanding spread across his face. "Damn!" he said, continuing to pour the wine. "Now I suppose she's vanished without a trace, leaving us to clean up the loose ends."

"Not exactly," said Solarin, reaching inside his shirt to extract an envelope. "She gave me this, addressed to Catherine. I was to give it to her when we arrived. Though I haven't opened it, I suspect it contains information of value to us all." He handed me the sealed envelope, which I was about to open when suddenly we were disturbed by a jarring sound—a sound that took me a moment to identify. It was the ringing of a telephone!

"I thought you didn't *have* a phone!" I looked at Nim with accusing eyes as he quickly set the bottle down and raced toward the area of the stoves and cupboards.

"I don't," he said, his voice tense as he extracted a key from his pocket and unlocked one of the cupboards. He pulled out something that looked very much like a phone, and it was ringing. "This phone belongs to someone else—a 'hot line,' you might say." He answered it. Solarin and I were on our feet.

"Mordecai!" I whispered, rushing across to where Nim stood speaking into the phone. "Lily must be there."

Nim looked at me gravely and handed me the phone. "Someone wants to chat with you," he said quietly, glancing at Solarin with an odd expression. I took the phone.

"Mordecai, it's Cat. Is Lily there?" I said.

"Darling!" boomed the voice that always made me hold the receiver away— Harry Rad! "So I understand you've had a successful trip down there with the Arabs! We'll get together and schmooze. But darling, I'm sorry to say something's come up. I'm here with Mordecai at his place. He phoned me to say Lily's called and was headed here from Grand Central Station. So of course I rushed right over. But she hasn't arrived. . . ."

I was dumbfounded. "I thought you and Mordecai weren't speaking to one another!" I cried into the phone.

"Darling, that's meshugge," said Harry soothingly. "Mordecai is my father. Of *course* I speak to him. I'm speaking to him right now—or at least he's listening."

"But Blanche said—"

"Ah, that's different," Harry explained. "Forgive me for saying such a thing, but my wife and brother-in-law, they're not very nice people. I've been afraid for Mordecai ever since I married Blanche Regine, if you understand my meaning. I'm the one who doesn't let him come by the house. . . ."

Blanche Regine. *Blanche Regine?!* Of course! What an idiot I'd been! Why on earth hadn't I seen it before? Blanche and Lily—Lily and Blanche—they both meant "white," didn't they? She'd named her daughter Lily, hoping she'd follow in her footsteps. Blanche Regine—the White Queen!

My head was swimming as I grasped the phone, Solarin and Nim standing there in silence. Of course it was Harry—it was Harry all along. Harry whom Nim had sent me to, as a client; Harry who'd pushed my friendship with his family; Harry who understood my computer expertise as well as Nim did. Harry who'd invited me to meet the fortune-teller—who in fact had insisted I'd come that night at New Year's Eve, and no other.

Then there was the night he'd invited me to his house for dinner—all that food and those hors d'oeuvres—keeping me there long enough for Solarin to slip into my apartment and leave that note! It was Harry who, very casually at that same dinner, had let his maid Valerie know I was headed for Algiers— Valerie, whose own mother was Therese, the telephone operator who'd worked for Kamel's father in Algiers; whose little brother Wahad lived in the Casbah and guarded the Black Queen!

It was Harry Saul had double-crossed by working for Blanche and Llewellyn. And maybe also Harry who'd dumped Saul's body in the East River so it looked like a simple mugging—perhaps not just to deceive the police, but to fool his own in-laws, too!

It was Harry, not Mordecai, who'd sent Lily to Algiers. Once he learned she'd been at that chess match, she was in danger not only from Hermanold—who was probably just a pawn—but from her own mother and uncle!

But finally, it was Harry who'd married Blanche—the White Queen—just as Mireille had persuaded Talleyrand to marry the Woman from India. But Talleyrand was only a Bishop!

"Harry," I said in shock, "you're the Black King!"

"Darling," he said placatingly over the line. I could almost see his droopy St. Bernard's face, his sad eyes. "Forgive me for keeping you in the dark like this. But now you understand the situation. If Lily's not with you . . ."

"I'll call you back," I told him. "I have to get off the phone."

I hung up and grabbed Nim, who was standing beside me, an expression of real fear on his face. "Dial your computer," I snapped. "I think I know where she went—but she said she'd leave a message if anything went wrong. I hope she hasn't done something rash."

Nim dialed the number, slapping on the modem switch when he got the connection. I clung to the receiver and in a few moments got the digitally reproduced voice of Lily provided by modern technology.

"I'm at the Palm Court at the Plaza." It was my imagination, but I thought I could hear the binary reproduction shaking like a real voice. "I went to my place to pick up the car keys we keep in that secretary in the living room. But my God—" The voice broke off. I could sense panic coming through the line. "You know that hideous lacquered desk of Llewellyn's with the brass handles?

They're not brass knobs—those are the pieces! Six of them, embedded in the cabinet. The bases project like knobs, but the pieces *themselves*—the top parts—are built into false panels in the drawers! Those drawers are always jammed, but I never thought—So I used a letter knife to open one, then got a hammer from the kitchen and smashed the panel apart. I got two pieces out, then I heard someone coming into the apartment. So I ran out the back and took the service elevator. My God, you've got to come at once. I can't go back there alone. . . ."

She hung up with a click. I waited for another message, but there wasn't any, so I threw the phone down.

"We've got to go," I told Nim and Solarin, who stood there anxiously. "I'll explain on the way."

"What about Harry?" said Nim as I stuffed Minnie's unread letter in my pocket and raced over to grab the pieces.

"I'll call him and tell him to meet us at the Plaza," I said. "You get the car started. Lily's found another cache of pieces."

It seemed like forever, slaloming along freeways and barreling through Manhattan traffic, before Nim's green Morgan screeched up in front of the Plaza, startling the pigeons that scattered in our path. I ran inside and searched the Palm Court, but Lily wasn't there. Harry had said he'd wait for us, but no one was in sight—I even checked the powder room.

I went running back outside, waving my arms, and jumped into the car.

"Something's wrong," I told the two of them. "The only reason Harry wouldn't have waited is if Lily wasn't here."

"Or someone else *was*," muttered Nim. "Someone was coming into the apartment just as she fled. They'd have seen she discovered the pieces, maybe they trailed her. They'd surely have left a greeting committee for Harry. . . ." He revved the engine in frustration. "Where would they go first—Mordecai's for the other nine pieces? Or the apartment?"

"Let's try the apartment," I urged. "It's closer. Besides, when I spoke to Harry before we left, I found I could set up a little greeting committee of my own." Nim looked at me in surprise. "Kamel Kader's in town," I said. Solarin squeezed my shoulder.

We all knew what it meant. Nine pieces at Mordecai's, the eight in my bag, and the six Lily said she'd seen at the apartment. That was enough to control the Game—and maybe to decipher the formula as well. Whoever won this round would have it cinched.

Nim pulled up before the apartment, jumped over the side, and tossed his keys to the astonished doorman. The three of us barreled inside without a word. I pushed the button for the elevator. The doorman was running after us.

"Has Mr. Rad come in yet?" I called over my shoulder as the doors swished open.

The doorman looked at me in surprise, then nodded.

"About ten minutes ago," he said. "With his brother-in-law. . . ."

That did it. We jumped into the elevator before he could speak further and were about to start up when something caught the corner of my eye. I put my hand out fast and stopped the doors. A little ball of fluff came barreling in. As I bent over to pick it up, I saw Lily plowing just behind across the lobby. I grabbed her and dragged her in. The doors closed, and we started up.

"They didn't get you!" I cried.

"No, but they got Harry," she said. "I was afraid to stay at the Palm Court, so I went outside with Carioca and waited near the park across the street. Harry was an idiot—he left his car at the apartment and *walked* down here to find me. It was him they followed, not me. I saw Llewellyn and Hermanold just behind him. They went right past me—looked right through me. They didn't *recognize* me!" she said in amazement. "I had Carioca stuffed in my bag with the two pieces I got. They're here." She patted her bag. My God, we were walking into this with all our ammunition. "I followed them back here and stayed across the street, not knowing what to do when they took him inside. Llewellyn was so close to Harry—maybe he had a gun."

The doors swished open, and we went down the hall, Carioca first. Lily was pulling out her key when the door opened and Blanche stood there in a shimmering white cocktail dress, still wearing that cool blond smile. She was holding a glass of champagne.

"Well, here we are—all together," she said smoothly, offering me her porcelain cheek to be pecked. I ignored it, so she turned to Lily. "Pick up that dog and put him in the study," she said coldly. "I think we've had enough incidents for one day."

"Just a minute," I said as Lily bent to pick up her dog. "We're not here for cocktails. What have you done with Harry?" I brushed past Blanche into the apartment I hadn't seen in six months. It hadn't changed, but now I saw it differently—the marble floor of the foyer laid out in checkered squares. The end game, I thought.

"He's fine," Blanche said, following me toward the wide marble steps that led down to the living room as Solarin, Nim, and Lily trooped in behind. Across the room Llewellyn knelt beside the lacquered red secretary, pulling apart the drawers Lily hadn't gotten to, extracting the remaining four pieces. There were chunks of wood lying all over the floor. He looked up as I crossed the vast room.

"Hello, my darling," said Llewellyn, rising to greet me. "I'm delighted to hear you got the pieces as I asked—only you haven't played the Game quite as one might have hoped. I understand you've switched sides. How sad. And I'd always been so fond of you."

"I was never on your side, Llewellyn," I said in disgust. "I want to see Harry. You're not leaving until I do. I know Hermanold's here, but we still outnumber you."

"Not really," said Blanche from the far side of the room, pouring herself more champagne. She tossed a glance at Lily, who was glaring at her, Carioca in her arms, then she came over to regard me with cold blue eyes. "There are a few friends of yours in the back—Mister Brodski of the KGB, who works in fact for me. And Sharrif—whom El-Marad was kind enough to fly over at my behest. They've been waiting ever so long for you to arrive here from Algiers, watching the house night and day. It seems you took the scenic route."

I shot a glance at Solarin and Nim. We should have expected something like this.

"What have you done with my father?" yelled Lily, coming up to Blanche with gritted teeth as Carioca growled at Llewellyn from his perch in her arms.

"He's tied up in a back room," Blanche said, toying with her ever-present strands of pearls. "He's perfectly safe, and will remain so if you all just listen to reason. I want the pieces. There's been enough violence—I'm sure we're all weary of it. Nothing will happen to anyone, if you just turn over the pieces to me."

Llewellyn extracted a gun from his jacket. "Not quite enough violence for me," he said calmly. "Why don't you let that little monster loose so I can do what I've always wished?"

Lily glared at him in horror. I put my hand on her arm as I glanced at Nim and Solarin, who'd moved out toward the walls in preparation. I thought I'd wasted enough time—my pieces were all in place.

"You obviously haven't been following the Game too closely," I told Blanche. "I have nineteen pieces. With the four you're about to give me, that makes twenty-three—enough to solve the formula and win." From the corner of my eye, I saw Nim smiling and nodding at me from across the room. Blanche stared at me in disbelief.

"You must be mad," she said abruptly. "My brother has a gun trained on you. My beloved husband—the Black King—is held hostage by three men in the other room. That's the object of the game—to pin the King."

"Not *this* Game," I told her as I started across the room toward the bar where Solarin stood. "You may as well resign. You don't know the objectives, the moves—or even the players. You aren't the only one who's planted a pawn— like Saul—inside your own household. You aren't the only one with allies in Russia and Algiers. . . ." I stood on the steps with my hand on the champagne bottle as I smiled at Blanche. Her normally pale skin had bled stark white. Llewellyn's gun was pointed at a part of my body I hoped would go on ticking, but I didn't think he'd pull the trigger until he heard the end. Solarin squeezed my elbow from behind.

"What are you saying?" said Blanche, biting her lip.

"When I called Harry and told him to go to the Plaza, he wasn't alone. He was with Mordecai—and Kamel Kader—and Valerie, your faithful maid, who works for us. *They* didn't go to the Plaza with Harry. They came here, through the service entrance. Why don't you have a look?"

Just then, all hell broke loose. Lily dropped Carioca on the floor, and he headed for Llewellyn, who wavered a second too long between Nim and the fuzzy dog. I grabbed the champagne bottle and hurled it across the room at Llewellyn's head just as he pulled the trigger and Nim doubled over. Then I was across the room, grabbing Llewellyn's hair and dragging him to the ground with all my weight.

As I wrestled with Llewellyn, from the corner of my eye I saw Hermanold come barreling into the room and Solarin trip him. I sank my teeth into Llewellyn's shoulder as Carioca did the same with his leg. I could hear Nim moaning on the floor a few inches away as Llewellyn struggled toward the gun. I grabbed the champagne bottle and smashed it down on his hand as I brought my knee up into his groin. He screamed, and I came up for air for a second. Blanche was headed for the marble steps, but Lily caught up with her, grabbed her by the pearl ropes, and gave them a good hard twist as Blanche struggled to claw her back. Her face turned dark.

Solarin grabbed Hermanold by the shirtfront, pulled him to his feet, and socked him in the jaw with a punch I didn't know chess players possessed. I caught all this in a flash, then I turned to dive for the gun as Llewellyn rolled about clutching his groin.

Gun in hand, I bent over Nim as Solarin raced across the room. "I'm fine," Nim gasped as Solarin touched his hip wound where a dark stain was forming. "Go to Harry!"

"You stay here," Solarin told me, pressing my shoulder. "I'll go back there." With a grave look at his brother, he sprinted across the room and up the stairs.

Hermanold lay sprawled across the steps, out cold. Llewellyn, a few feet from me, writhed screaming, clutching himself as Carioca still attacked his ankles, shredding the argyle socks. I was kneeling beside Nim, who was gasping heavily, holding his hand to the wet place on his hip where dark blood formed an ever-widening stain. Lily still wrestled with Blanche, whose broken pearls were scattered across the carpeting.

Noises and banging were coming from the back rooms as I bent over Nim.

"You'd better live," I told him under my breath. "After all you've put me through, I'd hate to lose you now before I can retaliate." His wound was small and deep, just a thin channel of flesh torn away from the side of his upper thigh.

Nim looked up at me and tried to smile. "Are you in love with Sascha?" he said.

I rolled my eyes at the ceiling and let out a sigh. "You've recovered," I told him, pulling him up to a sitting position and handing him the gun. "I think I'd better go make sure he's still alive."

I crossed the room on the double, grabbed Blanche by the hair, pulled her off Lily, and pointed to the gun in Nim's hand. "He'll use it," I explained.

Lily followed me up the steps and down the back hall, where the sounds had died away and things were suspiciously quiet. We tiptoed toward the study just as Kamel Kader stepped out the door. He saw us and smiled with his golden eyes, then took me by the hand.

"Well done," he said happily. "It appears the white team has resigned."

Lily and I pushed past into the study as Kamel went off down the hall toward the living room. There sat Harry, rubbing his head. Behind him stood Mordecai and Valerie the maid, who'd let them into the apartment through the back. Lily raced across the room and threw herself at Harry, weeping with joy. He stroked her hair as Mordecai winked at me across the room.

Glancing around quickly, I saw Solarin tying the last knot in the ropes that bound Sharrif. Brodski, the KGB man from the chess club, lay trussed beside him like a partridge. Solarin pushed the gag into Brodski's mouth and turned to me, grasping my shoulder.

"My brother?" he whispered.

"He'll be fine," I said.

"Cat darling," Harry called from behind my back, "thank you for saving my daughter's life." I turned to him, and Valerie smiled at me.

"I wish my little brozzaire were here to see zis!" she said, looking around. "He will be very sad—he like a good fight himself." I went over to give her a hug.

"We'll talk later," said Harry. "But now I'd like to say good-bye to my wife."

"I hate her," said Lily. "I would've killed her if Cat hadn't stopped me."

"No, you wouldn't, darling," said Harry, kissing her on the head. "No matter what else she may be, she's still your mother. You wouldn't be here if it weren't for her. Never forget that." He turned his sad droopy eyes to me. "And in a way, I'm as much to blame," he added. "I knew what she was when I married her. I married her for the Game."

He bent his head in sorrow and left the room. Mordecai patted Lily on the shoulder, looking at her through his thick, owlish glasses.

"The Game's not over yet," he said quietly. "In a way it's just begun."

Solarin had taken me by the arm and dragged me into the enormous kitchen behind the dining room of Harry's apartment. As the others cleaned up the mess, he pushed me against the gleaming copper table in the middle. His mouth on mine was so fierce and hot it seemed he wished to devour me as his hands moved down my body. All thought of what had passed outside, what was yet to come, had fled as the darkness of his passion filled me. I felt his teeth in my neck, his hands in my hair, as I struggled with dizziness. His tongue found mine again, and I moaned. At last he pulled away.

"I must return to Russia," he whispered in my ear. His lips were moving down my throat. "I must get the board. It's the only way this Game will truly end. . . ."

"I'm going with you," I said, drawing back to look him in the eye. He pulled me back into his arms again, kissing my eyes as I clung to him.

"Impossible," he murmured, his body trembling with the force of his emotion. "I'll come back—I promise. I swear it with every drop of blood. I shall never let you go."

Just then I heard the door open a crack, and we both turned, still locked in each other's embrace. Kamel stood in the doorway, and standing beside him, supported heavily against his shoulder—was Nim. He swayed against Kamel in the doorway, his face expressionless.

"Slava . . ." Solarin began, still gripping my arm with one hand as he stepped toward his brother.

"The party's over," said Nim, smiling a slow smile that contained both understanding and love. Kamel was looking at me with raised eyebrow as if to ask what was going on. "Come Sascha," Nim said. "It's time to finish the Game."

The white team—at least those we'd captured—were bound, trussed, and wrapped in white sheets. We carried them through the kitchen and took them down in the service elevator to Harry's limousine waiting in the garage. We put them all—Sharrif and Brodski, Hermanold, Llewellyn, and Blanche—in the roomy back compartment. Kamel and Valerie climbed in behind with the gun. Harry got in the driver's seat and, beside him, Nim. It wasn't yet dark, but through the tinted windows observers couldn't see the interior.

"We're taking them to Nim's place out on the point," Harry explained. "Then Kamel will pick up your sailboat and bring it around."

"We can load them in a rowboat right from my garden." Nim laughed, still clutching his hip. "No one lives near enough to see anything."

"What on earth will you *do* with them once they're on board?" I wanted to know.

"Valerie and I," said Kamel, "will take them out to sea. I'll arrange for an Algerian patrol boat to come out and meet us, once we're in international waters. The Algerian government will be very pleased to capture the conspirators who've plotted with Colonel Khaddafi against OPEC and planned to assassinate its members. In fact, it may well be true. I've been suspicious about the colonel's role in the Game ever since he inquired about *you* at the conference."

"What a wonderful idea." I laughed. "That should at least give us time to accomplish what we need without them getting in the way." Leaning over toward Valerie, I added, "When you get to Algiers, give your mother and Wahad a big hug for me."

"My brozzaire thinks you are very brave," said Valerie, taking my hand warmly. "He ask me to say he hope one day you will return to Algeria, too!"

So Harry, Kamel, and Nim set off for Long Island with hostages in tow. At least Sharrif—and even Blanche, the White Queen—would get to see the inside of the Algerian prison Lily and I had ourselves avoided so narrowly.

Solarin, Lily, Mordecai, and I took Nim's green Morgan. With the last four pieces we'd extracted from the secretary, we headed for Mordecai's apartment in the diamond district to assemble the pieces and begin the real work that lay ahead: deciphering the formula that had been sought by so many for so long. Lily drove, I sat in Solarin's lap once again, and Mordecai was jammed like a piece of luggage into the little crawlspace behind the seats, Carioca perched in *his* lap.

"Well, little dog," said Mordecai, stroking Carioca with a smile, "after all these adventures, you're practically a chess player yourself! And now we add to the eight pieces you've brought back from the desert, another unexpected six pieces captured from the white team. It's been a productive day."

"Plus the nine Minnie said *you* had," I added. "That makes twenty-three."

"Twenty-*six*," cackled Mordecai. "I also have the three that Minnie retrieved in Russia in 1951—which Ladislaus Nim and his father brought across the seas to America!"

"That's right!" I cried. "The nine you have are the ones Talleyrand buried in Vermont. But where did *our* eight come from—the ones Lily and I brought back from the desert?"

"Ah, that's right. There's something else I have for you, my dear," chirped the cheerful Mordecai. "It's at my apartment along with the pieces. Perhaps Nim told you that when Minnie bade him good-bye that night on the cliffs in Russia, she gave him some folded papers of great importance?"

"Yes," Solarin interjected. "Cut from a book. I saw her do it. I remember,

though I was only a child at the time. Was it the journal Minnie gave to
Catherine? From the moment she showed it to me, I wondered. . . ."

"Soon you won't have to wonder," Mordecai said cryptically. "You will
know. These pages, you see, reveal the final mystery. The secret of the Game."

We parked Nim's Morgan in a public garage at the end of the block and
went to Mordecai's apartment on foot. Solarin carried the collection of pieces,
which was now too heavy for anyone else to lift.

It was after eight o'clock and nearly dark in the diamond district. We went
past stores with iron gates across their facades. Newspapers blew across the empty
pavement. It was still Labor Day weekend, and everything was closed.

About halfway down the block, Mordecai stopped and unlocked a metal
grate. Inside was a long narrow stairway that led straight up toward the back
of the building. We followed him up into the twilight, where, at the landing,
he unlocked another door.

We went into an enormous loft where chandeliers hung from thirty-foot
ceilings. A bank of high windows at one end reflected these glittering prisms
of crystal when Mordecai threw on the lights. He crossed the room. Everywhere
were deep carpets in dark colors, beautiful shimmering trees and furniture spread
with furs, tables cluttered with objets d'art and books. It was what my old
apartment would've looked like, had it been bigger and I richer. Along one
whole wall hung a huge, magnificent tapestry that must have been as old as the
Montglane Service itself.

Solarin, Lily, and I took seats on the soft, deep sofas. On the table before
us a big chessboard had been set up. Lily swept away the pieces that were there,
and Solarin started to remove our pieces from the bag and set them on the board.

The pieces of the Montglane Service were too large even for the oversized
squares of Mordecai's alabaster board, but they looked magnificent, gleaming
beneath the chandelier's soft glow.

Mordecai pulled aside the tapestry and unlocked a huge safe that was built
into the brick. He extracted a large box containing twelve more pieces, which
Solarin rushed to help him carry.

When they were all set up, we studied them. There were the prancing horses
that were the Knights, the stately Bishops as elephants, camels with towerlike
chairs on their backs that served as Rooks. The gold King riding his pachyderm,
the Queen sitting in her sedan chair—all paved with jewels and detailed in
sculpted metals with a precision and grace no craftsman could have duplicated
in at least a thousand years. Only six pieces were absent: two silver pawns and
one gold, a golden Knight, a silver Bishop, and the White King—silver as well.

It was incredible, seeing them all together like that, shining in our midst. What fabulous mind had invented the idea of combining something so beautiful with something so deadly?

We pulled out the cloth and spread it on the large coffee table beside the board. My eyes were dazzled by the strangely glowing forms, the beautiful colors of the stones—emerald and sapphire, ruby and diamond, the yellow of citrine, light blue of aquamarine, and the pale green peridot that nearly matched Solarin's eyes. He reached over and pressed my hand as we sat there in silence.

Lily had pulled out the paper where we'd drawn our version of how the moves worked. Now she put it beside the cloth.

"There's something I think you should see," said Mordecai, who'd gone back to the safe. He returned to where I sat and handed me a small packet. I looked up into his eyes, magnified behind the thick glasses. His walnut face crumpled into a knowing smile. He held out his hand to Lily as if he expected her to rise. "Come, I want you to help me prepare some supper. We'll wait for your father and Nim to come back. They'll be hungry when they arrive. Meanwhile, our friend Cat can read what I've given her."

He dragged Lily off under protest to the kitchen. Solarin moved closer to me as I opened the packet and extracted a folded bundle of paper. As Solarin had guessed—the same kind of antique paper as in Mireille's ancient journal. Reaching over to take the original book from the bag that sat on the floor between us, I compared them. You could see where the paper had been cut and pulled away. I smiled at Solarin.

He slipped his arm around me as I leaned back into the soft lap of the sofa, unfolded the paper, and began to read. It was the last chapter in Mireille's journal. . . .

THE BLACK QUEEN'S TALE

The chestnut trees were blooming in Paris when I left Charles Maurice Talley-rand that spring of 1799, to return to England. It pained me to go, for I was again with child. A new life was beginning inside me, and with it the same seed of single-minded purpose—to finish the Game once and for all.

It would be four more years before I saw Maurice again. Four years in which the world was shaken and altered by many events. In France, Napoleon would return to overthrow the Directory and be named first consul—then consul for life. In Russia, Paul the First would be assassinated by a cadre of his own generals—and his mother's favorite lover, Plato Zubov. The mystical and mysterious Alexander—who'd stood with me in the forest beside the dying abbess—would now have access to that piece of the Montglane Service known as the Black Queen. The world I knew—England and France, Austria, Prussia, and Russia—would again go to war. And Talleyrand, the father of my children, would at last receive the papal dispensation I'd requested of him, to marry Catherine Noël Worlée Grand—the White Queen.

But I had in my possession the cloth, the drawing of the board, and the certain knowledge that seventeen pieces were nearly within my grasp. Not only the nine buried in Vermont—whose location I now knew—but also the eight: those seven of Madame Grand's and one belonging to Alexander. With this knowledge, I went to England—to Cambridge—where William Blake had told me the papers of Sir Isaac Newton were sequestered. Blake himself, who found almost morbid fascination in such things, secured me permission to study these works.

Boswell had died in May of 1795—and Philidor, that great chess master, had survived him by only three months. The old guard were dead—the White Queen's reluctant team dismantled by death. Before she had time to assemble a new one, I had to make my move.

It was just before Shahin and Charlot returned with Napoleon from Egypt— on October 4 of 1799, exactly six months after my own birthday—that I gave birth in London to a little girl. I christened her Elisa, after Elissa the Red, that great woman who'd founded the city of Carthage—and for whom Napoleon's own sister had been named. But I took to calling her Charlotte, not only for her father, Charles Maurice, and her brother, Charlot—but in memory of that other Charlotte who'd given her life in place of mine.

It was now, when Shahin and Charlot joined me in London, that the real work began. We labored by night over the ancient manuscripts of Newton, studying his many notes and experiments by candlelight. But all seemed in vain. After many months, I'd come to believe that even this great scientist had not discovered the secret. But then it occurred to me—perhaps I did not know what the secret really was.

"The Eight," I said aloud one night as we sat in the Cambridge rooms overlooking the kitchen gardens, the place where Newton himself had labored nearly a century ago. "What does the Eight really mean?"

"In Egypt," said Shahin, "they believed there were eight gods that preceded all the rest. In China they believe in the Eight Immortals. In India they think Krishna the Black—the eighth son—became an Immortal, too. An instrument of man's salvation. And the Buddhists believe in the Eightfold Path to Nirvana. There are many eights in the world's mythologies. . . ."

"But all mean the same thing," chimed in Charlot, my little son who was older than his years. "The alchemists were seeking more than just to change one metal into another. They wanted the same thing the Egyptians did when they built the pyramids—the same as the Babylonians who sacrificed children to their pagan gods. These alchemists always begin with a prayer to Hermes, who was not only the messenger who took dead souls to Hades, but was the god of healing as well. . . ."

"Shahin has fed you too much mysticism," I said. "What we're seeking here is a scientific formula."

"But Mother, that's it—don't you see?" replied Charlot. "That's why they invoke the god Hermes. In the first phase of the experiment—sixteen steps— they produce a reddish-black powder, a residue. They form it into a cake, which is called the philosophers' stone. In the second phase, they use this as a catalyst to transmute metals. In the third and final phase, they mix this powder with a special water, a water gathered from dew at a certain time of year—when the sun is between Taurot and the Belier, the Bull and the Ram. All the pictures in the books show this—it's just on your birthday—when the water that falls from the moon is very heavy. This is the time when the final phase begins."

"I don't understand," I said, confused. "What is this special water mixed with the powder of the philosophers' stone?"

"They call it al-Iksir," Shahin said softly. "When consumed, it brings health, long life, and heals all wounds."

"Mother," said Charlot, looking at me gravely, "it's the secret of immortality. The elixir of life."

Four years it took us to come to this juncture in the Game. But though we knew the formula's purpose, we still did not know how it was made.

It was August of 1803 when I arrived with Shahin and my two children at the spa of Bourbon-l'Archambault in central France, the town for which the Bourbon kings were named. The town where Maurice Talleyrand went to take the thermal waters on this same month each summer.

The spa was surrounded by ancient oaks, its long walks bordered in peonies heavy with bloom. As I stood that first morning on the path in the long linen robes one wore to take the waters, I waited there amidst the butterflies and flowers—and saw Maurice coming along down the path.

In the four years since I'd last seen him, he had changed. Though I was not yet thirty, he would soon be fifty—his handsome face webbed with fine lines, the curls of his unpowdered hair shot with silver in the morning sun. He saw me and stopped cold upon the path, his eyes never leaving my face. Those eyes that were still the intense, sparkling blue I remembered from that first morning I'd seen him in David's studio—with Valentine.

He came to me as if expecting to find me there, and put his hand in my hair as he gazed down at me.

"I shall never forgive you," were his first words, "for teaching me what love is, then leaving me to contend with it myself. Why have you never answered my letters? Why do you vanish, then reappear only long enough to break my heart again, just as it's nearly mended? Sometimes I find myself thinking of you—and wishing I'd never known you."

Then, in defiance of his words, he grasped me and pulled me to him in a passionate embrace, his lips moving from my mouth to my throat, my breast. As before, I felt the blinding force of his love sweep over me. Struggling against the desire I felt myself, I pulled away.

"I have come to collect on your promise," I told him in faint voice.

"I've done everything I promised—more than I promised," he told me bitterly. "I've sacrificed everything for you—my life, my freedom, perhaps my immortal soul. In the eyes of God, I'm still a priest. For you, I've married a woman I don't love, who can never bear me the children I want. While you, who've borne me two, have never let me glimpse them."

"They are here with me now," I told him. He watched me half in disbelief. "But first, where are the pieces of the White Queen?"

"The pieces," he said harshly. "Never fear, I have them. Extracted by trickery from a woman who loves me more than you ever have or will. Now you hold my children as hostage to get them from me. My God, that I should want you at all astounds me." He paused. The bitterness he felt could not be concealed, but it was mingled with a dark passion. "That I cannot live without you," he whispered, "suddenly seems the height of impossibility."

He trembled with the force of his emotion. His hands were on my face, my hair, his lips pressed to mine as we stood there on the public path, where people could come along at any moment. As always, the strength of his love was beyond bearing. My lips returned his kisses, my hands moved over the places where his robes had fallen open.

"This time," he whispered, "we shall not make a child—but I shall make you love me if it's the last thing I do."

Maurice's expression was more beatific than that of the holiest saint when—for the first time—he saw our children. We'd gone to the bathhouse at midnight, with Shahin guarding the door.

Charlot was now ten and already looked like the prophet Shahin had predicted he'd be, with his mass of red hair to his shoulders and the sparkling blue eyes of his father that seemed to see through time and space. At four, little Charlotte resembled Valentine at that age. It was she who captivated Talleyrand as we sat in the baths of Bourbon-l'Archambault in the steamy mineral waters.

"I want to take these children away with me," Talleyrand said at last, stroking Charlotte's fair hair as if he could not bear to let her go. "The life you insist upon leading is no life for a child. No one need know our relationship. I've acquired the estate of Valençay. I can give them their own titles and land. Let their origins remain a mystery. Only if you agree to this will I give you the pieces."

I knew he was right. What sort of mother could I be to them, when my life's direction had already been chosen by powers beyond my control? I could see in his eyes that Maurice loved them both even beyond my natural bond with them as the one who'd given them life. But there was another problem.

"Charlot must remain," I told him. "He was born in the eyes of the goddess—it is he who shall resolve the riddle. It was foretold." Charlot moved through the hot waters to Talleyrand and put his hand on his father's arm.

"You will be a great man," he told him, "a prince with many powers. You will live long, but you'll have no other children after us. You must take my sister, Charlotte—marry her into your family so her children will bond again with our blood. But I must return to the desert. My destiny is there. . . ."

Talleyrand looked at the little boy in amazement, but Charlot had not yet finished.

"You must cut your ties with Napoleon, for he is doomed to fall. If you do so, your own power will remain through many changes in the world. And you must do something else—for the Game. Get the Black Queen from Alexander of Russia. Tell him you come from me. With the seven you have already, that will make eight."

"Alexander?" said Talleyrand, looking at me through the thick steam. "Has he a piece as well? But why should he give it to me?"

"You'll give him Napoleon in return," Charlot replied.

Talleyrand did meet Alexander at the Conference of Erfurt. Whatever pact they made, everything Charlot had predicted came to pass. Napoleon fell, returned, and fell for good. In the end, he saw it was Talleyrand who had betrayed him. "Monsieur," he told him over breakfast one morning, in the eyes of all the court, "you are nothing but shit in a silk stocking." But Talleyrand had already secured the Russian piece—the Black Queen. With this, he gave me also something of value: a Knight's Tour done by the American, Benjamin Franklin, which purported to portray the formula.

I went with Shahin and Charlot to Grenoble with the eight pieces, the cloth, and the drawing the abbess had made of the board. There, in the south of France not far from where the Game had first begun, we found the famous physicist Jean Baptiste Joseph Fourier, whom Charlot and Shahin had met in Egypt. Though we had many pieces, we did not have the whole. It was thirty years before we deciphered the formula. But we did it at last.

There at night in the darkness of Fourier's laboratory, the four of us stood and watched the philosophers' stone forming in the crucible. Through thirty years and many failed attempts, at last we'd moved through all the sixteen phases as they were meant to be. The marriage of the Red King and the White Queen, it was called—the secret that had been lost for a thousand years. Calcination, oxidation, congelation, fixation, solution, digestion, distillation, evaporation, sublimation, separation, extraction, ceration, fermentation, putrefaction, propagation—and now projection. We watched the volatile gases rise from the crystals in the glass that shone like the constellations in the universe. The gases formed colors as they rose: midnight blue, purple, pink, magenta, red, orange, yellow, gold . . . The peacock's tail, they called it—the spectrum of visible wave lengths. And lower, the waves that could only be heard, not seen.

When it had dissolved and vanished, we saw the thick residue of reddish black coating the base of the glass. Scraping it away, we wrapped it in a bit of beeswax to drop it into the aqua philosophia—the heavy water.

Now only one question remained: Who would drink?

It was the year 1830 when we completed the formula. We knew from our books that such a drink could be lethal as well as life giving, if we'd done it wrong. There was another problem. If what we had was in fact the elixir, we must hide the pieces at once. To this end, I decided to return to the desert.

I crossed the sea again for what I feared might be the last time. At Algiers, I went with Shahin and Charlot to the Casbah. There was someone there I thought would be of use to me in my mission. I found him at last in a harem—a large canvas before him, and many women, veiled, reclining about him on divans. He turned to me, his blue eyes flashing, his dark hair disheveled, just as David had looked so many years before when we'd posed for him in his studio, Valentine and I. But this young painter resembled someone else far more than David—he was the very image of Charles Maurice Talleyrand.

"Your father has sent me to you," I told the young man, who was only a few years younger than Charlot.

The painter looked at me strangely. "You must be a medium." He smiled at me. "My father, Monsieur Delacroix, has been dead for many years." He twirled the paintbrush in his hand, anxious to get on with his work.

"I mean your natural father," I said as his face darkened into a glower. "I refer to Prince Talleyrand."

"Those rumors are quite unfounded," he told me curtly.

"I know differently," I said. "My name is Mireille, and I've come from France on a mission I need you for. This is my son, Charlot—your half brother. And Shahin, our guide. I want you to come with me to the desert, where I plan to restore something of great value and power to its native soil. I want to commission you to do a painting marking the spot—and warning all those who come near that it is protected by the gods."

Then I told him the tale.

It was weeks before we reached the Tassili. At last, in the secret cave, we found the place to hide the pieces. Eugene Delacroix scaled the wall as Charlot directed him where to draw the caduceus—and outside, the *labrys* form of the White Queen, which he added to the existing hunt scene.

When we'd completed our work, Shahin withdrew the vial of aqua philosophia and the pellet of powder we'd wrapped in beeswax so it would dissolve more slowly, as prescribed. We dissolved the pellet, and I looked at the vial I now held in my hand, as Shahin and Talleyrand's two sons looked on.

I remembered the words of Paracelsus, that great alchemist who once believed he had discovered the formula: "We shall be as gods," he said. I put the vial to my lips—and I drank.

When I'd finished reading this tale, I was shaking from head to foot. Solarin gripped my hand, his knuckles white as he sat beside me. The elixir of life—was that the formula? Was it possible something like that could exist?

My mind was racing. Solarin was pouring us brandy from a decanter on a nearby table. It was true, I thought, that genetic engineers had recently discovered the structure of DNA, the building block of life that, like the caduceus of Hermes, formed a double helix resembling the Eight. But nothing in ancient writings suggested this secret was known before. And how could something that transmuted metals also alter life?

My mind moved to the pieces—where they'd been buried. And I was more confused. Hadn't Minnie said she herself had placed them in the Tassili, beneath the caduceus, deep in the wall of the stone? How could she know precisely where they were, if Mireille had left them there nearly two hundred years ago?

Then I remembered the letter, the one Solarin had brought out of Algiers and given me at Nim's place—the letter from Minnie. With fumbling hand, I reached in my pocket and pulled it out, slashing it open as Solarin sat silently beside me, drinking his brandy. I could feel his eyes on me all the while.

I yanked the letter from the envelope and looked at it. Before I'd even started reading, cold horror ran down my spine. *The handwriting of the letter and the journal were the same!* Though the first was in modern English and the second in antique French, there was no way to duplicate those flowery scrolls of the sort that hadn't been used in hundreds of years.

I looked up at Solarin. He was staring at the letter in horror and disbelief.

Our eyes met, then slowly we turned again to the letter. I pressed it open on my lap, and we read:

> My dear Catherine,
>
> You now know a secret few people have ever learned. Even Alexander and Ladislaus have never guessed that I am not their grandmother at all, for twelve generations have passed since I gave birth to their ancestor—Charlot. Kamel's father, who married me only a year before his death, was in fact descended from my old friend Shahin, whose bones have lain in dust for over a hundred fifty years.
>
> Of course, you may imagine if you choose that I'm simply a mad old woman. Believe as you wish—you are the Black Queen now. You possess the parts of a secret both powerful and dangerous. Enough parts that you can solve the riddle, as I did, so many years ago. But will you? That is the choice you must now make, and make alone.
>
> If you want my advice, I suggest you destroy those pieces—melt them down so they'll never again be the cause of such misery and suffering as I've experienced all my life. What might be a great boon to mankind could also be a dreadful curse, as history has shown. Go forth, and do as you wish. My blessings go with you.
>
> Yours in God,
> Mireille

I sat with my eyes closed as Solarin pressed my hand in his. When I opened them, Mordecai was standing there, his arm wrapped around Lily protectively. Nim and Harry, whom I'd not heard return, were just behind him. They all came over, taking seats around the table where Solarin and I sat. At center were the pieces.

"What do you think of it?" asked Mordecai quietly.

Harry leaned over and patted my hand as I sat there shaking. "What if it were true?" he said.

"Then it would be the most dangerous thing imaginable," I said, still shaking. Though I didn't care to admit it, I believed it myself. "I think she's right. We should destroy those pieces."

"But you're the Black Queen now," said Lily. "You don't have to listen to her."

"Slava and I have both studied physics," Solarin added. "We have three times as many pieces as Mireille had when she deciphered the formula. Though we don't have the information contained in the board, we could solve it, I'm sure. I could get the board. . . ."

"Besides," Nim chimed in with a grin, holding his injured side, "I could use some of that stuff just now, to heal me of all my wounds."

I wondered how it would feel—to know you had the power to live two hundred years or more. To know that whatever happened to you, short of being dropped from an airplane, your wounds would heal, your diseases all be remedied.

But did I want to spend thirty years of *my* life trying to solve that formula? Though it might not take that long, I'd seen from Minnie's experience it had quickly turned to an obsession—something that ruined not only her life, but the lives of everyone she knew or touched. Did I want a long life at the expense of a happy one? By her own testimony, Minnie had lived two hundred years in terror and danger, even *after* she'd found the formula. No wonder she'd wanted to leave the Game.

It was my decision now. I looked at the pieces on the table. It would be easy enough to do. Minnie hadn't chosen Mordecai just because he was a chess master—he was a jeweler, too. Doubtless he had all the necessary equipment right here to analyze the pieces, find out what they were made of, and turn them into bijoux fit for a queen. But as I looked at them, I knew I could never bring myself to do it. They glowed with an inner life of their own. There was a bond between us—the Montglane Service and I—that I couldn't seem to cut.

I glanced up at the expectant faces watching me in silence. "I'm going to bury the pieces," I said slowly. "Lily, you'll help me; we make a good team. We'll take them somewhere—to the desert or the mountains—and Solarin will return to get the board. This Game has got to end. We'll put the Montglane Service away where no one will find it again for a thousand years."

"But in the end, it *will* be found again," Solarin said softly.

I turned to look at him, and something deep passed between us. He knew now what must happen—and I knew we might not see one another again for a very long time, if we carried out my decision.

"Maybe in a thousand years," I told him, "there'll be a nicer crop of humans on this planet—who'll know how to use a tool like this for the good of all, instead of a weapon for power. Or maybe by then scientists will have rediscovered the formula anyway. If the information in this service were no longer a secret, but common knowledge—the value of these pieces wouldn't even buy you a subway token."

"Then why not solve the formula now?" said Nim. "*Make* it common knowledge?"

Now he had cut to the bone—to the very heart of the matter. The problem was, how many people did I know whom I wanted to give eternal life? Not just evil people like Blanche and El-Marad, but ordinary crooks like those I'd worked with—Jock Upham and Jean Philippe Petard. Did I want people like *them* to live forever? Did *I* want to make the choice of whether they would or not?

Now I understood what Paracelsus had meant when he'd said, "We shall be as gods." These were decisions that had always been out of the hands of mortal men, whether you believed they were controlled by the gods, the totem spirits, or natural selection. If *we* were the ones with power to give or withhold something of that nature, we'd be playing with fire. And no matter how responsible we felt about its use or control, unless we kept it a dark secret forever as the ancient priests had done, we'd be in the same position as the scientists who invented the first "nuclear device."

"No," I said to Nim. I stood up and looked at the pieces glowing on the table—the pieces I'd risked my life for so often and so recklessly. As I stood there, I wondered if I could really do it, put them in the ground and never be tempted—never—to go searching for them and dig them up again. Harry was smiling at me, and as if he'd read my thoughts, he stood and came over to me.

"If anyone could do it, you could," he said, giving me a big bear hug. "That's why Minnie chose you above all. You see, darling, she thought you had the strength she never had—to resist the temptation of the power that comes with knowledge. . . ."

"My God, you make me sound like Savonarola, burning books," I told him. "All I'm doing is putting them out of harm's way for a while."

Mordecai had come back into the room with a big platter of delicatessen food that smelled delicious. He let Carioca out of the kitchen, where, from the appearance of the platter, he'd been "helping" with the food preparations.

We were all standing, stretching, moving about the big room—our voices resounding with the buoyancy that comes of being held down under insufferable pressure for so long and suddenly released. I was near Solarin and Nim, picking at the food, when Nim reached out and put his arm across my shoulders again. Solarin didn't seem to mind this time.

"We've just had a chat, Sascha and I," Nim told me. "You may not be in love with my brother, but he's in love with you. Beware of Russian passions— they can be all-consuming." He smiled at Solarin with a look of genuine love.

"I'm pretty hard to devour," I told him. "Besides, I feel the same way about him." Solarin looked at me in surprise—I don't know why. Though Nim's arm was still around me, Solarin grabbed me by the shoulders and planted a big kiss on my mouth.

"I won't keep him away for long," Nim told me, ruffling my hair. "I'm going to Russia with him, for the board. To lose your only brother once in life is enough. This time, if we go—we go together."

Mordecai came around, handing everyone a glass and pouring us champagne. When finished, he picked up Carioca and raised his own glass in a toast.

"To the Montglane Service," he said with his wizened smile. "May it rest in peace for a thousand thousand years!" We all drank to that, and there were cries of "Hear, Hear" from Harry.

"To Cat and Lily!" said Harry, raising his glass. "They've braved many dangers. May they live long in happiness and friendship. Even if they don't live forever, at least let every day be filled with joy." He beamed at me.

It was my turn. I raised my glass aloft and looked at their faces—the owlish Mordecai; Harry with his doglike eyes; Lily, tanned and toned; Nim, with the prophet's red hair but strange bicolored eyes, smiling at me as if he could read my thoughts. And Solarin, intense and alive, as he was beside a chessboard.

Here they all stood around me—my closest friends, people I genuinely loved. But people who were mortal, like me, and would decay in time. Our biological clocks would keep on ticking; nothing would slow the years. What we accomplished, we would have to do in under a hundred years—the span allotted for man. It had not always been that way. There were giants in the earth in those days, said the Bible: men of great power who lived seven or eight hundred years. Where had we gone wrong? When had we lost the knack? . . . I shook my head, held up my champagne glass, and smiled.

"To the Game," I said. "The game of kings . . . the most dangerous game: the eternal game. The Game we've just won—at least for another round. And to Minnie, who battled all her life to keep these pieces from the hands of those who'd use them wrongly, toward their own ends—evil and power over their fellow men. May she live on in peace wherever she is, and with our blessings. . . ."

"Hear, Hear," Harry called again, but I hadn't quite finished.

"And now that the Game is finished, and we've decided to bury the pieces," I added, "may we have the strength to resist all temptation to dig them up again!"

Everyone applauded wholeheartedly, and there was much backslapping as people downed their champagne. Almost as if we were trying to convince ourselves.

I put my glass to my lips and tipped it toward the sky. I felt the bubbles sliding down my throat—dry, stinging, perhaps a little bitter to swallow. As the last drops fell from the glass to my tongue, I wondered—only for an instant—what perhaps I'd never know. What would it taste like, what would it *feel* like, if that liquid sliding down my throat was not champagne. But the elixir of life.

END GAME

ABOUT THE AUTHOR

Katherine Neville was a Bank of America executive for several years, and as a computer expert installed systems for IBM, Honeywell, the Long Island Railroad, the Algerian Ministry of Industry and Energy, OPEC, and the U.S. Department of Energy. She has been a model and has dabbled in commercial photography and painting. She lives in the Bay area of California, where she is working on a new novel.